XENOPHON

VI

CYROPAEDIA

II

LCL 52

XENOPHON

IN SEVEN VOLUMES

VI

CYROPAEDIA

WITH AN ENGLISH TRANSLATION BY

WALTER MILLER

IN TWO VOLUMES

II

BOOKS V-VIII

HARVARD UNIVERSITY PRESS
CAMBRIDGE, MASSACHUSETTS
LONDON, ENGLAND

First published 1914
Reprinted 1932, 1943, 1953, 1961, 1968, 1979, 1989

ISBN 0-674-99058-7

Printed in Great Britain by St. Edmundsbury Press Ltd,
Bury St. Edmunds, Suffolk, on wood-free paper.
Bound by Hunter & Foulis Ltd, Edinburgh, Scotland.

CONTENTS

XENOPHON'S CYROPAEDIA

BOOK V

GOBRYAS AND GADATAS

E

I

1. Οἱ μὲν δὴ ταῦτ' ἔπραξάν τε καὶ ἔλεξαν. ὁ δὲ Κῦρος τὰ μὲν Κυαξάρου ἐκέλευσε διαλαβόντας φυλάττειν οὓς ᾔδει οἰκειοτάτους αὐτῷ ὄντας· καὶ ὅσα ἐμοὶ δίδοτε, ἡδέως, ἔφη, δέχομαι· χρήσεται δ' αὐτοῖς ὑμῶν ὁ ἀεὶ μάλιστα δεόμενος.

Φιλόμουσος δέ τις τῶν Μήδων εἶπε, Καὶ μὴν ἐγώ, ὦ Κῦρε, τῶν μουσουργῶν ἀκούσας ἑσπέρας ὧν σὺ νῦν ἔχεις, ἤκουσά τε ἡδέως κἄν μοι δῷς αὐτῶν μίαν, στρατεύεσθαι ἄν μοι δοκῶ ἥδιον ἢ οἴκοι μένειν.

Ὁ δὲ Κῦρος εἶπεν, Ἀλλ' ἐγώ, ἔφη, καὶ δίδωμί σοι καὶ χάριν οἶμαι σοὶ πλείω ἔχειν ὅτι ἐμὲ ᾔτησας ἢ σὺ ἐμοὶ ὅτι λαμβάνεις· οὕτως ἐγὼ ὑμῖν διψῶ χαρίζεσθαι.

Ταύτην μὲν οὖν ἔλαβεν ὁ αἰτήσας.

2. Καλέσας δὲ ὁ Κῦρος Ἀράσπαν Μῆδον, ὃς ἦν αὐτῷ ἐκ παιδὸς ἑταῖρος, ᾧ καὶ τὴν στολὴν ἐκδὺς ἔδωκε τὴν Μηδικήν, ὅτε παρὰ Ἀστυάγους εἰς Πέρσας ἀπῄει, τοῦτον ἐκέλευσε διαφυλάξαι αὐτῷ

2

BOOK V

I

1. Such were their words and deeds. Then Cyrus ordered the men whom he knew to be Cyaxares's most intimate friends to divide among themselves the keeping of the king's portion of the booty. "And what you offer me," he added, "I accept with pleasure; but it shall always be at the service of any one of you who at any time is most in need of it."

Cyrus's disposal of his prizes

"If you please, then, Cyrus," said one of the Medes who was fond of music, "when I listened last evening to the music-girls whom you now have, I was entranced; and if you will give me one of them, I should, I think, be more happy to go to war with you than to stay at home."

"Well," said Cyrus, "I will not only give her to you, but I believe that I am under greater obligation to you for your asking than you to me for receiving her; so thirsty am I to do you favours."

So he that asked received her.

2. Then Cyrus called to him Araspas, a Mede, who had been his friend from boyhood—the same one to whom he had given his Median robe when he laid it off as he was returning from Astyages's court to Persia—and bade him keep for him both the lady I. iv. 26

3

XENOPHON

τήν τε γυναῖκα καὶ τὴν σκηνήν· 3. ἦν δὲ αὕτη ἡ
γυνὴ τοῦ Ἀβραδάτου τοῦ Σουσίου· ὅτε δὲ ἡλίσκετο τὸ τῶν Ἀσσυρίων στρατόπεδον, ὁ ἀνὴρ
αὐτῆς οὐκ ἔτυχεν ἐν τῷ στρατοπέδῳ ὤν, ἀλλὰ
πρὸς τὸν τῶν Βακτρίων βασιλέα πρεσβεύων
ᾤχετο· ἔπεμψε δὲ αὐτὸν ὁ Ἀσσύριος περὶ συμ-
μαχίας· ξένος γὰρ ὢν ἐτύγχανε τῷ τῶν Βακτρίων
βασιλεῖ· ταύτην οὖν ἐκέλευσεν ὁ Κῦρος δια-
φυλάττειν τὸν Ἀράσπαν, ἕως ἂν αὐτὸς λάβῃ. 4.
κελευόμενος δὲ ὁ Ἀράσπας ἐπήρετο, Ἑώρακας δ᾽,
ἔφη, ὦ Κῦρε, τὴν γυναῖκα, ἥν με κελεύεις φυλάττειν;

Μὰ Δί᾽, ἔφη ὁ Κῦρος, οὐκ ἔγωγε.

Ἀλλ᾽ ἐγώ, ἔφη, ἡνίκα ἐξηροῦμέν σοι αὐτήν· καὶ
δῆτα, ὅτε μὲν εἰσήλθομεν εἰς τὴν σκηνὴν αὐτῆς, τὸ
πρῶτον οὐ διέγνωμεν αὐτήν· χαμαί τε γὰρ ἐκάθητο καὶ αἱ θεράπαιναι πᾶσαι περὶ αὐτήν· καὶ
τοίνυν ὁμοίαν ταῖς δούλαις εἶχε τὴν ἐσθῆτα· ἐπεὶ
δὲ γνῶναι βουλόμενοι ποία εἴη ἡ δέσποινα πάσας
περιεβλέψαμεν, ταχὺ πάνυ καὶ πασῶν ἐφαίνετο
διαφέρουσα τῶν ἄλλων, καίπερ καθημένη κεκα-
λυμμένη τε καὶ εἰς γῆν ὁρῶσα. 5. ὡς δὲ ἀναστῆ-
ναι αὐτὴν ἐκελεύσαμεν, συνανέστησαν μὲν αὐτῇ
ἅπασαι αἱ ἀμφ᾽ αὐτήν, διήνεγκε δ᾽ ἐνταῦθα πρῶτον μὲν τῷ μεγέθει, ἔπειτα δὲ καὶ τῇ ἀρετῇ καὶ τῇ
εὐσχημοσύνῃ καίπερ ἐν ταπεινῷ σχήματι ἑστη-
κυῖα. δῆλα δ᾽ ἦν αὐτῇ καὶ τὰ δάκρυά στάζοντα,
τὰ μὲν κατὰ τῶν πέπλων, τὰ δὲ καὶ ἐπὶ τοὺς
πόδας. 6. ὡς δ᾽ ἡμῶν ὁ γεραίτατος [1] εἶπε, Θάρρει, ὦ γύναι· καλὸν μὲν γὰρ κἀγαθὸν ἀκούομεν

---

[1] γεραίτατος F, most Edd. ; γεραίτερος xyD, Dindorf.

4

and the tent. 3. Now this woman was the wife of Abradatas of Susa; and when the Assyrian camp was taken, her husband happened not to be there, having gone on an embassy to the king of Bactria; for the Assyrian king had sent him thither to negotiate an alliance, because he chanced to be a guest-friend of the Bactrian king. This, then, was the lady that Cyrus placed in the charge of Araspas, until such a time as he himself should take her. 4. And when he received this commission Araspas asked: "And have you seen the lady, Cyrus, whom you give into my keeping?" said he. *Araspas describes Panthea*

"No, by Zeus," said Cyrus; "not I."

"But I have," said the other. "I saw her when we selected her for you. And when we went into her tent, upon my word, we did not at first distinguish her from the rest; for she sat upon the ground and all her handmaids sat around her. And she was dressed withal just like her servants; but when we looked round upon them all in our desire to make out which one was the mistress, at once her superiority to all the rest was evident, even though she sat veiled, with her head bowed to the earth. 5. But when we bade her rise, all her attendants stood up with her, and then was she conspicuous among them both for her stature and for her nobility and her grace, even though she stood there in lowly garb. And she could not hide her tears as they fell, some down her dress, some even to her feet. 6. Then, when the oldest man in our company said: 'Have no fear, lady; for

5

XENOPHON

καὶ τὸν σὸν ἄνδρα εἶναι· νῦν μέντοι ἐξαιροῦμεν
ἀνδρί σε εὖ ἴσθι ὅτι οὔτε τὸ εἶδος ἐκείνου χείρονι
οὔτε τὴν γνώμην οὔτε δύναμιν ἥττω ἔχοντι, ἀλλ'
ὡς ἡμεῖς γε νομίζομεν, εἴ τις καὶ ἄλλος ἀνήρ, καὶ
Κῦρος ἄξιός ἐστι θαυμάζεσθαι, οὗ σὺ ἔσει τὸ ἀπὸ
τοῦδε· ὡς οὖν τοῦτο ἤκουσεν ἡ γυνή, περικατερ-
ρήξατό τε τὸν ἄνωθεν πέπλον καὶ ἀνωδύρατο·
συνανεβόησαν δὲ καὶ αἱ δμωαί.

7. Ἐν τούτῳ δὲ ἐφάνη μὲν αὐτῆς τὸ πλεῖστον
μέρος τοῦ προσώπου, ἐφάνη δὲ ἡ δέρη καὶ αἱ
χεῖρες· καὶ εὖ ἴσθι, ἔφη, ὦ Κῦρε, ὡς ἐμοί τε ἔδοξε
καὶ τοῖς ἄλλοις ἅπασι τοῖς ἰδοῦσι μήπω φῦναι
μηδὲ γενέσθαι γυνὴ ἀπὸ θνητῶν τοιαύτη ἐν τῇ
Ἀσίᾳ· ἀλλὰ πάντως, ἔφη, καὶ σὺ θέασαι αὐτήν.

8. Καὶ ὁ Κῦρος ἔφη, [Ναὶ] [1] Μὰ Δία, πολύ γε
ἧττον, εἰ τοιαύτη ἐστὶν οἵαν σὺ λέγεις.

Τί δαί; ἔφη ὁ νεανίσκος.

Ὅτι, ἔφη, εἰ νυνὶ σοῦ ἀκούσας ὅτι καλή ἐστι
πεισθήσομαι ἐλθεῖν θεασόμενος, οὐδὲ πάνυ μοι
σχολῆς οὔσης, δέδοικα μὴ πολὺ θᾶττον ἐκείνη
αὖθις ἀναπείσῃ καὶ πάλιν ἐλθεῖν θεασόμενον· ἐκ
δὲ τούτου ἴσως ἂν ἀμελήσας ὧν με δεῖ πράττειν
καθήμην ἐκείνην θεώμενος.

9. Καὶ ὁ νεανίσκος ἀναγελάσας εἶπεν, Οἴει γάρ,
ἔφη, ὦ Κῦρε, ἱκανὸν εἶναι κάλλος ἀνθρώπου ἀναγκάζειν τὸν μὴ βουλόμενον πράττειν παρὰ τὸ
βέλτιστον; εἰ μέντοι, ἔφη, τοῦτο οὕτως ἐπεφύκει,
πάντας ἂν ἠνάγκαζεν ὁμοίως. 10. ὁρᾷς, ἔφη, τὸ
πῦρ, ὡς πάντας ὁμοίως κάει; πέφυκε γὰρ τοιοῦ-
τον· τῶν δὲ ·καλῶν τῶν μὲν ἐρῶσι τῶν δ' οὔ, καὶ

---

[1] ναὶ MSS., Dindorf, Breitenbach ; bracketed by Cobet,
Marchant, Gemoll.

6

though we understand that your husband also is a noble man, yet we are choosing you out for a man who, be assured, is not his inferior either in comeliness or intelligence or power, but, as we at least think, if there is any man in the world who deserves admiration, that man is Cyrus; and his you shall henceforth be.' Now when the lady heard that, she rent her outer garment from top to bottom and wept aloud; and her servants also cried aloud with her.

7. " And then we had vision of most of her face and vision of her neck and arms. And let me tell you, Cyrus," said he, " it seemed to me, as it did to all the rest who saw her, that there never was so beautiful a woman of mortal birth in Asia. But," he added, " you must by all means see her for yourself."

8. " No, by Zeus," said Cyrus; " and all the less, Cyrus declines to visit her if she is as beautiful as you say."

" Why so?" asked the young man.

" Because," said he, " if now I have heard from you that she is beautiful and am inclined just by your account of her to go and gaze on her, when I have no time to spare, I am afraid that she will herself much more readily persuade me to come again to gaze on her. And in consequence of that I might sit there, in neglect of my duties, idly gazing upon her."

9. " Why Cyrus," said the young man breaking into a laugh, " you do not think, do you, that human beauty is able to compel a man against his will to act contrary to his own best interests? Why," said he, " if that were a law of nature, it would compel us all alike. 10. Do you observe," said he, " how fire burns all alike? That is its nature. But of beautiful things we love some and some we do not; and one loves one, *Araspas maintains that love is a matter of will*

7

ἄλλος γε ἄλλου. ἐθελούσιον γάρ, ἔφη, ἐστί, καὶ
ἐρᾷ ἕκαστος ὧν ἂν βούληται. αὐτίκ᾽, ἔφη, οὐκ
ἐρᾷ ἀδελφὸς ἀδελφῆς, ἄλλος δὲ ταύτης, οὐδὲ
πατὴρ θυγατρός, ἄλλος δὲ ταύτης· καὶ γὰρ
φόβος καὶ νόμος ἱκανὸς ἔρωτα κωλύειν. 11. εἰ δέ
γ᾽, ἔφη, νόμος τεθείη μὴ ἐσθίοντας μὴ πεινῆν καὶ
μὴ πίνοντας μὴ διψῆν μηδὲ ῥιγοῦν τοῦ χειμῶνος
μηδὲ θάλπεσθαι τοῦ θέρους, οὐδεὶς ἂν νόμος[1]
δυνηθείη διαπράξασθαι ταῦτα πείθεσθαι ἀνθρώ-
πους· πεφύκασι γὰρ ὑπὸ τούτων κρατεῖσθαι. τὸ
δ᾽ ἐρᾶν ἐθελούσιόν ἐστιν· ἕκαστος γοῦν τῶν καθ᾽
ἑαυτὸν ἐρᾷ, ὥσπερ ἱματίων καὶ ὑποδημάτων.

12. Πῶς οὖν, ἔφη ὁ Κῦρος, εἰ ἐθελούσιόν ἐστι
τὸ ἐρασθῆναι, οὐ καὶ παύσασθαι ἔστιν ὅταν τις
βούληται; ἀλλ᾽ ἐγώ, ἔφη, ἑώρακα καὶ κλαίοντας
ὑπὸ λύπης δι᾽ ἔρωτα, καὶ δουλεύοντάς γε τοῖς ἐρωμένοις καὶ μάλα κακὸν νομίζοντας πρὶν ἐρᾶν τὸ
δουλεύειν, καὶ διδόντας γε πολλὰ ὧν οὐ βέλτιον
αὐτοῖς στέρεσθαι, καὶ εὐχομένους ὥσπερ καὶ
ἄλλης τινὸς νόσου ἀπαλλαγῆναι, καὶ οὐ δυναμένους μέντοι ἀπαλλάττεσθαι, ἀλλὰ δεδεμένους ἰσχυ-
ροτέρᾳ ἀνάγκῃ ἢ εἰ ἐν σιδήρῳ ἐδέδεντο. παρέχουσι
γοῦν ἑαυτοὺς τοῖς ἐρωμένοις πολλὰ καὶ εἰκῆ
ὑπηρετοῦντας· καὶ μέντοι οὐδ᾽ ἀποδιδράσκειν

---

[1] νόμος MSS. ; bracketed by Hug.

8

another another; for it is a matter of free will, and each one loves what he pleases. For example, a brother does not fall in love with his sister, but somebody else falls in love with her; neither does a father fall in love with his daughter, but somebody else does; for fear of God and the law of the land are sufficient to prevent such love. 11. But," he went on, "if a law should be passed forbidding those who did not eat to be hungry, those who did not drink to be thirsty, forbidding people to be cold in winter or hot in summer, no such law could ever bring men to obey its provisions, for they are so constituted by nature as to be subject to the control of such circumstances. But love is a matter of free will; at any rate, every one loves what suits his taste, as he does his clothes or shoes."

12. "How then, pray," said Cyrus, "if falling in love is a matter of free will, is it not possible for any one to stop whenever he pleases? But I have seen people in tears of sorrow because of love and in slavery to the objects of their love, even though they believed before they fell in love that slavery is a great evil; I have seen them give those objects of their love many things that they could ill afford to part with; and I have seen people praying to be delivered from love just as from any other disease, and, for all that, unable to be delivered from it, but fettered by a stronger necessity than if they had been fettered with shackles of iron. At any rate, they surrender themselves to those they love to perform for them many services blindly. And yet, in spite of all their misery, they do not attempt

Cyrus maintains that it is a kind of slavery

XENOPHON

ἐπιχειροῦσι, τοιαῦτα κακὰ ἔχοντες, ἀλλὰ καὶ
φυλάττουσι τοὺς ἐρωμένους μή ποι ἀποδρῶσι.

13. Καὶ ὁ νεανίσκος εἶπε πρὸς ταῦτα, Ποιοῦσι
γάρ, ἔφη, ταῦτα· εἰσὶ μέντοι, ἔφη, οἱ τοιοῦτοι
μοχθηροί· διόπερ οἶμαι καὶ εὔχονται μὲν ἀεὶ ὡς
ἄθλιοι ὄντες ἀποθανεῖν, μυρίων δ᾽ οὐσῶν μηχανῶν
ἀπαλλαγῆς τοῦ βίου οὐκ ἀπαλλάττονται. οἱ
αὐτοὶ δέ γε οὗτοι καὶ κλέπτειν ἐπιχειροῦσι καὶ
οὐκ ἀπέχονται τῶν ἀλλοτρίων, ἀλλ᾽ ἐπειδάν
τι ἁρπάσωσιν ἢ κλέψωσιν, ὁρᾷς ὅτι σὺ πρῶτος, ὡς οὐκ ἀναγκαῖον ὂν [1] τὸ κλέπτειν, αἰτιᾷ
τὸν κλέπτοντα καὶ ἁρπάζοντα, καὶ οὐ συγ-
γιγνώσκεις, ἀλλὰ κολάζεις. 14. οὕτω μέντοι,
ἔφη, καὶ οἱ καλοὶ οὐκ ἀναγκάζουσιν ἐρᾶν ἑαυτῶν
οὐδὲ ἐφίεσθαι ἀνθρώπους ὧν μὴ δεῖ, ἀλλὰ τὰ
μοχθηρὰ ἀνθρώπια πασῶν οἶμαι τῶν ἐπιθυμιῶν
ἀκρατῆ ἐστι, κἄπειτα ἔρωτα αἰτιῶνται· οἱ δέ γε
καλοὶ κἀγαθοὶ ἐπιθυμοῦντες καὶ χρυσίου καὶ ἵππων ἀγαθῶν καὶ γυναικῶν καλῶν, ὅμως πάντων
τούτων δύνανται ἀπέχεσθαι ὥστε μὴ ἅπτεσθαι
αὐτῶν παρὰ τὸ δίκαιον. 15. ἐγὼ γοῦν, ἔφη, ταύτην
ἑωρακὼς καὶ πάνυ καλῆς δοξάσης μοι εἶναι ὅμως
καὶ παρὰ σοί εἰμι καὶ ἱππεύω καὶ τἆλλα τὰ ἐμοὶ
προσήκοντα ἀποτελῶ.

16. Ναὶ μὰ Δί᾽, ἔφη ὁ Κῦρος· ἴσως γὰρ θᾶττον
ἀπῆλθες ἢ ἐν ὅσῳ χρόνῳ ἔρως πέφυκε συσκευάζεσθαι ἄνθρωπον. καὶ πυρὸς γάρ τοι ἔστι θιγόντα
μὴ εὐθὺς κάεσθαι καὶ τὰ ξύλα οὐκ εὐθὺς ἀναλάμ-

---

[1] ὂν added by Hug, Marchant, Gemoll.

to run away, but even watch their darlings to keep them from running away."

13. "Yes," the young man answered; "there are some who do so; but such are wretched weaklings, and because of their slavery, I think, they constantly pray that they may die, because they are so unhappy; but, though there are ten thousand possible ways of getting rid of life, they do not get rid of it. And this very same sort attempt also to steal and do not keep their hands off other people's property; but when they commit robbery or theft, you see that you are the first to accuse the thief and the robber, because it was not necessary to steal, and you do not pardon him, but you punish him. 14. Now in this same way, the beautiful do not compel people to fall in love with them nor to desire that which they should not, but there are some miserable apologies for men who are slaves to all sorts of passions, I think, and then they blame love. But the high-minded and the good, though they also have a desire for money and good horses and beautiful women, have the power to let all that alone so as not to touch anything beyond the limit of what is right. 15. At any rate," he added, "I have seen this lady and though she seemed to me surpassingly beautiful, still I am here with you, I practise horsemanship, and I do everything else that it is my duty to do."

16. "Aye, by Zeus," said Cyrus; "for you came away perhaps in less time than love takes, as its nature is, to get a man ensnared. For, you know, it is possible for a man to put his finger in the fire and not be burned at once, and wood does not burst at once into flame; still, for my part, I neither

Araspas claims that only the weakling is enslaved

πει· ὅμως δ᾽ ἔγωγε οὔτε πυρὸς ἑκὼν εἶναι ἅπτομαι
οὔτε τοὺς καλοὺς εἰσορῶ. οὐδέ γε σοὶ συμβουλεύω,
ἔφη, ὦ Ἀράσπα, ἐν τοῖς καλοῖς ἐᾶν τὴν ὄψιν
ἐνδιατρίβειν· ὡς τὸ μὲν πῦρ τοὺς ἁπτομένους κάει,
οἱ δὲ καλοὶ καὶ τοὺς ἄπωθεν θεωμένους ὑφάπτου-
σιν, ὥστε αἴθεσθαι τῷ ἔρωτι.

17. Θάρρει, ἔφη, ὦ Κῦρε· οὐδ᾽ ἐὰν μηδέποτε
παύσωμαι θεώμενος, οὐ μὴ κρατηθῶ ὥστε ποιεῖν
τι ὧν μὴ χρὴ ποιεῖν.

Κάλλιστα, ἔφη, λέγεις· φύλαττε τοίνυν, ἔφη,
ὥσπερ σε κελεύω καὶ ἐπιμέλου αὐτῆς· ἴσως γὰρ
ἂν πάνυ ἡμῖν ἐν καιρῷ γένοιτο αὕτη ἡ γυνή.

18. Τότε μὲν δὴ ταῦτα εἰπόντες διελύθησαν.

Ὁ δὲ νεανίσκος ἅμα μὲν ὁρῶν καλὴν τὴν
γυναῖκα, ἅμα δὲ αἰσθανόμενος τὴν καλοκἀγαθίαν
αὐτῆς, ἅμα δὲ θεραπεύων αὐτὴν καὶ οἰόμενος
χαρίζεσθαι αὐτῇ, ἅμα δὲ αἰσθανόμενος οὐκ ἀχά-
ριστον οὖσαν, ἀλλ᾽ ἐπιμελομένην διὰ τῶν αὑτῆς
οἰκετῶν ὡς καὶ εἰσιόντι εἴη αὐτῷ τὰ δέοντα καὶ
εἴ ποτε ἀσθενήσειεν, ὡς μηδενὸς ἐνδέοιτο, ἐκ
πάντων τούτων ἡλίσκετο ἔρωτι, καὶ ἴσως οὐδὲν
θαυμαστὸν ἔπασχε. καὶ ταῦτα μὲν δὴ οὕτως
ἐπράττετο.

19. Βουλόμενος δὲ ὁ Κῦρος ἐθελοντὰς μένειν
μεθ᾽ ἑαυτοῦ τούς τε Μήδους καὶ τοὺς συμμάχους,
συνεκάλεσε πάντας τοὺς ἐπικαιρίους· ἐπεὶ δὲ
συνῆλθον, ἔλεξε τοιάδε· 20. Ἄνδρες Μῆδοι καὶ
πάντες οἱ παρόντες, ἐγὼ ὑμᾶς οἶδα σαφῶς ὅτι
οὔτε χρημάτων δεόμενοι σὺν ἐμοὶ ἐξήλθετε οὔτε

put my hand into the fire nor look upon the beautiful, if I can help it. And I advise you, too, Araspas," said he, " not to let your eyes linger upon the fair; for fire, to be sure, burns only those who touch it, but beauty insidiously kindles a fire even in those who gaze upon it from afar, so that they are inflamed with passion."

17. " Never fear, Cyrus," said he, "even if I never cease to look upon her, I shall never be so overcome as to do anything that I ought not."

" Your professions," said he, " are most excellent. Keep her then, as I bid you, and take good care of her; for this lady may perhaps be of very great service to us when the time comes."

18. After this conversation, then, they separated. He falls in love And as the young man found the lady so beautiful and at the same time came to know her goodness and nobility of character, as he attended her and thought he pleased her, and then also as he saw that she was not ungrateful but always took care by the hands of her own servants not only that he should find whatever he needed when he came in, but that, if he ever fell sick, he should suffer no lack of attention—in consequence of all this, he fell desperately in love with her; and what happened to him was perhaps not at all surprising. Thus matters began to take this turn.

19. Cyrus, however, wishing to have his Medes Cyrus calls upon the Medes to answer Cyaxares and allies stay with him voluntarily, called a meeting of all his staff-officers, and when they were come together he spoke as follows: 20. " Men of Media and all here present, I am very sure that you came out with me, not because you desired to get money by it nor because you thought that in this you were

Κυαξάρῃ νομίζοντες τοῦτο ὑπηρετεῖν, ἀλλ' ἐμοὶ
βουλόμενοι τοῦτο χαρίζεσθαι καὶ ἐμὲ τιμῶντες
νυκτοπορεῖν καὶ κινδυνεύειν σὺν ἐμοὶ ἠθελήσατε.
21. καὶ χάριν τούτων ἐγὼ ὑμῖν ἔχω μέν, εἰ μὴ
ἀδικῶ· ἀποδιδόναι δὲ οὔπω ἀξίαν δύναμιν ἔχειν
μοι δοκῶ. καὶ τοῦτο μὲν οὐκ αἰσχύνομαι λέγων·
τὸ δ' ἐὰν μένητε παρ' ἐμοί, ἀποδώσω, εὖ ἴστε,
ἔφη, αἰσχυνοίμην ἂν εἰπεῖν· νομίζω γὰρ ἐμαυτὸν
ἐοικέναι λέγοντι ταῦτα ἕνεκα τοῦ ὑμᾶς μᾶλλον
ἐθέλειν παρ' ἐμοὶ καταμένειν. ἀντὶ δὲ τούτου τάδε
λέγω· ἐγὼ γὰρ ὑμῖν, κἂν ἤδη ἀπίητε Κυαξάρῃ
πειθόμενοι, ὅμως, ἂν ἀγαθόν τι πράξω, πειράσομαι
οὕτω ποιεῖν ὥστε καὶ ὑμᾶς ἐμὲ ἐπαινεῖν. 22. οὐ
γὰρ δὴ αὐτός γε ἄπειμι, ἀλλὰ καὶ Ὑρκανίοις οἷς
τοὺς ὅρκους καὶ τὰς δεξιὰς ἔδωκα ἐμπεδώσω καὶ
οὔποτε τούτους προδιδοὺς ἁλώσομαι, καὶ τῷ νῦν
διδόντι Γωβρύᾳ καὶ τείχη ἡμῖν καὶ χώραν
καὶ δύναμιν πειράσομαι ποιεῖν μὴ μεταμελῆσαι
τῆς πρὸς ἐμὲ ὁδοῦ. 23. καὶ τὸ μέγιστον δή,
θεῶν οὕτω διδόντων περιφανῶς ἀγαθὰ καὶ φο-
βοίμην ἂν αὐτοὺς καὶ αἰσχυνοίμην ἀπολιπὼν
ταῦτα εἰκῇ ἀπελθεῖν. ἐγὼ μὲν οὖν οὕτως, ἔφη,
ποιήσω· ὑμεῖς δὲ ὅπως γιγνώσκετε οὕτω καὶ
ποιεῖτε, καὶ ἐμοὶ εἴπατε ὅ τι ἂν ὑμῖν δοκῇ.
24. Ὁ μὲν οὕτως εἶπε. πρῶτος δ' ὁ φήσας ποτὲ
συγγενὴς τοῦ Κύρου εἶναι εἶπεν, Ἀλλ' ἐγὼ μέν,
ἔφη, ὦ βασιλεῦ· βασιλεὺς γὰρ ἔμοιγε δοκεῖς σὺ
φύσει πεφυκέναι οὐδὲν ἧττον ἢ ὁ ἐν τῷ σμήνει
φυόμενος τῶν μελιττῶν ἡγεμών· ἐκείνῳ τε γὰρ

doing Cyaxares a service; but it was to me that you wished to do this favour, and it was out of regard for me that you were willing to make the night-march and to brave dangers with me. 21. For this also I thank you—I should be in the wrong not to do so; but I do not think that I am as yet in a position to make you an adequate return, and this I am not ashamed to say. But let me assure you," said he, "that I should be ashamed to say 'if you will stay with me, I will make you a proper return;' for I think it would look as if I were saying it merely to make you more willing to stay with me. Instead of that, this is what I mean: even though you go back now in obedience to Cyaxares, still, if I achieve any success, I shall try so to act that you also will praise me. 22. For as to myself, I certainly am not going back, but I will be true to the oaths and the pledges which I gave the Hyrcanians, and I will never be caught playing them false; and I will also endeavour so to conduct myself that Gobryas, who is now offering us both his castle and his country and his forces, shall not repent his coming to us. 23. And above all, now that the gods are so manifestly blessing our efforts, I should fear to offend them, and I should be ashamed in their sight to go away without good reason and leave what they have bestowed. Thus, therefore, I propose to act," said he; "and do you also do as you judge to be best, and tell me what your decision is."

24. Thus he spoke. And the first one to reply was the man who had once upon a time claimed to be a kinsman of Cyrus. "For my part, O my king," said he—"for to me you seem to be a born king no less than is the sovereign of the bees in a hive.

Artabazus leads the movement to stay

I. iv. 27-28

αἱ μέλitται ἑκοῦσαι μὲν πείθονται, ὅπου δ' ἂν
μένῃ, οὐδεμία ἐντεῦθεν ἀπέρχεται· ἐὰν δέ ποι[1]
ἐξίῃ, οὐδεμία αὐτοῦ ἀπολείπεται. οὕτω δεινός
τις ἔρως αὐταῖς τοῦ ἄρχεσθαι ὑπ' ἐκείνου ἐγγί-
γνεται· 25. καὶ πρὸς σὲ δέ μοι δοκοῦσι παραπλη-
σίως πως οἱ ἄνθρωποι [οὕτω][2] διακεῖσθαι. καὶ
γὰρ εἰς Πέρσας ὅτε παρ' ἡμῶν ἀπῄεις, τίς
Μήδων ἢ νέος ἢ γέρων σοῦ ἀπελείφθη τὸ μή
σοι ἀκολουθεῖν ἔστε 'Αστυάγης ἡμᾶς ἀπέστρε-
ψεν; ἐπειδὴ δ' ἐκ Περσῶν βοηθὸς ἡμῖν ὡρμήθης,
σχεδὸν αὖ ἑωρῶμεν[3] τοὺς φίλους σου πάντας
ἐθελουσίους συνεπομένους. ὅτε δ' αὖ τῆς δεῦρο
στρατείας ἐπεθύμησας, πάντες σοι Μῆδοι ἑκόντες
ἠκολούθησαν. 26. νῦν δ' αὖ οὕτως ἔχομεν ὡς
σὺν μὲν σοὶ ὅμως καὶ ἐν τῇ πολεμίᾳ ὄντες
θαρροῦμεν, ἄνευ δὲ σοῦ καὶ οἴκαδε ἀπιέναι
φοβούμεθα. οἱ μὲν οὖν ἄλλοι ὅπως ποιήσουσιν αὐτοὶ ἐροῦσιν· ἐγὼ δέ, ὦ Κῦρε, καὶ ὧν
ἐγὼ κρατῶ καὶ μενοῦμεν παρὰ σοὶ καὶ ὁρῶντες
σὲ ἀνεξόμεθα καὶ καρτερήσομεν ὑπὸ σοῦ εὐεργε-
τούμενοι.

27. Ἐπὶ τούτῳ ἔλεξεν ὁ Τιγράνης ὧδε· Σύ,
ἔφη, ὦ Κῦρε, μήποτε θαυμάσῃς ἂν ἐγὼ σιωπῶ·
ἡ γὰρ ψυχή, ἔφη, οὐχ ὡς βουλεύσουσα παρε-
σκεύασται ἀλλ' ὡς ποιήσουσα ὅ τι ἂν παραγ-
γέλλῃς.

28. Ὁ δὲ Ὑρκάνιος εἶπεν, Ἀλλ' ἐγὼ μέν, ὦ
Μῆδοι, εἰ νῦν ἀπέλθοιτε, δαίμονος ἂν φαίην τὴν
ἐπιβουλὴν εἶναι τὸ μὴ ἐᾶσαι ὑμᾶς μέγα εὐδαί-

---

[1] ποι Dindorf, Edd. ; πρυ MSS.
[2] οὕτω MSS., most Edd. ; [οὕτω] Hug ; φιλῶς Gemoll.
[3] ἑωρῶμεν Camerarius, Edd. ; ὁρῶμεν MSS.

For as the bees always willingly obey the queen-bee and not one of them deserts the place where she stays; and as not one fails to follow her if she goes anywhere else—so marvellous a yearning to be ruled by her is innate to them; 25. so also do men seem to me to be drawn by something like the same sort of instinct toward you. And of that we have proof; for when you started to return from our country to Persia, what man of the Medes either young or old failed to follow you, until Astyages made us turn back? And when you hastened to our aid from Persia, we saw that almost all your friends followed with you of their own free will. Again, when you wished to come out on this expedition, all the Medes volunteered to follow you. 26. And now, too, this is our feeling, so that with you we are not afraid even in the enemy's land, while without you we are afraid even to return home. Now the rest may tell for themselves what they mean to do. But as for me, Cyrus, I, with the men whom I command, will remain with you and endure the sight of you and tolerate your goodness to us."

27. Following him, Tigranes spoke as follows: "Cyrus," said he, "you need never be surprised when I fail to speak. For my mind has been disciplined not to offer counsel but to do what you command."

28. "Well, Medes," said the Hyrcanian king, "if you should go away now, I should say that it was the plot of the evil one to prevent your becoming

μονας γενέσθαι· ἀνθρωπίνῃ δὲ γνώμῃ τίς ἂν ἢ
φευγόντων πολεμίων ἀποτρέποιτο ἢ ὅπλα παρα-
διδόντων οὐκ ἂν λαμβάνοι ἢ ἑαυτοὺς διδόντων
καὶ τὰ ἑαυτῶν οὐκ ἂν δέχοιτο, ἄλλως τε καὶ
τοῦ ἡγεμόνος ἡμῖν ὄντος τοιούτου ὃς ἐμοὶ δοκεῖ,
[ὡς]¹ ὄμνυμι ὑμῖν πάντας τοὺς θεούς, εὖ ποιῶν
ἡμᾶς μᾶλλον ἥδεσθαι ἢ ἑαυτὸν πλουτίζων.

29. Ἐπὶ τούτῳ πάντες οἱ Μῆδοι τοιάδ᾽ ἔλεγον·
Σύ, ὦ Κῦρε, καὶ ἐξήγαγες ἡμᾶς καὶ οἴκαδε, ὅταν
ἀπιέναι καιρὸς δοκῇ, σὺν σοὶ ἡμᾶς ἄγε.

Ὁ δὲ Κῦρος ταῦτα ἀκούσας ἐπηύξατο, Ἀλλ᾽,
ὦ Ζεῦ μέγιστε, αἰτοῦμαί σε, δὸς τοὺς ἐμὲ τιμῶντας
νικῆσαί με εὖ ποιοῦντα.

30. Ἐκ τούτου ἐκέλευσε τοὺς μὲν ἄλλους φυλακὰς καταστήσαντας ἀμφ᾽ αὑτοὺς ἤδη ἔχειν,
τοὺς δὲ Πέρσας διαλαβεῖν τὰς σκηνάς, τοῖς μὲν
ἱππεῦσι τὰς τούτοις πρεπούσας, τοῖς δὲ πεζοῖς
τὰς τούτοις ἀρκούσας· καὶ οὕτω καταστήσασθαι
ὅπως ποιοῦντες οἱ ἐν ταῖς σκηναῖς πάντα τὰ
δέοντα φέρωσιν εἰς τὰς τάξεις τοῖς Πέρσαις καὶ
τοὺς ἵππους τεθεραπευμένους παρέχωσι, Πέρσαις
δὲ μηδὲν ἄλλο ἢ ἔργον ἢ τὰ πρὸς τὸν πόλεμον
ἐκπονεῖν.

Ταύτην μὲν οὖν οὕτω διῆγον τὴν ἡμέραν.

¹ ὡς MSS. ; omitted by Schneider, Edd.

exceedingly blest. For, in all common sense, who would turn away from the enemy when they are in flight, or refuse to take their arms when they surrender them, or their persons and property when they offer them—especially under such a leader as we have ? For, I swear to you by all the gods, he seems to me happier in doing us kindnesses than in enriching himself."

29. Following him, all the Medes spoke to this effect : "It is you, Cyrus, that have brought us out here, and when you think the time to return has come, lead us back with you." The whole Median contingent stays with Cyrus

And when Cyrus heard that, he uttered this prayer : "Hear me, I beseech thee, O Zeus almighty, and grant that in service to them I may surpass the honour they show to me."

30. Thereupon he commanded the rest to station guards and after that to do for themselves whatever they pleased ; and the Persians he bade divide the tents among themselves—to the cavalry the ones appropriate to their use and to the infantry such as sufficed for their needs—and to arrange matters so that the commissaries in the tents should do all that was required of them, prepare everything necessary, and carry it to the quarters of the Persians, and have their horses groomed and fed, and that the Persians should have no duty other than to practise the arts of war.

Thus they spent that day.

II

1. Πρῲ δ᾽ ἀναστάντες ἐπορεύοντο πρὸς Γωβρύαν, Κῦρος μὲν ἐφ᾽ ἵππου καὶ οἱ Περσῶν
ἱππεῖς γεγενημένοι εἰς δισχιλίους· οἱ δὲ τὰ τούτων γέρρα καὶ τὰς κοπίδας ἔχοντες ἐπὶ τούτοις
εἵποντο, ἴσοι ὄντες τὸν ἀριθμόν· καὶ ἡ ἄλλη δὲ
στρατιὰ τεταγμένη ἐπορεύετο. ἕκαστον δ᾽ ἐκέλευσε τοῖς καινοῖς ἑαυτῶν θεράπουσιν εἰπεῖν ὅτι
ὅστις ἂν αὐτῶν ἢ τῶν ὀπισθοφυλάκων φαίνηται
ὄπισθεν ἢ τοῦ μετώπου πρόσθεν ἴῃ ἢ κατὰ τὰ[1]
πλάγια ἔξω τῶν ἐν τάξει ἰόντων[2] ἁλίσκηται,
κολασθήσεται.

2. Δευτεραῖοι δὲ ἀμφὶ δείλην γίγνονται πρὸς
τῷ Γωβρύου χωρίῳ, καὶ ὁρῶσιν ὑπερίσχυρόν
τε τὸ ἔρυμα καὶ ἐπὶ τῶν τειχῶν πάντα παρε-
σκευασμένα ὡς ἂν κράτιστα ἀπομάχοιτο· καὶ
βοῦς δὲ πολλοὺς καὶ πάμπολλα πρόβατα ὑπὸ
τὰ ἐρυμνὰ προσηγμένα ἑώρων.

3. Πέμψας δ᾽ ὁ Γωβρύας πρὸς τὸν Κῦρον
ἐκέλευσε περιελάσαντα ἰδεῖν ᾗ[3] ἡ πρόσοδος
εὐπετεστάτη, εἴσω δὲ πέμψαι πρὸς ἑαυτὸν τῶν
πιστῶν τινας, οἵτινες αὐτῷ[4] τὰ ἔνδον ἰδόντες
ἀπαγγελοῦσιν. 4. οὕτω δὴ ὁ Κῦρος αὐτὸς μὲν
τῷ ὄντι βουλόμενος ἰδεῖν εἴ που εἴη αἱρέσιμον
τὸ τεῖχος, εἰ ψευδὴς φαίνοιτο ὁ Γωβρύας, περιήλαυνε πάντοθεν, ἑώρα τε ἰσχυρότερα πάντα ἢ

---

[1] τὰ supplied by Pantazides, most Edd.; not in MSS.,
Dindorf.

[2] ἰόντων Pantazides, most Edd.; ὄντων MSS., Dindorf.

[3] ᾗ Camerarius, Edd.; εἰ MSS.

[4] αὐτῷ Stephanus, Edd.; αὐτῶν MSS.

II

I. RISING early the next morning they started— The Persian army visits Gobryas Cyrus, on horseback, with those of the Persians who had been transformed into cavalrymen, to the number of about two thousand—to visit Gobryas. And those who carried the horsemen's shields and sabres followed behind them, to the same number; the rest of the army also proceeded in its proper divisions. He ordered the horsemen, each one, to inform their new squires that if any one of them should be seen behind the rear-guard or get in front of the van or be found on the flanks outside the line of march, he should be punished.

2. Toward evening of the second day they arrived at Gobryas's castle; and they saw that the fortress was exceedingly strong and that everything was ready on the walls so that there might be most effective fighting from them. And they saw many cattle also and a great many sheep driven up under protection of the fortifications.

3. Then Gobryas sent to Cyrus and bade him ride around and see where access was most easy and send in some of his trusted officers to examine what was inside and report back to him what they saw. 4. So Cyrus, wishing, as a matter of fact, to Gobryas shows him his resources see for himself whether the fort could be stormed in case Gobryas should prove false, rode round on every side and saw that it was everywhere too strong for any one to approach. And those whom he had

XENOPHON

προσελθεῖν· οὓς δ' ἔπεμψε πρὸς Γωβρύαν, ἀπήγγελλον τῷ Κύρῳ ὅτι τοσαῦτα εἴη ἔνδον ἀγαθὰ ὅσα ἐπ' ἀνθρώπων γενεάν, ὡς σφίσι δοκεῖν, μὴ ἂν ἐπιλιπεῖν τοὺς ἔνδον ὄντας.

5. Ὁ μὲν δὴ Κῦρος ἐν φροντίδι ἦν ὅ τι ποτ' εἴη ταῦτα, ὁ δὲ Γωβρύας αὐτός τε ἐξήει πρὸς αὐτὸν καὶ τοὺς ἔνδοθεν πάντας ἐξῆγε φέροντας οἶνον, ἄλφιτα, ἄλευρα, ἄλλους δὲ ἐλαύνοντας βοῦς, αἶγας, οἷς, σῦς, καὶ εἴ τι βρωτόν, πάντα ἱκανὰ προσῆγον ὡς δειπνῆσαι πᾶσαν τὴν σὺν Κύρῳ στρατιάν. 6. οἱ μὲν δὴ ἐπὶ τούτῳ ταχθέντες διῄρουν τε ταῦτα καὶ ἐδειπνοποίουν. ὁ δὲ Γωβρύας, ἐπεὶ πάντες αὐτῷ οἱ ἄνδρες ἔξω ἦσαν, εἰσιέναι τὸν Κῦρον ἐκέλευσεν ὅπως νομίζοι ἀσφαλέστατα. προεισπέμψας οὖν ὁ Κῦρος προσκόπους καὶ δύναμιν καὶ αὐτὸς οὕτως εἰσῄει. ἐπεὶ δ' εἰσῆλθεν ἀναπεπταμένας τὰς πύλας ἔχων, παρεκάλει τοὺς φίλους πάντας καὶ ἄρχοντας τῶν μεθ' ἑαυτοῦ. 7. ἐπειδὴ δὲ ἔνδον ἦσαν, ἐκφέρων ὁ Γωβρύας φιάλας χρυσᾶς καὶ πρόχους καὶ κάλπιδας καὶ κόσμον παντοῖον καὶ δαρεικοὺς ἀμέτρους τινὰς καὶ πάντα καλὰ πολλά, τέλος τὴν θυγατέρα, δεινόν τι κάλλος καὶ μέγεθος, πενθικῶς δ' ἔχουσαν τοῦ ἀδελφοῦ τεθνηκότος, ἐξάγων ὧδε εἶπεν· Ἐγώ σοι, ὦ Κῦρε, τὰ μὲν χρήματα ταῦτα δωροῦμαι, τὴν δὲ θυγατέρα ταύτην ἐπιτρέπω διαθέσθαι ὅπως ἂν σὺ βούλῃ· ἱκετεύομεν δέ, ἐγὼ μὲν καὶ πρόσθεν τοῦ υἱοῦ, αὕτη δὲ νῦν τοῦ ἀδελφοῦ τιμωρὸν γενέσθαι σε.

8. Ὁ δὲ Κῦρος πρὸς ταῦτα εἶπεν, Ἀλλ' ἐγὼ σοὶ μὲν καὶ τότε ὑπεσχόμην ἀψευδοῦντός σου τιμωρήσειν εἰς δύναμιν· νῦν δὲ ὅτε ἀληθεύοντά σε

sent in to Gobryas brought back the report that there were provisions enough inside to last the garrison, as it seemed to them, for a whole generation.

5. Now Cyrus was pondering what all this meant, when Gobryas himself came out bringing with him all his followers; and some of them brought out with them wine and flour and barley-meal; others brought cattle, goats, sheep, swine, and all kinds of provisions—a plenty of everything for a dinner for Cyrus's whole army. 6. And they whose business it was apportioned it and set about preparing the meal. And when all his men were outside, Gobryas bade Cyrus enter, in whatever way he thought he might enter most safely. So Cyrus sent in ahead of him some scouts and a part of his forces, and then with this precaution he went in himself. And when he had gone in, keeping the gates wide open, he called to him all his friends and the officers of the troops with him. 7. And when they were inside, Gobryas brought out golden goblets, pitchers, and vases, all sorts of ornaments, an almost countless pile of darics, and all sorts of treasure in great quantities; and finally he brought out his daughter, a marvel of beauty and stature, but in mourning for her brother who was dead; IV. vi. 2 f. and he said: "These treasures, Cyrus, I present to you, and this my daughter I entrust to you to make what disposal of her you may see fit. But we make our prayer to you, I, as I have done already, that you avenge my son, and she that you be the avenger of her brother."

8. "Well," said Cyrus in reply to this, "I promised you even then that, assuming that you did not speak me false, I should do all in my power to avenge you; Cyrus renews his covenant with Gobryas

23

ὁρῶ, ἤδη ὀφείλω τὴν ὑπόσχεσιν, καὶ ταύτῃ ὑπισχνοῦμαι τὰ αὐτὰ ταῦτα σὺν θεοῖς ποιήσειν.

Καὶ τὰ μὲν χρήματα ταῦτα, ἔφη, ἐγὼ μὲν δέχομαι, δίδωμι δ' αὐτὰ τῇ παιδὶ ταύτῃ κἀκείνῳ ὃς ἂν γήμῃ αὐτήν. ἐν δὲ δῶρον ἄπειμι ἔχων παρὰ σοῦ ἀνθ' οὖ οὐδ' ἂν τὰ ἐν Βαβυλῶνι, [ἐκεῖ πλεῖστά ἐστιν,][1] οὐδὲ τὰ πανταχοῦ [ἀντὶ τούτου οὖ σύ μοι δεδώρησαι][2] ἥδιον ἂν ἔχων ἀπέλθοιμι.

9. Καὶ ὁ Γωβρύας θαυμάσας τε τί τοῦτ' εἴη καὶ ὑποπτεύσας μὴ τὴν θυγατέρα λέγοι, οὕτως ἤρετο· Καὶ τί τοῦτ' ἔστιν, ἔφη, ὦ Κῦρε;

Καὶ ὁ Κῦρος ἀπεκρίνατο, Ὅτι, ἔφη, ἐγώ, ὦ Γωβρύα, πολλοὺς μὲν οἶμαι εἶναι ἀνθρώπους οἳ οὔτε ἀσεβεῖν ἂν ἐθέλοιεν οὔτε ἀδικεῖν οὔτε ἂν ψεύδοιντο ἑκόντες εἶναι· διὰ δὲ τὸ μηδένα αὐτοῖς ἠθεληκέναι προέσθαι μήτε χρήματα πολλὰ μήτε τυραννίδα μήτε τείχη ἐρυμνὰ μήτε τέκνα ἀξιέραστα, ἀποθνήσκουσι πρότερον πρὶν δῆλοι γίγνεσθαι οἷοι ἦσαν· 10. ἐμοὶ δὲ σὺ νυνὶ καὶ τείχη ἐρυμνὰ καὶ πλοῦτον παντοδαπὸν καὶ δύναμιν τὴν σὴν καὶ θυγατέρα ἀξιόκτητον ἐγχειρίσας πεποίηκάς με δῆλον γενέσθαι πᾶσιν ἀνθρώποις ὅτι οὔτ' ἂν ἀσεβεῖν περὶ ξένους ἐθέλοιμι οὔτ' ἂν ἀδικεῖν χρημάτων ἕνεκα οὔτε συνθήκας ἂν ψευδοίμην ἑκὼν εἶναι. 11. τούτων ἐγώ, εὖ ἴσθι, ἕως ἂν ἀνὴρ δίκαιος ὦ καὶ δοκῶν εἶναι τοιοῦτος ἐπαινῶμαι ὑπ' ἀνθρώπων, οὔποτ' ἐπιλήσομαι, ἀλλὰ πειράσομαί σε ἀντιτιμῆσαι πᾶσι τοῖς καλοῖς.

[1] [ἐκεῖ πλεῖστά ἐστιν] Hug ; εἰ ἐκεῖ πλεῖστά ἐστιν MSS. ; [εἰ ἐκεῖ . . . ἐστιν] Hirschig ; εἰ καὶ πλεῖστά ἐστιν Dindorf.

[2] ἀντὶ . . . δεδώρησαι MSS. ; bracketed by Hirschig, most Edd.

and now, when I see that you are truthful, my promise is already due ; and I promise her likewise that with heaven's help I will fulfil my promise to the letter.

"Now as to these treasures," said he, "I accept them, but I give them again to your daughter here and the man who shall marry her. But one gift of yours will I take as I leave you, in place of which not even all the wealth of Babylon (and that is enormous)—no, not even all the wealth of all the world would send me away more happy than with this gift from you."

9. And Gobryas, wondering what he meant and suspecting that he meant his daughter, asked : " And what might that gift be, Cyrus ? "

"Gobryas," he replied, "it is this : I believe that there are many men who would not consent to be wicked or unjust or false, but they die before it is ever discovered what sort of men they are, simply because no one has ever seen fit to entrust them with great wealth or kingly power or mighty fortresses or lovely children ; 10. but you have now placed in my hands your fortress and all sorts of wealth, your forces and your precious child, and have thus given me an opportunity of showing to all the world that I would not do an act of wickedness against a friend or do a wrong for the sake of gain or willingly prove false to a covenant. 11. And so long as I am an honest man and receive men's approbation as bearing this reputation, I assure you that I shall never forget this proof of your confidence but shall try to show you all fair honour in return.

XENOPHON

12. Καὶ ἀνδρὸς δ', ἔφη, τῇ θυγατρὶ μὴ φοβοῦ ὡς ἀπορήσεις ἀξίου ταύτης· πολλοὶ γὰρ κἀγαθοὶ φίλοι εἰσὶν ἐμοί· ὧν τις γαμεῖ ταύτην· εἰ μέντοι χρήμαθ' ἕξει τοσαῦτα ὅσα σὺ δίδως ἢ καὶ ἄλλα πολλαπλάσια τούτων, οὐκ ἂν ἔχοιμι εἰπεῖν· σὺ μέντοι εὖ ἴσθι ὅτι εἰσί τινες αὐτῶν οἳ ὧν μὲν σὺ δίδως χρημάτων οὐδὲ μικρὸν τούτων ἕνεκά σε μᾶλλον θαυμάζουσιν· ἐμὲ δὲ ζηλοῦσι νυνὶ καὶ εὔχονται πᾶσι θεοῖς γενέσθαι ποτὲ ἐπιδείξασθαι ὡς πιστοὶ μέν εἰσιν οὐδὲν ἧττον ἐμοῦ τοῖς φίλοις, τοῖς δὲ πολεμίοις ὡς οὔποτ' ἂν ὑφεῖντο ζῶντες, εἰ μή τις θεὸς βλάπτοι· ἀντὶ δ' ἀρετῆς καὶ δόξης ἀγαθῆς ὅτι οὐδ' ἂν τὰ Σύρων πρὸς τοῖς σοῖς καὶ Ἀσσυρίων πάντα προέλοιντο· τοιούτους ἄνδρας εὖ ἴσθι ἐνταῦθα καθημένους.

13. Καὶ ὁ Γωβρύας εἶπε γελάσας, Πρὸς τῶν θεῶν, ἔφη, ὦ Κῦρε, δεῖξον δή μοι ποῦ οὗτοί εἰσιν, ἵνα σε τούτων τινὰ αἰτήσωμαι παῖδά μοι γενέσθαι.

Καὶ ὁ Κῦρος εἶπεν, Οὐδὲν ἐμοῦ σε δεήσει πυνθάνεσθαι, ἀλλ' ἂν σὺν ἡμῖν ἔπῃ, αὐτὸς σὺ ἕξεις καὶ ἄλλῳ δεικνύναι αὐτῶν ἕκαστον.

14. Τοσαῦτ' εἰπὼν δεξιάν τε λαβὼν τοῦ Γωβρύα καὶ ἀναστὰς ἐξῄει, καὶ τοὺς μεθ' αὑτοῦ ἐξῆγεν ἅπαντας· καὶ πολλὰ δεομένου τοῦ Γωβρύα ἔνδον δειπνεῖν οὐκ ἠθέλησεν, ἀλλ' ἐν τῷ στρατοπέδῳ ἐδείπνει καὶ τὸν Γωβρύαν σύνδειπνον παρέλαβεν.

15. ἐπὶ στιβάδος δὲ κατακλινεὶς ἤρετο αὐτὸν ὧδε·

26

12. "And as for your daughter," he continued, "do not fear that you shall fail to find a husband worthy of her; for I have many noble friends; some one of them will marry her. But whether he will have as much money as you are ready to give me or even many times as much, I could not say. Let me tell you, however, that there are some of them who do not admire you one whit the more for the money you have to offer; but with me they are vying now and praying to all the gods that it may be granted them one day to prove that they are not less faithful to their friends than I, and that so long as they live they would never yield to their enemies, unless some god should cross them. But their virtue and their good name they would not barter for all your wealth and the wealth of the Assyrians and Syrians to boot. Such men, let me tell you, are sitting here." *Cyrus's pledge for the daughter of Gobryas*

13. "By the gods, Cyrus," said Gobryas with a laugh, "please show me where they are, that I may ask you for one of them to be my son-in-law."

"There will be no need of your getting that information from me," answered Cyrus; "but, if you will go with us, you will be able yourself to point each one of them out to somebody else."

14. When he had thus spoken, he clasped Gobryas's right hand in his and rose to depart, taking with him all his followers. And though Gobryas urged him to dine in the castle, he declined, but dined in camp and took Gobryas with him as his guest. 15. And as he reclined upon a mat of straw he asked this question: "Tell me, *Gobryas is impressed by the simple life*

27

Εἰπέ μοι, ἔφη, ὦ Γωβρύα, πότερον οἴει σοὶ εἶναι
πλείω ἢ ἑκάστῳ ἡμῶν στρώματα;

Καὶ ὃς εἶπεν, Ὑμῖν νὴ Δί᾽ εὖ οἶδ᾽ ὅτι, ἔφη, καὶ
στρώματα πλείω ἐστὶ καὶ κλῖναι, καὶ οἰκία γε πολὺ μείζων ἢ ὑμετέρα τῆς ἐμῆς, οἵ γε οἰκίᾳ μὲν
χρῆσθε γῇ τε καὶ οὐρανῷ, κλῖναι δ᾽ ὑμῖν εἰσιν
ὁπόσαι εὐναὶ γένοιντ᾽ ἂν ἐπὶ γῆς· στρώματα δὲ
νομίζετε οὐχ ὅσα πρόβατα φύει [ἔρια],[1] ἀλλ᾽ ὅσα
ὄρη τε καὶ πεδία ἀνίησι.

16. Τὸ μὲν δὴ πρῶτον συνδειπνῶν αὐτοῖς ὁ
Γωβρύας καὶ ὁρῶν τὴν φαυλότητα τῶν παρα-
τιθεμένων βρωμάτων πολὺ σφᾶς ἐνόμιζεν ἐλευ-
θεριωτέρους εἶναι αὐτῶν· 17. ἐπεὶ δὲ κατενόησε
τὴν μετριότητα τῶν συσσίτων[2]—ἐπ᾽ οὐδενὶ γὰρ
βρώματι οὐδὲ πώματι Πέρσης ἀνὴρ τῶν πεπαι-
δευμένων οὔτ᾽ ἂν ὄμμασιν ἐκπεπληγμένος κατα-
φανὴς γένοιτο οὔτε ἁρπαγῇ οὔτε τῷ νῷ μὴ οὐχὶ
προσκοπεῖν ἅπερ ἂν καὶ μὴ ἐπὶ σίτῳ ὤν· ἀλλ᾽
ὥσπερ οἱ ἱππικοὶ διὰ τὸ μὴ ταράττεσθαι ἐπὶ τῶν
ἵππων δύνανται ἅμα ἱππεύοντες καὶ ὁρᾶν καὶ
ἀκούειν καὶ λέγειν τὸ δέον, οὕτω κἀκεῖνοι ἐν τῷ
σίτῳ οἴονται δεῖν φρόνιμοι καὶ μέτριοι φαίνεσθαι·
τὸ δὲ κεκινῆσθαι ὑπὸ τῶν βρωμάτων καὶ τῆς
πόσεως πάνυ αὐτοῖς ὑικὸν [καὶ θηριῶδες][3] δοκεῖ
εἶναι.

18. Ἐνενόησε δὲ αὐτῶν καὶ ὡς ἐπηρώτων ἀλλήλους τοιαῦτα οἷα ἐρωτηθῆναι ἥδιον ἢ μὴ καὶ

---

[1] ἔρια MSS., Breitenbach ; omitted by Dindorf, most Edd.
[2] συσσίτων Muretus, Edd. ; σίτων MSS.
[3] καὶ θηριῶδες MSS., Dindorf, Breitenbach, et al.; bracketed
by Cobet.

Gobryas, do you think you have more coverlets [1] than each one of us?"

"I am perfectly sure, by Zeus," the other answered, "that you have more coverlets and more couches, [1] and that your dwelling is much larger than mine; for you take heaven and earth for your dwelling, and you have as many couches as you can find resting-places on the ground, while you regard as your proper coverlets not wool that sheep produce, but whatever the mountains and plains bring forth."

16. Thus, as Gobryas dined with them for the first time and saw the simplicity of the food set before them, he thought his own people more refined than they. 17. But he soon perceived the temperance of the soldiers who sat at meat with him; for no Persian of the educated class would allow it to appear that he was captivated with any kind of food or drink, either with his eyes gloating over it, or with his hands greedy to get it, or with his thoughts so engrossed by it as to fail to observe things that would attract his attention if he were not at meat; but just as good horsemen do not lose their self-command when on horseback but can ride along and at the same time see and hear and say whatever they should, so also the educated Persians think that at their meals they ought to show themselves sensible and temperate; and to become excited over food or drink seems to them altogether swinish and bestial.

18. He noticed further about them that they asked one another such questions as people are more

Plain living and high thinking

[1] Costly coverlets and couches were a special feature of oriental luxury.

XENOPHON

ἔσκωπτον οἷα σκωφθῆναι ἥδιον ἢ μή· ἅ τε
ἔπαιζον ὡς πολὺ μὲν ὕβρεως ἀπῆν, πολὺ δὲ τοῦ
αἰσχρόν τι ποιεῖν, πολὺ δὲ τοῦ χαλεπαίνεσθαι
πρὸς ἀλλήλους. 19. μέγιστον δ' αὐτῷ ἔδοξεν
εἶναι τὸ ἐν στρατείᾳ ὄντας τῶν εἰς τὸν αὐτὸν κίνδυνον ἐμβαινόντων μηδενὸς οἴεσθαι δεῖν πλείω
παρατίθεσθαι, ἀλλὰ τοῦτο νομίζειν ἡδίστην εὐω-
χίαν εἶναι τοὺς συμμάχεσθαι μέλλοντας ὅτι βελτί-
στους παρασκευάζειν.

20. Ἡνίκα δὲ Γωβρύας ὡς εἰς οἶκον ἀπιὼν
ἀνίστατο, εἰπεῖν λέγεται, Οὐκέτι θαυμάζω, ὦ
Κῦρε, εἰ ἐκπώματα μὲν καὶ ἱμάτια καὶ χρυσίον
ἡμεῖς ὑμῶν πλείονα κεκτήμεθα, αὐτοὶ δὲ ἐλάτ-
τονος ὑμῶν ἄξιοί ἐσμεν. ἡμεῖς μὲν γὰρ ἐπιμελό-
μεθα ὅπως ἡμῖν ταῦτα ὡς πλεῖστα ἔσται, ὑμεῖς
δέ μοι δοκεῖτε ἐπιμέλεσθαι ὅπως αὐτοὶ ὡς
βέλτιστοι ἔσεσθε.

21. Ὁ μὲν ταῦτ' εἶπεν· ὁ δὲ Κῦρος, Ἄγ', ἔφη,
ὦ Γωβρύα, ὅπως πρῲ παρέσει ἔχων τοὺς ἱππέας
ἐξωπλισμένους, ἵνα καὶ τὴν δύναμίν σου ἴδωμεν,
καὶ ἅμα διὰ τῆς σῆς χώρας ἄξεις ἡμᾶς, ὅπως ἂν
εἰδῶμεν ἅ τε δεῖ φίλια καὶ πολέμια ἡμᾶς νομίζειν.

22. Τότε μὲν δὴ ταῦτ' εἰπόντες ἀπῆλθον ἑκάτερος ἐπὶ τὰ προσήκοντα.

Ἐπεὶ δὲ ἡμέρα ἐγένετο, παρῆν ὁ Γωβρύας
ἔχων τοὺς ἱππέας, καὶ ἡγεῖτο. ὁ δὲ Κῦρος, ὥσπερ
προσήκει ἀνδρὶ ἄρχοντι, οὐ μόνον τῷ πορεύεσθαι
τὴν ὁδὸν προσεῖχε τὸν νοῦν, ἀλλ' ἅμα προϊὼν
ἐπεσκοπεῖτο εἴ τι δυνατὸν εἴη τοὺς πολεμίους

pleased to be asked than not, that they indulged in
such banter as is more agreeable to hear than not;
he observed how far their jests were removed from in-
sult, how far they were from doing anything unbe-
coming, and how far from offending one another. 19.
But what seemed to him most extraordinary of all
was that when on active service they did not think
they ought to be served with a larger share than any
one else of those who were going into the same
dangers, but that they considered it the most sump-
tuous feast to make those who were to be their
comrades in arms as efficient as possible.

20. When Gobryas rose to go home, he is reported
to have said : " I am no longer surprised, Cyrus, that
while we possess more cups and clothing and gold
than you, we ourselves are worth less than you are.
For our whole thought is to have as much of those
things as possible, while your whole thought seems
to me to be that you may be yourselves as capable
as possible."

21. Thus he spoke ; and Cyrus answered : "Please
see to it, Gobryas, that you are here early in the
morning with your cavalry under arms, so that we
may see your forces, and then you shall lead us
through your country so that we may know what we
have to consider as belonging to our friends and
what as belonging to our enemies."

22. When they had thus spoken, they went away,
each to his own proper task.

When day dawned, Gobryas came with his cavalry
and led the way. But Cyrus, as became a general,
turned his thoughts not only upon the march, but at
the same time, as he proceeded, he kept studying
the situation to see whether it might be in any way

ἀσθενεστέρους ποιεῖν ἢ αὐτοὺς ἰσχυροτέρους.
23. καλέσας οὖν τὸν Ὑρκάνιον καὶ τὸν Γωβρύαν,
τούτους γὰρ ἐνόμιζεν εἰδέναι μάλιστα ὧν αὐτὸς
ᾤετο δεῖσθαι μαθεῖν, Ἐγώ τοι, ἔφη, ὦ ἄνδρες
φίλοι, οἶμαι σὺν ὑμῖν ἂν ὡς πιστοῖς βουλευόμενος[1] περὶ τοῦ πολέμου τοῦδε οὐκ ἂν ἐξαμαρτά-
νειν· ὁρῶ γὰρ ὅτι μᾶλλον ὑμῖν ἢ ἐμοὶ σκεπτέον
ὅπως ὁ Ἀσσύριος ἡμῶν μὴ ἐπικρατήσει. ἐμοὶ
μὲν γάρ, ἔφη, τῶνδε ἀποσφαλέντι ἔστιν ἴσως
καὶ ἄλλη ἀποστροφή· ὑμῖν δ᾽, εἰ οὗτος ἐπικρατήσει, ὁρῶ ἅμα πάντα τὰ ὄντα ἀλλότρια γιγνόμενα. 24. καὶ γὰρ ἐμοὶ μὲν πολέμιός ἐστιν,
οὐκ ἐμὲ μισῶν, ἀλλ᾽ οἰόμενος ἀσύμφορον ἑαυτῷ
μεγάλους εἶναι ἡμᾶς, καὶ στρατεύει[2] διὰ τοῦτο
ἐφ᾽ ἡμᾶς· ὑμᾶς δὲ καὶ μισεῖ, ἀδικεῖσθαι νομίζων
ὑφ᾽ ὑμῶν.

Πρὸς ταῦτα ἀπεκρίναντο ἀμφότεροι κατὰ ταὐτὰ
περαίνειν ὅ τι μέλλει, ὡς ταῦτ᾽ εἰδόσι σφίσι
καὶ μέλον αὐτοῖς ἰσχυρῶς ὅπη τὸ μέλλον ἀπο-
βήσοιτο. 25. Ἐνταῦθα δὴ ἤρξατο ὧδε· Λέξατε δή
μοι, ἔφη, ὑμᾶς νομίζει μόνους πολεμικῶς ἔχειν ὁ
Ἀσσύριος πρὸς ἑαυτόν, ἢ ἐπίστασθε καὶ ἄλλον
τινὰ αὐτῷ πολέμιον;

Ναὶ μὰ Δί᾽, ἔφη ὁ Ὑρκάνιος, πολεμιώτατοι
μέν εἰσιν αὐτῷ Καδούσιοι, ἔθνος πολύ τε καὶ
ἄλκιμον· Σάκαι γε μὴν ὅμοροι ἡμῖν, οἳ κακὰ
πολλὰ πεπόνθασιν ὑπὸ τοῦ Ἀσσυρίου· ἐπειρᾶτο
γὰρ κἀκείνους ὥσπερ καὶ ἡμᾶς καταστρέψασθαι.

---

[1] βουλευόμενος xyA, Edd. ; βουλευομένοις GH (taken into
my counsels).
[2] στρατεύει xzF, Edd.; ἐστράτευσε DG² (it was for this
reason that he began the war).

possible to make the enemy weaker or his own side stronger. 23. So he called Gobryas and the Hyrcanian king to him, for he supposed that they must know best what he thought he needed to learn, and said : "My dear friends, I think that I should be making no mistake to consult with you in regard to this war and to rely upon your trustworthiness. For I observe that you have greater need than I to see to it that the Assyrian shall not get the upper hand of us : if I am unsuccessful in this, I shall, perhaps, find some other place of refuge ; whereas in your case, I see that if he gains the upper hand, all that you have passes into other hands. 24. For, as for me, he is my enemy, not because he hates me, but because he imagines that it would be inimical to his interests for our nation to become great, and for that reason he is making war upon us ; but you he actually hates, for he thinks that you have done him wrong."

Cyrus consults with Gobryas and the Hyrcanian king

To this they both answered in the same way, that he should proceed with what he had to say, for they recognized the truth of what he had said and knew that it was a matter of vital concern to them how things turned out in the future. 25. Then he began as follows : "Tell me, then," said he, "does the Assyrian king believe that you are the only ones who are hostile to him, or do you know of any one else who is his enemy ?"

"Yes, by Zeus," said the Hyrcanian ; "the Cadusians, a large and powerful nation, are most bitter enemies of his ; and so are our neighbours, the Sacians, for they have suffered very severely at his hands ; for he attempted to subjugate them just as he did us."

Cyrus aims to effect a combination with other enemies of Assyria

33

XENOPHON

26. Οὐκοῦν, ἔφη, οἴεσθε νῦν αὐτοὺς ἀμφοτέρους ἡδέως ἂν ἐπιβῆναι μεθ᾽ ἡμῶν τῷ Ἀσσυρίῳ;

Ἔφασαν, Καὶ σφόδρ᾽ ἄν, εἰ πή γε δύναιντο συμμῖξαι.

Τί δ᾽, ἔφη, ἐν μέσῳ ἐστὶ τοῦ συμμῖξαι;

Ἀσσύριοι, ἔφασαν, τὸ αὐτὸ ἔθνος δι᾽ οὗπερ νυνὶ πορεύει.

27. Ἐπεὶ δὲ ταῦτα ἤκουσεν ὁ Κῦρος, Τί γάρ, ἔφη, ὦ Γωβρύα, οὐ σὺ τοῦ νεανίσκου τούτου ὃς νῦν εἰς τὴν βασιλείαν καθέστηκεν ὑπερηφανίαν πολλήν τινα τοῦ τρόπου κατηγορεῖς;

Τοιαῦτα γάρ, οἶμαι, ἔφη ὁ Γωβρύας, ἔπαθον ὑπ᾽ αὐτοῦ.

Πότερα δῆτα, ἔφη ὁ Κῦρος, εἰς σὲ μόνον τοιοῦτος ἐγένετο ἢ καὶ εἰς ἄλλους τινάς;

28. Νὴ Δί᾽, ἔφη ὁ Γωβρύας, καὶ εἰς ἄλλους γε· ἀλλὰ τοὺς μὲν ἀσθενοῦντας οἷα ὑβρίζει τί δεῖ λέγειν; ἑνὸς δὲ ἀνδρὸς πολὺ δυνατωτέρου ἢ ἐγὼ υἱόν, καὶ ἐκείνου ἑταῖρον ὄντα ὥσπερ τὸν ἐμόν, συμπίνοντα παρ᾽ ἑαυτῷ συλλαβὼν ἐξέτεμεν, ὡς μέν τινες ἔφασαν, ὅτι ἡ παλλακὴ αὐτοῦ ἐπῄνεσεν αὐτὸν ὡς καλὸς εἴη καὶ ἐμακάρισε τὴν μέλλουσαν αὐτῷ γυναῖκα ἔσεσθαι· ὡς δὲ αὐτὸς νῦν λέγει, ὅτι ἐπείρασεν αὐτοῦ τὴν παλλακίδα. καὶ νῦν οὗτος εὐνοῦχος μέν ἐστι, τὴν δ᾽ ἀρχὴν ἔχει, ἐπεὶ ὁ πατὴρ αὐτοῦ ἐτελεύτησεν.

29. Οὐκοῦν, ἔφη, οἴει ἂν καὶ τοῦτον ἡδέως ἡμᾶς ἰδεῖν, εἰ οἴοιτο ἑαυτῷ βοηθοὺς ἂν γενέσθαι;

34

26. "Well then," said he, "do you think that these two nations would like to join us in an attack upon the Assyrian?"

"Yes," they answered, "and right eagerly, if they could find a way to combine their forces with ours."

"And what is to hinder such a union of forces?" asked Cyrus.

"The Assyrians," they answered, "the same nation, through whose country you are now marching."

27. "But, Gobryas," said Cyrus, when he heard this, "do you not accuse this young fellow who has just come to the throne of cruel insolence of character?"

"That judgment, I think," said Gobryas," is warranted by my experience with him."

"Pray, are you the only man towards whom he has acted in this way," Cyrus asked, "or are there others also?"

28. "Aye, by Zeus," said Gobryas; "there are others also. But why should I recount his acts of insolence toward the weak? For once when he and the son of a man much more powerful than I were drinking together, a young man who, like my son, was his comrade, he had him seized and castrated; and the occasion, so some people said, was simply because his concubine had praised his friend, remarking how handsome he was and felicitating the woman who should be his wife; but the king himself now maintains that it was because the man had made advances toward his concubine. And so now he is a eunuch, but he has come into the kingdom, for his father is dead."

The king and Gadatas

29. "Well then," said Cyrus, "do you think that he also would be glad to see us, if he thought we could help him?"

35

XENOPHON

Εὖ μὲν οὖν, ἔφη, οἶδα, ὁ Γωβρύας· ἀλλ' ἰδεῖν
τοι αὐτὸν χαλεπόν ἐστιν, ὦ Κῦρε.

Πῶς; ἔφη ὁ Κῦρος.

῞Οτι εἰ μέλλει τις ἐκείνῳ συμμίξειν, παρ' αὐτὴν
τὴν Βαβυλῶνα δεῖ παριέναι.

30. Τί οὖν, ἔφη, τοῦτο χαλεπόν;

῞Οτι νὴ Δί', ἔφη ὁ Γωβρύας, οἶδα ἐξελθοῦσαν
ἂν [1] δύναμιν ἐξ αὐτῆς πολλαπλασίαν ἧς· σὺ
ἔχεις νῦν· εὖ δ' ἴσθι ὅτι καὶ δι' αὐτὸ τοῦτο ἧττόν
σοι νῦν ἢ τὸ πρότερον Ἀσσύριοι καὶ τὰ ὅπλα
ἀποφέρουσι καὶ τοὺς ἵππους ἀπάγουσιν, ὅτι τοῖς
ἰδοῦσιν αὐτῶν ὀλίγη ἔδοξεν εἶναι ἡ σὴ δύναμις·
καὶ ὁ λόγος οὗτος πολὺς ἤδη ἔσπαρται· δοκεῖ
δέ μοι, ἔφη, βέλτιον εἶναι φυλαττομένους πορεύεσθαι.

31. Καὶ ὁ Κῦρος ἀκούσας τοῦ Γωβρύου τοιαῦτα
τοιάδε πρὸς αὐτὸν ἔλεξε· Καλῶς μοι δοκεῖς
λέγειν, ὦ Γωβρύα, κελεύων ὡς ἀσφαλέστατα
τὰς πορείας ποιεῖσθαι. ἔγωγ' οὖν σκοπῶν οὐ
δύναμαι ἐννοῆσαι ἀσφαλεστέραν οὐδεμίαν πορείαν
ἡμῖν τοῦ [2] πρὸς αὐτὴν Βαβυλῶνα ἰέναι, εἰ ἐκεῖ
τῶν πολεμίων ἐστὶ τὸ κράτιστον. πολλοὶ μὲν
γάρ εἰσιν, ὡς σὺ φῇς· εἰ δὲ θαρρήσουσι, καὶ
δεινοὶ ἡμῖν, ὡς ἐγώ φημι, ἔσονται. 32. μὴ
ὁρῶντες μὲν οὖν ἡμᾶς, ἀλλ' οἰόμενοι ἀφανεῖς εἶναι
διὰ τὸ φοβεῖσθαι ἐκείνους, σάφ' ἴσθι, ἔφη, ὅτι
τοῦ μὲν φόβου ἀπαλλάξονται ὃς αὐτοῖς ἐνεγένετο,
θάρρος δ' ἐμφύσεται ἀντὶ τούτου τοσούτῳ μεῖζον
ὅσῳ ἂν πλείονα χρόνον ἡμᾶς μὴ ὁρῶσιν· ἢν δὲ

[1] ἂν added by Schaefer, Edd.; not in MSS.
[2] τοῦ Weckherlein, Dindorf, Breitenbach; τῆς MSS.,
Marchant (who writes, after Βαβυλῶνα, πορείας εἶναι), Gemoll.

36

"Think!" said Gobryas, "I am sure of it. But, Cyrus, it would be difficult to see him."

"Why?" asked Cyrus.

"Because, to effect a union of forces with him, one has to march along under the very walls of Babylon."

30. "Why, pray," said the other, "is that so difficult?"

"Because, by Zeus," said Gobryas, "I know that the forces that would come out of that city alone are many times as large as your own at present; and let me tell you that the Assyrians are now less inclined than heretofore to deliver up their arms and to bring in their horses to you for the very reason that to those of them who have seen your army it seemed a small one; and a rumour to this effect has now been widely spread abroad. And," he added, "I think we should do better to proceed cautiously." The Assyrians' terror of Cyrus is disappearing

31. "I think you are right, Gobryas, in admonishing us to march with the utmost caution," Cyrus made answer upon hearing this suggestion from him. "But when I think of it, I cannot conceive of any safer procedure for us than to march directly upon Babylon, if that is where the main body of the enemy's forces is. For they are, as you say, numerous; and if they take courage, they will also, as I say, give us cause to fear them. 32. However, if they do not see us and get the idea that we are keeping out of sight because we are afraid of them, then, let me assure you, they will recover from the fear with which we inspired them; and the longer we keep out of their sight, the greater the courage that will spring up within them in place of that fear. Cyrus proposes to march straight for Babylon

ἤδη ἴωμεν ἐπ᾽ αὐτούς, πολλοὺς μὲν αὐτῶν εὑρήσομεν ἔτι κλαίοντας τοὺς ἀποθανόντας ὑφ᾽ ἡμῶν,
πολλοὺς δ᾽ ἔτι τραύματα ἐπιδεδεμένους ἃ ὑπὸ
τῶν ἡμετέρων ἔλαβον, πάντας δ᾽ ἔτι μεμνημένους
τῆς μὲν τοῦδε τοῦ στρατεύματος τόλμης, τῆς
δ᾽ αὑτῶν φυγῆς τε καὶ συμφορᾶς. 33. εὖ δ᾽ ἴσθι,
ἔφη, ὦ Γωβρύα, [ἵνα καὶ τοῦτ᾽ εἰδῇς,] [1] οἱ πολλοὶ
ἄνθρωποι, ὅταν μὲν θαρρῶσιν, ἀνυπόστατον τὸ
φρόνημα παρέχονται· ὅταν δὲ δείσωσιν, ὅσῳ ἂν
πλείους ὦσι, τοσούτῳ μείζω καὶ ἐκπεπληγμένον
μᾶλλον τὸν φόβον κέκτηνται. 34. ἐκ πολλῶν
μὲν γὰρ καὶ κακῶν λόγων ηὐξημένος αὐτοῖς
πάρεστιν, ἐκ πολλῶν δὲ καὶ πονηρῶν σχημάτων,[2]
ἐκ πολλῶν δὲ καὶ δυσθύμων τε καὶ ἐξεστηκότων
προσώπων ἤθροισται. ὥσθ᾽ ὑπὸ τοῦ μεγέθους
οὐ ῥᾴδιον αὐτὸν ἐστιν οὔτε λόγοις κατασβέσαι
οὔτε προσάγοντα πολεμίοις μένος ἐμβαλεῖν οὔτε
ἀπάγοντα ἀναθρέψαι τὸ φρόνημα, ἀλλ᾽ ὅσῳ ἂν
μᾶλλον αὐτοῖς θαρρεῖν παρακελεύῃ, τοσούτῳ ἐν
δεινοτέροις ἡγοῦνται εἶναι.

35. Ἐκεῖνο μέντοι νὴ Δί᾽, ἔφη, σκεψώμεθα
ἀκριβῶς ὅπως ἔχει. εἰ μὲν γὰρ τὸ ἀπὸ τοῦδε
αἱ νῖκαι ἔσονται ἐν τοῖς πολεμικοῖς ἔργοις ὁπότεροι ἂν πλείονα ὄχλον ἀπαριθμήσωσιν, ὀρθῶς
καὶ σὺ φοβεῖ περὶ ἡμῶν καὶ ἡμεῖς τῷ ὄντι ἐν
δεινοῖς ἐσμεν· εἰ μέντοι ὥσπερ πρόσθεν διὰ τοὺς
εὖ μαχομένους ἔτι καὶ νῦν αἱ μάχαι κρίνονται,
θαρρῶν οὐδὲν ἂν σφαλείης· πολὺ μὲν γὰρ σὺν

---

[1] ἵνα . . . εἰδῇς xz, Dindorf, Breitenbach ; bracketed by
Schneider, Marchant, Gemoll ; εἶναι καὶ τοῦτο ἤδη ὡς yG[2].
[2] σχημάτων Toup (ad Longinus, p. 480), Gemoll ; χρωμάτων
xz, Dindorf, Breitenbach ; χρημάτων yG.

But if we march upon them at once, we shall find many of them still in tears over those whom we have slain, many still wearing bandages on the wounds they received from us, and all still mindful of the daring of this army of ours and of their own flight and defeat. 33. And let me assure you, Gobryas," he continued, " that your large bodies of men, when they are inspired with confidence, display a spirit that is irresistible ; but when once they are frightened, the greater their numbers are, the greater and more overpowering the panic that seizes them. 34. For it comes over them increased by the many faint-hearted words they hear and magnified by the many wretched figures and the many dejected and distorted coun-tenances they see ; and by reason of the large numbers it is not easy with a speech to quell the panic, nor by a charge against the enemy to inspire them with courage, nor by a retreat to rally their spirits ; but the more you try to encourage them to bravery, in so much the greater peril do they think they are.

35. " Again, by Zeus," said he, "let us consider Cyrus's grounds for confidence precisely how this matter stands : if, in future, victory on the field of battle is to rest with that side which counts the greater numbers, you have good reason to fear for us and we really are in danger. If, however, battles are still to be decided by good fighting as they have been before, it would not be at all amiss for you to be bold and confident ; for,

τοῖς θεοῖς πλείονας εὑρήσεις παρ' ἡμῖν τοὺς
θέλοντας μάχεσθαι ἢ παρ' ἐκείνοις· 36. ὡς δ'
ἔτι μᾶλλον θαρρῇς, καὶ τόδε κατανόησον· οἱ μὲν
γὰρ πολέμιοι πολὺ μὲν ἐλάττονές εἰσι νῦν ἢ πρὶν
ἡττηθῆναι ὑφ' ἡμῶν, πολὺ δ' ἐλάττονες ἢ ὅτε
ἀπέδρασαν ἡμᾶς· ἡμεῖς δὲ καὶ μείζονες νῦν, ἐπεὶ
νενικήκαμεν, καὶ ἰσχυρότεροι, ἐπεὶ ὑμεῖς ἡμῖν
προσεγένεσθε· μὴ γὰρ ἔτι ἀτίμαζε μηδὲ τοὺς
σούς, ἐπεὶ σὺν ἡμῖν εἰσι· σὺν γὰρ τοῖς νικῶσι,
σάφ' ἴσθι, ὦ Γωβρύα, θαρροῦντες καὶ οἱ ἀκό-
λουθοι ἕπονται.

37. Μὴ λανθανέτω δέ σε μηδὲ τοῦτο, ἔφη,
ὅτι ἔξεστι μὲν τοῖς πολεμίοις καὶ νῦν ἰδεῖν ἡμᾶς·
γοργότεροι δέ, σάφ' ἴσθι, οὐδαμῶς ἂν αὐτοῖς
φανείημεν ἢ ἰόντες ἐπ' ἐκείνους. ὡς οὖν ἐμοῦ
ταῦτα γιγνώσκοντος ἄγε ἡμᾶς εὐθὺ [τὴν ἐπὶ] [1]
Βαβυλῶνος.

III

1. Οὕτω μὲν δὴ πορευόμενοι τεταρταῖοι πρὸς
τοῖς ὁρίοις τῆς Γωβρύου χώρας ἐγένοντο. ὡς δὲ
ἐν τῇ πολεμίᾳ ἦν, κατέστησε λαβὼν ἐν τάξει
μεθ' ἑαυτοῦ τούς τε πεζοὺς καὶ τῶν ἱππέων
ὅσους ἐδόκει καλῶς αὐτῷ ἔχειν· τοὺς δ' ἄλλους
ἱππέας ἀφῆκε καταθεῖν, καὶ ἐκέλευσε τοὺς μὲν
ὅπλα ἔχοντας κατακαίνειν, τοὺς δ' ἄλλους καὶ
πρόβατα ὅσα ἂν λάβωσι πρὸς αὐτὸν ἄγειν.
ἐκέλευσε δὲ καὶ τοὺς Πέρσας συγκαταθεῖν· καὶ

---

[1] τὴν ἐπὶ MSS., Dindorf, Breitenbach; bracketed by
Cobet, Marchant; τὴν εὐθὺ [ἐπὶ] Gemoll.

please God, you will find far more men on our side who are eager to fight, than on theirs. 36. And to give yourself still more confidence, bethink you also of this: the enemy are much fewer now than they were before we defeated them, much weaker than when they fled before us; while we are bigger now since we have conquered and stronger since you have been added to us. For you must no longer undervalue your own men, now that they are with us; for be assured, Gobryas, that when they are with the victors, even those who follow the camp go along without a fear.

37. "And do not forget this either, that the enemy may find us even now, if they will. And, let me assure you, we could in no possible way strike more terror into them when they do see us, than by marching upon them. As this, therefore, is my conviction, lead us straight on to Babylon."

III

1. As they thus proceeded, they arrived on the fourth day at the boundaries of Gobryas's domains. And as soon as Cyrus was in the enemy's country, he arranged in regular order under his own command the infantry and as much of the cavalry as seemed to him best. The rest of the cavalry he sent out to forage, with orders to kill those who were under arms but to bring every one else to him, as well as any cattle they might take. The Persians he ordered to join the foraging party. And many of them

The Persians prove to Gobryas their generosity

41

ἧκον πολλοὶ μὲν αὐτῶν κατακεκυλισμένοι ἀπὸ
τῶν ἵππων, πολλοὶ δὲ καὶ λείαν πλείστην
ἄγοντες.

2. Ὡς δὲ παρῆν ἡ λεία, συγκαλέσας τούς τε
τῶν Μήδων ἄρχοντας καὶ τῶν Ὑρκανίων καὶ τοὺς
ὁμοτίμους ἔλεξεν ὧδε· Ἄνδρες φίλοι, ἐξένισεν
ἡμᾶς ἅπαντας πολλοῖς ἀγαθοῖς Γωβρύας. εἰ οὖν,
ἔφη, τοῖς θεοῖς ἐξελόντες [1] τὰ νομιζόμενα καὶ τῇ
στρατιᾷ τὰ ἱκανὰ τὴν ἄλλην τούτῳ δοίημεν λείαν,
ἆρ' ἄν, ἔφη, καλὸν ποιήσαιμεν τῷ εὐθὺς φανεροὶ
εἶναι ὅτι καὶ τοὺς εὖ ποιοῦντας πειρώμεθα νικᾶν
εὖ ποιοῦντες;

3. Ὡς δὲ τοῦτ' ἤκουσαν, πάντες μὲν ἐπῄνουν,
πάντες δ' ἐνεκωμίαζον· εἷς δὲ καὶ ἔλεξεν ὧδε·
Πάνυ, ἔφη, ὦ Κῦρε, τοῦτο ποιήσωμεν· καὶ γάρ
μοι δοκεῖ, ἔφη, ὁ Γωβρύας πτωχούς τινας ἡμᾶς
νομίζειν, ὅτι οὐ δαρεικῶν μεστοὶ ἥκομεν οὐδὲ ἐκ
χρυσῶν πίνομεν φιαλῶν· εἰ δὲ τοῦτο ποιήσομεν,
γνοίη ἄν, ἔφη, ὅτι ἔστιν ἐλευθερίους εἶναι καὶ
ἄνευ χρυσοῦ.

4. Ἄγε δή, ἔφη, τὰ τῶν θεῶν ἀποδόντες τοῖς
μάγοις καὶ ὅσα τῇ στρατιᾷ ἱκανὰ ἐξελόντες τἆλλα
καλέσαντες τὸν Γωβρύαν δότε αὐτῷ.

Οὕτω δὴ λαβόντες ἐκεῖνοι ὅσα ἔδει τἆλλα
ἔδοσαν τῷ Γωβρύᾳ.

5. Ἐκ τούτου δὴ ᾔει πρὸς Βαβυλῶνα παρατα-
ξάμενος ὥσπερ ὅτε ἡ μάχη ἦν. ὡς δ' οὐκ ἀντ-

---

[1] ἐξελόντες Aldine ed., Edd. ; ἀφελόντες MSS.

were thrown from their horses and came back, but many of them also came bringing a great quantity of plunder.

2. When all the booty was brought in, he called the peers and the officers of the Medes and Hyrcanians together and addressed them as follows: "My friends, Gobryas has entertained us all with great munificence. So, if we should set apart the share of the spoil ordained for the gods and a portion sufficient for the army and give the rest to him, should we not be doing the right thing? For we should be giving immediate proof that we are trying to outdo those who do good to us, in the good we do to them."

3. When they heard this they all signified their approval and applauded the proposition; and one of them also spoke as follows: "By all means, Cyrus," said he, "let us do that. And it would be a good stroke of policy, too; for it seems to me that Gobryas regards us as no better than a lot of beggars because we have not come here with our pockets full of darics and because we do not drink from golden goblets. And if we do this, then he would realize that it is possible for men to be gentlemen, even without gold."

4. "Come then," said Cyrus, "turn over to the magi what belongs to the gods, set apart for the army its share, and then call Gobryas in and give the rest to him."

So they set aside what was required and gave the rest to Gobryas.

5. After this Cyrus renewed his march upon Babylon, with his army in the same order as when the battle was fought. But as the Assyrians did The Assyrian refuses battle

ἐξῇσαν οἱ Ἀσσύριοι, ἐκέλευσεν ὁ Κῦρος τὸν
Γωβρύαν προσελάσαντα εἰπεῖν ὅτι εἰ βούλεται
ὁ βασιλεὺς ἐξιὼν ὑπὲρ τῆς χώρας μάχεσθαι, κἂν
αὐτὸς σὺν ἐκείνῳ μάχοιτο· εἰ δὲ μὴ ἀμυνεῖ τῇ
χώρᾳ, ὅτι ἀνάγκη τοῖς κρατοῦσι πείθεσθαι.

6. Ὁ μὲν δὴ Γωβρύας προσελάσας ἔνθα ἀσφαλὲς ἦν ταῦτα εἶπεν, ὁ δ᾽ αὐτῷ ἐξέπεμψεν ἀπο-
κρινούμενον τοιάδε· Δεσπότης ὁ σὸς λέγει, ὦ
Γωβρύα, οὐχ ὅτι ἀπέκτεινά σου τὸν υἱὸν μετα-
μέλει μοι, ἀλλ᾽ ὅτι οὐ καὶ σὲ προσαπέκτεινα.
μάχεσθαι δὲ ἐὰν βούλησθε, ἥκετε εἰς τριακοστὴν
ἡμέραν· νῦν δ᾽ οὔπω ἡμῖν σχολή· ἔτι γὰρ παρα-
σκευαζόμεθα.

7. Ὁ δὲ Γωβρύας εἶπεν, Ἀλλὰ μήποτέ σοι
λήξειεν αὕτη ἡ μεταμέλεια· δῆλον γὰρ ὅτι ἀνιῶ
σέ τι, ἐξ οὗ αὕτη σε ἡ μεταμέλεια ἔχει.

8. Ὁ μὲν δὴ Γωβρύας ἀπήγγειλε τὰ τοῦ
Ἀσσυρίου· ὁ δὲ Κῦρος ἀκούσας ταῦτα ἀπήγαγε
τὸ στράτευμα· καὶ καλέσας τὸν Γωβρύαν, Εἰπέ
μοι, ἔφη, οὐκ ἔλεγες μέντοι σὺ ὅτι τὸν ἐκτμηθέντα
ὑπὸ τοῦ Ἀσσυρίου οἴει ἂν σὺν ἡμῖν γενέσθαι;

Εὖ μὲν οὖν, ἔφη, δοκῶ εἰδέναι· πολλὰ γὰρ δὴ
ἔγωγε κἀκεῖνος ἐπαρρησιασάμεθα πρὸς ἀλλήλους.

9. Ὁπότε τοίνυν σοι δοκεῖ καλῶς ἔχειν, πρόσιθι
πρὸς αὐτόν· καὶ πρῶτον μὲν οὕτω ποίει ὅπως ἂν
αὐτοὶ λάθρα συνῆτε·[1] ἐπειδὰν δὲ συγγένῃ αὐτῷ,
ἐὰν γνῷς αὐτὸν φίλον βουλόμενον εἶναι, τοῦτο δεῖ
μηχανᾶσθαι ὅπως λάθῃ φίλος ὢν ἡμῖν· οὔτε γὰρ

---

[1] ὅπως ἂν αὐτοὶ λάθρα συνῆτε Muretus ; ὅπως ἂν αὐτοὶ ὅτι ἂν
λέγῃ εἰδῆτε yP, Marchant, Gemoll ; ὅπως ἂν οὗτος λέγῃ x ;
ὅπως ἂν αὐτὸς λέγῃ ᾖδη γε z ; ὅπως ἂν λέγῃ αὐτοὶ εἰδῆτε
Pantazides, Dindorf, Breitenbach.

not march out to meet them, Cyrus ordered Gobryas to ride up and say: "If the king wishes to come out and fight for his country, I myself would join him and fight for him too; but if the king will not protect his country, then I must needs submit to the victors."

6. Accordingly, Gobryas rode to a place where he could safely give his message; and the king sent out a messenger to deliver to Gobryas this reply: "This is your sovereign's response to you, Gobryas: 'I do not regret that I killed your son, but only that I did not kill you, too. And if you and your men wish to fight, come back a month from now. Just at present we have no time to fight, for we are still busy with our preparations.'"

7. "I only hope that this regret of yours may never cease," Gobryas replied; "for it is evident that I have been something of a thorn in your flesh, ever since you began to feel it."

8. Gobryas returned with the Assyrian king's reply, and when Cyrus heard it he drew off his army; then summoning Gobryas he said to him: "Tell me, you were saying, were you not, that you thought that the prince who was castrated by the Assyrian would be on our side?"

"Why, of course;" he replied, "I feel perfectly sure of it; for he and I have often talked together freely."

9. "Well then, when you think best, go to him; but first of all be sure that you meet him alone and in secret; and when you have conferred with him, if you see that he wishes to be our friend, you must manage to keep his friendship a secret. For in time

Cyrus plans to gain the secret support of Gadatas

45

ἂν φίλους τις ποιήσειεν ἄλλως πως πλείω ἀγαθὰ
ἐν πολέμῳ ἢ πολέμιος δοκῶν εἶναι οὔτ' ἂν ἐχθροὺς πλείω τις βλάψειεν ἄλλως πως ἢ φίλος
δοκῶν εἶναι.

10. Καὶ μήν, ἔφη ὁ Γωβρύας, οἶδ' ὅτι κἂν
πρίαιτο Γαδάτας τὸ μέγα τι ποιῆσαι κακὸν τὸν
νῦν βασιλέα Ἀσσυρίων. ἀλλ' ὅ τι ἂν δύναιτο,
τοῦτο δεῖ καὶ ἡμᾶς σκοπεῖν.

11. Λέγε δή μοι, ἔφη ὁ Κῦρος, εἰς τὸ φρούριον
τὸ πρὸ τῆς χώρας, ὅ φατε Ὑρκανίοις τε καὶ
Σάκαις ἐπιτετειχίσθαι τῇδε τῇ χώρᾳ πρόβολον
εἶναι τοῦ πολέμου, ἆρ' ἄν, ἔφη, οἴει ὑπὸ τοῦ
φρουράρχου παρεθῆναι τὸν εὐνοῦχον ἐλθόντα σὺν
δυνάμει;

Σαφῶς γ', ἔφη ὁ Γωβρύας, εἴπερ ἀνύποπτος
ὤν, ὥσπερ νῦν ἐστιν, ἀφίκοιτο πρὸς αὐτόν.

12. Οὐκοῦν, ἔφη, ἀνύποπτος ἂν εἴη, εἰ προσ-
βάλοιμι μὲν ἐγὼ πρὸς τὰ χωρία αὐτοῦ ὡς λαβεῖν
βουλόμενος, ἀπομάχοιτο δὲ ἐκεῖνος ἀνὰ κράτος·
καὶ λάβοιμι μὲν αὐτοῦ τι ἐγώ, ἀντιλάβοι δὲ
κἀκεῖνος ἡμῶν ἢ ἄλλους τινὰς ἢ καὶ ἀγγέλους
πεμπομένους ὑπ' ἐμοῦ πρὸς τούτους οὕς φατε
πολεμίους τῷ Ἀσσυρίῳ εἶναι· καὶ οἱ μὲν ληφθέντες λέγοιεν ὅτι ἐπὶ στράτευμα ἀπέρχονται καὶ
κλίμακας ὡς ἐπὶ τὸ φρούριον ἄξοντες, ὁ δ' εὐνοῦχος ἀκούσας προσποιήσαιτο προαγγεῖλαι βουλόμενος ταῦτα παρεῖναι.

13. Καὶ ὁ Γωβρύας εἶπεν ὅτι οὕτω μὲν γιγνο-

of war one could not in any way do more good to
one's friends than by seeming to be their enemy,
nor more harm to enemies than by seeming to be
their friend."

10. " Now mark my word," said Gobryas; " I am
sure that Gadatas would even pay for the opportunity
of doing the present Assyrian king some serious
harm. But what harm he could do it is for us on our
part to consider."

11. " Now tell me this," said Cyrus, " in regard
to the fort which stands upon the frontier of the
country and which you say was built to serve as a
base of operations against the Hyrcanians and the
Sacians and an outwork to protect this country in
time of war—do you think that the eunuch, if he
went there with his army, would be admitted by the
commandant ? "

" Yes ; certainly he would," said Gobryas, " if he
came to him as unsuspected as he now is."

12. " Then," answered Cyrus, " if I should make
an attack on his fortifications as if I wished to gain
possession of them, while he defended himself with
all his might ; and if I should take something of his
and he in turn should capture either some of our
other men or some of the messengers I send to
those who, you say, are enemies of the Assyrian
king ; and if these captives should say that they
had come out to get an army and ladders to use
against the fortress ; and if then the eunuch, on
hearing this, should pretend that he had come to
give warning ; under these conditions, he would be
unsuspected."

13. " Under such circumstances," answered
Gobryas, " the commandant would certainly admit

XENOPHON

μένων σαφῶς παρείη ἂν αὐτόν, καὶ δέοιτό γ᾽ ἂν αὐτοῦ μένειν ἕως ἀπέλθοις.

Οὐκοῦν, ἔφη ὁ Κῦρος, εἴ γε ἅπαξ εἰσέλθοι, δύναιτ᾽ ἂν ἡμῖν ὑποχείριον ποιῆσαι τὸ χωρίον;

14. Εἰκὸς γοῦν, ἔφη ὁ Γωβρύας, τὰ μὲν ἔνδον ἐκείνου συμπαρασκευάζοντος, τὰ δ᾽ ἔξωθεν σοῦ ἰσχυρότερα προσάγοντος.

Ἴθι οὖν, ἔφη, καὶ πειρῶ ταῦτα διδάξας καὶ διαπραξάμενος παρεῖναι· πιστὰ δὲ αὐτῷ οὐκ ἂν μείζω οὔτ᾽ εἴποις οὔτε δείξαις ὧν αὐτὸς σὺ τυγχάνεις παρ᾽ ἡμῶν εἰληφώς.

15. Ἐκ τούτου ᾤχετο μὲν ὁ Γωβρύας· ἄσμενος δὲ ἰδὼν αὐτὸν ὁ εὐνοῦχος συνωμολόγει τε πάντα καὶ συνέθετο ἃ ἔδει.

Ἐπεὶ δὲ ἀπήγγειλεν ὁ Γωβρύας ὅτι πάντα δοκοίη ἰσχυρῶς τῷ εὐνούχῳ τὰ ἐπισταλέντα, ἐκ τούτου τῇ ὑστεραίᾳ προσέβαλε μὲν ὁ Κῦρος, ἀπεμάχετο δὲ ὁ Γαδάτας. ἦν δὲ καὶ ὃ ἔλαβε χωρίον ὁ Κῦρος, ὁποῖον ἔφη ὁ Γαδάτας. 16. τῶν δὲ ἀγγέλων οὓς ἔπεμψεν ὁ Κῦρος προειπὼν ᾗ πορεύσοιντο, τοὺς μὲν εἴασεν ὁ Γαδάτας διαφεύγειν, ὅπως ἄγοιεν τὰ στρατεύματα καὶ τὰς κλίμακας κομίζοιεν· οὓς δ᾽ ἔλαβε, βασανίζων ἐναντίον πολλῶν, ὡς ἤκουσεν ἐφ᾽ ἃ ἔφασαν πορεύεσθαι, εὐθέως συσκευασάμενος ὡς ἐξαγγελῶν τῆς νυκτὸς ἐπορεύετο. 17. τέλος δὲ πιστευθεὶς ὡς βοηθὸς εἰσέρχεται εἰς τὸ φρούριον· καὶ τέως μὲν συμπαρεσκεύαζεν ὅ τι δύναιτο τῷ φρουράρχῳ· ἐπεὶ

48

him—aye, and would beg him to remain there until you went away."

"Well then," said Cyrus, "if he could but once get in, he would be in a position to put the fort in our hands?"

14. "That is at all events probable," answered Gobryas, "if he were within, helping with the preparations, while you on the outside made a vigorous attack."

"In that case," Cyrus replied, "go and try to explain these plans to him and win his coöperation and then return. And no better assurance of our good faith could you give him in word or deed than to show him what you happen to have received at our hands."

15. Thereupon Gobryas went away; and when the eunuch saw him, he gladly concurred in all the plans and settled with him the things they were to do.

So, when Gobryas reported back that all the proposals were heartily accepted by the eunuch, on the day following Cyrus made his attack and Gadatas his defence. And there was also a fort which Cyrus took, as Gadatas had indicated; 16. while of the messengers whom Cyrus sent with instructions which way to go, some Gadatas allowed to escape to bring the troops and fetch the ladders; but some he took and straitly examined in the presence of many witnesses, and when he heard from them the purpose of their journey, he made ready at once and set out in the night as if to give the alarm. 17. And the end was that he was trusted and entered the fort as an ally to defend it; and for a while he helped the commandant to the extent of his ability in making preparations; but when Cyrus came, he

Gadatas plays into Cyrus's hands

δὲ ὁ Κῦρος ἦλθε, καταλαμβάνει τὸ χωρίον συν-
εργοὺς ποιησάμενος καὶ τοὺς παρὰ τοῦ Κύρου
αἰχμαλώτους.

18. Ἐπεὶ δὲ τοῦτο ἐγένετο, εὐθὺς [Γαδάτας][1]
ὁ εὐνοῦχος τὰ ἔνδον καταστήσας ἐξῆλθε πρὸς
τὸν Κῦρον, καὶ τῷ νόμῳ προσκυνήσας εἶπε, Χαῖρε,
Κῦρε.

19. Ἀλλὰ ποιῶ ταῦτ᾽, ἔφη· σὺ γάρ με σὺν τοῖς
θεοῖς οὐ κελεύεις μόνον ἀλλὰ καὶ ἀναγκάζεις
χαίρειν. εὖ γὰρ ἴσθι, ἔφη, ὅτι ἐγὼ μέγα ποιοῦμαι
φίλιον τοῦτο τὸ χωρίον τοῖς ἐνθάδε συμμάχοις
καταλείπων· σοῦ δ᾽, ἔφη, ὦ Γαδάτα, ὁ Ἀσσύριος
παῖδας μέν, ὡς ἔοικε, τὸ ποιεῖσθαι ἀφείλετο, οὐ
μέντοι τό γε φίλους δύνασθαι κτᾶσθαι ἀπεστέ-
ρησεν· ἀλλ᾽ εὖ ἴσθι ὅτι ἡμᾶς τῷ ἔργῳ τούτῳ
φίλους πεποίησαι, οἵ σοι, ἐὰν δυνώμεθα, πειρασόμεθα μὴ χείρονες βοηθοὶ παραστῆναι ἢ εἰ παῖδας
ἐκγόνους ἐκέκτησο.

20. Ὁ μὲν ταῦτ᾽ ἔλεγεν. ἐν δὲ τούτῳ ὁ
Ὑρκάνιος ἄρτι ᾐσθημένος τὸ γεγενημένον προσθεὶ
τῷ Κύρῳ καὶ λαβὼν τὴν δεξιὰν αὐτοῦ εἶπεν,
Ὦ μέγα ἀγαθὸν σὺ τοῖς φίλοις Κῦρε, ὡς πολλήν
με τοῖς θεοῖς ποιεῖς χάριν ὀφείλειν ὅτι σοί με
συνήγαγον.

21. Ἴθι νῦν, ἔφη ὁ Κῦρος, καὶ λαβὼν τὸ χωρίον
οὗπερ ἕνεκά με ἀσπάζει διατίθει αὐτὸ οὕτως
ὡς ἂν τῷ ὑμετέρῳ φύλῳ πλείστου ἄξιον ᾖ καὶ
τοῖς ἄλλοις συμμάχοις, μάλιστα δ᾽, ἔφη, Γαδάτᾳ
τουτῳί,[2] ὃς ἡμῖν αὐτὸ λαβὼν παραδίδωσι.

---

[1] Γαδάτας MSS. ; bracketed by Zeune, Edd.
[2] τουτῳί Hirschig, Marchant, Gemoll ; τούτῳ MSS., Dindorf, Breitenbach.

made himself master of the place, employing also as his assistants in seizing it those men of Cyrus's whom he had taken prisoners.

Cyrus gains the desired stronghold

18. When this was accomplished, the eunuch, after setting things in order within the fort, came out and did him obeisance according to the custom and said: "Joy be with you, Cyrus!"

19. "So it is," said he; "for by the favour of the gods you not only bid me joy but even compel me to be joyful. For believe me, I consider it a great advantage to leave this place friendly to my allies in this country. From you, Gadatas," Cyrus went on, "the Assyrian has, it seems, taken away the power of begetting children, but at any rate he has not deprived you of the ability of acquiring friends. Let me assure you that by this deed you have made of us friends who will try, if we can, to stand by you and aid you no less efficiently than if we were your own children."

20. Thus he spoke; and at this juncture the Hyrcanian king, who had just heard what had happened, ran up to Cyrus and taking his right hand said to him: "O what a blessing you are to your friends, Cyrus, and what a debt of gratitude to the gods you lay upon me, because they have brought me into association with you!"

21. "Go then," said Cyrus, "take this fortress on account of which you congratulate me and so dispose of it that it may be of the most service to your people and to the rest of the allies, and especially," he added, "to Gadatas here, who gained possession of it and delivered it to us."

A base of operations established in the north-east

51

XENOPHON

22. Τί οὖν; ἔφη ὁ Ὑρκάνιος, ἐπειδὰν Καδούσιοι ἔλθωσι καὶ Σάκαι καὶ οἱ ἐμοὶ πολῖται, καλέσωμεν καὶ τούτων,[1] ἵνα κοινῇ βουλευσώμεθα πάντες ὅσοις προσήκει πῶς ἂν συμφορώτατα χρώμεθα τῷ φρουρίῳ;

23. Ταῦτα μὲν οὕτω συνήνεσεν ὁ Κῦρος· ἐπεὶ δὲ συνῆλθον οἷς ἔμελε περὶ τοῦ φρουρίου, ἐβουλεύσαντο κοινῇ φυλάττειν οἷσπερ ἀγαθὸν ἦν φίλιον ὄν, ὅπως αὐτοῖς μὲν πρόβολος εἴη πολέμου, τοῖς δ' Ἀσσυρίοις ἐπιτετειχισμένον.

24. Τούτων γενομένων πολὺ δὴ προθυμότερον καὶ πλείους καὶ Καδούσιοι συνεστρατεύοντο καὶ Σάκαι καὶ Ὑρκάνιοι· καὶ συνελέγη ἐντεῦθεν στράτευμα Καδουσίων μὲν πελτασταὶ εἰς δισμυρίους καὶ ἱππεῖς εἰς τετρακισχιλίους, Σακῶν δὲ τοξόται εἰς μυρίους καὶ ἱπποτοξόται εἰς δισχιλίους· καὶ Ὑρκάνιοι δὲ πεζούς τε ὁπόσους ἐδύναντο προσεξέπεμψαν καὶ ἱππέας ἐξεπλήρωσαν εἰς δισχιλίους· τὸ γὰρ πρόσθεν καταλελειμμένοι ἦσαν πλείους οἴκοι αὐτοῖς ἱππεῖς, ὅτι καὶ οἱ Καδούσιοι καὶ οἱ Σάκαι τοῖς Ἀσσυρίοις πολέμιοι ἦσαν.

25. Ὅσον δὲ χρόνον ἐκαθέζετο ὁ Κῦρος ἀμφὶ τὴν περὶ τὸ φρούριον οἰκονομίαν, τῶν Ἀσσυρίων τῶν κατὰ ταῦτα τὰ χωρία πολλοὶ μὲν ἀπῆγον ἵππους, πολλοὶ δὲ ἀπέφερον ὅπλα, φοβούμενοι ἤδη πάντας τοὺς προσχώρους.

26. Ἐκ δὲ τούτου προσέρχεται τῷ Κύρῳ ὁ Γαδάτας καὶ λέγει ὅτι ἥκουσιν αὐτῷ ἄγγελοι ὡς ὁ Ἀσσύριος, ἐπεὶ πύθοιτο τὰ περὶ τοῦ φρουρίου,

---

[1] τούτων Pantazides, most Edd.; τοῦτον MSS., Dindorf (i.e. the Hyrcanian).

22. "What then?" said the Hyrcanian. "When the Cadusians come and the Sacians and my people, are we to call in some of them also, that all of us who are concerned may consult together how we may use the fortress to the best advantage?"

23. To this plan Cyrus gave assent. And when all those who were interested in the fort were gathered together, they decided that it should be occupied in common by those to whose advantage it was to have it in the hands of friends, so that it might be an outwork for them in time of war and a base of operations against the Assyrians.

24. Because of this incident the Cadusians, Sacians, and Hyrcanians joined the expedition in greater numbers and with greatly increased zeal. And thereafter a new division was added to the army, consisting of Cadusians, about twenty thousand targeteers and about four thousand horsemen; of Sacians, about ten thousand bowmen and about two thousand mounted archers; while the Hyrcanians also sent as many more foot-soldiers as they could and filled up the ranks of their cavalry to the number of two thousand; for up to this time most of their cavalry had been left at home, because the Cadusians and the Sacians were enemies of the Assyrians.

25. Now during the time that Cyrus was busy with the arrangements about the fortress, many of the Assyrians of the country round about surrendered their horses and many laid down their arms, because now they were afraid of all their neighbours.

26. And after this, Gadatas came to Cyrus and said that messengers had come to him with the information that when the Assyrian king heard the *The king threatens to invade Gadatas's country*

53

χαλεπῶς τε ἐνέγκοι καὶ συσκευάζοιτο ὡς ἐμβα-
λῶν εἰς τὴν ἑαυτοῦ χώραν. ἐὰν οὖν ἀφῇς με, ὦ
Κῦρε, τὰ τείχη ἂν πειραθείην διασῶσαι, τῶν δ᾽
ἄλλων μείων λόγος.

27. Καὶ ὁ Κῦρος εἶπεν, Ἐὰν οὖν ἴῃς νῦν, πότε
ἔσει οἴκοι;

Καὶ ὁ Γαδάτας εἶπεν, Εἰς τρίτην δειπνήσω ἐν
τῇ ἡμετέρᾳ.

Ἦ καὶ τὸν Ἀσσύριον, ἔφη, οἴει ἐκεῖ ἤδη κατα-
λήψεσθαι;

Εὖ μὲν οὖν, ἔφη, οἶδα· σπεύσει γὰρ ἕως ἔτι
πρόσω δοκεῖς ἀπεῖναι.

28. Ἐγὼ δ᾽, ἔφη ὁ Κῦρος, ποσταῖος ἂν τῷ
στρατεύματι ἐκεῖσε ἀφικοίμην;

Πρὸς τοῦτο δὴ ὁ Γαδάτας λέγει, Πολὺ ἤδη, ὦ
δέσποτα, ἔχεις τὸ στράτευμα καὶ οὐκ ἂν δύναιο
μεῖον ἢ ἐν ἓξ ἢ ἑπτὰ ἡμέραις ἐλθεῖν πρὸς τὴν
ἐμὴν οἴκησιν.

Σὺ μὲν τοίνυν, ἔφη ὁ Κῦρος, ἄπιθι ὡς τάχιστα·
ἐγὼ δ᾽ ὡς ἂν δυνατὸν ᾖ πορεύσομαι.

29. Ὁ μὲν δὴ Γαδάτας ᾤχετο· ὁ δὲ Κῦρος συνεκάλεσε πάντας τοὺς ἄρχοντας τῶν συμμάχων·
καὶ ἤδη πολλοί τε ἐδόκουν καὶ καλοὶ κἀγαθοὶ
παρεῖναι· ἐν οἷς δὴ λέγει ὁ Κῦρος ταῦτα·

30. Ἄνδρες σύμμαχοι, Γαδάτας διέπραξεν ἃ
δοκεῖ πᾶσιν ἡμῖν πολλοῦ ἄξια εἶναι, καὶ ταῦτα
πρὶν καὶ ὁτιοῦν ἀγαθὸν ὑφ᾽ ἡμῶν παθεῖν. νῦν
δὲ ὁ Ἀσσύριος εἰς τὴν χώραν αὐτοῦ ἐμβαλεῖν
ἀγγέλλεται, δῆλον ὅτι ἅμα μὲν τιμωρεῖσθαι αὐτὸν
βουλόμενος, ὅτι δοκεῖ ὑπ᾽ αὐτοῦ μεγάλα βεβλά-
φθαι· ἅμα δὲ ἴσως κἀκεῖνο ἐννοεῖται ὡς εἰ οἱ μὲν
πρὸς ἡμᾶς ἀφιστάμενοι μηδὲν ὑπ᾽ ἐκείνου κακὸν

facts about the fortress, he was exceedingly wroth
and was preparing to invade his country. "If, then,
you will permit me to go, Cyrus, I should try to save
the fortified places ; the rest is of less account."

27. "If you start now," said Cyrus, "when shall
you reach home ?"

"The day after to-morrow," answered Gadatas, "I
shall dine in my own land."

"But you do not think, do you, that you will find
the Assyrian already there ?" said Cyrus.

"Nay, I am sure of it," he replied; "for he will
make haste while he thinks you are still far away."

28. "How many days," asked Cyrus, "do you
think it would take me with my army to get there ?"

"Sire," Gadatas made reply, "your army now is
large and you could not reach my residence in less
than six or seven days."

"Well," said Cyrus, "do you go as quickly as
possible, and I will follow as best I can."

29. So Gadatas went away, and Cyrus summoned
all the officers of the allies, and there seemed to be
there now many noble men and brave. In this
assembly, then, Cyrus spoke as follows :

30. "Friends and allies, Gadatas has done what
seems a very valuable service to us all, and that, too,
before receiving any favour whatsoever at our hands.
And now comes the report that the Assyrian is going
to invade his country, partly, as it seems plain, from
a wish to punish him because he thinks Gadatas has
done him a great wrong; and perhaps also he under-
stands that if those who desert him for us do not

Cyrus pro-
poses that
the whole
army go to
the relief of
Gadatas

πείσονται, οἱ δὲ σὺν ἐκείνῳ ὄντες ὑφ᾽ ἡμῶν ἀπο-
λοῦνται, ὅτι τάχιστα οὐδένα εἰκὸς σὺν αὐτῷ
βουλήσεσθαι εἶναι. 31. νῦν οὖν, ὦ ἄνδρες, καλόν
τι ἄν μοι δοκοῦμεν ποιῆσαι, εἰ προθύμως Γαδάτᾳ
βοηθήσαιμεν ἀνδρὶ εὐεργέτῃ· καὶ ἅμα δίκαια
ποιοῖμεν ἂν χάριν ἀποδιδόντες· ἀλλὰ μὴν καὶ
σύμφορά γ᾽ ἄν, ὡς ἐμοὶ δοκεῖ, πράξαιμεν ἡμῖν
αὐτοῖς. 32. εἰ γὰρ πᾶσι φαινοίμεθα τοὺς μὲν
κακῶς ποιοῦντας νικᾶν πειρώμενοι κακῶς ποιοῦντες, τοὺς δ᾽ εὐεργετοῦντας ἀγαθοῖς ὑπερβαλ-
λόμενοι, εἰκὸς ἐκ τῶν τοιούτων φίλους μὲν
πολλοὺς ἡμῖν βούλεσθαι γίγνεσθαι, ἐχθρὸν δὲ
μηδένα ἐπιθυμεῖν εἶναι.

33. Εἰ δὲ ἀμελῆσαι δόξαιμεν Γαδάτου, πρὸς
τῶν θεῶν ποίοις λόγοις ἂν ἄλλον πείθοιμεν χα-
ρίζεσθαί τι ἡμῖν; πῶς δ᾽ ἂν τολμῷμεν ἡμᾶς αὐτοὺς
ἐπαινεῖν; πῶς δ᾽ ἂν ἀντιβλέψαι τις ἡμῶν δύναιτο
Γαδάτᾳ, εἰ ἡττώμεθ᾽ αὐτοῦ εὖ ποιοῦντος τοσοῦτοι
ὄντες ἑνὸς ἀνδρὸς καὶ τούτου οὕτω διακειμένου;

34. Ὁ μὲν οὕτως εἶπεν· οἱ δὲ πάντες ἰσχυρῶς
συνεπῄνουν ταῦτα ποιεῖν.

Ἄγε τοίνυν, ἔφη, ἐπεὶ καὶ ὑμῖν συνδοκεῖ ταῦτα,
ἐπὶ μὲν τοῖς ὑποζυγίοις καὶ ὀχήμασι καταλίπω-
μεν ἕκαστοι τοὺς μετ᾽ αὐτῶν ἐπιτηδειοτάτους
πορεύεσθαι. Γωβρύας δ᾽ ἡμῖν ἀρχέτω αὐτῶν καὶ
ἡγείσθω αὐτοῖς· 35. καὶ γὰρ ὁδῶν ἔμπειρος καὶ
τἆλλα ἱκανός· ἡμεῖς δ᾽, ἔφη, καὶ ἵπποις τοῖς
δυνατωτάτοις καὶ ἀνδράσι πορευώμεθα, τἀπιτή-

suffer any harm at his hands, while those who follow
him are destroyed by us, the chances are that very
soon no one will be willing to stay with him. 31. So
now, my men, it seems to me that we should be
doing what is fair, if we gave Gadatas, our benefactor,
our heartiest assistance; and at the same time we
should be doing only what is right in paying a debt
of gratitude. But apart from that, it seems to me
that we should be gaining an advantage for ourselves.
32. For if we should show every one that we try to
surpass in doing harm those who do us harm, and
that we surpass in well-doing those who do well by
us, the consequences of such conduct would be that
many would wish to become our friends and not one
would desire to be our enemy.

The whole
army goes
to help
Gadatas

33. " But should we decide to abandon Gadatas,
with what arguments under heaven could we ever
persuade any one else to do us a favour? How
could we have the effrontery to approve our own
conduct? And how could any one of us look
Gadatas in the face, if, as numerous as we are, we
should be surpassed in well-doing by one man and
that one a man in such a plight as Gadatas is ? "

34. Thus he spoke, and all heartily agreed to do
as he said.

The army
accepts the
proposal

" Come then," he continued, " since you agree
with these suggestions, and first, let us leave men
in charge of the beasts of burden and the wagons,
each division appointing such of their number as are
best suited to go with them; and let Gobryas have
command of them in our place and be their guide;
35. for he is acquainted with the roads and in other
ways is qualified for that task. As for us, let us
proceed with the most able-bodied men and horses,

The order
of march

δεια τριῶν ἡμερῶν λαβόντες· ὅσῳ δ' ἂν κουφότε-
ρον συσκευασώμεθα καὶ εὐτελέστερον, τοσούτῳ
ἥδιον τὰς ἐπιούσας ἡμέρας ἀριστήσομέν τε καὶ
δειπνήσομεν καὶ καθευδήσομεν. 36. νῦν δ', ἔφη,
πορευώμεθα ὧδε· πρώτους μὲν ἄγε σύ, Χρυσάντα,
τοὺς θωρακοφόρους, ἐπεὶ ὁμαλή τε καὶ πλατεῖα ἡ
ὁδός ἐστι, τοὺς ταξιάρχους ἔχων ἐν μετώπῳ πάν-
τας· ἡ δὲ τάξις ἑκάστη ἐφ' ἑνὸς ἴτω· ἀθρόοι γὰρ
ὄντες καὶ τάχιστα καὶ ἀσφαλέστατα πορευοίμεθ'
ἄν. 37. τούτου δ' ἕνεκα, ἔφη, κελεύω τοὺς
θωρακοφόρους ἡγεῖσθαι ὅτι τοῦτο βραδύτατον[1]
ἐστι τοῦ στρατεύματος· τοῦ δὲ βραδύτατου[1]
ἡγουμένου ἀνάγκη ῥᾳδίως ἕπεσθαι πάντα τὰ θᾶττον ἰόντα· ὅταν δὲ τὸ τάχιστον ἡγῆται ἐν νυκτί,
οὐδέν ἐστι θαυμαστὸν καὶ διασπᾶσθαι τὰ στρα-
τεύματα· τὸ γὰρ προταχθὲν ἀποδιδράσκει.

38. Ἐπὶ δὲ τούτοις, ἔφη, Ἀρτάβαζος τοὺς
Περσῶν πελταστὰς καὶ τοξότας ἀγέτω· ἐπὶ δὲ
τούτοις Ἀνδαμύας ὁ Μῆδος τὸ Μήδων πεζόν·[2] ἐπὶ
δὲ τούτοις Ἔμβας τὸ Ἀρμενίων πεζόν·[2] ἐπὶ δὲ
τούτοις Ἀρτούχας Ὑρκανίους· ἐπὶ δὲ τούτοις
Θαμβράδας τὸ Σακῶν πεζόν·[2] ἐπὶ δὲ τούτοις
Δατάμας Καδουσίους. 39. ἀγόντων δὲ καὶ οὗτοι
πάντες ἐν μετώπῳ μὲν τοὺς ταξιάρχους ἔχοντες,
δεξιοὺς δὲ τοὺς πελταστάς, ἀριστεροὺς δὲ τοὺς
τοξότας τοῦ ἑαυτῶν πλαισίου· οὕτω γὰρ πορευόμενοι καὶ εὐχρηστότεροι γίγνονται. 40. ἐπὶ δὲ
τούτοις οἱ σκευοφόροι, ἔφη, πάντων ἐπέσθων· οἱ
δὲ ἄρχοντες αὐτῶν ἐπιμελέσθων ὅπως συνεσκευα-

----

[1] βραδύτατον (and βραδυτάτου) Cobet, Hirschig, Marchant,
Gemoll ; βαρύτατον (and βαρυτάτου) MSS., Dindorf, Breitenbach.   [2] πεζόν Dindorf, Edd. ; πεζικόν MSS.

taking with us three days' provisions. For the more lightly and simply equipped we go, the more we shall enjoy our luncheon and dinner and sleep in the days to follow. 36. And now let us march in the following order: Chrysantas, do you lead in the van the men armed with breastplates, for the road is smooth and wide. Have all your captains in front, each company following in single file; for, massed together, we can march with the greatest speed and the greatest safety. 37. And the reason why I direct the men armed with breastplates to lead the march is that they are the slowest portion of the army; and when the slowest lead, then all the more quickly moving troops can follow easily, as a matter of course. But when at night the light forces lead, it is not at all a strange thing for the line to be broken and a gap formed, for the vanguard outstrips the rear.

38. " Next let Artabazus follow at the head of the Persian targeteers and bowmen; following him, Andamyas, the Mede, in command of the Median infantry; next, Embas with the Armenian infantry; then, Artuchas with the Hyrcanians; he will be followed by Thambradas at the head of the Sacian infantry force and Datamas with that of the Cadusians. 39. Let these all lead the way with their captains in front, the targeteers on the right and the archers on the left of their own squares; for, marching thus, they are more easily handled. 40. Next to these the camp-followers of all the army are to follow; their officers should see to it that they have everything ready packed up before they sleep,

XENOPHON

σμένοι τε ὦσι πάντα πρὶν καθεύδειν καὶ πρῲ σὺν
τοῖς σκεύεσι παρῶσιν εἰς τὴν τεταγμένην χώραν
καὶ ὅπως κοσμίως ἕπωνται.

41. Ἐπὶ δὲ τοῖς σκευοφόροις, ἔφη, τοὺς Πέρσας
ἱππέας Μαδάτας ὁ Πέρσης ἀγέτω, ἔχων καὶ
οὗτος τοὺς ἑκατοντάρχους τῶν ἱππέων ἐν μετώπῳ·
ὁ δ' ἑκατόνταρχος τὴν τάξιν ἀγέτω εἰς ἕνα, ὥσπερ
οἱ πέζαρχοι. 42. ἐπὶ τούτοις Ῥαμβάκας ὁ Μῆδος
ὡσαύτως τοὺς ἑαυτοῦ ἱππέας· ἐπὶ τούτοις σύ, ὦ
Τιγράνη, τὸ σεαυτοῦ ἱππικόν· καὶ οἱ ἄλλοι δὲ ἵπ-
παρχοι μεθ' ὧν ἕκαστοι ἀφίκοντο πρὸς ἡμᾶς. ἐπὶ
τούτοις Σάκαι ἄγετε· ἔσχατοι δέ, ὥσπερ ἦλθον,
Καδούσιοι ἰόντων· Ἀλκεύνα, σὺ δὲ ὁ ἄγων
αὐτοὺς ἐπιμέλου τὸ νῦν εἶναι πάντων τῶν ὄπισθεν
καὶ μηδένα ἔα ὕστερον τῶν σῶν ἱππέων γίγνεσθαι.

43. Ἐπιμέλεσθε δὲ τοῦ σιωπῇ πορεύεσθαι οἵ
τε ἄρχοντες καὶ πάντες δὲ οἱ σωφρονοῦντες· διὰ
γὰρ τῶν ὤτων ἐν τῇ νυκτὶ ἀνάγκη μᾶλλον ἢ διὰ
τῶν ὀφθαλμῶν ἕκαστα καὶ αἰσθάνεσθαι καὶ πράτ-
τεσθαι· καὶ τὸ ταραχθῆναι δὲ ἐν τῇ νυκτὶ πολὺ
μεῖζόν ἐστι πρᾶγμα ἢ ἐν τῇ ἡμέρᾳ καὶ δυσκατα-
στατώτερον· 44. οὗ ἕνεκα ἥ τε σιωπὴ ἀσκητέα
καὶ ἡ τάξις φυλακτέα.

Τὰς δὲ νυκτερινὰς φυλακάς, ὅταν μέλλητε
νυκτὸς ἀναστήσεσθαι, χρὴ ὡς βραχυτάτας καὶ
πλείστας ποιεῖσθαι, ὡς μηδένα ἡ ἐν τῇ φυλακῇ
ἀγρυπνία πολλὴ οὖσα λυμαίνηται ἐν τῇ πορείᾳ·
ἡνίκα δ' ἂν ὥρα ᾖ πορεύεσθαι, σημαίνειν τῷ
κέρατι. 45. ὑμεῖς δ' ἔχοντες ἃ δεῖ ἕκαστοι πάρ-

and early in the morning let them be present with the baggage at the appointed place, ready to follow the march in proper order.

41. " After the camp-followers let Madatas, the Persian, bring up the Persian cavalry ; let him also arrange the cavalry captains in front, and let each captain lead his company in single file, just like the infantry officers. 42. After them will come Rhambacas, the Mede, with his cavalry in the same order ; after them you, Tigranes, with yours, and the rest of the cavalry officers, each with the forces with which he joined us. After them you Sacians are to fall in line ; and last of all, just as they came, the Cadusians will bring up the rear ; and you, Alceunas, who are their commander, for the present look out for all in the rear and do not allow any one to fall behind your horsemen.

43. " Take care to march in silence, both officers and all who are wise ; for in the night there is more need to use ears than eyes to secure information and to have things done. And to be thrown into confusion in the night is a much more serious matter than in the daytime and one more difficult to remedy. 44. Therefore let silence be maintained, and let the prescribed order be preserved.

" And the night watches, whenever you are to start off before daylight, must be made as short and as numerous as possible, so that want of sleep on account of doing sentinel duty may not be serious and exhaust the men for the march. And when the hour for starting comes, let the signal be given on the horn. 45. And then do you all, with whatever

εστε εἰς τὴν ἐπὶ Βαβυλῶνος ὁδόν· ὁ δ' ὁρμώ-
μενος ἀεὶ τῷ κατ' οὐρὰν παρεγγυάτω ἕπεσθαι.

46. Ἐκ τούτου δὴ ᾤχοντο ἐπὶ τὰς σκηνὰς καὶ
ἅμα ἀπιόντες διελέγοντο πρὸς ἀλλήλους ὡς μνη-
μονικῶς ὁ Κῦρος ὁπόσοις συνέταττε πᾶσιν[1]
ὀνομάζων ἐνετέλλετο. 47. ὁ δὲ Κῦρος ἐπιμελείᾳ
τοῦτο ἐποίει· πάνυ γὰρ αὐτῷ ἐδόκει θαυμαστὸν
εἶναι εἰ οἱ μὲν βάναυσοι ἴσασι τῆς ἑαυτοῦ τέχνης
ἕκαστος τῶν ἐργαλείων τὰ ὀνόματα, καὶ ὁ ἰατρὸς
δὲ οἶδε καὶ τῶν ὀργάνων καὶ τῶν φαρμάκων οἷς
χρῆται πάντων τὰ ὀνόματα, ὁ δὲ στρατηγὸς οὕτως
ἠλίθιος ἔσοιτο ὥστε οὐκ εἴσοιτο τῶν ὑφ' ἑαυτῷ
ἡγεμόνων τὰ ὀνόματα, οἷς ἀνάγκη ἐστὶν αὐτῷ
ὀργάνοις χρῆσθαι καὶ ὅταν καταλαβεῖν τι βούληται καὶ ὅταν φυλάξαι καὶ ὅταν θαρρῦναι καὶ
ὅταν φοβῆσαι· καὶ τιμῆσαι δὲ ὁπότε τινὰ βούλοιτο, πρέπον αὐτῷ ἐδόκει εἶναι ὀνομαστὶ προσαγορεύειν. 48. ἐδόκουν δ' αὐτῷ οἱ γιγνώσκεσθαι
δοκοῦντες ὑπὸ τοῦ ἄρχοντος καὶ τοῦ καλόν τι
ποιοῦντες ὁρᾶσθαι μᾶλλον ὀρέγεσθαι καὶ τοῦ
αἰσχρόν τι ποιεῖν μᾶλλον προθυμεῖσθαι ἀπέχεσθαι. 49. ἠλίθιον δὲ καὶ τοῦτ' ἐδόκει εἶναι αὐτῷ
τὸ ὁπότε τι βούλοιτο πραχθῆναι, οὕτω προστάτ-
τειν ὥσπερ ἐν οἴκῳ ἔνιοι δεσπόται προστάττουσιν,
Ἴτω τις ἐφ' ὕδωρ, Ξύλα τις σχισάτω· 50. οὕτω
γὰρ προσταττομένων εἰς ἀλλήλους τε ὁρᾶν πάντες
ἐδόκουν αὐτῷ καὶ οὐδεὶς περαίνειν τὸ προσταχθὲν
καὶ πάντες ἐν αἰτίᾳ εἶναι καὶ οὐδεὶς τῇ αἰτίᾳ
οὔτε αἰσχύνεσθαι οὔτε φοβεῖσθαι ὁμοίως διὰ
τὸ σὺν πολλοῖς αἰτίαν ἔχειν· διὰ ταῦτα δὴ πάντας

---

[1] πᾶσιν Heindorf, Edd. ; πῶς MSS.

is necessary, step out into the road to Babylon; and let each commander, as he gets his division in motion, pass the word to the man behind him to come on."

46. Hereupon they went to their tents, and, as they went, they remarked to one another what a good memory Cyrus had and how he called every one by name as he assigned them their places and gave them their instructions. 47. Now Cyrus made a study of this; for he thought it passing strange that, while every mechanic knows the names of the tools of his trade and the physician knows the names of all the instruments and medicines he uses, the general should be so foolish as not to know the names of the officers under him; and yet he must employ them as his instruments not only whenever he wishes to capture a place or defend one, but also whenever he wishes to inspire courage or fear. And whenever Cyrus wished to honour any one, it seemed to him proper to address him by name. 48. Furthermore, it seemed to him that those who were conscious of being personally known to their general exerted themselves more to be seen doing something good and were more ready to abstain from doing anything bad. 49. And when he wanted a thing done, he thought it foolish to give orders as do some masters in their homes: "Some one go get water!" "Some one split wood!" 50. for when orders are given in that way, all, he thought, looked at one another and no one carried out the order; all were to blame, but no one felt shame or fear as he should, because he shared the blame with many. It was for this reason, therefore, that he himself spoke to every one by name to whom

Cyrus's memory for names

63

ὠνόμαζεν αὐτὸς ὅτῳ τι προστάττοι. 51. καὶ
Κῦρος μὲν δὴ περὶ τούτων οὕτως ἐγίγνωσκεν.

Οἱ δὲ στρατιῶται τότε μὲν δειπνήσαντες καὶ
φυλακὰς καταστησάμενοι καὶ συσκευασάμενοι
πάντα ἃ ἔδει ἐκοιμήθησαν. 52. ἡνίκα δ᾽ ἦν ἐν
μέσῳ νυκτῶν, ἐσήμηνε τῷ κέρατι. Κῦρος δ᾽ εἰπὼν
τῷ Χρυσάντα ὅτι ἐπὶ τῇ ὁδῷ ὑπομενοίη ἐν τῷ
πρόσθεν τοῦ στρατεύματος ἐξῄει λαβὼν τοὺς
ἀμφ᾽ αὑτὸν ὑπηρέτας· βραχεῖ δὲ χρόνῳ ὕστερον
Χρυσάντας παρῆν ἄγων τοὺς θωρακοφόρους.
53. τούτῳ μὲν ὁ Κῦρος δοὺς ἡγεμόνας τῆς ὁδοῦ
πορεύεσθαι ἐκέλευεν ἡσύχως· οὐ γάρ πω ἐν ὁδῷ
πάντες ἦσαν·[1] αὐτὸς δὲ ἑστηκὼς ἐν τῇ ὁδῷ τὸν
μὲν προσιόντα προυπέμπετο ἐν τάξει, ἐπὶ δὲ
τὸν ὑστερίζοντα ἔπεμπε καλῶν. 54. ἐπεὶ δὲ
πάντες ἐν ὁδῷ ἦσαν, πρὸς μὲν Χρυσάνταν ἱππέας
ἔπεμψεν ἐροῦντας ὅτι ἐν ὁδῷ ἤδη πάντες· Ἄγε
οὖν ἤδη θᾶττον. 55. αὐτὸς δὲ παρελαύνων τὸν
ἵππον εἰς τὸ πρόσθεν ἥσυχος κατεθεᾶτο τὰς
τάξεις. καὶ οὓς μὲν ἴδοι εὐτάκτως καὶ σιωπῇ
ἰόντας, προσελαύνων αὐτοῖς τίνες τε εἶεν ἠρώτα
καὶ ἐπεὶ πύθοιτο ἐπῄνει· εἰ δέ τινας θορυβου-
μένους αἴσθοιτο, τὸ αἴτιον τούτου σκοπῶν κατα-
σβεννύναι τὴν ταραχὴν ἐπειρᾶτο.

56. Ἓν μόνον παραλέλειπται τῆς ἐν νυκτὶ
ἐπιμελείας αὐτοῦ, ὅτι πρὸ παντὸς τοῦ στρατεύματος πεζοὺς εὐζώνους οὐ πολλοὺς προύπεμπεν,
ἐφορωμένους ὑπὸ Χρυσάντα καὶ ἐφορῶντας αὐτόν,
ὡς ὠτακουστοῦντες καὶ εἴ πως ἄλλως δύναιντο
αἰσθάνεσθαί τι, σημαίνοιεν τῷ Χρυσάντα ὅ τι

[1] ἡσύχως . . . ἦσαν xz, Edd. ; ἥσυχον ἕως ἄγγελος ἔλθοι ὅτι
πάντες ἐν ὁδῷ yR.

he had any command to give. 51. Such, at least, was Cyrus's opinion about this matter.

The soldiers, however, then went to dinner, stationed sentinels, packed up everything they needed, and went to bed. 52. At midnight the signal horn sounded. Cyrus informed Chrysantas that he would wait for him on the road ahead of the army, took with him his aides-de-camp, and went on ; and a short time afterward Chrysantas came up at the head of his heavy-armed soldiers. 53. To him Cyrus turned over the guides and bade him advance leisurely, for the troops were not yet all on the way. He himself took his stand by the roadside, and as the troops came on he sent them forward in their order, and to those who were late he sent a messenger to bid them hasten. 54. And when they were all on the road, he sent some horsemen to Chrysantas to say that they were now all on the way; "Now then, double quick!" 55. He himself riding his horse leisurely along to the front inspected the ranks ; and to those whom he saw marching along in silence and in good order he would ride up and inquire who they were, and when he was informed he would praise them. But if he saw any in confusion, he would inquire into the cause of it and try to quiet the disorder.

56. Only one of his measures of precaution that night has been left unmentioned—namely, that he sent out in front of the main body of the army a few light-armed infantrymen to keep Chrysantas in sight and be kept in sight by him, to listen and gather information in whatever way they could, and report to Chrysantas what it seemed expedient that he

The midnight march

καιρὸς δοκοίη εἶναι· ἄρχων δὲ καὶ ἐπὶ τούτοις
ἦν ὃς καὶ τούτους ἐκόσμει, καὶ τὸ μὲν ἄξιον λόγου
ἐσήμαινε, τὸ δὲ μὴ οὐκ ἠνώχλει λέγων.

57. Τὴν μὲν δὴ νύκτα οὕτως ἐπορεύοντο· ἐπεὶ
δὲ ἡμέρα ἐγένετο, τοὺς μὲν Καδουσίων ἱππέας,
ὅτι αὐτῶν καὶ οἱ πεζοὶ ἐπορεύοντο ἔσχατοι, παρὰ
τούτοις κατέλιπεν, ὡς μηδ' οὗτοι ψιλοὶ ἱππέων
ἴοιεν· τοὺς δ' ἄλλους εἰς τὸ πρόσθεν παρελαύνειν
ἐκέλευσεν, ὅτι καὶ οἱ πολέμιοι ἐν τῷ πρόσθεν
ἦσαν, ὅπως εἴ τί που ἐναντιοῖτο αὐτῷ, ἀπαντῴη
ἔχων τὴν ἰσχὺν ἐν τάξει καὶ μάχοιτο, εἴ τέ τί
που φεύγον ὀφθείη, ὡς ἐξ ἑτοιμοτάτου διώκοι.
58. ἦσαν δὲ αὐτῷ ἀεὶ τεταγμένοι οὕς τε διώκειν
δέοι καὶ οὓς παρ' αὐτῷ μένειν· πᾶσαν δὲ τὴν
τάξιν λυθῆναι οὐδέποτε εἴα.

59. Κῦρος μὲν δὴ οὕτως ἦγε τὸ στράτευμα· οὐ
μέντοι αὐτός γε μιᾷ χώρᾳ ἐχρῆτο, ἀλλ' ἄλλοτε
ἀλλαχῇ περιελαύνων ἐφεώρα τε καὶ ἐπεμέλετο,
εἴ του δέοιντο.

Οἱ μὲν δὴ ἀμφὶ Κῦρον οὕτως ἐπορεύοντο.

IV

1. Ἐκ δὲ τοῦ Γαδάτου ἱππικοῦ τῶν δυνατῶν
τις ἀνδρῶν ἐπεὶ ἑώρα αὐτὸν ἀφεστηκότα ἀπὸ
τοῦ Ἀσσυρίου, ἐνόμισεν, εἴ τι οὗτος πάθοι, αὐτὸς
ἂν λαβεῖν παρὰ τοῦ Ἀσσυρίου πάντα τὰ Γαδάτου·

should know. There was also an officer in command of them who kept them in order, and what was of importance he communicated to Chrysantas, but he did not trouble him by reporting what was immaterial.

57. In this manner, therefore, they proceeded all night long; but when it became day, he left the cavalry of the Cadusians with their infantry (for these also were in the extreme rear), so that the latter might not be without the protection of cavalry; but the rest he ordered to ride up to the front, because the enemy were in front. He adopted this plan, in order that, if he happened to find any opposition, he might have his forces in fighting order to meet it, and that, if anything should be seen anywhere in flight, he might give chase with the utmost readiness. 58. He always kept drawn up in order one body of troops who were to pursue and another who were to stay with him; but he never suffered his main line to be broken.

59. Thus, then, Cyrus led his army; but he himself did not keep to the same position, but riding about, now here, now there, kept watch, and if they needed anything, he provided for it.

Thus, then, Cyrus and his army were proceeding.

The order by day

IV

1. Now there was a certain man among the officers of Gadatas's cavalry who, when he saw that his prince had revolted from the Assyrian, concluded that if some misfortune were to overtake Gadatas, he might himself obtain from the Assyrian all his chief's wealth

Conspiracy against Gadatas

οὕτω δὴ πέμπει τινὰ τῶν ἑαυτοῦ πιστῶν πρὸς
τὸν Ἀσσύριον καὶ κελεύει τὸν ἰόντα, εἰ καταλάβοι
ἤδη ἐν τῇ Γαδάτου χώρᾳ τὸ Ἀσσύριον στράτευμα,
λέγειν τῷ Ἀσσυρίῳ ὅτι εἰ βούλοιτο ἐνεδρεῦσαι,
λάβοι ἂν Γαδάταν καὶ τοὺς σὺν αὐτῷ. 2. δηλοῦν
δὲ ἐνετέλλετο ὅσην τε εἶχεν ὁ Γαδάτας δύναμιν
καὶ ὅτι Κῦρος οὐ συνέποιτο αὐτῷ· καὶ τὴν ὁδὸν
ἐδήλωσεν ᾗ προσιέναι μέλλοι. προσεπέστειλε
δὲ τοῖς αὐτοῦ οἰκέταις, ὡς πιστεύοιτο μᾶλλον,
καὶ τὸ τεῖχος ὃ ἐτύγχανεν αὐτὸς ἔχων ἐν τῇ
Γαδάτου χώρᾳ παραδοῦναι τῷ Ἀσσυρίῳ καὶ
τὰ ἐνόντα. ἥξειν δὲ καὶ αὐτὸς ἔφασκεν, εἰ μὲν
δύναιτο, ἀποκτείνας Γαδάταν, εἰ δὲ μή, ὡς σὺν
τῷ Ἀσσυρίῳ τὸ λοιπὸν ἐσόμενος.

3. Ἐπεὶ δὲ ὁ ἐπὶ ταῦτα ταχθεὶς ἐλαύνων ὡς
δυνατὸν ἦν τάχιστα ἀφικνεῖται πρὸς τὸν Ἀσσύριον καὶ ἐδήλωσεν ἐφ' ἃ ἥκοι, ἀκούσας ἐκεῖνος
τό τε χωρίον εὐθὺς παρέλαβε καὶ πολλὴν ἵππον
ἔχων καὶ ἅρματα ἐνήδρευεν ἐν κώμαις ἀθρόαις.

4. Ὁ δὲ Γαδάτας ὡς ἐγγὺς ἦν τούτων τῶν
κωμῶν, πέμπει τινὰς προδιερευνησομένους. ὁ δὲ
Ἀσσύριος ὡς ἔγνω προσιόντας τοὺς διερευνητάς,
φεύγειν κελεύει ἅρματα ἐξαναστάντα δύο ἢ τρία
καὶ ἵππους ὀλίγους, ὡς δὴ φοβηθέντας καὶ ὀλίγους
ὄντας. οἱ δὲ διερευνηταὶ ὡς εἶδον ταῦτα, αὐτοί
τε ἐδίωκον καὶ τῷ Γαδάτᾳ κατέσειον· καὶ ὃς

68

and power. With this in view, he sent one of his trusted friends to the Assyrian, instructing his messenger, in case he found the Assyrian army already in Gadatas's country, to tell their king that if he would lay an ambuscade, he would take Gadatas and his followers prisoners. 2. He furthermore commissioned him to explain how small an army Gadatas had and to make it clear that Cyrus was not with him; he also pointed out the road by which Gadatas was likely to return; and, that he might find fuller credence, he instructed his own subordinates to surrender to the Assyrian king, together with all that was in it, the fortress which he himself happened to be holding in Gadatas's country. He promised besides that he would come himself when he had slain Gadatas, if he could, but that, if he failed in the attempt, at least he would in future be on the king's side.

3. And the man who had been given this commission rode as fast as his horse could carry him; he came into the presence of the Assyrian king and made known the purpose of his coming. When the king heard it, he at once took possession of the fortress and with a large force of horse and chariots laid his ambuscade in a cluster of villages.

4. When Gadatas was not far from these villages, he sent some scouts on in advance to make a thorough search. And when the Assyrian was informed of the scouts' approach, he ordered two or three chariots and several horsemen to start up and gallop off as if they were affrighted and only a few in number. When the scouts saw that, they started in pursuit themselves and beckoned to Gadatas to come on. He, too, was deceived and started at full speed in

The plot almost succeeds

ἐξαπατηθεὶς διώκει ἀνὰ κράτος. οἱ δὲ Ἀσσύριοι,
ὡς ἐδόκει ἁλώσιμος εἶναι ὁ Γαδάτας, ἀνίστανται
ἐκ τῆς ἐνέδρας. 5. καὶ οἱ μὲν ἀμφὶ Γαδάταν
ἰδόντες ὥσπερ εἰκὸς ἔφευγον, οἱ δ᾽ αὖ ὥσπερ
εἰκὸς ἐδίωκον. καὶ ἐν τούτῳ ὁ ἐπιβουλεύων τῷ
Γαδάτᾳ παίει αὐτόν, καὶ καιρίας μὲν πληγῆς
ἁμαρτάνει, τύπτει δὲ αὐτὸν εἰς τὸν ὦμον καὶ
τιτρώσκει.

Ποιήσας δὲ τοῦτο ἐξίσταται, ἕως σὺν τοῖς
διώκουσιν ἐγένετο· ἐπεὶ δ᾽ ἐγνώσθη ὃς ἦν, ὁμοῦ
δὴ ὢν τοῖς Ἀσσυρίοις προθύμως ἐκτείνων τὸν
ἵππον σὺν τῷ βασιλεῖ ἐδίωκεν. 6. ἐνταῦθα δὴ
ἡλίσκοντο μὲν δῆλον ὅτι οἱ βραδυτάτους ἔχοντες
τοὺς ἵππους ὑπὸ τῶν ταχίστους·[1] ἤδη δὲ μάλα
πάντες πιεζόμενοι διὰ τὸ κατατετρῦσθαι ὑπὸ
τῆς πορείας οἱ τοῦ Γαδάτου ἱππεῖς καθορῶσι
τὸν Κῦρον προσιόντα σὺν τῷ στρατεύματι· δοκεῖν
δὲ χρὴ ἀσμένους καὶ ὥσπερ εἰς λιμένα ἐκ χειμῶνος προσφέρεσθαι αὐτούς. 7. ὁ δὲ Κῦρος τὸ
μὲν πρῶτον ἐθαύμασεν· ὡς δ᾽ ἔγνω τὸ πρᾶγμα,
ἕως πάντες ἐναντίοι ἤλαυνον, ἐναντίος καὶ αὐτὸς
ἐν τάξει ἦγε τὴν στρατιάν· ὡς δὲ γνόντες οἱ
πολέμιοι τὸ ὂν ἐτράποντο εἰς φυγήν, ἐνταῦθα
ὁ Κῦρος διώκειν ἐκέλευσε τοὺς πρὸς τοῦτο τεταγμένους, αὐτὸς δὲ σὺν τοῖς ἄλλοις εἵπετο ὡς
ᾤετο συμφέρειν. 8. ἐνταῦθα δὴ καὶ ἅρματα
ἡλίσκετο, ἔνια μὲν καὶ ἐκπιπτόντων τῶν ἡνιόχων,
τῶν μὲν ἐν τῇ ἀναστροφῇ, τῶν δὲ καὶ ἄλλως,
ἔνια δὲ καὶ περιτεμνόμενα ὑπὸ τῶν ἱππέων

---

[1] ταχίστους Cobet, most Edd. ; ταχίστων MSS., Dindorf,
Breitenbach.

pursuit. The Assyrians, in turn, when they thought Gadatas near enough to be taken, issued from their ambuscade. 5. And when Gadatas and his men saw this, they began to flee, as was natural; and the enemy, as was also natural, started in pursuit. At this juncture, the man who was plotting against Gadatas struck a blow at him but failed to inflict a mortal wound; still he smote him on the shoulder and wounded him.

When he had done this, he darted off to join the pursuing Assyrians; and when they recognized who he was, he took his place with them and urging his horse at full speed he joined with the king in the pursuit. 6. Then those who had the slowest horses were evidently being overtaken by those who had the fleetest; and just as Gadatas's men were becoming quite exhausted, because they were already jaded and worn out by their march, they saw Cyrus coming up with his army, and one may imagine that they rushed up to them with delight, like men putting into port out of a storm. 7. At first Cyrus was surprised; but when he comprehended the situation, he continued, while the enemy were all riding against him, to lead his army in battle order against them. But the enemy, recognizing the real state of affairs, turned and fled. Thereupon Cyrus ordered those who had been detailed for that purpose to start in pursuit, while he himself followed as he thought expedient. 8. Here chariots also were captured, some because the charioteers were thrown out, a part of them from wheeling around too sharply, others for other reasons, while some were intercepted by the cavalry and

Cyrus saves the day

7 I

XENOPHON

[ἠλίσκετο].[1] καὶ ἀποκτείνουσι δὲ ἄλλους τε πολλοὺς καὶ τὸν παίσαντα Γαδάταν. 9. τῶν μέντοι πεζῶν Ἀσσυρίων, οἳ ἔτυχον τὸ Γαδάτου χωρίον πολιορκοῦντες, οἱ μὲν εἰς τὸ τεῖχος κατέφυγον τὸ ἀπὸ Γαδάτου ἀποστάν, οἱ δὲ φθάσαντες εἰς πόλιν τινὰ τοῦ Ἀσσυρίου μεγάλην, ἔνθα καὶ αὐτὸς σὺν τοῖς ἵπποις καὶ τοῖς ἅρμασι κατέφυγεν ὁ Ἀσσύριος.

10. Κῦρος μὲν δὴ διαπραξάμενος ταῦτα ἐπαναχωρεῖ εἰς τὴν Γαδάτου χώραν· καὶ προστάξας οἷς ἔδει ἀμφὶ τὰ αἰχμάλωτα ἔχειν, εὐθὺς ἐπορεύετο, ὡς ἐπισκέψαιτο τὸν Γαδάταν πῶς ἔχοι ἐκ τοῦ τραύματος. πορευομένῳ δὲ αὐτῷ ὁ Γαδάτας ἐπιδεδεμένος ἤδη τὸ τραῦμα ἀπαντᾷ. ἰδὼν δὲ αὐτὸν ὁ Κῦρος ἥσθη τε καὶ εἶπεν, Ἐγὼ δὲ πρὸς σὲ ᾖα ἐπισκεψόμενος ὅπως ἔχεις.

11. Ἐγὼ δέ γ', ἔφη ὁ Γαδάτας, ναὶ μὰ τοὺς θεοὺς σὲ ἐπαναθεασόμενος ᾖα ὁποῖός τίς ποτε φαίνει ἰδεῖν ὁ τοιαύτην ψυχὴν ἔχων· ὅστις οὔτ' οἶδα ἔγωγε ὅ τι νῦν ἐμοῦ δεόμενος οὔτε μὴν ὑποσχόμενός γέ μοι ταῦτα πράξειν οὔτε εὖ πεπονθὼς ὑπ' ἐμοῦ εἴς γε τὸ ἴδιον οὐδ' ὁτιοῦν, ἀλλ' ὅτι τοὺς φίλους ἔδοξά σοί τι ὀνῆσαι, οὕτω μοι προθύμως ἐβοήθησας ὡς νῦν τὸ μὲν ἐπ' ἐμοὶ οἴχομαι, τὸ δ' ἐπὶ σοὶ σέσωσμαι. 12. οὐ μὰ τοὺς θεούς, ὦ Κῦρε, εἰ ἦν οἷος ἔφυν ἐξ ἀρχῆς καὶ ἐπαιδοποιησάμην, οὐκ οἶδ' ἂν εἰ ἐκτησάμην παῖδα τοιοῦτον περὶ ἐμέ· ἐπεὶ ἄλλους τε οἶδα παῖδας καὶ τοῦτον τὸν νῦν Ἀσσυρίων βασιλέα πολὺ πλείω ἤδη τὸν ἑαυτοῦ πατέρα ἀνιάσαντα ἢ σὲ νῦν δύναται ἀνιᾶν.

[1] ἠλίσκετο, MSS.; Hug; bracketed by Marchant, Gemoll.

taken. And many men were slain, and among them the man who had wounded Gadatas. 9. Of the Assyrian infantry, however, who happened to be besieging Gadatas's fortress, some fled to that fort which had been lost to Gadatas by betrayal, others had time to reach a large city of Assyria, in which the king himself with his horsemen and chariots also took refuge.

10. Now when Cyrus finished his pursuit of the enemy, he returned to Gadatas's country; and after he had given instructions to those whose duty it was to take care of the spoil, he went at once to visit Gadatas and see how his wound was. But as he was going, he was met by Gadatas with his wound already bandaged. And Cyrus was delighted at seeing him and said : "Why, I was coming to see how you were."

11. "And I, by the gods," said Gadatas, "was coming to gaze upon you again and see what you may look like, you who possess such a soul. For though I do not see what need you now have of my assistance, and though you made no promise to do this for me and have been put under no obligation whatever to me, at least no personal obligation, yet because you fancied that I had given some assistance to your friends, you have come so gallantly to my relief that at this moment, whereas by myself I am a lost man, by your goodness I am saved. 12. By the gods, Cyrus, if I were such a man as once I was and had children, I doubt if I could have had a child as kind to me as you have been; for I know that this present king of Assyria, like many another son that I have known, has caused his own father much more trouble than he can now cause you." Gadatas shows his gratitude

73

13. Καὶ ὁ Κῦρος πρὸς ταῦτα εἶπεν ὧδε· Ὦ Γαδάτα, ἦ πολὺ μεῖζον παρεὶς θαῦμα ἐμὲ νῦν θαυμάζεις.

Καὶ τί δὴ τοῦτ᾽ ἔστιν; ἔφη ὁ Γαδάτας.

Ὅτι τοσοῦτοι μέν, ἔφη, Περσῶν ἐσπούδασαν περὶ σέ, τοσοῦτοι δὲ Μήδων, τοσοῦτοι δὲ Ὑρκανίων, πάντες δὲ οἱ παρόντες Ἀρμενίων καὶ Σακῶν καὶ Καδουσίων.

14. Καὶ ὁ Γαδάτας ἐπηύξατο, Ἀλλ᾽, ὦ Ζεῦ, ἔφη, καὶ τούτοις πόλλ᾽ ἀγαθὰ δοῖεν οἱ θεοί, καὶ πλεῖστα τῷ αἰτίῳ τοῦ καὶ τούτους τοιούτους εἶναι. ὅπως μέντοι οὓς ἐπαινεῖς τούτους, ὦ Κῦρε, ξενίσωμεν καλῶς, δέχου τάδε ξένια οἷα ἐγὼ δοῦναι[1] δύναμαι.

Ἅμα δὲ προσῆγε πάμπολλα, ὥστε καὶ θύειν τὸν βουλόμενον καὶ ξενίζεσθαι πᾶν τὸ στράτευμα ἀξίως τῶν καλῶς πεποιημένων καὶ καλῶς συμβάντων.

15. Ὁ δὲ Καδούσιος ὠπισθοφυλάκει καὶ οὐ μετέσχε τῆς διώξεως· βουλόμενος δὲ καὶ αὐτὸς λαμπρόν τι ποιῆσαι, οὔτε ἀνακοινωσάμενος οὔτε εἰπὼν οὐδὲν Κύρῳ καταθεῖ τὴν πρὸς Βαβυλῶνα χώραν. διεσπασμένοις δὲ τοῖς ἵπποις αὐτοῦ ἀπιὼν ὁ Ἀσσύριος ἐκ τῆς ἑαυτοῦ πόλεως, οἷ[2] κατέφυγε, συντυγχάνει μάλα συντεταγμένον ἔχων τὸ ἑαυτοῦ στράτευμα. 16. ὡς δ᾽ ἔγνω μόνους ὄντας τοὺς Καδουσίους, ἐπιτίθεται, καὶ τόν τε ἄρχοντα τῶν Καδουσίων ἀποκτείνει καὶ ἄλλους

---

[1] δοῦναι supplied by Laar, most Edd.; not in MSS., Dindorf, Breitenbach.

[2] οἷ Dindorf, most Edd.; οὗ MSS., Breitenbach.

74

13. " You fail to notice a much greater wonder, Gadatas, when you now express your wonder at me," Cyrus made reply.

" And what is that, pray ? " asked Gadatas.

" That so many Persians have shown their interest in you," he answered, " and so many Medes and Hyrcanians, and all the Armenians, Sacians, and Cadusians here present."

14. " O Zeus," said Gadatas in prayer, " I pray that the gods may grant many blessings to them and most of all to him who is responsible for their being so generous toward me. But, Cyrus, in order that we may entertain handsomely these men whom you have been praising, accept as gifts of friendship these trifles, such as I can give."

At the same time he had a great many things brought out, so that any one who wished might sacrifice and that the whole army might be entertained in a manner worthy of their deeds of glory and the glorious issue.

15. The Cadusian prince had been guarding the rear and had no share in the pursuit ; so, wishing to do something brilliant on his own account, he went off, without consulting Cyrus or saying anything to him, to make a foray into the country toward Babylon. And as the Cadusian cavalry were scattered, the Assyrian, returning from his city in which he had taken refuge, came suddenly upon them with his own army in battle array. 16. And when he discovered that the Cadusians were alone, he made an attack, slew the commander of the Cadusians and many

The Cadusian fiasco

75

πολλούς, καὶ ἵππους τινὰς λαμβάνει τῶν Καδουσίων καὶ ἣν ἄγοντες λείαν ἐτύγχανον ἀφαιρεῖται.
καὶ ὁ μὲν Ἀσσύριος διώξας ἄχρι οὗ ἀσφαλὲς
ᾤετο εἶναι ἀπετράπετο· οἱ δὲ Καδούσιοι ἐσώζον-
το πρὸς τὸ στρατόπεδον ἀμφὶ δείλην οἱ πρῶτοι.

17. Κῦρος δὲ ὡς ᾔσθετο τὸ γεγονός, ἀπήντα τε
τοῖς Καδουσίοις καὶ ὅντινα ἴδοι τετρωμένον ἀνα-
λαμβάνων τοῦτον μὲν ὡς Γαδάταν ἔπεμπεν, ὅπως
θεραπεύοιτο, τοὺς δ' ἄλλους συγκατεσκήνου καὶ
ὅπως τἀπιτήδεια ἕξουσι συνεπεμέλετο, παραλαμ-
βάνων Περσῶν τῶν ὁμοτίμων συνεπιμελητάς· ἐν
γὰρ τοῖς τοιούτοις οἱ ἀγαθοὶ ἐπιπονεῖν ἐθέλουσι.
18. καὶ ἀνιώμενος μέντοι ἰσχυρῶς δῆλος ἦν, ὡς
καὶ τῶν ἄλλων δειπνούντων ἡνίκα ὥρα ἦν, Κῦρος
ἔτι σὺν τοῖς ὑπηρέταις καὶ τοῖς ἰατροῖς οὐδένα
ἑκὼν ἀτημέλητον παρέλειπεν, ἀλλ' ἢ αὐτόπτης
ἐφεώρα ἢ εἰ μὴ αὐτὸς ἐξανύτοι, πέμπων φανερὸς
ἦν τοὺς θεραπεύσοντας.

19. Καὶ τότε· μὲν οὕτως ἐκοιμήθησαν. ἅμα δὲ
τῇ ἡμέρᾳ κηρύξας συνιέναι τῶν μὲν ἄλλων τοὺς
ἄρχοντας, τοὺς δὲ Καδουσίους ἅπαντας, ἔλεξε
τοιάδε·

Ἄνδρες σύμμαχοι, ἀνθρώπινον τὸ γεγενημένον·
τὸ γὰρ ἁμαρτάνειν ἀνθρώπους ὄντας οὐδὲν οἶμαι
θαυμαστόν. ἄξιοί γε μέντοι ἐσμὲν τοῦ γεγενη-
μένου πράγματος τούτου ἀπολαῦσαί τι ἀγαθόν, τὸ
μαθεῖν μήποτε διασπᾶν ἀπὸ τοῦ ὅλου δύναμιν
ἀσθενεστέραν τῆς τῶν πολεμίων δυνάμεως. 20.
καὶ οὐ τοῦτο, ἔφη, λέγω ὡς οὐ δεῖ ποτε καὶ ἐλάτ-

others, took some of their horses, and recovered the spoil which they happened to be carrying off. He also pursued them as far as he thought was safe and then turned back. So the survivors of the Cadusians arrived at the camp, the first of them towards evening.

17. When Cyrus found out what had happened, he went out to meet them, and if he saw any one that was wounded he received him kindly and sent him on to Gadatas, that he might receive attention; the rest he helped into their tents and saw to it that they should have provisions, taking some of the Persian peers along to help him in looking after them. For under such circumstances, the good are ready 'to undertake extra labour. 18. Still Cyrus was evidently very much distressed, so that, when the rest went to dinner at the usual hour, he with his aides and the surgeons did not go; for he would not wittingly leave any uncared for, but either looked after them in person, or, if he did not succeed in doing that, he showed his personal interest by sending some one to attend to them. Cyrus cares for the survivors

19. Thus they went to sleep that evening. At daybreak he made proclamation for all the Cadusians and the officers of the rest to assemble; and he addressed them as follows: The lessons of the Cadusian blunder

" Friends and allies, that which has happened might happen to any man; for it is not at all strange, I think, for mortal man to err. Still it is worth our while to reap some benefit from this occurrence, the lesson never to detach from our main body a force weaker than the forces of the enemy. 20. I do not mean by that that we should never go off, if circumstances require it, with a still smaller de-

τονι ἔτι μορίῳ ἰέναι, ὅπου ἂν δέῃ, ἢ νῦν ὁ Καδούσιος ᾤχετο· ἀλλ' ἐάν τις κοινούμενος ὁρμᾶται τῷ
ἱκανῷ βοηθῆσαι, ἔστι μὲν ἀπατηθῆναι, ἔστι δὲ τῷ
ὑπομένοντι ἐξαπατήσαντι τοὺς πολεμίους ἄλλοσε
τρέψαι ἀπὸ τῶν ἐξεληλυθότων, ἔστι δὲ ἄλλα
παρέχοντα πράγματα τοῖς πολεμίοις τοῖς φίλοις
ἀσφάλειαν παρέχειν· καὶ οὕτω μὲν οὐδ' ὁ χωρὶς
ὢν ἀπέσται, ἀλλ' ἐξαρτήσεται τῆς ἰσχύος· ὁ δὲ
ἀπεληλυθὼς μὴ ἀνακοινωσάμενος, ὅπου ἂν ᾖ,
οὐδὲν διάφορον πάσχει ἢ εἰ μόνος ἐστρατεύετο.

21. Ἀλλ' ἀντὶ μὲν τούτου, ἔφη, ἐὰν θεὸς θέλῃ,
ἀμυνούμεθα τοὺς πολεμίους οὐκ εἰς μακράν. ἀλλ'
ἐπειδὰν τάχιστα ἀριστήσητε, ἄξω ὑμᾶς ἔνθα τὸ
πρᾶγμα ἐγένετο· καὶ ἅμα μὲν θάψομεν τοὺς
τελευτήσαντας, ἅμα δὲ δείξομεν τοῖς πολεμίοις
ἔνθα κρατῆσαι νομίζουσιν ἐνταῦθα ἄλλους αὐτῶν
κρείττους, ἢν θεὸς θέλῃ· καὶ ὅπως γε μηδὲ τὸ
χωρίον ἡδέως ὁρῶσιν ἔνθα κατέκανον ἡμῶν τοὺς
συμμάχους· ἐὰν δὲ μὴ ἀντεπεξίωσι,· καύσομεν
αὐτῶν τὰς κώμας καὶ δῃώσομεν τὴν χώραν, ἵνα
μὴ ἃ ἡμᾶς ἐποίησαν ὁρῶντες εὐφραίνωνται, ἀλλὰ
τὰ ἑαυτῶν κακὰ θεώμενοι ἀνιῶνται.

22. Οἱ μὲν οὖν ἄλλοι, ἔφη, ἀριστᾶτε ἰόντες·
ὑμεῖς δέ, ὦ Καδούσιοι, πρῶτον μὲν ἀπελθόντες
ἄρχοντα ὑμῶν αὐτῶν ἕλεσθε ᾗπερ ὑμῖν νόμος,
ὅστις ὑμῶν ἐπιμελήσεται σὺν τοῖς θεοῖς καὶ σὺν

tachment than that with which the Cadusian prince went. But if an officer, when he starts on an expedition, communicates his intention to one that is able to bring help, he may possibly fall into a trap, but then it is equally possible for the one who remains behind to entrap the enemy and turn them away from the detached corps; or he may annoy the enemy in some other way and so secure safety for his friends; and thus even those who are at a distance will not be out of reach but will keep in touch with the main body. But the man who goes off without communicating his purpose is in the same situation, no matter where he is, as if he were carrying on a campaign alone.

21. "But in return for this, we shall ere long, God willing, have our revenge on the enemy. So, as soon as you have had luncheon, I shall lead you to the place where this befell. There we shall not only bury the dead, but, God willing, on the very spot where the enemy think they have won a victory we will show them others better than they are. We shall at least let them have no satisfaction in looking even on the place where they slaughtered our allies. If they do not come out to meet us, we shall burn their villages and ravage their country, so that they may have no joy in viewing what they did to us but may be distressed at contemplating there their own misfortunes. Cyrus vows revenge

22. "The rest of you, therefore, go to luncheon. But you, Cadusians, go first and elect from your own number according to your custom a new general, who shall look out for your interests with the help of the gods and of us, if you have any need of our help

79

ἡμῖν, ἤν τι προσδέησθε· ἐπειδὰν δὲ ἔλησθε [καὶ ἀριστήσητε],[1] πέμψατε πρὸς ἐμὲ τὸν αἱρεθέντα.

23. Οἱ μὲν δὴ ταῦτ᾽ ἔπραξαν· ὁ δὲ Κῦρος ἐπεὶ ἐξήγαγε τὸ στράτευμα, κατέστησεν εἰς τάξιν τὸν ᾑρημένον ὑπὸ τῶν Καδουσίων καὶ ἐκέλευσε πλησίον αὑτοῦ ἄγειν τὴν τάξιν, Ὅπως, ἔφη, ἂν δυνώμεθα, ἀναθαρρύνωμεν τοὺς ἄνδρας. οὕτω δὴ ἐπορεύοντο· καὶ ἐλθόντες ἔθαπτον μὲν τοὺς Καδουσίους, ἐδῄουν δὲ τὴν χώραν. ποιήσαντες δὲ ταῦτα ἀπῆλθον τἀπιτήδεια ἐκ τῆς πολεμίας ἔχοντες πάλιν εἰς τὴν Γαδάτου.

24. Ἐννοήσας δὲ ὅτι οἱ πρὸς αὐτὸν ἀφεστηκότες ὄντες πλησίον Βαβυλῶνος κακῶς πείσονται, ἢν μὴ αὐτὸς ἀεὶ παρῇ, οὕτως ὅσους τε τῶν πολεμίων ἀφίει, τούτους ἐκέλευε λέγειν τῷ Ἀσσυρίῳ, καὶ αὐτὸς κήρυκα ἔπεμψε πρὸς αὐτὸν ταῦτα[2] λέγοντα, ὅτι ἕτοιμος εἴη τοὺς ἐργαζομένους τὴν γῆν ἐᾶν καὶ μὴ ἀδικεῖν, εἰ καὶ ἐκεῖνος βούλοιτο ἐᾶν ἐργάζεσθαι τοὺς τῶν πρὸς ἑαυτὸν ἀφεστηκότων ἐργάτας. 25. Καίτοι, ἔφη, σὺ μὲν ἢν καὶ δύνῃ κωλύειν, ὀλίγους τινὰς κωλύσεις· ὀλίγη γάρ ἐστι χώρα ἡ τῶν πρὸς ἐμὲ ἀφεστηκότων· ἐγὼ δὲ πολλὴν ἄν σοι χώραν ἐῴην ἐνεργὸν εἶναι. εἰς δὲ τὴν τοῦ καρποῦ κομιδήν, ἐὰν μὲν πόλεμος ᾖ, ὁ ἐπικρατῶν οἶμαι καρπώσεται· ἐὰν δὲ εἰρήνη, δῆλον, ἔφη, ὅτι σύ. ἐὰν μέντοι τις ἢ τῶν ἐμῶν ὅπλα ἀνταίρηται σοὶ ἢ τῶν σῶν ἐμοί, τούτους, ἔφη, ὡς ἂν δυνώμεθα ἑκάτεροι ἀμυνούμεθα.

[1] καὶ ἀριστήσητε MSS., earlier Edd.; bracketed by Hug, Gemoll; καὶ ἀριστήσατε after αἱρεθέντα Marchant.
[2] ταῦτα Dindorf, Edd.; ταῦτα MSS.

as well; and when you have made your choice,
send the man you have elected to me."

23. So they did as he bade. And when Cyrus led
the army out, he assigned the man elected by the
Cadusians his position and bade him lead his contingent near to himself, "in order," he said, "that we
may, if we can, put new courage into your men."
Thus, then, they proceeded; and when they came to
the place, they buried the Cadusians and ravaged
the country. And when they had done so they
returned again into the land of Gadatas, bringing
their supplies from the enemy's country.

24. And when he reflected that those who had
gone over to him would suffer severely, as they were
in the vicinity of Babylon, if he were not always at
hand, he ordered those of the enemy whom he
released to tell the Assyrian king (he also sent Cyrus pro-
a herald to bear the same message) that he was poses
ready to leave in peace the labourers tilling the land tection of
and to do them no harm, provided the king, on his the farms
part, would be willing to allow those farmers who
had transferred their allegiance to him to work their
farms. 25. "And yet," he had them say, "even if
you are able to hinder them, you will hinder but
few; for the country of those who have come over
to me is small; while the land under your
dominion that I should allow to be cultivated is
extensive. Then, as to the harvesting of the crops,
if there is war, the victor, I suppose, will do the
reaping; but if there is peace, it is evident that you
will do it. If, however, any of my adherents take up
arms against you, or any of yours against me, upon
such we will both execute vengeance according to
our ability."

26. Ταῦτα ἐπιστείλας τῷ κήρυκι ἔπεμψεν αὐτόν. οἱ δὲ Ἀσσύριοι ὡς ἤκουσαν ταῦτα, πάντα ἐποίουν πείθοντες τὸν βασιλέα συγχωρῆσαι ταῦτα καὶ ὅτι μικρότατον τοῦ πολέμου λιπεῖν. 27. καὶ ὁ Ἀσσύριος μέντοι εἴτε καὶ ὑπὸ τῶν ὁμοφύλων πεισθεὶς εἴτε καὶ αὐτὸς οὕτω βουληθεὶς συνήνεσε ταῦτα· καὶ ἐγένοντο συνθῆκαι τοῖς μὲν ἐργαζομένοις εἰρήνην εἶναι, τοῖς δ' ὁπλοφόροις πόλεμον.

28. Ταῦτα μὲν δὴ διεπέπρακτο περὶ τῶν ἐργατῶν ὁ Κῦρος· τὰς μέντοι νομὰς τῶν κτηνῶν τοὺς μὲν ἑαυτοῦ φίλους ἐκέλευσε καταθέσθαι, εἰ βούλοιντο, ἐν τῇ ἑαυτῶν ἐπικρατείᾳ· τὴν δὲ τῶν πολεμίων λείαν ἦγον ὁπόθεν δύναιντο, ὅπως εἴη ἡ στρατεία ἡδίων τοῖς συμμάχοις. οἱ μὲν γὰρ κίνδυνοι οἱ αὐτοὶ καὶ ἄνευ τοῦ λαμβάνειν τἀπιτήδεια, ἡ δ' ἐκ τῶν πολεμίων τροφὴ κουφοτέραν τὴν στρατείαν ἐδόκει παρέχειν.

29. Ἐπεὶ δὲ παρεσκευάζετο ἤδη ὁ Κῦρος ὡς ἀπιών, παρῆν ὁ Γαδάτας ἄλλα τε δῶρα πολλὰ καὶ παντοῖα φέρων καὶ ἄγων ὡς ἂν ἐξ οἴκου μεγάλου, καὶ ἵππους δὲ ἦγε πολλοὺς ἀφελόμενος τῶν ἑαυτοῦ ἱππέων οἷς ἠπιστήκει διὰ τὴν ἐπιβουλήν. 30. ὡς δ' ἐπλησίασεν, ἔλεξε τοιάδε· Ὦ Κῦρε, νῦν μέν σοι ἐγὼ ταῦτα δίδωμι ἐν τῷ παρόντι, καὶ χρῶ αὐτοῖς, ἐὰν δέῃ τι· νόμιζε δ', ἔφη, καὶ τἆλλα πάντα τἀμὰ σὰ εἶναι. οὔτε γὰρ ἔστιν οὔτ' ἔσται ποτὲ ὅτῳ ἐγὼ ἀπ' ἐμοῦ φύντι καταλείψω τὸν ἐμὸν οἶκον· ἀλλ' ἀνάγκη, ἔφη, σὺν ἐμοὶ τελευτῶντι πᾶν ἀποσβῆναι τὸ

26. This message he entrusted to the herald and sent him away. And when the Assyrians heard it, they did everything they could to persuade the king to accept the proposal, and to leave as little of the war as possible. 27. The Assyrian king, moreover, whether because he was persuaded by his countrymen or whether he himself also wished it so, agreed to the proposal; so a covenant was made to the effect that the farmers should have peace, but the men under arms war.

28. This concession Cyrus obtained for the farming classes. But as for the herds out grazing, he ordered his friends, if they wished, to drive them in and keep them in the territory under their own control; but the enemy's cattle they brought in as their legitimate prey from whatever quarter they could, so that the allies might be better pleased with the expedition. For the dangers were the same, even if they did not go foraging for provisions, while the burdens of war seemed lighter, if the army was to be fed at the enemy's cost.

29. When Cyrus was making preparations to depart, Gadatas came to him and brought many gifts of every sort, as might be expected from a wealthy house, and, most important of all, he brought many horses that he had taken from horsemen of his own whom he had come to distrust on account of the conspiracy against him. 30. When he came into Cyrus's presence he spoke as follows: "These gifts, Cyrus, I beg to offer you for the present; and do you accept them, if you have any use for them. But pray consider that everything else of mine is yours; for there is not and never can be a child of my own to whom I can leave my estates, but with my

Gadatas brings gifts to Cyrus

83

ἡμέτερον γένος καὶ ὄνομα. 31. καὶ ταῦτα, ἔφη,
ὦ Κῦρε, ὄμνυμί σοι θεούς, οἳ καὶ ὁρῶσι πάντα
καὶ ἀκούουσι πάντα, οὔτε ἄδικον οὔτ᾽ αἰσχρὸν
οὐδὲν οὔτ᾽ εἰπὼν οὔτε ποιήσας ἔπαθον.

Καὶ ἅμα ταῦτα λέγων κατεδάκρυσε τὴν ἑαυτοῦ
τύχην καὶ οὐκέτι ἐδυνήθη πλείω εἰπεῖν.

32. Καὶ ὁ Κῦρος ἀκούσας τοῦ μὲν πάθους
ᾤκτειρεν αὐτόν, ἔλεξε δὲ ὧδε· Ἀλλὰ τοὺς μὲν
ἵππους δέχομαι, ἔφη· σέ τε γὰρ ὠφελήσω εὐνουσ-
τέροις δοὺς αὐτοὺς ἢ οἳ νῦν σοι εἶχον, ὡς ἔοικεν,
ἐγώ τε οὐ δὴ πάλαι ἐπιθυμῶ, τὸ Περσῶν ἱππικὸν
θᾶττον ἐκπληρώσω εἰς τοὺς μυρίους ἱππέας· τὰ
δ᾽ ἄλλα χρήματα σὺ ἀπαγαγὼν φύλαττε, ἔστ᾽
ἂν ἐμὲ ἴδῃς[1] ἔχοντα ὥστε σοῦ μὴ ἡττᾶσθαι
ἀντιδωρούμενον· εἰ δὲ πλείω μοι δοὺς ἀπίοις
ἢ λαμβάνοις παρ᾽ ἐμοῦ, μὰ τοὺς θεοὺς οὐκ οἶδ᾽
ὅπως ἂν δυναίμην μὴ αἰσχύνεσθαι.

33. Πρὸς ταῦτα ὁ Γαδάτας εἶπεν, Ἀλλὰ ταῦτα
μέν, ἔφη, πιστεύω σοι· ὁρῶ γάρ σου τὸν τρόπον·
φυλάττειν μέντοι ὅρα εἰ ἐπιτήδειός εἰμι. 34. ἕως
μὲν γὰρ φίλοι ἦμεν τῷ Ἀσσυρίῳ, καλλίστη
ἐδόκει εἶναι ἡ τοῦ ἐμοῦ πατρὸς κτῆσις· τῆς
γὰρ μεγίστης πόλεως Βαβυλῶνος ἐγγὺς οὖσα
ὅσα μὲν ὠφελεῖσθαι ἔστιν ἀπὸ μεγάλης πόλεως,
ταῦτα ἀπελαύομεν, ὅσα δὲ ἐνοχλεῖσθαι, οἴκαδε
δεῦρ᾽ ἀπιόντες τούτων ἐκποδὼν ἦμεν· νῦν δ᾽ ἐπεὶ
ἐχθροί ἐσμεν, δῆλον ὅτι ἐπειδὰν σὺ ἀπέλθῃς,
καὶ αὐτοὶ ἐπιβουλευσόμεθα καὶ ὁ οἶκος ὅλος,
καὶ οἶμαι λυπηρῶς βιωσόμεθα ὅλως τοὺς ἐχθροὺς

[1] ἴδῃς y, Edd. ; εἰδῇς xz (know).

death our race and name must be altogether blotted out. 31. And by the gods, who see all things and hear all things, I swear to you, Cyrus, that it is not for anything wrong or base that I have said or done that I have suffered this affliction."

As he uttered these words he burst into tears over his lot and could say no more.

32. And Cyrus, as he listened, pitied him for his misfortune and answered him thus : " Your horses I accept; for I shall do you a service by giving them to men who are more loyal to you, it seems, than your own men who had them but now ; and for myself, I shall the sooner increase my Persian cavalry to full ten thousand horse, as I have been eager this long time to do. But do you take these other things away and keep them until you see me in possession of wealth enough so that I shall not be outdone in requiting you. For if, as we part, you should give me larger gifts than you receive from me, by the gods, I do not see how I could possibly help being ashamed."

33. " Well," said Gadatas in reply, " I can trust you for that ; for I know your ways. Still, bethink you whether I am in a position to keep these things safe for you. 34. For while we were friends to the Assyrian king, my father's estate seemed to me the finest in the world ; for it was so near to the mighty city of Babylon that we enjoyed all the advantages of a great city but could come back home and be rid of all its rush and worry. But now that we are his enemies, it is obvious that with your departure we ourselves and our whole house shall be the victims of plots ; and I think we shall lead an utterly miserable life, for we shall have our

Gadatas's relations with the Assyrian king

καὶ πλησίον ἔχοντες καὶ κρείττους ἡμῶν αὐτῶν
ὁρῶντες.

35. Τάχ' οὖν εἴποι τις ἄν· Καὶ τί δῆτα οὐχ
οὕτως ἐνενοοῦ πρὶν ἀποστῆναι; ὅτι, ὦ Κῦρε, ἡ
ψυχή μου διὰ τὸ ὑβρίσθαι καὶ ὀργίζεσθαι οὐ τὸ
ἀσφαλέστατον σκοποῦσα διῆγεν, ἀλλ' ἀεὶ τοῦτο
κυοῦσα, ἆρά ποτε ἔσται ἀποτίσασθαι τὸν καὶ
θεοῖς ἐχθρὸν καὶ ἀνθρώποις, ὃς διατελεῖ μισῶν,
οὐκ ἤν τίς τι αὐτὸν ἀδικῇ, ἀλλ' ἐάν τινα ὑπο-
πτεύσῃ βελτίονα ἑαυτοῦ εἶναι. 36. τοιγαροῦν
οἶμαι αὐτὸς πονηρὸς ὢν πᾶσι πονηροτέροις ἑαυτοῦ
συμμάχοις χρήσεται. ἐὰν δέ τις ἄρα καὶ βελτίων
αὐτοῦ φανῇ, θάρρει, ἔφη, ὦ Κῦρε, οὐδέν σε δεήσει
τῷ ἀγαθῷ ἀνδρὶ μάχεσθαι, ἀλλ' ἐκεῖνος τούτῳ
ἀρκέσει μηχανώμενος, ἕως ἂν ἕλῃ τὸν ἑαυτοῦ
βελτίονα. τοῦ μέντοι ἐμὲ ἀνιᾶν καὶ σὺν πονηροῖς
ῥᾳδίως οἶμαι κρείττων ἔσται.

37. Ἀκούσαντι ταῦτα τῷ Κύρῳ ἔδοξεν ἄξια
ἐπιμελείας λέγειν· καὶ εὐθὺς εἶπε, Τί οὖν, ἔφη,
ὦ Γαδάτα, οὐχὶ τὰ μὲν τείχη φυλακῇ ἐχυρὰ
ἐποιήσαμεν, ὅπως ἄν σοι σᾶ ᾖ χρῆσθαι ἀσφαλῶς,
ὁπόταν εἰς αὐτὰ ἴῃς· αὐτὸς δὲ σὺν ἡμῖν στρατεύει,
ἵνα ἢν οἱ θεοὶ ὥσπερ νῦν σὺν ἡμῖν ὦσιν, οὗτος
σὲ φοβῆται, ἀλλὰ μὴ σὺ τοῦτον; ὅ τι δὲ ἡδύ
σοι ὁρᾶν τῶν σῶν ἢ ὅτῳ συνὼν χαίρεις, ἔχων
σὺν σαυτῷ[1] πορεύου. καὶ σύ τ' ἂν ἐμοί, ὡς

[1] σαυτῷ Hertlein, most Edd.; ἑαυτῷ MSS., Dindorf,
Sauppe.

enemies close at hand and see them stronger than ourselves.

35. " Perhaps, then, some one might say : ' And why, pray, did you not think of that before you revolted ?' Because, Cyrus, on account of the outrage I had suffered and my consequent resentment, my soul was not looking out consistently for the safest course but was pregnant with this thought, whether it would ever be in my power to get revenge upon that enemy of gods and men, who cherishes an implacable hatred not so much toward the man who does him wrong as toward the one whom he suspects of being better than himself. 36. Therefore, since he is such a scoundrel himself, he will find no supporters but those who are worse scoundrels than himself. But if some one of them by any chance be found better than he, never fear, Cyrus, that you will have to fight that good man ; but he will take care of him, scheming unceasingly until he has got rid of that man who is better than himself. But as for me, he will, I think, even with worthless fellows easily be strong enough to harass me.

37. As Cyrus heard this, it seemed to him that Gadatas said something worthy of consideration ; so he answered at once : " Pray then, Gadatas," said he, " let us make the fortifications strong with garrisons and safe, that you may have confidence in their security, whenever you go into them ; and then do you take the field with us yourself so that, if the gods continue on our side as they now are, he may be afraid of you, not you of him. And bring with you whatsoever of yours you like to look at or to have with you, and come. It seems to me, too, that

γ᾽ ἐμοὶ δοκεῖ, πάνυ χρήσιμος εἴης, ἐγώ τε σοὶ
ὅσα ἂν δύνωμαι πειράσομαι.

38. Ἀκούσας ταῦτα ὁ Γαδάτας ἀνέπνευσέ τε
καὶ εἶπεν, Ἀρ᾽ οὖν, ἔφη, δυναίμην ἂν συσκευασάμενος φθάσαι πρίν σε ἐξιέναι; βούλομαι γάρ τοι,
ἔφη, καὶ τὴν μητέρα ἄγειν μετ᾽ ἐμαυτοῦ.

Ναὶ μὰ Δί᾽, ἔφη, φθάσεις[1] μέντοι. ἐγὼ γὰρ
ἐπισχήσω ἕως ἂν φῇς καλῶς ἔχειν.

39. Οὕτω δὴ ὁ Γαδάτας ἀπελθὼν φύλαξι
μὲν τὰ τείχη σὺν Κύρῳ ὠχυρώσατο, συνεσκευά-
σατο δὲ πάντα ὁπόσοις ἂν οἶκος μέγας καλῶς
οἰκοῖτο. ἤγετο δὲ καὶ τῶν ἑαυτοῦ τῶν τε πιστῶν
οἷς ἥδετο καὶ ὧν ἠπίστει πολλούς, ἀναγκάσας
τοὺς μὲν καὶ γυναῖκας ἄγειν, τοὺς δὲ καὶ ἀδελ-
φούς, ὡς δεδεμένους τούτοις κατέχοι αὐτούς.

40. Καὶ τὸν μὲν Γαδάταν εὐθὺς ὁ Κῦρος ἐν
τοῖς περὶ αὐτὸν ᾔει ἔχων καὶ ὁδῶν φραστῆρα
καὶ ὑδάτων καὶ χιλοῦ καὶ σίτου, ὡς εἴη ἐν [τοῖς][2]
ἀφθονωτάτοις στρατοπεδεύεσθαι.

41. Ἐπεὶ δὲ πορευόμενος καθεώρα τὴν τῶν
Βαβυλωνίων πόλιν καὶ ἔδοξεν αὐτῷ ἡ ὁδὸς ἣν
ᾔει παρ᾽ αὐτὸ τὸ τεῖχος φέρειν, καλέσας τὸν
Γωβρύαν καὶ τὸν Γαδάταν ἠρώτα εἰ εἴη ἄλλη
ὁδός, ὥστε μὴ πάνυ ἐγγὺς τοῦ τείχους ἄγειν.

42. Καὶ ὁ Γωβρύας εἶπεν, Εἰσὶ μέν, ὦ δέσποτα,
καὶ πολλαὶ ὁδοί· ἀλλ᾽ ἔγωγ᾽, ἔφη, ᾤμην καὶ
βούλεσθαι ἄν σε νῦν ὅτι ἐγγυτάτω τῆς πόλεως
ἄγειν, ἵνα καὶ ἐπιδείξαις αὐτῷ ὅτι τὸ στράτευμά
σου ἤδη πολύ τέ ἐστι καὶ καλόν· ἐπειδὴ καὶ ὅτε

---

[1] φθάσεις MSS., most Edd. ; φθήσει Hertlein, Hug.
[2] τοῖς MSS. ; [τοῖς] Dindorf[4], later Edd.

you would be very useful to me, and I shall try to be the same to you, as far as I can."

38. On hearing this, Gadatas breathed more freely and said: " Could I get things ready before you go? For, you see, I should like to take my mother with me." Gadatas makes common cause with Cyrus

"Yes, by Zeus," he answered, " you will have plenty of time; for I will hold back until you say it is all right."

39. Accordingly, Gadatas went away in company with Cyrus and strengthened the forts with garrisons and then packed up everything that a great house might need for comfort. And he brought with him many of his own loved and trusted friends and many also of those whom he distrusted, compelling some to bring along their wives, others their brothers and sisters, in order that he might keep them under control, when bound by such ties.

40. And from the first Cyrus kept Gadatas among those about him as he marched, to give him information in regard to roads and water, fodder and provisions, so that they might be able to camp where things were most abundant.

41. And when, as he proceeded, he came in sight of the city of Babylon and it seemed to him that the road which he was following led close by the walls, he called Gobryas and Gadatas to him and asked if there were not another road, so that they need not march right by the wall.

42. " Yes, sire," answered Gobryas; " in fact, there are many roads; but I supposed that you would surely wish to march as near to the city as possible, in order to show him that your army is now large and imposing; for even when you had a smaller

ἔλαττον εἶχες προσῆλθές τε πρὸς αὐτὸ τὸ τεῖχος
καὶ ἐθεᾶτο ἡμᾶς οὐ πολλοὺς ὄντας· νῦν δὲ εἰ
καὶ παρεσκευασμένος τί ἐστιν, ὥσπερ πρὸς σὲ
εἶπεν ὅτι παρασκευάζοιτο ὡς μαχούμενός σοι,
οἶδ᾽ ὅτι ἰδόντι αὐτῷ τὴν σὴν δύναμιν πάλιν
ἀπαρασκευότατα τὰ ἑαυτοῦ φανεῖται.

43. Καὶ ὁ Κῦρος πρὸς ταῦτα εἶπε, Δοκεῖς μοι,
ὦ Γωβρύα, θαυμάζειν ὅτι ἐν ᾧ μὲν χρόνῳ πολὺ
μείονα ἔχων στρατιὰν ἦλθον, πρὸς αὐτὸ τὸ τεῖχος
προσῆγον· νῦν δ᾽ ἐπεὶ πλείονα δύναμιν ἔχω, οὐκ
ἐθέλω ὑπ᾽ αὐτὰ τὰ τείχη ἄγειν. 44. ἀλλὰ μὴ θαύ-
μαζε· οὐ γὰρ τὸ αὐτό ἐστι προσάγειν τε καὶ
παράγειν. προσάγουσι μὲν γὰρ πάντες οὕτω
ταξάμενοι ὡς ἂν ἄριστοι εἶεν μάχεσθαι [καὶ
ἀπάγουσι δὲ οἱ σώφρονες ᾗ ἂν ἀσφαλέστατα, οὐχ
ᾗ ἂν τάχιστα ἀπέλθοιεν].[1] 45. παριέναι δὲ ἀνάγκη
ἐστὶν ἐκτεταμέναις μὲν ταῖς ἁμάξαις, ἀνειρμένοις[2]
δὲ καὶ τοῖς ἄλλοις σκευοφόροις ἐπὶ πολύ· ταῦτα
δὲ πάντα δεῖ προκεκαλύφθαι τοῖς ὁπλοφόροις καὶ
μηδαμῇ τοῖς πολεμίοις γυμνὰ ὅπλων τὰ σκευοφόρα
φαίνεσθαι. 46. ἀνάγκη οὖν οὕτω πορευομένων ἐπὶ
λεπτὸν καὶ ἀσθενὲς τὸ μάχιμον τετάχθαι· εἰ οὖν
βούλοιντο ἁθρόοι ἐκ τοῦ τείχους προσπεσεῖν πῃ,
ὅπῃ προσμίξειαν, πολὺ ἂν ἐρρωμενέστεροι[3] συμ-
μιγνύοιεν τῶν παριόντων· 47. καὶ τοῖς μὲν ἐπὶ
μακρὸν πορευομένοις μακραὶ καὶ αἱ ἐπιβοήθειαι,

[1] καὶ . . . ἀπέλθοιεν MSS., most Edd.; bracketed by Hug,
Marchant.
[2] ἀνειρμένοις Dindorf, recent Edd.; ἀνειργμένοις y, Suidas,
Sauppe; ἀνειργομένοις yzE[2].
[3] ἐρρωμενέστεροι Hertlein, recent Edd.; ἐρρωμενέστερον xy,
Dindorf, Breitenbach; ἐρρωμενεστέρων z.

force, you came right up to the very walls and he
saw that we had no great numbers. So now, even
if he really is to some extent prepared (for he
sent word to you that he was making preparations
to fight you), I am sure that, when he sees your
forces, his own will again seem to him extremely
ill-prepared."

43. "You seem to be surprised, Gobryas," said
Cyrus in answer, "that I marched right up to the
walls when I came with a much smaller army,
whereas now with a larger force I am unwilling to
march close up under the walls. 44. But do not be
surprised; for marching up to and marching by are
not the same thing. For every one leads up in
the order best for fighting [and the wise also
retreat in the safest possible way, and not in the
quickest], 45. but an army must needs march by
with the wagons in an extended line and with the
rest of the baggage vans in a long train. And
these must all be covered by soldiers, and the enemy
must never see the baggage wagons unprotected by
arms. 46. When people march in this way, therefore, they necessarily have the fighting men drawn
out in a thin, weak line. If, then, the enemy should
ever decide to sally out in a compact body from
their walls, on whichever part they came to close
quarters they would close with much greater force
than those have who are marching by. 47. Then,
too, those who are marching in a long column must
be a long distance from their supports, while the

Cyrus's
tactics in
passing
Babylon

XENOPHON

τοῖς δ' ἐκ τοῦ τείχους βραχὺ πρὸς τὸ ἐγγὺς καὶ προσδραμεῖν καὶ πάλιν ἀπελθεῖν.

48. Ἢν δὲ μὴ μεῖον ἀπέχοντες παρίωμεν ἢ ἐφ' ὅσον καὶ νῦν ἐκτεταμένοι πορευόμεθα, τὸ μὲν πλῆθος κατόψονται ἡμῶν· ὑπὸ δὲ τῶν παρυφασμένων ὅπλων πᾶς ὄχλος δεινὸς φαίνεται. 49. ἢν δ' οὖν τῷ ὄντι ἐπεξίωσί πη, ἐκ πολλοῦ προορῶντες αὐτοὺς οὐκ ἂν ἀπαράσκευοι λαμβανοίμεθα. μᾶλλον δέ, ὦ ἄνδρες, ἔφη, οὐδ' ἐπιχειρήσουσιν, ὁπόταν πρόσω δέῃ ἀπὸ τοῦ τείχους ἀπιέναι, ἢν μὴ τῷ ὅλῳ ὑπολάβωσι τοῦ παντὸς κρείττους εἶναι· φοβερὰ γὰρ ἡ ἀποχώρησις.

50. Ἐπεὶ δὲ ταῦτ' εἶπεν, ἔδοξέ τε ὀρθῶς τοῖς παροῦσι λέγειν καὶ ἦγεν ὁ Γωβρύας ὥσπερ ἐκέλευσε. παραμειβομένου δὲ τὴν πόλιν ·τοῦ στρατεύματος ἀεὶ τὸ ὑπολειπόμενον ἰσχυρότερον ποιούμενος ἀπεχώρει.

51. Ἐπεὶ δὲ πορευόμενος οὕτως ἐν ταῖς γιγνομέναις ἡμέραις ἀφικνεῖται εἰς τὰ μεθόρια τῶν Σύρων καὶ Μήδων, ἔνθενπερ ὥρμητο,[1] ἐνταῦθα δὴ τρία ὄντα τῶν Σύρων φρούρια, ἐν μὲν αὐτὸς τὸ ἀσθενέστατον βίᾳ προσβαλὼν ἔλαβε, τὼ δὲ δύο φρουρίω φοβῶν μὲν Κῦρος, πείθων δὲ Γαδάτας ἔπεισε παραδοῦναι τοὺς φυλάττοντας.

[1] ὥρμητο Hertlein, Edd. ; ὡρμᾶτο MSS.

townspeople have but a short way to go to make a dash on a force near them and again retire.

48. " On the other hand, if we march by at a distance from the walls not less than that at which we are now proceeding with our long extended line, they will have a view of our full numbers, to be sure, but behind the fringe of arms the whole host will look terrible. 49. Be that as it may, if they should really make a sally at any point, we should see them a long way off and not be caught unprepared ; or rather, I should say, friends, they will not so much as make the attempt when they have to go far from their walls, unless they judge that the whole of their force is superior to the whole of ours ; for a retreat is a perilous thing for them."

50. When he said this, those present agreed that what he said was right, and Gobryas led the way as he had directed. And as the army marched by the city, he constantly kept the part just passing the city the strongest, and so moved on.

51. Thus he continued his march and came in the usual number of days to the place on the boundaries between Media and Syria from which he had originally started. Of the three forts of the Syrians there, Cyrus in person assaulted one, the weakest, and took it by storm ; of the other two, Cyrus, by intimidation, brought the garrison of the one to surrender, and Gadatas, by persuasion, that of the other.

Cyrus captures three forts

XENOPHON

V

1. Ἐπεὶ δὲ ταῦτα διεπέπρακτο, πέμπει πρὸς Κυαξάρην καὶ ἐπέστελλεν αὐτῷ ἥκειν ἐπὶ τὸ στρατόπεδον, ὅπως περὶ τῶν φρουρίων ὧν εἰλήφεσαν βουλεύσαιντο ὅ τι χρήσαιντο, καὶ ὅπως θεασάμενος τὸ στράτευμα καὶ περὶ τῶν ἄλλων σύμβουλος γίγνοιτο ὅ τι δοκοίη ἐκ τούτου πράττειν· Ἐὰν δὲ κελεύῃ, εἰπέ, ἔφη, ὅτι ἐγὼ ἂν ὡς ἐκεῖνον ἰοίην συστρατοπεδευσόμενος. 2. Ὁ μὲν δὴ ἄγγελος ᾤχετο ταῦτ' ἀπαγγελῶν. ὁ δὲ Κῦρος ἐν τούτῳ ἐκέλευσε τὴν τοῦ Ἀσσυρίου σκηνήν, ἣν Κυαξάρῃ οἱ Μῆδοι ἐξεῖλον, ταύτην κατασκευάσαι ὡς βέλτιστα τῇ τε ἄλλῃ κατασκευῇ ἣν εἶχον καὶ τῷ γυναῖκα εἰσαγαγεῖν εἰς τὸν γυναικῶνα τῆς σκηνῆς καὶ σὺν ταύτῃ τὰς μουσουργούς, αἵπερ ἐξῃρημέναι ἦσαν Κυαξάρῃ. οἱ μὲν δὴ ταῦτ' ἔπραττον. 3. Ὁ δὲ πεμφθεὶς πρὸς τὸν Κυαξάρην ἐπεὶ ἔλεξε τὰ ἐντεταλμένα, ἀκούσας αὐτοῦ ὁ Κυαξάρης ἔγνω βέλτιον εἶναι τὸ στράτευμα μένειν ἐν τοῖς μεθορίοις. καὶ γὰρ οἱ Πέρσαι οὓς μετεπέμψατο ὁ Κῦρος ἧκον· ἦσαν δὲ μυριάδες τέτταρες τοξοτῶν καὶ πελταστῶν. 4. ὁρῶν οὖν καὶ τούτους σινομένους πολλὰ τὴν Μηδικήν, τούτων ἂν ἐδόκει ἥδιον ἀπαλλαγῆναι μᾶλλον ἢ ἄλλον ὄχλον εἰσδέξασθαι. ὁ μὲν δὴ ἐκ Περσῶν ἄγων τὸν στρατὸν ἐρόμενος τὸν Κυαξάρην κατὰ τὴν Κύρου ἐπιστολὴν εἴ τι δέοιτο τοῦ στρατοῦ, ἐπεὶ οὐκ ἔφη δεῖσθαι, αὐθημε-

94

V

1. WHEN this had been accomplished, he sent to Cyaxares and requested him to come to camp to hold a council of war concerning the disposition to be made of the forts which they had captured, and, after reviewing the army, to advise what steps he thought they ought to take next for the future conduct of the war. "But if he bids me," said he, "tell him that I would come and join camps with him." Cyrus requests Cyaxares to come

2. Accordingly, the messenger went away to deliver this message. Meanwhile Cyrus had given orders to bring out the tent of the Assyrian king which the Medes had selected for Cyaxares, to make it ready with all kinds of furnishings, and to conduct into the women's apartments of the tent the woman and with her the music-girls, who had been selected for Cyaxares. And this was done.

3. When the envoy to Cyaxares had delivered his message, Cyaxares gave it his attention and decided that it was better for the army to stay at the frontier. And there was the more reason, for the Persians whom Cyrus had sent for had come—forty thousand bowmen and peltasts. 4. And as he saw that these were a severe drain on the Median land, it seemed to him more desirable to get rid of the present army than to admit another host. So when the officer in command of the reinforcements from Persia inquired of Cyaxares, in accordance with the instructions he had had from Cyrus, whether he had any need of his army, he said "No"; and so this general went that same day at the head of his forces Reinforcements arrive from Persia IV. v. 31

ρόν, ἐπεὶ ἤκουσε παρόντα Κῦρον, ᾤχετο πρὸς
αὐτὸν ἄγων τὸ στράτευμα.

5. Ὁ δὲ Κυαξάρης ἐπορεύετο τῇ ὑστεραίᾳ σὺν
τοῖς παραμείνασιν ἱππεῦσι Μήδων· ὡς δ᾽ ᾔσθετο
ὁ Κῦρος προσιόντα αὐτόν, λαβὼν τούς τε τῶν
Περσῶν ἱππέας, πολλοὺς ἤδη ὄντας, καὶ τοὺς
Μήδους πάντας[1] καὶ τοὺς Ἀρμενίους καὶ τοὺς
Ὑρκανίους καὶ τῶν ἄλλων συμμάχων τοὺς εὐιπ-
ποτάτους τε καὶ εὐοπλοτάτους ἀπήντα, ἐπιδεικνὺς
τῷ Κυαξάρῃ τὴν δύναμιν. 6. ὁ δὲ Κυαξάρης
ἐπεὶ εἶδε σὺν μὲν τῷ Κύρῳ πολλούς τε καὶ καλοὺς
κἀγαθοὺς ἑπομένους, σὺν ἑαυτῷ δὲ ὀλίγην τε καὶ
ὀλίγου ἀξίαν θεραπείαν, ἄτιμόν τι αὐτῷ ἔδοξεν
εἶναι καὶ ἄχος αὐτὸν ἔλαβεν. ἐπεὶ δὲ καταβὰς
ἀπὸ τοῦ ἵππου ὁ Κῦρος προσῆλθεν ὡς φιλήσων
αὐτὸν κατὰ νόμον, ὁ Κυαξάρης κατέβη μὲν ἀπὸ
τοῦ ἵππου, ἀπεστράφη δέ· καὶ ἐφίλησε μὲν οὔ,
δακρύων δὲ φανερὸς ἦν.

7. Ἐκ τούτου δὴ ὁ Κῦρος τοὺς μὲν ἄλλους
πάντας ἀποστάντας ἐκέλευσεν ἀναπαύεσθαι·
αὐτὸς δὲ λαβόμενος τῆς δεξιᾶς τοῦ Κυαξάρου καὶ
ἀπαγαγὼν αὐτὸν τῆς ὁδοῦ ἔξω ὑπὸ φοίνικάς τινας,
τῶν τε Μηδικῶν πίλων ὑποβαλεῖν ἐκέλευσεν αὐτῷ
καὶ καθίσας αὐτὸν καὶ παρακαθισάμενος εἶπεν
ὧδε·

8. Εἰπέ μοι, ἔφη, πρὸς τῶν θεῶν, ὦ θεῖε, τί μοι
ὀργίζει καὶ τί χαλεπὸν ὁρῶν οὕτω χαλεπῶς
φέρεις;

Ἐνταῦθα δὴ ὁ Κυαξάρης ἀπεκρίνατο, Ὅτι, ὦ
Κῦρε, δοκῶν γε δὴ ἐφ᾽ ὅσον ἀνθρώπων μνήμη

---

[1] πάντας y, Edd. ; παρόντας xz, Zonaras (those who were
with him).

to Cyrus, for he heard that Cyrus was in that neighbourhood.

5. On the following day Cyaxares set out with the Median cavalry who had stayed with him, and when Cyrus learned that he was approaching, he went out to meet him with the Persian cavalry, which was now a large body; he took with him also all the Median, Armenian, and Hyrcanian horse, and those of the rest of the allies who were the best mounted and best armed; all these he took with him by way of displaying his forces to Cyaxares. 6. But when Cyaxares saw many fine, valiant men in the company of Cyrus, while his own escort was small and of little worth, he thought it a thing dishonourable, and grief gat hold on him. So when Cyrus dismounted from his horse and came up to him, intending to kiss him according to custom, Cyaxares dismounted from his horse but turned away. He refused to kiss him and could not conceal his tears. *Meeting between Cyrus and his uncle*

7. Thereupon Cyrus bade all the rest withdraw and wait. And he himself caught Cyaxares by the hand, led him to the shade of some palm-trees away from the road, ordered some Median rugs to be spread for him, and begged him to be seated; then sitting down beside him, he spoke as follows:

8. "In the name of all the gods, uncle," said he, "tell me why you are angry with me; and what do you find wrong that you take it so amiss?" *Cyaxares's jealous complaints*

"Because, Cyrus," Cyaxares then made answer, "while I am supposed to be the scion of a royal

ἐφικνεῖται καὶ τῶν πάλαι προγόνων καὶ πατρὸς
βασιλέως πεφυκέναι καὶ αὐτὸς βασιλεὺς νομιζό-
μενος εἶναι, ἐμαυτὸν μὲν ὁρῶ οὕτω ταπεινῶς καὶ
ἀναξίως ἐλαύνοντα, σὲ δὲ τῇ ἐμῇ θεραπείᾳ καὶ τῇ
ἄλλῃ δυνάμει μέγαν τε καὶ μεγαλοπρεπῆ παρόντα.
9. καὶ ταῦτα χαλεπὸν μὲν οἶμαι καὶ ὑπὸ πολεμίων
παθεῖν, πολὺ δ', ὦ Ζεῦ, χαλεπώτερον ὑφ' ὧν
ἥκιστα ἐχρῆν ταῦτα πεπονθέναι. ἐγὼ μὲν γὰρ
δοκῶ δεκάκις ἂν κατὰ τῆς γῆς καταδῦναι ἥδιον ἢ
ὀφθῆναι οὕτω ταπεινὸς καὶ ἰδεῖν τοὺς ἐμοὺς ἐμοῦ
ἀμελήσαντας καὶ ἐπεγγελῶντας ἐμοί. οὐ γὰρ
ἀγνοῶ τοῦτο, ἔφη, ὅτι οὐ σύ μου μόνον μείζων εἶ,
ἀλλὰ καὶ οἱ ἐμοὶ δοῦλοι ἰσχυρότεροι ἐμοῦ ὑπαντι-
άζουσί μοι καὶ κατεσκευασμένοι εἰσὶν ὥστε
δύνασθαι ποιῆσαι μᾶλλον ἐμὲ κακῶς ἢ παθεῖν ὑπ'
ἐμοῦ.

10. Καὶ ἅμα ταῦτα λέγων πολὺ ἔτι μᾶλλον
ἐκρατεῖτο ὑπὸ τῶν δακρύων, ὥστε καὶ τὸν Κῦρον
ἐπεσπάσατο ἐμπλησθῆναι δακρύων τὰ ὄμματα.
ἐπισχὼν δὲ μικρὸν ἔλεξε τοιάδε ὁ Κῦρος.

Ἀλλὰ ταῦτα μέν, ὦ Κυαξάρη, οὔτε λέγεις
ἀληθῆ οὔτε ὀρθῶς γιγνώσκεις, εἰ οἴει τῇ ἐμῇ
παρουσίᾳ Μήδους κατεσκευάσθαι ὥστε ἱκανοὺς
εἶναι σὲ κακῶς ποιεῖν. 11. τὸ μέντοι σε θυμοῦ-
σθαι καὶ φοβεῖν¹ αὐτοὺς οὐ² θαυμάζω· εἰ μέντοι
γε δικαίως ἢ ἀδίκως αὐτοῖς χαλεπαίνεις, παρήσω
τοῦτο· οἶδα γὰρ ὅτι βαρέως ἂν φέροις ἀκούων
ἐμοῦ ἀπολογουμένου ὑπὲρ αὐτῶν· τὸ μέντοι ἄνδρα
ἄρχοντα πᾶσιν ἅμα χαλεπαίνειν τοῖς ἀρχομένοις,
τοῦτο ἐμοὶ δοκεῖ μέγα ἁμάρτημα εἶναι. ἀνάγκη

¹ φοβεῖν Hug ; φοβεῖσθαι xy, other Edd. ; not in z.
² οὐ MSS. ; omitted by Pantazides, Hug.

father and of a line of ancestors who were kings of old as far back as the memory of man extends, and while I am called a king myself, still I see myself riding along with a mean and unworthy equipage, while you come before me great and magnificent in the eyes of my own retinue as well as the rest of your forces. 9. And this I think it a hard thing to suffer even at the enemy's hands and much harder, O Zeus, at the hands of those from whom I should least of all expect such treatment. For I think I should rather ten times sink into the earth than be seen so humiliated and see my own men disregarding me and laughing at me; for I am not ignorant of the fact not only that you are greater than I, but also that even my vassals come to meet me more powerful than I am myself and well enough equipped to do more harm to me than I can do to them."

10. And as he said this he was still more violently overcome with weeping, so that he affected Cyrus, too, till his eyes filled with tears. But after pausing for a moment Cyrus answered him as follows:

"Well, Cyaxares, in this you do not speak truly nor do you judge correctly, if you think that by my presence the Medes have been put in a position to do you harm; 11. but that you are angered and threaten them gives me no surprise. However, whether your anger against them is just or unjust, I will not stop to inquire; for I know that you would be offended to hear me speak in their defence. To me, however, it seems a serious error for a ruler to be angry with all his subjects at the same time; for, as

Cyrus reasons with his uncle

γὰρ διὰ τὸ πολλοὺς μὲν φοβεῖν πολλοὺς ἐχθροὺς
ποιεῖσθαι, διὰ δὲ τὸ πᾶσιν ἅμα χαλεπαίνειν πᾶσιν
αὐτοῖς ὁμόνοιαν ἐμβάλλειν. 12. ὧν ἕνεκα, εὖ ἴσθι,
ἐγὼ οὐκ ἀπέπεμπον ἄνευ ἐμαυτοῦ τούτους, φοβούμενος μή τι γένοιτο διὰ τὴν σὴν ὀργὴν ὅ τι πάντας
ἡμᾶς λυπήσοι. ταῦτα μὲν οὖν σὺν τοῖς θεοῖς ἐμοῦ
παρόντος ἀσφαλῶς ἔχει σοι.

Τὸ μέντοι σε νομίζειν ὑπ' ἐμοῦ ἀδικεῖσθαι,
τοῦτο ἐγὼ πάνυ χαλεπῶς φέρω, εἰ ἀσκῶν ὅσον
δύναμαι τοὺς φίλους ὡς πλεῖστα ἀγαθὰ ποιεῖν
ἔπειτα τἀναντία τούτου δοκῶ ἐξεργάζεσθαι.

13. Ἀλλὰ γάρ, ἔφη, μὴ οὕτως εἰκῇ ἡμᾶς
αὐτοὺς αἰτιώμεθα· ἀλλ', εἰ δυνατόν, σαφέστατα
κατίδωμεν ποῖόν ἐστι τὸ παρ' ἐμοῦ ἀδίκημα.
καὶ τὴν ἐν φίλοις δικαιοτάτην ὑπόθεσιν ἔχω
ὑποτιθέναι· ἐὰν γάρ τί σε φανῶ κακὸν πεποιηκώς,
ὁμολογῶ ἀδικεῖν· ἐὰν μέντοι μηδὲν φαίνωμαι
κακὸν πεποιηκὼς μηδὲ βουληθείς, οὐ καὶ σὺ
αὖ ὁμολογήσεις μηδὲν ὑπ' ἐμοῦ ἀδικεῖσθαι;

14. Ἀλλ' ἀνάγκη, ἔφη.

Ἐὰν δὲ δὴ καὶ ἀγαθά σοι πεπραχὼς δῆλος
ὦ καὶ προθυμούμενος πρᾶξαι ὡς ἐγὼ πλεῖστα
ἐδυνάμην, οὐκ ἂν καὶ ἐπαίνου σοι ἄξιος εἴην
μᾶλλον ἢ μέμψεως;

Δίκαιον γοῦν, ἔφη.

15. Ἄγε τοίνυν, ἔφη ὁ Κῦρος, σκοπῶμεν τὰ
ἐμοὶ πεπραγμένα πάντα καθ' ἓν ἕκαστον· οὕτω
γὰρ μάλιστα δῆλον ἔσται ὅ τι τε αὐτῶν ἀγαθόν
ἐστι καὶ ὅ τι κακόν. 16. ἀρξώμεθα δ', ἔφη,
ἐκ τῆσδε τῆς ἀρχῆς, εἰ καὶ σοὶ ἀρκούντως δοκεῖ

a matter of course, threatening many makes many enemies, and being angry with all at the same time inspires them all with a common sense of wrong. 12. It was for this reason, let me assure you, that I did not let them come back without me, for I was afraid that in consequence of your anger something might happen for which we should all be sorry. With the help of the gods, therefore, you are secured against that by my presence.

"As to your supposition that you have been wronged by me—I am exceedingly sorry, if, while I have been striving to the utmost of my ability to do as much good as possible to my friends, I seem after all to be accomplishing just the opposite.

13. "But enough of this; let us not thus idly accuse one another; but, if possible, let us examine what sort of wrong it is that has come from me. I am ready to make you a proposal, the fairest that can be made between friends: if it appear that I have done you harm, I confess that I am in the wrong; but if it turn out that I have done you no harm and intended none, will you then on your part confess that you have suffered no wrong at my hands?"

14. "Nay, I must," said he.

"And if it is demonstrated that I have done you good and have been eager to do as much for you as I could, pray should I not deserve your praise rather than your blame?"

"That is only fair," said he.

15. "Come, then," said Cyrus, "and let us consider all that I have done, all my acts one by one; for so it will be most clearly seen what is good and what is bad. 16. And let us begin, if you think it far enough back, with my assuming this command.

Cyrus reviews his own conduct

ἔχειν. σὺ γὰρ δήπου ἐπεὶ ᾔσθου πολλοὺς πολεμίους ἠθροισμένους, καὶ τούτους ἐπὶ σὲ καὶ τὴν
σὴν χώραν ὁρμωμένους, εὐθὺς ἔπεμπες πρός τε
τὸ Περσῶν κοινὸν συμμάχους αἰτούμενος καὶ
πρὸς ἐμὲ ἰδίᾳ δεόμενος πειρᾶσθαι αὐτὸν ἐμὲ
ἐλθεῖν ἡγούμενον, εἴ τινες Περσῶν ἴοιεν. οὔκουν[1]
ἐγὼ ἐπείσθην τε ταῦτα ὑπὸ σοῦ καὶ παρεγενόμην
ἄνδρας ἄγων σοι ὡς ἦν δυνατὸν πλείστους τε καὶ
ἀρίστους;

Ἦλθες γὰρ οὖν, ἔφη.

17. Ἐν τούτῳ τοίνυν, ἔφη, πρῶτόν μοι εἰπὲ
πότερον ἀδικίαν τινά μου πρὸς σὲ κατέγνως ἢ
μᾶλλον εὐεργεσίαν;

Δῆλον, ἔφη ὁ Κυαξάρης, ὅτι ἔκ γε τούτων
εὐεργεσίαν.

18. Τί γάρ, ἔφη, ἐπεὶ[2] οἱ πολέμιοι ἦλθον
καὶ διαγωνίζεσθαι ἔδει πρὸς αὐτούς, ἐν τούτῳ
κατενόησάς πού με ἢ πόνου ἀποστάντα ἤ τινος
κινδύνου φεισάμενον;

Οὐ μὰ τὸν Δί', ἔφη, οὐ μὲν δή.

19. Τί γάρ, ἐπεὶ τῆς[3] νίκης γενομένης σὺν
τοῖς θεοῖς ἡμετέρας καὶ ἀναχωρησάντων τῶν
πολεμίων παρεκάλουν ἐγώ σε ὅπως κοινῇ μὲν
αὐτοὺς διώκοιμεν, κοινῇ δὲ τιμωροίμεθα, κοινῇ
δὲ εἴ τι καλὸν κἀγαθὸν συμβαίνοι, τοῦτο καρποί-
μεθα, ἐν τούτοις ἔχεις τινά μου πλεονεξίαν
κατηγορῆσαι;

20. Ὁ μὲν δὴ Κυαξάρης πρὸς τοῦτο ἐσίγα·
ὁ δὲ Κῦρος πάλιν ἔλεγεν ὧδε· Ἀλλ' ἐπεὶ πρὸς

[1] οὔκουν Dindorf, Hug, Breitenbach, Marchant; οὐκοῦν
MSS., Gemoll.
[2] ἐπεὶ Schneider, Edd.; ἐπειδὴ yG²; εἰπὲ z; εἰπέ μοι x.
[3] τῆς Hertlein, Gemoll; not in MSS., most Edd.

Now, you remember, when you learned that the enemy had gathered in great numbers and that they were starting against you and your country, you at once sent to the Persian state to ask for help and to me personally to ask me to try to come myself at the head of the forces, if any of the Persians should come. Did I not comply with your request, and did I not come to you leading for your service as many and as valiant men as I could?"

"Yes," said he; "you certainly came."

17. "Well then," he answered, "tell me first whether in this you impute to me any wrong against you or do you not rather count it a benefit towards you?"

"Obviously," Cyaxares replied, "in that I see a benefit."

18. "Good, then," answered Cyrus; "and when the enemy came and we had to do battle with them, did you then see me ever shirking toil or avoiding danger?"

"No, by Zeus," said he; "I certainly did not."

19. "Furthermore, when with the help of the gods the victory was ours and the enemy retreated, when I urged you to come in order that we might together pursue them, together take vengeance upon them, and together reap the fruits of victory if any rich spoil should fall to our lot—can you charge me with any selfish purpose in that?"

20. To this Cyaxares said nothing. So Cyrus went on again: "Well, seeing that it suits you better

τοῦτο σιωπᾶν ἥδιόν σοι ἢ ἀποκρίνασθαι, τόδε
γ᾽, ἔφη, εἰπὲ εἴ τι ἀδικεῖσθαι ἐνόμισας ὅτι ἐπεί
σοι οὐκ ἀσφαλὲς ἐδόκει εἶναι τὸ διώκειν, σὲ
μὲν αὐτὸν ἀφῆκα τοῦ κινδύνου τούτου μετέχειν,
ἱππέας δὲ τῶν σῶν συμπέμψαι μοι ἐδεόμην
σου· εἰ γὰρ καὶ τοῦτο αἰτῶν ἠδίκουν, ἄλλως
τε καὶ προπαρεσχηκὼς ἐμαυτόν σοι σύμμαχον,
τοῦτ᾽ αὖ παρὰ σοῦ, ἔφη, ἐπιδεικνύσθω.

21. Ἐπεὶ δ᾽ αὖ καὶ πρὸς τοῦτο ἐσίγα ὁ Κυαξάρης, Ἀλλ᾽ εἰ μηδὲ τοῦτο, ἔφη, βούλει ἀποκρίνασθαι, σὺ δὲ τοὐντεῦθεν λέγε εἴ τι αὖ ἠδίκουν ὅτι σοῦ ἀποκριναμένου ἐμοὶ ὡς οὐκ ἂν
βούλοιο, εὐθυμουμένους ὁρῶν Μήδους, τούτου [1]
παύσας αὐτοὺς ἀναγκάζειν κινδυνεύσοντας ἰέναι,
εἴ τι αὖ σοι δοκῶ τοῦτο χαλεπὸν ποιῆσαι ὅτι
ἀμελήσας τοῦ ὀργίζεσθαί σοι ἐπὶ τούτοις πάλιν
ᾔτουν σε οὐ ἤδη οὔτε σοὶ μεῖον ὂν δοῦναι οὐδὲν
οὔτε ῥᾷον Μήδοις ἐπιταχθῆναι· τὸν γὰρ βουλόμενον δήπου ἕπεσθαι ᾔτησά σε δοῦναί μοι.

22. Οὐκοῦν τούτου τυχὼν παρὰ σοῦ οὐδὲν ἦν,
εἰ μὴ τούτους πείσαιμι. ἐλθὼν οὖν ἔπειθον
αὐτοὺς καὶ οὓς ἔπεισα τούτους ἔχων ἐπορευόμην
σοῦ ἐπιτρέψαντος. εἰ δὲ τοῦτο αἰτίας ἄξιον
νομίζεις, οὐδ᾽ ὅ τι ἂν διδῷς, ὡς ἔοικε, παρὰ σοῦ
δέχεσθαι ἀναίτιόν ἐστιν.

23. Οὐκοῦν ἐξωρμήσαμεν οὕτως· ἐπειδὴ δ᾽ ἐξ-
ήλθομεν, τί ἡμῖν πεπραγμένον οὐ φανερόν ἐστιν;
οὐ τὸ στρατόπεδον ἥλωκε τῶν πολεμίων; οὐ
τεθνᾶσι πολλοὶ τῶν ἐπὶ σὲ ἐλθόντων; ἀλλὰ
μὴν τῶν γε ζώντων ἐχθρῶν πολλοὶ μὲν ὅπλων

---

[1] τούτου Stephanus, Edd. ; τούτους MSS.

to be silent than to reply to this question, tell me
whether you thought you were wronged in any way
because, when you did not think it safe to pursue, I
excused you from a share in that peril and asked you
to let some of your cavalry go with me. For if I did
wrong also in asking that, and that, too, when I had
previously given you my own services as an ally, that
is yours to prove."

21. And as Cyaxares again said nothing, Cyrus
resumed: "Well, seeing that you do not choose
to answer that either, please tell me then if I did
you wrong in the next step I took: when you
answered that you saw that the Medes were enjoying
themselves and that you would not be willing to
disturb their pleasures and oblige them to go off into
dangers, then, far from being angry with you for that,
I asked you again for a favour than which, as I
knew, nothing was less for you to grant or easier for
you to require of the Medes: I asked you, as you
will remember, to allow any one who would to follow
me. Was there anything unfair, think you, in that?

22. "Well then, when I had obtained this concession from you, it amounted to nothing, unless I
were to gain their consent. So I went to see if I
could get their consent; and those whom I persuaded
I took with me, by your permission, on my expedition.
But if you think that deserving of blame, then, no
matter what you may offer, one may not, it seems,
accept it from you without blame.

23. "Thus, then, we started; and does not every
one know what we did when we were gone? Did
we not capture the enemy's camp? Are not many
of those who came against you slain? Aye, and of
the enemy still alive many have been deprived of

ἐστέρηνται, πολλοὶ δὲ ἵππων· χρήματά γε μὴν
τὰ τῶν φερόντων καὶ ἀγόντων τὰ σὰ πρόσθεν
νῦν ὁρᾷς τοὺς σοὺς φίλους καὶ ἔχοντας καὶ
ἄγοντας, τὰ μὲν σοί, τὰ δ' αὖ τοῖς ὑπὸ τὴν σὴν
ἀρχήν. 24. τὸ δὲ πάντων μέγιστον καὶ κάλλιστον, τὴν μὲν σὴν χώραν αὐξανομένην ὁρᾷς,
τὴν δὲ τῶν πολεμίων μειουμένην. καὶ τὰ μὲν
τῶν πολεμίων φρούρια ἐχόμενα, τὰ δὲ σὰ τὰ
πρότερον εἰς τὴν Σύρων ἐπικράτειαν συγκαταρρυέντα[1] νῦν τἀναντία σοὶ προσκεχωρηκότα· τούτων δὲ εἴ τι κακόν σοι ἢ εἴ τι μὴ ἀγαθόν σοι
μαθεῖν μὲν ἔγωγε βούλεσθαι οὐκ οἶδ' ὅπως ἂν
εἴποιμι· ἀκοῦσαι μέντοι γε οὐδὲν κωλύει. ἀλλὰ
λέγε ὅ τι γιγνώσκεις περὶ αὐτῶν.

25. Ὁ μὲν δὴ Κῦρος οὕτως εἰπὼν ἐπαύσατο·
ὁ δὲ Κυαξάρης ἔλεξε πρὸς ταῦτα τάδε· Ἀλλ',
ὦ Κῦρε, ὡς μὲν ταῦτα ἃ σὺ πεποίηκας κακά
ἐστιν οὐκ οἶδ' ὅπως χρὴ λέγειν· εὖ γε μέντοι,
ἔφη, ἴσθι ὅτι ταῦτα τἀγαθὰ τοιαῦτά ἐστιν οἷα
ὅσῳ πλείονα φαίνεται, τοσούτῳ μᾶλλον ἐμὲ
βαρύνει. 26. τήν τε γὰρ χώραν, ἔφη, ἐγὼ ἂν
τὴν σὴν ἐβουλόμην τῇ ἐμῇ δυνάμει μείζω ποιεῖν
μᾶλλον ἢ τὴν ἐμὴν ὑπὸ σοῦ ὁρᾶν οὕτως αὐξα-
νομένην· σοὶ μὲν γὰρ ταῦτα ποιοῦντι καλά,
ἐμοὶ δέ γέ ἐστί πῃ ταὐτὰ[2] ἀτιμίαν φέροντα.
27. καὶ χρήματα οὕτως ἄν μοι δοκῶ ἥδιόν σοι
δωρεῖσθαι ἢ παρὰ σοῦ οὕτω λαμβάνειν ὡς σὺ
νῦν ἐμοὶ δίδως· τούτοις γὰρ πλουτιζόμενος ὑπὸ

---

[1] συγκαταρρυέντα Hug; συγκυροῦντα xF (happening); συγ-
κατασπασθέντα AD, Dindorf, Breitenbach (demolished); συν-
τελοῦντα Herwerden, Marchant, Gemoll (contributing).

[2] ταὐτὰ Schneider, Edd.; ταῦτα yz; not in x.

their arms; many others of their horses; moreover, the belongings of those who before were robbing you and carrying off your property you now see in the hands of your friends and being brought in, some for you, some for those who are under your dominion. 24. But what is most important and best of all, you see your own territory increasing, that of the enemy diminishing; you see the enemy's fortresses in your possession, and your own, which had before all fallen under the Assyrian's power, now restored again to you. Now, I do not know that I can say that I should like to learn whether any one of these results is a bad thing or whether any one is not a good thing for you, but at any rate I have no objection to listening to what you have to say. So tell me what your judgment on the question is."

25. When he had thus spoken, Cyrus ceased, and Cyaxares answered as follows: "Well, Cyrus, I do not see how any one could say that what you have done is bad; but still, let me tell you, these services of yours are of such a nature that the more numerous they appear to be, the more they burden me. 26. For as to territory, I should rather extend yours by my power than see mine thus increased by you; for to you it brings glory to do this, but to me these same things somehow bring disgrace. 27. And as for money, it would be more agreeable for me to bestow it in this way upon you than to receive it from you under such circumstances as those under which you now offer it. For in being thus enriched

Cyaxares submits his grounds of complaint

σοῦ καὶ μᾶλλον αἰσθάνομαι οἷς πενέστερος γίγνο-
μαι. καὶ τούς γ᾽ ἐμοὺς ὑπηκόους ἰδὼν μικρά
γε ἀδικουμένους ὑπὸ σοῦ ἧττον ἂν δοκῶ λυπεῖσθαι ἢ νῦν ὁρῶν ὅτι μεγάλα ἀγαθὰ πεπόνθασιν
ὑπὸ σοῦ. 28. εἰ δέ σοι, ἔφη, ταῦτα δοκῶ ἀγνω-
μόνως ἐνθυμεῖσθαι, μὴ ἐν ἐμοὶ αὐτὰ ἀλλ᾽ εἰς
σὲ τρέψας πάντα καταθέασαι οἷά σοι φαίνεται.
τί γὰρ ἄν, εἴ τις κύνας, οὓς σὺ τρέφεις φυλακῆς
ἕνεκα σαυτοῦ τε καὶ τῶν σῶν, τούτους θεραπεύων
γνωριμωτέρους ἑαυτῷ ἢ σοὶ ποιήσειεν, ἆρ᾽ ἄν
σε εὐφράναι τούτῳ τῷ θεραπεύματι; 29. εἰ δὲ
τοῦτό σοι δοκεῖ μικρὸν εἶναι, ἐκεῖνο κατανόησον·
εἴ τις τοὺς σὲ θεραπεύοντας, οὓς σὺ καὶ φρουρᾶς
καὶ στρατείας ἕνεκα κέκτησαι, τούτους οὕτω
διατιθείη ὥστ᾽ ἐκείνου μᾶλλον ἢ σοῦ βούλεσθαι
εἶναι, ἆρ᾽ ἂν ἀντὶ ταύτης τῆς εὐεργεσίας χάριν
αὐτῷ εἰδείης; 30. τί δέ, ὃ μάλιστα ἄνθρωποι
ἀσπάζονταί τε καὶ θεραπεύουσιν οἰκειότατα, εἴ
τις τὴν γυναῖκα τὴν σὴν οὕτω θεραπεύσειεν
ὥστε φιλεῖν αὐτὴν μᾶλλον ποιήσειεν ἑαυτὸν ἢ
σέ, ἆρ᾽ ἄν σε τῇ εὐεργεσίᾳ ταύτῃ εὐφράναι;
πολλοῦ γ᾽ ἂν οἶμαι καὶ δέοι· ἀλλ᾽ εὖ οἶδ᾽ ὅτι
πάντων ἂν μάλιστα ἀδικοίη σε τοῦτο ποιήσας.

31. Ἵνα δὲ εἴπω καὶ τὸ μάλιστα τῷ ἐμῷ
πάθει ἐμφερές, εἴ τις οὓς σὺ ἤγαγες Πέρσας οὕτω
θεραπεύσειεν ὥστε αὐτῷ ἥδιον ἕπεσθαι ἢ σοί,
ἆρ᾽ ἂν φίλον αὐτὸν νομίζοις; οἶμαι μὲν οὔ, ἀλλὰ
πολεμιώτερον ἂν ἢ εἰ πολλοὺς αὐτῶν κατακάνοι.
32. τί δ᾽, εἴ τις τῶν σῶν φίλων φιλοφρόνως σου
εἰπόντος λαμβάνειν ὁπόσα ἐθέλοι εἶτα οὗτος[1]

---

[1] εἶτα οὗτος Hug ; εἰ y ; εἶτ᾽ αὐτοὶ C ; εἶτ᾽ αὐτὸς zE, Dindorf, Breitenbach, et al. ; εἶτα Marchant, Gemoll.

by you, I feel even more wherein I am made poorer. And I think I should be less displeased to see my subjects actually wronged a little by you than to see, as I do, that they have received great benefits from you. 28. But," he went on, "if it seems to you that it is unreasonable of me to take these things to heart, put yourself in my place and see in what light they appear to you. And tell me—if any one should pet your dogs, which you have been training for the protection of yourself and yours, and make them more familiar with himself than with you, would he please you with such petting? 29. Or if that seems to you a belittling comparison, think on this : if any one were to tamper with the attendants that you kept for your body-guard and for service in war, and so dispose them that they would rather be his than yours, would you be grateful to him for such kindness? 30. Again, let us take the object that men love most and most dearly cherish— suppose some one were to court your wife and make her love him more than yourself, would such kindness give you pleasure? Far from it, I think ; for I am sure that he who should be guilty of such conduct would be doing you the greatest of all injuries.

31. "But to quote an example most nearly akin to my own case—if any one should so treat the Persians whom you have brought here as to make them more glad to follow him than you, would you consider him your friend? I trow not; but you would consider him more of an enemy than if he were to slay many of them. 32. Or again, if you in your kindness of heart were to tell one of your friends to take what-

τοῦτο ἀκούσας λαβὼν οἴχοιτο ἅπαντα ὁπόσα
δύναιτο, καὶ αὐτὸς μέν γε τοῖς σοῖς πλουτοίη,
σὺ δὲ μηδὲ μετρίοις ἔχοις χρῆσθαι, ἆρ’ ἂν δύναιο
τὸν τοιοῦτον ἄμεμπτον φίλον νομίζειν;

33. Νῦν μέντοι ἐγώ, ὦ Κῦρε, εἰ μὴ ταῦτα
ἀλλὰ τοιαῦτα ὑπὸ σοῦ δοκῶ πεπονθέναι. σὺ
γὰρ ἀληθῆ λέγεις· εἰπόντος ἐμοῦ τοὺς ἐθέλοντας
ἄγειν λαβὼν ᾤχου πᾶσάν μου τὴν δύναμιν, ἐμὲ
δὲ ἔρημον κατέλιπες· καὶ νῦν ἃ ἔλαβες τῇ ἐμῇ
δυνάμει ἄγεις δή μοι καὶ τὴν ἐμὴν χώραν αὔξεις
[σὺν] [1] τῇ ἐμῇ ῥώμῃ· ἐγὼ δὲ δοκῶ οὐδὲν συναίτιος
ὢν τῶν ἀγαθῶν παρέχειν ἐμαυτὸν ὥσπερ γυνὴ
εὖ ποιεῖν, καὶ τοῖς τε ἄλλοις ἀνθρώποις καὶ
τοῖσδε τοῖς ἐμοῖς ὑπηκόοις σὺ μὲν ἀνὴρ φαίνει,
ἐγὼ δ’ οὐκ ἄξιος ἀρχῆς. 34. ταῦτά σοι δοκεῖ
εὐεργετήματ’ εἶναι, ὦ Κῦρε; εὖ ἴσθ’ ὅτι εἴ τι
ἐμοῦ ἐκήδου, οὐδενὸς ἂν οὕτω με ἀποστερεῖν
ἐφυλάττου ὡς ἀξιώματος καὶ τιμῆς. τί γὰρ
ἐμοὶ πλέον τὸ τὴν γῆν πλατύνεσθαι, αὐτὸν δὲ
ἀτιμάζεσθαι; οὐ γάρ τοι ἐγὼ Μήδων ἦρχον διὰ
τὸ κρείττων αὐτῶν πάντων εἶναι, ἀλλὰ μᾶλλον
διὰ τὸ αὐτοὺς τούτους ἀξιοῦν ἡμᾶς ἑαυτῶν πάντα
βελτίονας εἶναι.

35. Καὶ ὁ Κῦρος ἔτι λέγοντος αὐτοῦ ὑπολαβὼν
εἶπε, Πρὸς τῶν θεῶν, ἔφη, ὦ θεῖε, εἴ τι κἀγώ
σοι πρότερον ἐχαρισάμην, καὶ σὺ νῦν ἐμοὶ
χάρισαι ὃ ἂν δεηθῶ σου· παῦσαι, ἔφη, τὸ νῦν
εἶναι μεμφόμενός μοι· ἐπειδὰν δὲ πεῖραν ἡμῶν
λάβῃς πῶς ἔχομεν πρὸς σέ, ἐὰν μὲν δή σοι
φαίνηται τὰ ὑπ’ ἐμοῦ πεπραγμένα ἐπὶ τῷ σῷ

---

[1] σὺν MSS., Hug ; [σὺν] Hartmann, Gemoll.

ever of yours he wanted, and if he, accepting your offer, should make off with everything he could and enrich himself with what belonged to you, while you had not even enough left for moderate use, could you consider such a one a blameless friend?

33. "Well then, Cyrus, it seems to me that your treatment of me has been, if not that, at least something like that; for what you say is true: I told you to take those who wished to go with you, and off you went with my whole force and left me deserted. And now what you have taken with my forces you bring to me, forsooth, and with my own strength you increase my realm; and I, it seems, having no share in securing this good fortune, must submit like a mere woman to receive favours, and you are a hero in the eyes of all the world and especially of my subjects here, while I am not considered worthy of my crown. 34. Do you think that these are deeds of kindness, Cyrus? Let me tell you that if you had any regard for me, there is nothing of which you would be so careful not to rob me as my reputation and my honour. For what do I gain, if I have my realm extended wide and lose my own honour? For I was not made king of the Medes because I was more powerful than they all, but rather because they themselves accounted us to be in all things better than themselves."

35. "By the gods, uncle," said Cyrus, interrupting him before he had finished speaking, "if I have ever done you any favour before, please do me now the favour that I beg of you: desist from blaming me for the present, and when you have proof from us how we feel toward you, if it then appears that what I have done was done for your benefit, return

Cyaxares reconciled

ἀγαθῷ πεποιημένα, ἀσπαζομένου τέ μού σε
ἀντασπάζου με εὐεργέτην τε νόμιζε, ἐὰν δ᾽ ἐπὶ
θάτερα, τότε μοι μέμφου.

36. Ἀλλ᾽ ἴσως μέντοι, ἔφη ὁ Κυαξάρης, καλῶς
λέγεις· κἀγὼ οὕτω ποιήσω.

Τί οὖν; ἔφη ὁ Κῦρος, ἦ καὶ φιλήσω σε;

Εἰ σὺ βούλει, ἔφη.

Καὶ οὐκ ἀποστρέψει με ὥσπερ ἄρτι;

Οὐκ ἀποστρέψομαι, ἔφη.

Καὶ ὃς ἐφίλησεν αὐτόν.

37. Ὡς δὲ εἶδον οἱ Μῆδοί τε καὶ οἱ Πέρσαι
καὶ οἱ ἄλλοι, πᾶσι γὰρ ἔμελεν ὅ τι ἐκ τούτων
ἔσοιτο, εὐθὺς ἤσθησάν τε καὶ ἐφαιδρύνθησαν.
καὶ ὁ Κῦρος δὲ καὶ ὁ Κυαξάρης ἀναβάντες ἐπὶ
τοὺς ἵππους ἡγοῦντο, καὶ ἐπὶ μὲν τῷ Κυαξάρῃ
οἱ Μῆδοι εἵποντο, Κῦρος γὰρ αὐτοῖς οὕτως
ἐπένευσεν, ἐπὶ δὲ τῷ Κύρῳ οἱ Πέρσαι, οἱ δ᾽ ἄλλοι
ἐπὶ τούτοις.

38. Ἐπεὶ δὲ ἀφίκοντο ἐπὶ τὸ στρατόπεδον
καὶ κατέστησαν τὸν Κυαξάρην εἰς τὴν κατε-
σκευασμένην σκηνήν, οἷς μὲν ἐτέτακτο παρε-
σκεύαζον τἀπιτήδεια τῷ Κυαξάρῃ· 39. οἱ δὲ
Μῆδοι ὅσον χρόνον σχολὴν πρὸ δείπνου ἦγεν
ὁ Κυαξάρης ἦσαν πρὸς αὐτόν, οἱ μὲν καὶ αὐτοὶ
καθ᾽ ἑαυτούς, οἱ δὲ πλεῖστοι ὑπὸ Κύρου ἐγκέ-
λευστοι, δῶρα ἄγοντες, ὁ μέν τις οἰνοχόον καλόν,
ὁ δ᾽ ὀψοποιὸν ἀγαθόν, ὁ δ᾽ ἀρτοποιόν, ὁ δὲ μου-
σουργόν, ὁ δ᾽ ἔκπωμα,[1] ὁ δ᾽ ἐσθῆτα καλήν· πᾶς
δέ τις ὡς ἐπὶ τὸ πολὺ ἕν γέ τι ὧν εἰλήφει
ἐδωρεῖτο αὐτῷ· 40. ὥστε τὸν Κυαξάρην μετα-

---

[1] ὁ δ᾽ ἔκπωμα Hug ; ὁ δ᾽ ἐκπώματα, ὁ δ᾽ xy, Marchant, Gemoll;
οἱ δ᾽ ἐκπώματα zV, Dindorf, Breitenbach, Sauppe, et al.

my greeting when I greet you and consider me your benefactor; but if it seems the other way, then blame me."

36. "Well," said Cyaxares, "perhaps you are right after all; I will do so."

"Say then," said Cyrus, "may I kiss you, too?"

"If you please," said the other.

"And you will not turn away from me, as you did a little while ago?"

"No," said he.

So he kissed him.

37. And when the Medes and the Persians and the rest saw that, for they were all concerned to see what the outcome would be, they were satisfied and glad. Then Cyrus and Cyaxares mounted their horses and led the way, and the Medes followed after Cyaxares (for Cyrus gave them a nod so to do), the Persians fell in behind Cyrus, and the rest behind them.

38. And when they came to the camp and had lodged Cyaxares in the tent that had been made ready for him, they who had been detailed to do so supplied him with what he needed; 39. and as long as he had leisure before dinner, Cyaxares received calls from the Medes; some of them came of their own accord, but most of them went at the suggestion of Cyrus, taking presents with them—the one a handsome cup-bearer, another a fine cook, another a baker, another a musician, another a cup, another fine raiment; and every one of them, as a rule, presented him with at least one of the things that he had himself taken, 40. so that Cyaxares changed

He holds a reception

113

γιγνώσκειν ὡς οὔτε ὁ Κῦρος ἀφίστη αὐτοὺς ἀπ'
αὐτοῦ οὔθ' οἱ Μῆδοι ἧττόν τι αὐτῷ προσεῖχον
τὸν νοῦν ἢ καὶ πρόσθεν.

41. Ἐπεὶ δὲ δείπνου ὥρα ἦν, καλέσας ὁ Κυαξάρης ἠξίου τὸν Κῦρον διὰ χρόνου ἰδὼν [1] αὐτὸν
συνδειπνεῖν. ὁ δὲ Κῦρος ἔφη, Μὴ δὴ σὺ κέλευε,
ὦ Κυαξάρη· ἢ οὐχ ὁρᾷς ὅτι οὗτοι οἱ παρόντες
ὑφ' ἡμῶν πάντες ἐπαιρόμενοι πάρεισιν; οὔκουν
καλῶς ἂν πράττοιμι εἰ τούτων ἀμελῶν τὴν ἐμὴν
ἡδονὴν θεραπεύειν δοκοίην. ἀμελεῖσθαι δὲ δοκοῦντες στρατιῶται οἱ μὲν ἀγαθοὶ πολὺ ἀθυμό-
τεροι γίγνονται, οἱ δὲ πονηροὶ πολὺ ὑβριστότεροι.
42. ἀλλὰ σὺ μέν, ἔφη, ἄλλως τε καὶ ὁδὸν μακρὰν
ἥκων δείπνει ἤδη· καὶ εἴ τινές σε τιμῶσιν, ἀντασπάζου καὶ εὐώχει αὐτούς, ἵνα σε καὶ θαρρή-
σωσιν· ἐγὼ δ' ἀπιὼν ἐφ' ἅπερ λέγω τρέψομαι.
43. αὔριον δ', ἔφη, πρῲ δεῦρ' ἐπὶ τὰς σὰς θύρας
παρέσονται οἱ ἐπικαίριοι, ὅπως βουλευσώμεθα
πάντες σὺν σοὶ ὅ τι χρὴ ποιεῖν τὸ ἐκ τοῦδε.
σὺ δ' ἡμῖν ἔμβαλε βουλὴν [2] παρὼν περὶ τούτου
πότερον ἔτι δοκεῖ [3] στρατεύεσθαι ἢ καιρὸς ἤδη
διαλύειν τὴν στρατιάν.

44. Ἐκ τούτου ὁ μὲν Κυαξάρης ἀμφὶ δεῖπνον
εἶχεν, ὁ δὲ Κῦρος συλλέξας τοὺς ἱκανωτάτους
τῶν φίλων καὶ φρονεῖν καὶ συμπράττειν, εἴ τι
δέοι, ἔλεξε τοιάδε·

Ἄνδρες φίλοι, ἃ μὲν δὴ πρῶτα ηὐξάμεθα, πάρ-
εστι σὺν θεοῖς. ὅπῃ γὰρ ἂν πορευώμεθα, κρατοῦ-
μεν τῆς χώρας· καὶ μὲν δὴ τοὺς πολεμίους

---

[1] ἰδὼν Bothe, most Edd.; ἰδόντα MSS., Dindorf.
[2] βουλὴν supplied by Hug, Marchant, Gemoll; not in MSS.
or earlier Edd.   [3] δοκεῖ Ed. Junt., Edd.; δοκεῖς MSS.

his mind and realized that Cyrus was not alienating their affections from him and that the Medes were no less attentive to him than before.

41. And when the hour for dinner came, Cyaxares summoned Cyrus and asked him, as he had not seen him for a long time, to dine with him. But Cyrus answered: "Please, Cyaxares, do not ask me. Do you not see that all these who are here are here at our instance? I should not be doing right, then, if I should let them get the impression that I was neglecting them and pursuing my own pleasure. For when soldiers think they are being neglected, the good ones become much more despondent and the bad much more presuming. 42. But do you now go to dinner, especially as you have come a long way; and if any come to pay their respects to you, do you greet them kindly and entertain them well, so that they may feel confidence toward you also. For my part, I must go and attend to those matters of which I have been speaking to you. 43. And to-morrow morning my staff-officers will come with me to your headquarters, in order that we may all consult with you about what we should do next. Do you then and there lay before us the question whether it seems best to continue the campaign or whether it is now time to disband the armies."

44. After this Cyaxares attended to his dinner, while Cyrus collected those of his friends who were most able to think and to co-operate with him when occasion demanded, and addressed them as follows: Cyrus organizes for the continuance of the war

"My friends, with the help of the gods we have, you see, all that we prayed for at the first. For wherever we go, we are masters of the country. What is more, we see the enemy reduced, and our-

ὁρῶμεν μειουμένους, ἡμᾶς δὲ αὐτοὺς πλείονάς τε
καὶ ἰσχυροτέρους γιγνομένους. 45. εἰ δὲ ἡμῖν ἔτι
ἐθελήσειαν οἱ νῦν προσγεγενημένοι σύμμαχοι
παραμεῖναι, πολλῷ ἂν μᾶλλον ἀνύσαι δυναίμεθα
καὶ εἴ τι βιάσασθαι καιρὸς καὶ εἴ τι πεῖσαι δέοι.
ὅπως οὖν τὸ μένειν ὡς πλείστοις συνδοκῇ τῶν
συμμάχων, οὐδὲν μᾶλλον τοῦτο ἐμὸν ἔργον ἢ καὶ
ὑμέτερον μηχανᾶσθαι, 46. ἀλλ᾽ ὥσπερ καὶ ὅταν
μάχεσθαι δέῃ, ὁ πλείστους χειρωσάμενος ἀλκι-
μώτατος δοξάζεται εἶναι, οὕτω καὶ ὅταν πεῖσαι
δέῃ, ὁ πλείστους ὁμογνώμονας ἡμῖν ποιήσας οὗτος
δικαίως ἂν λεκτικώτατός τε καὶ πρακτικώτατος
κρίνοιτο ἂν εἶναι. 47. μὴ μέντοι ὡς λόγον ἡμῖν
ἐπιδειξόμενοι οἷον ἂν εἴπητε πρὸς ἕκαστον αὐτῶν
τοῦτο μελετᾶτε. ἀλλ᾽ ὡς τοὺς πεπεισμένους ὑφ᾽
ἑκάστου δήλους ἐσομένους οἷς ἂν πράττωσιν οὕτω
παρασκευάζεσθε. 48. καὶ ὑμεῖς μέν, ἔφη, τούτων
ἐπιμέλεσθε· ἐγὼ δὲ ὅπως ἂν ἔχοντες τἀπιτήδεια
ὅσον ἂν ἔγωγε δύνωμαι οἱ στρατιῶται περὶ τοῦ
στρατεύεσθαι βουλεύωνται τούτου πειράσομαι
ἐπιμέλεσθαι.

selves increased in both numbers and strength. 45. Now, if the allies we have gained would only stay on with us, we should be able to accomplish much more both by force, when occasion calls for it, and by persuasion, when that is needed; and it is not my business a whit more than it is yours to see to it that as many of the allies as possible agree to stay; 46. but just as, when we are called upon to fight, the one who conquers the greatest number has the glory of being considered the most valorous, so also when we are called upon to use persuasion, he that converts the greatest number to our opinion would justly be accounted at once the most eloquent and the most efficient. 47. Do not, however, aim at displaying to us the arguments that you will address to each one of them, but set to work with the feeling that those who are persuaded by any one of you will show what they are by what they do. 48. Do you, therefore, see to this. And I, for my part, will try to see to it, as far as I can, that the soldiers are supplied with all that they need, while they are deliberating about going on with the campaign.''

BOOK VI

ON THE EVE OF THE GREAT BATTLE

Z

I

1. Ταύτην μὲν δὴ τὴν ἡμέραν οὕτω διαγαγόντες καὶ δειπνήσαντες ἀνεπαύοντο. τῇ δ' ὑστεραίᾳ πρῲ ἧκον ἐπὶ τὰς Κυαξάρου θύρας πάντες οἱ σύμμαχοι. ἕως οὖν ὁ Κυαξάρης ἐκοσμεῖτο, ἀκούων ὅτι πολὺς ὄχλος ἐπὶ ταῖς θύραις εἴη, ἐν τούτῳ οἱ φίλοι τῷ Κύρῳ προσῆγον οἱ μὲν Καδουσίους δεομένους αὐτοῦ μένειν, οἱ δὲ Ὑρκανίους, ὁ δέ τις Σάκας, ὁ δέ τις καὶ Γωβρύαν· Ὑστάσπας δὲ Γαδάταν τὸν εὐνοῦχον προσῆγε, δεόμενον τοῦ Κύρου μένειν. 2. ἔνθα δὴ ὁ Κῦρος γιγνώσκων ὅτι Γαδάτας πάλαι ἀπωλώλει τῷ φόβῳ μὴ λυθείη ἡ στρατιά, ἐπιγελάσας εἶπεν, Ὦ Γαδάτα, δῆλος εἶ, ἔφη, ὑπὸ Ὑστάσπου τοῦδε πεπεισμένος ταῦτα γιγνώσκειν ἃ λέγεις. 3. καὶ ὁ Γαδάτας ἀνατείνας τὰς χεῖρας πρὸς τὸν οὐρανὸν ἀπώμοσεν ἦ μὴν μὴ ὑπὸ τοῦ Ὑστάσπου πεισθεὶς ταῦτα γιγνώσκειν· Ἀλλ' οἶδα, ἔφη, ὅτι ἢν ὑμεῖς ἀπέλθητε, ἔρρει τἀμὰ παντελῶς· διὰ ταῦτ', ἔφη, καὶ τούτῳ ἐγὼ αὐτὸς

120

BOOK VI

I

1. AFTER spending that day in the manner described, they dined and went to rest. Early on the following morning all the allies came to Cyaxares's headquarters. So while Cyaxares was attiring himself (for he heard that there was a large concourse of people at his doors), various friends were presenting the allies to Cyrus. One group brought the Cadusians, who begged him to stay; another, the Hyrcanians; some one brought forward the Sacians, and some one else, Gobryas; Hystaspas presented Gadatas, the eunuch, and he also begged Cyrus to remain. 2. Then Cyrus, though he realized that Gadatas had for some time been frightened almost to death for fear the army should be disbanded, laughing said: "It is clear, Gadatas, that Hystaspas here has been instigating you to the ideas that you have been expressing." 3. And Gadatas lifting up his hands toward heaven declared on his oath that he had not been influenced by Hystaspas to entertain those feelings. "But I know," said he, "that if you and your men go away, it is all over with me. For this reason, I introduced the subject with him

διελεγόμην, ἐρωτῶν εἰ εἰδείη τί ἐν νῷ ἔχεις [ὑπὲρ τῆς διαλύσεως τοῦ στρατεύματος][1] ποιεῖν.

4. Καὶ ὁ Κῦρος εἶπεν, Ἀδίκως ἄρα ἐγὼ Ὑστάσπαν τόνδε[2] καταιτιῶμαι.

Ἀδίκως μέντοι νὴ Δί, ἔφη ὁ Ὑστάσπας, ὦ Κῦρε· ἐγὼ γὰρ ἔλεγον τῷ Γαδάτᾳ τῷδε τοσοῦτον μόνον ὡς οὐχ οἷόν τέ σοι εἴη στρατεύεσθαι, λέγων ὅτι ὁ πατήρ σε μεταπέμπεται.

5. Καὶ ὁ Κῦρος, Τί λέγεις; ἔφη· καὶ σὺ τοῦτο ἐτόλμησας ἐξενεγκεῖν, εἴτ' ἐγὼ ἐβουλόμην εἴτε μή;

Ναὶ μὰ Δί, ἔφη· ὁρῶ γάρ σε ὑπερεπιθυμοῦντα ἐν Πέρσαις περίβλεπτον περιελθεῖν καὶ τῷ πατρὶ ἐπιδείξασθαι ᾗ ἕκαστα διεπράξω.

Ὁ δὲ Κῦρος ἔφη, Σὺ δ' οὐκ ἐπιθυμεῖς οἴκαδε ἀπελθεῖν;

Οὐ μὰ Δί, ἔφη, ὁ Ὑστάσπας, οὐδ' ἄπειμί γε, ἀλλὰ μένων στρατηγήσω, ἕως ἂν ποιήσω Γαδάταν τουτονὶ τοῦ Ἀσσυρίου δεσπότην.

6. Οἱ μὲν δὴ τοιαῦτα ἔπαιζον σπουδῇ πρὸς ἀλλήλους.

Ἐν δὲ τούτῳ Κυαξάρης σεμνῶς κεκοσμημένος ἐξῆλθε καὶ ἐπὶ θρόνου Μηδικοῦ ἐκαθέζετο. ὡς δὲ πάντες συνῆλθον οὓς ἔδει καὶ σιωπὴ ἐγένετο, ὁ Κυαξάρης ἔλεξεν ὧδε· Ἄνδρες σύμμαχοι, ἴσως, ἐπειδὴ παρὼν τυγχάνω καὶ πρεσβύτερός εἰμι Κύρου, εἰκὸς ἄρχειν με λόγου. νῦν οὖν δοκεῖ μοι εἶναι καιρὸς περὶ τούτου πρῶτον διαλέγεσθαι

[1] ὑπὲρ . . . στρατεύματος MSS., earlier Edd. ; bracketed by Hug, Marchant, Gemoll.

[2] Ὑστάσπαν τόνδε Hug, Marchant, Gemoll ; Ὑστάσπου τοῦδε xzV, Dindorf, Breitenbach, Hertlein ; Ὑστάσπην y.

of my own accord, asking him if he knew what it was your intention to do with reference to disbanding the army."

4. "I was wrong, then, as it seems," said Cyrus, "in accusing our friend Hystaspas."

"Aye, by Zeus, Cyrus, you were indeed," said Hystaspas. "For I was only remarking to our friend Gadatas that it was not possible for you to go on with the campaign; for I told him that your father was sending for you."

5. "What do you mean?" said Cyrus. "Did you dare to let that get out, whether I would or no?"

"Yes, by Zeus," he answered; "for I observe that you are exceedingly anxious to go around in Persia the cynosure of all eyes, and to parade before your father the way you have managed everything here."

"And do not you wish to go home yourself?" asked Cyrus.

"No, by Zeus," said Hystaspas; "and I am not going either; but I shall stay here and be general, until I have made our friend Gadatas master of the Assyrian."

6. Thus half-seriously did they jest with one another.

Meantime, Cyaxares came out in gorgeous attire and seated himself on a Median throne. And when all whose presence was required had assembled and silence prevailed, Cyaxares addressed them as follows: "Friends and allies, since I happen to be here and am older than Cyrus, it is perhaps proper for me to open the conference. To begin with, this seems to me to be an opportune time for us to discuss the

The conference on the continuance of the war

πότερον στρατεύεσθαι καιρὸς[1] ἔτι δοκεῖ [εἶναι][2] ἢ διαλύειν ἤδη τὴν στρατιάν· λεγέτω οὖν τις, ἔφη, περὶ αὐτοῦ τούτου ᾗ γιγνώσκει.

7. Ἐκ τούτου πρῶτος μὲν εἶπεν ὁ Ὑρκάνιος, Ἄνδρες σύμμαχοι, οὐκ οἶδα μὲν ἔγωγε εἴ τι δεῖ λόγων ὅπου αὐτὰ τὰ ἔργα δείκνυσι τὸ κράτιστον. πάντες γὰρ ἐπιστάμεθα ὅτι ὁμοῦ μὲν ὄντες[3] πλείω κακὰ τοὺς πολεμίους ποιοῦμεν ἢ πάσχομεν· ὅτε δὲ χωρὶς ἦμεν ἀλλήλων, ἐκεῖνοι ἡμῖν ἐχρῶντο ὡς ἐκείνοις ἦν ἥδιστον, ἡμῖν γε μὴν ὡς χαλεπώτατον.

8. Ἐπὶ τούτῳ ὁ Καδούσιος εἶπεν, Ἡμεῖς δὲ τί ἂν λέγοιμεν, ἔφη, περὶ τοῦ οἴκαδε ἀπελθόντες ἕκαστοι χωρὶς εἶναι, ὁπότε γε οὐδὲ στρατευομένοις, ὡς ἔοικε, χωρίζεσθαι συμφέρει; ἡμεῖς γοῦν οὐ πολὺν χρόνον δίχα τοῦ ὑμετέρου πλήθους στρατευσάμενοι δίκην ἔδομεν ὡς καὶ ὑμεῖς ἐπίστασθε.

9. Ἐπὶ τούτῳ Ἀρτάβαζος ὅ ποτε φήσας εἶναι Κύρου συγγενὴς ἔλεξε τοιάδε· Ἐγὼ δ᾽, ἔφη, ὦ Κυαξάρη, τοσοῦτον διαφέρομαι τοῖς πρόσθεν λέγουσιν· οὗτοι μὲν γάρ φασιν ὅτι δεῖ μένοντας στρατεύεσθαι, ἐγὼ δὲ λέγω ὅτι ὅτε μὲν οἴκοι ἦν, ἐστρατευόμην· 10. καὶ γὰρ ἐβοήθουν πολλάκις τῶν ἡμετέρων ἀγομένων καὶ περὶ τῶν ἡμετέρων φρουρίων ὡς ἐπιβουλευσομένων πολλάκις πράγματα εἶχον φοβούμενός τε καὶ φρουρῶν· καὶ ταῦτ᾽ ἔπραττον τὰ οἰκεῖα δαπανῶν. νῦν δ᾽ ἔχομεν[4] τὰ ἐκείνων φρούρια, οὐ φοβοῦμαι δὲ ἐκείνους, εὐωχοῦμαι δὲ τὰ ἐκείνων καὶ πίνω τὰ τῶν πολεμίων.

[1] καιρὸς xzV, Dindorf, Breitenbach; not in F; bracketed by Hug, Marchant, Gemoll.
[2] εἶναι MSS.; [εἶναι] Dindorf, Edd.
[3] μὲν ὄντες Jacobs, Edd.; μένοντες MSS.; μὲν μένοντες D.
[4] ἔχομεν E; ἔχο μὲν C; ἔχωμεν F; ἔχω μεν zV, most Edd.

question whether it is desirable to continue our campaign longer or at once to disband the armies. Any one, therefore, may express his opinion in regard to this question."

7. Thereupon the Hyrcanian was the first to speak: "Friends and comrades, I, for my part, cannot see what is the use of words, when the facts themselves point out the best course to follow. For we all know that when we are together, we do the enemy more harm than they do us; whereas as long as we were apart, they treated us as was most agreeable to them and most disagreeable to us."

8. After him the Cadusian spoke: "Why," said he, "should we talk about going back home and being separated from one another, since not even in the field, so it seems, is it well for us to get separated? At any rate, we not long ago went off on an expedition apart from your main body and paid for it, as you also know."

9. After him Artabazus, the one who once claimed I. iv. 27-28 to be a kinsman of Cyrus, made the following speech: "In one point, Cyaxares, I beg to differ from the previous speakers: they say that we must stay here and carry on the war; but I say that it was when I was at home that I was carrying on wars. 10. And I say truly; for I often had to go to the rescue when our property was being carried off; and when our fortresses were threatened, I often had trouble to defend them; I lived in constant fear and was kept continually on guard. And I fared thus at my own expense. But now we are in possession of their forts; I am in fear of them no longer; I revel in the good things of the enemy and drink what is

ὡς οὖν τὰ μὲν οἴκοι στρατείαν οὖσαν, τάδε δὲ
ἑορτήν, ἐμοὶ μὲν οὐ δοκεῖ, ἔφη, διαλύειν τήνδε τὴν
πανήγυριν.

11. Ἐπὶ τούτῳ ὁ Γωβρύας εἶπεν, Ἐγὼ δ', ὦ
ἄνδρες σύμμαχοι, μέχρι μὲν τοῦδε ἐπαινῶ τὴν
Κύρου δεξιάν· οὐδὲν γὰρ ψεύδεται ὧν ὑπέσχετο·
εἰ δ' ἄπεισιν ἐκ τῆς χώρας, δῆλον ὅτι ὁ μὲν Ἀσσύριος ἀναπνεύσεται,[1] οὐ τίνων ποινὰς ὧν τε ὑμᾶς
ἐπεχείρησεν ἀδικεῖν καὶ ὧν ἐμὲ ἐποίησεν· ἐγὼ δὲ
ἐν τῷ μέρει ἐκείνῳ πάλιν δώσω δίκην ὅτι ὑμῖν
φίλος ἐγενόμην.

12. Ἐπὶ τούτοις πᾶσι Κῦρος εἶπεν, Ὦ ἄνδρες,
οὐδ' ἐμὲ λανθάνει ὅτι ἐὰν μὲν διαλύωμεν τὸ στράτευμα, τὰ μὲν ἡμέτερα ἀσθενέστερα γίγνοιτ' ἄν,
τὰ δὲ τῶν πολεμίων πάλιν αὐξήσεται. ὅσοι τε
γὰρ αὐτῶν ὅπλα ἀφῄρηνται, ταχὺ ἄλλα ποιήσον-
ται· ὅσοι τε ἵππους ἀπεστέρηνται, ταχὺ πάλιν
ἄλλους ἵππους κτήσονται· ἀντὶ δὲ τῶν ἀποθα-
νόντων ἕτεροι ἐφηβήσουσι [καὶ ἐπιγενήσονται].[2]
ὥστε οὐδὲν θαυμαστὸν εἰ πάνυ ἐν τάχει πάλιν
ἡμῖν πράγματα παρέχειν δυνήσονται.

13. Τί δῆτα ἐγὼ Κυαξάρην ἐκέλευσα λόγον
ἐμβαλεῖν περὶ καταλύσεως τῆς στρατιᾶς; εὖ
ἴστε ὅτι φοβούμενος τὸ μέλλον. ὁρῶ γὰρ ἡμῖν
ἀντιπάλους προσιόντας οἷς ἡμεῖς, εἰ ὧδε στρατευσόμεθα, οὐ δυνησόμεθα μάχεσθαι. 14. προσέρχεται μὲν γὰρ δήπου χειμών, στέγαι δὲ εἰ καὶ
ἡμῖν αὐτοῖς εἰσιν, ἀλλὰ μὰ Δί' οὐχ ἵπποις οὐδὲ

[1] ἀναπνεύσεται Hertlein, Marchant, Gemoll ; ἀναπαύσεται
MSS., earlier Edd.

[2] καὶ ἐπιγενήσονται MSS., Dindorf, Breitenbach ; bracketed
by Schneider, later Edd.

theirs. Therefore, as life at home was warfare, while life here is a feast, I do not care to have this festal gathering break up."

11. After him Gobryas spoke : " Friends and comrades, up to the present time I have only praise for Cyrus's faithfulness ; for he has not proved untrue in anything that he has promised. But if he leaves the country now, it is evident that the Assyrian will take new heart without having to pay any penalty for the wrongs he has attempted to do us all and for those which he has done me ; and I, in my turn, shall pay to him the penalty for having been your friend."

12. Last of all Cyrus spoke : " I, too, am not un- Cyrus closes
aware, my friends, that if we disband the army, our the debate
own situation would again become weaker, while the enemy will again gather force. For as many of them as have been deprived of their arms will soon have new ones made, and as many as have been deprived of their horses will soon again procure others, while in place of those who have been killed others will have grown to young manhood to take their places. And so it will not be at all surprising, if in a very short time they are able again to give us trouble.

13. " Why then do you suppose I suggested to Cyaxares to bring up the question of disbanding the army? Let me tell you ; it was because I feared for the future ; for I see foes advancing against us that we shall never be able to cope with, if we go on campaigning in our present fashion. 14. For winter The battle
is coming, you know ; and even granting that we against cold
have shelter for ourselves, still, by Zeus, there will and hunger

θεράπουσιν οὐδὲ τῷ δήμῳ τῶν στρατιωτῶν, ὧν
ἄνευ ἡμεῖς οὐκ ἂν δυναίμεθα στρατεύεσθαι· τὰ δ'
ἐπιτήδεια ὅπου μὲν ἡμεῖς ἐληλύθαμεν ὑφ' ἡμῶν
ἀνήλωται· ὅποι δὲ μὴ ἀφίγμεθα, διὰ τὸ ἡμᾶς
φοβεῖσθαι ἀνακεκομισμένοι εἰσὶν εἰς ἐρύματα,
ὥστε αὐτοὶ μὲν ἔχειν, ἡμᾶς δὲ ταῦτα μὴ δύνασθαι
λαμβάνειν. 15. τίς οὖν οὕτως ἀγαθὸς ἢ τίς οὕτως
ἰσχυρὸς ὃς λιμῷ καὶ ῥίγει δύναιτ' ἂν μαχόμενος
στρατεύεσθαι; εἰ μὲν οὖν οὕτω στρατευσόμεθα,
ἐγὼ μέν φημι χρῆναι ἑκόντας ἡμᾶς καταλῦσαι τὴν
στρατιὰν μᾶλλον ἢ ἄκοντας ὑπ' ἀμηχανίας ἐξε-
λαθῆναι. εἰ δὲ βουλόμεθα ἔτι στρατεύεσθαι, τόδ'
ἐγὼ φημι χρῆναι ποιεῖν, ὡς τάχιστα πειρᾶσθαι
τῶν μὲν ἐκείνων ὀχυρῶν ὡς πλεῖστα παραιρεῖν,
ἡμῖν δ' αὐτοῖς ὡς πλεῖστα ὀχυρὰ ποιεῖσθαι· ἐὰν
γὰρ ταῦτα γένηται, τὰ μὲν ἐπιτήδεια πλείω ἕξου-
σιν ὁπότεροι ἂν πλείω δύνωνται λαβόντες ἀπο-
τίθεσθαι, πολιορκήσονται δὲ ὁπότεροι ἂν ἥττους
ὦσι. 16. νῦν δ' οὐδὲν διαφέρομεν τῶν ἐν τῷ
πελάγει πλεόντων· καὶ γὰρ ἐκεῖνοι πλέουσι μέν
ἀεί, τὸ δὲ πεπλευσμένον οὐδὲν οἰκειότερον τοῦ
ἀπλεύστου καταλείπουσιν. ἐὰν δὲ φρούρια ἡμῖν
γένηται, ταῦτα δὴ τοῖς μὲν πολεμίοις ἀλλοτριώσει
τὴν χώραν, ἡμῖν δ' ὑπ' εὐδίαν μᾶλλον πάντ'
ἔσται.

17. Ὁ δ' ἴσως ἄν τινες ὑμῶν φοβηθεῖεν, εἰ
δεήσει πόρρω τῆς ἑαυτῶν φρουρεῖν, μηδὲν τοῦτο
ὀκνήσητε. ἡμεῖς μὲν γὰρ ἐπείπερ καὶ ὡς οἴκοθεν
ἀποδημοῦμεν, φρουρήσειν ὑμῖν ἀναδεχόμεθα τὰ
ἐγγύτατα χωρία τῶν πολεμίων, ὑμεῖς δὲ τὰ πρόσ-

be none for our horses or for our attendants or for the rank and file of the army ; and without them we could not carry on the war. The provisions, wherever we have gone, we have consumed ; and where we have not gone, the people out of fear of us have conveyed them into their strongholds, so that they have them themselves, and we cannot get them. 15. Who then is so valiant and so strong that he can prosecute a war while battling against hunger and cold ? If, therefore, we propose to go on with the war as we have been doing, I maintain that we ought of our own free will to disband the army, rather than against our will to be driven out of the country by lack of means. But if we wish to go on with the war, this I say we must do : we must try as quickly as we may to get possession of as many as possible of their forts and build for ourselves as many as we can. For, if this is done, that side will have more provisions which is able to get and store up more, and those will be in a state of siege who are weaker. 16. As we are, we are not at all different from those who sail the seas : they keep on sailing continually, but they leave the waters over which they have sailed no more their own than those over which they have not sailed. But if we get fortresses, these will alienate the country from the enemy while everything will be smooth sailing for us.

Fortified posts in the enemy's country

17. " But perhaps some of you may fear that you will possibly have to do garrison duty far from your own country. You need have no hesitation on that score. For since we are far from home in any event, we will take it upon ourselves to do the garrison duty for you in the places nearest to the enemy ; but those parts of Assyria which are on your

ορα ὑμῖν αὐτοῖς τῆς Ἀσσυρίας ἐκεῖνα κτᾶσθε
καὶ ἐργάζεσθε. 18. ἐὰν γὰρ ἡμεῖς τὰ πλησίον[1]
αὐτῶν φρουροῦντες δυνώμεθα σώζεσθαι, ἐν πολλῇ
ὑμεῖς εἰρήνῃ ἔσεσθε οἱ τὰ πρόσω αὐτῶν ἔχοντες·
οὐ γὰρ οἶμαι δυνήσονται τῶν ἐγγὺς ἑαυτῶν ὄντων
ἀμελοῦντες τοῖς πρόσω ὑμῖν ἐπιβουλεύειν.

19. Ὡς δὲ ταῦτ' ἐρρήθη, οἵ τε ἄλλοι πάντες
ἀνιστάμενοι συμπροθυμήσεσθαι ταῦτ' ἔφασαν καὶ
Κυαξάρης. Γαδάτας δὲ καὶ Γωβρύας καὶ τεῖχος
ἑκάτερος αὐτῶν, ἢν ἐπιτρέψωσιν οἱ σύμμαχοι,
τειχιεῖσθαι ἔφασαν, ὥστε καὶ ταῦτα φίλια τοῖς
συμμάχοις ὑπάρχειν.

20. Ὁ οὖν Κῦρος ἐπεὶ πάντας ἑώρα προθύμους
ὄντας πράττειν ὅσα ἔλεξε, τέλος εἶπεν, Εἰ τοίνυν
περαίνειν βουλόμεθα ὅσα φαμὲν χρῆναι ποιεῖν, ὡς
τάχιστ' ἂν δέοι γενέσθαι μηχανὰς μὲν εἰς τὸ
καθαιρεῖν τὰ τῶν πολεμίων τείχη, τέκτονας δὲ εἰς
τὸ ἡμῖν ὀχυρὰ πυργοῦσθαι.

21. Ἐκ τούτου ὑπέσχετο ὁ μὲν Κυαξάρης μη-
χανὴν αὐτὸς ποιησάμενος παρέξειν, ἄλλην δὲ
Γαδάτας καὶ Γωβρύας, ἄλλην δὲ Τιγράνης· αὐτὸς
δὲ Κῦρος ἔφη δύο πειράσεσθαι ποιήσασθαι.
22. ἐπεὶ δὲ ταῦτ' ἔδοξεν, ἐπορίζοντο μὲν μηχανο-
ποιούς, παρεσκευάζοντο δ' ἕκαστοι εἰς τὰς μηχανὰς ὧν ἔδει· ἄνδρας δ' ἐπέστησαν οἳ ἐδόκουν
ἐπιτηδειότατοι εἶναι ἀμφὶ ταῦτ' ἔχειν.

23. Κῦρος δ' ἐπεὶ ἔγνω ὅτι διατριβὴ ἔσται
ἀμφὶ ταῦτα, ἐκάθισε τὸ στράτευμα ἔνθα ᾤετο

---

[1] πλησίον y, Edd. ; πλείω xzV (the greater part).

own borders—do you take possession of them and cultivate them. 18. For if we can safely guard what is near the enemy, you will enjoy a plenitude of peace in possession of the regions far away from them; for they, I trow, will not be able to neglect those who are close to them, while they lay schemes against those who are far away."

19. After these speeches all the rest, and Cyaxares with them, stood up and declared that they would be glad to co-operate with him in these plans. And Gadatas and Gobryas said that if the allies would permit them, they would each of them build a fortress, so that the allies should have these also on their side.

The unanimous decision for war

20. Accordingly, when Cyrus saw that all were ready to do whatever he suggested, he finally said: "Well then, if we wish to put into execution what we say we ought to do, we should as soon as possible procure siege-engines to demolish the enemy's forts, and builders to erect strong towers for our own defence."

21. Hereupon Cyaxares promised to have an engine made at his own expense and to put it at their disposal, Gadatas and Gobryas promised another, and Tigranes a third; Cyrus said that he would himself try to furnish two. 22. When this had been agreed upon, they set to work to procure engine-builders and to furnish whatever was needed for the construction of the engines; and they put in charge of it men whom they considered most competent to attend to this work.

Measures for strength and health

23. Since Cyrus realized that a long time would be required for the execution of these designs, he encamped with his army in a place which he thought

ὑγιεινότατον εἶναι καὶ εὐπροσοδώτατον ὅσα ἔδει
προσκομίζεσθαι· ὅσα τε ἐρυμνότητος προσεδεῖτο,
ἐποιήσατο, ὡς ἐν ἀσφαλεῖ οἱ ἀεὶ μένοντες εἶεν, εἴ
ποτε καὶ πρόσω τῇ ἰσχύι ἀποστρατοπεδεύοιτο.
24. πρὸς δὲ τούτοις ἐρωτῶν οὓς ᾤετο μάλιστα
εἰδέναι τὴν χώραν ὁπόθεν ἂν ὡς πλεῖστα ὠφελοῖ-
το τὸ στράτευμα, ἐξῆγεν ἀεὶ εἰς προνομάς, ἅμα
μὲν ὅπως ὅτι πλεῖστα λαμβάνοι τῇ στρατιᾷ
τἀπιτήδεια, ἅμα δ' ὅπως μᾶλλον ὑγιαίνοιεν καὶ
ἰσχύοιεν διαπονούμενοι ταῖς πορείαις, ἅμα δ' ὅπως
ἐν ταῖς ἀγωγαῖς τὰς τάξεις ὑπομιμνήσκοιντο.
25. Ὁ μὲν δὴ Κῦρος ἐν τούτοις ἦν.

Ἐκ δὲ Βαβυλῶνος οἱ αὐτόμολοι καὶ οἱ ἁλισκό-
μενοι ταῦτ'[1] ἔλεγον ὅτι ὁ Ἀσσύριος οἴχοιτο ἐπὶ
Λυδίας, πολλὰ τάλαντα χρυσίου καὶ ἀργυρίου
ἄγων καὶ ἄλλα κτήματα καὶ κόσμον παντοδαπόν.
26. ὁ μὲν οὖν ὄχλος τῶν στρατιωτῶν ἔλεγεν ὡς
ὑπεκτίθοιτο ἤδη τὰ χρήματα φοβούμενος· ὁ δὲ
Κῦρος γιγνώσκων ὅτι οἴχοιτο συστήσων εἴ τι
δύναιτο ἀντίπαλον ἑαυτῷ, ἀντιπαρεσκευάζετο ἐρ-
ρωμένως, ὡς μάχης ἔτι δεῆσον· ὥστ'[2] ἐξεπίμπλη
μὲν τὸ τῶν Περσῶν ἱππικόν, τοὺς μὲν ἐκ τῶν
αἰχμαλώτων, τοὺς δέ τινας καὶ παρὰ τῶν φίλων

[1] ταῦτ' Bothe, Edd. ; ταῦτ' MSS.
[2] ὥστ' Poppo, Edd. ; ὡς δ' xzV ; καὶ yV (corr.).

was most healthful and most readily accessible for conveying there everything that was necessary. And wherever any point needed further strengthening, he made provision that those who from time to time remained there should be in safety, even if he should be encamped at a distance with the main body of his forces. 24. But in addition to this, he made constant inquiry of those whom he thought likely to know about the country from what parts of it the army might get supplies as plentifully as possible and kept leading his men out on foraging expeditions; this he did partly that he might get supplies for the army in as great abundance as possible, partly that they might become inured to labour through these expeditions and might thus be in better health and strength, and partly that by such marches they might be enabled to keep their respective positions in mind.

25. Thus, then, Cyrus was occupied.

From Babylon a report was now brought by deserters and confirmed by his prisoners of war, that the Assyrian king had gone off in the direction of Lydia with many talents of gold and silver and with other treasures and jewels of every sort. 26. So it became general talk among the rank and file of the soldiers that he was already conveying his treasures to a place of safety because he was afraid. But Cyrus, recognizing that he had gone for the purpose of forming, if he could, a coalition against him, made vigorous counter preparation in the expectation that he would have to fight again. And so he set about bringing to its full complement the Persian cavalry, for which he obtained horses, some requisitioned from the captives, and a certain number

The king leaves Babylon

Cyrus increases his cavalry

λαμβάνων ἵππους· ταῦτα γὰρ παρὰ πάντων
ἐδέχετο καὶ ἀπεωθεῖτο οὐδέν, οὔτε εἴ τις ὅπλον
διδοίη καλὸν οὔτ' εἴ τις ἵππον.

27. Κατεσκευάζετο δὲ καὶ ἅρματα ἔκ τε τῶν
αἰχμαλώτων ἁρμάτων καὶ ἄλλοθεν ὁπόθεν ἐδύνατο. καὶ τὴν μὲν Τρωικὴν διφρείαν πρόσθεν
οὖσαν καὶ τὴν Κυρηναίων ἔτι καὶ νῦν ἁρματηλα-
σίαν κατέλυσε· τὸν γὰρ πρόσθεν χρόνον καὶ οἱ
ἐν τῇ Μηδίᾳ καὶ Συρίᾳ καὶ Ἀραβίᾳ καὶ πάντες οἱ
ἐν τῇ Ἀσίᾳ τοῖς ἅρμασιν οὕτως ἐχρῶντο ὥσπερ
νῦν οἱ Κυρηναῖοι. 28. ἔδοξε δ' αὐτῷ, ὃ κράτιστον
εἰκὸς ἦν εἶναι τῆς δυνάμεως, ὄντων τῶν βελτί-
στων ἐπὶ τοῖς ἅρμασι, τοῦτο ἐν ἀκροβολιστῶν μέρει
εἶναι καὶ εἰς τὸ κρατεῖν οὐδὲν μέγα [βάρος][1]
συμβάλλεσθαι. ἅρματα γὰρ τριακόσια τοὺς μὲν
μαχομένους παρέχεται τριακοσίους, ἵπποις δ'
οὗτοι χρῶνται διακοσίοις καὶ χιλίοις· ἡνίοχοι δ'
αὐτοῖς εἰσὶ μὲν ὡς εἰκὸς οἷς μάλιστα πιστεύουσιν,
οἱ βέλτιστοι· ἄλλοι δ' εἰσὶ τριακόσιοι οὗτοι,[2]
οἳ οὐδ' ὁτιοῦν τοὺς πολεμίους βλάπτουσι.
29. ταύτην μὲν οὖν τὴν διφρείαν κατέλυσεν· ἀντὶ
δὲ τούτου πολεμιστήρια κατεσκευάσατο ἅρματα
τροχοῖς τε ἰσχυροῖς, ὡς μὴ ῥαδίως συντρίβηται,
ἄξοσί τε μακροῖς· ἧττον γὰρ ἀνατρέπεται πάντα
τὰ πλατέα· τὸν δὲ δίφρον τοῖς ἡνιόχοις ἐποίησεν
ὥσπερ πύργον ἰσχυρῶν ξύλων· ὕψος δὲ τούτων
ἐστὶ μέχρι τῶν ἀγκώνων, ὡς δύνωνται ἡνιοχεῖ-
σθαι οἱ ἵπποι ὑπὲρ τῶν δίφρων· τοὺς δ' ἡνιόχους

[1] βάρος xz; bracketed by Hug, Marchant, Gemoll; μέρος
yV, Dindorf; omitted by Bornemann, Breitenbach.
[2] εἰσὶ τριακόσιοι οὗτοι Schneider, Breitenbach, Hug, Marchant; εἰς τριακοσίους οὗτοί εἰσι xz, Dindorf; εἰς τριακοσίους
οὗτοι δέ εἰσι y.

also presented to him by his friends ; for he accepted such gifts from every one and never refused anything, whether any one offered him a fine weapon or a horse.

27. Besides, with the chariots taken from the enemy and with whatever others he could get he equipped a corps of chariots of his own. The method of managing a chariot employed of old at Troy and that in vogue among the Cyrenaeans even unto this day he abolished; for in previous times people in Media and in Syria and in Arabia, and all the people in Asia used the chariot just as the Cyrenaeans now do. 28. But it seemed to him that inasmuch as the best men were mounted on the chariots, that part which might have been the chief strength of the army acted only the part of skirmishers and did not contribute anything of importance to the victory. For three hundred chariots call for three hundred combatants and require twelve hundred horses. And the fighting men must of course have as drivers the men in whom they have most confidence, that is, the best men to be had. That makes three hundred more, who do not do the enemy the least harm. 29. So he abolished this method of handling chariots, and in place of it he had chariots of war constructed with strong wheels, so that they might not easily be broken, and with long axles ; for anything broad is less likely to be overturned. The box for the driver he constructed out of strong timbers in the form of a turret ; and this rose in height to the drivers' elbows, so that they could manage the horses by reaching over the top of the box ; and, besides, he covered

Cyrus introduces a corps of chariots of war

ἐθωράκισε πάντα πλὴν τῶν ὀφθαλμῶν. 30. προσ-
έθηκε δὲ καὶ δρέπανα σιδηρᾶ ὡς διπήχη πρὸς
τοὺς ἄξονας ἔνθεν καὶ ἔνθεν τῶν τροχῶν καὶ ἄλλα
κάτω ὑπὸ τῷ ἄξονι εἰς τὴν γῆν βλέποντα, ὡς ἐμ-
βαλούντων εἰς τοὺς ἐναντίους τοῖς ἅρμασιν. ὡς
δὲ τότε Κῦρος ταῦτα κατεσκεύασεν, οὕτως ἔτι καὶ
νῦν τοῖς ἅρμασι χρῶνται οἱ ἐν τῇ βασιλέως
χώρᾳ.
Ἦσαν δὲ αὐτῷ καὶ κάμηλοι πολλαὶ παρά τε
τῶν φίλων συνειλεγμέναι καὶ αἱ[1] αἰχμάλωτοι
πᾶσαι συνηθροισμέναι.
31. Καὶ ταῦτα μὲν οὕτω συνεπεραίνετο.
Βουλόμενος δὲ κατάσκοπόν τινα πέμψαι ἐπὶ
Λυδίας καὶ μαθεῖν ὅ τι πράττοι ὁ Ἀσσύριος,
ἔδοξεν αὐτῷ ἐπιτήδειος εἶναι Ἀράσπας ἐλθεῖν
ἐπὶ τοῦτο ὁ φυλάττων τὴν καλὴν γυναῖκα. συνε-
βεβήκει γὰρ τῷ Ἀράσπᾳ τοιάδε· ληφθεὶς ἔρωτι
τῆς γυναικὸς ἠναγκάσθη προσενεγκεῖν λόγους
αὐτῇ περὶ συνουσίας. 32. ἡ δὲ ἀπέφησε μὲν
καὶ ἦν πιστὴ τῷ ἀνδρὶ καίπερ ἀπόντι· ἐφίλει
γὰρ αὐτὸν ἰσχυρῶς· οὐ μέντοι κατηγόρησε τοῦ
Ἀράσπου πρὸς τὸν Κῦρον, ὀκνοῦσα συμβαλεῖν
φίλους ἄνδρας. 33. ἐπεὶ δὲ ὁ Ἀράσπας δοκῶν
ὑπηρετήσειν τῷ τυχεῖν ἃ ἐβούλετο· ἠπείλησε
τῇ γυναικὶ ὅτι εἰ μὴ βούλοιτο ἑκοῦσα, ἄκουσα
ποιήσοι ταῦτα, ἐκ τούτου ἡ γυνή, ὡς ἔδεισε τὴν
βίαν, οὐκέτι κρύπτει, ἀλλὰ πέμπει τὸν εὐνοῦχον
πρὸς τὸν Κῦρον καὶ κελεύει λέξαι πάντα.
34. Ὁ δ᾽ ὡς ἤκουσεν, ἀναγελάσας ἐπὶ τῷ
κρείττονι τοῦ ἔρωτος φάσκοντι εἶναι, πέμπει
Ἀρτάβαζον σὺν τῷ εὐνούχῳ καὶ κελεύει αὐτῷ

---

[1] αἱ Dindorf, Edd. ; not in MSS.

the drivers with mail, all except their eyes. 30. On both sides of the wheels, moreover, he attached to the axles steel scythes about two cubits long and beneath the axles other scythes pointing down toward the ground ; this was so arranged with the intention of hurling the chariots into the midst of the enemy. And as Cyrus constructed them at that time, such even to this day are the chariots in use in the king's dominions.

He also had a large number of camels, some collected from among his friends and some taken in war, all brought together.

31. Thus these plans were being put into execution.

Now, he wished to send some one as a spy into Lydia to find out what the Assyrian was doing, and it seemed to him that Araspas, the guardian of the beautiful woman, was the proper person to go on this mission. Now Araspas's case had taken a turn like Araspas and this : he had fallen in love with the lady and could Panthea not resist the impulse to approach her with amorous proposals. 32. But she repulsed his advances and was true to her husband, although he was far away ; for she loved him devotedly. Still, she did not accuse Araspas to Cyrus, for she shrank from making trouble between friends. 33. But when Araspas, thinking that he should thus further the attainment of his desires, threatened the woman that he would use force if she would not submit willingly, then in fear of outrage the lady no longer kept it secret but She appeals sent her eunuch to Cyrus with instructions to tell him to Cyrus the whole story.

34. When Cyrus heard it he laughed outright at the man who had claimed to be superior to the passion of love ; and he sent Artabazus back with the

εἰπεῖν βιάζεσθαι μὲν μὴ τοιαύτην γυναῖκα, πείθειν δὲ εἰ δύναιτο, οὐκ ἔφη κωλύειν.

35. Ἐλθὼν δ' ὁ Ἀρτάβαζος πρὸς τὸν Ἀράσπαν ἐλοιδόρησεν αὐτόν, παρακαταθήκην ὀνομάζων τὴν γυναῖκα, ἀσέβειάν τε αὐτοῦ λέγων ἀδικίαν τε καὶ [1] ἀκράτειαν, ὥστε τὸν Ἀράσπαν πολλὰ μὲν δακρύειν ὑπὸ λύπης, καταδύεσθαι δ' ὑπὸ τῆς αἰσχύνης, ἀπολωλέναι δὲ τῷ φόβῳ μή τι καὶ πάθοι ὑπὸ Κύρου.

36. Ὁ οὖν Κῦρος καταμαθὼν ταῦτα ἐκάλεσεν αὐτὸν καὶ μόνος μόνῳ ἔλεξεν, Ὁρῶ σε, ἔφη, ὦ Ἀράσπα, φοβούμενόν τε ἐμὲ καὶ ἐν αἰσχύνῃ δεινῶς ἔχοντα. παῦσαι οὖν τούτων· ἐγὼ γὰρ θεούς τε ἀκούω ἔρωτος ἡττῆσθαι, ἀνθρώπους τε οἶδα καὶ μάλα δοκοῦντας φρονίμους εἶναι οἷα πεπόνθασιν ὑπ' ἔρωτος· καὶ αὐτὸς δ' ἐμαυτοῦ κατέγνων μὴ ἂν καρτερῆσαι ὥστε συνὼν καλοῖς ἀμελεῖν αὐτῶν. καὶ σοὶ δὲ τούτου τοῦ πράγματος ἐγὼ αἴτιός εἰμι· ἐγὼ γάρ σε συγκαθεῖρξα τούτῳ τῷ ἀμάχῳ πράγματι.

37. Καὶ ὁ Ἀράσπας ὑπολαβὼν εἶπεν, Ἀλλὰ σὺ μέν, ὦ Κῦρε, καὶ ταῦτα ὅμοιος εἶ οἷόσπερ καὶ τἆλλα, πρᾷός τε καὶ συγγνώμων τῶν ἀνθρωπίνων ἁμαρτημάτων· ἐμὲ δ', ἔφη, καὶ οἱ ἄλλοι ἄνθρωποι καταδύουσι τῷ ἄχει. ὡς γὰρ ὁ θροῦς διῆλθε τῆς ἐμῆς συμφορᾶς, οἱ μὲν ἐχθροὶ ἐφήδονταί μοι, οἱ δὲ φίλοι προσιόντες συμβουλεύουσιν ἐκποδὼν ἔχειν ἐμαυτόν, μή τι καὶ πάθω ὑπὸ σοῦ, ὡς ἠδικηκότος ἐμοῦ μεγάλα.

38. Καὶ ὁ Κῦρος εἶπεν, Εὖ τοίνυν ἴσθι, ὦ

[1] καὶ MSS., most Edd. ; τὴν Hartmann (calling his weakness ungodliness and sinfulness).

eunuch and bade him warn Araspas not to lay violent hands upon such a woman; but if he could win her consent, he himself would interpose no objection.

35. So, when Artabazus came to Araspas, he rebuked him severely, saying that the woman had been given to him in trust; and he dwelt upon his ungodliness, sinfulness, and sensuality, until Araspas shed bitter tears of contrition and was overwhelmed with shame and frightened to death lest Cyrus should punish him.

36. So, when Cyrus learned of this he sent for him and had a talk with him in private. "I see, Araspas," said he, "that you are afraid of me and terribly overcome with shame. Do not feel that way, pray; for I have heard say that even gods are victims of love; and as for mortals, I know what even some who are considered very discreet have suffered from love. And I had too poor an opinion of myself to suppose that I should have the strength of will to be thrown in contact with beauty and be indifferent to it. Besides, I am myself responsible for your condition, for it was I that shut you up with this irresistible creature." Cyrus discusses with Araspas his fall

37. "Aye, Cyrus," said Araspas, interrupting him, "you are in this, just as in everything else, gentle and forgiving of human errors. Other men make me ready to sink with my shame; for ever since the report of my fall got out, my enemies have been exulting over me, while my friends come to me and advise me to keep out of the way, for fear that you punish me for committing so great a wrong."

38. "Let me tell you then, Araspas," said Cyrus,

Ἀράσπα, ὅτι ταύτῃ τῇ δόξῃ οἷός τ' εἰ ἐμοί τε
ἰσχυρῶς χαρίσασθαι καὶ τοὺς συμμάχους μεγάλα
ὠφελῆσαι.

Εἰ γὰρ γένοιτο, ἔφη ὁ Ἀράσπας, ὅ τι ἐγώ σοι ἐν
καιρῷ ἂν γενοίμην [αὖ χρήσιμος].[1]

39. Εἰ τοίνυν, ἔφη, προσποιησάμενος ἐμὲ φεύγειν ἐθέλοις εἰς τοὺς πολεμίους ἐλθεῖν, οἶμαι ἄν
σε πιστευθῆναι ὑπὸ τῶν πολεμίων.

Ἔγωγε ναὶ μὰ Δί', ἔφη ὁ Ἀράσπας, καὶ ὑπὸ
τῶν φίλων οἶδα ὅτι ὡς σὲ πεφευγὼς λόγον ἂν
παρέχοιμι.

40. Ἔλθοις ἂν τοίνυν, ἔφη, ἡμῖν πάντα εἰδὼς
τὰ τῶν πολεμίων· οἶμαι δὲ καὶ λόγων καὶ βου-
λευμάτων κοινωνὸν ἄν σε ποιοῖντο διὰ τὸ πιστεύ-
ειν, ὥστε μηδὲ ἕν σε λεληθέναι ὧν βουλόμεθα
εἰδέναι.

Ὡς πορευσομένου, ἔφη, ἤδη νυνί· καὶ γὰρ
τοῦτο ἴσως ἓν τῶν πιστῶν ἔσται τὸ δοκεῖν με
ὑπὸ σοῦ μελλήσαντά τι παθεῖν ἐκπεφευγέναι.

41. Ἦ καὶ δυνήσει ἀπολιπεῖν, ἔφη, τὴν καλὴν
Πάνθειαν;

Δύο γάρ, ἔφη, ὦ Κῦρε, σαφῶς ἔχω ψυχάς· νῦν
τοῦτο πεφιλοσόφηκα μετὰ τοῦ ἀδίκου σοφιστοῦ
τοῦ Ἔρωτος. οὐ γὰρ δὴ μία γε οὖσα ἅμα ἀγαθή
τέ ἐστι καὶ κακή, οὐδ' ἅμα καλῶν τε καὶ αἰσχρῶν
ἔργων ἐρᾷ καὶ ταὐτὰ[2] ἅμα βούλεταί τε καὶ οὐ
βούλεται πράττειν, ἀλλὰ δῆλον ὅτι δύο ἐστὸν
ψυχά, καὶ ὅταν μὲν ἡ ἀγαθὴ κρατῇ, τὰ καλὰ

---

[1] αὖ χρήσιμος MSS. ; omitted by Weiske, Edd.
[2] ταὐτὰ Stephanus, Edd. ; ταῦτα MSS.

" that by reason of this very report which people have heard in regard to you, you are in a position to do me a very great favour and to be of great assistance to our allies."

" Would that some occasion might arise," answered Araspas, " in which I could be of service to you."

39. " If, then," said the other, " under pretence that you were fleeing from me you would go over into the enemy's country, I believe they would trust you." Cyrus sends him as a spy

" Aye, by Zeus," said Araspas, " and I know that even with my friends I could start the story that I was running away from you."

40. " Then you would return to us," said he, " with full information about the enemy's condition and plans. And I suppose that because of their trusting you they would make you a participant in their discussions and counsels, so that not a single thing that we wish to know would be hidden from you."

" Depend upon it," said he, " I will start at once ; and one of the circumstances that will gain my story credence will be the appearance that I have run away because I was likely to be punished by you."

41. " And will you be able to give up the beautiful Panthea ? " asked Cyrus.

" Yes, Cyrus," said he ; " for I evidently have two souls. I have now worked out this doctrine of philosophy in the school of that crooked sophist, Eros. For if the soul is one, it is not both good and bad at the same time, neither can it at the same time desire the right and the wrong, nor at the same time both will and not will to do the same things ; but it is obvious that there are two souls, and when the good one prevails, what is right is done ; but when the bad Doctrine of the duality of the soul

πράττεται, ὅταν δὲ ἦ πονηρά, τὰ αἰσχρὰ ἐπι-
χειρεῖται. νῦν δὲ ὡς σὲ σύμμαχον ἔλαβε, κρατεῖ
ἡ ἀγαθὴ καὶ πάνυ πολύ.

42. Εἰ τοίνυν καὶ σοὶ δοκεῖ πορεύεσθαι, ἔφη
ὁ Κῦρος, ὧδε χρὴ ποιεῖν, ἵνα κἀκείνοις πιστότερος
ἦς· ἐξάγγελλέ τε αὐτοῖς τὰ παρ' ἡμῶν, οὕτω τε
ἐξάγγελλε ὡς ἂν αὐτοῖς τὰ παρὰ σοῦ λεγόμενα
ἐμποδὼν μάλιστ' ἂν εἴη ὧν βούλονται πράττειν.
εἴη δ' ἂν ἐμποδών, εἰ ἡμᾶς φαίης παρασκευάζεσθαι
ἐμβαλεῖν ποι[1] τῆς ἐκείνων χώρας· ταῦτα γὰρ
ἀκούοντες ἧττον ἂν παντὶ σθένει ἀθροίζοιντο,
ἕκαστός τις φοβούμενος καὶ περὶ τῶν οἴκοι.
43. καὶ μένε, ἔφη, παρ' ἐκείνοις ὅτι πλεῖστον
χρόνον· ἃ γὰρ ἂν ποιῶσιν ὅταν ἐγγύτατα ἡμῶν
ὦσι, ταῦτα μάλιστα καιρὸς ἡμῖν εἰδέναι ἔσται.
συμβούλευε δ' αὐτοῖς καὶ ἐκτάττεσθαι ὅπῃ ἂν
δοκῇ κράτιστον εἶναι· ὅταν γὰρ σὺ ἀπέλθῃς
εἰδέναι δοκῶν τὴν τάξιν αὐτῶν, ἀναγκαῖον οὕτω
τετάχθαι αὐτοῖς· μετατάττεσθαι γὰρ ὀκνήσουσι,
καὶ ἤν πῃ ἄλλῃ μετατάττωνται ἐξ ὑπογύου,
ταράξονται.

44. Ἀράσπας μὲν δὴ οὕτως ἐξελθὼν καὶ συλλαβὼν τοὺς πιστοτάτους θεράποντας καὶ εἰπὼν
πρός τινας ἃ ᾤετο συμφέρειν τῷ πράγματι ᾤχετο.

45. Ἡ δὲ Πάνθεια ὡς ᾔσθετο οἰχόμενον τὸν
Ἀράσπαν, πέμψασα πρὸς τὸν Κῦρον εἶπε, Μὴ

---

[1] ποι Cobet, Hug. Marchant, Gemoll; που MSS., Dindorf,
Breitenbach.

one gains the ascendency, what is wrong is attempted. And now, since she has taken you to be her ally, it is the good soul that has gained the mastery, and that completely."

42. "Well then," answered Cyrus, "if you also have decided to go, this is what you must do so as to gain the more credence with them: tell them all about our affairs, but frame your account in such a way that your information will be the greatest possible hindrance to the success of their plans. And it would be a hindrance, if you should represent that we were making ready to invade their country at some point; for upon hearing this, they would be less likely to gather in full force, as each man would be afraid for his own possessions at home. 43. And stay with them as long as possible; for the most valuable information we can have will be in regard to what they are doing when they have come nearest to us. And advise them also to marshal themselves in whatever order seems best; for when you come away, it will be necessary for them to retain this order, even though they think you are familiar with it. For they will be slow to change it, and, if on the spur of the moment they make a change anywhere, they will be thrown into confusion." *Cyrus's final instructions to Araspas*

44. Then Araspas withdrew; he got together the most trusted of his attendants, told some of his friends such things as he thought would contribute to the success of his scheme, and was gone.

45. When Panthea learned that Araspas had gone away, she sent word to Cyrus, saying: "Do not be *Panthea sends for Abradatas*

143

λυποῦ, ὦ Κῦρε, ὅτι Ἀράσπας οἴχεται εἰς τοὺς
πολεμίους· ἢν γὰρ ἐμὲ ἐάσῃς πέμψαι πρὸς τὸν
ἐμὸν ἄνδρα, ἐγώ σοι ἀναδέχομαι ἥξειν πολὺ
Ἀράσπου πιστότερον φίλον· καὶ δύναμιν δὲ οἶδ'
ὅτι ὁπόσην ἂν δύνηται ἔχων παρέσται σοι. καὶ
γὰρ ὁ μὲν πατὴρ τοῦ νῦν βασιλεύοντος φίλος
ἦν αὐτῷ· ὁ δὲ νῦν βασιλεύων καὶ ἐπεχείρησέ
ποτε ἐμὲ καὶ τὸν ἄνδρα διασπάσαι ἀπ' ἀλλήλων·
ὑβριστὴν οὖν νομίζων αὐτὸν εὖ οἶδ' ὅτι ἄσμενος
ἂν πρὸς ἄνδρα οἷος εἶ ἀπαλλαγείη.

46. Ἀκούσας ταῦτα ὁ Κῦρος ἐκέλευε πέμπειν
πρὸς τὸν ἄνδρα· ἡ δ' ἔπεμψεν. ὡς δ' ἔγνω ὁ
Ἀβραδάτας τὰ παρὰ τῆς γυναικὸς σύμβολα,
καὶ τἆλλα δὲ ᾔσθετο ὡς εἶχεν, ἄσμενος πορεύεται
πρὸς τὸν Κῦρον ἵππους ἔχων ἀμφὶ τοὺς χιλίους.
ὡς δ' ἦν πρὸς τοῖς τῶν Περσῶν σκοποῖς, πέμπει
πρὸς τὸν Κῦρον εἰπὼν ὃς ἦν. ὁ δὲ Κῦρος εὐθὺς
ἄγειν κελεύει αὐτὸν πρὸς τὴν γυναῖκα. 47. ὡς
δ' εἰδέτην ἀλλήλους ἡ γυνὴ καὶ ὁ Ἀβραδάτας,
ἠσπάζοντο ἀλλήλους ὡς εἰκὸς ἐκ δυσελπίστων.
ἐκ τούτου δὴ λέγει ἡ Πάνθεια τοῦ Κύρου τὴν
ὁσιότητα καὶ τὴν σωφροσύνην καὶ τὴν πρὸς αὐτὴν
κατοίκτισιν.

Ὁ δὲ Ἀβραδάτας ἀκούσας εἶπε, Τί ἂν οὖν
ἐγὼ ποιῶν, ὦ Πάνθεια, χάριν Κύρῳ ὑπέρ τε σοῦ
καὶ ἐμαυτοῦ ἀποδοίην;

Τί δὲ ἄλλο, ἔφη ἡ Πάνθεια, ἢ πειρώμενος ὅμοιος
εἶναι περὶ ἐκεῖνον οἷόσπερ ἐκεῖνος περὶ σέ;

48. Ἐκ τούτου δὴ ἔρχεται πρὸς τὸν Κῦρον ὁ
Ἀβραδάτας· καὶ ὡς εἶδεν αὐτόν, λαβόμενος τῆς
δεξιᾶς εἶπεν, Ἀνθ' ὧν σὺ εὖ πεποίηκας ἡμᾶς, ὦ
Κῦρε, οὐκ ἔχω τί μεῖζον εἴπω ἢ ὅτι φίλον σοι

distressed, Cyrus, that Araspas has gone over to the
enemy; for if you will allow me to send to my
husband, I can guarantee you that a much more
faithful friend will come to you than Araspas was.
And what is more, I know that he will come to you
with as many troops as he can bring. For while the
father of the present king was his friend, this present
king once even attempted to separate me from my
husband. Inasmuch, therefore, as he considers the
king an insolent scoundrel, I am sure that he would
be glad to transfer his allegiance to such a man
as you."

46. When Cyrus heard that, he bade her send
word to her husband; and she did so. And when
Abradatas read the cipher message sent by his wife
and was informed how matters stood otherwise, he
joyfully proceeded with about a thousand horse to
join Cyrus. When he came up to the Persian sentries,
he sent to Cyrus to let him know who it was; and
Cyrus gave orders to take him at once to his wife.
47. And when Abradatas and his wife saw each other
they embraced each other with joy, as was natural,
considering they had not expected ever to meet again.
Thereafter Panthea told of Cyrus's piety and self-
restraint and of his compassion for her.

"Tell me, Panthea," said Abradatas when he heard
this, "what can I do to pay the debt of gratitude
that you and I owe to Cyrus?" *Abradatas makes common cause with Cyrus*

"What else, pray," said Panthea, "than to try to
be to him what he has been to you?"

48. Later Abradatas went to Cyrus. When he
saw him he took his right hand in his and said: "In
return for the kindnesses you have done us, Cyrus, I
do not know what more to say than that I offer

ἐμαυτὸν δίδωμι καὶ θεράποντα καὶ σύμμαχον·
καὶ ὅσα ἂν ὁρῶ σε σπουδάζοντα, συνεργὸς πειράσομαι γίγνεσθαι ὡς ἂν δύνωμαι κράτιστος.

49. Καὶ ὁ Κῦρος εἶπεν, Ἐγὼ δὲ δέχομαι· καὶ
νῦν μέν σε ἀφίημι, ἔφη, σὺν τῇ γυναικὶ δειπνεῖν·
αὖθις δὲ καὶ παρ' ἐμοὶ δεήσει σε σκηνοῦν σὺν τοῖς
σοῖς τε καὶ ἐμοῖς φίλοις.

50. Ἐκ τούτου ὁρῶν ὁ Ἀβραδάτας σπουδάζοντα τὸν Κῦρον περὶ τὰ δρεπανηφόρα ἅρματα
καὶ περὶ τοὺς τεθωρακισμένους ἵππους τε καὶ
ἱππέας, ἐπειρᾶτο συντελεῖν αὐτῷ εἰς τὰ ἑκατὸν
ἅρματα ἐκ τοῦ ἱππικοῦ τοῦ ἑαυτοῦ ὅμοια ἐκείνοις·[1]
αὐτὸς δὲ ὡς ἡγησόμενος αὐτῶν ἐπὶ τοῦ ἅρματος
παρεσκευάζετο. 51. συνεζεύξατο δὲ τὸ ἑαυτοῦ
ἅρμα τετράρρυμόν τε καὶ ἵππων ὀκτώ· [ἡ δὲ
Πάνθεια ἡ γυνὴ αὐτοῦ ἐκ τῶν ἑαυτῆς χρημάτων
χρυσοῦν τε αὐτῷ θώρακα ἐποιήσατο καὶ χρυσοῦν
κράνος, ὡσαύτως δὲ καὶ περιβραχιόνια.][2] τοὺς
δὲ ἵππους τοῦ ἅρματος χαλκοῖς πᾶσι προβλή-
μασι κατεσκευάσατο.

52. Ἀβραδάτας μὲν ταῦτα ἔπραττε· Κῦρος δὲ
ἰδὼν τὸ τετράρρυμον αὐτοῦ ἅρμα κατενόησεν
ὅτι οἷόν τε εἴη καὶ ὀκτάρρυμον ποιήσασθαι,
ὥστε ὀκτὼ ζεύγεσι βοῶν ἄγειν τῶν μηχανῶν
τὸ κατωτάτω[3] οἴκημα· ἦν δὲ τοῦτο τριώρυγον[4]

---

[1] ἐκείνοις Hug, Gemoll ; ἐκείνῳ MSS., most Edd. (for τοῖς
ἐκείνου).

[2] ἡ δὲ . . . περιβραχιόνια MSS., omitted by Bornemann
and Edd., as an obvious interpolation from VI. iv. 2.

[3] κατωτάτω Buttmann, Edd. ; κατώτατον MSS. ; omitted by
Herwerden, Marchant.

[4] τριώρυγον Dindorf, Edd.; τριοργυ(-ι D)ον yG[2] ; τὸ τριώρυον
xAH.

myself to you to be your friend, your servant, your ally. And in whatsoever enterprise I see you engage, I shall try to co-operate with you to the very best of my ability."

49. "And I accept your offer," said Cyrus. "And now I will take leave of you and let you go to dinner with your wife. Some other time you will be expected to dine at my headquarters with your friends and mine."

50. After this, as Abradatas observed that Cyrus was busily engaged with the scythe-bearing chariots and the mailed horses and riders, he tried to contribute from his own cavalry as many as a hundred chariots like them ; and he made ready to lead them in person upon his chariot. 51. He had the harnessing of his own chariot, moreover, arranged with four poles and eight horses abreast ; [and his wife, Panthea, with her own money had a golden corselet made for him and a helmet and armlet of gold ;] and he had the horses of his chariot equipped with armour of solid bronze.

52. Such was the work of Abradatas ; and when Cyrus saw his chariot with four poles, he conceived the idea that it was possible to make one even with eight poles, so as to move with eight yoke of oxen the lowest story of his movable towers ; including the wheels, this portion was about three fathoms

μάλιστα ἀπὸ τῆς γῆς σὺν τοῖς τροχοῖς. 53. τοιοῦτοι δὲ πύργοι σὺν τάξει ἀκολουθοῦντες ἐδόκουν
αὐτῷ μεγάλη μὲν ἐπικουρία γενέσθαι τῇ ἑαυτῶν
φάλαγγι, μεγάλη δὲ βλάβη τῇ τῶν πολεμίων
τάξει. ἐποίησε δὲ ἐπὶ τῶν οἰκημάτων καὶ περι-
δρόμους καὶ ἐπάλξεις· ἀνεβίβαζε δ' ἐπὶ τὸν
πύργον ἕκαστον ἄνδρας εἴκοσιν.

54. Ἐπεὶ δὲ πάντα συνειστήκει αὐτῷ τὰ περὶ
τοὺς πύργους, ἐλάμβανε τοῦ ἀγωγίου πεῖραν·
καὶ πολὺ ῥᾷον ἦγε τὰ ὀκτὼ ζεύγη τὸν πύργον
καὶ τοὺς ἐπ' αὐτῷ ἄνδρας ἢ τὸ σκευοφορικὸν
βάρος ἕκαστον τὸ ζεῦγος. σκευῶν μὲν γὰρ βάρος
ἀμφὶ τὰ πέντε καὶ εἴκοσι τάλαντα ἦν ζεύγει·
τοῦ δὲ πύργου, ὥσπερ τραγικῆς σκηνῆς τῶν
ξύλων πάχος ἐχόντων, καὶ εἴκοσιν ἀνδρῶν καὶ
ὅπλων, τούτων[1] ἐγένετο ἔλαττον ἢ πεντεκαίδεκα
τάλαντα ἑκάστῳ ζεύγει τὸ ἀγώγιον.

55. Ὡς δ' ἔγνω εὔπορον οὖσαν τὴν ἀγωγήν,
παρεσκευάζετο ὡς ἄξων τοὺς πύργους σὺν τῷ
στρατεύματι, νομίζων τὴν ἐν πολέμῳ πλεονεξίαν
ἅμα σωτηρίαν τε καὶ δικαιοσύνην εἶναι καὶ
εὐδαιμονίαν.

II

1. Ἦλθον δ' ἐν τούτῳ τῷ χρόνῳ καὶ παρὰ τοῦ
Ἰνδοῦ χρήματα ἄγοντες καὶ ἀπήγγελλον αὐτῷ
ὅτι ὁ Ἰνδὸς ἐπιστέλλει τοιάδε· Ἐγώ, ὦ Κῦρε,
ἥδομαι ὅτι μοι ἐπήγγειλας ὧν ἐδέου, καὶ βούλομαί σοι ξένος εἶναι καὶ πέμπω σοι χρήματα·

---

[1] τούτων Hutchinson, Edd. ; *harum turrium* Philelphus ;
τούτοις MSS.

high from the ground. 53. Moreover, when such towers were taken along with each division of the army, it seemed to him that they were a great help to his own phalanx and would occasion great loss to the ranks of the enemy. And on the different stories he constructed galleries also and battlements; and on each tower he stationed twenty men.

54. Now when all the appurtenances of his towers were put together, he made an experiment of their draught; and the eight yoke of oxen drew the tower with the men upon it more easily than each individual yoke could draw its *usual* load of baggage; for the load of baggage was about twenty-five talents[1] to the yoke; whereas the weight of the tower, on which the timbers were as thick as those of the tragic stage, together with the twenty men and their arms amounted to less than fifteen talents to each yoke of oxen.

55. Inasmuch, therefore, as he found that the hauling of the towers was easy, he made ready to take them with the army, for he thought that seizing an advantage in time of war was at once safety and justice and happiness.

II

1. At this juncture, representatives from the Indian king arrived with money; they announced also that the Indian king sent him the following message: "I am glad, Cyrus, that you let me know what you needed. I desire to be your friend, and I

Envoys from India are sent as spies

---

[1] That is, about 1400 pounds; the Attic talent is equivalent to 55¾ pounds avoirdupois.

κἂν ἄλλων δέῃ, μεταμέμπου. ἐπέσταλται δὲ τοῖς
παρ' ἐμοῦ ποιεῖν ὅ τι ἂν σὺ κελεύῃς.

2. Ἀκούσας δὲ ὁ Κῦρος εἶπε, Κελεύω τοίνυν
ὑμᾶς τοὺς μὲν ἄλλους μένοντας ἔνθα κατεσκηνώ-
κατε φυλάττειν τὰ χρήματα καὶ ζῆν ὅπως ὑμῖν
ἥδιστον· τρεῖς δέ μοι ἐλθόντες ὑμῶν εἰς τοὺς
πολεμίους ὡς παρὰ τοῦ Ἰνδοῦ περὶ συμμαχίας,
καὶ τἀκεῖ μαθόντες ὅ τι ἂν λέγωσί τε καὶ ποιῶσιν,
ὡς τάχιστα ἀπαγγείλατε ἐμοί τε καὶ τῷ Ἰνδῷ·
κἂν ταῦτά μοι καλῶς ὑπηρετήσητε, ἔτι μᾶλλον
ὑμῖν χάριν εἴσομαι τούτου ἢ ὅτι χρήματα πάρεστε ἄγοντες. καὶ γὰρ οἱ μὲν δούλοις ἐοικότες
κατάσκοποι οὐδὲν ἄλλο δύνανται εἰδότες ἀπαγ-
γέλλειν ἢ ὅσα πάντες ἴσασιν· οἱ δὲ οἷοίπερ ὑμεῖς
ἄνδρες πολλάκις καὶ τὰ βουλευόμενα καταμαν-
θάνουσιν.

3. Οἱ μὲν δὴ Ἰνδοὶ ἡδέως ἀκούσαντες καὶ
ξενισθέντες τότε παρὰ Κύρῳ, συσκευασάμενοι τῇ
ὑστεραίᾳ ἐπορεύοντο, ὑποσχόμενοι ἦ μὴν μαθόντες ὅσα ἂν δύνωνται πλεῖστα ἐκ τῶν πολεμίων
ἥξειν ὡς δυνατὸν τάχιστα.

4. Ὁ δὲ Κῦρος τά τε ἄλλα εἰς τὸν πόλεμον
παρεσκευάζετο μεγαλοπρεπῶς, ὡς δὴ ἀνὴρ οὐδὲν
μικρὸν ἐπινοῶν πράττειν, ἐπεμέλετο δὲ οὐ μόνον
ὧν ἔδοξε τοῖς συμμάχοις, ἀλλὰ καὶ ἔριν ἐνέβαλλε
πρὸς ἀλλήλους τοῖς φίλοις ὅπως αὐτοὶ ἕκαστοι
φανοῦνται καὶ εὐοπλότατοι καὶ ἱππικώτατοι καὶ
ἀκοντιστικώτατοι καὶ τοξικώτατοι καὶ φιλοπονώ-

am sending you the money, and if you need more, send for it. Moreover, my representatives have been instructed to do whatever you ask."

2. "Well then," said Cyrus, when he heard this, "I ask some of you to remain where you have been assigned quarters and keep guard of this money and live as best pleases you, while three of you will please go to the enemy on pretence of having been sent by the king of India to make an alliance between them and him; and when you have learned how things stand there, what they are doing and proposing to do, bring word of it as soon as possible to me and to your king. And if you perform this service acceptably, I shall be even more grateful to you for that than I am for your bringing the money with which you have come. And this is service which you are eminently fitted to perform; for spies disguised as slaves can give information of nothing more in their reports than what every one knows; whereas men in your capacity often discover even what is being planned."

3. The Indians were naturally pleased to hear this, and when they had been entertained by Cyrus, they made ready and set out on the following day with the solemn promise that when they had learned as much as they could they would return from the enemy's side with all possible dispatch.

4. The rest of his preparations for war Cyrus now continued on a magnificent scale, for he was planning no mean enterprise; and he provided not only for that which his allies had agreed upon but he also inspired his friends to rivalry among themselves, in order that each complement might strive to show its men the best armed soldiers, the most skilled horsemen, the best marksmen with spear or bow, and the

Further preparations for the conflict

τατοι. 5. ταῦτα δὲ ἐξειργάζετο ἐπὶ τὰς θήρας ἐξάγων καὶ τιμῶν τοὺς κρατίστους ἕκαστα· καὶ τοὺς ἄρχοντας δὲ οὓς ἑώρα ἐπιμελομένους τούτου ὅπως οἱ αὑτῶν¹ κράτιστοι ἔσονται στρατιῶται, καὶ τούτους ἐπαινῶν τε παρώξυνε καὶ χαριζόμενος αὐτοῖς ὅ τι δύναιτο. 6. εἰ δέ ποτε θυσίαν ποιοῖτο καὶ ἑορτὴν ἄγοι, καὶ ἐν ταύτῃ ὅσα πολέμου ἕνεκα μελετῶσιν ἄνθρωποι πάντων τούτων ἀγῶνας ἐποίει καὶ ἆθλα τοῖς νικῶσι μεγαλοπρεπῶς ἐδίδου, καὶ ἦν πολλὴ εὐθυμία ἐν τῷ στρατεύματι.

7. Τῷ δὲ Κύρῳ σχεδόν τι ἤδη ἀποτετελεσμένα ἦν ὅσα ἐβούλετο ἔχων στρατεύεσθαι πλὴν τῶν μηχανῶν. καὶ γὰρ οἱ Πέρσαι ἱππεῖς ἔκπλεω ἤδη ἦσαν εἰς τοὺς μυρίους, καὶ τὰ ἅρματα τὰ δρεπανηφόρα, ἅ τε αὐτὸς κατεσκεύαζεν, ἔκπλεω ἤδη ἦν εἰς τὰ ἑκατόν, ἅ τε Ἀβραδάτας ὁ Σούσιος ἐπεχείρησε κατασκευάζειν ὅμοια τοῖς Κύρου, καὶ ταῦτα ἔκπλεω ἦν εἰς ἄλλα ἑκατόν. 8. καὶ τὰ Μηδικὰ δὲ ἅρματα ἐπεπείκει Κῦρος Κυαξάρην εἰς τὸν αὐτὸν τρόπον τοῦτον μετασκευάσαι ἐκ τῆς Τρωικῆς καὶ Λιβυκῆς διφρείας· καὶ ἔκπλεω καὶ ταῦτα ἦν εἰς ἄλλα ἑκατόν. καὶ ἐπὶ τὰς καμήλους δὲ τεταγμένοι ἦσαν ἄνδρες δύο ἐφ᾽ ἑκάστην τοξόται. καὶ ὁ μὲν πλεῖστος στρατὸς οὕτως εἶχε τὴν γνώμην ὡς ἤδη παντελῶς κεκρατηκὼς καὶ οὐδὲν ὄντα τὰ τῶν πολεμίων.

9. Ἐπεὶ δὲ οὕτω διακειμένων ἦλθον οἱ Ἰνδοὶ ἐκ τῶν πολεμίων οὓς ἐπεπόμφει Κῦρος ἐπὶ κατασκοπήν, καὶ ἔλεγον ὅτι Κροῖσος μὲν ἡγεμὼν καὶ

¹ αὑτῶν Stephanus, Hug, Marchant, Gemoll ; αὐτῶν Dindorf (who ascribes his reading to Stephanus), Breitenbach ; αὐτοὶ xz ; αὐτοῦ yG².

most industrious workers. 5. And, as a means of accomplishing this, he took them out to hunt and rewarded those who were in each particular most efficient. Furthermore, those officers who, he saw, were eager to have their own soldiers most efficient he spurred on with praise and with whatever favours he could bestow. 6. And then, too, whenever he performed a sacrifice or celebrated a festival, he instituted in connection with it contests in all those events in which people train as a discipline for war, and to the victors he offered splendid prizes; and the whole camp was in the best of spirits.

7. Cyrus now had almost everything ready that he wished to have for his expedition except the engines of war. For the ranks of his Persian horse were now filled up to the number of ten thousand, the scythe-bearing chariots that he himself had had constructed had now reached the full number of one hundred, and those which Abradatas of Susa had undertaken to secure like those of Cyrus had also reached the full number of one hundred more. 8. And Cyrus had persuaded Cyaxares to transform the Median chariots also from the Trojan and Libyan type to this same style, and these amounted to another full hundred. For the camel corps, bowmen were detailed, two upon each camel. Thus the rank and file of the army generally cherished the feeling that the victory was already perfectly assured and that the enemy's side was as nothing.

9. While they were in this state of mind, the Indians that Cyrus had sent as spies to the enemy's camp returned with the report that Croesus had

The report of the Indian spies

στρατηγὸς πάντων ᾑρημένος εἴη τῶν πολεμίων,
δεδογμένον δ' εἴη πᾶσι τοῖς συμμάχοις βασιλεῦσι
πάσῃ τῇ δυνάμει ἕκαστον παρεῖναι, χρήματα δὲ
εἰσφέρειν πάμπολλα, ταῦτα δὲ τελεῖν καὶ μισθου-
μένους οὓς δύναιντο καὶ δωρουμένους οἷς δέοι, 10.
ἤδη δὲ καὶ μεμισθωμένους εἶναι πολλοὺς μὲν
Θρᾳκῶν μαχαιροφόρους, Αἰγυπτίους δὲ προσ-
πλεῖν, καὶ ἀριθμὸν ἔλεγον εἰς δώδεκα μυριάδας σὺν ἀσπίσι ποδήρεσι καὶ δόρασι μεγάλοις,
οἷάπερ καὶ νῦν ἔχουσι, καὶ κοπίσι· προσέτι
δὲ καὶ Κυπρίων στράτευμα· παρεῖναι δ' ἤδη
Κίλικας πάντας καὶ Φρύγας ἀμφοτέρους καὶ
Λυκάονας καὶ Παφλαγόνας καὶ Καππαδόκας καὶ
Ἀραβίους καὶ Φοίνικας καὶ σὺν τῷ Βαβυλῶνος
ἄρχοντι τοὺς Ἀσσυρίους, καὶ Ἴωνας δὲ καὶ
Αἰολέας καὶ σχεδὸν πάντας τοὺς Ἕλληνας τοὺς ἐν
τῇ Ἀσίᾳ ἐποικοῦντας σὺν Κροίσῳ ἠναγκάσθαι
ἕπεσθαι, πεπομφέναι δὲ Κροῖσον καὶ εἰς Λα-
κεδαίμονα περὶ συμμαχίας· 11. συλλέγεσθαι δὲ
τὸ στράτευμα ἀμφὶ τὸν Πακτωλὸν ποταμόν,
προϊέναι δὲ μέλλειν αὐτοὺς εἰς Θύμβραρα, ἔνθα
καὶ νῦν ὁ σύλλογος τῶν ὑπὸ βασιλέα βαρβάρων
τῶν κάτω [Συρίας],[1] καὶ ἀγορὰν πᾶσι παρηγγέλ-
θαι ἐνταῦθα κομίζειν.

Σχεδὸν δὲ τούτοις ταὐτὰ ἔλεγον καὶ οἱ αἰχ-
μάλωτοι· ἐπεμέλετο γὰρ καὶ τούτου ὁ Κῦρος ὅπως
ἁλίσκοιντο παρ' ὧν ἔμελλε πεύσεσθαί τι· ἔπεμπε
δὲ καὶ δούλοις ἐοικότας κατασκόπους ὡς αὐτο-
μόλους.

---

[1] Συρίας MSS., Dindorf ; [Συρίας] Lincke, most Edd.

been chosen field-marshal and commander-in-chief of all the enemy's hosts, that all the allied kings had decided to join him with their entire forces, to contribute vast sums of money, and to expend them in hiring what soldiers they could and in giving presents to those whom they were under obligations to reward. 10. They reported also that many Thracian swordsmen had already been hired and that Egyptians were under sail to join them, and they gave the number as one hundred and twenty thousand men armed with shields that came to their feet, with huge spears, such as they carry even to this day, and with sabres. Besides these, there was also the Cyprian army. The Cilicians were all present already, they said, as were also the contingents from both Phrygias, Lycaonia, Paphlagonia, Cappadocia, Arabia, and Phoenicia; the Assyrians were there under the king of Babylon; the Ionians also and the Aeolians and almost all the Greek colonists in Asia had been compelled to join Croesus, and Croesus had even sent to Lacedaemon to negotiate an alliance. 11. This army, they said, was being mustered at the River Pactolus, but it was their intention to advance to Thymbrara, where even to-day is the rendezvous of the king's barbarians from the interior. And a general call had been issued to bring provisions to market there.

The prisoners also told practically the same story as the Indian spies; for this was another thing that Cyrus always looked out for—that prisoners should be taken, from whom he was likely to gain some intelligence. And he used also to send out spies disguised as slaves to pretend that they were deserters from him.

12. Ὡς οὖν ταῦτα ἤκουσεν ὁ στρατὸς τοῦ Κύρου, ἐν φροντίδι τε ἐγένετο, ὥσπερ εἰκός, ἡσυχαίτεροί τε ἢ ὡς εἰώθεσαν διεφοίτων, [φαιδροί τε οὐ πάνυ ἐφαίνοντο,][1] ἐκυκλοῦντό τε καὶ μεστὰ ἦν πάντα ἀλλήλους ἐρωτώντων περὶ τούτων καὶ διαλεγομένων.

13. Ὡς δὲ ᾔσθετο ὁ Κῦρος φόβον διαθέοντα ἐν τῇ στρατιᾷ, συγκαλεῖ τούς τε ἄρχοντας τῶν στρατευμάτων καὶ πάντας ὁπόσων ἀθυμούντων ἐδόκει βλάβη τις γίγνεσθαι καὶ προθυμουμένων ὠφέλεια. προεῖπε δὲ τοῖς ὑπηρέταις, καὶ ἄλλος εἴ τις βούλοιτο τῶν ὁπλοφόρων προσίστασθαι[2] ἀκουσόμενος τῶν λόγων, μὴ κωλύειν. ἐπεὶ δὲ συνῆλθον, ἔλεξε τοιάδε·

14. Ἄνδρες σύμμαχοι, ἐγὼ τοίνυν ὑμᾶς συνεκάλεσα ἰδών τινας ὑμῶν, ἐπεὶ αἱ ἀγγελίαι ἦλθον ἐκ τῶν πολεμίων, πάνυ ἐοικότας πεφοβημένοις ἀνθρώποις. δοκεῖ γάρ μοι θαυμαστὸν εἶναι εἴ τις ὑμῶν ὅτι μὲν οἱ πολέμιοι συλλέγονται δέδοικεν, ὅτι δὲ ἡμεῖς πολὺ πλείους συνειλέγμεθα νῦν ἢ ὅτε ἐνικῶμεν ἐκείνους, πολὺ δὲ ἄμεινον σὺν θεοῖς παρεσκευάσμεθα νῦν ἢ πρόσθεν, ταῦτα δὲ ὁρῶντες οὐ θαρρεῖτε.

15. Ὦ πρὸς θεῶν, ἔφη, τί δῆτα ἂν ἐποιήσατε οἱ νῦν δεδοικότες, εἰ ἤγγελλόν τινες τὰ παρ᾽ ἡμῖν νῦν ὄντα ταῦτα ἀντίπαλα ἡμῖν προσιόντα, καὶ πρῶτον μὲν ἠκούετε, ἔφη, ὅτι οἱ πρότερον νικήσαντες ἡμᾶς οὗτοι πάλιν ἔρχονται ἔχοντες ἐν ταῖς ψυχαῖς ἣν τότε νίκην ἐκτήσαντο· ἔπειτα δὲ οἱ

[1] φαιδροί . . . ἐφαίνετο MSS., Edd. ; bracketed by Hug, Hartmann.

[2] προσίστασθαι Stephanus, Edd. ; προίστασθαι MSS.

12. When Cyrus's army heard this report, they were disturbed, as was natural; they went about more subdued than had been their wont, they gathered in groups, and every corner was full of people discussing the situation and asking one another's opinion. General alarm at the report

13. When Cyrus perceived that a panic was spreading through his army, he called together the officers of the different divisions and all others whose despondency he thought might cause injury and whose enthusiasm would be a help. And he sent word to his aides-de-camp that if any one else of the armed soldiers wished to attend the meeting and listen to the speeches, they should not hinder him. And when they had come together, he addressed them as follows:

14. "Friends and allies, I have called you together because I observed that when this news came from the enemy, some of you looked as if you were frightened. Now it seems strange to me that any of you should really be afraid because the enemy are mustering; but when you see that we are mustered in much larger numbers than we had when we defeated them and that we are now, thank heaven, much better equipped than we were then—it is strange that when you see this you are not filled with courage! Cyrus calms their fears

15. "What in the name of heaven, pray, would you who are now afraid have done, if the situation were reversed and some one told you that these forces that we have now were coming against us? And what, if you heard, in the first place, that those who had defeated us before were coming again, their hearts full of the victory they then gained; and, in

τότε ἐκκόψαντες τῶν τοξοτῶν καὶ ἀκοντιστῶν τὰς
ἀκροβολίσεις νῦν οὗτοι ἔρχονται καὶ ἄλλοι ὅμοιοι
τούτοις πολλαπλάσιοι· 16. ἔπειτα δὲ ὥσπερ
οὗτοι ὁπλισάμενοι τοὺς πεζοὺς τότ᾽ ἐνίκων, νῦν
οὕτω καὶ οἱ ἱππεῖς αὐτῶν παρεσκευασμένοι πρὸς
τοὺς ἱππέας προσέρχονται, καὶ τὰ μὲν τόξα καὶ
ἀκόντια ἀποδεδοκιμάκασι, παλτὸν δὲ ἓν ἰσχυρὸν
ἕκαστος λαβὼν προσελαύνειν διανενόηται ὡς ἐκ
χειρὸς τὴν μάχην ποιησόμενος· 17. ἔτι δὲ ἅρματα
ἔρχεται, ἃ οὐχ οὕτως ἑστήξει[1] ὥσπερ πρόσθεν
ἀπεστραμμένα ὥσπερ εἰς φυγήν, ἀλλ᾽ οἵ τε ἵπποι
εἰσὶ κατατεθωρακισμένοι οἱ ἐν τοῖς ἅρμασιν, οἵ τε
ἡνίοχοι ἐν πύργοις ἑστᾶσι ξυλίνοις τὰ ὑπερέχοντα
ἅπαντα συνεστεγασμένοι θώραξι καὶ κράνεσι,
δρέπανά τε σιδηρᾶ περὶ τοῖς ἄξοσι προσήρμοσται,
ὡς ἐλῶντες καὶ οὗτοι εὐθὺς εἰς τὰς τάξεις τῶν
ἐναντίων· 18. πρὸς δ᾽ ἔτι κάμηλοι εἰσὶν αὐτοῖς ἐφ᾽
ὧν προσελῶσιν, ὧν μίαν ἑκάστην ἑκατὸν ἵπποι
οὐκ ἂν ἀνάσχοιντο ἰδόντες· ἔτι δὲ πύργους προσίασιν ἔχοντες ἀφ᾽ ὧν τοῖς μὲν ἑαυτῶν ἀρήξουσιν,
ἡμᾶς δὲ βάλλοντες κωλύσουσι τοῖς ἐν τῷ ἰσο-
πέδῳ μάχεσθαι· 19. εἰ δὴ ταῦτα ἀπήγγελλέ τις
ὑμῖν ἐν τοῖς πολεμίοις ὄντα, οἱ νῦν φοβούμενοι
τί ἂν ἐποιήσατε; ὁπότε ἀπαγγελλομένων ὑμῖν
ὅτι Κροῖσος μὲν ᾕρηται τῶν πολεμίων στρατη-
γός, ὃς τοσούτῳ Σύρων κακίων ἐγένετο ὅσῳ
Σύροι μὲν μάχῃ ἡττηθέντες ἔφυγον, Κροῖσος δὲ
ἰδὼν Σύρους[2] ἡττημένους ἀντὶ τοῦ ἀρήγειν τοῖς

---

[1] ἑστήξει Elmsley, most Edd. ; ἑστήξεται MSS., Sauppe,
Breitenbach.
[2] Σύρους Hug ; not in MSS. or other Edd.

the second place, that those who before made short work of the skirmishing lines of bowmen and spearmen were now coming and others like them many times their number; 16. and, in the third place, that, equipped in the same armour in which they were armed when their infantry defeated our infantry, they have cavalry now coming to meet our cavalry; that they have rejected the bow and the javelin, and that each man has adopted one heavy lance and is resolved to ride up and fight hand to hand? 17. And again, what would you have done, if you heard that chariots are coming which are not, as before, to stand still facing back as if for flight, but that the horses harnessed to the chariots are covered with mail, while the drivers stand in wooden towers and the parts of their body not defended by the towers are completely panoplied in breast-plates and helmets; and that scythes of steel have been fitted to the axles, and that it is the intention to drive these also into the ranks of the enemy? 18. Or again, if you heard that they have camels on which they will ride up to us, and a hundred horses could not endure the sight of any one of them? And again, that they are coming with towers, from which they will protect their comrades and by throwing missiles hinder us from fighting in a fair field? 19. If any one reported to you that this was the condition of things among the enemy, what would you, who are now so frightened, have done, seeing that you were terrified when the report came that Croesus had been elected commander-in-chief of the enemy— Croesus, who was a worse coward than the Syrians; for the Syrians fled because they were defeated in the battle, whereas Croesus, instead of standing by his allies, beat a hasty retreat when he saw that they

and fills them with new enthusiasm

συμμάχοις φεύγων ᾤχετο· 20. ἔπειτα δὲ διαγ-
γέλλεται δήπου ὅτι αὐτοὶ μὲν οἱ πολέμιοι οὐχ
ἱκανοὶ ἡγοῦνται ὑμῖν εἶναι μάχεσθαι, ἄλλους δὲ
μισθοῦνται, ὡς ἄμεινον μαχουμένους ὑπὲρ σφῶν
ἢ αὐτοί. εἰ μέντοι τισὶ ταῦτα μὲν τοιαῦτα ὄντα
δεινὰ δοκεῖ εἶναι, τὰ δὲ ἡμέτερα φαῦλα, τούτους
ἐγώ φημι χρῆναι, ὦ ἄνδρες, ἀφεῖναι εἰς τοὺς
ἐναντίους· πολὺ γὰρ ἐκεῖ ὄντες πλείω ἂν ἡμᾶς ἢ
παρόντες ὠφελοῖεν.

21. Ἐπεὶ δὲ ταῦτα εἶπεν ὁ Κῦρος, ἀνέστη
Χρυσάντας ὁ Πέρσης καὶ ἔλεξεν ὧδε· Ὦ Κῦρε,
μὴ θαύμαζε εἴ τινες ἐσκυθρώπασαν ἀκούσαντες
τῶν ἀγγελλομένων· οὐ γὰρ φοβηθέντες οὕτω
διετέθησαν, ἀλλ' ἀχθεσθέντες· ὥσπερ γε, ἔφη,
εἴ τινων βουλομένων τε καὶ οἰομένων ἤδη ἀρι-
στήσειν ἐξαγγελθείη τι ἔργον ὃ ἀνάγκη εἴη πρὸ
τοῦ ἀρίστου ἐξεργάσασθαι, οὐδεὶς ἂν οἶμαι ἡσθείη
ἀκούσας· οὕτω τοίνυν καὶ ἡμεῖς ἤδη οἰόμενοι
πλουτήσειν, ἐπεὶ ἠκούσαμεν ὅτι ἐστὶ περίλοιπον
ἔργον ὃ δεῖ ἐξεργάσασθαι, συνεσκυθρωπάσαμεν,
οὐ φοβούμενοι, ἀλλὰ πεποιῆσθαι ἂν ἤδη καὶ
τοῦτο βουλόμενοι.

22. Ἀλλὰ γὰρ ἐπειδὴ οὐ περὶ Συρίας μόνον
ἀγωνιούμεθα, ὅπου σῖτος πολὺς καὶ πρόβατά
ἐστι καὶ φοίνικες οἱ καρποφόροι, ἀλλὰ καὶ περὶ
Λυδίας, ἔνθα πολὺς μὲν οἶνος, πολλὰ δὲ σῦκα,
πολὺ δὲ ἔλαιον, θάλαττα δὲ προσκλύζει καθ' ἣν
πλείω ἔρχεται ἢ ὅσα τις ἑώρακεν ἀγαθά, ταῦτα,

vere defeated? 20. And finally, you see, the
report is brought that the enemy do not feel that
they are strong enough to fight us by themselves, but
are hiring others in the hope that these will fight
for them more valiantly than they can for themselves. However, if there are any to whom the
situation over there—such as it is—seems formidable,
while our own condition seems contemptible, I say,
men, that we ought to send them over to the enemy,
for they would be much more useful to us over there
than in our ranks."

21. When Cyrus had finished his speech, Chrysan- Chrysantas
tas, the Persian, arose and spoke as follows: "Do explains
not wonder, Cyrus, that some looked disconsolate away the
when they heard the report; for it was not from fear fear
that they felt this, but from vexation—just as, if it
should be announced, when people are ready and
waiting to sit down to luncheon, that there is some
work that they must do before they may eat, not
one, I venture to say, would be pleased to hear it.
So we also, thinking we were just on the point of
getting rich, all put on a disconsolate look when we
heard that there was some work left over which we
must do; and it was not because we were frightened,
but because we wished that this, too, were already
accomplished.

22. " But our disappointment is past, seeing that
we are to contend not for Syria only, where there
is an abundance of grain and flocks and date-palms,
but for Lydia as well; for in that land there is an
abundance of wine and figs and olive oil, and its
shores are washed by the sea; and over its waters
more good things are brought than any one has ever
seen—when we think of that," said he, " we are no

ἔφη, ἐννοούμενοι οὐκέτι ἀχθόμεθα, ἀλλὰ θαρροῦμεν ὡς μάλιστα,[1] ἵνα θᾶττον καὶ τούτων τῶν
Λυδίων ἀγαθῶν ἀπολαύωμεν.

Ὁ μὲν οὕτως εἶπεν· οἱ δὲ σύμμαχοι πάντες
ἥσθησάν τε τῷ λόγῳ καὶ ἐπήνεσαν.

23. Καὶ μὲν δή, ἔφη ὁ Κῦρος, ὦ ἄνδρες, δοκεῖ
μοι ἰέναι ἐπ᾽ αὐτοὺς ὡς τάχιστα, ἵνα πρῶτον μὲν
αὐτοὺς φθάσωμεν ἀφικόμενοι, ἢν δυνώμεθα, ὅπου
τἀπιτήδεια αὐτοῖς συλλέγεται· ἔπειτα δὲ ὅσῳ ἂν
θᾶττον ἴωμεν, τοσούτῳ μείω μὲν τὰ παρόντα
εὑρήσομεν αὐτοῖς, πλείω δὲ τὰ ἀπόντα. 24. ἐγὼ
μὲν δὴ οὕτω λέγω· εἰ δέ τις ἄλλῃ πῃ γιγνώσκει ἢ
ἀσφαλέστερον εἶναι ἢ ῥᾷον ἡμῖν, διδασκέτω.

Ἐπεὶ δὲ συνηγόρευον μὲν πολλοὶ ὡς χρεὼν εἴη
ὅτι τάχιστα πορεύεσθαι ἐπὶ τοὺς πολεμίους,
ἀντέλεγε δὲ οὐδείς, ἐκ τούτου δὴ ὁ Κῦρος ἤρχετο
λόγου τοιοῦδε·

25. Ἄνδρες σύμμαχοι, αἱ μὲν ψυχαὶ καὶ τὰ
σώματα καὶ τὰ ὅπλα οἷς δεήσει χρῆσθαι ἐκ πολλοῦ ἡμῖν σὺν θεῷ παρεσκεύασται· νῦν δὲ τἀπιτήδεια δεῖ εἰς τὴν ὁδὸν συσκευάζεσθαι αὐτοῖς τε
ἡμῖν καὶ ὁπόσοις τετράποσι χρώμεθα μὴ μεῖον ἢ
εἴκοσιν ἡμερῶν. ἐγὼ γὰρ λογιζόμενος εὑρίσκω
πλέον[2] ἢ πεντεκαίδεκα ἡμερῶν ἐσομένην ὁδόν, ἐν
ᾗ οὐδὲν εὑρήσομεν τῶν ἐπιτηδείων· ἀνεσκεύασται
γὰρ τὰ μὲν ὑφ᾽ ἡμῶν, τὰ δὲ ὑπὸ τῶν πολεμίων
ὅσα ἐδύναντο. 26. συσκευάζεσθαι οὖν χρὴ σίτου
μὲν ἱκανόν· ἄνευ γὰρ τούτου οὔτε μάχεσθαι οὔτε
ζῆν δυναίμεθ᾽ ἄν· οἶνον δὲ τοσοῦτον ἕκαστον ἔχειν

---

[1] μάλιστα Dindorf, Edd. ; τάχιστα MSS.
[2] πλέον Dindorf[4], Marchant, Gemoll ; πλεόνων F, Dindorf[3],
Breitenbach ; πλέον ὃν DG[2].

longer vexed, but our courage rises to the highest point, with desire to come all the more quickly into the enjoyment of these good things in Lydia also."

Thus he spoke; and the allies were all pleased with his speech and applauded.

23. "And indeed, my friends," said Cyrus, " I propose that we move against them as soon as possible, in the first place that we may reach the place where their supplies are being collected, before they do, if we can; and in the second place, because the faster we march the less perfected we shall find their arrangements and the greater we shall find their deficiencies. 24. This, then, is my proposal; but if any one thinks that any other course would be safer or easier for us, let him inform us." *Cyrus proposes an immediate advance*

Many supported him, saying that it was expedient to proceed as soon as possible against the enemy, and no one opposed his plan; so Cyrus began to speak as follows :

25. " Friends and allies, our souls and bodies and the arms that we shall have to use have, with God's help, long since been made ready. And now for the march we must get together for ourselves and for the animals that we use provisions for not less than twenty days; for in reckoning it up, I find that there will be more than fifteen days' journey in which we shall find no provisions at all; for everything there has been made away with : the enemy took all that they could, and we have taken the rest. 26. Accordingly, we must put up and carry with us food enough; for without this we should be unable either to fight or to live. As for wine, each one ought to take along only enough to last till

χρὴ ὅσος ἱκανὸς ἔσται ἐθίσαι ἡμᾶς αὑτοὺς ὑδρο-
ποτεῖν· πολλὴ γὰρ ἔσται τῆς ὁδοῦ ἄοινος, εἰς ἣν
οὐδ' ἂν πάνυ πολὺν οἶνον συσκευασώμεθα, διαρ-
κέσει. 27. ὡς οὖν μὴ ἐξαπίνης ἄοινοι γενόμενοι
νοσήμασι περιπίπτωμεν, ὧδε χρὴ ποιεῖν· ἐπὶ μὲν
τῷ σίτῳ νῦν εὐθὺς ἀρχώμεθα πίνειν ὕδωρ· τοῦτο
γὰρ ἤδη ποιοῦντες οὐ πολὺ μεταβαλοῦμεν. 28. καὶ
γὰρ ὅστις ἀλφιτοσιτεῖ, ὕδατι μεμαγμένην [1] ἀεὶ τὴν
μᾶζαν ἐσθίει, καὶ ὅστις ἀρτοσιτεῖ, ὕδατι δεδευ-
μένον τὸν ἄρτον, καὶ τὰ ἑφθὰ δὲ πάντα μεθ' ὕδατος
τοῦ πλείστου ἐσκεύασται. μετὰ δὲ τὸν σῖτον ἂν
οἶνον ἐπιπίνωμεν, οὐδὲν μεῖον ἔχουσα ἡ ψυχὴ
ἀναπαύσεται. 29. ἔπειτα δὲ καὶ τοῦ μετὰ δεῖπνον
ἀφαιρεῖν χρή, ἕως ἂν λάθωμεν ὑδροπόται γενόμενοι. ἡ γὰρ κατὰ μικρὸν παράλλαξις πᾶσαν ποιεῖ
φύσιν ὑποφέρειν τὰς μεταβολάς· διδάσκει δὲ καὶ
ὁ θεός, ἀπάγων ἡμᾶς κατὰ μικρὸν ἔκ τε τοῦ χειμῶνος εἰς τὸ ἀνέχεσθαι ἰσχυρὰ θάλπη ἔκ τε τοῦ
θάλπους εἰς τὸν ἰσχυρὸν χειμῶνα· ὃν χρὴ μιμου-
μένους εἰς ὃ δεῖ ἐλθεῖν προειθισμένους ἡμᾶς
ἀφικνεῖσθαι.

30. Καὶ τὸ τῶν στρωμάτων δὲ βάρος εἰς τὰ-
πιτήδεια καταδαπανᾶτε· τὰ μὲν γὰρ ἐπιτήδεια
περιττεύοντα οὐκ ἄχρηστα ἔσται· στρωμάτων δὲ
ἐνδεηθέντες μὴ δείσητε ὡς οὐχ ἡδέως καθευδήσετε·
εἰ δὲ μή, ἐμὲ αἰτιᾶσθε. ἐσθὴς μέντοι ὅτῳ ἐστὶν
ἀφθονωτέρα παροῦσα, πολλὰ καὶ ὑγιαίνοντι καὶ
κάμνοντι ἐπικουρεῖ.

---

[1] μεμαγμένην Hemsterhuys, Dindorf [4], Marchant, Gemoll;
μεμιγμένην MSS., Dindorf [3], Breitenbach.

we accustom ourselves to drinking water; for the The wine habit to be broken off gradually
greater part of the march will be through a country
where there is no wine, and for that all the wine
we can carry will not suffice, even if we take along
a very great quantity. 27. That we may not,
therefore, fall a prey to sickness when we suddenly find ourselves deprived of wine, we must
take this course : let us now begin at once to drink
water at our meals, for by so doing we shall not
greatly change our manner of living. 28. For whoever eats barley bread always eats meal that
has been kneaded up with water, and whoever eats
wheaten bread eats of a loaf that was mixed with
water; and everything boiled is prepared with water
in very liberal quantities. So, if after the meal we
drink some wine, our soul will lack nothing and
find refreshment. 29. But later on we must also
gradually diminish the amount taken after dinner,
until unconsciously we have become teetotalers.
For gradual transition helps any nature to bear
changes. Why, God teaches us that, by leading
us gradually from winter to endure the burning
heat of summer, and from the heat of summer to
the rigours of winter; and we should imitate Him
and reach the end we would attain by accustoming
ourselves beforehand.

30. " For your heavy blankets you may substitute General directions for equip- ment
an equal weight of provisions; for excess of pro-
visions will not be useless. And do not be afraid
that you will not sleep soundly for want of your
blankets; if you do not, I will take the blame.
However, if any one has a generous supply of
clothing with him, that will be of good service to him
whether he be well or ill.

31. Ὄψα δὲ χρὴ συνεσκευάσθαι ὅσα ἐστὶν ὀξέα καὶ δριμέα καὶ ἁλμυρά· ταῦτα γὰρ ἐπὶ σῖτόν τε ἄγει καὶ ἐπὶ πλεῖστον ἀρκεῖ. ὅταν δ' ἐκβαίνωμεν εἰς ἀκέραια, ὅπου ἤδη εἰκὸς ἡμᾶς σῖτον λαμβάνειν, χειρομύλας χρὴ αὐτόθεν παρασκευάσασθαι αἷς σιτοποιησόμεθα· τοῦτο γὰρ κουφότατον τῶν σιτοποιικῶν ὀργάνων.

32. Συνεσκευάσθαι δὲ χρὴ καὶ ὧν ἀσθενοῦντες δέονται ἄνθρωποι. τούτων γὰρ ὁ μὲν ὄγκος μικρότατος, ἢν δὲ τύχῃ τοιαύτη γένηται, μάλιστα δεήσει.

Ἔχειν δὲ χρὴ καὶ ἱμάντας· τὰ γὰρ πλεῖστα καὶ ἀνθρώποις καὶ ἵπποις ἱμᾶσιν ἤρτηται· ὧν κατατριβομένων καὶ ῥηγνυμένων ἀνάγκη ἀργεῖν, ἢν μή τις ἔχῃ περίζυγα.

Ὅστις δὲ πεπαίδευται καὶ παλτὸν ξύσασθαι, ἀγαθὸν καὶ ξυήλης μὴ ἐπιλαθέσθαι. ἀγαθὸν δὲ καὶ ῥίνην φέρεσθαι· 33. ὁ γὰρ λόγχην ἀκονῶν ἐκεῖνος καὶ τὴν ψυχήν τι παρακονᾷ. ἔπεστι γάρ τις αἰσχύνη λόγχην ἀκονῶντα κακὸν εἶναι.

Ἔχειν δὲ χρὴ καὶ ξύλα περίπλεω [1] καὶ ἅρμασι καὶ ἁμάξαις· ἐν γὰρ πολλαῖς πράξεσι πολλὰ ἀνάγκη καὶ τὰ ἀπαγορεύοντα εἶναι. ἔχειν δὲ δεῖ καὶ τὰ ἀναγκαιότατα ὄργανα ἐπὶ ταῦτα πάντα· 34. οὐ γὰρ πανταχοῦ χειροτέχναι παραγίγνονται· τὸ δ' ἐφ' ἡμέραν ἀρκέσον ὀλίγοι τινὲς οἳ οὐχ ἱκανοὶ ποιῆσαι. ἔχειν δὲ χρὴ καὶ ἄμην καὶ σμινύην καθ' ἅμαξαν ἑκάστην, καὶ κατὰ τὸν νωτοφόρον δὲ ἀξίνην καὶ δρέπανον· ταῦτα γὰρ καὶ

---

[1] περίπλεω Dindorf[4], Marchant, Gemoll; περίπλεα MSS., Dindorf[3], Breitenbach.

31. "For meats, we must pack up and take along only such as are sharp, pungent, salty; for these not only stimulate the appetite but also afford the most lasting nourishment. And when we come out into a country that has not been plundered, where we are at once likely to find grain again, we must then have hand-mills ready made with which to prepare food, for these are the lightest of the implements used in making bread.

32. "Again, we must take with us the things that sick people need; for the weight they add is very small and, if we have a case of sickness, they will be very necessary.

Equipment for—
(1) hospital,

"We must also have plenty of straps; for nearly everything that men and horses have is fastened on with straps, and when these wear out or break, everything must come to a standstill, unless one has some extra ones.

(2) packs,

"And it will be a good thing for the man who has been taught how to smooth down a spear-shaft not to forget a rasp; and it will be well to bring along a file too; 33. for he that whets his spear whets his courage, in a way, at the same time; for a man must be overcome with shame to be whetting his spear and yet feel himself a coward.

(3) arms,

"We must also have a good supply of lumber for the chariots and the wagons, for from constant use many parts necessarily become defective. We must have also the most indispensable tools for all these purposes; 34. for we shall not find mechanics everywhere, and almost any one can make what will serve for a day. Besides these, we must have a shovel and mattock for every wagon, and for each pack-animal an axe and a sickle; for these are useful to each one

(4) vehicles,

ἰδίᾳ ἑκάστῳ χρήσιμα καὶ ὑπὲρ τοῦ κοινοῦ πολλάκις ὠφέλιμα γίγνεται.

35. Τὰ μὲν οὖν εἰς τροφὴν δέοντα οἱ ἡγεμόνες τῶν ὁπλοφόρων ἐξετάζετε τοὺς ὑφ᾽ ὑμῖν αὐτοῖς· οὐ γὰρ δεῖ παριέναι ὅτου ἄν τις τούτων ἐνδέηται· ἡμεῖς γὰρ τούτων ἐνδεεῖς ἐσόμεθα. ἃ δὲ κατὰ τὰ ὑποζύγια κελεύω ἔχειν, ὑμεῖς οἱ τῶν σκευοφόρων ἄρχοντες ἐξετάζετε, καὶ τὸν μὴ ἔχοντα κατασκευάζεσθαι ἀναγκάζετε.

36. Ὑμεῖς δ᾽ αὖ οἱ τῶν ὁδοποιῶν ἄρχοντες ἔχετε μὲν ἀπογεγραμμένους παρ᾽ ἐμοῦ τοὺς ἀποδεδοκιμασμένους καὶ τοὺς ἐκ τῶν ἀκοντιστῶν καὶ τοὺς ἐκ τῶν τοξοτῶν καὶ τοὺς ἐκ τῶν σφενδονητῶν· τούτων δὲ χρὴ τοὺς μὲν ἀπὸ τῶν ἀκοντιστῶν πέλεκυν ἔχοντας ξυλοκόπον ἀναγκάζειν στρατεύεσθαι, τοὺς δ᾽ ἀπὸ τῶν τοξοτῶν σμινύην, τοὺς δ᾽ ἀπὸ τῶν σφενδονητῶν ἄμην· τούτους δὲ ἔχοντας ταῦτα πρὸ τῶν ἁμαξῶν κατ᾽ ἴλας πορεύεσθαι, ὅπως ἤν τι δέῃ ὁδοποιίας, εὐθὺς ἐνεργοὶ ἦτε, καὶ ἐγὼ ἤν τι δέωμαι, ὅπως εἰδῶ ὅθεν δεῖ λαβόντα τούτοις χρῆσθαι.

37. Ἄξω δὲ καὶ τοὺς ἐν τῇ στρατιωτικῇ ἡλικίᾳ σὺν τοῖς ὀργάνοις χαλκέας τε καὶ τέκτονας καὶ σκυτοτόμους, ὅπως ἄν τι δέῃ καὶ τοιούτων τεχνῶν ἐν τῇ στρατιᾷ, μηδὲν ἐλλείπηται. οὗτοι δὲ ὁπλοφόρου μὲν τάξεως ἀπολελύσονται, ἃ δὲ ἐπίστανται, τῷ βουλομένῳ μισθοῦ ὑπηρετοῦντες ἐν τῷ τεταγμένῳ ἔσονται.

38. Ἢν δέ τις καὶ ἔμπορος βούληται ἕπεσθαι πωλεῖν τι βουλόμενος, τῶν μὲν προειρημένων

individually and often serviceable for the common good as well.

35. "As to what is needed for the commissariat, you officers of the armed soldiers must make inquiry of the men under you, for we must not overlook anything of this sort that any one may need; for it is we that shall feel the want of it, if it is lacking. In reference to what I order for the pack-animals, you officers of the baggage-train must inquire into the matter, and if any man is not properly provided, require him to procure what is lacking. *(5) commissary,*

36. "You superintendents of the engineering corps have here from me a list of the spearmen, the archers, and the slingers, whose names have been stricken from the roster. You must require those of them who were spearmen to carry on the march a woodcutter's axe, those who were bowmen a mattock, and those who were slingers a shovel. With these tools they are to march in squads ahead of the wagons, so that, in case there is any need of road-building, you may get to work without delay, and so that, if I require their services, I may know where to find them when the time comes. *(6) engineers*

37. "And finally I shall take along those of an age for military service who are smiths and carpenters and cobblers, in order that, if anything is wanted in the army in the line of their trades also, we may not suffer for lack of it. And they shall be relieved of assignments to duty under arms, but they shall occupy the position assigned to them and there ply their trades for pay at the order of whoever wishes their services. *Special arrangements for artisans*

38. "And any merchant who wishes to accompany us, seeking a market for his wares, may do so; but if *and merchants*

ἡμερῶν τἀπιτήδεια ἔχειν ἤν τι πωλῶν ἁλίσκηται,
πάντων στερήσεται· ἐπειδὰν δ' αὗται παρέλθωσιν
αἱ ἡμέραι, πωλήσει ὅπως ἂν βούληται. ὅστις
δ' ἂν τῶν ἐμπόρων πλείστην ἀγορὰν παρέχων
φαίνηται, οὗτος καὶ παρὰ τῶν συμμάχων καὶ
παρ' ἐμοῦ δώρων καὶ τιμῆς τεύξεται. 39. εἰ δέ
τις χρημάτων προσδεῖσθαι νομίζει εἰς ἐμπολήν,
γνωστῆρας ἐμοὶ προσαγαγὼν καὶ ἐγγυητὰς ἦ μὴν
πορεύσεσθαι[1] σὺν τῇ στρατιᾷ, λαμβανέτω ὧν
ἡμεῖς ἔχομεν.

Ἐγὼ μὲν δὴ ταῦτα προαγορεύω· εἰ δέ τίς
τι καὶ ἄλλο δέον ἐνορᾷ, πρὸς ἐμὲ σημαινέτω.

40. καὶ ὑμεῖς μὲν ἀπιόντες συσκευάζεσθε, ἐγὼ
δὲ θύσομαι ἐπὶ τῇ ὁρμῇ· ὅταν δὲ τὰ τῶν θεῶν
καλῶς ἔχῃ, σημανοῦμεν. παρεῖναι δὲ χρὴ ἅπαντας τὰ προειρημένα ἔχοντας εἰς τὴν τεταγμένην
χώραν πρὸς τοὺς ἡγεμόνας ἑαυτῶν. 41. ὑμεῖς
δὲ οἱ ἡγεμόνες τὴν ἑαυτοῦ ἕκαστος τάξιν εὐτρε-
πισάμενος πρὸς ἐμὲ πάντες συμβάλλετε, ἵνα
τὰς ἑαυτῶν ἕκαστοι χώρας καταμάθητε.

III

1. Ἀκούσαντες δὲ ταῦτα οἱ μὲν συνεσκευά-
ζοντο, ὁ δὲ Κῦρος ἐθύετο. ἐπεὶ δὲ καλὰ τὰ
ἱερὰ ἦν, ὡρμᾶτο σὺν τῷ στρατεύματι· καὶ τῇ

---

[1] πορεύσεσθαι Stephanus, Marchant, Gemoll ; πορεύεσθαι
MSS., Dindorf, Breitenbach.

he is caught trying to sell anything within the number of days for which the troops are ordered to furnish their own provisions, he shall have all his goods confiscated. But when those days are past, he may sell as he pleases. And the man who seems to offer the largest stock of goods shall receive rewards and preferment both from the allies and from myself. 39. And if any merchant thinks he needs more money for the purchase of supplies, let him bring me vouchers for his respectability and identity, and sureties as a pledge that he is really going with the army, and he shall receive a certain amount from the fund we have.

"These are the directions I have to give in advance. If any one thinks of anything else that we need, let him inform me of it.

40. "Now do you go and make ready, and I will sacrifice for a blessing upon our start; and when the omens from the gods are favourable, we shall give the signal, and all must come equipped with what has been prescribed and join their own commanders at the place appointed. 41. And all of you officers, when you have made ready each his own division, come to me that you may acquaint yourselves with your several positions."

III

1. WHEN they heard this they began to make ready for the march, and Cyrus proceeded to sacrifice; and when the omens of the sacrifice were favourable, he set out with the army. On the first day he left the

The advance begins

μὲν πρώτῃ ἡμέρᾳ ἐξεστρατοπεδεύσατο ὡς δυνατὸν
ἐγγύτατα, ὅπως εἴ τίς τι ἐπιλελησμένος εἴη,
μετέλθοι, καὶ εἴ τίς τι ἐνδεόμενος γνοίη, τοῦτο
ἐπιπαρασκευάσαιτο.

2. Κυαξάρης μὲν οὖν τῶν Μήδων ἔχων τὸ
τρίτον μέρος κατέμενεν, ὡς μηδὲ τὰ οἴκοι ἔρημα
εἴη. · ὁ δὲ Κῦρος ἐπορεύετο ὡς ἐδύνατο τάχιστα,
τοὺς ἱππέας μὲν πρώτους ἔχων, καὶ πρὸ τούτων
διερευνητὰς καὶ σκοποὺς ἀεὶ ἀναβιβάζων ἐπὶ
τὰ πρόσθεν εὐσκοπώτατα· μετὰ δὲ τούτους ἦγε
τὰ σκευοφόρα, ὅπου μὲν πεδινὸν εἴη, πολλοὺς
ὁρμαθοὺς ποιούμενος τῶν ἁμαξῶν καὶ τῶν σκευο-
φόρων· ὄπισθεν δὲ ἡ φάλαγξ ἐφεπομένη, εἴ τι
τῶν σκευοφόρων ὑπολείποιτο, οἱ προστυγχά-
νοντες τῶν ἀρχόντων ἐπεμέλοντο ὡς μὴ κω-
λύοιντο πορεύεσθαι. 3. ὅπου δὲ στενοτέρα εἴη
ἡ ὁδός, διὰ μέσου ποιούμενοι τὰ σκευοφόρα ἔνθεν
καὶ ἔνθεν ἐπορεύοντο οἱ ὁπλοφόροι· καὶ εἴ τι
ἐμποδίζοι, οἱ κατὰ ταῦτα γιγνόμενοι τῶν στρατιωτῶν ἐπεμέλοντο. ἐπορεύοντο δὲ ὡς τὰ πολλὰ
αἱ τάξεις παρ᾽ ἑαυταῖς ἔχουσαι τὰ σκευοφόρα·
ἐπετέτακτο γὰρ πᾶσι τοῖς σκευοφόροις κατὰ
τὴν ἑαυτῶν ἑκάστου¹ τάξιν ἰέναι, εἰ μή τι
ἀναγκαῖον ἀποκωλύοι. 4. καὶ σημεῖον δὲ ἔχων
ὁ τοῦ ταξιάρχου σκευοφόρος ἡγεῖτο γνωστὸν
τοῖς τῆς ἑαυτοῦ τάξεως· ὥστ᾽ ἀθρόοι ἐπορεύοντο,
ἐπεμέλοντό τε ἰσχυρῶς ἕκαστος τῶν ἑαυτοῦ ὡς
μὴ ὑπολείποιντο. καὶ οὕτω ποιούντων οὔτε ζητεῖν
ἔδει ἀλλήλους ἅμα τε παρόντα ἅπαντα καὶ σαῶ-

¹ ἑκάστους Hertlein, most Edd.; ἕκαστον D, Dindorf;
ἑκάστου xzF.

position he had occupied and encamped again as near as convenient to it. This he did, in order that, in case any one had forgotten anything, he might go back after it; and if any one discovered that he needed anything, he might still procure it.

2. Cyaxares, however, remained behind with one third of the Medes, so as not to leave the home country unprotected, while Cyrus, with the cavalry at the head of the line, marched as rapidly as possible; but he never failed to send patrols ahead, and scouts up to the heights commanding the widest view before them. After these he arranged the baggage train, and where the country was flat he arranged many lines of wagons and pack-animals abreast; the phalanx followed next, and if any part of the baggage train lagged behind, such of the officers as happened to be at hand took care that they and their men should not be retarded in their advance. 3. But when the road was narrower, the soldiers put the baggage in between their lines and marched on either side of it; and if they met with any hindrance, those of the soldiers who were near the place took the matter in hand. For the most part, the companies marched with their own baggage next to them; for the baggage captains had orders to go along with their own respective companies unless something unavoidable should prevent it. 4. And the baggage man of each captain went ahead bearing an ensign that was known to the men of his own company. They were thus enabled to march close together, and they were extremely careful, each of his own property, that nothing should be left behind. As they maintained this order, it was never necessary for them to look for one another, and at the same time everything was kept close at

The order of march

τερα ἦν καὶ θᾶττον τὰ δέοντα εἶχον οἱ στρατιῶται.

5. Ὡς δὲ οἱ προϊόντες σκοποὶ ἔδοξαν ἐν τῷ
πεδίῳ ὁρᾶν ἀνθρώπους λαμβάνοντας καὶ χιλὸν
καὶ ξύλα, καὶ ὑποζύγια δὲ ἑώρων ἕτερα τοιαῦτα
ἄγοντα, τὰ δὲ καὶ νεμόμενα, καὶ τὰ πρόσω αὖ
ἀφορῶντες ἐδόκουν καταμανθάνειν μετεωριζόμενον
ἢ καπνὸν ἢ κονιορτόν, ἐκ τούτων πάντων σχεδὸν
ἐγίγνωσκον ὅτι εἴη που πλησίον τὸ στράτευμα
τῶν πολεμίων. 6. εὐθὺς οὖν πέμπει τινὰ ὁ
σκόπαρχος[1] ἀγγελοῦντα ταῦτα τῷ Κύρῳ. ὁ δὲ
ἀκούσας ταῦτα ἐκείνους μὲν ἐκέλευσε μένοντας
ἐπὶ ταύταις ταῖς σκοπαῖς ὅ τι ἂν ἀεὶ καινὸν
ὁρῶσιν ἐξαγγέλλειν· τάξιν δ' ἔπεμψεν ἱππέων εἰς
τὸ πρόσθεν καὶ ἐκέλευσε πειραθῆναι συλλαβεῖν
τινας τῶν ἀνὰ τὸ πεδίον ἀνθρώπων, ὅπως σαφέ-
στερον μάθοιεν τὸ ὄν. οἱ μὲν δὴ ταχθέντες τοῦτο
ἔπραττον.

7. Αὐτὸς δὲ τὸ ἄλλο στράτευμα αὐτοῦ κατε-
χώριζεν, ὅπως παρασκευάσαιντο ὅσα ᾤετο χρῆναι
πρὶν πάνυ ὁμοῦ εἶναι. καὶ πρῶτον μὲν ἀριστᾶν
παρηγγύησεν, ἔπειτα δὲ μένοντας ἐν ταῖς τάξεσι
τὸ παραγγελλόμενον προνοεῖν· 8. ἐπεὶ δὲ ἠρί-
στησαν, συνεκάλεσε καὶ ἱππέων καὶ πεζῶν καὶ
ἁρμάτων ἡγεμόνας, καὶ τῶν μηχανῶν δὲ καὶ τῶν
σκευοφόρων τοὺς ἄρχοντας καὶ τῶν ἁρμαμαξῶν·
καὶ οὗτοι μὲν συνῇσαν. 9. οἱ δὲ καταδραμόντες
εἰς τὸ πεδίον συλλαβόντες ἀνθρώπους ἤγαγον· οἱ
δὲ ληφθέντες ἀνερωτώμενοι ὑπὸ τοῦ Κύρου ἔλεγον

---

[1] σκόπαρχος Dindorf, Edd. ; σκοπάρχης MSS.

hand and in greater safety, and the soldiers always obtained more promptly anything that was wanted.

5. Now the scouts who went forward thought they saw men getting fodder and fuel on the plain; and they also saw beasts of burden, some loaded with other supplies of that sort and others grazing. Then, as they looked further on into the distance, they thought that they detected smoke or a cloud of dust rising up. From all these evidences they pretty well recognised that the army of the enemy was somewhere in the neighbourhood. 6. Accordingly, the officer in command of the scouts at once sent a man to report the news to Cyrus; and when he heard it he ordered them to remain at their look-out place and send him reports from time to time of whatever they saw that was new. Moreover, he sent forward a company of cavalry with orders to try to capture some of the men moving up and down the plain, in order that he might learn more definitely the real state of affairs. Accordingly, those who received these orders proceeded to execute them.

The enemy is sighted

7. He himself halted the rest of the army there, so that they might make what preparations he considered necessary before they were in too close quarters. And he gave the word to take luncheon first and then to remain at their posts and be on the watch for orders. 8. So, when they had eaten, he summoned together the commanders of the cavalry, the infantry, and the chariot corps, and also the officers in charge of the engines, of the baggage train, and of the wagons, and they came. 9. And those who made the raid into the plain had captured some people and now brought them in; and the prisoners, when cross-questioned by Cyrus, said that

Cyrus gets information about the enemy

ὅτι ἀπὸ τοῦ στρατοπέδου εἶεν, προεληλυθότες ἐπὶ
χιλόν, οἱ δ' ἐπὶ ξύλα, παρελθόντες τὰς προφυλα-
κάς· διὰ γὰρ τὸ πλῆθος τοῦ στρατοῦ σπάνια πάντ'
εἶναι. 10. καὶ ὁ Κῦρος ταῦτα ἀκούσας, Πόσον δέ,
ἔφη, ἄπεστιν ἐνθένδε τὸ στράτευμα;

Οἱ δ' ἔλεγον, Ὡς δύο παρασάγγας.

Ἐπὶ τούτοις ἤρετο ὁ Κῦρος, Ἡμῶν δ', ἔφη,
λόγος τις ἦν παρ' αὐτοῖς;

Ναὶ μὰ Δί, ἔφασαν, καὶ πολύς γε ὡς ἐγγὺς ἤδη
εἴητε[1] προσιόντες.

Τί οὖν; ἔφη ὁ Κῦρος, ἦ καὶ ἔχαιρον ἀκούοντες
ἰόντας; τοῦτο δὲ ἐπήρετο τῶν παρόντων ἕνεκα.

Οὐ μὰ Δί, εἶπον ἐκεῖνοι, οὐ μὲν δὴ ἔχαιρον,
ἀλλὰ καὶ μάλα ἠνιῶντο.

11. Νῦν δ', ἔφη ὁ Κῦρος, τί ποιοῦσιν;

Ἐκτάττονται, ἔφασαν· καὶ ἐχθὲς δὲ καὶ τρίτην
ἡμέραν ταὐτὸ τοῦτ' ἔπραττον.

Ὁ δὲ τάττων, ἔφη ὁ Κῦρος, τίς ἐστιν;

Οἱ δὲ ἔφασαν, Αὐτός τε Κροῖσος καὶ σὺν αὐτῷ
Ἕλλην τις ἀνήρ, καὶ ἄλλος δέ τις Μῆδος· οὗτος
μέντοι ἐλέγετο φυγὰς εἶναι παρ' ὑμῶν.

Καὶ ὁ Κῦρος εἶπεν, Ἀλλ', ὦ Ζεῦ μέγιστε,
λαβεῖν μοι γένοιτο αὐτὸν ὡς ἐγὼ βούλομαι.

12. Ἐκ τούτου τοὺς μὲν αἰχμαλώτους ἀπάγειν
ἐκέλευσεν, εἰς δὲ τοὺς παρόντας ὡς λέξων τι
ἀνήγετο. ἐν τούτῳ δὲ παρῆν ἄλλος αὖ ἀπὸ τοῦ
σκοπάρχου, λέγων ὅτι ἱππέων τάξις μεγάλη ἐν
τῷ πεδίῳ προφαίνοιτο· καὶ ἡμεῖς μέν, ἔφη, εἰκά-

---

[1] εἴητε Dindorf[3], Hug, Breitenbach ; εἶτε Dindorf[4], Marchant, Gemoll ; ἦτε MSS.

they were from the camp and had come out after fodder, passing out beyond their advanced guards, while others had gone after fuel; for by reason of the vast numbers of their army, everything was scarce. 10. On hearing this, Cyrus asked: "How far from here is your army?"

"About two parasangs," they replied.

"Was there any talk about us over there?" Cyrus then asked.

"Yes, by Zeus," they answered, "a great deal, and to the effect that you were already close upon us in your advance."

"Tell me, then," said Cyrus, "were they glad when they heard we were coming?" This question he asked for the benefit of the bystanders.

"No, by Zeus," they answered; "they were not glad in the least, but were rather very much troubled."

11. "And what are they doing now?" asked Cyrus.

"They are being marshalled in battle array," they answered; "and yesterday and the day before they were doing the same."

"And the marshal," said Cyrus, "who is he?"

"Croesus himself," they replied, "and with him a Greek and some one else—a Mede; the latter, however, was said to be a deserter from your side."

"Grant, O Zeus almighty," said Cyrus, "that it be mine to get hold of him, as I desire!"

12. Then he ordered the prisoners to be led away, and turned to the bystanders as if to say something. But at that moment another messenger came from the captain of the scouts with word that a large body of cavalry was within sight on the plain. "And we presume," he added, "that they are coming with the

The enemy reconnoitres

ζομεν ἐλαύνειν αὐτοὺς βουλομένους ἰδεῖν τόδε τὸ
στράτευμα. καὶ γὰρ πρὸ τῆς τάξεως ταύτης
ἄλλοι ὡς τριάκοντα ἱππεῖς συχνὸν προελαύνουσι,[1]
καὶ μέντοι, ἔφη, κατ᾽ αὐτοὺς ἡμᾶς, ἴσως βουλόμενοι λαβεῖν, ἢν δύνωνται, τὴν σκοπήν· ἡμεῖς δ᾽
ἐσμὲν μία δεκὰς οἱ ἐπὶ ταύτης τῆς σκοπῆς.

13. Καὶ ὁ Κῦρος ἐκέλευσε τῶν περὶ αὐτὸν ἀεὶ
ὄντων ἱππέων ἐλάσαντας ὑπὸ τὴν σκοπὴν ἀδή-
λους τοῖς πολεμίοις ἀτρεμίαν ἔχειν. Ὅταν δ᾽,
ἔφη, ἡ δεκὰς ἡ ἡμετέρα λείπῃ τὴν σκοπήν, ἐξ-
αναστάντες ἐπίθεσθε τοῖς ἀναβαίνουσιν ἐπὶ τὴν
σκοπήν. ὡς δὲ ὑμᾶς μὴ λυπῶσιν οἱ ἀπὸ τῆς
μεγάλης τάξεως, ἀντέξελθε σύ, ἔφη, ὦ Ὑστάσπα,
τὴν χιλιοστὺν τῶν ἱππέων λαβὼν καὶ ἐπιφάνηθι
ἐναντίος τῇ τῶν πολεμίων τάξει. διώξῃς[2] δὲ
μηδαμῇ εἰς ἀφανές, ἀλλ᾽ ὅπως αἱ σκοπαί σοι δια-
μένωσιν ἐπιμεληθεὶς πάριθι. ἢν δ᾽ ἄρα ἀνατείναν-
τές τινες τὰς δεξιὰς προσελαύνωσιν ὑμῖν, δέχεσθε
φιλίως τοὺς ἄνδρας.

14. Ὁ μὲν δὴ Ὑστάσπας ἀπιὼν ὡπλίζετο· οἱ
δ᾽ ὑπηρέται ἤλαυνον εὐθὺς ὡς ἐκέλευσεν. ἀπαντᾷ
δ᾽ αὐτοῖς καὶ δὴ ἐντὸς τῶν σκοπῶν σὺν τοῖς
θεράπουσιν ὁ πεμφθεὶς πάλαι κατάσκοπος, ὁ
φύλαξ τῆς Σουσίδος γυναικός. 15. ὁ μὲν οὖν
Κῦρος ὡς ἤκουσεν, ἀναπηδήσας ἐκ τῆς ἕδρας
ὑπήντα τε αὐτῷ καὶ ἐδεξιοῦτο· οἱ δὲ ἄλλοι
ὥσπερ εἰκὸς μηδὲν εἰδότας[3] ἐκπεπληγμένοι ἦσαν

---

[1] προελαύνουσι Stephanus, Edd.; προσελαύνουσι MSS.

[2] διώξῃς Hug, Marchant, Gemoll; διώξει Dindorf; διώξεις
MSS., Breitenbach.

[3] εἰδότας Schliack, Marchant, Gemoll; εἰδότες MSS., Hug,
Dindorf, Breitenbach.

intention of reconnoitring the army here. And we have good reasons for the suspicion, for at a considerable distance in advance of this company about thirty other horsemen are riding forward; as a matter of fact, they are riding in the direction of our party, aiming perhaps, if possible, to get possession of our look-out point; and we who are holding this particular point are only ten in number."

13. So Cyrus ordered a detachment of the horsemen who formed his body-guard to ride up to the foot of the place of look-out and to remain quiet there out of sight of the enemy. "But," he added, "when our ten leave the look-out place, rush up and attack the enemy as they come up it. But that the horsemen of the large battalion may not bring you to grief, do you, Hystaspas," said he to that officer, "take your regiment of cavalry, go out against them, and show yourself over against the enemy's battalion. But do not by any means allow yourself to pursue into places that you do not know, but when you have made sure that the look-out stations remain in your possession, come back. And if any ride toward you, holding up their right hands, receive them as friends."

14. Accordingly, Hystaspas went away and donned Araspas returns his armour; the men from Cyrus's body-guard rode off at once, as he had ordered. And just within the picket line there met them, with his attendants, the man who had been sent some time since as a spy, the guardian of the lady of Susa. 15. So when Cyrus heard this, he sprang up from his seat, went to meet him, and welcomed him cordially; and the rest, knowing nothing of the facts, were naturally

τῷ πράγματι, ἕως Κῦρος εἶπεν, Ἄνδρες φίλοι,
ἥκει ἡμῖν ἀνὴρ ἄριστος. νῦν γὰρ ἤδη πάντας
ἀνθρώπους δεῖ εἰδέναι τὰ τούτου ἔργα. οὗτος
οὔτε αἰσχροῦ ἡττηθεὶς οὐδενὸς ᾤχετο οὔτ' ἐμὲ
φοβηθείς, ἀλλ' ὑπ' ἐμοῦ πεμφθεὶς ὅπως ἡμῖν
μαθὼν τὰ τῶν πολεμίων σαφῶς τὰ ὄντα ἐξαγ-
γείλειεν. 16. ἃ μὲν οὖν ἐγώ σοι ὑπεσχόμην, ὦ
Ἀράσπα, μέμνημαί τε καὶ ἀποδώσω σὺν τούτοις
πᾶσι. δίκαιον δὲ καὶ ὑμᾶς ἅπαντας, ὦ ἄνδρες,
τοῦτον τιμᾶν ὡς ἀγαθὸν ἄνδρα· ἐπὶ γὰρ τῷ
ἡμετέρῳ ἀγαθῷ καὶ ἐκινδύνευσε καὶ αἰτίαν ὑπ-
έσχεν, ᾗ ἐβαρύνετο.

17. Ἐκ τούτου δὴ πάντες ἠσπάζοντο τὸν
Ἀράσπαν καὶ ἐδεξιοῦντο. εἰπόντος δὲ Κύρου ὅτι
τούτων μὲν τοίνυν εἴη ἅλις, Ἃ δὲ καιρὸς ἡμῖν
εἰδέναι, ταῦτ,' ἔφη, διηγοῦ, ὦ Ἀράσπα· καὶ μηδὲν
ἐλάττου τοῦ ἀληθοῦς μηδὲ μείου τὰ τῶν πολεμίων.
κρεῖττον γὰρ μείζω οἰηθέντας μείονα ἰδεῖν ἢ μείω
ἀκούσαντας ἰσχυρότερα εὑρίσκειν.

18. Καὶ μήν, ἔφη ὁ Ἀράσπας, ὡς ἂν ἀσφαλέ-
στατά γε εἰδείην ὁπόσον τὸ στράτευμά ἐστιν
ἐποίουν· συνεξέταττον γὰρ παρὼν αὐτός.[1]

Σὺ μὲν ἄρα, ἔφη ὁ Κῦρος, οὐ τὸ πλῆθος μόνον
οἶσθα, ἀλλὰ καὶ τὴν τάξιν αὐτῶν.

Ἐγὼ μὲν ναὶ μὰ Δί', ἔφη ὁ Ἀράσπας, καὶ ὡς
διανοοῦνται τὴν μάχην ποιεῖσθαι.

Ἀλλ' ὅμως, ἔφη ὁ Κῦρος, τὸ πλῆθος ἡμῖν πρῶτον εἰπὲ ἐν κεφαλαίῳ.

---

[1] αὐτός Cobet, most Edd. ; αὐτοῖς xz, Dindorf ; αὐτούς y.

astonished at his actions until Cyrus said: "My friends, here has come a man most loyal; for now all the world must know at once what he has done. He went away not because his disgrace was too great for him to bear, nor because he feared my displeasure, but because I sent him to discover for us the exact condition of the enemy and to report to us the true state of affairs. 16. And now, Araspas, I have not forgotten what I promised you, and I will fulfil it, and all these men shall help me; for it is only right, my friends, that you also should all honour him as a valiant man. For, for our general good, he has risked his life and borne the stigma that was put upon him."

17. Then all embraced Araspas and gave him a hearty welcome. But Cyrus, remarking that there had been enough of that, added, "Tell us, Araspas, what it is of the first importance for us to know; and do not detract anything from the truth nor underrate the real strength of the enemy. For it is better for us to think it greater and find it less than to hear that it is less and find it really more formidable."

18. "Aye," said Araspas, "but I did take steps to get the most accurate information about the size of their army; for I was present in person and helped to draw it up in battle order." He delivers his report

"And so," said Cyrus, "you are acquainted not only with their numbers but also with their order of battle."

"Yes, by Zeus," answered Araspas, "I am; and I know also how they are planning to conduct the battle."

"Good," said Cyrus; "still, tell us first, in round numbers, how many of them there are."

19. Ἐκεῖνοι τοίνυν, ἔφη, πάντες τεταγμένοι ἐπὶ τριάκοντα τὸ βάθος καὶ πεζοὶ καὶ ἱππεῖς πλὴν τῶν Αἰγυπτίων ἐπέχουσιν[1] ἀμφὶ τὰ τετταράκοντα στάδια· πάνυ γάρ μοι, ἔφη, ἐμέλησεν ὥστε εἰδέναι ὁπόσον κατεῖχον χωρίον.

20. Οἱ δ᾽ Αἰγύπτιοι, ἔφη ὁ Κῦρος, πῶς εἰσι τεταγμένοι; ὅτι εἶπας, Πλὴν τῶν Αἰγυπτίων.

Τούτους δὲ οἱ μυρίαρχοι ἔταττον εἰς ἑκατὸν πανταχῇ τὴν μυριοστὺν ἑκάστην· τοῦτον γὰρ σφίσι καὶ οἴκοι νόμον ἔφασαν εἶναι τῶν τάξεων. καὶ ὁ Κροῖσος μέντοι μάλα ἄκων συνεχώρησεν αὐτοῖς οὕτω τάττεσθαι· ἐβούλετο γὰρ ὅτι πλεῖστον ὑπερφαλαγγῆσαι τοῦ σοῦ στρατεύματος.

Πρὸς τί δή, ἔφη ὁ Κῦρος, τοῦτο ἐπιθυμῶν;

Ὡς ναὶ μὰ Δί᾽, ἔφη, τῷ περιττῷ κυκλωσόμενος. καὶ ὁ Κῦρος εἶπεν, Ἀλλ᾽ οὗτοι[2] ἂν εἰδεῖεν εἰ οἱ κυκλούμενοι κυκλωθεῖεν. 21. ἀλλ᾽ ἃ μὲν παρὰ σοῦ καιρὸς μαθεῖν, ἀκηκόαμεν· ὑμᾶς δὲ χρή, ὦ ἄνδρες, οὕτω ποιεῖν· νῦν μὲν ἐπειδὰν ἐνθένδε ἀπέλθητε, ἐπισκέψασθε καὶ τὰ τῶν ἵππων καὶ τὰ ὑμῶν αὐτῶν ὅπλα· πολλάκις γὰρ μικροῦ ἐνδείᾳ καὶ ἀνὴρ καὶ ἵππος καὶ ἅρμα ἀχρεῖον γίγνεται· αὔριον δὲ πρῴ, ἕως ἂν ἐγὼ θύωμαι, πρῶτον μὲν χρὴ ἀριστῆσαι καὶ ἄνδρας καὶ ἵππους, ὅπως ὅ

[1] ἐπέχουσιν Leonclav, Edd.; ἀπέχουσιν D; οὗτοι δ᾽ ἀμφέχουσιν xAHV; οὗτοι δ᾽ ἀπέχουσιν G; ἔχουσιν F.
[2] οὗτοι Brodaeus, Hug, Marchant, Gemoll; οὗτοι MSS., Dindorf, Breitenbach.

19. "Well," he replied, "with the exception of the Egyptians, they are all drawn up thirty deep, both foot and horse, and their front extends about forty stadia; for I took especial pains to find out how much space they covered."[1] The enemy's order of battle

20. "And how are the Egyptians drawn up?" asked Cyrus; "for you said 'with the exception of the Egyptians.'"

"The brigadier-generals drew them up—each one ten thousand men, a hundred square; for this, they said, was their manner of arranging their order of battle at home. And Croesus consented to their being so drawn up, but very reluctantly, for he wished to outflank your army as much as possible."

"And what is his object in doing that, pray?" asked Cyrus.

"In order, by Zeus," he replied, "to surround you with the part that extends beyond your line."

"Well," said Cyrus, "they may have an opportunity to find out whether the surrounders may not be surrounded. 21. Now we have heard from you what it is of the first importance for us to learn. And you, my men, must carry out the following programme: when you leave me, look at once to your own accoutrement and that of your horses; for often, for want of a trifle, man or horse or chariot becomes useless. And early to-morrow morning, during the time that I shall be sacrificing, first you must all breakfast, both men and horses, so that we may not Cyrus outlines his order of battle

[1] The stadium is 600 feet; the ancient soldier was normally allowed 3 feet. That makes a front of 200 men per stadium, 8,000 for the entire front. That means, as they stood 30 deep, 240,000 in the army, and with the Egyptians 360,000.

τι ἂν πράττειν ἀεὶ καιρὸς ἦ μὴ τούτου ἡμῖ
ἐνδέη.

Ἔπειτα δὲ σύ, ἔφη, ὦ Ἀρσάμα, . . . ,[1] τὸ δεξιὸ
κέρας ἔχε ὥσπερ καὶ ἔχετε,[2] καὶ οἱ ἄλλοι μυρίαρ
χοι ἧπερ νῦν ἔχετε· ὁμοῦ δὲ τοῦ ἀγῶνος ὄντο
οὐδενὶ ἅρματι καιρὸς ἵππους μεταζευγνύναι
παραγγείλατε δὲ τοῖς ταξιάρχοις καὶ λοχαγοῖς ἐπ
φάλαγγος καθίστασθαι εἰς δύο ἔχοντας ἕκαστο
τὸν λόχον. [ὁ δὲ λόχος ἦν ἕκαστος εἴκοσι
τέτταρες.][3]

22. Καί τις εἶπε τῶν μυριάρχων, Καὶ δοκοῦμέ
σοι, ἔφη, ὦ Κῦρε, ἱκανῶς ἕξειν εἰς τοσούτου
τεταγμένοι πρὸς οὕτω βαθεῖαν φάλαγγα;

Καὶ ὁ Κῦρος εἶπεν, Αἱ δὲ βαθύτεραι φάλαγγε
ἢ ὡς ἐξικνεῖσθαι τοῖς ὅπλοις τῶν ἐναντίων τί σοι
ἔφη, δοκοῦσιν ἢ τοὺς πολεμίους βλάπτειν ἢ τοὺ
συμμάχους ὠφελεῖν; 23. ἐγὼ μὲν γάρ, ἔφη, τοὺ
εἰς ἑκατὸν τούτους ὁπλίτας εἰς μυρίους ἂν μᾶλλο
βουλοίμην τετάχθαι· οὕτω γὰρ ἂν ἐλαχίστοι
μαχοίμεθα. ἐξ ὅσων μέντοι ἐγὼ τὴν φάλαγγ
βαθυνῶ οἴομαι ὅλην ἐνεργὸν καὶ σύμμαχον ποι
ήσειν αὐτὴν ἑαυτῇ. 24. ἀκοντιστὰς μὲν ἐπὶ τοῖ
θωρακοφόροις τάξω, ἐπὶ δὲ τοῖς ἀκοντισταῖς τοὺ
τοξότας. τούτους γὰρ πρωτοστάτας τί ἄν τις
τάττοι, οἳ καὶ αὐτοὶ ὁμολογοῦσι μηδεμίαν μάχη
ἂν ὑπομεῖναι ἐκ χειρός; προβεβλημένοι δὲ τοὺ

---

[1] Ἀρσάμα, . . . , Pantazides, Hug, Marchant, Gemoll (th
missing words would be something like τὸ ἀριστερόν, σὺ δέ
ὦ Χρυσάντα) ; Ἀράσπα MSS.. Dindorf, Breitenbach.

[2] καὶ ἔχετε Pantazides, Hug, Marchant, Gemoll ; καὶ ἔχει
xzV, Dindorf, Breitenbach ; κατέχεις y.

[3] ὁ δὲ . . . τέτταρες MSS., Edd. ; seems an obvious gloss.

[4] τί ἄν τις Marchant ; τοι ἄν τις z ; πῶς ἄν τις cod. Med.

fail in anything that it may be of importance for us to do in any exigency.

"And then do you, Arsamas," said he, . . . "and you [Chrysantas] take charge of the right wing, as you always have done, and the rest of you brigadier-generals take the posts you now have. When the race is on, it is not the time for any chariot to change horses. So instruct your captains and lieutenants to form a line with each separate platoon two deep." [Now each platoon contained twenty-four men.]

22. "And do you think, Cyrus," said one of the generals, "that drawn up with lines so shallow we shall be a match for so deep a phalanx?"

"When phalanxes are too deep to reach the enemy with weapons," answered Cyrus, "how do you think they can either hurt their enemy or help their friends? 23. For my part, I would rather have these hoplites who are arranged in columns a hundred deep drawn up ten thousand deep; for in that case we should have very few to fight against. According to the depth that I shall give my line of battle, I think I shall bring the entire line into action and make it everywhere mutually helpful. 24. I shall bring up the spearmen immediately behind the heavy-armed troops, and the bowmen immediately behind the spearmen; for why should any one put in the front ranks those who themselves acknowledge that they could never withstand the shock of battle in a hand-to-hand encounter? But with the heavy-

He explains the advantages of his plan

Dindorf, Breitenbach, Gemoll ; ἄν τις xyV ; τίς ἂν Stephanus, Hug.

θωρακοφόρους μενοῦσί τε, καὶ οἱ μὲν ἀκοντίζοντες,
οἱ δὲ τοξεύοντες, ὑπὲρ τῶν πρόσθεν πάντων
λυμανοῦνται τοὺς πολεμίους. ὅ τι δ' ἂν κακ-
ουργῇ τις τοὺς ἐναντίους, δῆλον ὅτι παντὶ τούτῳ
τοὺς συμμάχους κουφίζει. 25. τελευταίους μέντοι
στήσω τοὺς ἐπὶ πᾶσι καλουμένους. ὥσπερ γὰρ
οἰκίας οὔτε ἄνευ λιθολογήματος ὀχυροῦ οὔτε
ἄνευ τῶν στέγην ποιούντων οὐδὲν ὄφελος, οὕτως
οὐδὲ φάλαγγος οὔτ' ἄνευ τῶν πρώτων οὔτ' ἄνευ
τῶν τελευταίων, εἰ μὴ ἀγαθοὶ ἔσονται, ὄφελος
οὐδέν.

26. ᾿Αλλ' ὑμεῖς τ᾽, ἔφη, ὡς παραγγέλλω τάτ-
τεσθε, καὶ ὑμεῖς οἱ τῶν πελταστῶν ἄρχοντες ἐπὶ
τούτοις ὡσαύτως τοὺς λόχους καθίστατε, καὶ
ὑμεῖς οἱ τῶν τοξοτῶν ἐπὶ τοῖς πελτασταῖς
ὡσαύτως.

27. Σὺ δέ, ὃς τῶν ἐπὶ πᾶσιν ἄρχεις, τελευταίους
ἔχων τοὺς ἄνδρας παράγγελλε τοῖς σαυτοῦ
ἐφορᾶν τε ἑκάστῳ τοὺς καθ' αὑτὸν καὶ τοῖς μὲν
τὸ δέον ποιοῦσιν ἐπικελεύειν, τοῖς δὲ μαλακυνο-
μένοις ἀπειλεῖν ἰσχυρῶς· ἢν δέ τις στρέφηται
προδιδόναι θέλων, θανάτῳ ζημιοῦν. ἔργον γάρ
ἐστι τοῖς μὲν πρωτοστάταις θαρρύνειν τοὺς ἑπομένους καὶ λόγῳ καὶ ἔργῳ· ὑμᾶς δὲ δεῖ τοὺς ἐπὶ
πᾶσι τεταγμένους πλείω φόβον παρέχειν τοῖς
κακοῖς τοῦ ἀπὸ τῶν πολεμίων.

28. Καὶ ὑμεῖς μὲν ταῦτα ποιεῖτε. σὺ δέ, ὦ
Εὐφράτα, ὃς ἄρχεις τῶν ἐπὶ ταῖς μηχαναῖς, οὕτω
ποίει ὅπως τὰ ζεύγη τὰ τοὺς πύργους ἄγοντα

armed troops as a shield in front of them, they will stand their ground ; and the one division with their spears, the other with their arrows will rain destruction upon the enemy, over the heads of all the lines in front.　And whatever harm any one does to the enemy, in all this he obviously lightens the task of his comrades.　25. Behind all the rest I shall station the so-called rear-guard of veteran reserves. For just as a house, without a strong foundation or without the things that make a roof, is good for nothing, so likewise a phalanx is good for nothing, unless both front and rear are composed of valiant men.

26. " Do you, therefore, take your positions as I direct, and you also, the officers of the light-armed troops, bring up your platoons immediately behind them, and you, the officers of the archery, fall in, in the same way, directly behind the light-armed troops.

27. " Now you, the commander of the rear-guard, as you are behind all the rest with your men, issue orders to your own division that each man watch those immediately in front of him, encourage those who are doing their duty, threaten violently those who lag behind, and punish with death any one who turns his back with traitorous intent.　For it is the duty of the men in the front ranks with word and deed to encourage those who follow them, while it is your business, who occupy the rear, to inspire the cowardly with greater fear than the enemy does.

He gives his final directions

28. " That is what you have to attend to.　Now you, Euphratas, who are commander of the division in charge of the engines, manage to have the teams that draw the towers follow as close as possible behind

ἕψεται ὡς ἐγγύτατα τῆς φάλαγγος. 29. σὺ δ',
ὦ Δαοῦχε, ὃς ἄρχεις τῶν σκευοφόρων, ἐπὶ τοῖς
πύργοις ἄγε πάντα τὸν τοιοῦτον στρατόν· οἱ δὲ
ὑπηρέται σου ἰσχυρῶς κολαζόντων τοὺς προϊόντας
τοῦ καιροῦ ἢ λειπομένους.

30. Σὺ δέ, ὦ Καρδοῦχε, ὃς ἄρχεις τῶν ἁρμαμαξῶν αἳ ἄγουσι τὰς γυναῖκας, κατάστησον
αὐτὰς τελευταίας ἐπὶ τοῖς σκευοφόροις. ἑπόμενα
γὰρ ταῦτα πάντα καὶ πλήθους δόξαν παρέξει καὶ
ἐνεδρεύειν ἡμῖν ἐξουσία ἔσται, καὶ τοὺς πολεμίους,[1] ἢν κυκλοῦσθαι πειρῶνται, μείζω τὴν
περιβολὴν ἀναγκάσει ποιεῖσθαι· ὅσῳ δ' ἂν
μεῖζον χωρίον περιβάλλωνται, τοσούτῳ ἀνάγκη
αὐτοὺς ἀσθενεστέρους γίγνεσθαι.

31. Καὶ ὑμεῖς μὲν οὕτω ποιεῖτε· σὺ δέ, ὦ
Ἀρτάοζε καὶ Ἀρταγέρσα [τὴν][2] χιλιοστὺν ἑκάτερος τῶν σὺν ὑμῖν πεζῶν ἐπὶ τούτοις ἔχετε.
32. καὶ σύ, ὦ Φαρνοῦχε καὶ Ἀσιαδάτα, τὴν τῶν
ἱππέων χιλιοστὺν ἧς ἑκάτερος ἄρχει ὑμῶν μὴ
συγκατατάττετε εἰς τὴν φάλαγγα, ἀλλ' ὄπισθεν
τῶν ἁρμαμαξῶν ἐξοπλίσθητε καθ' ὑμᾶς αὐτούς·
ἔπειτα πρὸς ἐμὲ ἥκετε σὺν τοῖς ἄλλοις ἡγεμόσιν.
οὕτω δὲ δεῖ ὑμᾶς παρεσκευάσθαι ὡς πρώτους
δεῆσον ἀγωνίζεσθαι.

33. Καὶ σὺ δὲ ὁ ἄρχων τῶν ἐπὶ ταῖς καμήλοις
ἀνδρῶν, ὄπισθεν τῶν ἁρμαμαξῶν ἐκτάττου· ποίει
δ' ὅ τι ἄν σοι παραγγέλλῃ Ἀρταγέρσης.

34. Ὑμεῖς δ' οἱ τῶν ἁρμάτων ἡγεμόνες δια-
κληρωσάμενοι, ὁ μὲν λαχὼν ὑμῶν πρὸ τῆς
φάλαγγος τὰ μεθ' ἑαυτοῦ ἑκατὸν ἔχων ἅρματα

---

[1] τοὺς πολεμίους Schneider, Edd. ; τοῖς πολεμίοις MSS.
[2] τὴν MSS., Hug; [τὴν] Gemoll.

the phalanx. 29. And you, Daüchus, who have command of the baggage-train, bring up all your division of the army next after the towers, and let your adjutants punish severely those who advance or fall behind further than is expedient.

30. "And you, Carduchus, who have charge of the carriages which convey the women, bring them up in the rear next after the baggage-train. For, if all this follows, it will give an impression of numbers and will afford us an opportunity for an ambuscade; and if the enemy try to surround us, they will have to make a wider circuit; and the greater the circuit they have to make, the weaker they must necessarily make their line.

31. "That is your course to pursue. But do you, Artaozus and Artagerses, have each of you a regiment of your infantry behind the carriages. 32. And you, Pharnuchus and Asiadatas, keep each of you the regiment of cavalry under your command out of the main line and take your stand by yourselves behind the carriages, and then come to me with the rest of the officers. You must be just as fully ready, though in the rear, as if you were to be the first to have to join battle.

33. "And you, the commander of the men on camels, take your position also behind the women's carriages and do whatever Artagerses commands you.

34. "And finally, do you officers of the chariot forces cast lots, and let the one to whose lot it falls bring up his hundred chariots in front of the main

καταστησάτω· αἱ δ' ἕτεραι ἑκατοστύες τῶν ἁρμάτων, ἡ μὲν κατὰ τὸ δεξιὸν πλευρὸν τῆς στρατιᾶς
στοιχοῦσα ἐπέσθω τῇ φάλαγγι ἐπὶ κέρως, ἡ δὲ
κατὰ τὸ εὐώνυμον.

35. Κῦρος μὲν οὕτω διέταττεν.

Ἀβραδάτας δὲ ὁ Σούσων βασιλεὺς εἶπεν,
Ἐγώ σοι, Κῦρε, ἐθελούσιος ὑφίσταμαι τὴν κατὰ
πρόσωπον τῆς ἀντίας φάλαγγος τάξιν ἔχειν, εἰ
μή τί σοι ἄλλο δοκεῖ.

36. Καὶ ὁ Κῦρος ἀγασθεὶς αὐτὸν καὶ δεξιωσάμενος ἐπήρετο τοὺς ἐπὶ τοῖς ἄλλοις ἅρμασι
Πέρσας, Ἦ καὶ ὑμεῖς, ἔφη, ταῦτα συγχωρεῖτε;
ἐπεὶ δ' ἐκεῖνοι ἀπεκρίναντο ὅτι οὐ καλὸν εἴη ταῦτα
ὑφίεσθαι, διεκλήρωσεν αὐτούς, καὶ ἔλαχεν ὁ
Ἀβραδάτας ᾗπερ ὑφίστατο, καὶ ἐγένετο κατὰ
τοὺς Αἰγυπτίους.

37. Τότε μὲν δὴ ἀπιόντες καὶ ἐπιμεληθέντες
ὧν προεῖπον ἐδειπνοποιοῦντο καὶ φυλακὰς καταστησάμενοι ἐκοιμήθησαν.

IV

1. Τῇ δ' ὑστεραίᾳ πρῲ Κῦρος μὲν ἐθύετο, ὁ δ'
ἄλλος στρατὸς ἀριστήσας καὶ σπονδὰς ποιησάμενος ἐξωπλίζετο πολλοῖς μὲν καὶ καλοῖς χιτῶσι,
πολλοῖς δὲ καὶ καλοῖς θώραξι καὶ κράνεσιν·
ὥπλιζον δὲ καὶ ἵππους προμετωπιδίοις καὶ
προστερνιδίοις· καὶ τοὺς μὲν μονίππους παραμηριδίοις, τοὺς δ' ὑπὸ τοῖς ἅρμασιν ὄντας παρα-
πλευριδίοις· ὥστε ἤστραπτε μὲν χαλκῷ, ἤνθει δὲ
φοινικίσι πᾶσα ἡ στρατιά.

line; of the other two hundred, one shall take its place in line upon the right flank of the army, the other on the left, and follow the phalanx each in single file."

35. Thus did Cyrus plan his order of battle.

But Abradatas, the king of Susa, said: "I will gladly volunteer to hold for you the post immediately in front of the enemy's phalanx, Cyrus, unless you have some better plan." Abradatas asks for the post of danger

36. And Cyrus admired his spirit and clasped his hand, and turning to the Persians in command of the other chariots he asked: "Do you consent to this?" But they answered that it was inconsistent with their idea of honour to yield the place to him; accordingly, he had them cast lots; and Abradatas was assigned by lot to the place for which he had volunteered, and took his place over against the Egyptians.

37. This done, they went away, and when they had attended to the details of all that I have mentioned, they went to dinner; and then they stationed their pickets and went to bed.

IV

1. EARLY on the following day Cyrus was sacrificing, and the rest of the army, after breakfasting and pouring libations, proceeded to array themselves with many fine tunics and corselets and helms. And they armed their horses also with frontlets and breast-plates; the saddle-horses also they armed with thigh-pieces and the chariot teams with side-armour. And so the whole army flashed with bronze and was resplendent in purple. They pre-pare for battle

2. Καὶ τῷ Ἀβραδάτᾳ δὲ τὸ †τετράρρυμον ἅρμα
καὶ ἵππων ὀκτὼ παγκάλως ἐκεκόσμητο. ἐπεὶ
ἔμελλε τὸν λινοῦν θώρακα, ὃς ἐπιχώριος ἦν αὐτοῖς
ἐνδύεσθαι, προσφέρει αὐτῷ ἡ Πάνθεια χρυσοῦν¹
καὶ χρυσοῦν κράνος καὶ περιβραχιόνια καὶ ψέλι
πλατέα περὶ τοὺς καρποὺς τῶν χειρῶν καὶ χιτῶνα
πορφυροῦν ποδήρη στολιδωτὸν τὰ κάτω καὶ λόφον
ὑακινθινοβαφῆ. ταῦτα δ᾽ ἐποιήσατο λάθρᾳ τοῦ
ἀνδρὸς ἐκμετρησαμένη τὰ ἐκείνου ὅπλα. 3. ὁ δὲ
ἰδὼν ἐθαύμασέ τε καὶ ἐπήρετο τὴν Πάνθειαν, Οὐ
δήπου, ὦ γύναι, συγκόψασα τὸν σαυτῆς κόσμον
τὰ ὅπλα μοι ἐποιήσω;

Μὰ Δί, ἔφη ἡ Πάνθεια, οὔκουν τόν γε πλείστου
ἄξιον· σὺ γὰρ ἔμοιγε, ἢν καὶ τοῖς ἄλλοις φανῇς
οἷόσπερ ἐμοὶ δοκεῖς εἶναι, μέγιστος κόσμος ἔσει.

Ταῦτα δὲ λέγουσα ἅμα ἐνέδυε τὰ ὅπλα, καὶ
λανθάνειν μὲν ἐπειρᾶτο, ἐλείβετο δὲ αὐτῇ τὰ
δάκρυα κατὰ τῶν παρειῶν.

4. Ἐπεὶ δὲ καὶ πρόσθεν ὢν ἀξιοθέατος
Ἀβραδάτας ὡπλίσθη τοῖς ὅπλοις τούτοις, ἐφάνη
μὲν κάλλιστος καὶ ἐλευθεριώτατος, ἅτε καὶ τῆς
φύσεως ὑπαρχούσης· λαβὼν δὲ παρὰ τοῦ ὑφη-
νιόχου τὰς ἡνίας παρεσκευάζετο ὡς ἀναβησόμενος
ἤδη ἐπὶ τὸ ἅρμα. 5. ἐν δὲ τούτῳ ἡ Πάνθεια
ἀποχωρῆσαι κελεύσασα τοὺς παρόντας πάντα
ἔλεξεν, Ἀλλ᾽ ὅτι μέν, ὦ Ἀβραδάτα, εἴ τις καὶ
ἄλλη πώποτε γυνὴ τὸν ἑαυτῆς ἄνδρα μεῖζον τῆς
ἑαυτῆς ψυχῆς ἐτίμησεν, οἶμαί σε γιγνώσκειν ὅτι
καὶ ἐγὼ μία τούτων εἰμί. τί οὖν ἐμὲ δεῖ καθ᾽
ἕκαστον λέγειν; τὰ γὰρ ἔργα οἶμαί σοι πιθανώ-

¹ χρυσοῦν supplied by Meyer, Edd. ; not in MSS.

2. And Abradatas's chariot with its four poles and eight horses was adorned most handsomely; and when he came to put on his linen corselet, such as they used in his country, Panthea brought him one of gold, also a helmet, arm-pieces, broad bracelets for his wrists—all of gold—and a purple tunic that hung down in folds to his feet, and a helmet-plume of hyacinth dye. All these she had had made without her husband's knowledge, taking the measure for them from his armour. 3. And when he saw them he was astonished and turning to Panthea, he asked: " Tell me, wife, you did not break your own jewels to pieces, did you, to have this armour made for me ? " Panthea arrays Abradatas for the battle

" No, by Zeus," answered Panthea, "at any rate, not my most precious jewel ; for you, if you appear to others as you seem to me, shall be my noblest jewel."

With these words, she began to put the armour on him, and though she tried to conceal them, the tears stole down her cheeks.

4. And when Abradatas was armed in his panoply he looked most handsome and noble, for he had been favoured by nature and, even unadorned, was well worth looking at ; and taking the reins from his groom he was now making ready to mount his chariot. 5. But at this moment Panthea bade all who stood near to retire and then she said : " Abradatas, if ever any woman loved her husband more than her own life, I think you know that I, too, am such a one. Why, then, should I tell of these things one by one? For I think that my conduct has given you better proof of She exhorts him to bravery

τερα παρεσχῆσθαι τῶν νῦν ἄν¹ λεχθέντων
λόγων. 6. ὅμως δὲ οὕτως ἔχουσα πρὸς σὲ ὥσπερ
σὺ οἶσθα, ἐπομνύω σοι τὴν ἐμὴν καὶ σὴν φιλίαν
ἦ μὴν ἐγὼ βούλεσθαι ἂν μετὰ σοῦ ἀνδρὸς ἀγαθοῦ
γενομένου κοινῇ γῆν ἐπιέσασθαι μᾶλλον ἢ ζῆν
μετ' αἰσχυνομένου αἰσχυνομένη· οὕτως ἐγὼ καὶ
σὲ τῶν καλλίστων καὶ ἐμαυτὴν ἠξίωκα. 7. καὶ
Κύρῳ δὲ μεγάλην τινὰ δοκῶ ἡμᾶς χάριν ὀφείλειν,
ὅτι με αἰχμάλωτον γενομένην καὶ ἐξαιρεθεῖσαν
ἑαυτῷ οὔτε με ὡς δούλην ἠξίωσε κεκτῆσθαι οὔτε
ὡς ἐλευθέραν ἐν ἀτίμῳ ὀνόματι, διεφύλαξε δὲ σοὶ
ὥσπερ ἀδελφοῦ γυναῖκα λαβών. 8. πρὸς δὲ καὶ
ὅτε Ἀράσπας ἀπέστη αὐτοῦ ὁ ἐμὲ φυλάττων,
ὑπεσχόμην αὐτῷ, εἴ με ἐάσειε πρὸς σὲ πέμψαι,
ἥξειν αὐτῷ σὲ πολὺ Ἀράσπου ἄνδρα καὶ πιστότερον καὶ ἀμείνονα.

9. Ἡ μὲν ταῦτα εἶπεν· ὁ δὲ Ἀβραδάτας ἀγασθεὶς τοῖς λόγοις καὶ θιγὼν αὐτῆς τῆς κεφαλῆς
ἀναβλέψας εἰς τὸν οὐρανὸν ἐπηύξατο, Ἀλλ', ὦ
Ζεῦ μέγιστε, δός μοι φανῆναι ἀξίῳ μὲν Πανθείας
ἀνδρί, ἀξίῳ δὲ Κύρου φίλῳ τοῦ ἡμᾶς τιμήσαντος.

Ταῦτ' εἰπὼν κατὰ τὰς θύρας τοῦ ἁρματείου
δίφρου ἀνέβαινεν ἐπὶ τὸ ἅρμα. 10. ἐπεὶ δὲ ἀνα-
βάντος αὐτοῦ κατέκλεισε τὸν δίφρον ὁ ὑφηνίοχος,
οὐκ ἔχουσα ἡ Πάνθεια πῶς ἂν ἔτι ἄλλως ἀσπά-
σαιτο αὐτόν, κατεφίλησε τὸν δίφρον· καὶ τῷ μὲν
προῄει ἤδη τὸ ἅρμα, ἡ δὲ λαθοῦσα αὐτὸν συν-
εφείπετο, ἕως ἐπιστραφεὶς καὶ ἰδὼν αὐτὴν ὁ
Ἀβραδάτας εἶπε, Θάρρει, Πάνθεια, καὶ χαῖρε
καὶ ἄπιθι ἤδη.

¹ ἄν supplied by Cobet, Hertlein, Gemoll ; not in MSS.,
Dindorf, Breitenbach, Marchant, Hug.

it than any words I now might say. 6. Still, with the affection that you know I have for you, I swear to you by my love for you and yours for me that, of a truth, I would far rather go down into the earth with you, if you approve yourself a gallant soldier, than live disgraced with one disgraced : so worthy of the noblest lot have I deemed both you and myself. 7. And to Cyrus I think we owe a very large debt of gratitude, because, when I was his prisoner and allotted to him, he did not choose to keep me either as his slave or as a freewoman under a dishonourable name, but took me and kept me for you as one would a brother's wife. 8. And then, too, when Araspas, who had been charged with my keeping, deserted him, I promised him that if he would let me send to you, a far better and truer friend than Araspas would come to him, in you."

9. Thus she spoke; and Abradatas, touched by her words, laid his hand upon her head and lifting up his eyes toward heaven prayed, saying : " Grant me, I pray, almighty Zeus, that I may show myself a husband worthy of Panthea and a friend worthy of Cyrus, who has shown us honour."

As he said this, he mounted his car by the doors in the chariot-box. 10. And when he had entered and the groom closed the box, Panthea, not knowing how else she could now kiss him good-bye, touched her lips to the chariot-box. And then at once his chariot rolled away, but she followed after, unknown to him, until Abradatas turned round·and saw her and said : " Have a brave heart, Panthea, and farewell ! And now go back."

The parting

11. Ἐκ τούτου δὴ οἱ εὐνοῦχοι καὶ αἱ θεράπαιναι λαβοῦσαι ἀπῆγον αὐτὴν εἰς τὴν ἁρμάμαξαν
καὶ κατακλίναντες κατεκάλυψαν τῇ σκηνῇ. οἱ δὲ
ἄνθρωποι, καλοῦ ὄντος τοῦ θεάματος τοῦ τε
Ἀβραδάτου καὶ τοῦ ἅρματος, οὐ πρόσθεν ἐδύναντο θεάσασθαι αὐτὸν πρὶν ἡ Πάνθεια ἀπῆλθεν.
12. Ὡς δ' ἐκεκαλλιερήκει μὲν ὁ Κῦρος, ἡ δὲ
στρατιὰ παρετέτακτο αὐτῷ ὥσπερ παρήγγειλε,
κατέχων σκοπὰς ἄλλας πρὸ ἄλλων συνεκάλεσε
τοὺς ἡγεμόνας καὶ ἔλεξεν ὧδε· 13. Ἄνδρες φίλοι
καὶ σύμμαχοι, τὰ μὲν ἱερὰ οἱ θεοὶ ἡμῖν φαίνουσιν
οἷάπερ ὅτε τὴν πρόσθεν νίκην ἔδοσαν· ὑμᾶς δ'
ἐγὼ βούλομαι ἀναμνῆσαι ὧν μοι δοκεῖτε μεμνη-
μένοι πολὺ ἂν εὐθυμότεροι εἰς τὸν ἀγῶνα ἰέναι.
14. ἠσκήκατε μὲν γὰρ τὰ εἰς τὸν πόλεμον πολὺ
μᾶλλον τῶν πολεμίων, συντέτραφθε δὲ καὶ συν-
τέταχθε ἐν τῷ αὐτῷ πολὺ πλείω ἤδη χρόνον ἢ οἱ
πολέμιοι καὶ συννενικήκατε μετ' ἀλλήλων· τῶν δὲ
πολεμίων οἱ πολλοὶ συνήττηνται μεθ' αὑτῶν. οἱ
δὲ ἀμάχητοι ἑκατέρων οἱ μὲν τῶν πολεμίων ἴσασιν
ὅτι προδότας τοὺς παραστάτας ἔχουσιν, ὑμεῖς δὲ
οἱ μεθ' ἡμῶν ἴστε ὅτι μετ' ἐθελόντων τοῖς συμμάχοις ἀρήγειν μάχεσθε. 15. εἰκὸς δὲ τοὺς μὲν
πιστεύοντας ἀλλήλοις ὁμόνως[1] μάχεσθαι μένοντας,
τοὺς δὲ ἀπιστοῦντας ἀναγκαῖον βουλεύεσθαι πῶς
ἂν ἕκαστοι τάχιστα ἐκποδὼν γένοιντο.

---

[1] ὁμόνως Dindorf, most Edd.; ὁμονόως MSS., Sauppe,
Hertlein.

11. Then the eunuchs and maid-servants took her and conducted her to her carriage, where they bade her recline, and hid her completely from view with the hood of the carriage. And the people, beautiful as was the sight of Abradatas and his chariot, had no eyes for him, until Panthea was gone.

12. Now when Cyrus found the omens from his sacrifice favourable, and when his army was arranged as he had instructed, he had posts of observation occupied, one in advance of another, and then called his generals together and addressed them as follows:

13. "Friends and allies, the gods have sent us omens from the sacrifice just like those we had when they gave the former victory into our hands. So I wish to remind you of some things which, if you will remember them, I think will make you go into battle with much stouter hearts. 14. On the one hand, you have received much better training in the arts of war than the enemy, you have lived together and drilled together in the same place for a much longer time now than they, and together you have won a victory; most of the enemy, on the other hand, have together suffered defeat. Some on both sides, however, were not in the battle; among these our enemies know that they have traitors by their sides, while you who are with us know that you are doing battle in company with those who are glad to stand by their comrades. 15. And it is a matter of course that those who trust one another will stand their ground and fight with one heart and mind, and that those who distrust each other will necessarily be scheming, each how he may get out of the way as quickly as possible.

Cyrus analyses the situation

XENOPHON

16. Ἴωμεν δή, ὦ ἄνδρες, ἐπὶ τοὺς πολεμίους, ἅρματα μὲν ἔχοντες ὡπλισμένα πρὸς ἄοπλα τὰ τῶν πολεμίων, ὡς δ' αὔτως καὶ ἱππέας καὶ ἵππους ὡπλισμένους πρὸς ἀόπλους, ὡς ἐκ χειρὸς μάχεσθαι. 17. πεζοῖς δὲ τοῖς μὲν ἄλλοις οἷς καὶ πρόσθεν μαχεῖσθε, Αἰγύπτιοι δὲ ὁμοίως μὲν ὡπλισμένοι εἰσίν, ὁμοίως δὲ τεταγμένοι· τάς τε γὰρ ἀσπίδας μείζους ἔχουσιν ἢ ὡς ποιεῖν τι καὶ ὁρᾶν, τεταγμένοι τε εἰς ἑκατὸν δῆλον ὅτι κωλύσουσιν ἀλλήλους μάχεσθαι πλὴν πάνυ ὀλίγων. 18. εἰ δὲ ὠθοῦντες ἐξώσειν πιστεύουσιν, ἵπποις αὐτοὺς πρῶτον δεήσει ἀντέχειν καὶ σιδήρῳ ὑφ' ἵππων ἰσχυριζομένῳ· ἢν δέ τις αὐτῶν καὶ ὑπομείνῃ, πῶς ἅμα δυνήσεται ἱππομαχεῖν τε καὶ φαλαγγομαχεῖν καὶ πυργομαχεῖν; καὶ γὰρ οἱ ἀπὸ τῶν πύργων ἡμῖν μὲν ἐπαρήξουσι, τοὺς δὲ πολεμίους παίοντες ἀμηχανεῖν ἀντὶ τοῦ μάχεσθαι ποιήσουσιν.

19. Εἰ δέ τινος ἔτι ἐνδεῖσθαι δοκεῖτε, πρὸς ἐμὲ λέγετε· σὺν γὰρ θεοῖς οὐδενὸς ἀπορήσομεν. καὶ εἰ μέν τις εἰπεῖν τι βούλεται, λεξάτω· εἰ δὲ μή, ἐλθόντες πρὸς τὰ ἱερὰ καὶ προσευξάμενοι οἷς ἐθύσαμεν θεοῖς ἴτε ἐπὶ τὰς τάξεις· 20. καὶ ἕκαστος ὑμῶν ὑπομιμνησκέτω τοὺς μεθ' αὑτοῦ ἅπερ ἐγὼ ὑμᾶς, καὶ ἐπιδεικνύτω τις τοῖς ἀρχομένοις ἑαυτὸν ἄξιον ἀρχῆς, ἄφοβον δεικνὺς καὶ σχῆμα καὶ πρόσωπον καὶ λόγους.

16. "Therefore, my men, let us go against the enemy; to fight in a hand-to-hand encounter, with our chariots armed, against theirs unarmed; and our horses and riders in like manner armed, against theirs unarmed. 17. The infantry that you will fight against, you have fought before—all but the Egyptians; and they are armed and drawn up alike badly; for with those big shields which they have they cannot do anything or see anything; and drawn up a hundred deep, it is clear that they will hinder one another from fighting—all except a few. 18. But if they believe that by rushing they will rush us off the field, they will first have to sustain the charge of horses and of steel driven upon them by the force of horses; and if any of them should hold his ground, how will he be able to fight at the same time against cavalry and phalanxes and towers? And that he will have to do, for those upon our towers will come to our aid and raining their missiles upon the enemy will drive them to distraction rather than to fighting.

19. "Still, if you think we need anything more, tell me; for with the help of the gods, we shall lack for nothing. So, if any one wishes to make any remarks, let him speak. If not, do you go to the place of sacrifice and pray to the gods to whom we have sacrificed and then go back to your posts. 20. And each one of you remind his own men of what I have called to your attention, and let each man prove to those whom he commands that he is himself worthy of command, by showing himself fearless in his bearing, in his countenance, and in his words."

BOOK VII

THE GREAT BATTLE

THE FALL OF SARDIS AND BABYLON

Z

I.

1. Οἱ μὲν δὴ εὐξάμενοι τοῖς θεοῖς ἀπῆσαν πρὸς τὰς τάξεις· τῷ δὲ Κύρῳ καὶ τοῖς ἀμφ' αὐτὸν προσήνεγκαν οἱ θεράποντες ἐμφαγεῖν καὶ πιεῖν ἔτι οὖσιν ἀμφὶ τὰ ἱερά. ὁ δὲ Κῦρος ὥσπερ εἶχεν ἑστηκὼς ἀπαρξάμενος ἠρίστα καὶ μετεδίδου ἀεὶ τῷ μάλιστα δεομένῳ· καὶ σπείσας καὶ εὐξάμενος ἔπιε, καὶ οἱ ἄλλοι δὲ οἱ περὶ αὐτὸν οὕτως ἐποίουν. μετὰ δὲ ταῦτα αἰτησάμενος Δία πατρῷον ἡγεμόνα εἶναι καὶ σύμμαχον ἀνέβαινεν ἐπὶ τὸν ἵππον καὶ τοὺς ἀμφ' αὐτὸν ἐκέλευεν. 2. ὡπλισμένοι δὲ πάντες ἦσαν οἱ περὶ τὸν Κῦρον τοῖς αὐτοῖς Κύρῳ ὅπλοις, χιτῶσι φοινικοῖς, θώραξι χαλκοῖς, κράνεσι χαλκοῖς, λόφοις λευκοῖς, μαχαίραις, παλτῷ κρανεΐνῳ ἑνὶ ἕκαστος· οἱ δὲ ἵπποι προμετωπιδίοις καὶ προστερνιδίοις καὶ παραμηριδίοις[1] χαλκοῖς· τὰ δ' αὐτὰ ταῦτα παραμηρίδια ἦν καὶ τῷ ἀνδρί· τοσοῦτον μόνον διέφερε τὰ Κύρου ὅπλα ὅτι τὰ μὲν ἄλλα ἐκέχριτο τῷ χρυσοειδεῖ χρώματι, τὰ δὲ Κύρου ὅπλα ὥσπερ κάτοπτρον ἐξέλαμπεν.

---

[1] παραμηριδίοις Weiske, Edd.; παραπλευριδίοις yG²; not in xzV.

BOOK VII

I

1. So when they had prayed to the gods they went back to their posts; and while Cyrus and his staff were still engaged with the sacrifice, their attendants brought them meat and drink. And Cyrus remained standing just as he was and first offered to the gods a part and then began his breakfast, and kept giving a share of it also from time to time to any one who most needed it. And when he had poured a libation and prayed, he drank; and the rest, his staff-officers, followed his example. After that, he prayed to ancestral Zeus to be their guide and helper and then mounted his horse and bade his staff do the same. 2. Now all Cyrus's staff were panoplied in armour the same as his: purple tunics, bronze corselets, bronze helmets with white plumes, and sabres; and each had a single spear with a shaft of cornel wood. Their horses were armed with frontlets, breast-pieces, and thigh-pieces of bronze; these served to protect the thighs of the rider as well. The arms of Cyrus differed from those of the rest in this only, that while the rest were overlaid with the ordinary gold colour, Cyrus's arms flashed like a mirror.

3. Ἐπεὶ δὲ ἀνέβη καὶ ἔστη ἀποβλέπων ᾗπερ ἔμελλε πορεύεσθαι, βροντὴ δεξιὰ ἐφθέγξατο· ὁ δ' εἶπεν, Ἑψόμεθά σοι, ὦ Ζεῦ μέγιστε. καὶ ὡρμᾶτο ἐν μὲν¹ δεξιᾷ ἔχων Χρυσάνταν τὸν ἵππαρχον καὶ τοὺς ἱππέας, ἐν ἀριστερᾷ δὲ Ἀρσάμαν καὶ τοὺς πεζούς. 4. παρηγγύησε δὲ παρορᾶν πρὸς τὸ σημεῖον καὶ ἐν ἴσῳ ἕπεσθαι· ἦν δὲ αὐτῷ τὸ σημεῖον ἀετὸς χρυσοῦς ἐπὶ δόρατος μακροῦ ἀνατεταμένος. καὶ νῦν δ' ἔτι τοῦτο τὸ σημεῖον τῷ Περσῶν βασιλεῖ διαμένει.

Πρὶν δὲ ὁρᾶν τοὺς πολεμίους εἰς τρὶς ἀνέπαυσε τὸ στράτευμα. 5. ἐπεὶ δὲ προεληλύθεσαν ὡς εἴκοσι σταδίους, ἤρχοντο ἤδη τὸ τῶν πολεμίων στράτευμα ἀντιπροσιὸν καθορᾶν.² ὡς δ' ἐν τῷ καταφανεῖ πάντες ἀλλήλοις ἐγένοντο καὶ ἔγνωσαν οἱ πολέμιοι πολὺ ἑκατέρωθεν ὑπερφαλαγγοῦντες, στήσαντες τὴν αὑτῶν φάλαγγα, οὐ γὰρ ἔστιν ἄλλως κυκλοῦσθαι, ἐπέκαμπτον εἰς κύκλωσιν, ὥσπερ γάμμα ἑκατέρωθεν τὴν ἑαυτῶν τάξιν ποιήσαντες, ὡς πάντοθεν ἅμα μάχοιντο. 6. ὁ δὲ Κῦρος ὁρῶν ταῦτα οὐδέν τι μᾶλλον ἀφίστατο, ἀλλ' ὡσαύτως ἡγεῖτο.

Κατανοῶν δὲ ὡς πρόσω τὸν καμπτῆρα ἑκατέρωθεν ἐποιήσαντο περὶ ὃν κάμπτοντες ἀνέτεινον

---

¹ ἐν μὲν Dindorf, Edd. ; μὲν ἐν MSS.
² καθορᾶν Dindorf⁴, Hug, Marchant, Gemoll ; παρορᾶν MSS., Dindorf³, Breitenbach.

3. Then, when he had mounted his horse and sat looking off in the direction he was to take, there was a clap of thunder on the right. "Almighty Zeus, we will follow thee," he cried, and started, with Chrysantas, the master of the horse, and the cavalry on the right, and on the left Arsamas and the infantry. 4. And he gave orders to keep an eye upon his ensign and advance in even step. Now his ensign was a golden eagle with outspread wings mounted upon a long shaft. And this continues even unto this day as the ensign of the Persian king. ^{His army moves forward}

Before they came in sight of the enemy, he halted the army as many as three times. 5. But when they had advanced about twenty stadia, then they began to get sight of the enemy's army coming on to meet them. And when they were all in sight of one another and the enemy became aware that they greatly outflanked the Persians on both sides, Croesus halted his centre—for otherwise it is impossible to execute a surrounding manœuvre—and began to wheel the wings around to encompass the Persians, thus making his own lines on either flank in form like a gamma,[1] so as to close in and attack on all three sides at once. 6. But Cyrus, although he saw this movement, did not any the more recede but led on just as before. ^{Croesus begins his flanking movement}

"Do you observe, Chrysantas, where the wings are drawing off to form their angle with the centre?" he asked, as he noticed at what a distance from the centre column on both sides they made their turning point, and how far they were pushing

---

[1] Thus : Γ ⌐.

τὰ κέρατα, Ἐννοεῖς, ἔφη, ὦ Χρυσάντα, ἔνθα τὴν
ἐπικαμπὴν ποιοῦνται;

Πάνυ γε, ἔφη ὁ Χρυσάντας, καὶ θαυμάζω γε·
πολὺ γάρ μοι δοκοῦσιν ἀποσπᾶν τὰ κέρατα ἀπὸ
τῆς ἑαυτῶν φάλαγγος.

Ναὶ μὰ Δί', ἔφη ὁ Κῦρος, καὶ ἀπό γε τῆς
ἡμετέρας.

7. Τί δὴ τοῦτο;

Δῆλον ὅτι φοβούμενοι μὴ ἢν ἐγγὺς ἡμῶν γένηται τὰ κέρατα τῆς φάλαγγος ἔτι πρόσω οὔσης,
ἐπιθώμεθα αὐτοῖς.

Ἔπειτ', ἔφη ὁ Χρυσάντας, πῶς δυνήσονται
ὠφελεῖν οἱ ἕτεροι τοὺς ἑτέρους οὕτω πολὺ ἀπέχοντες ἀλλήλων;

Ἀλλὰ δῆλον, ἔφη ὁ Κῦρος, ὅτι ἡνίκα ἂν γένηται τὰ κέρατα ἀναβαίνοντα κατ' ἀντιπέρας τῶν
πλαγίων τοῦ ἡμετέρου στρατεύματος, στραφέντες
ὡς εἰς φάλαγγα ἅμα πάντοθεν ἡμῖν προσίασιν,
ὡς ἅμα πάντοθεν μαχούμενοι.

8. Οὐκοῦν, ἔφη ὁ Χρυσάντας, εὖ σοι δοκοῦσι
βουλεύεσθαι;

Πρός γε ἃ ὁρῶσι· πρὸς δὲ ἃ οὐχ ὁρῶσιν ἔτι
κάκιον ἢ εἰ κατὰ κέρας προσῆσαν. ἀλλὰ σὺ μέν,
ἔφη, ὦ Ἀρσάμα, ἡγοῦ τῷ πεζῷ ἠρέμα ὥσπερ
ἐμὲ ὁρᾷς· καὶ σύ, ὦ Χρυσάντα, ἐν ἴσῳ τούτῳ τὸ
ἱππικὸν ἔχων συμπαρέπου. ἐγὼ δὲ ἄπειμι ἐκεῖσε
ὅθεν μοι δοκεῖ καιρὸς εἶναι ἄρχεσθαι τῆς μάχης·
ἅμα δὲ παριὼν ἐπισκέψομαι ἕκαστα πῶς ἡμῖν
ἔχει. 9. ἐπειδὰν δ' ἐκεῖ γένωμαι, ὅταν ἤδη ὁμοῦ
προσιόντες ἀλλήλοις γιγνώμεθα, παιᾶνα ἐξάρξω,
ὑμεῖς δὲ ἐπείγεσθε. ἡνίκα δ' ἂν ἡμεῖς ἐγχειρῶμεν

forward their wings in executing their flanking movement.

"Indeed I do," answered Chrysantas, "and I am surprised, too; for it strikes me that they are drawing their wings a long way off from their centre."

"Aye, by Zeus," said Cyrus, "and from ours, too."

7. "What, pray, is the reason for that?"

"Evidently because they are afraid their wings will get too close to us while their centre is still far away and that we shall thus close with them."

"Then," said Chrysantas, "how will the one division be able to support the other, when they are so far apart?"

"Well," answered Cyrus, "it is obvious that just as soon as the wings now advancing in column get directly opposite the flanks of our army, they will face about so as to form front and then advance upon us from all three sides simultaneously; for it is their intention to close in on us on all sides at once."

8. "Well," said Chrysantas, "do you then think their plan a good one?"

"Yes; to meet what they see. But in the face of what they do not see, it is even worse than if they were coming on in column. But do you, Arsamas," said he, "lead on your infantry slowly, just as you see me moving; and you, Chrysantas, follow along with the cavalry in an even line with him; meanwhile I shall go to the point where it seems to me most advantageous to open the battle; and at the same time, as I pass along, I will take observations and see how everything is with our side. 9. But when I reach the spot, and as soon as in our advance we are near enough together, I will begin the pæan, and then do you press on. And the moment we come to close

Cyrus gives orders how to meet it

τοῖς πολεμίοις, αἰσθήσεσθε μέν, οὐ γὰρ οἶμαι
ὀλίγος θόρυβος ἔσται, ὁρμήσεται δὲ τηνικαῦτα
Ἀβραδάτας ἤδη σὺν τοῖς ἅρμασιν εἰς τοὺς ἐναν-
τίους· οὕτω γὰρ αὐτῷ εἰρήσεται· ὑμᾶς δὲ χρὴ
ἕπεσθαι ἐχομένους ὅτι μάλιστα τῶν ἁρμάτων.
οὕτω γὰρ μάλιστα τοῖς πολεμίοις τεταραγμένοις
ἐπιπεσούμεθα. παρέσομαι δὲ κἀγὼ ᾗ ἂν δύνωμαι
τάχιστα διώκων τοὺς ἄνδρας, ἢν οἱ θεοὶ θέλωσι.

10. Ταῦτ᾽ εἰπὼν καὶ σύνθημα παρεγγυήσας
Ζεὺς σωτὴρ καὶ ἡγεμὼν ἐπορεύετο. μεταξὺ δὲ τῶν
ἁρμάτων καὶ τῶν θωρακοφόρων διαπορευόμενος
ὁπότε προσβλέψειέ τινας τῶν ἐν ταῖς τάξεσι, τότε
μὲν εἶπεν ἄν, Ὦ ἄνδρες, ὡς ἡδὺ ὑμῶν τὰ πρόσωπα
θεάσασθαι. τοτὲ δ᾽ αὖ ἐν ἄλλοις ἂν ἔλεξεν, Ἆρα,
ἐννοεῖτε, ἄνδρες, ὅτι ὁ νῦν ἀγών ἐστιν οὐ μόνον
περὶ τῆς τήμερον νίκης, ἀλλὰ καὶ περὶ τῆς πρόσθεν ἣν νενικήκατε καὶ περὶ πάσης εὐδαιμονίας;
11. ἐν ἄλλοις δ᾽ ἂν παριὼν[1] εἶπεν, Ὦ ἄνδρες, τὸ
ἀπὸ τοῦδε οὐδέν ποτε ἔτι θεοὺς αἰτιατέον ἔσται·
παραδεδώκασι γὰρ ἡμῖν πολλά τε καὶ ἀγαθὰ
κτήσασθαι. ἀλλ᾽ ἄνδρες[2] ἀγαθοὶ γενώμεθα. 12.
κατ᾽ ἄλλους δ᾽ αὖ τοιάδε· Ὦ ἄνδρες, εἰς τίνα
ποτ᾽ ἂν καλλίονα ἔρανον ἀλλήλους παρακαλέ-
σαιμεν ἢ εἰς τόνδε; νῦν γὰρ ἔξεστιν ἀγαθοῖς ἀνδράσι γενομένοις πολλὰ κἀγαθὰ ἀλλήλοις εἰσενεγ-
κεῖν. 13. κατ᾽ ἄλλους δ᾽ αὖ, Ἐπίστασθε μέν,

---

[1] παριὼν Hug, Marchant, Gemoll; προσιὼν xzV; προϊὼν y,
earlier Edd.

[2] ἄνδρες Dindorf, most Edd.; ὦ ἄνδρες MSS., Breitenbach.

quarters with the enemy, you will perceive it, for there will be no little noise, I presume ; and at the same moment Abradatas will charge with his chariots upon the enemy's lines—for so he will be instructed to do—and you must follow him, keeping as close as possible behind the chariots. For in this way we shall best throw the enemy into confusion and then fall upon them. And I also shall be there as soon as I can, please God, to join in the pursuit."

10. When he had spoken these words, he passed along the lines the watchword, ZEUS OUR SAVIOUR AND GUIDE, and rode on. And as he passed between the lines of chariots and heavy-armed infantry and bestowed a glance upon some of those in the lines, he would say : "What a pleasure it is, my friends, to look into your faces." And then again in the presence of others he would say : "I trust you remember, men, that in the present battle not only is to-day's victory at stake, but also the first victory you won and all our future success." 11. Before still others, as he passed along, he would remark : "For all time to come, my men, we shall never have any more fault to find with the gods ; for they have given us the opportunity of winning many blessings. So let us prove ourselves valiant men." 12. Passing still others he said : "To what fairer common feast [1] could we ever invite each other, my men, than to this one ? For now by showing ourselves brave men we may each contribute many good things for our mutual benefit." 13. Passing others he would say : "I suppose

[margin: He encourages his men]

---

[1] A "common feast," ἔρανος, was a feast where all the participants contributed an equal share — a pic-nic. The ἔρανος might also be a society or club in which all the members contributed equally to some public cause.

οἶμαι, ὦ ἄνδρες, ὅτι νῦν ἆθλα πρόκειται τοῖς
νικῶσι μὲν διώκειν, παίειν, κατακαίνειν, ἀγαθὰ
ἔχειν, καλὰ ἀκούειν, ἐλευθέροις εἶναι, ἄρχειν· τοῖς
δὲ κακοῖς δῆλον ὅτι τἀναντία τούτων. ὅστις οὖν
αὐτὸν φιλεῖ, μετ' ἐμοῦ μαχέσθω· ἐγὼ γὰρ
κακὸν οὐδὲν οὐδ' αἰσχρὸν ἑκὼν εἶναι προσήσομαι.
14. ὁπότε δ' αὖ γένοιτο κατά τινας τῶν πρόσθεν
συμμαχεσαμένων, εἶπεν ἄν, Πρὸς δὲ ὑμᾶς, ὦ
ἄνδρες, τί δεῖ λέγειν; ἐπίστασθε γὰρ οἵαν τε οἱ
ἀγαθοὶ ἐν ταῖς μάχαις ἡμέραν ἄγουσι καὶ οἵαν οἱ
κακοί.

15. Ὡς δὲ παριὼν κατὰ Ἀβραδάταν ἐγένετο,
ἔστη· καὶ ὁ Ἀβραδάτας παραδοὺς τῷ ὑφηνιόχῳ
τὰς ἡνίας προσῆλθεν αὐτῷ· προσέδραμον δὲ καὶ
ἄλλοι τῶν πλησίον τεταγμένων καὶ πεζῶν καὶ
ἁρματηλατῶν. ὁ δ' αὖ Κῦρος ἐν τοῖς παραγεγενη-
μένοις ἔλεξεν, Ὁ μὲν θεός, ὦ Ἀβραδάτα, ὥσπερ
σὺ ἠξίους, συνηξίωσέ σε καὶ τοὺς σὺν σοὶ πρωτοστάτας εἶναι τῶν συμμάχων· σὺ δὲ τοῦτο
μέμνησο, ὅταν δέῃ σε ἤδη ἀγωνίζεσθαι, ὅτι Πέρσαι
οἵ τε θεασόμενοι ὑμᾶς ἔσονται καὶ οἱ ἑψόμενοι
ὑμῖν καὶ οὐκ ἐάσοντες ἐρήμους ὑμᾶς ἀγωνίζεσθαι.

16. Καὶ ὁ Ἀβραδάτας εἶπεν, Ἀλλὰ τὰ μὲν καθ'
ἡμᾶς ἔμοιγε δοκεῖ, ὦ Κῦρε, καλῶς ἔχειν· ἀλλὰ τὰ
πλάγια λυπεῖ με, ὅτι τὰ μὲν τῶν πολεμίων κέρατα
ἰσχυρὰ ὁρῶ ἀνατεινόμενα καὶ ἅρμασι καὶ παν-
τοδαπῇ στρατιᾷ· ἡμέτερον δ' οὐδὲν ἄλλο αὐτοῖς
ἀντιτέτακται ἢ ἅρματα· ὥστ' ἔγωγ', ἔφη, εἰ μὴ
ἔλαχον τήνδε τὴν τάξιν, ᾐσχυνόμην ἂν ἐνθάδε ὤν·
οὕτω πολύ μοι δοκῶ ἐν ἀσφαλεστάτῳ εἶναι.

17. Καὶ ὁ Κῦρος εἶπεν, Ἀλλ' εἰ τὰ παρὰ σοὶ
καλῶς ἔχει, θάρρει ὑπὲρ ἐκείνων· ἐγὼ γάρ σοι σὺν

that you understand, men, that pursuing, dealing blows and death, plunder, fame, freedom, power—all these are now held up as prizes for the victors; the cowardly, of course, have the reverse of all this. Whoever, therefore, cares for himself, let him fight with me; for I will never bring myself to do anything base or cowardly, if I can help it." 14. But whenever he came past any of those who had fought under him before, he would say : "What need to say anything to you, my men? For you know how the brave celebrate a day in battle, and how cowards."

15. And as he passed along and came to Abradatas, he stopped; and Abradatas, handing the reins to his groom, came toward him, and others also of those whose positions were near, both foot and chariot-drivers, ran up. And then to the company gathered about him Cyrus said : "Abradatas, God has approved your request that you and your men should take the front ranks among the allies. So now remember this, when presently it becomes necessary for you to enter the conflict, that Persians will not only be your witnesses but will also follow you and will not let you go into the conflict unsupported." *His last interview with Abradatas*

16. "Well," answered Abradatas, "to me at least our part of the army seems to be all right; but I am anxious for the flanks; for I see the enemy's wings stretching out strong with chariots and troops of every description, while in the centre there is nothing opposed to our side except chariots; and so if I had not obtained this position by lot, I should, for my part, be ashamed of being here, so much the safest position do I think I occupy."

17. "Well," said Cyrus, "if your part is all right, never fear for the others; for with the help of the *His confidence in the outcome*

θεοῖς ἔρημα τῶν πολεμίων τὰ πλάγια ταῦτα ἀπο-
δείξω. καὶ σὺ μὴ πρότερον ἔμβαλλε τοῖς ἐναντίοις,
διαμαρτύρομαι, πρὶν ἂν φεύγοντας τούτους οὓς νῦν
φοβεῖ θεάσῃ· τοιαῦτα δ' ἐμεγαληγόρει, μελλούσης
τῆς μάχης γίγνεσθαι· ἄλλως δ' οὐ μάλα μεγαλή-
γορος ἦν. "Οταν μέντοι ἴδῃς τούτους φεύγοντας,
ἐμέ τε ἤδη παρεῖναι νόμιζε καὶ ὅρμα εἰς τοὺς
ἄνδρας· καὶ σὺ γὰρ τότε τοῖς μὲν ἐναντίοις κακί-
στοις ἂν χρήσαιο, τοῖς δὲ μετὰ σαυτοῦ ἀρίστοις.

18. Ἀλλ' ἕως ἔτι σοι σχολή, ὦ Ἀβραδάτα,
πάντως παρελάσας παρὰ τὰ σαυτοῦ ἅρματα
παρακάλει τοὺς σὺν σοὶ εἰς τὴν ἐμβολήν, τῷ μὲν
προσώπῳ παραθαρρύνων, ταῖς δ' ἐλπίσιν ἐπικου-
φίζων. ὅπως δὲ κράτιστοι φανεῖσθε τῶν ἐπὶ τοῖς
ἅρμασι, φιλονικίαν αὐτοῖς ἔμβαλλε· καὶ γάρ, εὖ
ἴσθι, ἢν τάδε εὖ γένηται, πάντες ἐροῦσι τὸ λοιπὸν
μηδὲν εἶναι κερδαλεώτερον ἀρετῆς.

Ὁ μὲν δὴ Ἀβραδάτας ἀναβὰς παρήλαυνε καὶ
ταῦτ' ἐποίει.

19. Ὁ δ' αὖ Κῦρος παριὼν ὡς ἐγένετο πρὸς τῷ
εὐωνύμῳ, ἔνθα ὁ Ὑστάσπας τοὺς ἡμίσεις ἔχων ἦν
τῶν Περσῶν ἱππέων, ὀνομάσας αὐτὸν εἶπεν, Ὦ
Ὑστάσπα, νῦν ὁρᾷς ἔργον τῆς σῆς ταχυεργίας·
νῦν γὰρ ἢν φθάσωμεν τοὺς πολεμίους κατακανόν-
τες, οὐδεὶς ἡμῶν ἀποθανεῖται.

20. Καὶ ὁ Ὑστάσπας ἐπιγελάσας εἶπεν, Ἀλλὰ περὶ μὲν τῶν ἐξ ἐναντίας ἡμῖν μελήσει, τοὺς δ'
ἐκ πλαγίου σὺ ἄλλοις πρόσταξον, ὅπως μηδ'
οὗτοι σχολάζωσι.

Καὶ ὁ Κῦρος εἶπεν, Ἀλλ' ἐπί γε τούτους ἐγὼ
αὐτὸς παρέρχομαι· ἀλλ', ὦ Ὑστάσπα, τόδε μέ-

gods I will clear those flanks of enemies for you.
And do not you hurl yourself upon the opposing
ranks, I adjure you, until you see in flight those
whom you now fear." Cyrus indulged in such boastful
speech only on the eve of battle; at other times he
was never boastful at all; and he went on : " But
when you see them in flight, then be sure that I am
already at hand, and charge upon those fellows; for
at that moment you will find your opponents most
cowardly and your own men valiant.

18. " But now, Abradatas, while you have time, by
all means ride along your line of chariots and exhort
your men to the charge, cheering them by your own
looks and buoying them up with hopes. Furthermore, inspire them with a spirit of rivalry that you
and your division may prove yourselves the best of
the charioteers. And that will be worth while ; for
be assured that if we are successful to-day, all men in
future will say that nothing is more profitable than
valour."

Abradatas accordingly mounted and drove along
and did as Cyrus had suggested.

19. And as Cyrus passed along again, he came to ^{He exhorts}
the left wing, where Hystaspas was with half the ^{other officers :}
Persian cavalry ; he called to him and said : " Now, ^{(1) Hystas-}
Hystaspas, you see some use for your speed ; for now, ^{pas,}
if we can kill the enemy before they kill us, not one
of us will perish."

20. " Well," said Hystaspas laughing, " we will
take care of those opposite us ; assign those on the
flank to another division, so that they also may have
something to do."

" Why," said Cyrus, " I am going on to them myself.
But remember this, Hystaspas, no matter to which of

μνησο, ὅτῳ ἂν ἡμῶν ὁ θεὸς νίκην διδῷ, ἤν τί που
μένῃ πολέμιον, πρὸς τὸ μαχόμενον ἀεὶ συμβάλ-
λωμεν.

21. Ταῦτ' εἰπὼν προῄει. ἐπεὶ δὲ κατὰ τὸ πλευρὸν παριὼν ἐγένετο καὶ κατὰ τὸν ἄρχοντα τῶν
ταύτῃ ἁρμάτων, πρὸς τοῦτον ἔλεξεν, Ἐγὼ δὲ
ἔρχομαι ὑμῖν ἐπικουρήσων, ἀλλ' ὁπόταν αἴσθησθε
ἡμᾶς ἐπιτιθεμένους κατ' ἄκρον, τότε καὶ ὑμεῖς
πειρᾶσθε ἅμα διὰ τῶν πολεμίων ἐλαύνειν· πολὺ
γὰρ ἐν ἀσφαλεστέρῳ ἔσεσθε ἔξω γενόμενοι ἢ
ἔνδον ἀπολαμβανόμενοι.

22. Ἐπεὶ δ' αὖ παριὼν ἐγένετο ὄπισθεν τῶν
ἁρμαμαξῶν, Ἀρταγέρσαν μὲν καὶ Φαρνοῦχον ἐκέλευσεν ἔχοντας τήν τε τῶν πεζῶν χιλιοστὺν καὶ
τὴν τῶν ἱππέων μένειν αὐτοῦ. Ἐπειδὰν δ', ἔφη,
αἰσθάνησθε ἐμοῦ ἐπιτιθεμένου τοῖς κατὰ τὸ δεξιὸν
κέρας, τότε καὶ ὑμεῖς τοῖς καθ' ὑμᾶς ἐπιχειρεῖτε
μαχεῖσθε δ', ἔφη, πρὸς κέρας, ὥσπερ[1] ἀσθενέστατον στράτευμα γίγνεται, φάλαγγα δ' ἔχοντες,
ὥσπερ ἂν ἰσχυρότατοι εἴητε. καὶ εἰσὶ μέν, ὡς
ὁρᾶτε, τῶν πολεμίων ἱππεῖς οἱ ἔσχατοι· πάντως
δὲ πρόετε πρὸς αὐτοὺς τὴν τῶν καμήλων τάξιν,
καὶ εὖ ἴστε ὅτι καὶ πρὶν μάχεσθαι γελοίους τοὺς
πολεμίους θεάσεσθε.

23. Ὁ μὲν δὴ Κῦρος ταῦτα διαπραξάμενος ἐπὶ
τὸ δεξιὸν παρῄει· ὁ δὲ Κροῖσος νομίσας ἤδη
ἐγγύτερον εἶναι τῶν πολεμίων τὴν φάλαγγα σὺν
ᾗ αὐτὸς ἐπορεύετο ἢ τὰ ἀνατεινόμενα κέρατα, ἦρε
τοῖς κέρασι σημεῖον μηκέτι ἄνω πορεύεσθαι, ἀλλ'
αὐτοῦ ἐν χώρᾳ στραφῆναι. ὡς δ' ἔστησαν ἀντία

---

[1] ὥσπερ MSS., most Edd.; Castalio's suggestion ᾗπερ is
adopted by Marchant, Gemoll.

us God gives the victory first, if afterwards anything is left of any part of the enemy, let us all engage any force that still continues the fight."

21. Thus he spoke and passed on. And as he went along the flank, he came to the general in command of the chariots there and to him he said : "Yes, I am coming to help you ; but when you see us charging on the extremity of the enemy's wing, then do you try at the same time to break through their lines ; for you will be in a much securer position if you get clear through than if you are enclosed within their lines." (2) the commander of the chariots,

22. And as he passed on again and came behind the women's carriages, he ordered Artagerses and Pharnuchus with their respective regiments of infantry and cavalry to stay there. "But," said he, "when you see me charging against those opposite our right wing, do you also attack those opposite you. And you will be in a phalanx—the formation in which you would be strongest—and take the enemy on their flank, the position in which an army is weakest. And, as you see, their cavalry stands furthest out ; so by all means send against them the brigade of camels, and be assured that even before the battle begins you will see the enemy in a ridiculous plight." (3) Pheraulas and Artagerses

23. When Cyrus had completed his round of the troops, he passed on to the right wing. And Croesus, thinking that the centre, which he commanded in person, was already nearer to the enemy than the wings that were spreading out beyond, gave a signal to his wings not to go out any further but to halt and face about. And when they had halted, and stood Croesus orders his attack ;

πρὸς τὸ τοῦ Κύρου στράτευμα ὁρῶντες, ἐσήμηνεν
αὐτοῖς πορεύεσθαι πρὸς τοὺς πολεμίους. 24. κα
οὕτω δὴ προσῆσαν τρεῖς φάλαγγες ἐπὶ τὸ Κύρου
στράτευμα, ἡ μὲν μία κατὰ πρόσωπον, τὼ δὲ δύο
ἡ μὲν κατὰ τὸ δεξιόν, ἡ δὲ κατὰ τὸ εὐώνυμον
ὥστε πολὺν φόβον παρεῖναι πάσῃ τῇ Κύρου
στρατιᾷ. ὥσπερ γὰρ μικρὸν πλινθίον ἐν μεγάλῳ
τεθέν, οὕτω καὶ τὸ Κύρου στράτευμα πάντοθεν
περιείχετο ὑπὸ τῶν πολεμίων καὶ ἱππεῦσι κα
ὁπλίταις καὶ πελτοφόροις καὶ τοξόταις καὶ ἅρμασι πλὴν ἐξόπισθεν. 25. ὅμως δὲ ὡς[1] ὁ Κῦρος
[ἐπεὶ][2] παρήγγειλεν, ἐστράφησαν πάντες ἀντι-
πρόσωποι τοῖς πολεμίοις· καὶ ἦν μὲν πολλὴ παν-
ταχόθεν σιγὴ ὑπὸ τοῦ τὸ μέλλον ὀκνεῖν· ἡνίκα δὲ
ἔδοξε τῷ Κύρῳ καιρὸς εἶναι, ἐξῆρχε παιᾶνα, συνε-
πήχησε δὲ πᾶς ὁ στρατός. 26. μετὰ δὲ τοῦτο τῷ
Ἐνυαλίῳ τε ἅμα ἐπηλάλαξαν καὶ ἐξανίσταται ὁ
Κῦρος, καὶ εὐθὺς μὲν μετὰ τῶν ἱππέων λαβὼν
πλαγίους τοὺς πολεμίους ὁμόσε αὐτοῖς τὴν ταχίστην συνεμίγνυ· οἱ δὲ πεζοὶ αὐτῷ συντεταγμένοι
ταχὺ ἐφείποντο, καὶ περιεπτύσσοντο ἔνθεν καὶ
ἔνθεν, ὥστε πολὺ ἐπλεονέκτει· φάλαγγι γὰρ κατὰ
κέρας προσέβαλλεν· ὥστε ταχὺ ἰσχυρὰ φυγὴ
ἐγένετο τοῖς πολεμίοις.

---

[1] ὡς Hug, Marchant, Gemoll ; καὶ MSS., earlier Edd.
[2] ἐπεὶ MSS., earlier Edd. ; bracketed by Hug, Marchant, Gemoll.

facing Cyrus's army, Croesus gave them the signal to advance against the foe. 24. And so the three phalanxes advanced upon the army of Cyrus, one from in front, the other two against his wings, one from the right, the other from the left; in consequence, great fear came upon all his army. For just like a little tile set inside a large one,[1] Cyrus's army was encompassed by the enemy on every side, except the rear, with horsemen and hoplites, with targeteers and bowmen and chariots. 25. Still, when Cyrus gave the command, they all turned and faced the enemy. And deep silence reigned on every hand because of their apprehension as to what was coming. Then, when it seemed to Cyrus to be just the right time, he began the paean and all the army joined in the chant. 26. After it was finished, together they raised the battle-shout to Enyalius, and in that instant Cyrus dashed forward; and at once he hurled his cavalry upon the enemy's flank and in a moment he was engaged with them hand to hand. With a rapid movement the infantry followed him in good order and began to envelop the enemy on this side and on that, so that he had them at a great disadvantage; for he clashed with a phalanx against their flank; and as a result, the enemy soon were in headlong flight.

but Cyrus anticipates him on the right,

[1] The point of Xenophon's simile is clear, when we recall the marble tiling of the temple roofs of his time; the situation was like this:

27. Ὡς δὲ ᾔσθετο Ἀρταγέρσης ἐν ἔργῳ ὄντα τὸν Κῦρον, ἐπιτίθεται καὶ αὐτὸς κατὰ τὰ εὐώνυμα, προεὶς τὰς καμήλους ὥσπερ Κῦρος ἐκέλευσεν. οἱ δὲ ἵπποι αὐτὰς ἐκ πάνυ πολλοῦ οὐκ ἐδέχοντο, ἀλλ᾽ οἱ μὲν ἔκφρονες γιγνόμενοι ἔφευγον, οἱ δ᾽ ἐξήλλοντο, οἱ δ᾽ ἐνέπιπτον ἀλλήλοις. τοιαῦτα γὰρ πάσχουσιν ἵπποι ὑπὸ καμήλων. 28. ὁ δὲ Ἀρταγέρσης συντεταγμένους ἔχων τοὺς μεθ᾽ ἑαυτοῦ ταραττομένοις ἐπέκειτο· καὶ τὰ ἅρματα δὲ κατὰ τὸ δεξιὸν καὶ τὸ εὐώνυμον ἅμα ἐνέβαλλε. καὶ πολλοὶ μὲν τὰ ἅρματα φεύγοντες ὑπὸ τῶν κατὰ κέρας ἑπομένων ἀπέθνησκον, πολλοὶ δὲ τούτους φεύγοντες ὑπὸ τῶν ἁρμάτων ἡλίσκοντο.

29. Καὶ ὁ Ἀβραδάτας δὲ οὐκέτι ἔμελλεν, ἀλλ᾽ ἀναβοήσας, Ἄνδρες φίλοι, ἔπεσθε, ἐνίει οὐδὲν φειδόμενος τῶν ἵππων, ἀλλ᾽ ἰσχυρῶς ἐξαιμάττων τῷ κέντρῳ· συνεξώρμησαν δὲ καὶ οἱ ἄλλοι ἁρματηλάται. καὶ τὰ μὲν ἅρματα ἔφευγεν αὐτοὺς εὐθύς, τὰ μὲν καὶ ἀναλαβόντα τοὺς παραβάτας, τὰ δὲ καὶ ἀπολιπόντα.

30. Ὁ δὲ Ἀβραδάτας ἀντικρὺ διᾴττων[1] εἰς τὴν τῶν Αἰγυπτίων φάλαγγα ἐμβάλλει· συνεισέβαλον δὲ αὐτῷ καὶ οἱ ἐγγύτατα τεταγμένοι. πολλαχοῦ μὲν οὖν καὶ ἄλλοθι δῆλον ὡς οὐκ ἔστιν ἰσχυροτέρα φάλαγξ ἢ ὅταν ἐκ φίλων συμμάχων ἠθροισμένη ᾖ, καὶ ἐν τούτῳ δὲ ἐδήλωσεν. οἱ μὲν γὰρ ἑταῖροί τε αὐτοῦ καὶ ὁμοτρά-

---

[1] διᾴττων F, Hug, Marchant Gemoll; δι᾽ αὐτῶν xzDV, Dindorf, Breitenbach.

27. As soon as Artagerses saw Cyrus in action, he delivered his attack on the enemy's left, putting forward the camels, as Cyrus had directed. But while the camels were still a great way off, the horses gave way before them; some took fright and ran away, others began to rear, while others plunged into one another; for such is the usual effect that camels produce upon horses. 28. And Artagerses, with his men in order, fell upon them in their confusion; and at the same moment the chariots also charged on both the right and the left. And many in their flight from the chariots were slain by the cavalry following up their attack upon the flank, and many also trying to escape from the cavalry were caught by the chariots.

29. And Abradatas also lost no more time, but shouting, "Now, friends, follow me," he swept forward, showing no mercy to his horses but drawing blood from them in streams with every stroke of the lash. And the rest of the chariot-drivers also rushed forward with him. And the opposing chariots at once broke into flight before them; some, as they fled, took up their dismounted [1] fighting men, others left theirs behind.

30. But Abradatas plunged directly through them and hurled himself upon the Egyptian phalanx; and the nearest of those who were arrayed with him also joined in the charge. Now, it has been demonstrated on many other occasions that there is no stronger phalanx than that which is composed of comrades that are close friends; and it was shown to be true on this occasion. For it was only the personal friends and mess-mates of Abradatas who pressed home the

Margin notes: Artagerses on the left. Abradatas charges to his death.

[1] Compare III. iii. 60; VI. i. 27.

πεζοὶ συνεισέβαλον· οἱ δ' ἄλλοι ἡνίοχοι ὡς εἶδον
ὑπομένοντας πολλῷ στίφει τοὺς Αἰγυπτίους,
ἐξέκλιναν κατὰ τὰ φεύγοντα ἅρματα καὶ τούτοις
ἐφείποντο. 31. οἱ δὲ ἀμφὶ Ἀβραδάταν ᾗ μὲν
ἐνέβαλλον, ἅτε οὐ δυναμένων διαχάσασθαι τῶν
Αἰγυπτίων διὰ τὸ μένειν τοὺς ἔνθεν καὶ ἔνθεν
αὐτῶν, τοὺς μὲν ὀρθοὺς τῇ ῥύμῃ τῇ τῶν ἵππων
παίοντες ἀνέτρεπον, τοὺς δὲ πίπτοντας κατη-
λόων καὶ αὐτοὺς καὶ ὅπλα καὶ ἵπποις καὶ
τροχοῖς.[1] ὅτου δ' ἐπιλάβοιτο τὰ δρέπανα, πάντα
βίᾳ διεκόπτετο καὶ ὅπλα καὶ σώματα.
    32. Ἐν δὲ τῷ ἀδιηγήτῳ τούτῳ ταράχῳ ὑπὸ
τῶν παντοδαπῶν σωρευμάτων ἐξαλλομένων τῶν
τροχῶν ἐκπίπτει ὁ Ἀβραδάτας καὶ ἄλλοι δὲ
τῶν συνεισβαλόντων, καὶ οὗτοι μὲν ἐνταῦθα
ἄνδρες ἀγαθοὶ γενόμενοι κατεκόπησαν καὶ ἀπέ-
θανον.
    Οἱ δὲ Πέρσαι συνεπισπόμενοι, ᾗ μὲν ὁ Ἀβρα-
δάτας ἐνέβαλε καὶ οἱ σὺν αὐτῷ, ταύτῃ ἐπεισ-
πεσόντες τεταραγμένους ἐφόνευον, ᾗ δὲ ἀπαθεῖς
ἐγένοντο οἱ Αἰγύπτιοι, πολλοὶ δ' οὗτοι ἦσαν,
ἐχώρουν ἐναντίοι τοῖς Πέρσαις. 33. ἔνθα δὴ
δεινὴ μάχη ἦν καὶ δοράτων καὶ ξυστῶν καὶ
μαχαιρῶν· ἐπλεονέκτουν μέντοι οἱ Αἰγύπτιοι καὶ
πλήθει καὶ τοῖς ὅπλοις. τά τε γὰρ δόρατα ἰσχυρὰ
καὶ μακρὰ ἔτι καὶ νῦν ἔχουσιν, αἵ τε ἀσπίδες
πολὺ μᾶλλον τῶν θωράκων καὶ τῶν γέρρων καὶ
στεγάζουσι τὰ σώματα, καὶ πρὸς τὸ ὠθεῖσθαι
συνεργάζονται πρὸς τοῖς ὤμοις οὖσαι. συγκλεί-

[1] ἵπποις καὶ τροχοῖς Camerarius, Edd. ; ἵππους καὶ τροχούς
MSS.

charge with him, while the rest of the charioteers, when they saw that the Egyptians with their dense throng withstood them, turned aside after the fleeing chariots and pursued them. 31. But in the place where Abradatas and his companions charged, the Egyptians could not make an opening for them because the men on either side of them stood firm; consequently, those of the enemy who stood upright were struck in the furious charge of the horses and overthrown, and those who fell were crushed to pieces by the horses and the wheels, they and their arms; and whatever was caught in the scythes—everything, arms and men, was horribly mangled.

32. As in this indescribable confusion the wheels bounded over the heaps of every sort, Abradatas and others of those who went with him into the charge were thrown to the ground, and there, though they proved themselves men of valour, they were cut down and slain.

Then the Persians, following up the attack at the point where Abradatas and his men had made their charge, made havoc of the enemy in their confusion; but where the Egyptians were still unharmed—and there were many such—they advanced to oppose the Persians. 33. Here, then, was a dreadful conflict with spears and lances and swords. The Egyptians, however, had the advantage both in numbers and in weapons; for the spears that they use even unto this day are long and powerful, and their shields cover their bodies much more effectually than corselets and targets, and as they rest against the shoulder they are a help in shoving. So, locking their shields to-

The Persians charge the Egyptian phalanx

σαντες οὖν τὰς ἀσπίδας ἐχώρουν καὶ ἐώθουν.
34. οἱ δὲ Πέρσαι οὐκ ἐδύναντο ἀντέχειν, ἅτε
ἐν ἄκραις ταῖς χερσὶ τὰ γέρρα ἔχοντες, ἀλλ᾽
ἐπὶ πόδα ἀνεχάζοντο παίοντες καὶ παιόμενοι,
ἕως ὑπὸ ταῖς μηχαναῖς ἐγένοντο. ἐπεὶ μέντοι
ἐνταῦθα ἦλθον, ἐπαίοντο αὖθις οἱ Αἰγύπτιοι ἀπὸ
τῶν πύργων· καὶ οἱ ἐπὶ πᾶσι δὲ οὐκ εἴων φεύγειν
οὔτε τοὺς τοξότας οὔτε τοὺς ἀκοντιστάς, ἀλλ᾽
ἀνατεταμένοι τὰς μαχαίρας ἠνάγκαζον καὶ τοξεύειν καὶ ἀκοντίζειν. 35. ἦν δὲ πολὺς μὲν
ἀνδρῶν φόνος, πολὺς δὲ κτύπος ὅπλων καὶ βελῶν
παντοδαπῶν, πολλὴ δὲ βοὴ τῶν μὲν ἀνακα-
λούντων ἀλλήλους, τῶν δὲ παρακελευομένων, τῶν
δὲ θεοὺς ἐπικαλουμένων.

36. Ἐν δὲ τούτῳ Κῦρος διώκων τοὺς καθ᾽
αὑτὸν παραγίγνεται. ὡς δ᾽ εἶδε τοὺς Πέρσας
ἐκ τῆς χώρας ἐωσμένους, ἤλγησέ τε καὶ γνοὺς
ὅτι οὐδαμῶς ἂν θᾶττον σχοίη τοὺς πολεμίους
τῆς εἰς τὸ πρόσθεν προόδου ἢ εἰ[1] εἰς τὸ ὄπισθεν
περιελάσειεν αὐτῶν, παραγγείλας ἕπεσθαι τοῖς
μεθ᾽ αὑτοῦ περιήλαυνεν εἰς τὸ ὄπισθεν· καὶ
εἰσπεσόντες παίουσιν ἀφορῶντας[2] καὶ πολλοὺς
κατακαίνουσιν. 37. οἱ δὲ Αἰγύπτιοι ὡς ᾔσθοντο,
ἐβόων τε ὅτι ὄπισθεν οἱ πολέμιοι καὶ ἐστρέφοντο
ἐν ταῖς πληγαῖς. καὶ ἐνταῦθα δὴ φύρδην ἐμάχοντο καὶ πεζοὶ καὶ ἱππεῖς, πεπτωκὼς δέ τις
ὑπὸ τῷ Κύρου ἵππῳ καὶ πατούμενος παίει εἰς
τὴν γαστέρα τῇ μαχαίρᾳ τὸν ἵππον αὐτοῦ· ὁ
δὲ ἵππος πληγεὶς σφαδᾴζων ἀποσείεται τὸν

---

[1] εἰ Philelphus, Edd.; not in MSS.
[2] ἀφορῶντας MSS., Hug, Dindorf, Breitenbach, Marchant;
ἀποροῦντας Madvig, Gemoll (in their distress).

ether, they advanced and shoved. 34. And because the Persians had to hold out their little shields clutched in their hands, they were unable to hold the line, but were forced back foot by foot, giving and taking blows, until they came up under cover of the moving towers. When they reached that point, the Egyptians in turn received a volley from the towers; and the forces in the extreme rear would not allow any retreat on the part of either archers or lancers, but with drawn swords they compelled them to shoot and hurl. 35. Then there was a dreadful carnage, an awful din of arms and missiles of every sort, and a great tumult of men, as they called to one another for aid, or exhorted one another, or invoked the gods.

36. At this juncture Cyrus came up in pursuit of the part that had been opposed to him; and when he saw that the Persians had been forced from their position, he was grieved; but as he realized that he could in no way check the enemy's progress more quickly than by marching around behind them, he ordered his men to follow him and rode around to the rear. There he fell upon the enemy as they faced the other way and smote them and slew many of them. 37. And when the Egyptians became aware of their position they shouted out that the enemy was in their rear, and amidst the blows they faced about. And then they fought promiscuously both foot and horse; and a certain man, who had fallen under Cyrus's horse and was under the animal's heels, struck the horse in the belly with his sword. And the horse thus wounded plunged convulsively and threw Cyrus

Cyrus falls upon their rear

Κῦρον. 38. ἔνθα δὴ ἔγνω ἄν τις ὅσου ἄξιο
εἴη τὸ φιλεῖσθαι ἄρχοντα ὑπὸ τῶν περὶ αὐτόν
εὐθὺς γὰρ ἀνεβόησάν τε πάντες καὶ προσπεσόντε
ἐμάχοντο, ἐώθουν, ἐωθοῦντο, ἔπαιον, ἐπαίοντο
καταπηδήσας δέ τις ἀπὸ τοῦ ἵππου τῶν το
Κύρου ὑπηρετῶν ἀναβάλλει αὐτὸν ἐπὶ τὸν ἑαυτοῦ
ἵππον. 39. ὡς δ' ἀνέβη ὁ Κῦρος, κατεῖδε πάντοθεν
ἤδη παιομένους τοὺς Αἰγυπτίους· καὶ γὰρ Ὑστά
σπας ἤδη παρῆν σὺν τοῖς Περσῶν ἱππεῦσι κα
Χρυσάντας. ἀλλὰ τούτους ἐμβάλλειν μὲν οὐκέτ
εἴα εἰς τὴν φάλαγγα τῶν Αἰγυπτίων, ἔξωθεν
δὲ τοξεύειν καὶ ἀκοντίζειν ἐκέλευεν.

Ὡς δ' ἐγένετο περιελαύνων παρὰ τὰς μηχανάς
ἔδοξεν αὐτῷ ἀναβῆναι ἐπὶ τῶν πύργων τινὰ κα
κατασκέψασθαι εἴ πῃ καὶ ἄλλο τι μένοι τῶν
πολεμίων καὶ μάχοιτο. [1] 40. ἐπεὶ δὲ ἀνέβη, κατεῖδ
μεστὸν τὸ πεδίον ἵππων, ἀνθρώπων, ἁρμάτων
φευγόντων, διωκόντων, κρατούντων, κρατουμένων
μένον δ' οὐδαμοῦ οὐδὲν ἔτι ἐδύνατο κατιδεῖν πλὴ
τὸ τῶν Αἰγυπτίων· οὗτοι δὲ ἐπειδὴ ἠποροῦντο
πάντοθεν κύκλον ποιησάμενοι, ὥστε ὁρᾶσθαι τὰ
ὅπλα, ὑπὸ ταῖς ἀσπίσιν ἐκάθηντο· καὶ ἐποίου
μὲν οὐδὲν ἔτι, ἔπασχον δὲ πολλὰ καὶ δεινά.

41. Ἀγασθεὶς δὲ ὁ Κῦρος αὐτοὺς καὶ οἰκτείρω
ὅτι ἀγαθοὶ ἄνδρες ὄντες ἀπώλλυντο, ἀνεχώρισε
πάντας τοὺς περιμαχομένους καὶ μάχεσθαι οὐδένα
ἔτι εἴα. πέμπει δὲ πρὸς αὐτοὺς κήρυκα ἐρωτῶν

---

[1] ἀνεχώρισε Edd.; ἀνεχώρησε MSS.

ff. 38. Then one might have realized how much it is worth to an officer to be loved by his men; for they all at once cried out and leaping forward they fought, shoved and were shoved, gave and received blows. And one of his aides-de-camp leaped down from his own horse and helped him mount upon it; 39. and when Cyrus had mounted he saw that the Egyptians were now assailed on every side; for Hystaspas also and Chrysantas had now come up with the Persian cavalry. But he did not permit them yet to charge into the Egyptian phalanx, but bade them shoot and hurl from a distance.

And when, as he rode round, he came to the engines, he decided to ascend one of the towers and take a view to see if anywhere any part of the enemy's forces were making a stand to fight. 40. And when he had ascended the tower, he looked down upon the field full of horses and men and chariots, some fleeing, some pursuing, some victorious, others vanquished; but nowhere could he discover any division that was still standing its ground, except that of the Egyptians; and they, inasmuch as they found themselves in a desperate condition, formed in a complete circle and crouched behind their shields, so that only their weapons were visible; but they were no longer accomplishing anything, but were suffering very heavy loss.

Cyrus surveys the field from a movable tower

41. And Cyrus, filled with admiration for their conduct and moved to pity for them that men as brave as they were should be slain, drew off all those who were fighting around the ring and allowed no one to fight any more. Then he sent a herald to them to ask whether they all wished to die for

He spares the Egyptians

πότερα βούλονται ἀπολέσθαι πάντες ὑπὲρ τῶν
προδεδωκότων αὐτοὺς ἢ σωθῆναι ἄνδρες ἀγαθοὶ
δοκοῦντες εἶναι.

Οἱ δ' ἀπεκρίναντο, Πῶς δ' ἂν ἡμεῖς σωθείημεν
ἄνδρες ἀγαθοὶ δοκοῦντες εἶναι;

42. Ὁ δὲ Κῦρος πάλιν ἔλεγεν, Ὅτι ἡμεῖς ὑμᾶς
ὁρῶμεν μόνους καὶ μένοντας καὶ μάχεσθαι ἐθέλοντας.

Ἀλλὰ τοὐντεῦθεν, ἔφασαν οἱ Αἰγύπτιοι, τί
καλὸν ἂν ποιοῦντες σωθείημεν;

Καὶ ὁ Κῦρος αὖ πρὸς τοῦτο εἶπεν, [Εἰ τῶν τε
συμμαχομένων μηδένα προδόντες σωθείητε][1] Τά
τε ὅπλα παραδόντες φίλοι τε γενόμενοι τοῖς αἱρου-
μένοις ὑμᾶς σῶσαι, ἐξὸν ἀπολέσαι.

43. Ἀκούσαντες ταῦτα ἐπήροντο, Ἢν δὲ γενώ-
μεθά σοι φίλοι, τί ἡμῖν ἀξιώσεις χρῆσθαι;

Ἀπεκρίνατο ὁ Κῦρος, Εὖ ποιεῖν καὶ εὖ πάσχειν.

Ἐπηρώτων πάλιν οἱ Αἰγύπτιοι, Τίνα εὐεργεσίαν;

Πρὸς τοῦτο εἶπεν ὁ Κῦρος, Μισθὸν μὲν ὑμῖν
δοίην ἂν πλείονα ἢ νῦν ἐλαμβάνετε ὅσον ἂν χρόνον
πόλεμος ᾖ· εἰρήνης δὲ γενομένης τῷ βουλομένῳ
ὑμῶν μένειν παρ' ἐμοὶ χώραν τε δώσω καὶ πόλεις
καὶ γυναῖκας καὶ οἰκέτας.

44. Ἀκούσαντες ταῦτα οἱ Αἰγύπτιοι τὸ μὲν
ἐπὶ Κροῖσον συστρατεύειν ἀφελεῖν σφίσιν ἐδε-
ήθησαν· τούτῳ γὰρ μόνῳ γιγνώσκεσθαι ἔφασαν·
τὰ δ' ἄλλα συνομολογήσαντες ἔδοσαν πίστιν καὶ
ἔλαβον.

[1] Εἰ . . . σωθείητε MSS., earlier Edd.; bracketed by Hug,
Marchant, Gemoll [*If you could save your lives without betraying any of your friends*].

those who had treacherously deserted them or to save their lives and at the same time be accounted brave men.

"How could we save our lives," they answered, "and at the same time be accounted brave men?"

42. "You can," Cyrus replied, "because we are witnesses that you are the only ones who stood your ground and were willing to fight."

"Well," answered the Egyptians, "granting that, what can we do consistently with honour to save our lives?"

"You could surrender your arms," Cyrus answered again, "and become friends of those who choose to save you, when it is in their power to destroy you."

43. "And if we become your friends," they asked on hearing that, "how will you see fit to deal with us?"

"I will do you favours and expect favours from you," answered Cyrus.

"What sort of favours?" asked the Egyptians in turn.

"As long as the war continues," Cyrus made answer to this, "I would give you larger pay than you were now receiving; and when peace is made, to those of you who care to stay with me I will give lands and cities and wives and servants." *and wins their allegiance*

44. On hearing this, the Egyptians begged to be excused from taking part in any campaign against Croesus, for with him alone, they said, they were acquainted; all other stipulations they accepted, and gave and received pledges of good faith.

45. Καὶ οἱ Αἰγύπτιοί τε οἱ καταμείναντες τότε
ἔτι καὶ νῦν βασιλεῖ πιστοὶ διαμένουσι, Κύρός τε
πόλεις αὐτοῖς ἔδωκε, τὰς μὲν ἄνω, αἳ ἔτι καὶ νῦν
πόλεις Αἰγυπτίων καλοῦνται, Λάρισαν δὲ καὶ
Κυλλήνην παρὰ Κύμην πλησίον θαλάττης, ἃς ἔτι
καὶ νῦν οἱ ἀπ' ἐκείνων ἔχουσι.

Ταῦτα δὲ διαπραξάμενος ὁ Κῦρος ἤδη σκοταῖος
ἀναγαγὼν ἐστρατοπεδεύσατο ἐν Θυμβράροις.

46. Ἐν δὲ τῇ μάχῃ τῶν πολεμίων Αἰγύπτιοι
μόνοι ηὐδοκίμησαν, τῶν δὲ σὺν Κύρῳ τὸ Περσῶν
ἱππικὸν κράτιστον ἔδοξεν εἶναι· ὥστ' ἔτι καὶ νῦν
διαμένει ἡ ὅπλισις ἣν τότε Κῦρος τοῖς ἱππεῦσι
κατεσκεύασεν.

47. Ηὐδοκίμησε δὲ ἰσχυρῶς καὶ τὰ δρεπανηφόρα ἅρματα· ὥστε καὶ τοῦτο ἔτι καὶ νῦν διαμένει
τὸ πολεμιστήριον τῷ ἀεὶ βασιλεύοντι.

48. Αἱ μέντοι κάμηλοι ἐφόβουν μόνον τοὺς
ἵππους, οὐ μέντοι κατέκαινόν γε οἱ ἐπ' αὐτῶν
ἱππεῖς,[1] οὐδ' αὐτοί γε ἀπέθνησκον ὑπὸ ἱππέων·
οὐδεὶς γὰρ ἵππος ἐπέλαζε. 49. καὶ χρήσιμον μὲν
ἐδόκει εἶναι· ἀλλὰ γὰρ οὔτε τρέφειν οὐδεὶς ἐθέλει
καλὸς κἀγαθὸς κάμηλον ὥστ' ἐποχεῖσθαι, οὔτε
μελετᾶν ὡς πολεμήσων ἀπὸ τούτων. οὕτω δὴ
ἀπολαβοῦσαι πάλιν τὸ ἑαυτῶν σχῆμα ἐν τοῖς
σκευοφόροις διάγουσι.

---

[1] ἱππεῖς MSS., most Edd.; ἱππέας Gemoll.

45. And the Egyptians who then stayed in the country have continued loyal subjects to the king even unto this day; and Cyrus gave them cities, some in the interior, which even to this day are called Egyptian cities, and besides these Larissa and Cyllene near Cyme on the coast; and their descendants dwell there even unto this day.

When he had accomplished this, it was already dark; and Cyrus led back his forces and encamped in Thymbrara.

46. The Egyptians were the only ones of all the enemy that distinguished themselves in the battle, while of those under Cyrus the Persian cavalry seemed to be the most efficient. And therefore the equipment which Cyrus had then provided for his cavalry continues in use even to our own times.

Observations on the battle

47. The scythe-bearing chariots also won extraordinary distinction, so that this military device also has been retained even to our day by each successive king.

48. The camels, however, did nothing more than frighten the horses; their riders could neither kill any one nor be killed by any of the enemy's cavalry, for not a horse would come near them. 49. What they did do seemed useful enough; but be that as it may, no gentleman is willing to keep a camel for riding or to practise for fighting in war upon one. And so they have again taken their proper position and do service among the pack-animals.

II

1. Καὶ οἱ μὲν ἀμφὶ τὸν Κῦρον δειπνοποιησάμενοι καὶ φυλακὰς καταστησάμενοι, ὥσπερ ἔδει, ἐκοιμήθησαν. Κροῖσος μέντοι εὐθὺς ἐπὶ Σάρδεων ἔφευγε σὺν τῷ στρατεύματι· τὰ δ' ἄλλα φῦλα ὅποι¹ ἐδύνατο προσωτάτω ἐν τῇ νυκτὶ τῆς ἐπ' οἶκον ὁδοῦ ἕκαστος ἀπεχώρει.

2. Ἐπειδὴ δὲ ἡμέρα ἐγένετο, εὐθὺς ἐπὶ Σάρδεις ἦγε Κῦρος. ὡς δ' ἐγένετο πρὸς τῷ τείχει τῷ ἐν Σάρδεσι, τάς τε μηχανὰς ἀνίστη ὡς προσβαλῶν πρὸς τὸ τεῖχος καὶ κλίμακας παρεσκευάζετο. 3. ταῦτα δὲ ποιῶν κατὰ τὰ ἀποτομώτατα δοκοῦντα εἶναι τοῦ Σαρδιανῶν ἐρύματος τῆς ἐπιούσης νυκτὸς ἀναβιβάζει Χαλδαίους τε καὶ Πέρσας. ἡγήσατο δ' αὐτοῖς ἀνὴρ Πέρσης δοῦλος γεγενημένος τῶν ἐν τῇ ἀκροπόλει τινὸς φρουρῶν καὶ καταμεμαθηκὼς κατάβασιν εἰς τὸν ποταμὸν καὶ ἀνάβασιν τὴν αὐτήν.

4. Ὡς δ' ἐγένετο τοῦτο δῆλον ὅτι εἴχετο τὰ ἄκρα, πάντες δὴ ἔφευγον οἱ Λυδοὶ ἀπὸ τῶν τειχῶν ὅποι¹ ἐδύνατο ἕκαστος τῆς πόλεως. Κῦρος δὲ ἅμα τῇ ἡμέρᾳ εἰσῄει εἰς τὴν πόλιν καὶ παρήγγειλεν ἐκ τῆς τάξεως μηδένα κινεῖσθαι. 5. ὁ δὲ Κροῖσος κατακλεισάμενος ἐν τοῖς βασιλείοις Κῦρον ἐβόα· ὁ δὲ Κῦρος τοῦ μὲν Κροίσου φύλακας κατέλιπεν, αὐτὸς δὲ ἀπαγαγὼν πρὸς τὴν ἐχομένην ἄκραν ὡς εἶδε τοὺς μὲν Πέρσας φυλάττοντας τὴν ἄκραν, ὥσπερ ἔδει, τὰ δὲ τῶν Χαλδαίων ὅπλα ἔρημα, κατεδεδραμήκεσαν γὰρ ἁρπασόμενοι τὰ ἐκ τῶν

¹ ὅποι xzE, most Edd.; ὅπῃ C.

230

II

1. WHEN Cyrus and his men had finished dinner and stationed guards, as was necessary, they went to rest. As for Croesus and his army, they fled straight towards Sardis, while the other contingents got away, each man as far as he could under cover of the night on his way toward home.

2. When daylight came, Cyrus led his army The capture straight on against Sardis. And as soon as he came of Sardis up to the walls of the city, he set up his engines as if intending to assault it and made ready his scaling ladders. 3. But though he did this, in the course of the following night he sent some Chaldaeans and Persians to climb up by what was considered the most precipitous side of the Sardian citadel. The way was shown them by a Persian who had been the slave of one of the guards of the acropolis and had discovered a way down to the river and up again by the same route.

4. When it became known that the citadel was taken, all the Lydians immediately fled from the walls to whatever part of the city they could. And Cyrus at daybreak entered the city and gave orders that not a man of his should stir from his post. 5. But Croesus shut himself up in his palace and called for Cyrus. Cyrus, however, left behind a guard to watch Croesus, while he himself drew off his army to the citadel now in his possession; for he saw that the Persians were holding guard over it, as it was The their duty to do, but that the quarters of the Chal- Chaldaeans' daeans were deserted, for they had run down into discipline

οἰκιῶν, εὐθὺς συνεκάλεσεν αὐτῶν τοὺς ἄρχοντας
καὶ εἶπεν αὐτοῖς ἀπιέναι ἐκ τοῦ στρατεύματος ὡς
τάχιστα. 6. Οὐ γὰρ ἄν, ἔφη, ἀνασχοίμην πλεο-
νεκτοῦντας ὁρῶν τοὺς ἀτακτοῦντας. καὶ εὖ μὲν,
ἔφη, ἐπίστασθε ὅτι παρεσκευαζόμην ἐγὼ ὑμᾶς
τοὺς ἐμοὶ συστρατευομένους πᾶσι Χαλδαίοις
μακαριστοὺς ποιῆσαι· νῦν δ', ἔφη, μὴ θαυμάζετε
ἤν τις καὶ ἀπιοῦσιν ὑμῖν κρείττων ἐντύχῃ.

7. Ἀκούσαντες ταῦτα οἱ Χαλδαῖοι ἔδεισάν τε
καὶ ἱκέτευον παύσασθαι ὀργιζόμενον καὶ τὰ
χρήματα πάντα ἀποδώσειν ἔφασαν. ὁ δ' εἶπεν
ὅτι οὐδὲν αὐτῶν δέοιτο. Ἀλλ' εἴ με, ἔφη, βού-
λεσθε παύσασθαι ἀχθόμενον, ἀπόδοτε πάντα ὅσα
ἐλάβετε τοῖς διαφυλάξασι τὴν ἄκραν. ἢν γὰρ
αἴσθωνται οἱ ἄλλοι στρατιῶται ὅτι πλεονεκτοῦσιν
οἱ εὔτακτοι γενόμενοι, πάντα μοι καλῶς ἕξει.

8. Οἱ μὲν δὴ Χαλδαῖοι οὕτως ἐποίησαν ὡς
ἐκέλευσεν ὁ Κῦρος· καὶ ἔλαβον οἱ πειθόμενοι
πολλὰ καὶ παντοῖα χρήματα. ὁ δὲ Κῦρος κατα-
στρατοπεδεύσας τοὺς ἑαυτοῦ, ὅπου ἐδόκει ἐπιτη-
δειότατον εἶναι τῆς πόλεως, μένειν ἐπὶ τοῖς ὅπλοις
παρήγγειλε καὶ ἀριστοποιεῖσθαι.

9. Ταῦτα δὲ διαπραξάμενος ἀγαγεῖν ἐκέλευσεν
αὐτῷ[1] τὸν Κροῖσον. ὁ δὲ Κροῖσος ὡς εἶδε τὸν
Κῦρον, Χαῖρε, ὦ δέσποτα, ἔφη· τοῦτο γὰρ ἡ τύχη
καὶ ἔχειν τὸ ἀπὸ τοῦδε δίδωσι σοὶ καὶ ἐμοὶ
προσαγορεύειν.

10. Καὶ σύ γε, ἔφη, ὦ Κροῖσε, ἐπείπερ ἄνθρω-

---

[1] αὐτῷ F, Edd.; αὑτῷ xzDV.

the city to get plunder from the houses. He at once called their officers together and told them to leave his army with all speed. 6. "For," said he, "I could not endure to see men who are guilty of insubordination better off than others. And let me tell you," he added, "that I was getting ready to make you Chaldaeans who have been helping in my campaigns objects of envy in the eyes of all other Chaldaeans; but, as it is, you need not be surprised if some one who is your superior in strength should fall in with you, even as you go away."

7. When they heard this, the Chaldaeans were afraid; they besought him to lay aside his wrath and promised to give up their plunder. But he said he did not want it. "But," said he, "if you wish me to forget my displeasure, surrender all that you have taken to those who have not relaxed their guard of the citadel. For if the rest of the soldiers find out that those who have been obedient to orders are better off than the rest, everything will be as I wish." *Good discipline rewarded*

8. The Chaldaeans, accordingly, did as Cyrus bade; and the obedient received a large amount of spoil of every description. And Cyrus encamped his men in that part of the city where he deemed it most convenient, ordering them to stay in their quarters and take luncheon there.

9. When he had attended to this, he ordered Croesus to be brought before him. And when Croesus saw Cyrus, he said: "I salute you, my sovereign lord; for fortune grants that henceforth you should bear this title and I address you by it." *Croesus before Cyrus*

10. "And I you, Croesus; for we are both men.

ποί γέ ἐσμεν ἀμφότεροι. ἀτάρ, ἔφη, ὦ Κροῖσε, ἆρ' ἄν τί μοι ἐθελήσαις συμβουλεῦσαι;

Καὶ βουλοίμην γ' ἄν, ἔφη, ὦ Κῦρε, ἀγαθόν τί σοι εὑρεῖν· τοῦτο γὰρ ἂν οἶμαι ἀγαθὸν κἀμοὶ γενέσθαι.

11. Ἄκουσον τοίνυν, ἔφη, ὦ Κροῖσε· ἐγὼ γὰρ ὁρῶν τοὺς στρατιώτας πολλὰ πεπονηκότας καὶ πολλὰ κεκινδυνευκότας καὶ νῦν νομίζοντας πόλιν ἔχειν τὴν πλουσιωτάτην ἐν τῇ Ἀσίᾳ μετὰ Βαβυλῶνα, ἀξιῶ ὠφεληθῆναι τοὺς στρατιώτας. γιγνώσκω γάρ, ἔφη, ὅτι εἰ μή τινα καρπὸν λήψονται τῶν πόνων, οὐ δυνήσομαι αὐτοὺς πολὺν χρόνον πειθομένους ἔχειν. διαρπάσαι μὲν οὖν αὐτοῖς ἐφεῖναι τὴν πόλιν οὐ βούλομαι· τήν τε γὰρ πόλιν νομίζω ἂν διαφθαρῆναι, ἔν τε τῇ ἁρπαγῇ εὖ οἶδ' ὅτι οἱ πονηρότατοι πλεονεκτήσειαν ἄν.

12. Ἀκούσας ταῦτα ὁ Κροῖσος ἔλεξεν, Ἀλλ' ἐμέ, ἔφη, ἔασον λέξαι πρὸς οὓς ἂν ἐγὼ Λυδῶν ἔλθω[1] ὅτι διαπέπραγμαι παρὰ σοῦ μὴ ποιῆσαι ἁρπαγὴν μηδὲ ἐᾶσαι ἀφανισθῆναι παῖδας καὶ γυναῖκας· ὑπεσχόμην δέ σοι ἀντὶ τούτων ἦ μὴν παρ' ἑκόντων Λυδῶν ἔσεσθαι πᾶν ὅ τι καλὸν κἀγαθόν ἐστιν ἐν Σάρδεσιν. 13. ἢν γὰρ ταῦτα ἀκούσωσιν, οἶδ' ὅτι ἥξει σοι πᾶν ὅ τι ἐστὶν ἐνθάδε καλὸν κτῆμα ἀνδρὶ καὶ γυναικί· καὶ ὁμοίως εἰς νέωτα πολλῶν καὶ καλῶν πάλιν σοι πλήρης ἡ πόλις ἔσται· ἢν δὲ διαρπάσῃς, καὶ αἱ τέχναι σοι, ἅς πηγάς φασι τῶν καλῶν εἶναι, διεφθαρμέναι ἔσονται. 14. ἐξέσται δέ σοι ἰδόντι ταῦτα ἐλθόντα ἔτι καὶ περὶ τῆς ἁρπαγῆς βουλεύ-

[1] ἔλθω Hug, Marchant; (ἐ)θέλω MSS., Dindorf, Sauppe, Breitenbach; ἔλωμαι Gemoll.

But, Croesus," he added, "would you be willing to give me a bit of advice?"

"Aye, Cyrus," said he; "I wish I could find something of practical value to say to you. For that, I think, would prove good for me as well."

11. "Listen, then, Croesus," said he. "I observe that my soldiers have gone through many toils and dangers and now are thinking that they are in possession of the richest city in Asia, next to Babylon; and I think that they deserve some reward. For I know that if they do not reap some fruit of their labours, I shall not be able to keep them in obedience very long. Now, I do not wish to abandon the city to them to plunder; for I believe that then the city would be destroyed, and I am sure that in the pillaging the worst men would get the largest share."

Cyrus proposes to spare Sardis

12. "Well," said Croesus on hearing these words, "permit me to say to any Lydians that I meet that I have secured from you the promise not to permit any pillaging nor to allow the women and children to be carried off, and that I, in return for that, have given you my solemn promise that you should get from the Lydians of their own free will everything there is of beauty or value in Sardis. 13. For when they hear this, I am sure that whatever fair possession man or woman has will come to you; and next year you will again find the city just as full of wealth as it is now; whereas, if you pillage it completely, you will find even the industrial arts utterly ruined; and they say that these are the fountain of wealth. 14. But when you have seen what is brought in, you will still have the privilege of deciding about

σασθαι. πρῶτον δ᾽, ἔφη, ἐπὶ τοὺς ἐμοὺς θησαυροὺς πέμπε καὶ παραλαμβανόντων[1] οἱ σοὶ φύλακες παρὰ τῶν ἐμῶν φυλάκων.

Ταῦτα μὲν δὴ ἅπαντα οὕτω συνῄνεσε ποιεῖν ὁ
Κῦρος ὥσπερ ἔλεξεν ὁ Κροῖσος.

15. Τάδε δέ μοι πάντως, ἔφη, ὦ Κροῖσε, λέξον
πῶς σοι ἀποβέβηκε τὰ ἐκ τοῦ ἐν Δελφοῖς χρη-
στηρίου· σοὶ γὰρ δὴ λέγεται πάνυ γε τεθερα-
πεῦσθαι ὁ Ἀπόλλων καί σε πάντα ἐκείνῳ πειθό-
μενον πράττειν.

16. Ἐβουλόμην ἄν, ἔφη, ὦ Κῦρε, οὕτως ἔχειν·
νῦν δὲ πάντα τἀναντία εὐθὺς ἐξ ἀρχῆς πράττων
προσηνέχθην τῷ Ἀπόλλωνι.

Πῶς δέ; ἔφη ὁ Κῦρος· δίδασκε· πάνυ γὰρ
παράδοξα λέγεις.

17. Ὅτι πρῶτον μέν, ἔφη, ἀμελήσας ἐρωτᾶν
τὸν θεόν, εἴ τι ἐδεόμην, ἀπεπειρώμην αὐτοῦ εἰ
δύναιτο ἀληθεύειν. τοῦτο δ᾽, ἔφη, μὴ ὅτι θεός,
ἀλλὰ καὶ ἄνθρωποι καλοὶ κἀγαθοί, ἐπειδὰν γνῶ-
σιν ἀπιστούμενοι, οὐ φιλοῦσι τοὺς ἀπιστοῦντας.
18. ἐπεὶ μέντοι ἔγνω καὶ μάλ᾽ ἄτοπα ἐμοῦ ποιοῦντος, καίπερ[2] πρόσω Δελφῶν ἀπέχοντος, οὕτω
δὴ πέμπω περὶ παίδων. 19. ὁ δέ μοι τὸ μὲν πρῶτον
οὐδ᾽ ἀπεκρίνατο· ἐπεὶ δ᾽ ἐγὼ πολλὰ μὲν πέμπων
ἀναθήματα χρυσᾶ, πολλὰ δ᾽ ἀργυρᾶ, πάμπολλα
δὲ θύων ἐξιλασάμην ποτὲ αὐτόν, ὡς ἐδόκουν, τότε
δή μοι ἀποκρίνεται ἐρωτῶντι τί ἄν μοι ποιήσαντι
παῖδες γένοιντο· ὁ δὲ εἶπεν ὅτι ἔσοιντο. 20. καὶ
ἐγένοντο μέν, οὐδὲ γὰρ οὐδὲ τοῦτο ἐψεύσατο,

---

[1] παραλαμβανόντων Bishop, Dindorf, Edd.; παραλαμβανέτωσαν
MSS.
[2] καίπερ Hug, Marchant, Gemoll; καί MSS., earlier Edd.

plundering the city. And first of all," he went on, "send to my treasuries and let your guards obtain from my guards what is there."

All this, accordingly, Cyrus agreed to have done as Croesus suggested.

15. "But pray tell me, Croesus," he resumed, "what has come of your responses from the oracle at Delphi? For it is said that Apollo has received much service from you and that everything that you do is done in obedience to him." *Croesus and the Pythian oracle*

16. "I would it were so, Cyrus," he answered. "But as it is; I have from the very beginning behaved toward Apollo in a way contrary to all that he has advised."

"How so?" asked Cyrus; "please explain; for your statement sounds very strange."

17. "At first," he answered, "instead of asking the god for the particular favour I needed, I proceeded to put him to the test to see if he could tell the truth. And when even men, if they are gentlemen—to say nothing of a god—discover that they are mistrusted, they have no love for those who mistrust them. 18. However, as he knew even about the gross absurdities I was engaged in, far as I was from Delphi,[1] I then sent to him to inquire if I should have male issue. 19. And at first he did not even answer me; but when I had at last propitiated him, as I thought, by sending many offerings of gold and many of silver and by sacrificing very many victims, then he did answer my question as to what I should do to have sons; and he said that I should have them. 20. And I had; for not even in this did he speak falsely; but those

---

[1] See Index, *s.v.* Croesus, note.

γενόμενοι δὲ οὐδὲν ὤνησαν. ὁ μὲν γὰρ κωφὸς ὢν
διετέλει, ὁ δὲ ἄριστος γενόμενος ἐν ἀκμῇ τοῦ βίου
ἀπώλετο. πιεζόμενος δὲ ταῖς περὶ τοὺς παῖδας
συμφοραῖς πάλιν πέμπω καὶ ἐπερωτῶ τὸν θεὸν τί
ἂν ποιῶν τὸν λοιπὸν βίον εὐδαιμονέστατα δια-
τελέσαιμι· ὁ δέ μοι ἀπεκρίνατο·

Σαυτὸν γιγνώσκων εὐδαίμων, Κροῖσε, περάσεις.

21. ἐγὼ δ' ἀκούσας τὴν μαντείαν ἥσθην· ἐνόμιζον
γὰρ τὸ ῥᾷστόν μοι αὐτὸν προστάξαντα τὴν εὐδαιμονίαν διδόναι. ἄλλους μὲν γὰρ γιγνώσκειν τοὺς
μὲν οἷόν τ' εἶναι τοὺς δ' οὔ· ἑαυτὸν δὲ ὅστις ἐστὶ
πάντα τινὰ ἐνόμιζον ἄνθρωπον εἰδέναι.

22. Καὶ τὸν μετὰ ταῦτα δὴ χρόνον, ἕως μὲν
εἶχον ἡσυχίαν, οὐδὲν ἐνεκάλουν μετὰ τὸν τοῦ
παιδὸς θάνατον ταῖς τύχαις· ἐπειδὴ δὲ ἀνεπείσθην
ὑπὸ τοῦ Ἀσσυρίου ἐφ' ὑμᾶς στρατεύεσθαι, εἰς
πάντα κίνδυνον ἦλθον· ἐσώθην μέντοι οὐδὲν κακὸν λαβών. οὐκ αἰτιῶμαι δὲ οὐδὲ τάδε τὸν θεόν.
ἐπεὶ γὰρ ἔγνων ἐμαυτὸν μὴ ἱκανὸν ὑμῖν μάχεσθαι,
ἀσφαλῶς σὺν τῷ θεῷ ἀπῆλθον καὶ αὐτὸς καὶ οἱ
σὺν ἐμοί.

23. Νῦν δ' αὖ πάλιν ὑπό τε πλούτου τοῦ
παρόντος διαθρυπτόμενος καὶ ὑπὸ τῶν δεομένων
μου προστάτην γενέσθαι καὶ ὑπὸ τῶν δώρων ὧν
ἐδίδοσάν μοι καὶ ὑπ' ἀνθρώπων,[1] οἵ με κολακεύ-
οντες ἔλεγον ὡς εἰ ἐγὼ ἐθέλοιμι ἄρχειν, πάντες ἂν
ἐμοὶ πείθοιντο καὶ μέγιστος ἂν εἴην ἀνθρώπων,

---

[1] καὶ ὑπὸ τῶν δώρων . . . ἀνθρώπων bracketed by Gemoll.

that were born to me have been no joy to me. For the one has continued dumb until now, and the other, the better of the two, was killed in the flower of his youth. Then, overwhelmed by the afflictions I suffered in connection with my sons, I sent again and inquired of the god what I should do to pass the rest of my life most happily ; and he answered me : The secret of a happy life

‘ Knowing thyself, O Croesus—thus shalt thou live and be happy.’ [1]

21. And when I heard this response, I was glad ; for I thought that it was the easiest task in the world that he was laying upon me as the condition to happiness. For in the case of others, it is possible to know some ; and some, one cannot know ; but I thought that everybody knows who and what he himself is.

22. " For the succeeding years, as long as I lived at peace, I had no complaint to make of my fortunes after the death of my son. But when I was persuaded by the Assyrian king to take the field against you, I fell into every sort of danger. However, I was saved without having suffered any harm. Here again I have no fault to find with the god. For when I recognized that I was not your match in battle, with his help I got off in safety, both I and my men.

23. " And lately again, spoiled by the wealth I had and by those who were begging me to become their leader, by the gifts they gave me and by the people who flattered me, saying that if I would consent to take command they would all obey me and I should be the greatest of men—puffed up by

[1] There is a reference to the famous inscription on the temple at Delphi—γνῶθι σεαυτόν.

ὑπὸ τοιούτων δὲ λόγων ἀναφυσώμενος, ὡς εἵλοντό
με πάντες οἱ κύκλῳ βασιλεῖς προστάτην τοῦ πολέμου, ὑπεδεξάμην τὴν στρατηγίαν, ὡς ἱκανὸς ὢν
μέγιστος γενέσθαι, ἀγνοῶν ἄρα ἐμαυτόν, 24. ὅτι
σοὶ ἀντιπολεμεῖν ἱκανὸς ᾤμην εἶναι, πρῶτον μὲν
ἐκ θεῶν γεγονότι, ἔπειτα δὲ διὰ βασιλέων πεφυ-
κότι, ἔπειτα δ᾽ ἐκ παιδὸς ἀρετὴν ἀσκοῦντι· τῶν δ᾽
ἐμῶν προγόνων ἀκούω τὸν πρῶτον βασιλεύσαντα
ἅμα τε βασιλέα καὶ ἐλεύθερον γενέσθαι. ταῦτ᾽
οὖν ἀγνοήσας δικαίως, ἔφη, ἔχω τὴν δίκην.

25. Ἀλλὰ νῦν δή, ἔφη, ὦ Κῦρε, γιγνώσκω μὲν
ἐμαυτόν· σὺ δ᾽, ἔφη, ἔτι δοκεῖς ἀληθεύειν τὸν
Ἀπόλλω ὡς εὐδαίμων ἔσομαι γιγνώσκων ἐμαυτόν;
σὲ δὲ ἐρωτῶ διὰ τοῦτο ὅτι ἄριστ᾽ ἄν μοι δοκεῖς
εἰκάσαι τοῦτο ἐν τῷ παρόντι· καὶ γὰρ δύνασαι
ποιῆσαι.

26. Καὶ ὁ Κῦρος εἶπε, Βουλήν μοι δὸς περὶ
τούτου, ὦ Κροῖσε· ἐγὼ γάρ σου ἐννοῶν τὴν πρόσθεν εὐδαιμονίαν οἰκτείρω τέ σε καὶ ἀποδίδωμι
ἤδη γυναῖκά τε ἔχειν ἣν εἶχες καὶ τὰς θυγατέρας,
ἀκούω γάρ σοι εἶναι, καὶ τοὺς φίλους καὶ τοὺς
θεράποντας καὶ τράπεζαν σὺν οἷάπερ ἐζῆτε·[1]
μάχας δέ σοι καὶ πολέμους ἀφαιρῶ.

27. Μὰ Δία μηδὲν τοίνυν, ἔφη ὁ Κροῖσος, σὺ
ἐμοὶ ἔτι βουλεύου ἀποκρίνασθαι περὶ τῆς ἐμῆς
εὐδαιμονίας· ἐγὼ γὰρ ἤδη σοι λέγω, ἢν ταῦτά μοι
ποιήσῃς ἃ λέγεις, ὅτι ἣν ἄλλοι τε μακαριωτάτην

---

[1] ἐζῆτε Edd.; ἐζῶτε xzDV ; ἔζωτε F.

such words, when all the princes round about chose me to be their leader in the war, I accepted the command, deeming myself fit to be the greatest; but, as it seems, I did not know myself. 24. For I thought I was capable of carrying on war against you; but I was no match for you; for you are in the first place a scion of the gods and in the second place the descendant of an unbroken line of kings, and finally you have been practising virtue from your childhood on, while the first of my ancestors to wear a crown, I am told, was at the same time king and freedman.[1] Therefore, as I was thus without knowledge, I have my just deserts.

25. "But, Cyrus," said he, "I know myself now. But do you think Apollo's declaration still holds true, that if I know myself I shall be happy? I ask you this for the reason that under the present circumstances it seems to me you can judge best; for you are also in a position to fulfil it."

26. "You must give me time to consider this, Croesus," Cyrus replied; "for when I think of your happiness hitherto, I am sorry for you, and I now restore to you your wife, whom you once had, your daughters (for I understand you have daughters), your friends, your servants, and the table that you and yours used to enjoy. But wars and battles I must forbid you." *Cyrus restores to Croesus his household*

27. "In the name of Zeus," said Croesus, "pray do not trouble yourself further to answer me in regard to my happiness; for I assure you even now that if you do for me what you say you will, I, too, shall have and enjoy that life which others have always

---

[1] Gyges, the shepherd king of Lydia.

XENOPHON

ἐνόμιζον εἶναι βιοτὴν καὶ ἐγὼ συνεγίγνωσκον
αὐτοῖς, ταύτην καὶ ἐγὼ νῦν ἔχων διάξω.

28. Καὶ ὁ Κῦρος εἶπε, Τίς δὴ ὁ ἔχων ταύτην
τὴν μακαρίαν βιοτήν;

Ἡ ἐμὴ γυνή, εἶπεν, ὦ Κῦρε· ἐκείνη γὰρ τῶν
μὲν ἀγαθῶν καὶ τῶν μαλακῶν καὶ εὐφροσυνῶν
πασῶν ἐμοὶ τὸ ἴσον μετεῖχε, φροντίδων δὲ ὅπως
ταῦτα ἔσται καὶ πολέμου καὶ μάχης οὐ μετῆν
αὐτῇ. οὕτω δὴ καὶ σὺ δοκεῖς ἐμὲ κατασκευάζειν
ὥσπερ ἐγὼ ἦν ἐφίλουν μάλιστα ἀνθρώπων, ὥστε
τῷ Ἀπόλλωνι ἄλλα μοι δοκῶ χαριστήρια ὀφει-
λήσειν.

29. Ἀκούσας δ' ὁ Κῦρος τοὺς λόγους αὐτοῦ
ἐθαύμασε μὲν τὴν εὐθυμίαν, ἦγε δὲ τὸ λοιπὸν ὅποι
καὶ αὐτὸς πορεύοιτο, εἴτε ἄρα καὶ χρήσιμόν τι
νομίζων αὐτὸν εἶναι εἴτε καὶ ἀσφαλέστερον οὕτως
ἡγούμενος.

III

1. Καὶ τότε μὲν οὕτως ἐκοιμήθησαν. τῇ δ' ὑστεραίᾳ καλέσας ὁ Κῦρος τοὺς φίλους καὶ τοὺς ἡγεμόνας τοῦ στρατεύματος, τοὺς μὲν αὐτῶν ἔταξε
τοὺς θησαυροὺς παραλαμβάνειν, τοὺς δ' ἐκέλευσεν
ὁπόσα παραδοίη Κροῖσος χρήματα, πρῶτον μὲν
τοῖς θεοῖς ἐξελεῖν ὁποῖ ἂν οἱ μάγοι ἐξηγῶνται,
ἔπειτα τἆλλα χρήματα παραδεχομένους ἐν ζυγά-
στροις στήσαντας ἐφ' ἁμαξῶν ἐπισκευάσαι καὶ
διαλαχόντας τὰς ἁμάξας κομίζειν ὅποιπερ ἂν αὐτοὶ

considered most blissful ; and I have agreed with
them."

28. "And who is it," asked Cyrus, "that enjoys
such a life of bliss ? "

"My wife, Cyrus," said he. "For she always
shared equally with me my wealth and the luxuries
and all the good cheer that it brought, but she had
no share in the anxieties of securing it nor in war or
battle. So, then, you seem to be putting me in the
same position as I did her whom I loved more than
all the world, so that I feel that I shall owe Apollo
new thank-offerings."

29. At hearing these words Cyrus wondered at his
good spirits, and after that he always used to take
Croesus with him wherever he went, whether, as
may well have been, because he thought Croesus was
of some service to him, or whether he considered
that this was the safer course.

III

1. Such was their interview, and then they went
to rest. And on the following day Cyrus summoned
his friends and the general officers of his army. He
appointed some of them to take charge of the
treasures and others he ordered first to select from
the valuables that Croesus delivered such a portion
for the gods as the magi should designate ; the rest
they should then take into their own charge and
put in chests, and these they should pack upon the
wagons ; they should then divide the wagons by
lot and convey them whithersoever they themselves
might go ; then, when the time came, the treasure

Cyrus takes
the Lydian
treasures

πορεύωνται, ἵνα ὅπου καιρὸς εἴη διαλαμβάνοιεν
ἕκαστοι τὰ ἄξια. 2. οἱ μὲν δὴ 'ταῦτ' ἐποίουν.

Ὁ δὲ Κῦρος καλέσας τινὰς τῶν παρόντων
ὑπηρετῶν, Εἴπατέ μοι, ἔφη, ἑωράκέ τις ὑμῶν
'Αβραδάταν; θαυμάζω γάρ, ἔφη, ὅτι πρόσθεν
θαμίζων ἐφ' ἡμᾶς νῦν οὐδαμοῦ φαίνεται.

3. Τῶν οὖν ὑπηρετῶν τις ἀπεκρίνατο ὅτι Ὦ
δέσποτα, οὐ ζῇ, ἀλλ' ἐν τῇ μάχῃ ἀπέθανεν ἐμ-
βαλὼν τὸ ἅρμα εἰς τοὺς Αἰγυπτίους· οἱ δ' ἄλλοι
πλὴν τῶν ἑταίρων αὐτοῦ ἐξέκλιναν, ὥς φασιν,
ἐπεὶ τὸ στῖφος εἶδον τὸ τῶν Αἰγυπτίων. 4. καὶ
νῦν γε ἔφη, λέγεται αὐτοῦ ἡ γυνὴ ἀνελομένη τὸν
νεκρὸν καὶ ἐνθεμένη εἰς τὴν ἁρμάμαξαν, ἐν ᾗπερ
αὐτὴ ὠχεῖτο, προσκεκομικέναι αὐτὸν ἐνθάδε ποι
πρὸς τὸν Πακτωλὸν ποταμόν. 5. καὶ τοὺς μὲν
εὐνούχους καὶ τοὺς θεράποντας αὐτοῦ ὀρύττειν
φασὶν ἐπὶ λόφου τινὸς θήκην τῷ τελευτήσαντι·
τὴν δὲ γυναῖκα λέγουσιν ὡς κάθηται χαμαὶ κεκο-
σμηκυῖα οἷς εἶχε τὸν ἄνδρα, τὴν κεφαλὴν αὐτοῦ
ἔχουσα ἐπὶ τοῖς γόνασι.

6. Ταῦτα ἀκούσας ὁ Κῦρος ἐπαίσατο ἄρα τὸν
μηρὸν καὶ εὐθὺς ἀναπηδήσας ἐπὶ τὸν ἵππον λαβὼν
χιλίους ἱππέας ἤλαυνεν ἐπὶ τὸ πάθος. 7. Γαδάταν δὲ καὶ Γωβρύαν ἐκέλευσεν ὅ τι δύναιντο
λαβόντας καλὸν κόσμημα ἀνδρὶ φίλῳ καὶ ἀγαθῷ
τετελευτηκότι μεταδιώκειν· καὶ ὅστις εἶχε τὰς
ἑπομένας ἀγέλας, καὶ βοῦς καὶ ἵππους εἶπε τούτῳ
καὶ ἅμα πρόβατα πολλὰ ἐλαύνειν ὅπου[1] ἂν αὐτὸν
πυνθάνηται ὄντα, ὡς ἐπισφαγείη τῷ 'Αβραδάτᾳ.

---

[1] ὅπου Priscian, Hug, Gemoll ; ὅπη xG, Dindorf, Breitenbach, Marchant ; ὅποι yAHV.

should be divided, and each man should receive his share according to his deserts. 2. The officers, accordingly, proceeded to follow his instructions.

And when he had called to him certain of his aides who were present, Cyrus said: "Tell me, has any one of you seen Abradatas? For I wonder why, in view of the fact that he used often to come to us, he is now nowhere to be seen."

3. "Sire," answered one of the aides, "he is no longer alive, but he fell in the battle as he hurled his chariot against the ranks of the Egyptians, while the rest, they say, all but himself and his companions, turned aside when they saw the dense host of the Egyptians. 4. And even now his wife, I am told, has taken up his body for burial, placed it in the carriage in which she herself used to ride, and brought it to some place here by the River Pactolus. 5. And his eunuchs and servants, so they say, are digging a grave upon a certain hill for his dead body. But his wife, they say, has decked her husband with what she possessed and now sits upon the ground, holding his head in her lap." He learns the death Abradatas

6. Upon hearing this, Cyrus smote his thigh, mounted his horse at once, and rode with a regiment of cavalry to the scene of sorrow. 7. He left orders for Gadatas and Gobryas to follow him with the most beautiful ornaments they could get for the man, who had fallen beloved and brave. And he ordered those who had in charge the herds that were taken with the army to bring both cattle and horses and many sheep besides to the place where they should hear that he was, that he might sacrifice them in honour of Abradatas.

8. Ἐπεὶ δὲ εἶδε τὴν γυναῖκα χαμαὶ καθημένην
καὶ τὸν νεκρὸν κείμενον, ἐδάκρυσέ τε ἐπὶ τῷ πάθει
καὶ εἶπε, Φεῦ, ὦ ἀγαθὴ καὶ πιστὴ ψυχή, οἴχει δὴ
ἀπολιπὼν ἡμᾶς· καὶ ἅμα ἐδεξιοῦτο αὐτὸν καὶ ἡ
χεὶρ τοῦ νεκροῦ ἐπηκολούθησεν· ἀπεκέκοπτο γὰρ
κοπίδι ὑπὸ τῶν Αἰγυπτίων. 9. ὁ δὲ ἰδὼν πολὺ ἔτι
μᾶλλον ἤλγησε· καὶ ἡ γυνὴ δὲ ἀνωδύρατο καὶ
δεξαμένη δὴ παρὰ τοῦ Κύρου ἐφίλησέ τε τὴν
χεῖρα καὶ πάλιν ὡς οἷόν τ' ἦν προσήρμοσε, καὶ
εἶπε, 10. Καὶ τἆλλά τοι, ὦ Κῦρε, οὕτως ἔχει·
ἀλλὰ τί δεῖ σε ὁρᾶν; καὶ ταῦτα, ἔφη, οἶδ' ὅτι δι'
ἐμὲ οὐχ ἥκιστα ἔπαθεν, ἴσως δὲ καὶ διὰ σέ, ὦ
Κῦρε, οὐδὲν ἧττον. ἐγώ τε γὰρ ἡ μώρα πολλὰ
διεκελευόμην αὐτῷ οὕτω ποιεῖν, ὅπως σοι φίλος
ἄξιος γενήσοιτο·[1] αὐτός τε οἶδ' ὅτι οὗτος οὐ τοῦτο
ἐνενόει ὅ τι πείσοιτο, ἀλλὰ τί ἄν σοι ποιήσας
χαρίσαιτο. καὶ γὰρ οὖν, ἔφη, αὐτὸς μὲν ἀμέμ-
πτως τετελεύτηκεν, ἐγὼ δ' ἡ παρακελευομένη
ζῶσα παρακάθημαι.

11. Καὶ ὁ Κῦρος χρόνον μέν τινα σιωπῇ κατε-
δάκρυσεν, ἔπειτα δὲ ἐφθέγξατο, Ἀλλ' οὗτος μὲν
δή, ὦ γύναι, ἔχει τὸ κάλλιστον τέλος· νικῶν γὰρ
τετελεύτηκε· σὺ δὲ λαβοῦσα τοῖσδε ἐπικόσμει
αὐτὸν τοῖς παρ' ἐμοῦ· παρῆν δὲ ὁ Γωβρύας καὶ ὁ
Γαδάτας πολὺν καὶ καλὸν κόσμον φέροντες·
ἔπειτα δ', ἔφη, ἴσθι ὅτι οὐδὲ τἆλλα ἄτιμος ἔσται,
ἀλλὰ καὶ τὸ μνῆμα πολλοὶ χώσουσιν ἀξίως ἡμῶν
καὶ ἐπισφαγήσεται αὐτῷ ὅσα εἰκὸς ἀνδρὶ ἀγαθῷ.
12. Καὶ σὺ δ', ἔφη, οὐκ ἔρημος ἔσει, ἀλλ' ἐγώ

---

[1] γενήσοιτο F, Hug, Marchant, Gemoll ; λόγου φανείη xzV,
Zonaras, Dindorf, Breitenbach (show himself a friend worth
mentioning).

8. And when he saw the lady sitting upon the ground and the corpse lying there, he wept over his loss and said : " Alas, O brave and faithful soul, hast thou then gone and left us ? " And with the words he clasped his hand, and the dead man's hand came away in his grasp ; for the wrist had been severed by a sabre in the hands of an Egyptian. 9. And Cyrus was still more deeply moved at seeing this ; and the wife wept aloud ; but taking the hand from Cyrus, she kissed it and fitted it on again as best she could and said : 10. " The rest of his limbs also you will find in the same condition, Cyrus ; but why should you see it ? And I am in no small degree to blame that he has suffered so, and you, Cyrus, perhaps not less than I. For it was I that, in my folly, urged him to do his best to show himself a worthy friend to you ; and as for him, I know that he never had a thought of what might happen to him, but only of what he could do to please you. And so," she said, " he has indeed died a blameless death, while I who urged him to it sit here alive ! " Panthea mourns over her dead

11. For some time Cyrus wept in silence and then he said aloud : " Well, lady, he indeed has met the fairest of ends, for he has died in the very hour of victory ; but do you accept these gifts from me "—for Gobryas and Gadatas had come with many beautiful ornaments—"and deck him with them. And then, let me assure you that in other ways also he shall not want for honours, but many hands shall rear to him a monument worthy of us, and sacrifice shall be made over it, such as will befit a man so valiant. Cyrus tries to comfort her

12. " And you," he continued, " shall not be left

σε καὶ σωφροσύνης ἔνεκα καὶ πάσης ἀρετῆς κα
τἄλλα τιμήσω καὶ συστήσω ὅστις ἀποκομιεῖ σ
ὅποι ἂν αὐτὴ ἐθέλῃς· μόνον, ἔφη, δήλωσον πρὸ
ἐμὲ πρὸς ὅντινα χρήζεις κομισθῆναι.

13. Καὶ ἡ Πάνθεια εἶπεν, Ἀλλὰ θάρρει, ἔφη
ὦ Κῦρε, οὐ μή σε κρύψω πρὸς ὅντινα βούλομα
ἀφικέσθαι.

14. Ὁ μὲν δὴ ταῦτ' εἰπὼν ἀπῄει, κατοικτείρω
τήν τε γυναῖκα οἵου ἀνδρὸς στέροιτο καὶ τὸ
ἄνδρα οἵαν γυναῖκα καταλιπὼν οὐκέτ' ὄψοιτο. ἱ
δὲ γυνὴ τοὺς μὲν εὐνούχους ἐκέλευσεν ἀποστῆναι
ἕως ἄν, ἔφη, τόνδ' ἐγὼ ὀδύρωμαι ὡς βούλομαι· τῇ
δὲ τροφῷ εἶπε παραμένειν, καὶ ἐπέταξεν αὐτῇ
ἐπειδὰν ἀποθάνῃ, περικαλύψαι αὐτήν τε καὶ τὸ
ἄνδρα ἑνὶ ἱματίῳ. ἡ δὲ τροφὸς πολλὰ ἱκετεύουσα
μὴ ποιεῖν τοῦτο, ἐπεὶ οὐδὲν ἤνυτε[1] καὶ χαλε
παίνουσαν ἑώρα, ἐκάθητο κλαίουσα. ἡ δὲ ἀκινάκη
πάλαι παρεσκευασμένον σπασαμένη σφάττει ἑαυ
τὴν καὶ ἐπιθεῖσα ἐπὶ τὰ στέρνα τοῦ ἀνδρὸς τὴ
ἑαυτῆς κεφαλὴν ἀπέθνησκεν.

Ἡ δὲ τροφὸς ἀνωλοφύρατό τε καὶ περιεκά
λυπτεν ἄμφω ὥσπερ ἡ Πάνθεια ἐπέστειλεν.

15. Ὁ δὲ Κῦρος ὡς ᾔσθετο τὸ ἔργον τῆς γυ
ναικός, ἐκπλαγεὶς ἵεται, εἴ τι δύναιτο βοηθῆσαι
οἱ δὲ εὐνοῦχοι ἰδόντες τὸ γεγενημένον, τρεῖς ὄντε
σπασάμενοι κἀκεῖνοι τοὺς ἀκινάκας ἀποσφάτ
τονται οὗπερ ἔταξεν αὐτοὺς ἑστηκότες.

[1] ἤνυτε Dindorf, Edd.; ἤνυε xzDV ; ἤνυσε F.

friendless, but on account of your goodness and all your worth, I shall show you all honour; and besides, I will commend to you some one to escort you to the place where you yourself desire to go. Only let me know to whom you wish to be conducted."

13. "Ah, Cyrus," Panthea answered, "do not fear; I shall never hide from you who it is to whom I wish to go."

14. When he had said this, Cyrus went away, his heart full of pity for the woman, as he thought what a husband she had lost, and for the man, that he must leave such a wife and never see her more. The lady then desired the eunuchs to retire, "until," she said, "I have bewailed my husband here, as I desire." But her nurse she told to stay with her, and she charged her to cover her and her husband, when she, too, was dead, with the same cloak. The nurse, however, pleaded earnestly with her not to do so; but when her prayers proved of no avail and she saw her mistress becoming angered, she sat down and burst into tears. Panthea then drew out a dagger, with which she had provided herself long before, and plunged it into her heart, and laying her head upon her husband's bosom she breathed her last. *Panthea's death*

Then the nurse wailed aloud and covered them both, even as Panthea had directed.

15. When Cyrus heard what the woman had done, he was filled with dismay and hastened to the place to see if he could bring any help. And when the eunuchs, three in number, beheld what had occurred, they also, standing in the spot where she had ordered them to stand, drew their daggers and drove them into their own breasts.

XENOPHON

[Καὶ νῦν τὸ μνῆμα μέχρι τοῦ νῦν τῶν εὐνούχων κεχῶσθαι λέγεται· καὶ ἐπὶ μὲν τῇ ἄνω
στήλῃ τοῦ ἀνδρὸς καὶ τῆς γυναικὸς ἐπιγεγράφθαι
φασὶ τὰ ὀνόματα, Σύρια γράμματα, κάτω δὲ
εἶναι τρεῖς λέγουσι στήλας καὶ ἐπιγεγράφθαι
ΣΚΗΠΤΟΥΧΩΝ.][1]

16. Ὁ δὲ Κῦρος ὡς ἐπλησίασε τῷ πάθει ἀγα-
σθείς τε τὴν γυναῖκα καὶ κατολοφυράμενος ἀπῄει·
καὶ τούτων μὲν ᾗ εἰκὸς ἐπεμελήθη ὡς τύχοιεν
πάντων τῶν καλῶν, καὶ τὸ μνῆμα ὑπερμέγεθες
ἐχώσθη, ὥς φασιν.

IV

1. Ἐκ δὲ τούτου στασιάζοντες οἱ Κᾶρες καὶ
πολεμοῦντες πρὸς ἀλλήλους, ἅτε τὰς οἰκήσεις
ἔχοντες ἐν ἐχυροῖς χωρίοις, ἑκάτεροι ἐπεκαλοῦντο
τὸν Κῦρον. ὁ δὲ Κῦρος αὐτὸς μὲν μένων ἐν
Σάρδεσι μηχανὰς ἐποιεῖτο καὶ κριούς, ὡς τῶν
μὴ πειθομένων ἐρείψων τὰ τείχη, Ἀδούσιον δὲ
ἄνδρα Πέρσην καὶ τἆλλα οὐκ ἄφρονα οὐδ᾽ ἀπό-
λεμον, καὶ πάνυ δὴ εὔχαριν, πέμπει ἐπὶ τὴν
Καρίαν στράτευμα δούς· καὶ Κίλικες δὲ καὶ
Κύπριοι πάνυ προθύμως αὐτῷ συνεστράτευσαν.
2. ὧν ἕνεκα οὐδ᾽ ἔπεμψε πώποτε Πέρσην σατράπην οὔτε Κιλίκων οὔτε Κυπρίων, ἀλλ᾽ ἤρκουν
αὐτῷ ἀεὶ οἱ ἐπιχώριοι βασιλεύοντες· δασμὸν
μέντοι ἐλάμβανε καὶ στρατιᾶς ὁπότε δέοιτο
ἐπήγγελλεν αὐτοῖς.

[1] καὶ νῦν : . . ΣΚΗΠΤΟΥΧΩΝ MSS.; omitted by Dindorf,
omitted or bracketed by Edd.

[And now even to this day, it is said, the monument Their of the eunuchs is still standing; and they say that monument the names of the husband and wife are inscribed in Assyrian letters upon the slab above; and below, it is said, are three slabs with the inscription THE MACE-BEARERS.[1]]

16. And when Cyrus drew near to the place of sorrow he marvelled at the woman; and having made lament over her, he went his way. He also took care that they should find all due honours, and the monument reared over them was, as they say, exceeding great.

IV

1. THEN the Carians fell into strife and civil war Adusius with one another; they were intrenched in strong- settles a holds, and both sides called upon Cyrus for assistance. civil war in So while Cyrus himself stayed in Sardis to make siege- Caria engines and battering rams to demolish the walls of such as should refuse to submit, he entrusted an army to Adusius, a Persian who was not lacking in judgment generally and not unskilled in war, and who was besides a very courteous gentleman, and sent him into Caria; and the Cilicians and Cyprians also joined most heartily in this expedition. 2. Because of their enthusiastic allegiance he never sent a Persian satrap to govern either the Cilicians or the Cyprians, but was always satisfied with their native princes. Tribute, however, he did receive from them, and whenever he needed forces he made a requisition upon them for troops.

[1] Staff-bearers—apparently court officials, bearing a "staff" of office; mentioned again VIII. i. 38; VIII. iii. 15; *Anab.* I. vi. 11.

3. Ὁ δὲ Ἀδούσιος ἄγων τὸ στράτευμα ἐπὶ τὴν Καρίαν ἦλθε, καὶ ἀπ᾽ ἀμφοτέρων τῶν Καρῶν παρῆσαν πρὸς αὐτὸν ἕτοιμοι ὄντες δέχεσθαι εἰς τὰ τείχη ἐπὶ κακῷ τῶν ἀντιστασιαζόντων· ὁ δὲ Ἀδούσιος πρὸς ἀμφοτέρους ταὐτὰ ἐποίει· δικαιότερά τε ἔφη λέγειν τούτους ὁποτέροις διαλέγοιτο, λαθεῖν τε ἔφη δεῖν τοὺς ἐναντίους φίλους σφᾶς γενομένους, ὡς δὴ οὕτως ἂν μᾶλλον ἐπιπεσὼν ἀπαρασκεύοις τοῖς ἐναντίοις. πιστὰ δ᾽ ἠξίου γενέσθαι, καὶ τοὺς μὲν Κᾶρας ὀμόσαι ἀδόλως τε δέξεσθαι[1] εἰς τὰ τείχη σφᾶς καὶ ἐπ᾽ ἀγαθῷ τῷ Κύρου καὶ Περσῶν· αὐτὸς δὲ ὀμόσαι θέλειν ἀδόλως εἰσιέναι εἰς τὰ τείχη καὶ ἐπ᾽ ἀγαθῷ τῶν δεχομένων. 4. ταῦτα δὲ ποιήσας ἀμφοτέροις λάθρα ἑκατέρων νύκτα συνέθετο τὴν αὐτήν, καὶ ἐν ταύτῃ εἰσήλασέ τε[2] εἰς τὰ τείχη καὶ παρέλαβε τὰ ἐρύματα ἀμφοτέρων. ἅμα δὲ τῇ ἡμέρᾳ καθεζόμενος εἰς τὸ μέσον σὺν τῇ στρατιᾷ ἐκάλεσεν ἑκατέρων τοὺς ἐπικαιρίους. οἱ δὲ ἰδόντες ἀλλήλους ἠχθέσθησαν, νομίζοντες ἐξηπατῆσθαι ἀμφότεροι. 5. ὁ μέντοι Ἀδούσιος ἔλεξε τοιάδε·

Ἐγὼ ὑμῖν, ὦ ἄνδρες, ὤμοσα ἀδόλως εἰσιέναι εἰς τὰ τείχη καὶ ἐπ᾽ ἀγαθῷ τῶν δεχομένων. εἰ μὲν οὖν ἀπολῶ ὁποτέρους ὑμῶν, νομίζω ἐπὶ κακῷ εἰσεληλυθέναι Καρῶν· ἢν δὲ εἰρήνην ὑμῖν ποιήσω καὶ ἀσφάλειαν ἐργάζεσθαι ἀμφοτέροις τὴν γῆν, νομίζω ὑμῖν ἐπ᾽ ἀγαθῷ παρεῖναι. νῦν οὖν χρὴ

---

[1] δέξεσθαι Dindorf, Madvig, Edd.; δέξασθαι MSS.
[2] ἠσήλασέ τε Hug (ἠσήλασε Leonclav; εἰσῆλθέ τε Cobet), Marchant, Gemoll; εἰσήλατο zV, Dindorf, Breitenbach; εἰσήλλατο x; εἰσῆλθεν y.

3. Adusius now set out for Caria at the head of his army; and there came to him representatives from both parties of the Carians, ready to receive him into their walls to the injury of the rival faction. But Adusius treated both sides alike: with whichever party he conferred, he said they were more in the right, but they must not let their opponents know that he and they had become friends, alleging that he would thus be more likely to fall upon those opponents unprepared. Moreover, he demanded from the Carians pledges of good faith and made them swear to receive him without treachery within their walls to the advantage of Cyrus and the Persians, and he himself consented to give his oath that he would without treachery enter their walls for the advantage of those who admitted him. 4. And when he had done this, he made appointments with both parties for the same night—each party without the other's knowledge—and on that night he marched inside the walls and took possession of the strongholds of both. At day-break he took his stand with his army between the two and summoned the leaders of the two factions. And when they saw one another they were indignant, for they both thought they had been duped. 5. Adusius, however, addressed them as follows:

"Gentlemen, I gave you my oath that I would without treachery enter your walls for the advantage of those who admitted me. If, therefore, I destroy either party of you, I think that I have come in to the injury of the Carians; whereas, if I can secure peace for you and security for all to till the fields, I think I am here for your advantage. Now, therefore,

Peace is established between the factions

ἀπὸ τῆσδε τῆς ἡμέρας ἐπιμίγνυσθαί τε ἀλλήλοις
φιλικῶς, ἐργάζεσθαί τε τὴν γῆν ἀδεῶς, διδόναι
τε τέκνα καὶ λαμβάνειν παρ' ἀλλήλων. ἢν δὲ
παρὰ ταῦτα ἀδικεῖν τις ἐπιχειρῇ, τούτοις Κῦρός
τε καὶ ἡμεῖς πολέμιοι ἐσόμεθα.

6. Ἐκ τούτου πύλαι μὲν ἀνεῳγμέναι ἦσαν τῶν
τειχῶν, μεσταὶ δὲ αἱ ὁδοὶ πορευομένων παρ'
ἀλλήλους, μεστοὶ δὲ οἱ χῶροι ἐργαζομένων·
ἑορτὰς δὲ κοινῇ ἦγον, εἰρήνης δὲ καὶ εὐφροσύνης
πάντα πλέα ἦν.

7. Ἐν δὲ τούτῳ ἧκον παρὰ Κύρου ἐρωτῶντες
εἴ τι στρατιᾶς προσδέοιτο ἢ μηχανημάτων· ὁ δὲ
Ἀδούσιος ἀπεκρίνατο ὅτι καὶ τῇ παρούσῃ ἐξείη
ἄλλοσε χρῆσθαι στρατιᾷ· καὶ ἅμα ταῦτα λέγων
ἀπῆγε τὸ στράτευμα, φρουροὺς ἐν ταῖς ἄκραις
καταλιπών. οἱ δὲ Κᾶρες ἱκέτευον μένειν αὐτόν·
ἐπεὶ δὲ οὐκ ἤθελε, προσέπεμψαν πρὸς Κῦρον
δεόμενοι πέμψαι Ἀδούσιον σφίσι σατράπην.

8. Ὁ δὲ Κῦρος ἐν τούτῳ ἀπεστάλκει Ὑστάσπαν
στράτευμα ἄγοντα ἐπὶ Φρυγίαν τὴν περὶ Ἑλλήσ-
ποντον· ἐπεὶ δ' ἧκεν ὁ Ἀδούσιος, μετάγειν αὐτὸν
ἐκέλευσεν ᾗπερ ὁ Ὑστάσπας προῴχετο, ὅπως
μᾶλλον πείθοιντο τῷ Ὑστάσπᾳ, ἀκούσαντες
ἄλλο στράτευμα προσιόν.

9. Οἱ μὲν οὖν Ἕλληνες οἱ ἐπὶ θαλάττῃ οἰκοῦντες
πολλὰ δῶρα δόντες διεπράξαντο ὥστε εἰς μὲν τὰ
τείχη βαρβάρους μὴ δέχεσθαι, δασμὸν δὲ ἀποφέρειν[1] καὶ στρατεύειν ὅποι Κῦρος ἐπαγγέλλοι.

---

[1] ἀποφέρειν Zonaras, Edd.; ὑποφέρειν MSS.

from this day you must live together like friends, till your lands without fear of one another, and intermarry your children one party with the other; and if any one in defiance of these regulations attempts to make trouble, Cyrus, and we with him, will be that man's enemies."

6. After that, the gates of the city were opened, the streets filled up with people passing to and fro, and the farms with labourers; they celebrated their festivals together, and peace and joy reigned everywhere.

7. At this juncture messengers came to him from Cyrus to ask if he needed any more troops or engines; but Adusius answered that even the army he had with him was at the disposal of Cyrus to employ elsewhere. And with those words he started to lead back his army, leaving only garrisons upon the citadels. But the Carians pleaded with him to stay; and when he refused, they sent to Cyrus to petition him to send Adusius to be their satrap.

8. Cyrus had meanwhile sent off Hystaspas in command of an expedition against the Phrygia that lies along the Hellespont. So when Adusius returned, he directed him to march on in the direction Hystaspas had taken, that they might submit to Hystaspas more readily when they heard that another army was on the way. *The conquest of the lesser Phrygia*

9. Now the Greeks who dwelt by the sea gave many gifts and secured an agreement to the effect that while they should not receive the barbarians [1] within their walls, they would yet pay tribute and serve under him in the field wherever Cyrus should direct.

---

[1] "Barbarians," from the Greek point of view; that is, Persians.

10. ὁ δὲ τῶν Φρυγῶν βασιλεὺς παρεσκευάζετο μὲν ὡς καθέξων τὰ ἐρυμνὰ καὶ οὐ πεισόμενος καὶ παρήγγελλεν οὕτως· ἐπεὶ δὲ ἀφίσταντο αὐτοῦ οἱ ὕπαρχοι καὶ ἔρημος ἐγίγνετο, τελευτῶν εἰς χεῖρας ἦλθεν Ὑστάσπᾳ ἐπὶ τῇ Κύρου δίκῃ. καὶ ὁ Ὑστάσπας καταλιπὼν ἐν ταῖς ἄκραις ἰσχυρὰς Περσῶν φρουρὰς ἀπῄει ἄγων σὺν τοῖς ἑαυτοῦ καὶ Φρυγῶν πολλοὺς ἱππέας καὶ πελταστάς. 11. ὁ δὲ Κῦρος ἐπέστελλεν Ἀδουσίῳ συμμίξαντα πρὸς Ὑστάσπαν τοὺς μὲν ἑλομένους Φρυγῶν τὰ σφέτερα σὺν τοῖς ὅπλοις ἄγειν, τοὺς δὲ ἐπιθυμήσαντας πολεμεῖν τούτων ἀφελομένους τοὺς ἵππους καὶ τὰ ὅπλα σφενδόνας ἔχοντας πάντας κελεύειν ἕπεσθαι. 12. οὗτοι μὲν δὴ ταῦτ᾽ ἐποίουν.

Κῦρος δὲ ὡρμᾶτο ἐκ Σάρδεων, φρουρὰν μὲν πεζὴν καταλιπὼν πολλὴν ἐν Σάρδεσι, Κροῖσον δὲ ἔχων, ἄγων δὲ πολλὰς ἁμάξας πολλῶν καὶ παντοδαπῶν χρημάτων. ἧκε δὲ καὶ ὁ Κροῖσος γεγραμμένα ἔχων ἀκριβῶς ὅσα ἐν ἑκάστῃ ἦν τῇ ἁμάξῃ· καὶ διδοὺς τῷ Κύρῳ τὰ γράμματα εἶπε, Ταῦτ᾽, ἔφη, ἔχων, ὦ Κῦρε, εἴσει τόν τέ σοι ὀρθῶς ἀποδιδόντα ἃ ἄγει καὶ τὸν μή.

13. Καὶ ὁ Κῦρος ἔλεξεν, Ἀλλὰ σὺ μὲν καλῶς ποιεῖς,[1] ὦ Κροῖσε, προνοῶν· ἔμοιγε μέντοι ἄξουσι τὰ χρήματα οἵπερ καὶ ἔχειν αὐτὰ ἄξιοί εἰσιν· ὥστε ἤν τι καὶ κλέψωσι, τῶν ἑαυτῶν κλέψονται.

Καὶ ἅμα ταῦτα λέγων ἔδωκε τὰ γράμματα τοῖς

---

[1] ποιεῖς xy, Hug, Marchant, Gemoll ; ἐποίεις zVe, Dindorf, Sauppe, Breitenbach ; ἐποίησας Zonaras.

10. But the king of Phrygia made preparations to keep possession of his forts and not to submit, and he gave orders to that effect. When, however, his subordinate officers deserted and he was left alone, he finally surrendered to Hystaspas on condition that Cyrus should be his judge and arbiter. And Hystaspas, leaving strong garrisons of Persians upon the citadels, went back with his own army reinforced with many Phrygian horsemen and peltasts. 11. Besides, Cyrus had given Adusius instructions to join Hystaspas and bring with them armed those Phrygians who had voluntarily taken their side, but to take their horses and arms away from those who had shown fight, and to make all such follow, armed with nothing but slings. 12. Accordingly, they were thus engaged in executing these orders.

But Cyrus, leaving behind a large garrison of foot-soldiers, started from Sardis in company with Croesus; and he took with him many wagons loaded with valuables of every sort. And Croesus also had come with an accurate inventory of what was in each wagon; and as he handed the lists to Cyrus he said: "From this, Cyrus, you may know who renders to you in full that of which he has charge and who does not." *Cyrus starts from Sardis*

13. "Aye, Croesus," answered Cyrus; "you do well to take this precaution. As far as I am concerned, however, those shall have charge of the valuables who also deserve to own them; so that if they embezzle anything, they will be embezzling from what is their own."

With these words, he gave the inventories to his

φίλοις καὶ τοῖς ἄρχουσιν, ὅπως εἰδεῖεν τῶν ἐπι-
τρόπων οἵ τε σῶα[1] αὐτοῖς ἀποδιδοῖεν οἵ τε μή.

14. Ἦγε δὲ καὶ Λυδῶν οὓς μὲν ἑώρα καλλωπι-
ζομένους καὶ ὅπλοις καὶ ἵπποις καὶ ἅρμασι καὶ
πάντα πειρωμένους ποιεῖν ὅ τι ᾤοντο αὐτῷ
χαριεῖσθαι, τούτους μὲν σὺν τοῖς ὅπλοις· οὓς δὲ
ἑώρα ἀχαρίτως ἑπομένους, τοὺς μὲν ἵππους αὐτῶν
παρέδωκε Πέρσαις τοῖς πρώτοις συστρατευομέ-
νοις, τὰ δὲ ὅπλα κατέκαυσε· σφενδόνας δὲ καὶ τούτους ἠνάγκασεν ἔχοντας ἕπεσθαι. 15. καὶ πάντας
δὲ τοὺς ἀόπλους τῶν ὑποχειρίων γενομένων σφεν-
δονᾶν ἠνάγκαζε μελετᾶν, νομίζων τοῦτο τὸ ὅπλον
δουλικώτατον εἶναι· σὺν μὲν γὰρ ἄλλῃ δυνάμει
μάλα ἔστιν ἔνθα ἰσχυρῶς ὠφελοῦσι σφενδονῆται
παρόντες, αὐτοὶ δὲ καθ' αὑτοὺς οὐδ' ἂν οἱ πάντες
σφενδονῆται μείνειαν πάνυ ὀλίγους ὁμόσε ἰόντας
σὺν ὅπλοις ἀγχεμάχοις.

16. Προϊὼν δὲ τὴν ἐπὶ Βαβυλῶνος κατεστρέψατο μὲν Φρύγας τοὺς ἐν τῇ μεγάλῃ Φρυγίᾳ,
κατεστρέψατο δὲ Καππαδόκας, ὑποχειρίους δ'
ἐποιήσατο Ἀραβίους. ἐξώπλισε[2] δὲ ἀπὸ πάντων
τούτων Περσῶν μὲν ἱππέας οὐ μεῖον τετρακισμυ-
ρίους, πολλοὺς δὲ ἵππους τῶν αἰχμαλώτων καὶ

---

[1] σῶα MSS., Breitenbach, Marchant, Gemoll; σᾶ Dindorf,
Hug.
[2] ἐξώπλισε xyG², Hug, Marchant; ἐξέπλησε zG¹V, Dindorf,
Breitenbach, Hertlein, Gemoll (*he filled up the number*).

friends and officers, that they might be able to tell who of the overseers delivered everything safe and who of them failed.

14. He took with him also such of the Lydians as he saw taking a pride in the fine appearance of their arms and horses and chariots and trying to do everything that they thought would please him; these he permitted to retain their arms. But if he saw any following with bad grace, he turned their horses over to those Persians who had been the first to engage in his service; he had their arms burned, and these men, too, he required to follow with nothing but slings. 15. And of those who had been made subjects he required all who were unarmed to practise with the sling, for he considered this weapon to be the one most fitting for a slave. For in conjunction with other forces there are occasions when the presence of slingers is of very effective assistance, but by themselves alone not all the slingers in the world could stand against a very few men who came into a hand-to-hand encounter with them with weapons suited for close combat.

16. On the way to Babylon he subdued Greater Phrygia and Cappadocia and reduced the Arabians to submission. From all these he secured armour for not less than forty thousand Persian horsemen, and many horses taken from the prisoners he dis-

He marches still conquering to Babylon

259

πᾶσι τοῖς συμμάχοις διέδωκε· καὶ πρὸς Βαβυλῶνα ἀφίκετο παμπόλλους μὲν ἱππέας ἔχων,
παμπόλλους δὲ τοξότας καὶ ἀκοντιστάς, σφενδο-
νήτας δὲ ἀναριθμήτους.

V

1. Ἐπεὶ δὲ πρὸς Βαβυλῶνι ἦν ὁ Κῦρος, περι-
έστησε μὲν πᾶν τὸ στράτευμα περὶ τὴν πόλιν,
ἔπειτα αὐτὸς περιήλαυνε τὴν πόλιν σὺν τοῖς
φίλοις τε καὶ ἐπικαιρίοις τῶν συμμάχων. 2. ἐπεὶ
δὲ κατεθεάσατο τὰ τείχη, ἀπάγειν παρεσκευάσατο τὴν στρατιὰν ἀπὸ τῆς πόλεως· ἐξελθὼν
δέ τις αὐτόμολος εἶπεν ὅτι ἐπιτίθεσθαι μέλλοιεν
αὐτῷ, ὁπότε ἀπάγοι τὸ στράτευμα· καταθεωμέ-
νοις γάρ, ἔφη, αὐτοῖς ἀπὸ τοῦ τείχους ἀσθενὴς
ἐδόκει εἶναι ἡ φάλαγξ· καὶ οὐδὲν θαυμαστὸν
ἦν οὕτως ἔχειν· περὶ γὰρ πολὺ τεῖχος κυκλουμένοις[1] ἀνάγκη ἦν ἐπ' ὀλίγων[2] τὸ βάθος γενέσθαι
τὴν φάλαγγα.

3. Ἀκούσας οὖν ὁ Κῦρος ταῦτα, στὰς κατὰ
μέσον τῆς αὑτοῦ στρατιᾶς σὺν τοῖς περὶ αὐτὸν
παρήγγειλεν ἀπὸ τοῦ ἄκρου ἑκατέρωθεν τοὺς
ὁπλίτας ἀναπτύσσοντας τὴν φάλαγγα ἀπιέναι
παρὰ τὸ ἑστηκὸς τοῦ στρατεύματος, ἕως γένοιτο
ἑκατέρωθεν τὸ ἄκρον κατ' αὐτὸν καὶ κατὰ τὸ
μέσον. 4. οὕτως οὖν ποιούντων οἵ τε μένοντες

---

[1] κυκλουμένοις Bornemann, recent Edd.; κυκλουμένους MSS.,
earlier Edd.
[2] ὀλίγων Hertlein, Edd.; ὀλίγον MSS.

tributed among all the divisions of his allies. And thus he arrived before Babylon with a great host of cavalry, and a great host of bowmen and spearmen, and a multitude of slingers that was beyond number.

V

1. WHEN Cyrus appeared before Babylon he stationed his whole force about the city and then rode around it himself in company with his friends and the staff-officers of the allies; 2. but when he had taken a survey of the walls, he prepared to draw off his army from the city. But a deserter came out and told him that they were going to attack him as soon as he began to draw his army off. "For," the man went on, "your lines looked weak to those who observed them from the walls." And it was no wonder that they appeared so; for, encompassing walls of such extent,[1] the lines necessarily had but little depth.

3. On hearing this, therefore, Cyrus took his place with his body-guard in the centre of his army and gave orders that the hoplites should fold back the phalanx from the extremity of either wing and move toward each other behind the main body, which had been halted, until each of the extreme wings should meet in a line with him, that is, in the centre.[2] 4. By

Cyrus surrounds Babylon

He retires from the wall

---

[1] See Index, s.v. Babylon, note.
[2] See Appendix I.

εὐθὺς θαρραλεώτεροι ἐγίγνοντο ἐπὶ διπλασίων τὸ
βάθος γιγνόμενοι, οἵ τ᾽ ἀπιόντες ὡσαύτως θαρρα-
λεώτεροι· εὐθὺς γὰρ οἱ μένοντες ἀντ᾽[1] αὐτῶν
πρὸς τοὺς πολεμίους ἐγίγνοντο. ἐπεὶ δὲ πορευόμενοι ἑκατέρωθεν συνῆψαν τὰ ἄκρα, ἔστησαν
ἰσχυρότεροι γεγενημένοι, οἵ τε ἀπεληλυθότες διὰ
τοὺς ἔμπροσθεν, οἵ τ᾽ ἔμπροσθεν διὰ τοὺς ὄπισθεν
προσγεγενημένους. 5. ἀναπτυχθείσης δ᾽ οὕτω τῆς
φάλαγγος ἀνάγκη τοὺς πρώτους ἀρίστους εἶναι
καὶ τοὺς τελευταίους, ἐν μέσῳ δὲ τοὺς κακίστους
τετάχθαι· ἡ δ᾽ οὕτως ἔχουσα τάξις καὶ πρὸς
τὸ μάχεσθαι ἐδόκει εὖ παρεσκευάσθαι καὶ πρὸς
τὸ μὴ φεύγειν. καὶ οἱ ἱππεῖς δὲ καὶ οἱ γυμνῆτες
οἱ ἀπὸ τῶν κεράτων ἀεὶ ἐγγύτερον ἐγίγνοντο
τοῦ ἄρχοντος τοσούτῳ ὅσῳ ἡ φάλαγξ βραχυτέρα
ἐγίγνετο ἀναδιπλουμένη. 6. ἐπεὶ δὲ οὕτω συν-
εσπειράθησαν, ἀπῆσαν, ἕως μὲν ἐξικνεῖτο τὰ βέλη
ἀπὸ τοῦ τείχους, ἐπὶ πόδα· ἐπεὶ δὲ ἔξω βελῶν
ἐγένοντο, στραφέντες, καὶ τὸ μὲν πρῶτον ὀλίγα
βήματα προϊόντες μετεβάλλοντο[2] ἐπ᾽ ἀσπίδα
καὶ ἵσταντο πρὸς τὸ τεῖχος βλέποντες· ὅσῳ δὲ
προσωτέρω ἐγίγνοντο, τόσῳ δὲ μανότερον μετεβάλλοντο. ἐπεὶ δ᾽ ἐν τῷ ἀσφαλεῖ ἐδόκουν εἶναι,
συνεῖρον ἀπιόντες, ἔστ᾽ ἐπὶ ταῖς σκηναῖς ἐγένοντο.

---

[1] ἀντ᾽ supplied by Hertlein, Edd.; not in MSS.
[2] μετεβάλλοντο xyV, Dindorf, Breitenbach, Gemoll; μετε-
βάλοντο z, Hug, Marchant.

this manœuvre the men that remained standing in their places were at once given more courage, for the depth of the line was thus doubled; and those who had fallen back were likewise rendered more courageous, for thus those troops which had been kept standing had now come to face the enemy, and not they. But when, as they marched in from both sides, the ends came together, they stood thus mutually strengthened—those who had shifted their position were supported by those in front of them, those in front by the men behind them. 5. And when the phalanx was thus folded back, the front ranks and the rear were of necessity composed of the most valiant men and the poorest were drawn up between them. And this arrangement of the lines seemed well adapted both for fighting and for keeping the men from flight; and the cavalry and the light-armed troops upon the wings were in each case brought as much nearer to the commander as the phalanx was shorter when doubled. 6. And when they had thus closed up, they retired backward as long as they were within range of the missiles from the wall; but when they were out of range, they would face about and go forward at first only a few steps and wheel to the left and stand facing the wall; and the further off they got, the less often did they thus wheel around; and when they seemed to be out of all danger, they marched off without stopping until they arrived at their tents.

7. Ἐπεὶ δὲ κατεστρατοπεδεύσαντο, συνεκάλεσεν ὁ Κῦρος τοὺς ἐπικαιρίους καὶ ἔλεξεν, Ἄνδρες σύμμαχοι, τεθεάμεθα μὲν κύκλῳ τὴν πόλιν· ἐγὼ δὲ ὅπως μὲν ἄν τις τείχη οὕτως ἰσχυρὰ καὶ ὑψηλὰ προσμαχόμενος ἕλοι οὐκ ἐνορᾶν μοι δοκῶ· ὅσῳ δὲ πλείους ἄνθρωποι ἐν τῇ πόλει εἰσίν, ἐπείπερ οὐ μάχονται ἐξιόντες, τοσούτῳ ἂν θᾶττον λιμῷ αὐτοὺς ἡγοῦμαι ἁλῶναι. εἰ μή τιν' οὖν ἄλλον τρόπον ἔχετε λέγειν, τούτῳ πολιορκητέους φημὶ εἶναι τοὺς ἄνδρας.

8. Καὶ ὁ Χρυσάντας εἶπεν, Ὁ δὲ ποταμός, ἔφη, οὗτος οὐ διὰ μέσης τῆς πόλεως ῥεῖ πλάτος ἔχων πλεῖον ἢ ἐπὶ δύο στάδια;

Ναὶ μὰ Δί', ἔφη ὁ Γωβρύας, καὶ βάθος γ' ὡς οὐδ' ἂν δύο ἄνδρες ὁ ἕτερος ἐπὶ τοῦ ἑτέρου ἑστηκὼς τοῦ ὕδατος ὑπερέχοιεν· ὥστε τῷ ποταμῷ ἔτι ἰσχυροτέρα ἐστὶν ἡ πόλις ἢ τοῖς τείχεσι.

9. Καὶ ὁ Κῦρος, Ταῦτα μέν, ἔφη, ὦ Χρυσάντα, ἐῶμεν ὅσα κρείττω ἐστὶ τῆς ἡμετέρας δυνάμεως· διαμετρησαμένους δὲ χρὴ ὡς τάχιστα τὸ μέρος ἑκάστους [1] ἡμῶν ὀρύττειν τάφρον ὡς πλατυτάτην καὶ βαθυτάτην, ὅπως ὅτι ἐλαχίστων ἡμῖν τῶν φυλάκων δέῃ.

10. Οὕτω δὴ κύκλῳ διαμετρήσας περὶ τὸ τεῖχος, ἀπολιπὼν ὅσον τύρσεσι μεγάλαις ἀπὸ τοῦ

---

[1] ἑκάστους Madvig, Breitenbach, Hug, Marchant, Gemoll; ἑκάστου xzFV, Dindorf; ἕκαστον D.

7. When they had encamped, Cyrus called to- Cyrus plans for a siege
gether his staff-officers and said : " Friends and allies,
we have viewed the city on every side. But I am
sure I cannot see how any one could take by
storm walls so massive and so hïgh; but the more
men there are in the city, the sooner they can, I
think, be brought by famine to capitulate, seeing
that they will not come out and fight. Therefore,
unless you have some other method to suggest, I
propose that we use this method of laying siege to
those gentlemen."

8. "But," said Chrysantas, "does not this river
flow through the midst of the city? And it is
more than two stadia in width."

"Aye, by Zeus," said Gobryas, "and its depth is
such that two men, one standing . on the other's
shoulders, would not reach the surface of the water,
so that the city is better defended by the river than
by its walls."

9. "Chrysantas," Cyrus answered, "let us not He proposes to divert the Euphrates
trouble ourselves with that which is beyond our
powers ; but we must apportion the work among
ourselves as quickly as possible, to each contingent
its proper share, and dig a ditch as wide and as deep
as possible, so that we may require only as many men
on guard as are absolutely indispensable."

10. Accordingly, he took measurements in a circle
round about the city, leaving just enough room by
the river for the erection of large towers, and began

ποταμοῦ, ὤρυττεν ἔνθεν καὶ ἔνθεν τοῦ τείχους τάφρον ὑπερμεγέθη, καὶ τὴν γῆν ἀνέβαλλον πρὸς ἑαυτούς. 11. καὶ πρῶτον μὲν πύργους ἐπὶ τῷ ποταμῷ ᾠκοδόμει, φοίνιξι θεμελιώσας οὐ μεῖον ἢ πλεθριαίοις—εἰσὶ γὰρ καὶ μείζονες ἢ τοσοῦτοι τὸ μῆκος πεφυκότες· καὶ γὰρ δὴ πιεζόμενοι οἱ φοίνικες ὑπὸ βάρους ἄνω κυρτοῦνται, ὥσπερ οἱ ὄνοι οἱ κανθήλιοι· 12. τούτους δ᾽ ὑπετίθει τούτου ἕνεκα [ὅπως ὅτι μάλιστα ἐοίκοι πολιορκήσειν παρασκευαζομένῳ],[1] ὡς εἰ καὶ διαφύγοι ὁ ποταμὸς εἰς τὴν τάφρον, μὴ ἀνέλοι τοὺς πύργους. ἀνίστη δὲ καὶ ἄλλους πολλοὺς πύργους ἐπὶ τῆς ἀμβολάδος γῆς, ὅπως ὅτι πλεῖστα φυλακτήρια εἴη.

13. Οἱ μὲν δὴ ταῦτ᾽ ἐποίουν· οἱ δ᾽ ἐν τῷ τείχει κατεγέλων τῆς πολιορκίας, ὡς ἔχοντες τἀπιτήδεια πλέον ἢ εἴκοσιν ἐτῶν.

Ἀκούσας δὲ ταῦτα ὁ Κῦρος τὸ στράτευμα κατένειμε δώδεκα μέρη, ὡς μῆνα τοῦ ἐνιαυτοῦ ἕκαστον τὸ μέρος φυλάξον. 14. οἱ δὲ αὖ Βαβυλώνιοι ἀκούσαντες ταῦτα πολὺ ἔτι μᾶλλον κατεγέλων, ἐννοούμενοι εἰ σφᾶς Φρύγες καὶ Λυδοὶ καὶ Ἀράβιοι καὶ Καππαδόκαι φυλάξοιεν, οὓς σφίσιν ἐνόμιζον πάντας εὐμενεστέρους εἶναι ἢ Πέρσαις.

15. Καὶ αἱ μὲν τάφροι ἤδη ὀρωρυγμέναι ἦσαν. ὁ δὲ Κῦρος ἐπειδὴ ἑορτὴν τοιαύτην ἐν τῇ Βαβυλῶνι ἤκουσεν εἶναι, ἐν ᾗ πάντες Βαβυλώνιοι ὅλην τὴν νύκτα πίνουσι καὶ κωμάζουσιν, ἐν ταύτῃ, ἐπειδὴ τάχιστα συνεσκότασε, λαβὼν πολλοὺς

---

[1] ὅπως . . . παρασκευαζομένῳ MSS. ; bracketed by Breitenbach, Hug, Marchant, Gemoll ; Dindorf brackets τούτους . . . πύργους.

on either side of the city to dig an immense trench ; and the earth from it they threw up on their own side of the ditch. 11. First of all, he began to build towers by the river, laying his foundations with the trunks of date-palms not less than a hundred feet long—and they grow even taller than that. And they were good material for this purpose, for it is a well known fact that date-palms, when under heavy pressure, bend upward like the backs of pack-asses. 12. These he used as "mud-sills," in order that, even if the river should break into his trench above, it might not carry his towers away. And he erected many other towers besides upon the breast-works of earth, so that he might have as many watch-towers as possible.

13. Thus, then, his men were employed, while the enemy upon the walls laughed his siege-works to scorn, in the belief that they had provisions enough for more than twenty years.

Upon hearing of this, Cyrus divided his army into twelve parts as if intending each part to be responsible for sentry duty during one month of each year ; 14. but the Babylonians, in their turn, when they heard of that, laughed much more scornfully still, at the thought of Phrygians and Lydians and Arabians and Cappadocians keeping guard against them, for they considered all these to be more friendly to them than to the Persians.

15. At last the ditches were completed. Then, *The river is turned* when he heard that a certain festival had come round in Babylon, during which all Babylon was accustomed to drink and revel all night long, Cyrus took a large number of men, just as soon as it was dark, and

XENOPHON

ἀνθρώπους ἀνεστόμωσε τὰς τάφρους πρὸς τὸν
ποταμόν. 16. ὡς δὲ τοῦτο ἐγένετο, τὸ ὕδωρ κατὰ
τὰς τάφρους ἐχώρει ἐν τῇ νυκτί, ἡ δὲ διὰ τῆς
πόλεως τοῦ ποταμοῦ ὁδὸς πορεύσιμος ἀνθρώποις
ἐγίγνετο.

17. Ὡς δὲ τὸ τοῦ ποταμοῦ οὕτως ἐπορσύνετο,
παρηγγύησεν ὁ Κῦρος Πέρσαις χιλιάρχοις καὶ
πεζῶν καὶ ἱππέων εἰς δύο ἄγοντας τὴν χιλιοστὺν
παρεῖναι πρὸς αὑτόν, τοὺς δὲ ἄλλους συμμάχους
κατ᾽ οὐρὰν τούτων ἕπεσθαι ᾗπερ πρόσθεν τεταγμένους. 18. οἱ μὲν δὴ παρῆσαν· ὁ δὲ καταβι-
βάσας εἰς τὸ ξηρὸν τοῦ ποταμοῦ τοὺς ὑπηρέτας
καὶ πεζοὺς καὶ ἱππέας, ἐκέλευσε σκέψασθαι εἰ
πορεύσιμον εἴη τὸ ἔδαφος τοῦ ποταμοῦ. 19. ἐπεὶ
δὲ ἀπήγγειλαν ὅτι πορεύσιμον εἴη, ἐνταῦθα δὴ
συγκαλέσας τοὺς ἡγεμόνας τῶν πεζῶν καὶ ἱππέων
ἔλεξε τοιάδε·

20. Ἄνδρες, ἔφη, φίλοι, ὁ μὲν ποταμὸς ἡμῖν
παρακεχώρηκε τῆς εἰς τὴν πόλιν ὁδοῦ. ἡμεῖς δὲ
θαρροῦντες εἰσίωμεν μηδὲν φοβούμενοι εἴσω, ἐννοούμενοι ὅτι οὗτοι ἐφ᾽ οὓς νῦν πορευσόμεθα ἐκεῖνοί
εἰσιν οὓς ἡμεῖς καὶ συμμάχους πρὸς ἑαυτοῖς ἔχοντας καὶ ἐγρηγορότας ἅπαντας καὶ νήφοντας καὶ
ἐξωπλισμένους καὶ συντεταγμένους ἐνικῶμεν·
21. νῦν δ᾽ ἐπ᾽ αὐτοὺς ἴμεν ἐν ᾧ πολλοὶ μὲν αὐτῶν
καθεύδουσι, πολλοὶ δ᾽ αὐτῶν μεθύουσι, πάντες δ᾽
ἀσύντακτοί εἰσιν· ὅταν δὲ αἴσθωνται ἡμᾶς ἔνδον
ὄντας, πολὺ ἔτι μᾶλλον ἢ νῦν ἀχρεῖοι ἔσονται ὑπὸ
τοῦ ἐκπεπλῆχθαι.

22. Εἰ δέ τις τοῦτο ἐννοεῖται, ὃ δὴ λέγεται
φοβερὸν εἶναι τοῖς εἰς πόλιν εἰσιοῦσι, μὴ ἐπὶ
τὰ τέγη ἀναβάντες βάλλωσιν ἔνθεν καὶ ἔνθεν,
268

opened up the heads of the trenches at the river.
16. As soon as that was done, the water flowed down
through the ditches in the night, and the bed of the
river, where it traversed the city, became passable
for men.

17. When the problem of the river was thus
solved, Cyrus gave orders to his Persian colonels,
infantry and cavalry, to marshal their regiments two
abreast and come to him, and the rest, the allies, to
follow in their rear, drawn up as before. 18. They
came, according to orders, and he bade his aides,
both foot and horse, get into the dry channel of the
river and see if it was possible to march in the bed
of the river. 19. And when they brought back word
that it was, he called together the generals of both
infantry and cavalry and spoke as follows:

20. "My friends," said he, "the river has made
way for us and given us an entrance into the city. Cyrus issues
instructions
Let us, therefore, enter in with dauntless hearts, for entering
fearing nothing and remembering that those the city
against whom we are now to march are the same
men that we have repeatedly defeated, and that,
too, when they were all drawn up in battle line
with their allies at their side, and when they were
all wide awake and sober and fully armed; 21.
whereas now we are going to fall upon them at a
time when many of them are asleep, many drunk,
and none of them in battle array. And when they
find out that we are inside the walls, in their panic
fright they will be much more helpless still than
they are now.

22. "But if any one is apprehensive of that
which is said to be a source of terror to those
invading a city—namely, that the people may go up

XENOPHON

τοῦτο μάλιστα θαρρεῖτε· ἢν γὰρ ἀναβῶσί τινες
ἐπὶ τὰς οἰκίας, ἔχομεν σύμμαχον θεὸν Ἥφαιστον.
εὔφλεκτα δὲ τὰ πρόθυρα αὐτῶν, φοίνικος μὲν
αἱ θύραι πεποιημέναι, ἀσφάλτῳ δὲ ὑπεκκαύματι
κεχριμέναι.[1] 23. ἡμεῖς δὲ αὖ πολλὴν δᾷδα ἔχομεν, ἢ ταχὺ πολὺ πῦρ τέξεται, πολλὴν δὲ πίτταν
καὶ στυππεῖον, ἃ ταχὺ παρακαλεῖ πολλὴν φλόγα·
ὥστε ἀνάγκην εἶναι ἢ φεύγειν ταχὺ τοὺς ἀπὸ
τῶν οἰκιῶν ἢ ταχὺ κατακεκαῦσθαι.

24. Ἀλλ' ἄγετε λαμβάνετε τὰ ὅπλα· ἡγήσομαι
δὲ ἐγὼ σὺν τοῖς θεοῖς. ὑμεῖς δ', ἔφη, ὦ Γαδάτα
καὶ Γωβρύα, δείκνυτε τὰς ὁδούς· ἴστε γάρ· ὅταν
δ' ἐντὸς γενώμεθα, τὴν ταχίστην ἄγετε ἐπὶ τὰ
βασίλεια.

25. Καὶ μήν, ἔφασαν οἱ ἀμφὶ τὸν Γωβρύαν,
οὐδὲν ἂν εἴη θαυμαστὸν εἰ καὶ ἄκλειστοι αἱ
πύλαι αἱ τοῦ βασιλείου εἶεν ὡς ἐν κώμῳ· δειπνεῖ[2]
γὰρ ἡ πόλις πᾶσα τῇδε τῇ νυκτί. φυλακῇ μέντοι
πρὸ τῶν πυλῶν ἐντευξόμεθα· ἔστι γὰρ ἀεὶ τεταγμένη.

Οὐκ ἂν μέλλειν[3] δέοι, ἔφη ὁ Κῦρος, ἀλλ'
ἰέναι, ἵνα ἀπαρασκεύους ὡς μάλιστα λάβωμεν
τοὺς ἄνδρας.

26. Ἐπεὶ δὲ ταῦτα ἐρρήθη, ἐπορεύοντο· τῶν
δὲ ἀπαντώντων οἱ μὲν ἀπέθνησκον παιόμενοι,
οἱ δὲ ἔφευγον πάλιν εἴσω, οἱ δὲ ἐβόων· οἱ δ'
ἀμφὶ τὸν Γωβρύαν συνεβόων αὐτοῖς, ὡς κωμασταὶ

---

[1] κεχριμέναι Cobet, most Edd. ; κεχρισμέναι MSS., Breitenbach.

[2] ὡς . . . δειπνεῖ Hug ; ὡς . . . δοκεῖ xzV, Dindorf, Breitenbach ; κωμοδοκεῖ y ; κωμάζει Stephanus, Marchant, Gemoll.

[3] ἂν μέλλειν Muret, Edd.; ἀμελεῖν z ; ἂν ἀμελεῖν xy.

on the house-tops and hurl down missiles right and left, you need not be in the least afraid of that; for if any do go up upon their houses, we have a god on our side, Hephaestus. And their porticoes are very inflammable, for the doors are made of palm-wood and covered with bituminous varnish which will burn like tinder; 23. while we, on our side, have plenty of pine-wood for torches, which will quickly produce a mighty conflagration; we have also plenty of pitch and tow, which will quickly spread the flames everywhere, so that those upon the house-tops must either quickly leave their posts or quickly be consumed.

24. "But come, to arms! and with the help of the gods I will lead you on. And do you, Gadatas and Gobryas, show the streets, for you are familiar with them. And when we get inside the walls, lead us by the quickest route to the royal palace."

25. "Aye," answered Gobryas and his staff, "in view of the revelry, it would not be at all surprising if the gates leading to the palace were open, for all the city is feasting this night. Still, we shall find a guard before the gates, for one is always posted there."

"We must lose no time, then," said Cyrus. "Forward, that we may catch the men as unprepared as we can."

26. When these words were spoken, they advanced. Babylon falls And of those they met on the way, some fell by their swords, some fled back into their houses, some shouted to them; and Gobryas and his men shouted

ὄντες καὶ αὐτοί· καὶ ἰόντες ᾗ ἐδύναντο [ὡς]¹
τάχιστα ἐπὶ τοῖς βασιλείοις ἐγένοντο. 27. καὶ
οἱ μὲν σὺν τῷ Γωβρύᾳ καὶ Γαδάτᾳ τεταγμένοι
κεκλειμένας εὑρίσκουσι τὰς πύλας τοῦ βασιλείου·
οἱ δὲ ἐπὶ τοὺς φύλακας ταχθέντες ἐπεισπίπτουσιν
αὐτοῖς πίνουσι πρὸς φῶς πολύ, καὶ εὐθὺς ὡς
πολεμίοις ἐχρῶντο αὐτοῖς. 28. ὡς δὲ κραυγὴ
καὶ κτύπος ἐγίγνετο, αἰσθόμενοι οἱ ἔνδον τοῦ
θορύβου, κελεύσαντος τοῦ βασιλέως σκέψασθαι
τί εἴη τὸ πρᾶγμα, ἐκθέουσί τινες ἀνοίξαντες τὰς
πύλας. 29. οἱ δ᾽ ἀμφὶ τὸν Γαδάταν ὡς εἶδον
τὰς πύλας χαλώσας εἰσπίπτουσι καὶ τοῖς πάλιν
φεύγουσιν εἴσω ἐφεπόμενοι καὶ παίοντες ἀφικνοῦνται πρὸς τὸν βασιλέα· καὶ ἤδη ἑστηκότα
αὐτὸν καὶ ἐσπασμένον ὃν εἶχεν ἀκινάκην εὑρίσκουσι. 30. καὶ τοῦτον μὲν οἱ σὺν Γαδάτᾳ
καὶ Γωβρύᾳ ἐχειροῦντο· καὶ οἱ σὺν αὐτῷ δὲ
ἀπέθνησκον, ὁ μὲν προβαλόμενός τι, ὁ δὲ φεύγων,
ὁ δέ γε καὶ ἀμυνόμενος ὅτῳ ἐδύνατο.

31. Ὁ δὲ Κῦρος διέπεμπε τὰς τῶν ἱππέων
τάξεις κατὰ τὰς ὁδοὺς καὶ προεῖπεν οὓς μὲν
ἔξω λαμβάνοιεν κατακαίνειν, τοὺς δ᾽ ἐν ταῖς
οἰκίαις κηρύττειν τοὺς Συριστὶ ἐπισταμένους
ἔνδον μένειν· εἰ δέ τις ἔξω ληφθείη, ὅτι θανα-
τώσοιτο.

32. Οἱ μὲν δὴ ταῦτ᾽ ἐποίουν. Γαδάτας δὲ
καὶ Γωβρύας ἧκον· καὶ θεοὺς μὲν πρῶτον προσ-
εκύνουν, ὅτι τετιμωρημένοι ἦσαν τὸν ἀνόσιον
βασιλέα, ἔπειτα δὲ Κύρου κατεφίλουν καὶ χεῖρας

¹ ὡς MSS.; [ὡς] Hug, Etonensis 1613, Edd.

back to them, as if they were fellow-revellers. They advanced as fast as they could and were soon at the palace. 27. And Gobryas and Gadatas and their troops found the gates leading to the palace locked, and those who had been appointed to attack the guard fell upon them as they were drinking by a blazing fire, and without waiting they dealt with them as with foes. 28. But, as a noise and tumult ensued, those within heard the uproar, and at the king's command to see what the matter was, some of them opened the gates and ran out. 29. And when Gadatas and his men saw the gates open they dashed in in pursuit of the others as they fled back into the palace, and dealing blows right and left they came into the presence of the king; and they found him already risen with his dagger in his hand. 30. And Gadatas and Gobryas and their followers overpowered him; and those about the king perished also, one where he had sought some shelter, another while running away, another while actually trying to defend himself with whatever he could. *Gobryas and Gadatas avenge their wrongs*

31. Cyrus then sent the companies of cavalry around through the streets and gave them orders to cut down all whom they found out of doors, while he directed those who understood Assyrian to proclaim to those in their houses that they should stay there, for if any one should be caught outside, he would be put to death.

32. While they were thus occupied, Gadatas and Gobryas came up; and first of all they did homage to the gods, seeing that they had avenged themselves

καὶ πόδας, πολλὰ δακρύοντες ἅμα χαρᾷ [καὶ
εὐφραινόμενοι].[1]

33. Ἐπεὶ δὲ ἡμέρα ἐγένετο καὶ ᾔσθοντο οἱ τὰς
ἄκρας ἔχοντες ἑαλωκυῖάν τε τὴν πόλιν καὶ τὸν
βασιλέα τεθνηκότα, παραδιδόασι καὶ τὰς ἄκρας.
34. ὁ δὲ Κῦρος τὰς μὲν ἄκρας εὐθὺς παρελάμβανε
καὶ φρουράρχους τε καὶ φρουροὺς εἰς ταύτας
ἀνέπεμπε, τοὺς δὲ τεθνηκότας θάπτειν ἐφῆκε τοῖς
προσήκουσι· τοὺς δὲ κήρυκας κηρύττειν ἐκέλευσεν ἀποφέρειν πάντας τὰ ὅπλα Βαβυλωνίους·
ὅπου δὲ ληφθήσοιτο ὅπλα ἐν οἰκίᾳ, προηγόρευεν
ὡς πάντες οἱ ἔνδον ἀποθανοῖντο. οἱ μὲν δὴ
ἀπέφερον, ὁ δὲ Κῦρος ταῦτα μὲν εἰς τὰς ἄκρας
κατέθετο, ὡς εἴη ἕτοιμα, εἴ τί ποτε δέοι χρῆσθαι.

35. Ἐπεὶ δὲ ταῦτ' ἐπέπρακτο, πρῶτον μὲν τοὺς
μάγους καλέσας, ὡς δοριαλώτου τῆς πόλεως
οὔσης ἀκροθίνια τοῖς θεοῖς καὶ τεμένη ἐκέλευσεν
ἐξελεῖν· ἐκ τούτου δὲ καὶ οἰκίας διεδίδου καὶ
ἀρχεῖα τούτοις οὕσπερ κοινῶνας ἐνόμιζε τῶν κατα-
πεπραγμένων· οὕτω δὲ διένειμεν ὥσπερ ἐδέδοκτο
τὰ κράτιστα τοῖς ἀρίστοις. εἰ δέ τις οἴοιτο μεῖον
ἔχειν, διδάσκειν προσιόντας ἐκέλευε.

36. Προεῖπε δὲ Βαβυλωνίοις μὲν τὴν γῆν ἐργάζεσθαι καὶ τοὺς δασμοὺς ἀποφέρειν καὶ θεραπεύειν τούτους οἷς ἕκαστοι αὐτῶν ἐδόθησαν·
Πέρσας δὲ τοὺς κοινῶνας καὶ τῶν συμμάχων ὅσοι

[1] καὶ εὐφραινόμενοι MSS., Dindorf, Breitenbach ; bracketed
by Lincke, Hug, Marchant, Gemoll.

upon the wicked king, and then they kissed Cyrus's hands and his feet with many tears of joy.

33. And when day dawned and those in possession of the citadels discovered that the city was taken and the king slain, they surrendered the citadels, too. The entire city yields to Cyrus
34. And Cyrus at once took possession of the citadels and sent up to them guards and officers of the guards. As for the dead, he gave their relatives permission to bury them. He furthermore ordered the heralds to make proclamation that all Babylonians deliver up their arms; and he ordered that wherever arms should be found in any house, all the occupants should be put to the sword. So they delivered up their arms and Cyrus stored them in the citadels, so that they might be ready if he ever needed them for use.

35. When all this was finished, he first called the magi and requested them, inasmuch as the city had been taken by the sword, to select sanctuaries and the first fruits of the booty for the gods. Next he distributed the private houses and official residences among those whom he considered to have had a share in what had been achieved; and he made the division in the way that had been decided upon— the best to the most meritorious. And if any one thought he had less than he should, he bade him come and explain his reasons for thinking so.

36. He ordered the Babylonians, moreover, to go on tilling their lands, to pay their tribute, and to serve those to whom they had severally been assigned; and he directed the Persians who had shared in the expedition and as many of the allies as chose

μένειν ἡροῦντο παρ' αὐτῷ ὡς δεσπότας ὧν ἔλαβον
προηγόρευε διαλέγεσθαι.

37. Ἐκ δὲ τούτου ἐπιθυμῶν ὁ Κῦρος ἤδη
κατασκευάσασθαι καὶ αὐτὸς ὡς βασιλεῖ ἡγεῖτο
πρέπειν, ἔδοξεν αὐτῷ τοῦτο σὺν τῇ τῶν φίλων
γνώμῃ ποιῆσαι, ὡς ὅτι ἥκιστα ἂν ἐπιφθόνως
σπάνιός τε καὶ σεμνὸς φανείη. ὧδε οὖν ἐμηχανᾶτο τοῦτο. ἅμα τῇ ἡμέρᾳ στὰς ὅπου ἐδόκει
ἐπιτήδειον εἶναι προσεδέχετο τὸν βουλόμενον
λέγειν τι καὶ ἀποκρινάμενος ἀπέπεμπεν. 38. οἱ δ'
ἄνθρωποι ὡς ἔγνωσαν ὅτι προσδέχοιτο, ἧκον
ἀμήχανοι τὸ πλῆθος· καὶ ὠθουμένων περὶ τοῦ
προσελθεῖν μηχανή τε πολλὴ καὶ μάχη ἦν.
39. οἱ δὲ ὑπηρέται ὡς ἐδύναντο διακρίνοντες
προσίεσαν.[1]

Ὁπότε δέ τις καὶ τῶν φίλων διωσάμενος τὸν
ὄχλον προφανείη, προτείνων ὁ Κῦρος τὴν χεῖρα
προσήγετο αὐτοὺς καὶ οὕτως ἔλεγεν· Ἄνδρες
φίλοι, περιμένετε, ἕως ἂν[2] τὸν ὄχλον διωσώ-
μεθα· ἔπειτα δὲ καθ' ἡσυχίαν· συγγενησόμεθα.
οἱ μὲν δὴ φίλοι περιέμενον, ὁ δ' ὄχλος πλείων καὶ
πλείων ἐπέρρει, ὥστ' ἔφθασεν ἑσπέρα γενομένη
πρὶν τοῖς φίλοις αὐτὸν σχολάσαι [καὶ][3] συγγε-
νέσθαι. 40. οὕτω δὴ ὁ Κῦρος λέγει, Ὥρα,[4] ἔφη, ὦ
ἄνδρες, νῦν μὲν [καιρὸς][5] διαλυθῆναι· αὔριον δὲ
πρῲ ἔλθετε· καὶ γὰρ ἐγὼ βούλομαι ὑμῖν τι
διαλεχθῆναι.

---

[1] προσίεσαν Stephanus, Edd.; προσήεσαν MSS.
[2] ἂν Hertlein, Hug, Marchant, Gemoll; not in MSS.,
Dindorf, Breitenbach.
[3] καὶ MSS., Edd.; bracketed by Gemoll.
[4] Ὥρα Cobet, most Edd.; ἆρα or ἄρα MSS., Breitenbach.
[5] καιρὸς MSS. ; omitted by Cobet, Edd.

to remain with him to address those who had fallen
to their share as a master would his servants.

37. After this, Cyrus conceived a desire to establish
himself as he thought became a king, but he decided
to do it with the approval of his friends, in such a
way that his public appearances should be rare and
solemn and yet excite as little jealousy as possible.
So he adopted the following plan : at day-break he
would take his station in a place that seemed to him
to be adapted to the purpose and there receive all
who had any matter to bring before him, give them
an answer, and send them away. 38. But when
people learned that he was holding audience, they
came in an unmanageable throng, and as they
crowded up to get in there was no end of trickery
and contention. 39. And his attendants would admit
them, making the best discrimination they could.

But whenever any of his personal friends managed
to push their way through the throng and catch his
eye, Cyrus would stretch out his hand, draw them
up to him, and say : " Just wait, friends, until we get
rid of the crowd, and then we will enjoy each other's
company quietly." So his friends would wait, but the
throng would stream in greater and greater, so that
evening would set in before he had leisure to share
his friends' company. 40. So Cyrus would say :
" Gentlemen, it is now time to separate ; come to-
morrow morning ; for I, too, have something to talk
over with you."

Cyrus holds court

His personal friends are crowded out

XENOPHON

Ἀκούσαντες ταῦτα οἱ φίλοι ἄσμενοι ὤχοντο
ἀποθέοντες, δίκην δεδωκότες ὑπὸ πάντων τῶν
ἀναγκαίων. καὶ τότε μὲν οὕτως ἐκοιμήθησαν.

41. Τῇ δ' ὑστεραίᾳ ὁ μὲν Κῦρος παρῆν εἰς τὸ
αὐτὸ χωρίον, ἀνθρώπων δὲ πολὺ πλεῖον πλῆθος
περιειστήκει βουλομένων προσιέναι, καὶ πολὺ
πρότερον ἢ οἱ φίλοι παρῆσαν. ὁ οὖν Κῦρος
περιστησάμενος τῶν ξυστοφόρων Περσῶν κύκλον
μέγαν εἶπε μηδένα παριέναι ἢ τοὺς φίλους τε καὶ
ἄρχοντας τῶν Περσῶν τε καὶ τῶν συμμάχων.
42. ἐπεὶ δὲ συνῆλθον οὗτοι, ἔλεξεν ὁ Κῦρος
αὐτοῖς τοιάδε· Ἄνδρες φίλοι καὶ σύμμαχοι, τοῖς
μὲν θεοῖς οὐδὲν ἂν ἔχοιμεν μέμψασθαι τὸ μὴ
οὐχὶ μέχρι τοῦδε πάντα ὅσα ηὐχόμεθα καταπε-
πραχέναι. εἰ μέντοι τοιοῦτον ἔσται τὸ μεγάλα
πράττειν ὥστε μὴ οἷόν τ' εἶναι μήτε ἀμφ' αὑτὸ
σχολὴν ἔχειν μήτε μετὰ τῶν φίλων εὐφρανθῆναι,
ἐγὼ μὲν χαίρειν ταύτην τὴν εὐδαιμονίαν κελεύω.
43. ἐνενοήσατε γάρ, ἔφη, καὶ χθὲς δήπου ὅτι ἔωθεν
ἀρξάμενοι ἀκούειν τῶν προσιόντων οὐκ ἐλήξαμεν
πρόσθεν ἑσπέρας· καὶ νῦν ὁρᾶτε τούτους ἄλλους
πλείονας τῶν χθὲς παρόντας [1] ὡς πράγματα ἡμῖν
παρέξοντας. 44. εἰ οὖν τις τούτοις ὑφέξει ἑαυτόν,
λογίζομαι μικρὸν μέν τι ὑμῖν μέρος ἐμοῦ μετεσό-
μενον, μικρὸν δέ τι ἐμοὶ ὑμῶν· ἐμαυτοῦ μέντο
σαφῶς οἶδ' ὅτι οὐδ' ὁτιοῦν μοι μετέσται.

45. Ἔτι δ', ἔφη, καὶ ἄλλο ὁρῶ γελοῖον πρᾶγμα
ἐγὼ γὰρ δήπου ὑμῖν μὲν ὥσπερ εἰκὸς διάκειμαι
τούτων δὲ τῶν περιεστηκότων ἤ τινα ἢ οὐδένα

---

[1] παρόντας yG, Edd.; παρόντων xAHV.

278

Upon hearing this, his friends gladly departed, running from his presence, for they had paid the penalty for ignoring all the wants of nature. Thus then they went to rest.

41. On the following day, Cyrus went to the same place and long before his friends came, there was a much greater crowd of people standing there desiring audience with him. So Cyrus stationed a large circle of Persian lancers about him and gave orders that no one should be admitted except his friends and the officers of the Persians and the allies. 42. And when they had come together, Cyrus addressed them as follows: "Friends and allies, we cannot possibly find any fault with the gods that all that we wished for so far has not been fulfilled. However, if great success is to have such consequences that a man is not to be able to have some leisure for himself nor time to enjoy himself with his friends, I am ready to bid farewell to that sort of happiness. 43. For yesterday, too, you saw, of course, that although we began at dawn to give audience to those who came to see us, we did not get through before evening; and now you see that these others, who are here in greater numbers than came yesterday, will give us even more trouble. 44. If, therefore, one is to sacrifice oneself to such affairs, I reckon that you will have but a small part in my society or I in yours; while in myself I know that I shall certainly have no part at all.

45. "I see also," he went on, "still another absurd feature in all this: while my affection for you is, as you know, what it naturally ought to be, of these

He discusses organization of his court

οἶδα,[1] καὶ οὗτοι πάντες οὕτω παρεσκευασμένοι
εἰσὶν ὡς, ἢν νικῶσιν ὑμᾶς ὠθοῦντες, πρότεροι ἃ
βούλονται ὑμῶν παρ' ἐμοῦ διαπραξόμενοι. ἐγὼ
δὲ ἠξίουν τοὺς τοιούτους, εἴ τίς τι ἐμοῦ δέοιτο,
θεραπεύειν ὑμᾶς τοὺς ἐμοὺς φίλους δεομένους
προσαγωγῆς.

46. Ἴσως ἂν οὖν εἴποι τις, τί δῆτα οὐχ οὕτως
ἐξ ἀρχῆς παρεσκευασάμην, ἀλλὰ παρεῖχον ἐν τῷ
μέσῳ ἐμαυτόν. ὅτι τὰ τοῦ πολέμου τοιαῦτα
ἐγίγνωσκον ὄντα ὡς μὴ ὑστερίζειν δέον τὸν ἄρχοντα μήτε τῷ εἰδέναι ἃ δεῖ μήτε τῷ πράττειν
ἂν καιρὸς ᾖ· τοὺς δὲ σπανίους ἰδεῖν στρατηγοὺς
πολλὰ ἐνόμιζον ὧν δεῖ πραχθῆναι παριέναι.

47. Νῦν δ' ἐπειδὴ καὶ ὁ φιλοπονώτατος πόλεμος
ἀναπέπαυται, δοκεῖ μοι καὶ ἡ ἐμὴ ψυχὴ ἀναπαύ-
σεώς τινος ἀξιοῦν τυγχάνειν. ὡς οὖν ἐμοῦ ἀπο-
ροῦντος ὅ τι ἂν τύχοιμι ποιῶν ὥστε καλῶς ἔχειν
τά τε ἡμέτερα καὶ τὰ τῶν ἄλλων ὧν ἡμᾶς δεῖ
ἐπιμέλεσθαι, συμβουλευέτω ὅ τι τις ὁρᾷ συμφο-
ρώτατον.

48. Κῦρος μὲν οὕτως εἶπεν· ἀνίσταται δ' ἐπ'
αὐτῷ Ἀρτάβαζος ὁ συγγενής ποτε φήσας εἶναι
καὶ εἶπεν, Ἦ καλῶς, ἔφη, ἐποίησας, ὦ Κῦρε,
ἄρξας τοῦ λόγου. ἐγὼ γὰρ ἔτι νέου μὲν ὄντος
σοῦ πάνυ ἀρξάμενος ἐπεθύμουν φίλος γενέσθαι,
ὁρῶν δέ σε οὐδὲν δεόμενον ἐμοῦ κατώκνουν σοι
προσιέναι. 49. ἐπεὶ δ' ἔτυχές ποτε καὶ ἐμοῦ δεηθεὶς [προθύμως] [2] ἐξαγγεῖλαι πρὸς Μήδους τὰ

---

[1] οἶδα z, Edd.; γιγνώσκω y; εἶδον X.
[2] προθύμως MSS., earlier Edd.; [προθύμως] Hug, later Edd.

who stand about here I know few or none; and yet all these have made up their minds that if they can get ahead of you in crowding in, they will obtain what they wish from me before you can. Now what I expected all such to do, if any one wanted anything from me, was to get into favour with you as my friends and ask you for an introduction.

46. " Perhaps some one may ask why I did not adopt this arrangement in the beginning instead of making myself accessible to all. It was, I answer, because I realized that the demands of war made it necessary for a commander not to be behind others in finding out what he ought to know nor in doing what it is expedient that he should do. And I thought generals who were seldom to be seen often neglected much that needed to be done.

47. " But now that this most toilsome war is really over, it seems to me that I, too, am entitled to find some relaxation of spirit. So, while I am in doubt as to what I could do to harmonize our interests and those of the others for whom we must care, let any one who sees what is to the best advantage give me a word of counsel."

48. Thus Cyrus spoke. After him Artabazus arose —the man who had once claimed to be his kinsman— and said: " I am very glad, Cyrus, that you have opened this discussion. For when you were still a lad, I was very anxious even from the first to be a friend of yours; but when I saw that I could be of no use to you, I shrank from approaching you. 49. But when you once happened to need even my services to publish among the Medes the concession

Artabazus reviews his own relations with Cyrus

IV. i. 21-24

παρὰ Κυαξάρου, ἐλογιζόμην, εἰ ταῦτα προθύμως
σοι συλλάβοιμι, ὡς οἰκεῖός τέ σοι ἐσοίμην καὶ
ἐξέσοιτό μοι διαλέγεσθαί σοι ὁπόσον χρόνον βουλοίμην. κἀκεῖνα μὲν δὴ ἐπράχθη ὥστε σε
ἐπαινεῖν.

50. Μετὰ τοῦτο Ὑρκάνιοι μὲν πρῶτοι φίλοι
ἡμῖν ἐγένοντο καὶ μάλα πεινῶσι συμμάχων· ὥστε
μόνον οὐκ ἐν ταῖς ἀγκάλαις περιεφέρομεν αὐτοὺς
ἀγαπῶντες. μετὰ δὲ τοῦτο ἐπεὶ ἑάλω τὸ πολέμιον
στρατόπεδον, οὐκ οἶμαι σχολή σοι ἦν ἀμφ' ἐμὲ
ἔχειν· καὶ ἐγώ σοι συνεγίγνωσκον. 51. ἐκ δὲ
τούτου Γωβρύας ἡμῖν φίλος ἐγένετο, καὶ ἐγὼ ἔχαι-
ρον· καὶ αὖθις Γαδάτας· καὶ ἤδη ἔργον σοῦ ἦν
μεταλαβεῖν· ἐπεί γε μέντοι καὶ Σάκαι καὶ
Καδούσιοι σύμμαχοι ἐγεγένηντο, θεραπεύειν εἰκότως ἔδει τούτους· καὶ γὰρ οὗτοι σὲ ἐθεράπευον.

52. Ὡς δ' ἤλθομεν πάλιν ἔνθεν ὡρμήθημεν,
ὁρῶν σε ἀμφ' ἵππους ἔχοντα, ἀμφ' ἅρματα,
ἀμφὶ μηχανάς, ἡγούμην, ἐπεὶ ἀπὸ τούτων σχο-
λάσαις, τότε σε καὶ ἀμφ' ἐμὲ ἕξειν σχολήν.
ὥς γε μέντοι ἦλθεν ἡ δεινὴ ἀγγελία τὸ πάντας
ἀνθρώπους ἐφ' ἡμᾶς συλλέγεσθαι, ἐγίγνωσκον ὅτι
ταῦτα μέγιστα εἴη· εἰ δὲ ταῦτα καλῶς γένοιτο,
εὖ ἤδη ἐδόκουν εἰδέναι ὅτι πολλὴ ἔσοιτο ἀφθονία
τῆς ἐμῆς καὶ [τῆς]¹ σῆς συνουσίας.

53. Καὶ νῦν δὴ νενικήκαμέν τε τὴν μεγάλην
μάχην καὶ Σάρδεις καὶ Κροῖσον ὑποχείριον ἔχομεν
καὶ Βαβυλῶνα ᾑρήκαμεν καὶ πάντας² κατεστράμ-

---

¹ τῆς MSS., Breitenbach; omitted by Dindorf, Hug,
Marchant, Gemoll.
² πάντας xy, Hug, Marchant, Gemoll; πάντα z, Dindorf,
Breitenbach.

obtained from Cyaxares, I reasoned that, if I gave you my earnest support in this, I then might be your intimate friend and talk with you as much as I pleased. Now that particular commission was executed in such a way as to call for your approval.

50. "After that, the Hyrcanians were the first to become our friends, and at a time, too, when we were very hungry for allies, so that in our affection for them we all but carried them around in our arms. And after that, when the enemy's camp was taken, you did not have any time to concern yourself about me, I suppose, and I did not blame you. 51. Next, Gobryas became our friend, and I was glad; and then Gadatas; and then it was hard work to get any share of your attention. When, however, both the Sacians and the Cadusians had become our allies, you must needs show them proper attention, for they also were attentive to you.

52. "When we came back to the place from which His hopes we had started, I saw you busy with horses and too long chariots and engines, but I thought that as soon as deferred you had leisure from these distractions you would have some time to think of me. Still, when the terrible news came that the whole world was assembling against us, I realized that that was a matter of paramount importance; but if it should turn out successfully, then at last I thought I might be sure that the intercourse between me and you would be unstinted.

53. "And now we have won the great battle and have Sardis and Croesus in subjection; we have taken Babylon and subjugated everything; and yet

μεθα, καὶ μὰ τὸν Μίθρην ἐγώ τοι ἐχθές, εἰ μὴ
πολλοῖς διεπύκτευσα, οὐκ ἂν ἐδυνάμην σοι προσελθεῖν. ἐπεί γε μέντοι ἐδεξιώσω με καὶ παρὰ σοὶ
ἐκέλευσας μένειν, ἤδη περίβλεπτος ἦν, ὅτι μετὰ
σοῦ ἄσιτος καὶ ἄποτος διημέρευον. 54. νῦν οὖν
εἰ μὲν ἔσται πῃ ὅπως οἱ πλείστου ἄξιοι γεγενημένοι πλεῖστόν σου μέρος μεθέξομεν· εἰ δὲ μή,
πάλιν αὖ ἐγὼ ἐθέλω παρὰ σοῦ ἐξαγγέλλειν
ἀπιέναι πάντας ἀπὸ σοῦ πλὴν ἡμῶν τῶν ἐξ ἀρχῆς
φίλων.

55. Ἐπὶ τούτῳ ἐγέλασε μὲν ὁ Κῦρος καὶ ἄλλοι
πολλοί· Χρυσάντας δ' ἀνέστη ὁ Πέρσης καὶ ἔλεξεν
ὧδε· Ἀλλὰ τὸ μὲν πρόσθεν, ὦ Κῦρε, εἰκότως ἐν
τῷ φανερῷ σαυτὸν παρεῖχες, δι' ἅ τε αὐτὸς εἶπας [1]
καὶ ὅτι οὐχ ἡμᾶς σοι μάλιστα ἦν θεραπευτέον.
ἡμεῖς μὲν γὰρ καὶ ἡμῶν αὐτῶν ἕνεκα παρῆμεν· τὸ
δὲ πλῆθος ἔδει ἀνακτᾶσθαι ἐκ παντὸς τρόπου,
ὅπως ὅτι ἥδιστα συμπονεῖν καὶ συγκινδυνεύειν
ἡμῖν ἐθέλοιεν. 56. νῦν δ' ἐπεὶ οὐ τούτῳ τῷ τρόπῳ
μόνον ἄρχεις, ἀλλὰ καὶ ἄλλως [2] ἀνακτᾶσθαι
δύνασαι οὓς καιρὸς εἴη, ἤδη καὶ οἰκίας σε τυχεῖν
ἄξιον· ἢ τί ἀπολαύσαις ἂν τῆς ἀρχῆς, εἰ μόνος
ἄμοιρος εἴης ἑστίας, οὗ οὔτε ὁσιώτερον χωρίον ἐν
ἀνθρώποις οὔτε ἥδιον οὔτε οἰκειότερόν ἐστιν οὐδέν;
ἔπειτα δ', ἔφη, οὐκ ἂν οἴει καὶ ἡμᾶς αἰσχύνεσθαι,

[1] εἶπας Dindorf, Breitenbach, Hug, Marchant; εἶπες MSS.,
Gemoll.
[2] οὐ . . . ἄλλως Hug; οὐχ οὕτω τρόπον (-ου DG[1]) μονον ἔχεις
ἀλλὰ καὶ ἄλλους xy; οὖν τρόπῳ μόνῳ ἔχεις κ.τ.λ. z; οὐχ οὕτω
τρόπῳ μόνῳ ἔχεις V; no two editors seem to agree on the
restoration of this corrupt passage.

yesterday, by Mithras, if I had not fought my way through the crowd with my fists, I vow I could not have got near you. However, when you took me by the hand and bade me stay by you, I was the object of all envious eyes, for having spent a whole day with you—without a thing to eat or drink. 54. If, therefore, it can now be so arranged that we, who have proved ourselves most deserving, shall have the largest share of your company, well and good; if not, I am ready once again to make a proclamation in your name to the effect that all shall keep away from you, except us who have been your friends from the beginning."

55. At this Cyrus laughed as did many others. Then Chrysantas, the Persian, rose and spoke as follows: "Well, Cyrus, it was hitherto quite proper for you to make yourself approachable, for the reasons you have yourself assigned and also because we were not the ones whose favour you most needed to win; for we were with you for our own sakes. But it was imperative for you in every way to win the affections of the multitude, so that they might consent to toil and risk their lives with us as gladly as possible. 56. But now, seeing that you do not hold your power by this method alone but are in a position in still other ways to win the hearts of those whom it is of advantage for you to win, it is meet that you should now have a home. Else what enjoyment would you have of your power, if you alone were to have no hearth and home of your own? For there is no spot on earth more sacred, more sweet, or more dear than that. And finally," he said, "do you not think that we also should be ashamed to see you

Chrysantas proposes a royal home for Cyrus

εἰ σὲ μὲν ὁρῶμεν ἔξω καρτεροῦντα, αὐτοὶ δ' ἐν
οἰκίαις εἶμεν καὶ σοῦ δοκοίημεν πλεονεκτεῖν;

57. Ἐπεὶ δὲ Χρυσάντας ταῦτα ἔλεξε, συνηγόρευον αὐτῷ κατὰ ταὐτὰ[1] πολλοί. ἐκ τούτου δὴ
εἰσέρχεται εἰς τὰ βασίλεια, καὶ τὰ ἐκ Σάρδεων
χρήματα ἐνταῦθ' οἱ ἄγοντες ἀπέδοσαν. ἐπεὶ δ'
εἰσῆλθεν ὁ Κῦρος, πρῶτον μὲν Ἑστίᾳ ἔθυσεν,
ἔπειτα Διὶ βασιλεῖ καὶ εἴ τινι ἄλλῳ θεῷ οἱ μάγοι
ἐξηγοῦντο.

58. Ποιήσας δὲ ταῦτα τἆλλα ἤδη ἤρχετο
διοικεῖν. ἐννοῶν δὲ τὸ αὑτοῦ πρᾶγμα ὅτι ἐπιχει-
ροίη μὲν ἄρχειν πολλῶν ἀνθρώπων, παρασκευάζοιτο δὲ οἰκεῖν ἐν πόλει τῇ μεγίστῃ τῶν φα-
νερῶν, αὕτη δ' οὕτως ἔχοι αὐτῷ ὡς πολεμιωτάτη
ἂν γένοιτο ἀνδρὶ πόλις, ταῦτα δὴ λογιζόμενος
φυλακῆς περὶ τὸ σῶμα ἡγήσατο δεῖσθαι.
59. γνοὺς δ' ὅτι οὐδαμοῦ ἄνθρωποι εὐχειρωτότεροί
εἰσιν ἢ ἐν σίτοις καὶ ποτοῖς καὶ λουτροῖς καὶ κοίτῃ
καὶ ὕπνῳ, ἐσκόπει τίνας ἂν ἐν τούτοις περὶ ἑαυτὸν
πιστοτάτους ἔχοι. ἐνόμισε δὲ μὴ ἂν γενέσθαι
ποτὲ πιστὸν ἄνθρωπον ὅστις ἄλλον μᾶλλον φιλή-
σοι τοῦ τῆς φυλακῆς δεομένου. 60. τοὺς μὲν
οὖν ἔχοντας παῖδας ἢ γυναῖκας συναρμοττούσας
ἢ παιδικὰ ἔγνω φύσει[2] ἠναγκάσθαι ταῦτα μάλιστα
φιλεῖν· τοὺς δ' εὐνούχους ὁρῶν πάντων τούτων
στερομένους ἡγήσατο τούτους ἂν περὶ πλείστου
ποιεῖσθαι οἵτινες δύναιντο πλουτίζειν μάλιστα
αὐτοὺς καὶ βοηθεῖν, εἴ τι ἀδικοῖντο, καὶ τιμὰς

---

[1] ταὐτὰ Muretus, Edd.; ταῦτα MSS.
[2] φύσει MSS., Edd.; φύσει ἂν Hug.

iving in discomfort, out of doors, while we ourselves
ived in houses and seemed to be better off than
you?"

57. When Chrysantas had finished his speech, Cyrus
many supported him in the same tenor. After that, moves into
Cyrus moved into the royal palace, and those who the palace
had charge of the treasures brought from Sardis
delivered them there. And after he took possession,
Cyrus sacrificed first to Hestia, then to sovereign
Zeus, and then to any other god that the magi
suggested.

58. This done, he began at once to organize the
rest of his court. And as he considered his own
situation, that he was undertaking to hold sway over
many people, and preparing to dwell in the greatest
of all famous cities, and that that city was as hostile
to him as a city could be to any man—as he reflected
on this, he decided that he needed a body-guard.
59. And as he realized that men are nowhere an easier He selects
prey to violence than when at meals or at wine, in his body-
the bath, or in bed and asleep, he looked around to guard
see who were the most faithful men that he could
have around him at such times; and he held that no
man was ever faithful who loved any one else better
than the one who needed his protection. 60. Those,
therefore, who had children or congenial wives or
sweethearts, such he believed were by nature con-
strained to love them best. But as he observed that
eunuchs were not susceptible to any such affections,
he thought that they would esteem most highly
those who were in the best position to make them
rich and to stand by them, if ever they were wronged,

περιάπτειν αὐτοῖς· τούτοις [1] δ᾽ εὐεργετοῦντα
ὑπερβάλλειν αὐτὸν οὐδέν᾽ ἂν ἡγεῖτο δύνασθαι.
61. πρὸς δὲ τούτοις ἄδοξοι ὄντες οἱ εὐνοῦχοι παρὰ
τοῖς ἄλλοις ἀνθρώποις καὶ διὰ τοῦτο δεσπότου
ἐπικούρου προσδέονται· οὐδεὶς γὰρ ἀνὴρ ὅστις
οὐκ ἂν ἀξιώσειεν εὐνούχου πλέον ἔχειν ἐν παντί,
εἰ μή τι ἄλλο κρεῖττον ἀπείργοι· δεσπότῃ δὲ
πιστὸν ὄντα οὐδὲν κωλύει πρωτεύειν καὶ τὸν
εὐνοῦχον. 62. ὃ δ᾽ ἂν μάλιστά τις οἰηθείη, ἀνάλκιδας τοὺς εὐνούχους γίγνεσθαι, οὐδὲ τοῦτο
ἐφαίνετο αὐτῷ. ἐτεκμαίρετο δὲ καὶ ἐκ τῶν ἄλλων
ζῴων ὅτι οἵ τε ὑβρισταὶ ἵπποι ἐκτεμνόμενοι τοῦ
μὲν δάκνειν καὶ ὑβρίζειν ἀποπαύονται, πολεμικοὶ
δὲ οὐδὲν ἧττον γίγνονται, οἵ τε ταῦροι ἐκτεμνόμενοι τοῦ μὲν μέγα φρονεῖν καὶ ἀπειθεῖν ὑφίενται,
τοῦ δ᾽ ἰσχύειν καὶ ἐργάζεσθαι οὐ στερίσκονται,
καὶ οἱ κύνες δὲ ὡσαύτως τοῦ μὲν ἀπολείπειν τοὺς
δεσπότας ἀποπαύονται ἐκτεμνόμενοι, φυλάττειν
δὲ καὶ εἰς θήραν οὐδὲν κακίους γίγνονται. 63. καὶ
οἵ γε ἄνθρωποι ὡσαύτως ἠρεμέστεροι γίγνονται
στερισκόμενοι ταύτης τῆς ἐπιθυμίας, οὐ μέντοι
ἀμελέστεροί γε τῶν προσταττομένων, οὐδ᾽ ἧττόν τι
ἱππικοί, οὐδὲ ἧττόν τι ἀκοντιστικοί, οὐδὲ ἧττον
φιλότιμοι. 64. κατάδηλοι δ᾽ ἐγίγνοντο καὶ ἐν τοῖς
πολέμοις καὶ ἐν ταῖς θήραις ὅτι ἔσῳζον τὸ φιλό-
νικον ἐν ταῖς ψυχαῖς. τοῦ δὲ πιστοὶ εἶναι ἐν τῇ
φθορᾷ τῶν δεσποτῶν μάλιστα βάσανον ἐδίδοσαν·
οὐδένες γὰρ πιστότερα ἔργα ἀπεδείκνυντο ἐν ταῖς
δεσποτικαῖς συμφοραῖς τῶν εὐνούχων. 65. εἰ δέ

---

[1] τούτοις Pantazides, Hug, Marchant, Gemoll; τούτους
MSS., Dindorf, Breitenbach.

and to place them in offices of honour; and no one, he thought, could surpass him in bestowing favours of that kind. 61. Besides, inasmuch as eunuchs are objects of contempt to the rest of mankind, for this reason, if for no other, they need a master who will be their patron; for there is no man who would not think that he had a right to take advantage of a eunuch at every opportunity unless there were some higher power to prevent his doing so; but there is no reason why even a eunuch should not be superior to all others in fidelity to his master. 62. But he did not admit what many might very easily be inclined to suppose, that eunuchs are weaklings; and he drew this conclusion also from the case of other animals: for instance, vicious horses, when gelded, stop biting and prancing about, to be sure, but are none the less fit for service in war; and bulls, when castrated, lose somewhat of their high spirit and unruliness but are not deprived of their strength or capacity for work. And in the same way dogs, when castrated, stop running away from their masters, but are no less useful for watching or hunting. 63. And men, too, in the same way, become gentler when deprived of this desire, but not less careful of that which is entrusted to them; they are not made any less efficient horsemen, or any less skilful lancers, or less ambitious men. 64. On the contrary, they showed both in times of war and in hunting that they still preserved in their souls a spirit of rivalry; and of their fidelity they gave the best proof upon the fall of their masters, for no one ever performed acts of greater fidelity in his master's misfortunes than eunuchs do. 65. And if it is thought with some

τι ἄρα τῆς τοῦ σώματος ἰσχύος μειοῦσθαι δοκοῦ
σιν, ὁ σίδηρος ἀνισοῖ τοὺς ἀσθενεῖς τοῖς ἰσχυροῖ
ἐν τῷ πολέμῳ. ταῦτα δὴ γιγνώσκων ἀρξάμενο
ἀπὸ τῶν θυρωρῶν πάντας τοὺς περὶ τὸ ἑαυτο
σῶμα θεραπευτῆρας ἐποιήσατο εὐνούχους.

66. Ἡγησάμενος δὲ οὐχ ἱκανὴν εἶναι τὴν φυ
λακὴν ταύτην πρὸς τὸ πλῆθος τῶν δυσμενῶ
ἐχόντων, ἐσκόπει τίνας τῶν ἄλλων ἂν πιστοτάτου
περὶ τὸ βασίλειον φύλακας λάβοι. 67. εἰδὼς οὖ
Πέρσας τοὺς οἴκοι κακοβιωτάτους μὲν ὄντας δι
πενίαν, ἐπιπονώτατα δὲ ζῶντας διὰ τὴν τῆς χώρα
τραχύτητα καὶ διὰ τὸ αὐτουργοὺς εἶναι, τούτου
ἐνόμισε μάλιστ' ἂν ἀγαπᾶν τὴν παρ' ἑαυτῷ δί
αιταν. 68. λαμβάνει οὖν τούτων μυρίους δορυ
φόρους, οἳ κύκλῳ μὲν νυκτὸς καὶ ἡμέρας ἐφύ
λαττον περὶ τὰ βασίλεια, ὁπότε ἐπὶ χώρας εἴη
ὁπότε δὲ ἐξίοι ποι,[1] ἔνθεν καὶ ἔνθεν τεταγμένο
ἐπορεύοντο.

69. Νομίσας δὲ καὶ Βαβυλῶνος ὅλης φύλακα
δεῖν εἶναι ἱκανούς, εἴτ' ἐπιδημῶν αὐτὸς τυγχάνο
εἴτε καὶ ἀποδημῶν, κατέστησε καὶ ἐν Βαβυλῶ
φρουροὺς ἱκανούς· μισθὸν δὲ καὶ τούτοις Βαβυ
λωνίους ἔταξε παρέχειν, βουλόμενος αὐτοὺς ὡ
ἀμηχανωτάτους εἶναι, ὅπως ὅτι ταπεινότατοι κα
εὐκαθεκτότατοι εἶεν.

70. Αὕτη μὲν δὴ ἡ περὶ αὐτόν τε φυλακὴ καὶ
ἐν Βαβυλῶνι τότε κατασταθεῖσα καὶ νῦν ἔτ
οὕτως ἔχουσα διαμένει. σκοπῶν δ' ὅπως ἂν καὶ
πᾶσα ἀρχὴ κατέχοιτο καὶ ἄλλη ἔτι προσγίγνοιτο.

[1] ποι Schneider, most Edd.; που MSS., Breitenbach.

justice that they are inferior in bodily strength, yet on the field of battle steel makes the weak equal to the strong. Recognizing these facts, he selected eunuchs for every post of personal service to him, from the door-keepers up.

66. But, as he deemed this guard insufficient in view of the multitude of those who bore him ill-will, he looked around to see whom he could find among the rest who would be the most trustworthy guards about the palace. 67. Now he knew that the Persians on account of their poverty lived in the greatest privation at home and were accustomed to a life of the hardest toil, because their country was rugged and they had to work with their own hands; so he believed that they would especially welcome life with him. 68. Accordingly, he took from among them ten thousand spearmen, who kept guard about the palace day and night, whenever he was in residence; but whenever he went away anywhere, they went along drawn up in order on either side of him. *The palace guard*

69. And since he considered that all Babylon, too, stood in need of adequate protection, whether he himself happened to be at home or abroad, he stationed there also an adequate garrison, and he arranged that the Babylonians should furnish the money for their wages, for it was his aim that this people should be as destitute of resources as possible, so that they might be as submissive and as easily restrained as possible. *The city guards*

70. This guard that he then established about himself and in the city of Babylon is maintained on the same footing even to this day. And as he studied how his whole empire might be held together and at

ἡγήσατο τοὺς μισθοφόρους τούτους οὐ[1] τοσοῦτον
βελτίονας τῶν ὑπηκόων εἶναι ὅσον ἐλάττονας·
τοὺς δὲ ἀγαθοὺς ἄνδρας ἐγίγνωσκε συνεκτέον
εἶναι, οἵπερ σὺν τοῖς θεοῖς τὸ κρατεῖν παρέσχον,
καὶ ἐπιμελητέον ὅπως μὴ ἀνήσουσι[2] τὴν τῆς
ἀρετῆς ἄσκησιν. 71. ὅπως δὲ μὴ ἐπιτάττειν
αὐτοῖς δοκοίη, ἀλλὰ γνόντες καὶ αὐτοὶ ταῦτα
ἄριστα εἶναι οὕτως ἐμμένοιέν τε καὶ ἐπιμέλοιντο
τῆς ἀρετῆς, συνέλεξε τούς τε ὁμοτίμους καὶ
πάντας ὁπόσοι ἐπικαίριοι ἦσαν καὶ ἀξιοχρεώτατοι
αὐτῷ ἐδόκουν κοινωνοὶ εἶναι καὶ πόνων καὶ ἀγαθῶν. 72. ἐπεὶ δὲ συνῆλθον, ἔλεξε τοιάδε·

Ἄνδρες φίλοι καὶ σύμμαχοι, τοῖς μὲν θεοῖς
μεγίστη χάρις ὅτι ἔδοσαν ἡμῖν τυχεῖν ὧν ἐνομί-
ζομεν ἄξιοι εἶναι. νῦν μὲν γὰρ δὴ ἔχομεν καὶ
γῆν πολλὴν καὶ ἀγαθὴν καὶ οἵτινες ταύτην ἐργα-
ζόμενοι θρέψουσιν ἡμᾶς· ἔχομεν δὲ καὶ οἰκίας
καὶ ἐν ταύταις κατασκευάς. 73. καὶ μηδείς γε
ὑμῶν ἔχων ταῦτα νομισάτω ἀλλότρια ἔχειν·
νόμος γὰρ ἐν πᾶσιν ἀνθρώποις ἀίδιός ἐστιν, ὅταν
πολεμούντων πόλις ἁλῷ, τῶν ἑλόντων εἶναι καὶ
τὰ σώματα τῶν ἐν τῇ πόλει καὶ τὰ χρήματα.
οὔκουν ἀδικίᾳ γε ἕξετε ὅ τι ἂν ἔχητε, ἀλλὰ
φιλανθρωπίᾳ οὐκ ἀφαιρήσεσθε, ἤν τι ἐᾶτε ἔχειν
αὐτούς.

74. Τὸ μέντοι ἐκ τοῦδε οὕτως ἐγὼ γιγνώσκω
ὅτι εἰ μὲν τρεψόμεθα ἐπὶ ῥᾳδιουργίαν καὶ τὴν
τῶν κακῶν ἀνθρώπων ἡδυπάθειαν, οἳ νομίζουσι

---

[1] οὐ MSS., Edd.; δεῖν Gemoll (they must be as much braver
as they are fewer).

[2] μὴ ἀνήσουσι Muretus, Edd.; μηνύσωσι MSS.

the same time enlarged, he reflected that these
mercenaries were not so much better men than
those he had made subject as they were inferior
in number; and he realized that the brave men,
who with the aid of the gods had brought him
victory, must be kept together and that care must
be exercised that they should not abandon their
practice of virtue. 71. But in order that he might
not seem to be issuing orders to them, but that
they also might of themselves recognize that this
was the best course for them and so abide in
virtue and cultivate it, he collected the peers and all
who were men of influence, together with such as
seemed to him most worthy sharers of his toil and its
rewards; 72. and when they had come together he
addressed them as follows:

"Friends and allies, thanks be above all to the gods
that they have vouchsafed to us to obtain all that we
thought we deserved. For now we are in possession
of broad and fertile lands and of subjects to support
us by tilling them; we have houses also and furniture
in them. 73. And let not one of you think that in
having these things he has what does not belong to
him; for it is a law established for all time among
all men that when a city is taken in war, the persons
and the property of the inhabitants thereof belong
to the captors. It will, therefore, be no injustice
for you to keep what you have, but if you let them
keep anything, it will be only out of generosity that
you do not take it away.

74. "As for the future, however, it is my judgment
that if we turn to idleness and the luxurious self-
indulgence of men of coarse natures, who count toil

Cyrus advocates the old morals for his new empire

τὸ μὲν πονεῖν ἀθλιότητα, τὸ δὲ ἀπόνως βιοτεύειν
εὐδαιμονίαν,[1] ταχὺ ἡμᾶς φημι ὀλίγου ἀξίους ἡμῖν
αὐτοῖς ἔσεσθαι καὶ ταχὺ πάντων τῶν ἀγαθῶν
στερήσεσθαι. 75. οὐ γάρ τοι τὸ ἀγαθοὺς ἄνδρας γενέσθαι τοῦτο ἀρκεῖ ὥστε καὶ διατελεῖν,
ἢν μή τις αὐτοῦ διὰ τέλους ἐπιμέληται· ἀλλὰ
ὥσπερ καὶ αἱ ἄλλαι τέχναι ἀμεληθεῖσαι μείονος
ἄξιαι γίγνονται καὶ τὰ σώματά γε τὰ εὖ ἔχοντα,
ὁπόταν τις αὐτὰ ἀνῇ ἐπὶ ῥᾳδιουργίαν, πονήρως
πάλιν ἔχει, οὕτω καὶ ἡ σωφροσύνη καὶ ἡ ἐγ-
κράτεια καὶ ἡ ἀλκή, ὁπόταν τις αὐτῶν ἀνῇ τὴν
ἄσκησιν, ἐκ τούτου εἰς τὴν πονηρίαν πάλιν τρέπεται. 76. οὔκουν δεῖ ἀμελεῖν οὐδ' ἐπὶ τὸ αὐτίκα
ἡδὺ προϊέναι αὐτούς.[2] μέγα μὲν γὰρ οἶμαι ἔργον
καὶ τὸ ἀρχὴν καταπρᾶξαι, πολὺ δ' ἔτι μεῖζον τὸ
λαβόντα διασώσασθαι. τὸ μὲν γὰρ λαβεῖν
πολλάκις τῷ τόλμαν μόνον παρασχομένῳ ἐγένετο,
τὸ δὲ λαβόντα κατέχειν οὐκέτι τοῦτο ἄνευ σωφροσύνης οὐδ' ἄνευ ἐγκρατείας οὐδ' ἄνευ πολλῆς
ἐπιμελείας γίγνεται.

77. Ἃ χρὴ γιγνώσκοντας νῦν πολὺ μᾶλλον
ἀσκεῖν τὴν ἀρετὴν ἢ πρὶν τάδε τἀγαθὰ κτήσασθαι, εὖ εἰδότας ὅτι ὅταν πλεῖστά τις ἔχῃ,
τότε πλεῖστοι καὶ φθονοῦσι καὶ ἐπιβουλεύουσι
καὶ πολέμιοι γίγνονται, ἄλλως τε κἂν παρ'
ἀκόντων τά τε κτήματα καὶ τὴν θεραπείαν
ὥσπερ ἡμεῖς ἔχῃ.

Τοὺς μὲν οὖν θεοὺς οἴεσθαι χρὴ σὺν ἡμῖν
ἔσεσθαι· οὐ γὰρ ἐπιβουλεύσαντες ἀδίκως ἔχο-

---

[1] εὐδαιμονίαν Wecklein, Marchant, Gemoll; ἡδυπάθειαν
MSS., earlier Edd.
[2] αὐτούς Edd.; αὑτούς MSS.

misery and living without toil happiness, we shall soon
be of little account in our own eyes and shall soon
lose all the blessings that we have. 75. For, to have
quitted yourselves once like valiant men does not, we
know, assure the perpetuity of valour, unless you
devote yourselves to it to the end; but, just as skill
in other arts retrogrades if neglected, and as bodies,
too, that were once in good condition change and
deteriorate as soon as the owners relax into idleness,
so also self-control and temperance and strength will
take a backward turn to vice as soon as one ceases to
cultivate them. 76. Therefore, we dare not become
careless nor give ourselves up to the enjoyment
of the present moment; for, while I think it is a
great thing to have won an empire, it is a still greater
thing to preserve it after it has been won.
For to win falls often to the lot of one who has
shown nothing but daring; but to win and hold—
that is no longer a possibility without the exercise
of self-control, temperance, and unflagging care.

77. "Recognizing all this, we ought to practise He empha-
virtue even more than we did before we secured Persians'
these advantages, for we may be sure that the more need
a man has, the more people will envy him and plot
against him and become his enemies, particularly if,
as in our case, he draws his wealth and service from
unwilling hands.

"We must, therefore, believe that the gods will
be on our side; for we have not come unjustly into

μεν, ἀλλ᾽ ἐπιβουλευθέντες ἐτιμωρησάμεθα. 78.
τὸ μέντοι μετὰ τοῦτο κράτιστον ἡμῖν αὐτοῖς
παρασκευαστέον· τοῦτο δ᾽ ἐστὶ τὸ βελτίονας
ὄντας τῶν ἀρχομένων ἄρχειν ἀξιοῦν. θάλπους
μὲν οὖν καὶ ψύχους καὶ σίτων καὶ ποτῶν καὶ
πόνων καὶ ὕπνου ἀνάγκη καὶ τοῖς δούλοις μετα-
διδόναι· μεταδιδόντας γε μέντοι πειρᾶσθαι δεῖ
ἐν τούτοις πρῶτον βελτίονας αὐτῶν φαίνεσθαι.
79. πολεμικῆς δ᾽ ἐπιστήμης καὶ μελέτης παντάπασιν οὐ μεταδοτέον τούτοις, οὕστινας ἐργάτας
ἡμετέρους καὶ δασμοφόρους βουλόμεθα καταστήσασθαι, ἀλλ᾽ αὐτοὺς δεῖ τούτοις τοῖς ἀσκήμασι
πλεονεκτεῖν, γιγνώσκοντας ὅτι ἐλευθερίας ταῦτα
ὄργανα καὶ εὐδαιμονίας οἱ θεοὶ τοῖς ἀνθρώποις
ἀπέδειξαν· καὶ ὥσπερ γε ἐκείνους τὰ ὅπλα
ἀφῃρήμεθα, οὕτως ἡμᾶς αὐτοὺς δεῖ μήποτ᾽ ἐρήμους ὅπλων γίγνεσθαι, εὖ εἰδότας ὅτι τοῖς ἀεὶ
ἐγγυτάτω τῶν ὅπλων οὖσι τούτοις καὶ οἰκειότατά
ἐστιν ἃν βούλωνται.
  80. Εἰ δέ τις τοιαῦτα ἐννοεῖται, τί δῆτα ἡμῖν
ὄφελος καταπρᾶξαι ἃ ἐπεθυμοῦμεν, εἰ ἔτι δεήσει
καρτερεῖν καὶ πεινῶντας καὶ διψῶντας καὶ πο-
νοῦντας καὶ ἐπιμελομένους, ἐκεῖνο δεῖ καταμαθεῖν
ὅτι τοσούτῳ τἀγαθὰ μᾶλλον εὐφραίνει ὅσῳ ἂν
μᾶλλον προπονήσας τις ἐπ᾽ αὐτὰ ἴῃ[1] οἱ γὰρ
πόνοι ὄψον τοῖς ἀγαθοῖς· ἄνευ δὲ τοῦ δεόμενον
τυγχάνειν τινὸς οὐδὲν οὕτω πολυτελῶς παρα-
σκευασθείη ἂν ὥσθ᾽ ἡδὺ εἶναι.
  81. Εἰ δὲ ὧν μὲν μάλιστα ἄνθρωποι ἐπιθυ-
μοῦσιν ὁ δαίμων ἡμῖν ταῦτα συμπαρεσκεύακεν,

---

[1] ἴῃ V corr. Cobet, Hug, Marchant, Gemoll; ἀπίῃ Dindorf,
Breitenbach; εἴη y; ἀπίοι xzε.

our possessions through plotting against others, but plotted against we have avenged ourselves. 78. But that which is next in importance after the favour of the gods we must get for ourselves—namely, we must claim the right to rule over our subjects only on the ground that we are their betters. Now the conditions of heat and cold, food and drink, toil and rest, we must share even with our slaves. But though we share with them, we must above all try to show ourselves their betters in such matters; 79. but the science and practice of war we need not share at all with those whom we wish to put in the position of workmen or tributaries to us, but we must maintain our superiority in these accomplishments, as we recognize in these the means to liberty and happiness that the gods have given to men. And just as we have taken their arms away from them, so surely must we never be without our own, for we know that the nearer to their arms men constantly are, the more completely at their command is their every wish.

80 " But if any one is revolving in his mind any such question as this—' of what earthly use it is to us to have attained to the goal of our ambitions if we still have to endure hunger and thirst, toil and care '—he must take this lesson to heart: that good things bring the greater pleasure, in proportion to the toil one undergoes beforehand to attain them; for toil gives a relish to good things; and nothing, however sumptuously prepared, could give pleasure unless a man get it when he needs it. The secret of happiness

81. " Now if God has helped us to obtain that which men most desire, and if any one will so order these

ὡς δ' ἂν ἥδιστα ταῦτα φαίνοιτο αὐτός τις αὑτῷ
[ταῦτα] [1] παρασκευάσει, ὁ τοιοῦτος ἀνὴρ τοσούτῳ
πλεονεκτήσει τῶν ἐνδεεστέρων βίου ὡς πεινήσας
τῶν ἡδίστων σίτων τεύξεται καὶ διψήσας τῶν
ἡδίστων ποτῶν ἀπολαύσεται καὶ δεηθεὶς ἀνα-
παύσεως ὡς ἥδιστον ἀναπαύσεται.

82. Ὧν ἕνεκά φημι χρῆναι νῦν ἐπιταθῆναι
ἡμᾶς εἰς ἀνδραγαθίαν, ὅπως τῶν τε ἀγαθῶν
ᾗ ἄριστον καὶ ἥδιστον ἀπολαύσωμεν καὶ ὅπως
τοῦ πάντων χαλεπωτάτου ἄπειροι γενώμεθα.
οὐ γὰρ τὸ μὴ λαβεῖν τἀγαθὰ οὕτω χαλεπὸν
ὥσπερ τὸ λαβόντα στερηθῆναι λυπηρόν.

83. Ἐννοήσατε δὲ κἀκεῖνο τίνα πρόφασιν
ἔχοντες ἂν προσιοίμεθα [2] κακίονες ἢ πρόσθεν
γενέσθαι. πότερον ὅτι ἄρχομεν; ἀλλ' οὐ δήπου
τὸν ἄρχοντα τῶν ἀρχομένων πονηρότερον προσήκει εἶναι. ἀλλ' ὅτι εὐδαιμονέστεροι δοκοῦμεν νῦν
ἢ πρότερον εἶναι; ἔπειτα τῇ εὐδαιμονίᾳ φήσει
τις τὴν κακίαν ἐπιπρέπειν; ἀλλ' ὅτι ἐπεὶ κεκτήμεθα δούλους, τούτους κολάσομεν, [3] ἢν πονηροὶ
ὦσι; 84. καὶ τί προσήκει αὐτὸν ὄντα πονηρὸν
πονηρίας ἕνεκα ἢ βλακείας ἄλλους κολάζειν;

Ἐννοεῖτε δὲ καὶ τοῦτο ὅτι τρέφειν μὲν παρεσκευάσμεθα πολλοὺς καὶ τῶν ἡμετέρων οἴκων
φύλακας καὶ τῶν σωμάτων· αἰσχρὸν δὲ πῶς
οὐκ ἂν εἴη, εἰ δι' ἄλλους μὲν δορυφόρους τῆς
σωτηρίας οἰησόμεθα χρῆναι τυγχάνειν, αὐτοὶ

[1] ταῦτα MSS., Dindorf, Breitenbach; [ταῦτα] Brown, Hug,
Marchant, Gemoll.
[2] προσιοίμεθα Schneider, most Edd.; προσιέμεθα xzV, Breitenbach; προειλό(-ώ D)μεθα y.
[3] κολάσομεν D, Edd.; κολάσωμεν xzFV.

results for himself that they shall give as great pleasure as possible, such a man will have this advantage over those who are not so well supplied with the means of living: when hungry he will enjoy the most dainty food, and when thirsty he will enjoy the finest drinks, and when in need of rest he will find it most refreshing.

82. "Wherefore I maintain that we should now strain every nerve after manliness, so that we may enjoy our success in the best and most delightful manner and have no experience in that which is hardest of all. For failure to obtain good things is not so hard as the loss of them, when once obtained, is painful.

83. "And think of this also: what excuse should we offer for allowing ourselves to become less deserving than before? That we are rulers? But, you know, it is not proper for the ruler to be worse than his subjects. Or that we seem to be more fortunate than before? Will any one then maintain that vice is the proper ornament for good fortune? Or shall we plead that since we have slaves, we will punish them, if they are bad? 84. Why, what propriety is there in any one's punishing others for viciousness or indolence, when he himself is bad?

"And think also on this: we have made arrangements to keep many men to guard our homes and our lives; and how would it be otherwise than base in us to think that we have a right to enjoy security protected by other men's spears, while we ourselves

Virtue the strongest safeguard

δὲ ἡμῖν αὐτοῖς οὐ δορυφορήσομεν; καὶ μὴν εὖ
γε δεῖ εἰδέναι ὅτι οὐκ ἔστιν ἄλλη φυλακὴ τοιαύτη
οἵα αὐτόν τινα καλὸν κἀγαθὸν ὑπάρχειν· τοῦτο
γὰρ δεῖ συμπαρομαρτεῖν· τῷ δ' ἀρετῆς ἐρήμῳ
οὐδὲ ἄλλο καλῶς ἔχειν οὐδὲν προσήκει.

85. Τί οὖν φημι χρῆναι ποιεῖν καὶ ποῦ τὴν
ἀρετὴν ἀσκεῖν καὶ ποῦ τὴν μελέτην ποιεῖσθαι;
οὐδὲν καινόν, ὦ ἄνδρες, ἐρῶ· ἀλλ' ὥσπερ ἐν
Πέρσαις ἐπὶ τοῖς ἀρχείοις οἱ ὁμότιμοι διάγουσιν,
οὕτω καὶ ἡμᾶς φημι χρῆναι ἐνθάδε ὄντας τοὺς
ὁμοτίμους πάνθ' ὅσαπερ[1] κἀκεῖ ἐπιτηδεύειν, καὶ
ὑμᾶς τε ἐμὲ ὁρῶντας κατανοεῖν παρόντας εἰ
ἐπιμελόμενος ὧν δεῖ διάξω, ἐγώ τε ὑμᾶς κατανοῶν θεάσομαι, καὶ οὓς ἂν ὁρῶ τὰ καλὰ καὶ
τἀγαθὰ ἐπιτηδεύοντας, τούτους τιμήσω. 86. καὶ
τοὺς παῖδας δέ, οἳ[2] ἂν ἡμῶν γίγνωνται, ἐνθάδε
παιδεύωμεν· αὐτοί τε γὰρ βελτίονες ἐσόμεθα,
βουλόμενοι τοῖς παισὶν ὡς βέλτιστα παρα-
δείγματα ἡμᾶς αὐτοὺς παρέχειν, οἵ τε παῖδες
οὐδ' ἂν εἰ βούλοιντο ῥαδίως πονηροὶ γένοιντο,
αἰσχρὸν μὲν μηδὲν μήτε ὁρῶντες μήτε ἀκούοντες,
ἐν δὲ καλοῖς κἀγαθοῖς ἐπιτηδεύμασι διημερεύοντες.

[1] πάνθ' ὅσαπερ Dindorf[4], Hug ; πάντα ἅπερ Stephanus, Dindorf[3], Marchant, Gemoll ; πάντας ἅπερ MSS., Breitenbach.
[2] οἳ xy, Hug, Marchant, Gemoll ; οἷς zV, Dindorf, Breitenbach (to whomsoever of us sons may be born).

do not take up the spear for our own defence? And yet we must be fully aware that there is no such safeguard as for a man to be good and brave himself; this guard must be ever at our side. But if a man lack virtue, neither is it fitting that aught else be well with him.

85. "What, then, do I propose that we should do, wherein practise virtue, and where apply the practice? I have nothing new to tell you, my men; but just as in Persia the peers spend their time at the government buildings, so here also we peers must practise the same things as we did there; you must be in your places and watch me to see if I continue to do what I ought, and I will watch to see the same in you, and whomsoever I see pursuing what is good and honourable, him will I honour. 86. And as for our boys, as many as shall be born to us, let us educate them here. For we ourselves shall be better, if we aim to set before the boys as good examples as we can in ourselves; and the boys could not easily turn out bad, even if they should wish to, if they neither see nor hear anything vicious but spend their days in good and noble pursuits."

The Persian discipline in Babylon I. ii. 4 ff.

BOOK VIII

THE ORGANIZATION OF THE EMPIRE

THE DEATH OF CYRUS

Η

I

1. Κῦρος μὲν οὖν οὕτως εἶπεν· ἀνέστη δ' ἐπ' αὐτῷ Χρυσάντας καὶ εἶπεν ὧδε· Ἀλλὰ πολλάκις μὲν δή, ὦ ἄνδρες, καὶ ἄλλοτε κατενόησα ὅτι ἄρχων ἀγαθὸς οὐδὲν διαφέρει πατρὸς ἀγαθοῦ· οἵ τε γὰρ πατέρες προνοοῦσι τῶν παίδων ὅπως μήποτε αὐτοὺς τἀγαθὰ ἐπιλείψει, Κῦρός τέ μοι δοκεῖ νῦν συμβουλεύειν ἡμῖν ἀφ' ὧν μάλιστ' ἂν εὐδαιμονοῦντες διατελοῖμεν· ὃ δέ μοι δοκεῖ ἐνδεέστερον ἢ ὡς ἐχρῆν δηλῶσαι, τοῦτο ἐγὼ πειράσομαι τοὺς μὴ εἰδότας διδάξαι. 2. ἐννοήσατε γὰρ δὴ τίς ἂν πόλις πολεμία ὑπὸ μὴ πειθομένων ἁλοίη· τίς δ' ἂν φιλία ὑπὸ μὴ πειθομένων διαφυλαχθείη· ποῖον δ' ἂν ἀπειθούντων στράτευμα νίκης τύχοι· πῶς δ' ἂν μᾶλλον ἐν μάχαις ἡττῷντο ἄνθρωποι ἢ ἐπειδὰν ἄρξωνται ἰδίᾳ ἕκαστος περὶ τῆς αὑτοῦ σωτηρίας βουλεύεσθαι· τί δ' ἂν ἄλλο ἀγαθὸν τελεσθείη ὑπὸ μὴ πειθομένων τοῖς κρείττοσι· ποῖαι δὲ πόλεις νομίμως ἂν οἰκήσειαν ἢ ποῖοι οἶκοι σωθείησαν· πῶς δ' ἂν νῆες ὅποι δεῖ ἀφίκοιντο·

304

BOOK VIII

I

1. Such was Cyrus's address; and after him Chrysantas rose and spoke as follows: "Well, gentlemen, I have noticed often enough before now that a good ruler is not at all different from a good father. For as fathers provide for their children so that they may never be in want of the good things of life, so Cyrus seems to me now to be giving us counsel how we may best continue in prosperity. But there is one thing that he has not stated so clearly, it seems to me, as he should have done, and that I will try to present to any who do not know about it. 2. Bethink you, then, of this: what city that is hostile could be taken or what city that is friendly could be preserved by soldiers who are insubordinate? What army of disobedient men could gain a victory? How could men be more easily defeated in battle than when they begin to think each of his own individual safety? And what possible success could be achieved by such as do not obey their superiors? What state could be administered according to its laws, or what private establishments could be maintained, and how could ships arrive at their destination?

3. Ἡμεῖς δὲ ἃ νῦν ἀγαθὰ ἔχομεν διὰ τί ἄλλο μᾶλλον κατεπράξαμεν ἢ διὰ τὸ πείθεσθαι τῷ ἄρχοντι; διὰ τοῦτο γὰρ καὶ νυκτὸς καὶ ἡμέρας ταχὺ μὲν ὅποι ἔδει παρεγιγνόμεθα, ἀθρόοι δὲ τῷ ἄρχοντι ἑπόμενοι ἀνυπόστατοι ἦμεν, τῶν δ' ἐπιταχθέντων οὐδὲν ἡμιτελὲς κατελείπομεν. · εἰ τοίνυν μέγιστον ἀγαθὸν τὸ πειθαρχεῖν φαίνεται εἰς τὸ καταπράττειν τἀγαθά, οὕτως εὖ ἴστε ὅτι τὸ αὐτὸ τοῦτο καὶ εἰς τὸ διασώζειν ἃ δεῖ μέγιστον ἀγαθόν ἐστι.

4. Καὶ πρόσθεν μὲν δὴ πολλοὶ ἡμῶν ἦρχον μὲν οὐδενός, ἤρχοντο δέ· νῦν δὲ κατεσκεύασθε οὕτω πάντες οἱ παρόντες ὥστε ἄρχετε οἱ μὲν πλειόνων, οἱ δὲ μειόνων. ὥσπερ τοίνυν αὐτοὶ ἀξιώσετε ἄρχειν τῶν ὑφ' ὑμῖν, οὕτω καὶ αὐτοὶ πειθώμεθα οἷς ἂν ἡμᾶς καθήκῃ. τοσοῦτον δὲ διαφέρειν δεῖ τῶν δούλων ὅσον οἱ μὲν δοῦλοι ἄκοντες τοῖς δεσπόταις ὑπηρετοῦσιν, ἡμᾶς δ', εἴπερ ἀξιοῦμεν ἐλεύθεροι εἶναι, ἑκόντας δεῖ ποιεῖν ὃ πλείστου ἄξιον φαίνεται εἶναι. εὑρήσετε δ', ἔφη, καὶ ἔνθα ἄνευ μοναρχίας πόλις οἰκεῖται, τὴν μάλιστα τοῖς ἄρχουσιν ἐθέλουσαν πείθεσθαι ταύτην ἥκιστα τῶν πολεμίων ἀναγκαζομένην ὑπακούειν.[1]

5. Παρῶμέν τε οὖν, ὥσπερ Κῦρος κελεύει, ἐπὶ τόδε τὸ ἀρχεῖον, ἀσκῶμέν τε δι' ὧν μάλιστα δυνησόμεθα κατέχειν ἃ δεῖ, παρέχωμέν τε ἡμᾶς αὐτοὺς χρῆσθαι Κύρῳ ὅ τι ἂν δέῃ. καὶ τοῦτο γὰρ εὖ εἰδέναι χρὴ ὅτι οὐ μὴ δυνήσεται Κῦρος

---

[1] ὑπακούειν MSS., most Edd.; ἀκούειν Cobet, Hug.

3. "And as for us, how have we secured the good things we now have, except by obedience to our commander? For by that course we always quickly reached our required destination, whether by day or by night, and following our commander in close array we were invincible, and we left half done none of the tasks committed to us. If, therefore, obedience to one's commander is, as it seems, the first essential to achieving success, then you may be sure that this same course is the first essential to ensuring its permanence.

4. "Heretofore, you know, many of us had no command but were under command; but now all of you here are so situated that you have command, some of larger, some of smaller divisions. Therefore, as you yourselves will expect to exercise authority over those under your command, so let us also give our obedience to those whom it is our duty to obey. And we must distinguish ourselves from slaves in this way, that, whereas slaves serve their masters against their wills, we, if indeed we claim to be free, must do of our own free will all that seems to be of the first importance. And you will find that among states, even when the government is not a monarchy, that state which most readily obeys its officers is least likely to be compelled to submit to its enemies. *and the need of obedience to Cyrus*

5. "Let us, therefore, present ourselves before our ruler's headquarters yonder, as Cyrus bids; let us devote ourselves to those pursuits by which we shall best be able to hold fast to that which we ought, and let us offer ourselves for whatever service Cyrus may need us for. And this trust will not be abused, for we may be sure that Cyrus will never be able to *Duty of attendance at court*

307

εὑρεῖν ὅ τι αὑτῷ μὲν ἐπ' ἀγαθῷ χρήσεται, ἡμῖν δὲ
οὔ, ἐπείπερ τά γε αὐτὰ ἡμῖν συμφέρει καὶ οἱ
αὐτοί εἰσιν ἡμῖν πολέμιοι.

6. Ἐπεὶ δὲ ταῦτα εἶπε Χρυσάντας, οὕτω δὴ
καὶ ἄλλοι ἀνίσταντο πολλοὶ καὶ Περσῶν καὶ τῶν
συμμάχων συνεροῦντες· καὶ ἔδοξε τοὺς ἐντίμους
ἀεὶ παρεῖναι ἐπὶ θύρας καὶ παρέχειν αὑτοὺς
χρῆσθαι ὅ τι ἂν βούληται, ἕως ἀφείη Κῦρος. ὡς
δὲ τότε ἔδοξεν, οὕτω καὶ νῦν ἔτι ποιοῦσιν οἱ κατὰ
τὴν Ἀσίαν ὑπὸ βασιλεῖ ὄντες, θεραπεύουσι τὰς
τῶν ἀρχόντων θύρας. 7. ὡς δ' ἐν τῷ λόγῳ
δεδήλωται Κῦρος καταστησάμενος εἰς τὸ διαφυ-
λάττειν αὑτῷ τε καὶ Πέρσαις τὴν ἀρχήν, ταὐτὰ
καὶ οἱ μετ' ἐκεῖνον βασιλεῖς νόμιμα ἔτι καὶ νῦν
διατελοῦσι ποιοῦντες. 8. οὕτω δ' ἔχει καὶ ταῦτα
ὥσπερ καὶ τἆλλα· ὅταν μὲν ὁ ἐπιστάτης βελτίων
γένηται, καθαρώτερον τὰ νόμιμα πράττεται· ὅταν
δὲ χείρων, φαυλότερον.

Ἐφοίτων μὲν οὖν ἐπὶ τὰς θύρας Κύρου οἱ
ἔντιμοι σὺν τοῖς ἵπποις καὶ ταῖς αἰχμαῖς, συνδόξαν
πᾶσι τοῖς ἀρίστοις τῶν συγκαταστρεψαμένων τὴν
ἀρχήν.

9. Κῦρος δ' ἐπὶ μὲν τἆλλα καθίστη ἄλλους
ἐπιμελητάς, καὶ ἦσαν αὑτῷ καὶ προσόδων ἀπο-
δεκτῆρες καὶ δαπανημάτων δοτῆρες καὶ ἔργων
ἐπιστάται καὶ κτημάτων φύλακες καὶ τῶν εἰς
τὴν δίαιταν ἐπιτηδείων ἐπιμεληταί· καὶ ἵππων
δὲ καὶ κυνῶν ἐπιμελητὰς καθίστη οὓς ἐνόμιζε
καὶ ταῦτα τὰ βοσκήματα βέλτιστ' ἂν παρέχειν
αὑτῷ χρῆσθαι.

find anything in which he can employ us for his own advantage and not equally for ours; for we have common interests and we have common enemies."

6. When Chrysantas had finished this address, Policies adopted many others also both of the Persians and the allies rose to support him. They passed a resolution that the nobles should always be in attendance at court and be in readiness for whatever service Cyrus wished until he should dismiss them. And as they then resolved, so even unto this day those who are the subjects of the great king in Asia continue to do— they are constantly in attendance at the court of their princes. 7. And the institutions which Cyrus inaugurated as a means of securing the kingdom permanently to himself and the Persians, as has been set forth in the foregoing narrative, these the succeeding kings have preserved unchanged even to this day. 8. And it is the same with these as with everything else: whenever the officer in charge is better, the administration of the institutions is purer; but when he is worse, the administration is more corrupt.

Accordingly, the nobles came to Cyrus's court with their horses and their spears, for so it had been decreed by the best of those who with him had made the conquest of the kingdom.

9. Cyrus next appointed officers to have charge of Cyrus appoints many officers the various departments; for example, tax-collectors, paymasters, boards of public works, keepers of his estates, and stewards of his commissary department. He appointed also as superintendents of his horses and hounds those who he thought would keep these creatures in a condition most efficient for his use.

10. Οὓς δὲ συμφύλακας τῆς εὐδαιμονίας οἱ ᾤετο χρῆναι ἔχειν, τούτους ὅπως ὡς βέλτιστοι ἔσοιντο οὐκέτι τούτου τὴν ἐπιμέλειαν ἄλλοις προσέταττεν, ἀλλ' αὑτοῦ ἐνόμιζε τοῦτο ἔργον εἶναι. ᾔδει γὰρ ὅτι, εἴ τι μάχης ποτὲ δεήσοι, ἐκ τούτων αὑτῷ καὶ παραστάτας καὶ ἐπιστάτας ληπτέον εἴη, σὺν οἷσπερ οἱ μέγιστοι κίνδυνοι· καὶ ταξιάρχους δὲ καὶ πεζῶν καὶ ἱππέων ἐγίγνωσκεν ἐκ τούτων καταστατέον εἶναι. 11. εἰ δὲ δέοι καὶ στρατηγῶν που ἄνευ αὑτοῦ, ᾔδει ὅτι ἐκ τούτων πεμπτέον εἴη· καὶ πόλεων δὲ καὶ ὅλων ἐθνῶν φύλαξι καὶ σατράπαις ᾔδει ὅτι τούτων τισὶν εἴη χρηστέον καὶ πρέσβεις γε τούτων τινὰς πεμπτέον, ὅπερ ἐν τοῖς μεγίστοις ἡγεῖτο εἶναι εἰς τὸ ἄνευ πολέμου τυγχάνειν ὧν δέοιτο.

12. Μὴ ὄντων μὲν οὖν οἵων δεῖ δι' ὧν αἱ μέγισται καὶ πλεῖσται πράξεις ἔμελλον εἶναι, κακῶς ἡγεῖτο τὰ αὑτοῦ ἕξειν. εἰ δ' οὗτοι εἶεν οἵους δέοι, πάντα ἐνόμιζε καλῶς ἔσεσθαι. ἐνέδυ μὲν οὖν οὕτω γνοὺς εἰς ταύτην τὴν ἐπιμέλειαν· ἐνόμιζε δὲ τὴν αὐτὴν καὶ αὑτῷ ἄσκησιν εἶναι τῆς ἀρετῆς. οὐ γὰρ ᾤετο οἷόν τε εἶναι μὴ αὐτόν τινα ὄντα οἷον δεῖ ἄλλους παρορμᾶν ἐπὶ τὰ καλὰ καὶ ἀγαθὰ ἔργα.

13. Ὡς δὲ ταῦτα διενοήθη, ἡγήσατο σχολῆς

10. But he did not in the same way leave to others the precaution of seeing that those whom he thought he ought to have as his associates in establishing the permanence of his success should be the ablest men available, but he considered that this responsibility was his own. For he knew that if ever there should be occasion for fighting, he would then have to select from their number men to stand beside and behind him, men in whose company also he would have to meet the greatest dangers ; from their number likewise he knew that he would have to appoint his captains both of foot and of horse. 11. Besides, if generals should be needed where he himself could not be, he knew that they would have to be commissioned from among that same number. And he knew that he must employ some of these to be governors and satraps of cities or of whole nations, and that he must send others on embassies— an office which he considered of the very first importance for obtaining without war whatever he might want.

12. If, therefore, those by whom the most numerous and most important affairs of state were to be transacted were not what they ought to be, he thought that his government would be a failure. But if they were all that they ought to be, he believed that everything would succeed. In this conviction, therefore, he took upon himself this charge ; and he determined that the same practice of virtue should be his as well. For he thought that it was not possible for him to incite others to good and noble deeds, if he were not himself such as he ought to be. The importance of wise appointments

13. When he had arrived at this conclusion, he

πρῶτον δεῖν, εἰ μέλλοι δυνήσεσθαι τῶν κρατίστων
ἐπιμελεῖσθαι.[1] τὸ μὲν οὖν προσόδων ἀμελεῖν οὐχ
οἷόν τε ἐνόμιζεν εἶναι, προνοῶν ὅτι πολλὰ καὶ
τελεῖν ἀνάγκη ἔσοιτο εἰς μεγάλην ἀρχήν· τὸ δ᾽
αὖ πολλῶν κτημάτων ὄντων ἀμφὶ ταῦτα αὐτὸν
ἀεὶ ἔχειν ᾔδει ὅτι ἀσχολίαν παρέξοι τῆς τῶν ὅλων
σωτηρίας ἐπιμελεῖσθαι.[1]

14. Οὕτω δὴ σκοπῶν, ὅπως ἂν τά τε οἰκονομικὰ
καλῶς ἔχοι καὶ ἡ σχολὴ γένοιτο, κατενόησέ πως
τὴν στρατιωτικὴν σύνταξιν. ὡς γὰρ τὰ πολλὰ
δεκάδαρχοι μὲν δεκαδέων ἐπιμέλονται, λοχαγοὶ δὲ
δεκαδάρχων, χιλίαρχοι δὲ λοχαγῶν, μυρίαρχοι δὲ
χιλιάρχων, καὶ οὕτως οὐδεὶς ἀτημέλητος γίγνεται,
οὐδ᾽ ἢν πάνυ πολλαὶ μυριάδες ἀνθρώπων ὦσι, καὶ
ὅταν ὁ στρατηγὸς βούληται χρήσασθαί τι τῇ
στρατιᾷ, ἀρκεῖ ἢν τοῖς μυριάρχοις παραγγείλῃ·
15. ὥσπερ οὖν ταῦτ᾽ ἔχει, οὕτω καὶ ὁ Κῦρος συν-
εκεφαλαιώσατο τὰς οἰκονομικὰς πράξεις· ὥστε
καὶ τῷ Κύρῳ ἐγένετο ὀλίγοις διαλεγομένῳ μηδὲν
τῶν οἰκείων ἀτημελήτως ἔχειν· καὶ ἐκ τούτου
ἤδη σχολὴν ἦγε πλείω ἢ ἄλλος μιᾶς οἰκίας καὶ
μιᾶς νεὼς ἐπιμελόμενος.

Οὕτω δὴ καταστησάμενος τὸ αὑτοῦ ἐδίδαξε καὶ
τοὺς περὶ αὑτὸν ταύτῃ τῇ καταστάσει χρῆσθαι.

16. Τὴν μὲν δὴ σχολὴν οὕτω κατεσκευάσατο
αὑτῷ τε καὶ τοῖς περὶ αὑτόν, ἤρχετο δ᾽ ἐπιστατεῖν

---

[1] ἐπιμελεῖσθαι MSS., most Edd.; ἐπιμέλεσθαι Hug.

thought, first of all, that he needed leisure if he were to be able to confine his attention to affairs of paramount importance. He decided, then, that it was out of the question for him to neglect the revenues, for he foresaw that there would necessarily be enormous expenses connected with a vast empire ; and on the other hand, he knew that for him to be constantly engaged in giving his personal attention to his manifold possessions would leave him with no time to care for the welfare of the whole realm.

14. As he thus pondered how the business of administration might be successfully conducted and how he still might have the desired leisure, he some- how happened to think of his military organization : in general, the sergeants care for the ten men under them, the lieutenants for the sergeants, the colonels for the lieutenants, the generals for the colonels, and thus no one is uncared for, even though there be many brigades ; and when the commander-in-chief wishes to do anything with his army, it is sufficient for him to issue his commands only to his brigadier-generals. 15. On this same model, then, Cyrus centralized the administrative functions also. And so it was possible for him, by communicating with only a few officers, to have no part of his administration uncared for. In this way he now enjoyed more leisure than one who has care of a single household or a single ship.

He models his civil service after the army

When he had thus organized his own functions in the government, he instructed those about him to follow the same plan of organization.

16. In this way, then, he secured leisure for himself and for his ministers ; and then he began to

τοῦ εἶναι οἵους δεῖ τοὺς κοινῶνας. πρῶτον μὲν
ὁπόσοι ὄντες ἱκανοὶ ἄλλων ἐργαζομένων τρέφε-
σθαι μὴ παρεῖεν ἐπὶ τὰς θύρας, τούτους ἐπεζήτει,
νομίζων τοὺς μὲν παρόντας οὐκ ἂν ἐθέλειν οὔτε
κακὸν οὔτε αἰσχρὸν οὐδὲν πράττειν καὶ διὰ τὸ
παρ' ἄρχοντι εἶναι καὶ διὰ τὸ εἰδέναι ὅτι ὁρῶντ' ἂν
ὅ τι πράττοιεν ὑπὸ τῶν βελτίστων· οἱ δὲ μὴ
παρεῖεν, τούτους ἡγεῖτο ἢ ἀκρατείᾳ τινὶ ἢ ἀδικίᾳ
ἢ ἀμελείᾳ ἀπεῖναι.

17. Τοῦτο οὖν πρῶτον διηγησόμεθα ὡς προσ-
ηνάγκαζε τοὺς τοιούτους παρεῖναι. τῶν γὰρ παρ'
ἑαυτῷ μάλιστα φίλων ἐκέλευσεν ἄν τινα λαβεῖν
τὰ τοῦ μὴ φοιτῶντος, φάσκοντα λαμβάνειν τὰ
ἑαυτοῦ. ἐπεὶ οὖν τοῦτο γένοιτο, ἧκον ἂν εὐθὺς οἱ
στερόμενοι ὡς ἠδικημένοι. 18. ὁ δὲ Κῦρος πολὺν
μὲν χρόνον οὐκ ἐσχόλαζε τοῖς τοιούτοις ὑπακούειν·
ἐπεὶ δὲ ἀκούσειεν αὐτῶν, πολὺν χρόνον ἀνεβάλ-
λετο τὴν διαδικασίαν. ταῦτα δὲ ποιῶν ἡγεῖτο
προσεθίζειν αὐτοὺς θεραπεύειν, ἧττον δὲ ἐχθρῶς ἢ
εἰ αὐτὸς κολάζων ἠνάγκαζε παρεῖναι.

19. Εἷς μὲν τρόπος διδασκαλίας ἦν αὐτῷ οὗτος
τοῦ παρεῖναι· ἄλλος δὲ τὸ τὰ ῥᾷστα καὶ κερδα-
λεώτατα τοῖς παροῦσι προστάττειν· ἄλλος δὲ τὸ
μηδέν ποτε τοῖς ἀποῦσι νέμειν· 20. ὁ δὲ δὴ

take measures that his associates in power should be such as they ought to be. In the first place, if any of those who were able to live by the labours of others failed to attend at court, he made inquiry after them; for he thought that those who came would not be willing to do anything dishonourable or immoral, partly because they were in the presence of their sovereign and partly also because they knew that, whatever they did, they would be under the eyes of the best men there; whereas, in the case of those who did not, come he believed that they absented themselves because they were guilty of some form of intemperance or injustice or neglect of duty.

17. We will describe first, therefore, the manner in which he obliged all such to come; he would direct some one of the best friends he had at court to seize some of the property of the man who did not present himself and to declare that he was taking only what was his own. So, whenever this happened, those who lost their effects would come to him to complain that they had been wronged. 18. Cyrus, however, would not be at leisure for a long time to give such men a hearing, and when he did give them a hearing he would postpone the trial for a long time. By so doing he thought he would accustom them to pay their court and that he would thus excite less ill-feeling than he would if he compelled them to come by imposing penalties.

How he enforced the discipline

19. That was one of his methods of training them to attend. Another was to give those who did attend the easiest and the most profitable employment; and another was never to distribute any favours among those who failed to attend. 20. But the

μέγιστος τρόπος τῆς ἀνάγκης ἦν, εἰ τούτων μηδέν
τις ὑπακούοι, ἀφελόμενος ἂν τοῦτον ἃ ἔχοι ἄλλῳ
ἐδίδου ὃν ᾤετο [δύνασθαι] [1] ἂν ἐν τῷ δέοντι
παρεῖναι· καὶ οὕτως ἐγίγνετο αὐτῷ φίλος χρήσιμος ἀντὶ ἀχρήστου. ἐπιζητεῖ δὲ καὶ ὁ νῦν
βασιλεύς, ἤν τις ἀπῇ οἷς παρεῖναι καθήκει.

21. Τοῖς μὲν δὴ μὴ παροῦσιν οὕτω προσεφέρετο·
τοὺς δὲ παρέχοντας ἑαυτοὺς ἐνόμισε μάλιστ᾽ ἂν
ἐπὶ τὰ καλὰ κἀγαθὰ ἐπαίρειν, ἐπείπερ ἄρχων ἦν
αὐτῶν, εἰ αὐτὸς ἑαυτὸν ἐπιδεικνύειν πειρῷτο τοῖς
ἀρχομένοις πάντων μάλιστα κεκοσμημένον τῇ
ἀρετῇ. 22. αἰσθάνεσθαι μὲν γὰρ ἐδόκει καὶ διὰ
τοὺς γραφομένους νόμους βελτίους γιγνομένους
ἀνθρώπους· τὸν δὲ ἀγαθὸν ἄρχοντα βλέποντα
νόμον ἀνθρώποις ἐνόμισεν, ὅτι καὶ τάττειν ἱκανός
ἐστι καὶ ὁρᾶν τὸν ἀτακτοῦντα καὶ κολάζειν.

23. Οὕτω δὴ γιγνώσκων πρῶτον μὲν τὰ περὶ
τοὺς θεοὺς μᾶλλον ἐκπονοῦντα ἐπεδείκνυ ἑαυτὸν
ἐν τούτῳ τῷ χρόνῳ, ἐπεὶ εὐδαιμονέστερος ἦν.
καὶ τότε πρῶτον κατεστάθησαν οἱ μάγοι . . . . [2]
ὑμνεῖν τε ἀεὶ ἅμα τῇ ἡμέρᾳ τοὺς θεοὺς καὶ
θύειν ἀν᾽ ἑκάστην ἡμέραν οἷς οἱ μάγοι θεοῖς
εἴποιεν. 24. οὕτω δὴ τὰ τότε κατασταθέντα
ἔτι καὶ νῦν διαμένει παρὰ τῷ ἀεὶ ὄντι βασιλεῖ.
ταῦτ᾽ οὖν πρῶτον ἐμιμοῦντο αὐτὸν καὶ οἱ ἄλλοι
Πέρσαι, νομίζοντες καὶ αὐτοὶ εὐδαιμονέστεροι
ἔσεσθαι, ἢν θεραπεύωσι τοὺς θεούς, ὥσπερ ὁ

[1] δύνασθαι MSS., Dindorf, Breitenbach ; [δύνασθαι] Nitsche,
Hug, Marchant, Gemoll.
[2] Lacuna discovered by Hug, adopted by Marchant, Gemoll.
(ἐκ τούτου δὲ αὐτὸς ἤρχετο—and in consequence of this he
himself began).

surest way of compulsion was this : if a man paid no
attention to any of these three methods, he would
take away all that he had and give it to some one
else who he thought would present himself when he
was wanted ; and thus he would get a useful friend
in exchange for a useless one. And the king to-day
likewise makes inquiries if any one absents himself
whose duty it is to be present.

21. Thus, then, he dealt with those who failed *Cyrus*
to attend at court. But in those who did present *resolves to*
themselves he believed that he could in no way more *be a model*
effectively inspire a desire for the beautiful and the *in*
good than by endeavouring, as their sovereign, to set
before his subjects a perfect model of virtue in his
own person. 22. For he thought he perceived that
men are made better through even the written law,
while the good ruler he regarded as a law with eyes
for men, because he is able not only to give com-
mandments but also to see the transgressor and
punish him.

23. In this conviction, he showed himself in the *(1) religion,*
first place more devout in his worship of the gods,
now that he was more fortunate ; and then for the
first time the college of magi was instituted . . .
and he never failed to sing hymns to the gods
at daybreak and to sacrifice daily to whatsoever
deities the magi directed. 24. Thus the institutions
established by him at that time have continued in
force with each successive king even to this day. In
this respect, therefore, the rest of the Persians also
imitated him from the first ; for they believed that
they would be more sure of good fortune if they
revered the gods just as he did who was their

εὐδαιμονέστατός τε ὢν καὶ ἄρχων· καὶ Κύρῳ
δ᾽ ἂν ἡγοῦντο ταῦτα ποιοῦντες ἀρέσκειν. 25. ὁ
δὲ Κῦρος τὴν τῶν μεθ᾽ αὑτοῦ εὐσέβειαν καὶ
ἑαυτῷ ἀγαθὸν ἐνόμιζε, λογιζόμενος ὥσπερ οἱ
πλεῖν αἱρούμενοι μετὰ τῶν εὐσεβῶν μᾶλλον ἢ
μετὰ τῶν ἠσεβηκέναι τι δοκούντων. πρὸς δὲ
τούτοις ἐλογίζετο ὡς εἰ πάντες οἱ κοινῶνες θεο-
σεβεῖς εἶεν, ἧττον ἂν αὐτοὺς ἐθέλειν περί τε
ἀλλήλους ἀνόσιόν τι ποιεῖν καὶ περὶ ἑαυτόν,
εὐεργέτης νομίζων εἶναι τῶν κοινώνων. 26. ἐμ-
φανίζων δὲ καὶ τοῦτο ὅτι περὶ πολλοῦ ἐποιεῖτο
μηδένα μήτε φίλον ἀδικεῖν μήτε σύμμαχον, ἀλλὰ
τὸ δίκαιον ἰσχυρῶς ὁρῶν, μᾶλλον καὶ τοὺς ἄλλους
ᾤετ᾽ ἂν τῶν μὲν αἰσχρῶν κερδῶν ἀπέχεσθαι,
διὰ τοῦ δικαίου δ᾽ ἐθέλειν πορεύεσθαι. 27. καὶ
αἰδοῦς δ᾽ ἂν ἡγεῖτο μᾶλλον πάντας ἐμπιμπλάναι,
εἰ αὐτὸς φανερὸς εἴη πάντας οὕτως αἰδούμενος
ὡς μήτ᾽ εἰπεῖν ἂν μήτε ποιῆσαι μηδὲν αἰσχρόν.
28. ἐτεκμαίρετο δὲ τοῦτο οὕτως ἕξειν ἐκ τοῦδε·
μὴ γὰρ ὅτι ἄρχοντα, ἀλλὰ καὶ οὓς οὐ φοβοῦνται,
μᾶλλον τοὺς αἰδουμένους αἰδοῦνται τῶν ἀναιδῶν
οἱ ἄνθρωποι· καὶ γυναῖκας δὲ ἃς ἂν αἰδουμένας
αἰσθάνωνται, ἀνταιδεῖσθαι μᾶλλον ἐθέλουσιν
ὁρῶντες.

29. Τὸ δ᾽ αὖ πείθεσθαι οὕτω μάλιστ᾽ ἂν ᾤετο
ἔμμονον εἶναι τοῖς περὶ αὑτόν, εἰ τοὺς ἀπρο-
φασίστως πειθομένους φανερὸς εἴη μᾶλλον τιμῶν
τῶν τὰς μεγίστας ἀρετὰς καὶ ἐπιπονωτάτας δο-

overeign and the most fortunate of all; and they
thought also that in doing this they would please
Cyrus. 25. And Cyrus considered that the piety of
his friends was a good thing for him, too; for he
reasoned as they do who prefer, when embarking on
a voyage, to set sail with pious companions rather
than with those who are believed to have committed
some impiety. And besides, he reasoned that if all
his associates were god-fearing men, they would be
less inclined to commit crime against one another or
against himself, for he considered himself their benefactor; 26. and if he made it plain how important he (2) upright-
held it to be to wrong no one of his friends or allies, ness,
and if he always paid scrupulous regard to what was
upright, others also, he thought, would be more likely
to abstain from improper gains and to endeavour to
make their way by upright methods. 27. And he (3) consider-
thought that he should be more likely to inspire in ateness,
all respect for others, if he himself were seen to show
such respect for all as not to say or do anything
improper. 28. And that this would be the result
he concluded from the following observation: people
have more respect for those who have such respect
for others than they have for those who have not;
they show it toward even those whom they do not
fear—to say nothing of what they would show toward
their kings; and women also whom they see showing
respect for others they are more inclined to look
upon in turn with respect.

29. And again, obedience he thought would be (4) obedi-
most deeply impressed upon his attendants, if he ence,
showed that he honoured those who unhesitatingly
obeyed more than those who thought they exhibited

κούντων παρέχεσθαι. γιγνώσκων δ' οὕτω κα
ποιῶν διετέλει.

30. Καὶ σωφροσύνην δ' αὐτοῦ[1] ἐπιδεικνὺ
μᾶλλον ἐποίει καὶ ταύτην πάντας ἀσκεῖν. ὅται
γὰρ ὁρῶσιν, ᾧ μάλιστα ἔξεστιν ὑβρίζειν, τούτοι
σωφρονοῦντα, οὕτω μᾶλλον οἵ γε ἀσθενέστεροι
ἐθέλουσιν οὐδὲν ὑβριστικὸν ποιοῦντες φανεροὶ
εἶναι. 31. [διῄρει δὲ αἰδῶ καὶ σωφροσύνην τῇδε,
ὡς τοὺς μὲν αἰδουμένους τὰ ἐν τῷ φανερῷ αἰσχρὰ
φεύγοντας, τοὺς δὲ σώφρονας καὶ τὰ ἐν τῷ
ἀφανεῖ.][2] 32. καὶ ἐγκράτειαν δὲ οὕτω μάλιστ
ἂν ᾤετο ἀσκεῖσθαι, εἰ αὐτὸς ἐπιδεικνύοι ἑαυτὸν
μὴ ὑπὸ τῶν παραυτίκα ἡδονῶν ἑλκόμενον ἀπὸ
τῶν ἀγαθῶν, ἀλλὰ προπονεῖν ἐθέλοντα πρῶτον
σὺν τῷ καλῷ τῶν εὐφροσυνῶν.

33. Τοιγαροῦν τοιοῦτος ὢν ἐποίησεν ἐπὶ ταῖς
θύραις πολλὴν μὲν τῶν χειρόνων εὐταξίαν, ὑπει-
κόντων τοῖς ἀμείνοσι, πολλὴν δ' αἰδῶ καὶ εὐκο-
σμίαν πρὸς ἀλλήλους. ἐπέγνως δ' ἂν ἐκεῖ οὐδένα
οὔτε ὀργιζόμενον κραυγῇ οὔτε χαίροντα ὑβρι-
στικῷ γέλωτι, ἀλλὰ ἰδὼν ἂν αὐτοὺς ἡγήσω τῷ
ὄντι εἰς κάλλος ζῆν.

34. Τοιαῦτα μὲν δὴ ποιοῦντες καὶ ὁρῶντες ἐπὶ
θύραις διῆγον. τῆς πολεμικῆς δ' ἕνεκα ἀσκήσεως
ἐπὶ θήραν ἐξῆγεν οὕσπερ ἀσκεῖν ταῦτα ᾤετο
χρῆναι, ταύτην ἡγούμενος καὶ ὅλως ἀρίστην

---

[1] αὑτοῦ Edd.; αὐτοῦ MSS.
[2] διῄρει . . . ἀφανεῖ MSS., Dindorf, Breitenbach ; bracketed
by Nitsche, Hug, Marchant, Gemoll.

the greatest and most elaborate virtues. And thus
he continued throughout to judge and to act.

30. And by making his own self-control an example, (5) temper-
he disposed all to practise that virtue more diligently. ance
For when the weaker members of society see that one
who is in a position where he may indulge himself to
excess is still under self-control, they naturally strive
all the more not to be found guilty of any excessive
indulgence. 31. [Moreover, he distinguished between considerateness and self-control in this way:
the considerate are those who avoid what is offensive
when seen; the self-controlled avoid that which is
offensive, even when unseen.] 32. And he thought
that temperance could be best inculcated, if he
showed that he himselr was never carried away from
the pursuit of the good by any pleasures of the
moment, but that he was willing to labour first for
the attainment of refined pleasures.

33. To sum up, then, by setting such an example
Cyrus secured at court great correctness of conduct
on the part of his subordinates, who gave precedence
to their superiors; and thus he also secured from
them a great degree of respect and politeness toward
one another. And among them you would never
have detected any one raising his voice in anger or
giving vent to his delight in boisterous laughter;
but on seeing them you would have judged that they
were in truth making a noble life their aim.

34. Such was what they did and such what they The chase as
witnessed day by day at court. With a view to training a means of
in the arts of war, Cyrus used to take out hunting discipline
those who he thought ought to have such practice,
for he held that this was altogether the best

ἄσκησιν πολεμικῶν εἶναι, καὶ ἱππικῆς δὲ ἀληθε
στάτην. 35. καὶ γὰρ ἐπόχους ἐν παντοδαποῖ
χωρίοις αὕτη μάλιστα ἀποδείκνυσι διὰ τὸ θη
ρίοις φεύγουσιν ἐφέπεσθαι, καὶ ἀπὸ τῶν ἵππω
ἐνεργοὺς αὕτη μάλιστα ἀπεργάζεται διὰ τὴ
τοῦ λαμβάνειν φιλοτιμίαν καὶ ἐπιθυμίαν. 36. κα
τὴν ἐγκράτειαν δὲ καὶ πόνους καὶ ψύχη κα
θάλπη καὶ λιμὸν καὶ δίψος δύνασθαι φέρει
ἐνταῦθα μάλιστα προσείθιζε τοὺς κοινῶνας. κα
νῦν δ' ἔτι βασιλεὺς καὶ οἱ ἄλλοι οἱ περὶ βασιλέ
ταῦτα ποιοῦντες διατελοῦσιν.

37. Ὅτι μὲν οὖν οὐκ ᾤετο προσήκειν οὐδε
ἀρχῆς ὅστις μὴ βελτίων εἴη τῶν ἀρχομένων κα
τοῖς προειρημένοις πᾶσι δῆλον, καὶ ὅτι οὕτω
ἀσκῶν τοὺς περὶ αὐτὸν πολὺ μάλιστα αὐτὸ
ἐξεπόνει καὶ τὴν ἐγκράτειαν καὶ τὰς πολεμικὰ
τέχνας καὶ [τὰς]¹ μελέτας. 38. καὶ γὰρ ἐπὶ θήρα
τοὺς μὲν ἄλλους ἐξῆγεν, ὁπότε μὴ μένειν ἀνάγκη
τις εἴη· αὐτὸς δὲ καὶ ὁπότε ἀνάγκη εἴη, οἴκο
ἐθήρα τὰ ἐν τοῖς παραδείσοις θηρία τρεφόμενα· κα
οὔτ' αὐτός ποτε πρὶν ἱδρῶσαι δεῖπνον ᾑρεῖτο οὔτε
ἵπποις ἀγυμνάστοις σῖτον ἐνέβαλλε· συμπαρε
κάλει δὲ καὶ εἰς ταύτην τὴν θήραν τοὺς περὶ
αὐτὸν σκηπτούχους. 39. τοιγαροῦν πολὺ μὲ
αὐτὸς διέφερεν ἐν πᾶσι τοῖς καλοῖς ἔργοις, πολὺ
δὲ οἱ περὶ ἐκεῖνον, διὰ τὴν ἀεὶ μελέτην. παρά-
δειγμα μὲν δὴ τοιοῦτον ἑαυτὸν παρείχετο.

Πρὸς δὲ τούτῳ καὶ τῶν ἄλλων οὕστινας μάλιστα

¹ τὰς MSS., Dindorf³, Breitenbach; [τὰς] Dindorf⁴, Hertlein, Hug, Marchant, Gemoll.

training in military science and also the truest in horsemanship. 35. For it is the exercise best adapted to give riders a firm seat in all sorts of places, because they have to pursue the animals wherever they may run; and it is also the best exercise to make them active on horseback because of their rivalry and eagerness to get the game. 36. By this same exercise, too, he was best able to accustom his associates to temperance and the endurance of hardship, to heat and cold, to hunger and thirst. And even to this day the king and the rest that make up his retinue continue to engage in the same sport.

37. From all that has been said, therefore, it is evident that he believed that no one had any right to rule who was not better than his subjects; and it is evident, too, that in thus drilling those about him he himself got his own best training both in temperance and in the arts and pursuits of war. 38. For he not only used to take the others out hunting, whenever there was no need of his staying at home, but even when there was some need of his staying at home, he would himself hunt the animals that were kept in the parks. And he never dined without first having got himself into a sweat, nor would he have any food given to his horses without their having first been duly exercised; and to these hunts he would invite also the mace-bearers in attendance upon him. 39. The result of all this constant training was that he and his associates greatly excelled in all manly exercises. Such an example did he furnish by his own personal conduct. _{Excellence encouraged}

And besides this, he used to reward with gifts and

ὁρῴη τὰ καλὰ διώκοντας, τούτους καὶ δώροις
καὶ ἀρχαῖς καὶ ἕδραις καὶ πάσαις τιμαῖς ἐγέραιρεν·
ὥστε πολλὴν πᾶσι φιλοτιμίαν ἐνέβαλλεν ὅπως
ἕκαστος ὅτι ἄριστος φανήσοιτο Κύρῳ.

40. Καταμαθεῖν δὲ τοῦ Κύρου δοκοῦμεν ὡς οὐ
τούτῳ μόνῳ ἐνόμιζε χρῆναι τοὺς ἄρχοντας τῶν
ἀρχομένων διαφέρειν, τῷ βελτίονας αὐτῶν εἶναι,
ἀλλὰ καὶ καταγοητεύειν ᾤετο χρῆναι αὐτούς.
στολήν τε γοῦν εἵλετο τὴν Μηδικὴν αὐτός τε
φορεῖν καὶ τοὺς κοινῶνας ταύτην ἔπεισεν ἐν-
δύεσθαι· αὕτη γὰρ αὐτῷ συγκρύπτειν ἐδόκει εἴ
τίς τι ἐν τῷ σώματι ἐνδεὲς ἔχοι, καὶ καλλί-
στους καὶ μεγίστους ἐπιδεικνύναι τοὺς φοροῦντας.
41. καὶ γὰρ τὰ ὑποδήματα τοιαῦτα ἔχουσιν ἐν
οἷς μάλιστα λαθεῖν ἔστι καὶ ὑποτιθεμένους τι,
ὥστε δοκεῖν μείζους εἶναι ἢ εἰσί. καὶ ὑποχρίεσθαι
δὲ τοὺς ὀφθαλμοὺς προσίετο, ὡς εὐοφθαλμότεροι
φαίνοιντο ἢ εἰσί, καὶ ἐντρίβεσθαι, ὡς εὐχροώτεροι
ὁρῷντο ἢ πεφύκασιν.

42. Ἐμελέτησε δὲ καὶ ὡς μὴ πτύοντες μηδὲ
ἀπομυττόμενοι φανεροὶ εἶεν, μηδὲ μεταστρεφόμενοι
ἐπὶ θέαν μηδενός, ὡς οὐδὲν θαυμάζοντες. πάντα
δὲ ταῦτα ᾤετο φέρειν τι εἰς τὸ δυσκαταφρονητο-
τέρους φαίνεσθαι τοῖς ἀρχομένοις.

43. Οὓς μὲν δὴ ἄρχειν ᾤετο χρῆναι, δι᾽ ἑαυτοῦ
οὕτω κατεσκεύασε καὶ μελέτῃ καὶ τῷ σεμνῶς
προεστάναι αὐτῶν· οὓς δ᾽ αὖ κατεσκεύαζεν εἰς τὸ
δουλεύειν, τούτους οὔτε μελετᾶν τῶν ἐλευθερίων

positions of authority and seats of honour and all
sorts of preferment others whom he saw devoting
themselves most eagerly to the attainment of
excellence ; and thus he inspired in all an earnest
ambition, each striving to appear as deserving as he
could in the eyes of Cyrus.

40. We think, furthermore, that we have observed *He adopts the Median costume*
in Cyrus that he held the opinion that a ruler ought
to excel his subjects not only in point of being
actually better than they, but that he ought also to
cast a sort of spell upon them. At any rate, he chose
to wear the Median dress himself and persuaded
his associates also to adopt it ; for he thought
that if any one had any personal defect, that dress
would help to conceal it, and that it made the
wearer look very tall and very handsome. 41. For
they have shoes of such a form that without being detected the wearer can easily put something into the
soles so as to make him look taller than he is.
He encouraged also the fashion of pencilling the
eyes, that they might seem more lustrous than they
are, and of using cosmetics to make the complexion
look better than nature made it.

42. He trained his associates also not to spit or to
wipe the nose in public, and not to turn round to look
at anything, as being men who wondered at nothing.
All this he thought contributed, in some measure, to
their appearing to their subjects men who could not
lightly be despised.

43. Those, therefore, who he thought ought to be *His policy toward the servant class*
in authority he thus prepared in his own school by
careful training as well as by the respect which he
commanded as their leader ; those, on the other
hand, whom he was training to be servants he did

πόνων οὐδένα παρώρμα οὔθ' ὅπλα κεκτῆσθαι
ἐπέτρεπεν· ἐπεμέλετο δὲ ὅπως μήτε ἄσιτοι μήτε
ἄποτοί ποτε ἔσοιντο ἐλευθερίων ἕνεκα μελετη-
μάτων. 44. καὶ γὰρ ὁπότε ἐλαύνοιεν τὰ θηρία τοῖς
ἱππεῦσιν εἰς τὰ πεδία, φέρεσθαι σῖτον εἰς θήραν
τούτοις ἐπέτρεπε, τῶν δὲ ἐλευθέρων οὐδενί· καὶ
ὁπότε πορεία εἴη, ἦγεν αὐτοὺς πρὸς τὰ ὕδατα
ὥσπερ τὰ ὑποζύγια. καὶ ὁπότε δὲ ὥρα εἴη
ἀρίστου, ἀνέμενεν αὐτοὺς ἔστε ἐμφάγοιέν τι, ὡς
μὴ βουλιμιῷεν· ὥστε καὶ οὗτοι αὐτὸν ὥσπερ οἱ
ἄριστοι πατέρα ἐκάλουν, ὅτι ἐπεμέλετο αὐτῶν
[ὅπως ἀναμφιλόγως ἀεὶ ἀνδράποδα διατελοῖεν].[1]

45. Τῇ μὲν δὴ ὅλῃ Περσῶν ἀρχῇ οὕτω τὴν
ἀσφάλειαν κατεσκεύαζεν. ἑαυτῷ δὲ ὅτι μὲν οὐχ
ὑπὸ τῶν καταστραφέντων κίνδυνος εἴη παθεῖν τι
ἰσχυρῶς ἐθάρρει· καὶ γὰρ ἀνάλκιδας ἡγεῖτο εἶναι
αὐτοὺς καὶ ἀσυντάκτους ὄντας ἑώρα, καὶ πρὸς
τούτοις οὐδ' ἐπλησίαζε τούτων οὐδεὶς αὐτῷ οὔτε
νυκτὸς οὔτε ἡμέρας. 46. οὓς δὲ κρατίστους τε
ἡγεῖτο καὶ ὡπλισμένους καὶ ἀθρόους ὄντας ἑώρα
—καὶ τοὺς μὲν αὐτῶν ᾔδει ἱππέων ἡγεμόνας
ὄντας, τοὺς δὲ πεζῶν· πολλοὺς δὲ αὐτῶν καὶ
φρονήματα ἔχοντας ᾐσθάνετο ὡς ἱκανοὺς ὄντας
ἄρχειν· καὶ τοῖς φύλαξι δὲ αὐτοῦ οὗτοι μάλιστα

---

[1] ὅπως . . . διατελοῖεν MSS., most Edd.; bracketed by
Cobet, Hug.

not encourage to practise any of the exercises of freemen ; neither did he allow them to own weapons ; but he took care that they should not suffer any deprivation in food or drink on account of the exercises in which they served the freemen. 44. And he managed it in this way : whenever they were to drive the animals down into the plains for the horsemen, he allowed those of the lower classes, but none of the freemen, to take food with them on the hunt ; and whenever there was an expedition to make, he would lead the serving men to water, just as he did the beasts of burden. And again, when it was time for luncheon, he would wait for them until they could get something to eat, so that they should not get so ravenously hungry. And so this class also called him "father," just as the nobles did, for he provided for them well [so that they might spend all their lives as slaves, without a protest].

45. Thus he secured for the whole Persian empire the necessary stability ; and as for himself, he was perfectly confident that there was no danger of his suffering aught at the hands of those whom he had subdued. And the ground of his confidence was this— that he believed them to be powerless and he saw that they were unorganized ; and besides that, not one of them came near him either by night or by day. 46. But there were some whom he considered very powerful and whom he saw well armed and well organized ; and some of them, he knew, had cavalry under their command, others infantry ; and he was aware that many of them had the assurance to think that they were competent to rule ; and these not only came in very close touch with his guards but

His personal security

ἐπλησίαζον, καὶ αὐτῷ δὲ τῷ Κύρῳ τούτων πολλοὶ
πολλάκις συνεμίγνυσαν· ἀνάγκη γὰρ ἦν, ὅ τι
καὶ χρῆσθαι ἔμελλεν αὐτοῖς—ὑπὸ τούτων οὖν
καὶ κίνδυνος ἦν αὐτὸν μάλιστα παθεῖν τι κατὰ
πολλοὺς τρόπους.

47. Σκοπῶν οὖν ὅπως ἂν αὐτῷ καὶ τὰ ἀπὸ
τούτων ἀκίνδυνα γένοιτο, τὸ μὲν περιελέσθαι
αὐτῶν τὰ ὅπλα καὶ ἀπολέμους ποιῆσαι ἀπεδοκί-
μασε, καὶ ἄδικον ἡγούμενος καὶ κατάλυσιν τῆς
ἀρχῆς ταύτην νομίζων· τὸ δ᾽ αὖ μὴ προσίεσθαι
αὐτοὺς καὶ τὸ ἀπιστοῦντα φανερὸν εἶναι ἀρχὴν
ἡγήσατο πολέμου. 48. ἐν δὲ ἀντὶ πάντων τούτων
ἔγνω καὶ κράτιστον εἶναι πρὸς τὴν ἑαυτοῦ ἀσφάλειαν καὶ κάλλιστον, εἰ δύναιτο ποιῆσαι τοὺς
κρατίστους ἑαυτῷ μᾶλλον φίλους ἢ ἀλλήλοις. ὡς
οὖν ἐπὶ τὸ φιλεῖσθαι δοκεῖ ἡμῖν ἐλθεῖν, τοῦτο
πειρασόμεθα διηγήσασθαι.

II

1. Πρῶτον μὲν γὰρ διὰ παντὸς ἀεὶ τοῦ χρόνου
φιλανθρωπίαν τῆς ψυχῆς ὡς ἐδύνατο μάλιστα
ἐνεφάνιζεν, ἡγούμενος, ὥσπερ οὐ ῥάδιόν ἐστι
φιλεῖν τοὺς μισεῖν δοκοῦντας οὐδ᾽ εὐνοεῖν τοῖς
κακόνοις, οὕτω καὶ τοὺς γνωσθέντας ὡς φιλοῦσι
καὶ εὐνοοῦσιν, οὐκ ἂν δύνασθαι μισεῖσθαι ὑπὸ
τῶν φιλεῖσθαι ἡγουμένων.

2. Ἕως μὲν οὖν χρήμασιν ἀδυνατώτερος ἦν
εὐεργετεῖν, τῷ τε προνοεῖν τῶν συνόντων καὶ τῷ

many of them came frequently in contact with Cyrus himself, and this was unavoidable if he was to make any use of them—this, then, was the quarter from which there was the greatest danger that something might happen to him in any one of many ways.

47. So, as he cast about in his mind how to remove any danger that might arise from them also, he rejected the thought of disarming them and making them incapable of war; for he decided that that would be unjust, and besides he thought that this would be destruction to his empire. On the other hand, he believed that to refuse to admit them to his presence or to show that he mistrusted them would lead at once to hostilities. 48. But better than any of these ways, he recognized that there was one course that would be at once the most honourable and the most conducive to his own personal security, and that was, if possible, to make those powerful nobles better friends to himself than to one another. We shall, therefore, attempt to explain the method that he seems to have taken to gain their friendship.

II

1. In the first place, then, he showed at all times as great kindness of heart as he could; for he believed that just as it is not easy to love those who seem to hate us, or to cherish good-will toward those who bear us ill-will, in the same way those who are known to love and to cherish good-will could not be hated by those who believe themselves loved.

2. During the time, therefore, when he was not yet quite able to do favours through gifts of money,

How Cyrus made himself popular

προπονεῖν καὶ τῷ συνηδόμενος μὲν ἐπὶ τοῖς ἀγαθοῖς φανερὸς εἶναι, συναχθόμενος δ' ἐπὶ τοῖς
κακοῖς, τούτοις ἐπειρᾶτο τὴν φιλίαν θηρεύειν·
ἐπειδὴ δὲ ἐγένετο αὐτῷ ὥστε χρήμασιν εὐεργετεῖν,
δοκεῖ ἡμῖν γνῶναι πρῶτον μὲν ὡς εὐεργέτημα
ἀνθρώποις πρὸς ἀλλήλους οὐδέν ἐστιν ἀπὸ τῆς
αὐτῆς δαπάνης ἐπιχαριτώτερον ἢ σίτων καὶ ποτῶν
μετάδοσις. 3. τοῦτο δ' οὕτω νομίσας πρῶτον
μὲν ἐπὶ τὴν αὑτοῦ τράπεζαν συνέταξεν ὅπως οἷς
αὐτὸς σιτοῖτο σίτοις, τούτοις ὅμοια ἀεὶ παρατί-
θοιτο αὐτῷ ἱκανὰ παμπόλλοις ἀνθρώποις· ὅσα
δὲ παρατεθείη, ταῦτα πάντα, πλὴν οἷς αὐτὸς καὶ
οἱ σύνδειπνοι χρήσαιντο, διεδίδου οἷς δὴ βούλοιτο
τῶν φίλων μνήμην ἐνδείκνυσθαι ἢ φιλοφροσύνην.
διέπεμπε δὲ καὶ τούτοις οὓς ἀγασθείη ἢ ἐν φυ-
λακαῖς ἢ ἐν θεραπείαις ἢ ἐν αἰστισινοῦν πρά-
ξεσιν, ἐνσημαινόμενος ὅτι οὐκ ἂν λανθάνοιεν
χαρίζεσθαι βουλόμενοι.

4. Ἐτίμα δὲ καὶ τῶν οἰκετῶν ἀπὸ τῆς τραπέζης ὁπότε τινὰ ἐπαινέσειε· καὶ τὸν πάντα
δὲ σῖτον τῶν οἰκετῶν ἐπὶ τὴν αὑτοῦ τράπεζαν
ἐπετίθετο, οἰόμενος ὥσπερ καὶ τοῖς κυσὶν ἐμποιεῖν
τινα καὶ τοῦτο εὔνοιαν. εἰ δὲ καὶ θεραπεύεσθαί
τινα βούλοιτο τῶν φίλων ὑπὸ πολλῶν, καὶ τούτοις ἔπεμπεν ἀπὸ τραπέζης· καὶ νῦν γὰρ ἔτι
οἷς ἂν ὁρῶσι πεμπόμενα ἀπὸ τῆς βασιλέως τραπέζης, τούτους πάντες μᾶλλον θεραπεύουσι, νομίζοντες αὐτοὺς ἐντίμους εἶναι καὶ ἱκανοὺς δια-

he tried to win the love of those about him by taking forethought for them and labouring for them and showing that he rejoiced with them in their good fortune and sympathized with them in their mishaps; and after he found himself in a position to do favours with money, he seems to us to have recog- The nearest way to a man's heart nized from the start that there is no kindness which men can show one another, with the same amount of expenditure, more acceptable than sharing meat and drink with them. 3. In this belief, he first of all arranged that there should be placed upon his own table a quantity of food, like that of which he himself regularly partook, sufficient for a very large number of people; and all of that which was served to him, except what he and his companions at table consumed, he distributed among those of his friends to whom he wished to send remembrances or good wishes. And he used to send such presents around to those also whose services on garrison duty or in attendance upon him or in any other way met with his approval; in this way he let them see that he did not fail to observe their wish to please him.

4. He used also to honour with presents from his table any one of his servants whom he took occasion to commend; and he had all of his servants' food served from his own table, for he thought that this would implant in them a certain amount of good-will, just as it does in dogs. And if he wished to have any one of his friends courted by the multitude, to such a one he would send presents from his table. And that device proved effective; for even to this day everybody pays more diligent court to those to whom they see things sent from the royal table; for they think that such persons must be in high favour

πράττειν, ἤν τι δέωνται. ἔτι δὲ καὶ οὐ τούτων
μόνον ἕνεκα τῶν εἰρημένων εὐφραίνει τὰ πεμπόμενα παρὰ βασιλέως, ἀλλὰ τῷ ὄντι καὶ ἡδονῇ
πολὺ διαφέρει τὰ ἀπὸ τῆς βασιλέως τραπέζης.
5. καὶ τοῦτο μέντοι οὕτως ἔχειν οὐδέν τι θαυ-
μαστόν· ὥσπερ γὰρ καὶ αἱ ἄλλαι τέχναι διαφερόντως ἐν ταῖς μεγάλαις πόλεσιν ἐξειργασμέναι
εἰσί, κατὰ τὸν αὐτὸν τρόπον καὶ τὰ παρὰ βασιλεῖ
σῖτα πολὺ διαφερόντως ἐκπεπόνηται. ἐν μὲν γὰρ
ταῖς μικραῖς πόλεσιν οἱ αὐτοὶ ποιοῦσι κλίνην,
θύραν, ἄροτρον, τράπεζαν, πολλάκις δ' ὁ αὐτὸς
οὗτος καὶ οἰκοδομεῖ, καὶ ἀγαπᾷ ἢν καὶ οὕτως
ἱκανοὺς αὐτὸν τρέφειν ἐργοδότας λαμβάνῃ· ἀδύ-
νατον οὖν πολλὰ τεχνώμενον ἄνθρωπον πάντα
καλῶς ποιεῖν. ἐν δὲ ταῖς μεγάλαις πόλεσι διὰ τὸ
πολλοὺς ἑκάστου δεῖσθαι ἀρκεῖ καὶ μία ἑκάστῳ
τέχνη εἰς τὸ τρέφεσθαι· πολλάκις δὲ οὐδ' ὅλη
μία· ἀλλ' ὑποδήματα ποιεῖ ὁ μὲν ἀνδρεῖα, ὁ δὲ
γυναικεῖα· ἔστι δὲ ἔνθα καὶ ὑποδήματα ὁ μὲν
νευρορραφῶν μόνον τρέφεται, ὁ δὲ σχίζων, ὁ δὲ
χιτῶνας μόνον συντέμνων, ὁ δέ γε τούτων οὐδὲν
ποιῶν ἀλλὰ συντιθεὶς ταῦτα. ἀνάγκη οὖν τὸν
ἐν βραχυτάτῳ διατρίβοντα ἔργῳ τοῦτον καὶ
ἄριστα δὴ ἠναγκάσθαι[1] τοῦτο ποιεῖν.
6. Τὸ αὐτὸ δὲ τοῦτο πέπονθε καὶ τὰ ἀμφὶ
τὴν δίαιταν. ᾧ μὲν γὰρ ὁ αὐτὸς κλίνην στρών-
νυσι, τράπεζαν κοσμεῖ, μάττει, ὄψα ἄλλοτε ἀλ-

---

[1] δὴ ἠναγκάσθαι Hertlein, Sauppe, Hug, Marchant; διηναγ-
κάσθαι xzV, Dindorf, Breitenbach; διενεγκάσθαι y; δύνασθαι
Gemoll.

and in a position to secure for them anything they may want. Moreover, it is not for these reasons only that that which is sent by the king gives delight, but the food that is sent from the king's board really is much superior in the gratification also that it gives. 5. That this, however, should be so is no marvel. For just as all other arts are developed to superior excellence in large cities, in that same way the food at the king's palace is also elaborately prepared with superior excellence. For in small towns the same workman makes chairs and doors and plows and tables, and often this same artisan builds houses, and even so he is thankful if he can only find employment enough to support him. And it is, of course, impossible for a man of many trades to be proficient in all of them. In large cities, on the other hand, inasmuch as many people have demands to make upon each branch of industry, one trade alone, and very often even less than a whole trade, is enough to support a man: one man, for instance, makes shoes for men, and another for women; and there are places even where one man earns a living by only stitching shoes, another by cutting them out, another by sewing the uppers together, while there is another who performs none of these operations but only assembles the parts. It follows, therefore, as a matter of course, that he who devotes himself to a very highly specialized line of work is bound to do it in the best possible manner.

6. Exactly the same thing holds true also in reference to the kitchen: in any establishment where one and the same man arranges the dining couches, lays the table, bakes the bread, prepares now one sort of dish

Specialization desirable even in the kitchen

333

λοῖα ποιεῖ, ἀνάγκη οἶμαι τούτῳ, ὡς ἂν ἕκαστον
προχωρῇ, οὕτως ἔχειν· ὅπου δὲ ἱκανὸν ἔργον ἑνὶ
ἕψειν κρέα, ἄλλῳ ὀπτᾶν, ἄλλῳ δὲ ἰχθὺν ἕψειν,
ἄλλῳ ὀπτᾶν, ἄλλῳ ἄρτους ποιεῖν, καὶ μηδὲ
τούτους παντοδαπούς, ἀλλ' ἀρκεῖ ἐὰν ἐν εἶδος εὐδοκιμοῦν παρέχῃ, ἀνάγκη οἶμαι καὶ ταῦτα
οὕτω ποιούμενα πολὺ διαφερόντως ἐξειργάσθαι
ἕκαστον.

7. Τῇ μὲν δὴ τῶν σίτων θεραπείᾳ τοιαῦτα
ποιῶν πολὺ ὑπερεβάλλετο πάντας· ὡς δὲ καὶ
τοῖς ἄλλοις πᾶσι θεραπεύων πολὺ ἐκράτει, τοῦτο
νῦν διηγήσομαι· πολὺ γὰρ διενεγκὼν ἀνθρώπων
τῷ πλείστας προσόδους λαμβάνειν πολὺ ἔτι
πλέον διήνεγκε τῷ πλεῖστα ἀνθρώπων δωρεῖσθαι.
κατῆρξε μὲν οὖν τούτου Κῦρος, διαμένει δ' ἔτι
καὶ νῦν τοῖς βασιλεῦσιν ἡ πολυδωρία.   8. τίνι
μὲν γὰρ φίλοι πλουσιώτεροι ὄντες φανεροὶ ἢ
Περσῶν βασιλεῖ; τίς δὲ κοσμῶν κάλλιον φαίνεται στολαῖς τοὺς περὶ αὑτὸν[1] ἢ βασιλεύς;
τίνος δὲ δῶρα γιγνώσκεται ὥσπερ ἔνια τῶν
βασιλέως, ψέλια καὶ στρεπτοὶ καὶ ἵπποι χρυσοχάλινοι; οὐ γὰρ δὴ ἔξεστιν ἐκεῖ ταῦτα ἔχειν
ᾧ ἂν μὴ βασιλεὺς δῷ.   9. τίς δ' ἄλλος λέγεται
δώρων μεγέθει ποιεῖν αἱρεῖσθαι αὑτὸν καὶ ἀντ'
ἀδελφῶν καὶ ἀντὶ πατέρων καὶ ἀντὶ παίδων;
τίς δ'· ἄλλος ἐδυνάσθη ἐχθροὺς ἀπέχοντας πολλῶν μηνῶν ὁδὸν τιμωρεῖσθαι ὡς Περσῶν βασιλεύς; τίς δ' ἄλλος καταστρεψάμενος ἀρχὴν ὑπὸ

---

[1] αὑτὸν Edd.; αὐτὸν MSS.

and now another, he must necessarily have things go as they may ; but where it is all one man can do to stew meats and another to roast them, for one man to boil fish and another to bake them, for another to make bread and not every sort at that, but where it suffices if he makes one kind that has a high reputation—everything that is prepared in such a kitchen will, I think, necessarily be worked out with superior excellence.

7. Accordingly, Cyrus far surpassed all others in the art of making much of his friends by gifts of food. And how he far surpassed in every other way of courting favour, I will now explain. Though he far exceeded all other men in the amount of the revenues he received, yet he excelled still more in the quantity of presents he made. It was Cyrus, therefore, who began the practice of lavish giving, and among the kings it continues even to this day. 8. For who has richer friends to show than the Persian king ? Who is there that is known to adorn his friends with more beautiful robes than does the king ? Whose gifts are so readily recognized as some of those which the king gives, such as bracelets, necklaces, and horses with gold-studded bridles ? For, as everybody knows, no one over there is allowed to have such things except those to whom the king has given them. And of whom else is it said that by the munificence of his gifts he makes himself preferred above even brothers and parents and children ? Who else was ever in a position like the Persian king to punish enemies who were distant a journey of many months ? And who, besides

Cyrus lavish in his gifts

335

τῶν ἀρχομένων πατὴρ καλούμενος ἀπέθανεν ἢ
Κῦρος; τοῦτο δὲ τοὔνομα δῆλον ὅτι εὐεργετοῦντός
ἐστι μᾶλλον ἢ ἀφαιρουμένου. 10. κατεμάθομεν
δὲ ὡς καὶ τοὺς βασιλέως καλουμένους ὀφθαλμοὺς
καὶ τὰ βασιλέως ὦτα οὐκ ἄλλως ἐκτήσατο ἢ
τῷ δωρεῖσθαί τε καὶ τιμᾶν· τοὺς γὰρ ἀπαγγεί-
λαντας ὅσα καιρὸς αὐτῷ εἴη πεπύσθαι μεγάλως
εὐεργετῶν πολλοὺς ἐποίησεν ἀνθρώπους καὶ ὠτα-
κουστεῖν καὶ διοπτεύειν τί ἂν ἀγγείλαντες ὠφε-
λήσειαν βασιλέα. 11. ἐκ τούτου δὴ καὶ πολλοὶ
ἐνομίσθησαν βασιλέως ὀφθαλμοὶ καὶ πολλὰ ὦτα.
εἰ δέ τις οἴεται ἕνα αἱρετὸν εἶναι ὀφθαλμὸν
βασιλεῖ, οὐκ ὀρθῶς οἴεται· ὀλίγα γὰρ εἷς γ' ἂν
ἴδοι καὶ εἷς ἀκούσειε· καὶ τοῖς ἄλλοις ὥσπερ
ἀμελεῖν ἂν παρηγγελμένον[1] εἴη, εἰ ἑνὶ τοῦτο
προστεταγμένον εἴη· πρὸς δὲ καὶ ὅντινα γιγνώ-
σκοιεν ὀφθαλμὸν ὄντα, τοῦτον ἂν εἰδεῖεν ὅτι
φυλάττεσθαι δεῖ. ἀλλ' οὐχ οὕτως ἔχει, ἀλλὰ
τοῦ φάσκοντος ἀκοῦσαί τι ἢ ἰδεῖν ἄξιον ἐπιμελείας παντὸς βασιλεὺς ἀκούει. 12. οὕτω δὴ
πολλὰ μὲν βασιλέως ὦτα, πολλοὶ δ' ὀφθαλμοὶ
νομίζονται· καὶ φοβοῦνται πανταχοῦ λέγειν τὰ
μὴ σύμφορα βασιλεῖ, ὥσπερ αὐτοῦ ἀκούοντος,
καὶ ποιεῖν ἃ μὴ σύμφορα, ὥσπερ αὐτοῦ παρόντος.
οὔκουν ὅπως μνησθῆναι ἄν τις ἐτόλμησε πρός
τινα περὶ Κύρου φλαῦρόν τι, ἀλλ' ὡς ἐν
ὀφθαλμοῖς πᾶσι καὶ ὠσὶ βασιλέως τοῖς ἀεὶ
παροῦσιν οὕτως ἕκαστος διέκειτο. τὸ δὲ οὕτω

---

[1] παρηγγελμένον Weckherlin, Dindorf[4], Hug, Marchant,
Gemoll ; παραγγελ(λ)όμενον MSS., Dindorf[3], Breitenbach.

Cyrus, ever gained an empire by conquest and even
to his death was called "father" by the people he
had subdued? For that name obviously belongs to
a benefactor rather than to a despoiler. 10. Moreover, we have discovered that he acquired the so-
called "king's eyes" and "king's ears" in no other
way than by bestowing presents and honours ; for
by rewarding liberally those who reported to him
whatever it was to his interest to hear, he prompted
many men to make it their business to use their eyes
and ears to spy out what they could report to the
king to his advantage. 11. As a natural result of
this, many "eyes" and many "ears" were ascribed
to the king. But if any one thinks that the king
selected one man to be his "eye," he is wrong ; for
one only would see and one would hear but little ;
and it would have amounted to ordering all the rest
to pay no attention, if one only had been appointed
to see and hear. Besides, if people knew that a
certain man was the "eye," they would know that
they must beware of him. But such is not the case ;
for the king listens to anybody who may claim to
have heard or seen anything worthy of attention.
12. And thus the saying comes about, "The king
has many ears and many eyes" ; and people are
everywhere afraid to say anything to the discredit of
the king, just as if he himself were listening ; or to
do anything to harm him, just as if he were present.
Not only, therefore, would no one have ventured to
say anything derogatory of Cyrus to any one else, but
every one conducted himself at all times just as if
those who were within hearing were so many eyes
and ears of the king. I do not know what better

The "king's
eyes'
and "king's
ears"

Hdt. i. 114 ;
Aesch. Pers.
980

337

διακεῖσθαι τοὺς ἀνθρώπους πρὸς αὐτὸν ἐγὼ μὲν
οὐκ οἶδα ὅ τι ἄν τις αἰτιάσαιτο μᾶλλον ἢ ὅτι
μεγάλα ἤθελεν ἀντὶ μικρῶν εὐεργετεῖν.

13. Καὶ τὸ μὲν δὴ μεγέθει δώρων ὑπερβάλλειν
πλουσιώτατον ὄντα οὐ θαυμαστόν· τὸ δὲ τῇ θεραπείᾳ καὶ τῇ ἐπιμελείᾳ τῶν φίλων βασιλεύοντα
περιγίγνεσθαι, τοῦτο ἀξιολογώτερον. ἐκεῖνος
τοίνυν λέγεται κατάδηλος εἶναι μηδενὶ ἂν οὕτως
αἰσχυνθεὶς ἡττώμενος ὡς φίλων θεραπείᾳ· 14. καὶ
λόγος δὲ αὐτοῦ ἀπομνημονεύεται ὡς λέγοι παρα-
πλήσια ἔργα εἶναι νομέως ἀγαθοῦ καὶ βασιλέως
ἀγαθοῦ· τόν τε γὰρ νομέα χρῆναι ἔφη εὐδαίμονα
τὰ κτήνη ποιοῦντα χρῆσθαι αὐτοῖς, ἣ δὴ προβάτων εὐδαιμονία, τόν τε βασιλέα ὡσαύτως
εὐδαίμονας πόλεις καὶ ἀνθρώπους ποιοῦντα χρῆσθαι αὐτοῖς. οὐδὲν οὖν θαυμαστόν, εἴπερ ταύτην
εἶχε τὴν γνώμην, τὸ φιλονίκως ἔχειν πάντων
ἀνθρώπων θεραπείᾳ περιγίγνεσθαι. 15. καλὸν
δ' ἐπίδειγμα καὶ τοῦτο λέγεται Κῦρος ἐπιδεῖξαι
Κροίσῳ, ὅτε ἐνουθέτει αὐτὸν ὡς διὰ τὸ πολλὰ
διδόναι πένης ἔσοιτο, ἐξὸν αὐτῷ θησαυροὺς χρυσοῦ πλείστους ἑνί γε ἀνδρὶ ἐν τῷ οἴκῳ καταθέσθαι.

Καὶ τὸν Κῦρον λέγεται ἐρέσθαι, Καὶ πόσα ἂν
ἤδη οἴει μοι χρήματα εἶναι, εἰ συνέλεγον χρυσίον
ὥσπερ σὺ κελεύεις ἐξ ὅτου ἐν τῇ ἀρχῇ εἰμι;

16. Καὶ τὸν Κροῖσον εἰπεῖν πολύν τινα ἀριθμόν.
Καὶ τὸν Κῦρον πρὸς ταῦτα, Ἄγε δή, φάναι, ὦ

reason any one could assign for this attitude toward him on the part of people generally than that it was his policy to do large favours in return for small ones.

13. That he, the richest man of all, should excel in the munificence of his presents is not surprising; but for him, the king, to exceed all others in thoughtful attention to his friends and in care for them, that is more remarkable; and it is said to have been no secret that there was nothing wherein he would have been so much ashamed of being outdone as in attention to his friends. 14. People quote a remark of his to the effect that the duties of a good shepherd and of a good king were very much alike; a good shepherd ought, while deriving benefit from his flocks, to make them happy (so far as sheep can be said to have happiness), and in the same way a king ought to make his people and his cities happy, if he would derive benefits from them. Seeing that he held this theory, it is not at all surprising that he was ambitious to surpass all other men in attention to his friends. 15. And, among other proofs, Cyrus is said to have given Croesus one splendid practical demonstration of the correctness of this theory, when the latter warned him that by giving so much away he would make himself poor, whereas he was in a position to lay up in his house more treasures of gold than any other man.

Cyrus excelled in generosity

Cyrus's theory of wealth *vs.* that of Croesus

"And how much gold, pray," Cyrus is said to have asked, "do you think I should have by this time, if I had been amassing it, as you propose, ever since I have been in power?"

16. Croesus named some large sum.

"Well, then, Croesus," said Cyrus in reply, "send

Κροῖσε, σύμπεμψον ἄνδρα σὺν Ὑστάσπᾳ τουτῳὶ[1] ὅτῳ σὺ πιστεύεις μάλιστα. σὺ δέ, ὦ Ὑστάσπα, ἔφη, περιελθὼν πρὸς τοὺς φίλους λέγε αὐτοῖς ὅτι δέομαι χρυσίου πρὸς πρᾶξίν τινα· καὶ γὰρ τῷ ὄντι προσδέομαι· καὶ κέλευε αὐτοὺς ὁπόσα ἂν ἕκαστος δύναιτο πορίσαι μοι χρήματα γράψαντας καὶ κατασημηναμένους δοῦναι τὴν ἐπιστολὴν τῷ Κροίσου θεράποντι φέρειν.

17. Ταῦτα δὲ ὅσα ἔλεγε καὶ γράψας καὶ σημηνάμενος ἐδίδου τῷ Ὑστάσπᾳ φέρειν πρὸς τοὺς φίλους· ἐνέγραψε δὲ πρὸς πάντας καὶ Ὑστάσπαν ὡς φίλον αὐτοῦ δέχεσθαι.

Ἐπεὶ δὲ περιῆλθε καὶ ἤνεγκεν ὁ Κροίσου θεράπων τὰς ἐπιστολάς, ὁ δὴ Ὑστάσπας εἶπεν, Ὦ Κῦρε βασιλεῦ, καὶ ἐμοὶ ἤδη χρὴ ὡς πλουσίῳ χρῆσθαι· πάμπολλα γὰρ ἔχων πάρειμι δῶρα διὰ τὰ σὰ γράμματα.

18. Καὶ ὁ Κῦρος εἶπεν, Εἷς μὲν τοίνυν καὶ οὗτος ἤδη θησαυρὸς ἡμῖν, ὦ Κροῖσε· τοὺς δ᾽ ἄλλους καταθεῶ καὶ λόγισαι πόσα ἐστὶν ἕτοιμα χρήματα, ἤν τι δέωμαι χρῆσθαι.

Λέγεται δὴ λογιζόμενος ὁ Κροῖσος πολλαπλάσια εὑρεῖν ἢ ἔφη Κύρῳ ἂν εἶναι ἐν τοῖς θησαυροῖς ἤδη, εἰ συνέλεγεν. 19. ἐπεὶ δὲ τοῦτο φανερὸν ἐγένετο, εἰπεῖν λέγεται ὁ Κῦρος, Ὁρᾷς, φάναι, ὦ Κροῖσε, ὡς εἰσὶ καὶ ἐμοὶ θησαυροί; ἀλλὰ σὺ μὲν κελεύεις με παρ᾽ ἐμοὶ αὐτοὺς συλλέγοντα φθονεῖσθαί τε δι᾽ αὐτοὺς καὶ μισεῖσθαι, καὶ φύλακας αὐτοῖς ἐφιστάντα μισθοφόρους τού-

___
[1] τουτῳὶ Hertlein, Hug, Marchant, Gemoll ; τούτῳ MSS., Dindorf, Breitenbach.

along with Hystaspas here a man in whom you
have most confidence. And you, Hystaspas," said
he to him, " go the round of my friends and tell
them that I need money for a certain enterprise ;
for, in truth, I do need more. And bid them write
down the amount they could each let me have, and
affix their seals to each subscription, and give it to
Croesus's messenger to deliver here."

17. And when he had written down what he had
said, he sealed the letter and gave it to Hystaspas
to carry to his friends. And he included in it also a
request that they all receive Hystaspas as his friend.

And when he had made the round and Croesus's
messenger had brought in the subscriptions, Hystaspas said : " King Cyrus, you should treat me also
henceforth as a rich man ; for, thanks to your letter,
I have come back with a great number of presents."

18. " Even in this man, Croesus," said Cyrus, " we
have one treasure-house already. But as for the rest
of my friends, look over the list, and add up the
amounts, and see how much money is ready for me,
if I need any for my use."

Then Croesus is said to have added it up and
to have found that there was many times as much
subscribed as he had told Cyrus he should have
in his treasury by this time, if he had been amassing
it. 19. And when this became apparent, Cyrus is
said to have remarked : " Do you observe, Croesus, Cyrus also
that I, too, have my treasures ? But you are pro- has his
posing to me to get them together and hoard them treasures
in my palace, to put hired watchmen in charge of
everything and to trust to them, and on account of
those hoards to be envied and hated. I, on the

τοῖς πιστεύειν· ἐγὼ δὲ τοὺς φίλους πλουσίους
ποιῶν τούτους μοι νομίζω θησαυροὺς καὶ φύλακας
ἅμα ἐμοῦ τε καὶ τῶν ἡμετέρων ἀγαθῶν πιστο-
τέρους εἶναι ἢ εἰ φρουροὺς μισθοφόρους ἐπεστησά-
μην.   20. καὶ ἄλλο δέ σοι ἐρῶ· ἐγὼ γάρ, ὦ
Κροῖσε, ὃ μὲν οἱ θεοὶ δόντες εἰς τὰς ψυχὰς
τοῖς ἀνθρώποις ἐποίησαν ὁμοίως πένητας πάντας,
τούτου μὲν οὐδ' αὐτὸς δύναμαι περιγενέσθαι, ἀλλ'
εἰμὶ ἄπληστος κἀγὼ ὥσπερ οἱ ἄλλοι χρημάτων.
21. τῇδέ γε μέντοι διαφέρειν μοι δοκῶ τῶν πλείστων ὅτι οἱ μὲν ἐπειδὰν τῶν ἀρκούντων περιττὰ
κτήσωνται, τὰ μὲν αὐτῶν κατορύττουσι, τὰ δὲ
κατασήπουσι, τὰ δὲ ἀριθμοῦντες καὶ μετροῦντες
καὶ ἱστάντες καὶ διαψύχοντες καὶ φυλάττοντες
πράγματα ἔχουσι, καὶ ὅμως ἔνδον ἔχοντες τοσαῦτα
οὔτε ἐσθίουσι πλείω ἢ δύνανται φέρειν, διαρρα-
γεῖεν γὰρ ἄν, οὔτ' ἀμφιέννυνται πλείω ἢ δύνανται
φέρειν, ἀποπνιγεῖεν γὰρ ἄν, ἀλλὰ τὰ περιττὰ
χρήματα πράγματα ἔχουσιν·   22. ἐγὼ δ' ὑπηρετῶ
μὲν τοῖς θεοῖς καὶ ὀρέγομαι ἀεὶ πλειόνων· ἐπειδὰν
δὲ κτήσωμαι, ἂν ἴδω[1] περιττὰ ὄντα τῶν ἐμοὶ
ἀρκούντων, τούτοις τάς τ' ἐνδείας τῶν φίλων
ἐξακοῦμαι[2] καὶ πλουτίζων καὶ εὐεργετῶν ἀνθρώπους εὔνοιαν ἐξ αὐτῶν κτῶμαι καὶ φιλίαν, καὶ ἐκ
τούτων καρποῦμαι ἀσφάλειαν καὶ εὔκλειαν· ἃ
οὔτε κατασήπεται οὔτε ὑπερπληροῦντα λυμαί-
νεται, ἀλλὰ ἡ εὔκλεια ὅσῳ ἂν πλείων ᾖ, τοσούτῳ
καὶ μείζων καὶ καλλίων καὶ κουφοτέρα φέρειν

[1] ἴδω xV, Edd.; εἰδῶ yz (know).
[2] ἐξακοῦμαι F, Edd.; ἐξαρκοῦμαι xz (I come to the relief
of); ἐξασκοῦμαι D.

other hand, believe that if I make my friends rich I shall have treasures in them and at the same time more trusty watchers both of my person and of our common fortunes than any hired guards I could put in charge. 20. And one more thing I must tell you: even I cannot eradicate from myself that passion for wealth which the gods have put into the human soul and by which they have made us all poor alike, but I, too, am as insatiate of wealth as other people are. 21. However, I think I am different from most people, in that others, when they have acquired more than a sufficiency, bury some of their treasure and allow some to decay, and some they weary themselves with counting, measuring, weighing, airing, and watching; and though they have so much at home, they never eat more than they can hold, for they would burst if they did, and they never wear more than they can carry, for they would be suffocated if they did; they only find their superfluous treasure a burden. 22. But I follow the leading of the gods and am always grasping after more. But when I have obtained what I see is more than enough for my needs, I use it to satisfy the wants of my friends; and by enriching men and doing them kindnesses I win with my superfluous wealth their friendship and loyalty, and from that I reap as my reward security and good fame—possessions that never decay or do injury from overloading the recipient; but the more one has of good fame, the greater and more attractive and lighter to

Why Cyrus wanted wealth

γίγνεται, πολλάκις δὲ καὶ τοὺς φέροντας αὐτὴν
κουφοτέρους παρέχεται.

23. Ὅπως δὲ καὶ τοῦτο εἰδῇς, ἔφη, ὦ Κροῖσε,
ἐγὼ οὐ τοὺς πλεῖστα ἔχοντας καὶ φυλάττοντας
πλεῖστα εὐδαιμονεστάτους ἡγοῦμαι· οἱ γὰρ τὰ
τείχη φυλάττοντες οὕτως ἂν εὐδαιμονέστατοι
εἴησαν· πάντα γὰρ τὰ ἐν ταῖς πόλεσι φυλάττου-
σιν· ἀλλ' ὃς ἂν κτᾶσθαί τε πλεῖστα δύνηται σὺν
τῷ δικαίῳ καὶ χρῆσθαι δὲ πλείστοις σὺν τῷ καλῷ,
τοῦτον ἐγὼ εὐδαιμονέστατον νομίζω [καὶ τὰ
χρήματα].[1]

Καὶ ταῦτα μὲν δὴ φανερὸς ἦν ὥσπερ[2] ἔλεγε καὶ
πράττων.

24. Πρὸς δὲ τούτοις κατανοήσας τοὺς πολλοὺς
τῶν ἀνθρώπων ὅτι ἦν μὲν ὑγιαίνοντες διατελῶσι,
παρασκευάζονται ὅπως ἕξουσι τἀπιτήδεια καὶ
κατατίθενται τὰ χρήσιμα εἰς τὴν τῶν ὑγιαινόντων
δίαιταν· ὅπως δὲ ἦν ἀσθενήσωσι τὰ σύμφορα
παρέσται, τούτου οὐ πάνυ ἐπιμελομένους ἑώρα·
ἔδοξεν οὖν καὶ ταῦτα ἐκπονῆσαι αὐτῷ, καὶ τούς
τε ἰατροὺς[3] τοὺς ἀρίστους συνεκομίσατο πρὸς
αὐτὸν τῷ τελεῖν ἐθέλειν καὶ ὁπόσα ἢ ὄργανα
χρήσιμα ἔφη τις ἂν αὐτῶν γενέσθαι ἢ φάρμακα
ἢ σῖτα ἢ ποτά, οὐδὲν τούτων ὅ τι οὐχὶ παρα-
σκευάσας ἐθησαύριζε παρ' αὑτῷ. 25. καὶ ὁπότε
δέ τις ἀσθενήσειε τῶν θεραπεύεσθαι ἐπικαιρίων,
ἐπεσκόπει καὶ παρεῖχε πάντα ὅτου ἔδει. καὶ τοῖς

---

[1] καὶ τὰ χρήματα MSS.; bracketed by Schneider, Weiske,
Edd.

[2] ὥσπερ Hertlein, Edd.; καὶ MSS.

[3] καὶ τούς τε ἰατροὺς Hug; καὶ ἰατρούς τε y, Marchant,
Gemoll; τούς τε ἰατροὺς xzV, Dindorf, Breitenbach.

bear it becomes, and often, too, it makes those who bear it lighter of heart.

23. " And let me tell you, Croesus," he continued, " I do not consider those the happiest who have the most and keep guard of the most; for if that were so, those would be the happiest who keep guard on the city walls, for they keep guard of everything in the city. But the one who can honestly acquire the most and use the most to noble ends, him I count most happy."

And it was evident that he practised what he preached.

24. Besides this, he had observed that most people in days of health and strength make preparations that they may have the necessaries of life, and they lay up for themselves what will serve to supply the wants of healthy people; but he saw that they made no provision at all for such things as would be serviceable in case of sickness. He resolved, there-fore, to work out these problems, and to that end he spared no expense to collect about him the very best physicians and surgeons and all the instruments and drugs and articles of food and drink that any one of them said would be useful—there were none ot these things that he did not procure and keep in store at his palace. 25. And whenever any one fell sick in whose recovery he was interested, he would visit him and provide for him whatever was needed. And he was grateful to the physicians

Cyrus establishes a board of health and a medical dispensary

ἰατροῖς δὲ χάριν ᾔδει, ὁπότε τις ἰάσαιτό τινα τῶν
παρ' ἐκείνου λαμβάνων.

26. Ταῦτα μὲν δὴ καὶ τοιαῦτα πολλὰ ἐμηχανᾶτο πρὸς τὸ πρωτεύειν παρ' οἷς ἐβούλετο
ἑαυτὸν φιλεῖσθαι.

Ὧν δὲ προηγόρευέ τε ἀγῶνας καὶ ἆθλα πρου-
τίθει, φιλονικίας ἐμποιεῖν βουλόμενος περὶ τῶν
καλῶν κἀγαθῶν ἔργων, ταῦτα τῷ μὲν Κύρῳ
ἔπαινον παρεῖχεν ὅτι ἐπεμέλετο ὅπως ἀσκοῖτο
ἡ ἀρετή· τοῖς μέντοι ἀρίστοις οἱ ἀγῶνες οὗτοι
πρὸς ἀλλήλους καὶ ἔριδας καὶ φιλονικίας ἐνέβαλλον.

27. Πρὸς δὲ τούτοις ὥσπερ νόμον κατεστήσατο
ὁ Κῦρος, ὅσα διακρίσεως δέοιτο εἴτε δίκῃ εἴτε
ἀγωνίσματι, τοὺς δεομένους διακρίσεως συντρέχειν
τοῖς κριταῖς. δῆλον οὖν ὅτι ἐστοχάζοντο μὲν οἱ
ἀνταγωνιζόμενοί τι ἀμφότεροι τῶν κρατίστων καὶ
τῶν μάλιστα φίλων κριτῶν· ὁ δὲ μὴ νικῶν τοῖς
μὲν νικῶσιν ἐφθόνει, τοὺς δὲ μὴ ἑαυτὸν κρίνοντας
ἐμίσει· ὁ δ' αὖ νικῶν τῷ δικαίῳ προσεποιεῖτο
νικᾶν, ὥστε χάριν οὐδενὶ ἡγεῖτο ὀφείλειν.

28. Καὶ οἱ πρωτεύειν δὲ βουλόμενοι φιλίᾳ παρὰ
Κύρῳ, ὥσπερ ἄλλοι ἐν πόλεσι, καὶ οὗτοι ἐπιφθόνως πρὸς ἀλλήλους εἶχον, ὥσθ' οἱ πλείονες
ἐκποδὼν ἐβούλοντο ὁ ἕτερος τὸν ἕτερον γενέσθαι
μᾶλλον ἢ συνέπραξαν ἄν τι ἀλλήλοις ἀγαθόν.

Καὶ ταῦτα μὲν δεδήλωται ὡς ἐμηχανᾶτο τοὺς
κρατίστους αὐτὸν μᾶλλον πάντας φιλεῖν ἢ ἀλλήλους.

also, whenever any of them took any of his medical stores and with them effected a cure.

26. These and many other such arts he employed in order to hold the first place in the affections of those by whom he wished to be beloved.

And the games, in which Cyrus used to announce contests and to offer prizes from a desire to inspire in his people a spirit of emulation in what was beautiful and good—these games also brought him praise, because his aim was to secure practice in excellence. But these contests also stirred up contentions and jealousies among the nobles.

27. Besides this, Cyrus had made a regulation that was practically a law, that, in any matter that required adjudication, whether it was a civil action or a contest for a prize, those who asked for such adjudication must concur in the choice of judges. It was, therefore, a matter of course that each of the contestants aimed to secure the most influential men as judges and such as were most friendly to himself. The one who did not win was always jealous of those who did, and disliked those of the judges who did not vote in his favour; on the other hand, the one who did win claimed that he had won by virtue of the justice of his cause, and so he thought he owed no thanks to anybody. *How Cyrus guarded against coalitions*

28. And those also who wished to hold the first place in the affections of Cyrus were jealous of one another, just like other people (even in republics), so that in most cases the one would have wished to get the other out of the way sooner than to join with him in any work to their mutual interest.

Thus it has been shown how he contrived that the most influential citizens should love him more than they did each other.

III

1. Νῦν δὲ ἤδη διηγησόμεθα ὡς τὸ πρῶτον
ἐξήλασε Κῦρος ἐκ τῶν βασιλείων· καὶ γὰρ αὐτῆς
τῆς ἐξελάσεως ἡ σεμνότης ἡμῖν δοκεῖ μία τῶν
τεχνῶν εἶναι τῶν μεμηχανημένων τὴν ἀρχὴν μὴ
εὐκαταφρόνητον εἶναι. πρῶτον μὲν οὖν πρὸ τῆς
ἐξελάσεως εἰσκαλέσας πρὸς αὐτὸν τοὺς τὰς ἀρχὰς
ἔχοντας Περσῶν τε καὶ τῶν ἄλλων συμμάχων
διέδωκεν αὐτοῖς τὰς Μηδικὰς στολάς· καὶ τότε
πρῶτον Πέρσαι Μηδικὴν στολὴν ἐνέδυσαν· διαδι-
δούς τε ἅμα τάδε ἔλεγεν αὐτοῖς ὅτι ἐλάσαι βούλοιτο
εἰς τὰ τεμένη τὰ τοῖς θεοῖς ἐξῃρημένα καὶ θῦσαι
μετ᾽ ἐκείνων. 2. Πάρεστε οὖν, ἔφη, ἐπὶ τὰς θύρας
κοσμηθέντες ταῖς στολαῖς ταύταις πρὶν ἥλιον
ἀνατέλλειν, καὶ καθίστασθε ὡς ἂν ὑμῖν Φεραύλας
ὁ Πέρσης ἐξαγγείλῃ παρ᾽ ἐμοῦ· καὶ ἐπειδάν, ἔφη,
ἐγὼ ἡγῶμαι, ἕπεσθε ἐν τῇ ῥηθείσῃ χώρᾳ. ἢν δ᾽
ἄρα τινὶ δοκῇ ὑμῶν ἄλλῃ κάλλιον εἶναι ἢ ὡς ἂν
νῦν ἐλαύνωμεν, ἐπειδὰν πάλιν ἔλθωμεν, διδασκέτω
με· ὅπῃ γὰρ ἂν κάλλιστον καὶ ἄριστον ὑμῖν [1] δοκῇ
εἶναι, ταύτῃ ἕκαστα δεῖ καταστήσασθαι.

3. Ἐπεὶ δὲ τοῖς κρατίστοις διέδωκε τὰς καλ-
λίστας στολάς, ἐξέφερε δὴ καὶ ἄλλας Μηδικὰς
στολάς, παμπόλλας γὰρ παρεσκευάσατο, οὐδὲν
φειδόμενος οὔτε πορφυρίδων οὔτε ὀρφνίνων οὔτε
φοινικίδων οὔτε καρυκίνων ἱματίων· νείμας δὲ
τούτων τὸ μέρος ἑκάστῳ τῶν ἡγεμόνων ἐκέλευσεν
αὐτοὺς τούτοις κοσμεῖν τοὺς αὐτῶν φίλους, ὥσπερ,
ἔφη, ἐγὼ ὑμᾶς κοσμῶ.

---

[1] ὑμῖν EDG, Edd.; ἡμῖν CFAHV.

III

1. NEXT we shall describe how Cyrus for the first time drove forth in state from his palace; and that is in place here, for the magnificence of his appearance in state seems to us to have been one of the arts that he devised to make his government command respect. Accordingly, before he started out, he called to him those of the Persians and of the allies who held office, and distributed Median robes among them (and this was the first time that the Persians put on the Median robe); and as he distributed them he said that he wished to proceed in state to the sanctuaries that had been selected for the gods, and to offer sacrifice there with his friends. 2. "Come, therefore, to court before sunrise, dressed in these robes," said he, "and form in line as Pheraulas, the Persian, shall direct in my name; and when I lead the way, follow me in the order assigned to you. But if any one of you thinks that some other way would be better than that in which we shall now proceed, let him inform me as soon as we return, for everything must be arranged as you think best and most becoming."

3. And when he had distributed among the noblest the most beautiful garments, he brought out other Median robes, for he had had a great many made, with no stint of purple or sable or red or scarlet or crimson cloaks. He apportioned to each one of his officers his proper share of them, and he bade them adorn their friends with them, "just as I," said he, "have been adorning you."

Cyrus plans to appear in state

4. Καί τις τῶν παρόντων ἐπήρετο αὐτόν, Σὺ δέ, ὦ Κῦρε, ἔφη, πότε κοσμήσει;

Ὁ δ᾽ ἀπεκρίνατο, Οὐ γὰρ νῦν, ἔφη, δοκῶ ὑμῖν αὐτὸς κοσμεῖσθαι ὑμᾶς κοσμῶν; ἀμέλει, ἔφη, ἢν δύνωμαι ὑμᾶς τοὺς φίλους εὖ ποιεῖν, ὁποίαν ἂν ἔχων στολὴν τυγχάνω, ἐν ταύτῃ καλὸς φανοῦμαι.

5. Οὕτω δὴ οἱ μὲν ἀπελθόντες μεταπεμπόμενοι τοὺς φίλους ἐκόσμουν ταῖς στολαῖς.

Ὁ δὲ Κῦρος νομίζων Φεραύλαν τὸν ἐκ τῶν δημοτῶν καὶ συνετὸν εἶναι καὶ φιλόκαλον καὶ εὔτακτον καὶ τοῦ χαρίζεσθαι αὐτῷ οὐκ ἀμελῆ, ὅς ποτε καὶ περὶ τοῦ τιμᾶσθαι ἕκαστον κατὰ τὴν ἀξίαν συνεῖπε, τοῦτον δὴ καλέσας συνεβουλεύετο αὐτῷ πῶς ἂν τοῖς μὲν εὔνοις κάλλιστα ἰδεῖν ποιοῖτο τὴν ἐξέλασιν, τοῖς δὲ δυσμενέσι φοβερώτατα. 6. ἐπεὶ δὲ σκοπούντοιν αὐτοῖν ταὐτὰ συνέδοξεν, ἐκέλευσε τὸν Φεραύλαν ἐπιμεληθῆναι ὅπως ἂν οὕτω γένηται αὔριον ἡ ἐξέλασις ὥσπερ ἔδοξε καλῶς ἔχειν. Εἴρηκα δέ, ἔφη, ἐγὼ πάντας πείθεσθαί σοι περὶ τῆς ἐν τῇ ἐξελάσει τάξεως· ὅπως δ᾽ ἂν ἥδιον παραγγέλλοντός σου ἀκούωσι, φέρε λαβών, ἔφη, χιτῶνας μὲν τουτουσὶ τοῖς τῶν δορυφόρων ἡγεμόσι, κασᾶς [1] δὲ τούσδε τοὺς ἐφιππίους τοῖς τῶν ἱππέων ἡγεμόσι, δὸς δὲ καὶ τῶν ἁρμάτων τοῖς ἡγεμόσιν ἄλλους τούσδε χιτῶνας.

Ὁ μὲν δὴ ἔφερε λαβών· 7. οἱ δὲ ἡγεμόνες ἐπεὶ

---

[1] κασᾶς Brodaeus, Edd.; καλέσας MSS.

4. "And you, Cyrus," asked one of those present, "when will you adorn yourself?"

"Why, do I not seem to you to be adorned myself when I adorn you?" he answered. "Be sure that if I can treat you, my friends, properly, I shall look well, no matter what sort of dress I happen to have on."

5. So they went away, sent for their friends, and adorned them with the robes.

Now Cyrus believed Pheraulas, that man of the common people, to be intelligent, to have an eye for beauty and order, and to be not indisposed to please him; (this was the same Pheraulas who had once supported his proposal that each man should be honoured in accordance with his merit;) so he called him in and with him planned how to arrange the procession in a manner that should prove most splendid in the eyes of his loyal friends and most intimidating to those who were disaffected. 6. And when after careful study they agreed on the arrangement, he bade Pheraulas see that the procession take place on the morrow exactly as they had decided was best. "And I have issued orders," said he, "that everybody shall obey you in regard to the ordering of the procession; but, in order that they may the more readily follow your directions, take these tunics here and give them to the officers of the lancers, and these cavalry mantles here to the commanders of the horse; and give the officers of the chariot forces also these other tunics."

So he took them and carried them away. 7. And when the officers one after another saw him, they

Pheraulas is made grand marshal

II. iii. 7 ff.

ἴδοιεν αὐτόν, ἔλεγον, Μέγας δὴ σύγε, ὦ Φεραύλα,
ὁπότε γε καὶ ἡμῖν προστάξεις ἂν δέῃ ποιεῖν.

Οὐ μὰ Δί', ἔφη ὁ Φεραύλας, οὐ μόνον γε, ὡς
ἔοικεν, ἀλλὰ καὶ συσκευοφορήσω· νῦν γοῦν φέρω
τῷδε δύο κασᾶ, τὸν μὲν σοί, τὸν δὲ ἄλλῳ· σὺ
μέντοι τούτων λαβὲ ὁπότερον βούλει.

8. Ἐκ τούτου δὴ ὁ μὲν λαμβάνων τὸν κασᾶν
τοῦ μὲν φθόνου ἐπελέληστο, εὐθὺς δὲ συνεβουλεύετο αὐτῷ ὁπότερον λαμβάνοι· ὁ δὲ συμβου-
λεύσας ἂν ὁπότερος βελτίων εἴη καὶ εἰπών,
Ἢν μου κατηγορήσῃς ὅτι αἵρεσίν σοι ἔδωκα,
εἰς αὖθις ὅταν διακονῶ, ἑτέρῳ χρήσει μοι δια-
κόνῳ, ὁ μὲν δὴ Φεραύλας οὕτω διαδοὺς ᾗ ἐτάχθη
εὐθὺς ἐπεμέλετο τῶν εἰς τὴν ἐξέλασιν ὅπως
ὡς κάλλιστα ἕκαστα ἔξοι.

9. Ἡνίκα δ' ἡ ὑστεραία ἧκε, καθαρὰ μὲν ἦν
πάντα πρὸ ἡμέρας, στοῖχοι δὲ εἱστήκεσαν ἔνθεν
καὶ ἔνθεν τῆς ὁδοῦ, ὥσπερ καὶ νῦν ἔτι ἵστανται
ᾗ ἂν βασιλεὺς μέλλῃ ἐλαύνειν· ὧν ἐντὸς οὐδενὶ
ἔστιν εἰσιέναι τῶν μὴ τετιμημένων· μαστιγοφόροι
δὲ καθέστασαν οἳ ἔπαιον, εἴ τις ἐνοχλοίη.

Ἕστασαν δὲ πρῶτον μὲν τῶν δορυφόρων εἰς
τετρακισχιλίους ἔμπροσθεν τῶν πυλῶν εἰς τέτταρας, δισχίλιοι δ' ἑκατέρωθεν τῶν πυλῶν.
10. καὶ οἱ ἱππεῖς δὲ πάντες παρῆσαν κατα-
βεβηκότες ἀπὸ τῶν ἵππων, καὶ διειρκότες τὰς

would say: "You must be a great man, Pheraulas, seeing that you are to command even us what we must do."

"No, by Zeus," Pheraulas would answer; "not only not that, so it seems, but I am even to be one of the porters; at any rate, I am now carrying these two mantles here, the one for you, the other for some one else. You, however, shall have your choice."

8. With that, of course, the man who was receiving the mantle would at once forget about his jealousy and presently be asking his advice which one to choose. And he would give his advice as to which one was better and say: "If you betray that I have given you your choice, you will find me a different sort of servant the next time I come to serve." And when Pheraulas had distributed everything as he had been instructed to do, he at once began to arrange for the procession that it might be as splendid as possible in every detail.

9. When the next day dawned, everything was in order before sunrise; rows of soldiers stood on this side of the street and on that, just as even to this day the Persians stand, where the king is to pass; and within these lines no one may enter except those who hold positions of honour. And policemen with whips in their hands were stationed there, who struck any one who tried to crowd in.

First in order, in front of the gates stood about four thousand lancers, four deep, and two thousand on either side the gates. 10. And all the cavalrymen had alighted and stood there beside their horses, and they all had their hands thrust through

The formation of the line of the procession

χεῖρας διὰ τῶν κανδύων, ὥσπερ καὶ νῦν ἔτι
διείρουσιν, ὅταν ὁρᾷ βασιλεύς. ἕστασαν δὲ
Πέρσαι μὲν ἐκ δεξιᾶς, οἱ δὲ ἄλλοι σύμμαχοι
ἐξ ἀριστερᾶς τῆς ὁδοῦ, καὶ τὰ ἅρματα ὡσαύτως
τὰ ἡμίσεα ἑκατέρωθεν.

11. Ἐπεὶ δ᾽ ἀνεπετάννυντο αἱ τοῦ βασιλείου
πύλαι, πρῶτον μὲν ἤγοντο τῷ Διὶ ταῦροι πάγκα-
λοι εἰς τέτταρας καὶ οἷς τῶν ἄλλων θεῶν οἱ
μάγοι ἐξηγοῦντο· πολὺ γὰρ οἴονται Πέρσαι
χρῆναι τοῖς περὶ τοὺς θεοὺς μᾶλλον τεχνίταις
χρῆσθαι ἢ περὶ τἄλλα. 12. μετὰ δὲ τοὺς βοῦς
ἵπποι ἤγοντο θῦμα τῷ Ἡλίῳ· μετὰ δὲ τούτους
ἐξήγετο ἅρμα λευκὸν χρυσόζυγον ἐστεμμένον
Διὸς ἱερόν· μετὰ δὲ τοῦτο Ἡλίου ἅρμα λευκὸν
καὶ τοῦτο ἐστεμμένον ὥσπερ τὸ πρόσθεν· μετὰ
δὲ τοῦτο ἄλλο τρίτον ἅρμα ἐξήγετο, φοινικίσι
καταπεπταμένοι οἱ ἵπποι, καὶ πῦρ ὄπισθεν
αὐτοῦ ἐπ᾽ ἐσχάρας μεγάλης ἄνδρες εἵποντο
φέροντες.

13. Ἐπὶ δὲ τούτοις ἤδη αὐτὸς ἐκ τῶν πυλῶν
προυφαίνετο ὁ Κῦρος ἐφ᾽ ἅρματος ὀρθὴν ἔχων
τὴν τιάραν καὶ χιτῶνα πορφυροῦν μεσόλευκον,
ἄλλῳ δ᾽ οὐκ ἔξεστι μεσόλευκον ἔχειν, καὶ περὶ
τοῖς σκέλεσιν ἀναξυρίδας ὑσγινοβαφεῖς, καὶ κάν-
δυν ὁλοπόρφυρον. εἶχε δὲ καὶ διάδημα περὶ
τῇ τιάρᾳ· καὶ οἱ συγγενεῖς δὲ αὐτοῦ τὸ αὐτὸ
τοῦτο σημεῖον εἶχον, καὶ νῦν τὸ αὐτὸ τοῦτο
ἔχουσι. 14. τὰς δὲ χεῖρας ἔξω τῶν χειρίδων

the sleeves of their doublets,[1] just as they do even to this day when the king sees them. The Persians stood on the right side of the street, the others, the allies, on the left, and the chariots were arranged in the same way, half on either side.

11. Then, when the palace gates were thrown open, there were led out at the head of the procession four abreast some exceptionally handsome bulls for Zeus and for the other gods as the magi directed; for the Persians think that they ought much more scrupulously to be guided by those whose profession is with things divine than they are by those in other professions. 12. Next after the bulls came horses, a sacrifice for the Sun; and after them came a chariot sacred to Zeus; it was drawn by white horses with a yoke of gold and wreathed with garlands; and next, for the Sun, a chariot drawn by white horses and wreathed with garlands like the other. After that came a third chariot with horses covered with purple trappings, and behind it followed men carrying fire on a great altar.

13. Next after these Cyrus himself upon a chariot appeared in the gates wearing his tiara upright, a purple tunic shot with white (no one but the king may wear such a one), trousers of scarlet dye about his legs, and a mantle all of purple. He had also a fillet about his tiara, and his kinsmen also had the same mark of distinction, and they retain it even now. 14. His hands he kept outside his sleeves.[1] With

Cyrus appears in the procession

---

[1] The Persians were obliged, in the presence of the king, to thrust their hands inside the sleeves of their doublets in token of their submission to royalty: moreover, with the hands thus withdrawn, no act of violence was possible. Cyrus, the Younger, is said to have had two of his kinsmen executed for their failure to observe this regulation. (*Hellenica* II. i. 8.)

εἶχε. παρωχεῖτο δὲ αὐτῷ ἡνίοχος μέγας μέν, μείων δ' ἐκείνου εἴτε καὶ τῷ ὄντι εἴτε καὶ ὁπωσοῦν· μείζων δ' ἐφάνη πολὺ Κῦρος.

Ἰδόντες δὲ πάντες προσεκύνησαν, εἴτε καὶ ἄρξαι τινὲς κεκελευσμένοι εἴτε καὶ ἐκπλαγέντες τῇ παρασκευῇ καὶ τῷ δόξαι μέγαν τε καὶ καλὸν φανῆναι τὸν Κῦρον. πρόσθεν δὲ Περσῶν οὐδεὶς Κῦρον προσεκύνει.

15. Ἐπεὶ δὲ προῄει τὸ τοῦ Κύρου ἅρμα, προηγοῦντο μὲν οἱ τετρακισχίλιοι δορυφόροι, παρείποντο δὲ οἱ δισχίλιοι ἑκατέρωθεν τοῦ ἅρματος· ἐφείποντο δὲ οἱ περὶ αὐτὸν σκηπτοῦχοι ἐφ' ἵππων κεκοσμημένοι σὺν τοῖς παλτοῖς ἀμφὶ τοὺς τριακοσίους. 16. οἱ δ' αὖ τῷ Κύρῳ τρεφόμενοι ἵπποι παρήγοντο χρυσοχάλινοι, ῥαβδωτοῖς ἱματίοις καταπεπταμένοι, ἀμφὶ τοὺς διακοσίους· ἐπὶ δὲ τούτοις δισχίλιοι ξυστοφόροι· ἐπὶ δὲ τούτοις ἱππεῖς οἱ πρῶτοι γενόμενοι μύριοι, εἰς ἑκατὸν πανταχῇ τεταγμένοι· ἡγεῖτο δ' αὐτῶν Χρυσάντας. 17. ἐπὶ δὲ τούτοις μύριοι ἄλλοι Περσῶν ἱππεῖς τεταγμένοι ὡσαύτως, ἡγεῖτο δ' αὐτῶν Ὑστάσπας· ἐπὶ δὲ τούτοις ἄλλοι μύριοι ὡσαύτως, ἡγεῖτο δ' αὐτῶν Δατάμας· ἐπὶ δὲ τούτοις τοσοῦτοι[1] ἄλλοι, ἡγεῖτο δ' αὐτῶν Γαδάτας· 18. ἐπὶ δὲ τούτοις Μῆδοι ἱππεῖς, ἐπὶ δὲ τούτοις Ἀρμένιοι, μετὰ δὲ τούτους Ὑρκάνιοι, μετὰ δὲ τούτους Καδούσιοι, ἐπὶ δὲ τούτοις Σάκαι· μετὰ δὲ τοὺς ἱππέας ἅρματα ἐπὶ τεττάρων τεταγμένα, ἡγεῖτο δ' αὐτῶν Ἀρταβάτας Πέρσης.

---

[1] τοσοῦτοι Hertlein, Hug; not in MSS. or most Edd.

him rode a charioteer, who was tall, but neither in reality nor in appearance so tall as he ; at all events, Cyrus looked much taller.

And when they saw him, they all prostrated themselves before him, either because some had been instructed to begin this act of homage, or because they were overcome by the splendour of his presence, or because Cyrus appeared so great and so goodly to look upon ; at any rate, no one of the Persians had ever prostrated himself before Cyrus before.

15. Then, when Cyrus's chariot had come forth, the four thousand lancers took the lead, and the two thousand fell in line on either side of his chariot ; and his mace-bearers, about three hundred in number, followed next in gala attire, mounted, and equipped with their customary javelins. 16. Next came Cyrus's private stud of horses, about two hundred in all, led along with gold-mounted bridles and covered over with embroidered housings. Behind these came two thousand spearmen, and after them the original ten thousand Persian cavalry, drawn up in a square with a hundred on each side ; and Chrysantas was in command of them. 17. Behind them came ten thousand other Persian horsemen arranged in the same way with Hystaspas in command, and after them ten thousand more in the same formation with Datamas as their commander ; following them, as many more with Gadatas in command. 18. And then followed in succession the cavalry of the Medes, Armenians, Hyrcanians, Cadusians, and Sacians ; and behind the cavalry came the chariots ranged four abreast, and Artabatas, a Persian, had command of them.

The procession itself

XENOPHON

19. Πορευομένου δὲ αὐτοῦ πάμπολλοι ἄνθρωποι
παρείποντο ἔξω τῶν σημείων, δεόμενοι Κύρου
ἄλλος ἄλλης πράξεως. πέμψας οὖν πρὸς αὐτοὺς
τῶν σκηπτούχων τινάς, οἳ παρείποντο αὐτῷ τρεῖς
ἑκατέρωθεν τοῦ ἅρματος αὐτοῦ τούτου ἕνεκα τοῦ
διαγγέλλειν, ἐκέλευσεν εἰπεῖν αὐτοῖς, εἴ τίς τι
αὐτοῦ δέοιτο, διδάσκειν τῶν ἱππάρχων τινὰ ὅ τι
τις βούλοιτο, ἐκείνους δ' ἔφη πρὸς αὐτὸν ἐρεῖν.
οἱ μὲν δὴ ἀπιόντες εὐθὺς κατὰ τοὺς ἱππέας
ἐπορεύοντο καὶ ἐβουλεύοντο τίνι ἕκαστος προσίοι.
20. Ὁ δὲ Κῦρος οὓς ἐβούλετο μάλιστα θεραπεύεσθαι τῶν φίλων ὑπὸ τῶν ἀνθρώπων, τούτους
πέμπων τινὰ πρὸς αὐτὸν¹ ἐκάλει καθ' ἕνα ἕκαστον
καὶ ἔλεγεν αὐτοῖς οὕτως· Ἤν τις ὑμᾶς διδάσκῃ
τι τούτων τῶν παρεπομένων, ὃς μὲν ἂν μηδὲν δοκῇ
ὑμῖν λέγειν, μὴ προσέχετε αὐτῷ τὸν νοῦν· ὃς δ'
ἂν δικαίων δεῖσθαι δοκῇ, εἰσαγγέλλετε πρὸς ἐμέ,
ἵνα κοινῇ βουλευόμενοι διαπράττωμεν αὐτοῖς.
21. Οἱ μὲν δὴ ἄλλοι, ἐπεὶ καλέσειεν, ἀνὰ κράτος
ἐλαύνοντες ὑπήκουον, συναύξοντες τὴν ἀρχὴν τῷ
Κύρῳ καὶ ἐνδεικνύμενοι ὅτι σφόδρα πείθοιντο·
Δαϊφέρνης δέ τις ἦν σολοικότερος ἄνθρωπος τῷ
τρόπῳ, ὃς ᾤετο, εἰ μὴ ταχὺ ὑπακούοι, ἐλευθερώ-
τερος ἂν φαίνεσθαι. 22. αἰσθόμενος οὖν ὁ Κῦρος
τοῦτο, πρὶν προσελθεῖν αὐτὸν καὶ διαλεχθῆναι
αὐτῷ, ὑποπέμψας τινὰ τῶν σκηπτούχων εἰπεῖν

¹ αὐτὸν Edd.; αὑτὸν MSS.

358

19. And as he proceeded, a great throng of people followed outside the lines with petitions to present to Cyrus, one about one matter, another about another. So he sent to them some of his mace-bearers, who followed, three on either side of his chariot, for the express purpose of carrying messages for him; and he bade them say that if any one wanted anything of him, he should make his wish known to some one of his cavalry officers and they, he said, would inform him. So the people at once fell back and made their way along the lines of cavalry, each considering what officer he should approach.

How Cyrus received petitions

20. From time to time Cyrus would send some one to call to him one by one those of his friends whom he wished to have most courted by the people, and would say to them: "If any one of the people following the procession tries to bring anything to your attention, if you do not think he has anything worth while to say, pay no attention to him; but if any one seems to you to ask what is fair, come and tell me, so that we may consult together and grant the petition."

21. And whenever he sent such summons, the men would ride up at full speed to answer it, thereby magnifying the majesty of Cyrus's authority and at the same time showing their eagerness to obey. There was but one exception: a certain Daïphernes, a fellow rather boorish in his manners, thought that he would show more independence if he did not obey at once. 22. Cyrus noticed this; and so, before Daïphernes came and talked with him, he sent one of his mace-bearers privately to say that he had no

Discourtesy toward the king rebuked

ἐκέλευσε πρὸς αὐτὸν ὅτι οὐδὲν ἔτι δέοιτο· καὶ τὸ
λοιπὸν οὐκ ἐκάλει. 23. ὡς δ' ὁ ὕστερον κληθεὶς
αὐτοῦ πρότερος αὐτῷ προσήλασεν, ὁ Κῦρος καὶ
ἵππον αὐτῷ ἔδωκε τῶν παρεπομένων καὶ ἐκέλευσε
τῶν σκηπτούχων τινὰ συναπαγαγεῖν αὐτῷ ὅποι[1]
κελεύσειε. τοῖς δὲ ἰδοῦσιν ἔντιμόν τι τοῦτο ἔδοξεν
εἶναι, καὶ πολὺ πλείονες ἐκ τούτου αὐτὸν ἐθεράπευον ἀνθρώπων.

24. Ἐπεὶ δὲ ἀφίκοντο πρὸς τὰ τεμένη, ἔθυσαν
τῷ Διὶ καὶ ὡλοκαύτησαν τοὺς ταύρους· ἔπειτα τῷ
Ἡλίῳ καὶ ὡλοκαύτησαν τοὺς ἵππους· ἔπειτα Γῇ
σφάξαντες ὡς ἐξηγήσαντο οἱ μάγοι ἐποίησαν·
ἔπειτα δὲ ἥρωσι τοῖς Συρίαν ἔχουσι. 25. μετὰ δὲ
ταῦτα καλοῦ ὄντος τοῦ χωρίου ἔδειξε τέρμα ὡς
ἐπὶ πέντε σταδίων χωρίου, καὶ εἶπε κατὰ φῦλα
ἀνὰ κράτος ἐνταῦθα ἀφεῖναι τοὺς ἵππους. σὺν
μὲν οὖν τοῖς Πέρσαις αὐτὸς ἤλασε καὶ ἐνίκα πολύ·
μάλιστα γὰρ ἐμεμελήκει αὐτῷ ἱππικῆς· Μήδων
δὲ Ἀρτάβαζος ἐνίκα· Κῦρος γὰρ αὐτῷ τὸν ἵππον
ἐδεδώκει· Σύρων δὲ τῶν ἀποστάντων[2] ὁ Γαδάτας·
Ἀρμενίων δὲ Τιγράνης· Ὑρκανίων δὲ ὁ υἱὸς τοῦ
ἱππάρχου· Σακῶν δὲ ἰδιώτης ἀνὴρ ἀπέλιπεν ἄρα
τῷ ἵππῳ τοὺς ἄλλους ἵππους ἐγγὺς τῷ ἡμίσει τοῦ
δρόμου. 26. ἔνθα δὴ λέγεται ὁ Κῦρος ἐρέσθαι τὸν
νεανίσκον εἰ δέξαιτ' ἂν βασιλείαν ἀντὶ τοῦ ἵππου.

Τὸν δ' ἀποκρίνασθαι ὅτι Βασιλείαν μὲν οὐκ

---

[1] ὅποι Dindorf, most Edd.; ὅπου yz, Breitenbach ; ὅπῃ x.
[2] τῶν ἀποστάντων Madvig, recent Edd.; ὁ προστατῶν xzV,
Dindorf, τῶν πάντων y.

more need of him ; and he did not send for him again.
23. But when a man who was summoned later than
Daïphernes rode up to him sooner than he, Cyrus
gave him one of the horses that were being led in
the procession and gave orders to one of the mace-
bearers to have it led away for him wherever he
should direct. And to those who saw it it seemed
to be a mark of great honour, and as a consequence
of that event many more people paid court to that
man.

24. So, when they came to the sanctuaries, they
performed the sacrifice to Zeus and made a holocaust
of the bulls ; then they gave the horses to the flames
in honour of the Sun ; next they did sacrifice to the
Earth, as the magi directed, and lastly to the tutelary
heroes of Syria. 25. And after that, as the locality
seemed adapted to the purpose, he pointed out a
goal about five stadia distant and commanded the
riders, nation by nation, to put their horses at full
speed toward it. Accordingly, he himself rode with
the Persians and came in far ahead of the rest, for he
had given especial attention to horsemanship. Among
the Medes, Artabazus won the race, for the horse
he had was a gift from Cyrus ; among the Assyrians
who had revolted to him, Gadatas secured the first
place ; among the Armenians, Tigranes ; and among
the Hyrcanians, the son of the master of the horse ;
but among the Sacians a certain private soldier with
his horse actually outdistanced the rest by nearly
half the course. 26. Thereupon Cyrus is said to have
asked the young man if he would take a kingdom
for his horse.

"No," answered he ; "I would not take a king-

The sacrifice and the races

ἂν δεξαίμην, χάριν δὲ ἀνδρὶ ἀγαθῷ καταθέσθαι
δεξαίμην ἄν.

27. Καὶ ὁ Κῦρος εἶπε, Καὶ μὴν ἐγὼ δεῖξαί σοι
ἐθέλω ἔνθα κἂν μύων βάλῃς, οὐκ ἂν ἁμάρτοις
ἀνδρὸς ἀγαθοῦ.

Πάντως τοίνυν, ὁ Σάκας ἔφη, δεῖξόν μοι· ὡς
βαλῶ γε ταύτῃ τῇ βώλῳ, ἔφη ἀνελόμενος.

28. Καὶ ὁ μὲν Κῦρος δείκνυσιν αὐτῷ ὅπου
ἦσαν πλεῖστοι τῶν φίλων· ὁ δὲ καταμύων ἵησι
τῇ βώλῳ καὶ παρελαύνοντος Φεραύλα τυγχάνει·
ἔτυχε γὰρ ὁ Φεραύλας παραγγέλλων τι τακτὸς
παρὰ τοῦ Κύρου· βληθεὶς δὲ οὐδὲ μετεστράφη,
ἀλλ' ᾤχετο ἐφ' ὅπερ ἐτάχθη.

29. Ἀναβλέψας δὲ ὁ Σάκας ἐρωτᾷ τίνος
ἔτυχεν.

Οὐ μὰ τὸν Δί', ἔφη, οὐδενὸς τῶν παρόντων.

Ἀλλ' οὐ μέντοι, ἔφη ὁ νεανίσκος, τῶν γε
ἀπόντων.

Ναὶ μὰ Δί', ἔφη ὁ Κῦρος, σύγε ἐκείνου τοῦ
παρὰ τὰ ἅρματα ταχὺ ἐλαύνοντος τὸν ἵππον.

Καὶ πῶς, ἔφη, οὐδὲ μεταστρέφεται;

30. Καὶ ὁ Κῦρος ἔφη, Μαινόμενος γάρ τίς
ἐστιν, ὡς ἔοικεν.

Ἀκούσας ὁ νεανίσκος ᾤχετο σκεψόμενος τίς
εἴη· καὶ εὑρίσκει τὸν Φεραύλαν γῆς τε κατάπλεων
τὸ γένειον καὶ αἵματος· ἐρρύη[1] γὰρ αὐτῷ ἐκ
τῆς ῥινὸς βληθέντι. ἐπεὶ δὲ προσῆλθεν, ἤρετο
αὐτὸν εἰ βληθείη.

---

[1] ἐρρύη zDGH, most Edd.; ἔρρει x, Gemoll (*was still
flowing*); ἐρρύει F.

dom for him, but I would take the chance of laying up a store of gratitude with a brave man."

27. "Aye," said Cyrus, "and I will show you where you could not fail to hit a brave man, even if you throw with your eyes shut."

Pheraulas gets a blow and a horse

"All right, then," said the Sacian; "show me; and I will throw this clod here." And with that he picked one up.

28. And Cyrus pointed out to him the place where most of his friends were. And the other, shutting his eyes, let fly with the clod and hit Pheraulas as he was riding by; for Pheraulas happened to be carrying some message under orders from Cyrus. But though he was hit, he did not so much as turn around but went on to attend to his commission.

29. The Sacian opened his eyes and asked whom he had hit.

"None of those here, by Zeus," said Cyrus.

"Well, surely it was not one of those who are not here," said the youth.

"Yes, by Zeus," said Cyrus, "it was; you hit that man who is riding so fast along the line of chariots yonder."

"And why does he not even turn around?" said the youth.

30. "Because he is crazy, I should think," answered Cyrus.

On hearing this, the young man went to find out who it was. And he found Pheraulas with his chin covered with dirt and blood, for the blood had flowed from his nose where he had been struck; and when he came up to him he asked him if he had been hit.

31. Ὁ δὲ ἀπεκρίνατο, Ὡς ὁρᾷς.

Δίδωμι τοίνυν σοι, ἔφη, τοῦτον τὸν ἵππον.

Ὁ δ' ἐπήρετο, Ἀντὶ τοῦ;

Ἐκ τούτου δὴ διηγεῖτο ὁ Σάκας τὸ πρᾶγμα, καὶ τέλος εἶπε, Καὶ οἶμαί γε οὐχ ἡμαρτηκέναι ἀνδρὸς ἀγαθοῦ.

32. Καὶ ὁ Φεραύλας εἶπεν, Ἀλλὰ πλουσιωτέρῳ μὲν ἄν, εἰ ἐσωφρόνεις, ἢ ἐμοὶ ἐδίδους· νῦν δὲ κἀγὼ δέξομαι. ἐπεύχομαι δέ, ἔφη, τοῖς θεοῖς, οἵπερ με ἐποίησαν βληθῆναι ὑπὸ σοῦ, δοῦναί μοι ποιῆσαι μὴ μεταμέλειν σοι τῆς ἐμῆς δωρεᾶς. καὶ νῦν μέν, ἔφη, ἀπέλα, ἀναβὰς ἐπὶ τὸν ἐμὸν ἵππον· αὖθις δ' ἐγὼ παρέσομαι πρὸς σέ.

Οἱ μὲν δὴ οὕτω διηλλάξαντο.

Καδουσίων δὲ ἐνίκα Ῥαθίνης.

33. Ἀφίει δὲ καὶ τὰ ἅρματα καθ' ἕκαστον· τοῖς δὲ νικῶσι πᾶσιν ἐδίδου βοῦς τε, ὅπως ἂν θύσαντες ἑστιῷντο, καὶ ἐκπώματα. τὸν μὲν οὖν βοῦν ἔλαβε καὶ αὐτὸς τὸ νικητήριον· τῶν δ' ἐκπωμάτων τὸ αὐτοῦ μέρος Φεραύλᾳ ἔδωκεν, ὅτι καλῶς ἔδοξεν αὐτῷ τὴν ἐκ τοῦ βασιλείου ἔλασιν διατάξαι.

34. Οὕτω δὴ τότε ὑπὸ Κύρου κατασταθεῖσα ἡ βασιλέως ἔλασις οὕτως ἔτι καὶ νῦν διαμένει,[1] πλὴν τὰ ἱερὰ ἄπεστιν, ὅταν μὴ θύῃ.

Ὡς δὲ ταῦτα τέλος εἶχεν, ἀφικνοῦνται πάλιν εἰς τὴν πόλιν, καὶ ἐσκήνησαν, οἷς μὲν ἐδόθησαν οἰκίαι, κατ' οἰκίας, οἷς δὲ μή, ἐν τάξει.

---

[1] οὕτω δὴ . . . διαμένει Hug, Marchant, Gemoll ; οὕτω δὴ η (ἡ not in y) τότε ὑπὸ Κ. κ. ἔλασις (ἡ ἔ. y) οὕτω ἔτι κ. ν. διαμένει ἡ βασιλέως ἔλασις xyzV (but οὕτω . . . ἔλασις is not in G ; ἡ βασιλέως ἔλασις is not in D).

31. "As you see," he answered.

"Well then," said the other, "I will make you a present of this horse."

"What for?" asked Pheraulas.

Then the Sacian related the circumstances and finally said: "And in my opinion, at least, I have not failed to hit a brave man."

32. "But you would give him to a richer man than I, if you were wise," answered Pheraulas. "Still, even as it is, I will accept him. And I pray the gods, who have caused me to receive your blow, to grant me to see that you never regret your gift to me. And now," said he, "mount my horse and ride away; I will join you presently."

Thus they made the exchange.

Of the Cadusians, Rhathines was the winner.

33. The chariots also he allowed to race by divisions; to all the winners he gave cups and cattle, so that they might sacrifice and have a banquet. He himself, then, took the ox as his prize, but his share of the cups he gave to Pheraulas because he thought that that officer, as grand marshal, had managed the procession from the palace admirably. The chariot race

34. The procession of the king, therefore, as thus instituted by Cyrus, continues even so unto this day, except that the victims are omitted when the king does not offer sacrifice.

When it was all over, they went back to the city to their lodgings—those to whom houses had been given, to their homes; those who had none, to their company's quarters. The procession comes to an end

35. Καλέσας δὲ καὶ ὁ Φεραύλας τὸν Σάκαν τὸν δόντα τὸν ἵππον ἐξένιζε, καὶ τἆλλα τε παρεῖχεν ἔκπλεω, καὶ ἐπεὶ ἐδεδειπνήκεσαν, τὰ ἐκπώματα αὐτῷ ἃ ἔλαβε παρὰ Κύρου ἐμπιμπλὰς προύπινε καὶ ἐδωρεῖτο.

36. Καὶ ὁ Σάκας ὁρῶν πολλὴν μὲν καὶ καλὴν στρωμνήν, πολλὴν δὲ καὶ καλὴν κατασκευήν, καὶ οἰκέτας δὲ πολλούς, Εἰπέ μοι, ἔφη, ὦ Φεραύλα, ἦ καὶ οἴκοι τῶν πλουσίων ἦσθα;

37. Καὶ ὁ Φεραύλας εἶπε, Ποίων πλουσίων; τῶν μὲν οὖν σαφῶς ἀποχειροβιώτων.[1] ἐμὲ γάρ τοι ὁ πατὴρ τὴν μὲν τῶν παίδων παιδείαν γλίσχρως αὐτὸς ἐργαζόμενος καὶ τρέφων ἐπαίδευεν· ἐπεὶ δὲ μειράκιον ἐγενόμην, οὐ δυνάμενος τρέφειν ἀργόν, εἰς ἀγρὸν ἀπαγαγὼν ἐκέλευσεν ἐργάζεσθαι. 38. ἔνθα δὴ ἐγὼ ἀντέτρεφον ἐκεῖνον, ἕως ἔζη, αὐτὸς σκάπτων καὶ σπείρων καὶ μάλα μικρὸν γῄδιον, οὐ μέντοι πονηρόν γε, ἀλλὰ πάντων δικαιότατον· ὅ τι γὰρ λάβοι σπέρμα, καλῶς καὶ δικαίως ἀπεδίδου αὐτό τε καὶ τόκον οὐδέν τι πολύν· ἤδη δέ ποτε ὑπὸ γενναιότητος καὶ διπλάσια ἀπέδωκεν ὧν ἔλαβεν. οἴκοι μὲν οὖν ἔγωγε οὕτως ἔζων· νῦν δὲ ταῦτα πάντα ἃ ὁρᾷς Κῦρός μοι ἔδωκε.

39. Καὶ ὁ Σάκας εἶπεν, Ὦ μακάριε σὺ τά τε ἄλλα καὶ αὐτὸ τοῦτο ὅτι ἐκ πένητος πλούσιος

---

[1] ἀποχειροβιώτων zED, most Edd.; ἀποχειροβιότων CF, Hug.

35. Pheraulas invited to his house the Sacian
also, who had given him his horse, and entertained
his new friend there and made bountiful provision
for him in every way; and when they had dined,
he filled up the cups that he had received from
Cyrus, drank to his health, and then gave him the
cups.

36. And when the Sacian saw the many beautiful
coverlets, the many beautiful pieces of furniture, and
the large number of servants, he said: "Pray tell
me, Pheraulas, were you a rich man at home,
too?"

37. "Rich, indeed!" answered Pheraulas; "nay
rather, as everybody knows, one of those who lived
by the labour of their hands. To be sure, my father,
who supported us by hard labour and close economy
on his own part, managed to give me the education of
the boys; but when I became a young man, he could
not support me in idleness, and so he took me off
to the farm and put me to work. 38. And there,
as long as he lived, I, in turn, supported him by
digging and planting a very little plot of ground. It
was really not such a very bad plot of ground, but, on
the contrary, the most honest; for all the seed that
it received it returned fairly and honestly, and yet
with no very great amount of interest. And sometimes, in a fit of generosity, it would even return to
me twice as much as it received. Thus, then, I used
to live at home; but now everything that you see
has been given to me by Cyrus."

39. "What a happy fellow you must be," said the
Sacian, "for every reason, but particularly because
from being poor you have become rich. For you

γεγένησαι· πολὺ γὰρ οἶμαί σε καὶ διὰ τοῦτο ἥδιον πλουτεῖν ὅτι πεινήσας χρημάτων ἐπλούτησας.[1]

40. Καὶ ὁ Φεραύλας εἶπεν, Ἦ γὰρ οὕτως, ὦ Σάκα, ὑπολαμβάνεις ὡς ἐγὼ νῦν τοσούτῳ ἥδιον ζῶ ὅσῳ πλείω κέκτημαι; οὐκ οἶσθα, ἔφη, ὅτι ἐσθίω μὲν καὶ πίνω καὶ καθεύδω οὐδ᾽ ὁτιοῦν νῦν ἥδιον ἢ τότε ὅτε πένης ἦν. ὅτι δὲ ταῦτα πολλά ἐστι, τοσοῦτον κερδαίνω, πλείω μὲν φυλάττειν δεῖ, πλείω δὲ ἄλλοις διανέμειν, πλειόνων δὲ ἐπιμελόμενον πράγματα ἔχειν. 41. νῦν γὰρ δὴ ἐμὲ πολλοὶ μὲν οἰκέται σῖτον αἰτοῦσι, πολλοὶ δὲ πιεῖν, πολλοὶ δὲ ἱμάτια· οἱ δὲ ἰατρῶν δέονται· ἥκει δέ τις ἢ τῶν προβάτων λελυκωμένα φέρων ἢ τῶν βοῶν κατακεκρημνισμένα ἢ νόσον φάσκων ἐμπεπτωκέναι τοῖς κτήνεσιν· ὥστε μοι δοκῶ, ἔφη ὁ Φεραύλας, νῦν διὰ τὸ πολλὰ ἔχειν πλείω λυπεῖσθαι ἢ πρόσθεν διὰ τὸ ὀλίγα ἔχειν.

42. Καὶ ὁ Σάκας, Ἀλλὰ ναὶ μὰ Δί᾽, ἔφη, ὅταν σῶα[2] ᾖ, πολλὰ ὁρῶν πολλαπλάσια ἐμοῦ εὐφραίνει.

Καὶ ὁ Φεραύλας εἶπεν, Οὗτοι, ὦ Σάκα, οὕτως ἡδύ ἐστι τὸ ἔχειν χρήματα ὡς ἀνιαρὸν τὸ ἀποβάλλειν. γνώσει δ᾽ ὅτι ἐγὼ ἀληθῆ λέγω· τῶν μὲν γὰρ πλουτούντων οὐδεὶς ἀναγκάζεται ὑφ᾽ ἡδονῆς ἀγρυπνεῖν, τῶν δὲ ἀποβαλλόντων τι ὄψει οὐδένα δυνάμενον καθεύδειν ὑπὸ λύπης.

43. Μὰ Δί᾽, ἔφη ὁ Σάκας, οὐδέ γε τῶν λαμβανόντων τι νυστάζοντα οὐδένα ἂν ἴδοις ὑφ᾽ ἡδονῆς.

[1] ἐπλούτησας Hertlein, recent Edd.; πεπλούτηκας MSS., Dindorf, Breitenbach.
[2] σῶα MSS., Marchant, Gemoll; σᾶ Dindorf, Hug.

must enjoy your riches much more, I think, for the very reason that it was only after being hungry for wealth that you became rich."

40. "Why, do you actually suppose, my Sacian friend," answered Pheraulas, "that the more I own, the more happily I live? You are not aware," he went on, "that it gives me not one whit more pleasure to eat and drink and sleep now than it did when I was poor. My only gain from having so much is that I am obliged to take care of more, distribute more to others, and have the trouble of looking after more than I used to have. 41. For now many domestics look to me for food, many for drink, and many for clothes, while some need doctors; and one comes to me with a tale about sheep attacked by wolves, or of oxen killed by falling over a precipice, or to say that some disease has broken out among the cattle. And so it looks to me," said Pheraulas, "as if I had more trouble now through possessing much than I used to have from possessing little."

He complains of the burden of riches

42. "But still, by Zeus," said the Sacian, "when everything is going well, you must at the sight of so many blessings be many times as happy as I."

"The pleasure that the possession of wealth gives, my good Sacian," said Pheraulas, "is not nearly so great as the pain that is caused by its loss. And you shall be convinced that what I say is true: for not one of thóse who are rich is made sleepless for joy, but of those who lose anything you will not see one who is able to sleep for grief."

43. "Not so, by Zeus," said the Sacian; "but of those who get anything not one could you see who gets a wink of sleep for very joy."

44. Ἀληθῆ, ἔφη, λέγεις· εἰ γάρ τοι τὸ ἔχειν οὕτως ὥσπερ τὸ λαμβάνειν ἡδὺ ἦν, πολὺ ἂν διέφερον εὐδαιμονίᾳ οἱ πλούσιοι τῶν πενήτων. καὶ ἀνάγκη δέ τοί ἐστιν, ἔφη, ὦ Σάκα, τὸν πολλὰ ἔχοντα πολλὰ καὶ δαπανᾶν καὶ εἰς θεοὺς καὶ εἰς φίλους καὶ εἰς ξένους· ὅστις οὖν ἰσχυρῶς χρήμασιν ἥδεται, εὖ ἴσθι τοῦτον καὶ δαπανῶντα ἰσχυρῶς ἀνιᾶσθαι.

45. Ναὶ[1] μὰ Δί', ἔφη ὁ Σάκας· ἀλλ' οὐκ ἐγὼ τούτων εἰμί, ἀλλὰ καὶ εὐδαιμονίαν τοῦτο νομίζω τὸ πολλὰ ἔχοντα πολλὰ καὶ δαπανᾶν.

46. Τί οὖν, ἔφη, πρὸς τῶν θεῶν, ὁ Φεραύλας, οὐχὶ σύγε αὐτίκα μάλα εὐδαίμων ἐγένου καὶ ἐμὲ εὐδαίμονα ἐποίησας; λαβὼν γάρ, ἔφη, ταῦτα πάντα κέκτησο, καὶ χρῶ ὅπως βούλει αὐτοῖς· ἐμὲ δὲ μηδὲν ἄλλο ἢ ὥσπερ ξένον τρέφε, καὶ ἔτι εὐτελέστερον ἢ ξένον· ἀρκέσει γάρ μοι ὅ τι ἂν καὶ σὺ ἔχῃς τούτων μετέχειν.

47. Παίζεις, ἔφη ὁ Σάκας.

Καὶ ὁ Φεραύλας ὀμόσας εἶπεν ἦ μὴν σπουδῇ λέγειν. καὶ ἄλλα γέ σοι, ὦ Σάκα, προσδιαπράξομαι παρὰ Κύρου, μήτε θύρας τὰς Κύρου θεραπεύειν μήτε στρατεύεσθαι· ἀλλὰ σὺ μὲν πλουτῶν οἴκοι μένε· ἐγὼ δὲ ταῦτα ποιήσω καὶ ὑπὲρ σοῦ καὶ ὑπὲρ ἐμοῦ· καὶ ἐάν τι ἀγαθὸν προσλαμβάνω διὰ τὴν Κύρου θεραπείαν ἢ καὶ ἀπὸ στρατείας τινός, οἴσω πρὸς σέ, ἵνα ἔτι πλειόνων ἄρχῃς· μόνον, ἔφη, ἐμὲ ἀπόλυσον ταύτης τῆς ἐπιμελείας· ἢν γὰρ ἐγὼ

---

[1] Ναὶ added by Hertlein, recent Edd.; not in MSS., earlier Edd.

44. "True," said the other; "for, you see, if having were as pleasant as getting, the rich would be incomparably happier than the poor. But, you see, my good Sacian, it is also a matter of course that he who has much should also spend much both in the service of the gods and for his friends and for the strangers within his gates. Let me assure you, therefore, that any one who takes inordinate pleasure in the possession of money is also inordinately distressed at having to part with it."

45. "Aye, by Zeus," answered the Sacian; "but I am not one of that sort; my idea of happiness is both to have much and also to spend much."

46. "In the name of the gods, then," said Pheraulas, "please make yourself happy at once and make me happy, too! Take all this and own it and use it as you wish. And as for me, you need do no more than keep me as a guest—aye, even more sparingly than a guest, for I shall be content to share whatever you have." *Pheraulas gets rid of his burden of wealth*

47. "You are joking," said the Sacian.

But Pheraulas assured him with an oath that he was really in earnest in what he proposed. "And I will get you other favours besides from Cyrus, my Sacian—exemption from attending at court and from serving in the field; you may just stay at home with your wealth. I will attend to those other duties for you as well as for myself; and if I secure anything more of value either through my attendance upon Cyrus or from some campaign, I will bring it to you, so that you may have still more wealth at your command. Only deliver me from this care. For if you

σχολὴν ἄγω ἀπὸ τούτων, ἐμοί τέ σε οἶμαι πολλὰ
καὶ Κύρῳ χρήσιμον ἔσεσθαι.

48. Τούτων οὕτω ῥηθέντων ταῦτα συνέθεντο
καὶ ταῦτα ἐποίουν. καὶ ὁ μὲν ἡγεῖτο εὐδαίμων
γεγενῆσθαι, ὅτι πολλῶν ἦρχε χρημάτων· ὁ δ' αὖ
ἐνόμιζε μακαριώτατος εἶναι, ὅτι ἐπίτροπον ἕξοι,
σχολὴν παρέχοντα¹ πράττειν ὅ τι ἂν αὐτῷ
ἡδὺ ᾖ.

49. Ἦν δὲ τοῦ Φεραύλα ὁ τρόπος φιλέταιρός
τε καὶ θεραπεύειν οὐδὲν ἡδὺ αὐτῷ οὕτως ἐδόκει
εἶναι οὐδ' ὠφέλιμον ὡς ἀνθρώπους. καὶ γὰρ
βέλτιστον πάντων τῶν ζῴων ἡγεῖτο ἄνθρωπον
εἶναι καὶ εὐχαριστότατον, ὅτι ἑώρα τούς τε
ἐπαινουμένους ὑπό τινος ἀντεπαινοῦντας τούτους
προθύμως τοῖς τε χαριζομένοις πειρωμένους ἀντι-
χαρίζεσθαι, καὶ οὓς γνοῖεν εὐνοϊκῶς ἔχοντας,
τούτοις ἀντευνοοῦντας, καὶ οὓς εἰδεῖεν φιλοῦντας
αὐτούς, τούτους μισεῖν οὐ δυναμένους, καὶ γονέας
δὲ πολὺ μᾶλλον ἀντιθεραπεύειν πάντων τῶν ζῴων
ἐθέλοντας καὶ ζῶντας καὶ τελευτήσαντας· τὰ δ'
ἄλλα πάντα ζῷα καὶ ἀχαριστότερα καὶ ἀγνω-
μονέστερα ἀνθρώπων ἐγίγνωσκεν εἶναι. 50. οὕτω
δὴ ὅ τε Φεραύλας ὑπερήδετο ὅτι ἐξέσοιτο αὐτῷ
ἀπαλλαγέντι τῆς τῶν ἄλλων κτημάτων ἐπιμελείας ἀμφὶ τοὺς φίλους ἔχειν, ὅ τε Σάκας ὅτι
ἔμελλε πολλὰ ἔχων πολλοῖς χρήσεσθαι. ἐφίλει
δὲ ὁ μὲν Σάκας τὸν Φεραύλαν, ὅτι προσέφερέ τι
ἀεί· ὁ δὲ τὸν Σάκαν, ὅτι παραλαμβάνειν πάντα

¹ παρέχοντα xzV, Edd.; παρέξοντα y.

will relieve me of its burden, I think you will do a great service also to Cyrus as well as to myself."

48. When they had thus talked things over together, they came to an agreement according to this last suggestion and proceeded to act upon it. And the one thought that he had been made a happy man because he had command of great riches, while the other considered himself most blessed because he was to have a steward who would give him leisure to do only whatever was pleasant to him.

49. Now, Pheraulas was naturally a " good fellow," *He delights to serve others* and nothing seemed to him so pleasant or so useful as to serve other people. For he held man to be the best and most grateful of all creatures, since he saw that when people are praised by any one they are very glad to praise him in turn ; and when any one does them a favour, they try to do him one in return ; when they recognize that any one is kindly disposed toward them they return his good-will ; and when they know that any one loves them they cannot dislike him ; and he noticed especially that they strive more earnestly than any other creature to return the loving care of parents both during their parents' lifetime and after their death ; whereas all other creatures, he knew, were both more thankless and more unfeeling than man. 50. And so Pheraulas was *An unusual partnership* greatly delighted to think that he could be rid of the care of all his worldly goods and devote himself to his friends ; and the Sacian, on his part, was delighted to think that he was to have much and enjoy much. And the Sacian loved Pheraulas because he was always bringing him something more ; and Pheraulas loved the Sacian because he

ἤθελε καὶ ἀεὶ πλειόνων ἐπιμελόμενος οὐδὲν μᾶλλον αὐτῷ ἀσχολίαν παρεῖχε.

Καὶ οὗτοι μὲν δὴ οὕτω διῆγον.

IV

1. Θύσας δὲ καὶ ὁ Κῦρος νικητήρια ἑστιῶν
ἐκάλεσε τῶν φίλων οἳ μάλιστ᾽ αὐτὸν αὔξειν τε
βουλόμενοι φανεροὶ ἦσαν καὶ τιμῶντες εὐνοϊκώ-
τατα. συνεκάλεσε δὲ αὐτοῖς καὶ Ἀρτάβαζον τὸν
Μῆδον καὶ Τιγράνην τὸν Ἀρμένιον καὶ τὸν
Ὑρκάνιον ἵππαρχον καὶ Γωβρύαν. 2. Γαδάτας
δὲ τῶν σκηπτούχων ἦρχεν αὐτῷ, καὶ ᾗ ἐκεῖνος
διεκόσμησεν ἡ πᾶσα ἔνδον δίαιτα καθειστήκει·
καὶ ὁπότε μὲν συνδειπνοῖέν τινες, οὐδ᾽ ἐκάθιζε
Γαδάτας, ἀλλ᾽ ἐπεμέλετο· ὁπότε δὲ αὐτοὶ εἶεν,
καὶ συνεδείπνει· ἥδετο γὰρ αὐτῷ συνών· ἀντὶ δὲ
τούτων πολλοῖς καὶ μεγάλοις ἐτιμᾶτο ὑπὸ τοῦ
Κύρου, διὰ δὲ Κῦρον καὶ ὑπ᾽ ἄλλων.
3. Ὡς δ᾽ ἦλθον οἱ κληθέντες ἐπὶ τὸ δεῖπνον,
οὐχ ὅπου ἔτυχεν ἕκαστον ἐκάθιζεν, ἀλλ᾽ ὃν μὲν
μάλιστα ἐτίμα, παρὰ τὴν ἀριστερὰν χεῖρα, ὡς
εὐεπιβουλευτοτέρας ταύτης οὔσης ἢ τῆς δεξιᾶς, τὸν
δὲ δεύτερον παρὰ τὴν δεξιάν, τὸν δὲ τρίτον πάλιν
παρὰ τὴν ἀριστεράν, τὸν δὲ τέταρτον παρὰ τὴν
δεξιάν· καὶ ἢν πλείονες ὦσιν, ὡσαύτως. 4. σα-
φηνίζεσθαι δὲ ὡς ἕκαστον ἐτίμα διὰ[1] τοῦτο ἐδόκει

---

[1] διὰ Dindorf, Hug, Marchant, Gemoll; not in MSS.,
other Edd.

was willing to take charge of everything; and though the Sacian had continually more in his charge, none the more did he trouble Pheraulas about it.

Thus these two continued to live.

IV

1. WHEN Cyrus had sacrificed and was celebrating his victory with a banquet, he invited in those of his friends who showed that they were most desirous of magnifying his rule and of honouring him most loyally. He invited with them Artabazus the Mede, Tigranes the Armenian, Gobryas, and the commander of the Hyrcanian horse. 2. Now Gadatas was the chief of the mace-bearers, and the whole household was managed as he directed. Whenever guests dined with Cyrus, Gadatas did not even take his seat, but attended upon them. But when they were by themselves, he would dine with Cyrus, for Cyrus enjoyed his company. And in return for his services he received many valuable presents from Cyrus himself and, through Cyrus's influence, from others also.

3. So when invited guests came to dinner, he did not assign them their seats at random, but he seated on Cyrus's left the one for whom he had the highest regard, for the left side was more readily exposed to treacherous designs than the right; and the one who was second in esteem he seated on his right, the third again on the left, the fourth on the right, and so on, if there were more. 4. For he thought it a good plan to show publicly how much regard he had

A royal banquet

Order of preferment at Cyrus's dinners

αὐτῷ ἀγαθὸν εἶναι, ὅτι ὅπου μὲν οἴονται ἄνθρωποι
τὸν κρατιστεύοντα μήτε κηρυχθήσεσθαι μήτε
ἆθλα λήψεσθαι, δῆλοί εἰσιν ἐνταῦθα οὐ φιλονίκως
πρὸς ἀλλήλους ἔχοντες· ὅπου δὲ μάλιστα πλε-
ονεκτῶν ὁ κράτιστος φαίνεται, ἐνταῦθα προθυμό-
τατα φανεροί εἰσιν ἀγωνιζόμενοι πάντες.

5. Καὶ ὁ Κῦρος δὲ οὕτως ἐσαφήνιζε μὲν τοὺς
κρατιστεύοντας παρ' ἑαυτῷ, εὐθὺς ἀρξάμενος
ἐξ ἕδρας καὶ παραστάσεως. οὐ μέντοι ἀθά-
νατον τὴν ταχθεῖσαν ἕδραν κατεστήσατο, ἀλλὰ
νόμιμον ἐποιήσατο καὶ ἀγαθοῖς ἔργοις προ-
βῆναι εἰς τὴν τιμιωτέραν ἕδραν, καὶ εἴ τις ῥᾳδι-
ουργοίη, ἀναχωρῆσαι εἰς τὴν ἀτιμοτέραν.   τὸν
δὲ πρωτεύοντα ἐν ἕδρᾳ ᾐσχύνετο μὴ οὐ πλεῖστα
καὶ ἀγαθὰ ἔχοντα παρ' αὐτοῦ φαίνεσθαι.   καὶ
ταῦτα δὲ ἐπὶ Κύρου γενόμενα οὕτως ἔτι καὶ νῦν
διαμένοντα αἰσθανόμεθα.

6. Ἐπεὶ δὲ ἐδείπνουν, ἐδόκει τῷ Γωβρύᾳ τὸ
μὲν πολλὰ ἕκαστα εἶναι οὐδέν τι θαυμαστὸν παρ'
ἀνδρὶ πολλῶν ἄρχοντι· τὸ δὲ τὸν Κῦρον οὕτω
μεγάλα πράττοντα, εἴ τι ἡδὺ δόξειε λαβεῖν, μηδὲν
τούτων μόνον καταδαπανᾶν, ἀλλ' ἔργον ἔχειν
δεόμενον[1] τούτου κοινωνεῖν τοὺς παρόντας,[2] πολλάκις δὲ καὶ τῶν ἀπόντων φίλων ἔστιν οἷς ἑώρα
πέμποντα ταῦτα αὐτὸν οἷς ἡσθεὶς τύχοι· 7. ὥστε
ἐπεὶ ἐδεδειπνήκεσαν καὶ πάντα τὰ λοιπὰ[3] πολλὰ
ὄντα διεπεπόμφει ὁ Κῦρος ἀπὸ τῆς τραπέζης,

---

[1] δεόμενον zV, Dindorf, Breitenbach ; τὸν δεόμενον y,
Cobet ; αὐτὸν δεόμενον Richards, Gemoll ; τῶν ἐδομένων x ;
αὐτὸν ἐδόμενον (when he was about to eat) Marchant.

[2] τοὺς παρόντας MSS., most Edd.; [τοὺς π.] Cobet, Hug.

[3] λοιπὰ added by Hug, Marchant, Gemoll ; not in MSS.,
other Edd.

for each one, because where people feel that the one who merits most will neither have his praise proclaimed nor receive a prize, there is no emulation among them; but where the most deserving is seen to receive the most preferment, there all are seen to contend most eagerly for the first place.

5. Accordingly, Cyrus thus made public recognition of those who stood first in his esteem, beginning even with the places they took when sitting or standing in his company. He did not, however, assign the appointed place permanently, but he made it a rule that by noble deeds any one might advance to a more honoured seat, and that if any one should conduct himself ill he should go back to one less honoured. And Cyrus felt it a discredit to himself, if the one who sat in the seat of highest honour was not also seen to receive the greatest number of good things at his hands. And we observe, furthermore, that this custom introduced in the time of Cyrus continues in force even to our own times.

6. Now, when they were at dinner, it struck Gobryas as not at all surprising that there was a great abundance of everything upon the table of a man who ruled over wide domains; but what did excite his wonder was that Cyrus, who enjoyed so great good fortune, should never consume by himself any delicacy that he might receive, but took pains to ask his guests to share it, and that he often saw him send even to some of his friends who were not there something that he happened to like very much himself. 7. And so when the dinner was over and Cyrus had sent around to others all that was left from the meal—and there was a great deal left—Gobryas

Cyrus's generosity

377

XENOPHON

εἶπεν ἄρα ὁ Γωβρύας, ᾿Αλλ᾿, ἐγώ, ὦ Κῦρε, πρόσθεν μὲν ἡγούμην τούτῳ σε πλεῖστον διαφέρειν
ἀνθρώπων τῷ στρατηγικώτατον εἶναι· νῦν δὲ
θεοὺς ὄμνυμι ἦ μὴν ἐμοὶ δοκεῖν πλέον σε διαφέρειν
φιλανθρωπίᾳ ἢ στρατηγίᾳ.

8. Νὴ Δί᾿, ἔφη ὁ Κῦρος· καὶ μὲν δὴ καὶ ἐπι-
δείκνυμαι τὰ ἔργα πολὺ ἥδιον φιλανθρωπίας ἢ
στρατηγίας.

Πῶς δή; ἔφη ὁ Γωβρύας.

῞Οτι, ἔφη, τὰ μὲν κακῶς ποιοῦντα ἀνθρώπους
δεῖ ἐπιδείκνυσθαι, τὰ δὲ εὖ.

9. ᾿Εκ τούτου δὴ ἐπεὶ ὑπέπινον, ἤρετο ὁ
῾Υστάσπας τὸν Κῦρον, ᾿Αρ᾿ ἄν, ἔφη, ὦ Κῦρε,
ἀχθεσθείης μοι, εἴ σε ἐροίμην ὃ βούλομαί σου
πυθέσθαι;

᾿Αλλὰ ναὶ μὰ τοὺς θεούς, ἔφη, τοὐναντίον τούτου ἀχθοίμην ἄν σοι, εἰ αἰσθοίμην σιωπῶντα ἃ
βούλοιο ἐρέσθαι.

Λέγε δή μοι, ἔφη, ἤδη πώποτε καλέσαντός σου
οὐκ ἦλθον;

Εὐφήμει, ἔφη ὁ Κῦρος.

᾿Αλλ᾿ ὑπακούων σχολῇ ὑπήκουσα;

Οὐδὲ τοῦτο.

Προσταχθὲν δέ τι ἤδη σοι οὐκ ἔπραξα;

Οὐκ αἰτιῶμαι, ἔφη.

῝Ο δὲ πράττοιμι, ἔστιν ὅ τι πώποτε οὐ προθύμως ἢ οὐχ ἡδομένως πράττοντά με κατέγνως;

Τοῦτο δὴ πάντων ἥκιστα, ἔφη ὁ Κῦρος.

could not help remarking: " Well, Cyrus, I used to think that you surpassed all other men in that you were the greatest general; and now, I swear by the gods, you seem actually to excel even more in kindness than in generalship."

8. " Aye, by Zeus," answered Cyrus; "and what is more, I assure you that I take much more pleasure in showing forth my deeds of kindness than ever I did in my deeds of generalship."

" How so? " asked Gobryas.

" Because," said he, " in the one field, one must necessarily do harm to men; in the other, only good."

9. Later, when they were drinking after their meal, Hystaspas asked: " Pray, Cyrus, would you be displeased with me, if I were to ask you something that I wish to know from you? " *Why Hystaspas felt slighted*

" Why, no; by the gods, no," he answered; "on the contrary, I should be displeased with you if I found that you refrained from asking something that you wished to ask."

" Tell me, then," said the other, " did I ever fail to come when you sent for me? "

" Hush! " [1] said Cyrus.

" Or, obeying, did I ever obey reluctantly? "

" No; nor that."

" Or did I ever fail to do your bidding in anything? "

" I make no such accusation," answered Cyrus.

" And is there anything I did that you found me doing otherwise than eagerly or cheerfully? "

" That, least of all," answered Cyrus.

[1] The Greek says: "Speak words of good omen"—*i.e.*, preserve auspicious silence.

10. Τίνος μὴν ἕνεκα, ἔφη, πρὸς τῶν θεῶν, ὦ Κῦρε, Χρυσάνταν ἔγραψας ὥστε εἰς τὴν τιμιωτέραν ἐμοῦ χώραν ἱδρυθῆναι;

Ἦ λέγω; ἔφη ὁ Κῦρος.

Πάντως, ἔφη ὁ Ὑστάσπας.

Καὶ σὺ αὖ οὐκ ἀχθέσει¹ μοι ἀκούων τἀληθῆ;

11. Ἡσθήσομαι μὲν οὖν, ἔφη, ἢν εἰδῶ ὅτι οὐκ ἀδικοῦμαι.

Χρυσάντας τοίνυν, ἔφη, οὑτοσὶ πρῶτον μὲν οὐ κλῆσιν ἀνέμενεν, ἀλλὰ πρὶν καλεῖσθαι παρῆν τῶν ἡμετέρων ἕνεκα· ἔπειτα δὲ οὐ τὸ κελευόμενον μόνον, ἀλλὰ καὶ ὅ τι αὐτὸς γνοίη ἄμεινον εἶναι πεπραγμένον ἡμῖν τοῦτο ἔπραττεν. ὁπότε δὲ εἰπεῖν τι δέοι εἰς τοὺς συμμάχους, ἃ μὲν ἐμὲ ᾤετο πρέπειν λέγειν ἐμοὶ συνεβούλευεν· ἃ δὲ ἐμὲ αἴσθοιτο βουλόμενον μὲν εἰδέναι τοὺς συμμάχους, αὐτὸν δέ με αἰσχυνόμενον περὶ ἐμαυτοῦ λέγειν, ταῦτα οὗτος λέγων ὡς ἑαυτοῦ γνώμην ἀπεφαίνετο· ὥστ᾽ ἔν γε τούτοις τί κωλύει αὐτὸν καὶ ἐμοῦ ἐμοὶ κρείττονα εἶναι; καὶ ἑαυτῷ μὲν ἀεί φησι πάντα τὰ παρόντα ἀρκεῖν, ἐμοὶ δὲ ἀεὶ φανερός ἐστι σκοπῶν τί ἂν προσγενόμενον ὀνήσειεν, ἐπί τε τοῖς ἐμοῖς καλοῖς πολὺ μᾶλλον ἐμοῦ ἀγάλλεται καὶ ἥδεται.

12. Πρὸς ταῦτα ὁ Ὑστάσπας εἶπε, Νὴ τὴν Ἥραν, ὦ Κῦρε, ἥδομαί γε ταῦτά σε ἐρωτήσας.

Τί μάλιστα; ἔφη ὁ Κῦρος.

¹ ἀχθέσει most Edd.; ἀχθεσθήσῃ(-ει F) MSS., Breitenbach.

10. "Then why, in heaven's name, Cyrus," he said, "did you put Chrysantas down for a more honourable place than mine?"

"Am I really to tell you?" asked Cyrus.

"By all means," answered Hystaspas.

"And you, on your part, will not be angry with me when you hear the truth?"

11. "Nay rather," said he, "I shall be more than glad, if I find that I am not being slighted."

"Well then," said Cyrus, "in the first place, Chrysantas here did not wait to be sent for, but presented himself for our service even before he was called; and in the second place, he has always done not only what was ordered but all that he himself saw was better for us to have done. Again, whenever it was necessary to send some communication to the allies, he would give me advice as to what he thought proper for me to say; and whenever he saw that I wished the allies to know about something, but that I felt some hesitation in saying anything about myself, he would always make it known to them, giving it as his own opinion. And so, in these matters at least, what reason is there why he should not be of more use to me even than I am myself? And finally, he always insists that what he has is enough for him, while he is manifestly always on the lookout for some new acquisition that would be of advantage to me, and takes much more pleasure and joy in my good fortune than I do myself."

12. "By Hera," said Hystaspas in reply, "I am glad at any rate that I asked you this question, Cyrus."

"Why so, pray?" asked Cyrus.

Why Cyrus preferred Chrysantas

Ὅτι κἀγὼ πειράσομαι ταῦτα ποιεῖν· ἓν μόνον, ἔφη, ἀγνοῶ, πῶς ἂν εἴην δῆλος χαίρων ἐπὶ τοῖς σοῖς ἀγαθοῖς· πότερον κροτεῖν δεῖ τὼ χεῖρε ἢ γελᾶν ἢ τί ποιεῖν.

Καὶ ὁ Ἀρτάβαζος εἶπεν, Ὀρχεῖσθαι δεῖ τὸ Περσικόν.

Ἐπὶ τούτοις μὲν δὴ γέλως ἐγένετο. 13. Προϊόντος δὲ τοῦ συμποσίου ὁ Κῦρος τὸν Γωβρύαν ἐπήρετο, Εἰπέ μοι, ἔφη, ὦ Γωβρύα, νῦν ἂν δοκεῖς ἥδιον τῶνδέ τῳ τὴν θυγατέρα δοῦναι ἢ ὅτε τὸ πρῶτον ἡμῖν συνεγένου;

Οὐκοῦν, ἔφη ὁ Γωβρύας, κἀγὼ τἀληθῆ λέγω;

Νὴ Δί᾽, ἔφη ὁ Κῦρος, ὡς ψεύδους γε οὐδεμία ἐρώτησις δεῖται.

Εὖ τοίνυν, ἔφη, ἴσθι ὅτι νῦν ἂν πολὺ ἥδιον.

Ἦ καὶ ἔχοις ἄν, ἔφη ὁ Κῦρος, εἰπεῖν διότι;

14. Ἔγωγε.

Λέγε δή.

Ὅτι τότε μὲν ἑώρων τοὺς πόνους καὶ τοὺς κινδύνους εὐθύμως αὐτοὺς φέροντας, νῦν δὲ ὁρῶ αὐτοὺς τἀγαθὰ σωφρόνως φέροντας. δοκεῖ δέ μοι, ὦ Κῦρε, χαλεπώτερον εἶναι εὑρεῖν ἄνδρα τἀγαθὰ καλῶς φέροντα ἢ τὰ κακά· τὰ μὲν γὰρ

"Because I too shall try to do as he does," said
he. "Only I am not sure about one thing—I do not
know how I could show that I rejoice at your good
fortune. Am I to clap my hands or laugh or what
must I do?"

"You must dance the Persian dance,"[1] suggested
Artabazus.

At this, of course, there was a laugh. 13. But, as Hystaspas asks for the daughter of Gobryas
the banquet proceeded, Cyrus put this question to
Gobryas: "Tell me, Gobryas," said he, "would you
be more ready to consent now to give your daughter
to one of my friends here than you were when first
you joined us?"

"Well," answered Gobryas, "shall I also tell the
truth?"

"Aye, by Zeus," answered Cyrus; "surely no
question calls for a falsehood."

"Well, then," he replied, "I should consent much
more readily now, I assure you."

"And would you mind telling us why?" asked
Cyrus.

"Certainly not."

"Tell us, then."

14. "Because, while at that time I saw them bear
toils and dangers with cheerfulness, now I see them
bear their good fortune with self-control. And to
me, Cyrus, it seems harder to find a man who can
bear good fortune well than one who can bear misfortune well; for it is the former that engenders

[1] What the "Persian dance" was is not known; hence
we miss the whole point of the joke. Obviously, however,
it was a dance with many gesticulations. At all events,
Artabazus introduces his jest about the dance only to cut
short the maudlin talk of Hystaspas.

ὕβριν τοῖς πολλοῖς, τὰ δὲ σωφροσύνην τοῖς πᾶσιν ἐμποιεῖ.

15. Καὶ ὁ Κῦρος εἶπεν, Ἤκουσας, ὦ Ὑστάσπα, Γωβρύου τὸ ῥῆμα;

Ναὶ μὰ Δί᾽, ἔφη· καὶ ἐὰν πολλὰ τοιαῦτά γε λέγῃ, πολὺ μᾶλλόν με τῆς θυγατρὸς μνηστῆρα λήψεται ἢ ἐὰν ἐκπώματα πολλά μοι ἐπιδεικνύῃ.

16. Ἦ μήν, ἔφη ὁ Γωβρύας, πολλά γέ μοί ἐστι τοιαῦτα συγγεγραμμένα, ὧν ἐγώ σοι οὐ φθονήσω, ἢν τὴν θυγατέρα μου γυναῖκα λαμβάνῃς· τὰ δ᾽ ἐκπώματα, ἔφη, ἐπειδὴ οὐκ ἀνέχεσθαί μοι φαίνει, οὐκ οἶδ᾽ εἰ Χρυσάντᾳ τουτῳὶ[1] δῶ, ἐπεὶ καὶ τὴν ἕδραν σου ὑφήρπασε.

17. Καὶ μὲν δή, ἔφη ὁ Κῦρος, ὦ Ὑστάσπα, καὶ οἱ ἄλλοι δὲ οἱ παρόντες, ἢν ἐμοὶ λέγητε, ὅταν τις ὑμῶν γαμεῖν ἐπιχειρήσῃ, γνώσεσθε ὁποῖός τις κἀγὼ συνεργὸς ὑμῖν ἔσομαι.

18. Καὶ ὁ Γωβρύας εἶπεν, Ἢν δέ τις ἐκδοῦναι βούληται θυγατέρα, πρὸς τίνα δεῖ λέγειν;

Πρὸς ἐμέ, ἔφη ὁ Κῦρος, καὶ τοῦτο· πάνυ γάρ, ἔφη, δεινός εἰμι ταύτην τὴν τέχνην.

Ποίαν; ἔφη ὁ Χρυσάντας.

19. Τὸ γνῶναι ὁποῖος ἂν γάμος ἑκάστῳ συναρμόσειε.

Καὶ ὁ Χρυσάντας ἔφη, Λέγε δὴ πρὸς τῶν θεῶν ποίαν τινά μοι γυναῖκα οἴει συναρμόσειν κάλλιστα.

20. Πρῶτον μέν, ἔφη, μικράν· μικρὸς γὰρ καὶ αὐτὸς εἶ· εἰ δὲ μεγάλην γαμεῖς, ἤν ποτε βούλῃ

---

[1] τουτῳὶ Hertlein, later Edd.; τούτῳ MSS., earlier Edd.

arrogance in most men; it is the latter that inspires in all men self-control."

15. "Hystaspas, did you hear that saying of Gobryas?" asked Cyrus.

"Yes, by Zeus," he answered; "and if he has many such things to say, he will find me a suitor for his daughter's hand much sooner than he would if he should exhibit to me a great number of goblets."

16. "I promise you," said Gobryas, "that I have a great number of such saws written down, and I will not begrudge them to you, if you get my daughter to be your wife. But as to the goblets," said he, "inasmuch as you do not seem to appreciate them, I rather think I shall give them to Chrysantas here, since he also has usurped your place at table."

17. "And what is more, Hystaspas—yes, and you others here," said Cyrus, "if you will let me know whenever any one of you is proposing to marry, you will discover what manner of assistant I, too, shall be to you." Cyrus sets up a matrimonial bureau

18. "And if any one has a daughter to give in marriage," said Gobryas, "to whom is he to apply?"

"To me," said Cyrus; "for I am exceedingly skilled in that art."

"What art?" asked Chrysantas.

19. "In knowing what sort of match would suit each one of you."

"Tell me, then, for heaven's sake," said Chrysantas, "what sort of wife you think would suit me best."

20. "In the first place," said he, "she must be small; for you are small yourself; and if you marry a tall woman and wish to kiss her when she is

αὐτὴν ὀρθὴν φιλῆσαι, προσάλλεσθαί σε δεήσει ὥσπερ τὰ κυνάρια.

Τοῦτο μὲν δή, ἔφη, ὀρθῶς προνοεῖς· καὶ γὰρ οὐδ᾽ ὁπωστιοῦν ἁλτικός εἰμι.

21. Ἔπειτα δ᾽, ἔφη, σιμὴ ἄν σοι ἰσχυρῶς συμφέροι.

Πρὸς τί δὴ αὖ τοῦτο;

Ὅτι, ἔφη, σὺ γρυπὸς εἶ· πρὸς οὖν τὴν σιμότητα σάφ᾽ ἴσθι ὅτι ἡ γρυπότης ἄριστ᾽ ἂν προσαρμόσειε.

Λέγεις σύ, ἔφη, ὡς καὶ τῷ εὖ δεδειπνηκότι ὥσπερ καὶ ἐγὼ νῦν ἄδειπνος ἂν συναρμόττοι.[1]

Ναὶ μὰ Δί᾽, ἔφη ὁ Κῦρος· τῶν μὲν γὰρ μεστῶν γρυπὴ ἡ γαστὴρ γίγνεται, τῶν δὲ ἀδείπνων σιμή.

22. Καὶ ὁ Χρυσάντας ἔφη, Ψυχρῷ δ᾽ ἄν, πρὸς τῶν θεῶν, βασιλεῖ ἔχοις ἂν εἰπεῖν ποία τις συνοίσει;

Ἐνταῦθα μὲν δὴ ὅ τε Κῦρος ἐξεγέλασε καὶ οἱ ἄλλοι ὁμοίως.

23. Γελώντων δὲ ἅμα εἶπεν ὁ Ὑστάσπας, Πολύ γ᾽, ἔφη, μάλιστα τούτου σε, ὦ Κῦρε, ζηλῶ ἐν τῇ βασιλείᾳ.

Τίνος; ἔφη ὁ Κῦρος.

Ὅτι δύνασαι καὶ ψυχρὸς ὢν γέλωτα παρέχειν.

Καὶ ὁ Κῦρος εἶπεν, Ἔπειτα οὐκ ἂν πρίαιό γε παμπόλλου ὥστε σοὶ ταῦτ᾽ εἰρῆσθαι, καὶ

---

[1] συναρμόττοι Dindorf, most Edd.; συναρμόζοι xy, Sauppe; συναρμόσοι z.

standing up straight, you will have to jump for it, like a puppy."

"You are quite right in that provision for me," said he; "and I should never get my kiss, for I am no jumper at all."

21. "And in the next place," Cyrus went on, "a snub-nosed woman would suit you admirably."

"Why so?"

"Because," was the answer, "your own nose is so hooked; and hookedness, I assure you, would be the very proper mate for snubbiness."

"Do you mean to say also," said the other, "that a supperless wife would suit one who has had a good dinner, like me now?"

"Aye, by Zeus," answered Cyrus; "for the stomach of one who has eaten heartily bows out, but that of one who has not eaten bows in."

22. "Then, in heaven's name," said Chrysantas, Cyrus's "frigid" jokes "could you tell us what sort of wife would suit a frigid king?" [1]

At this, of course, Cyrus burst out laughing, as did also all the rest.

23. "I envy you for that, Cyrus," said Hystaspas while they were still laughing, "more than for anything else in your kingdom."

"Envy me for what?" asked Cyrus.

"Why, that, frigid as you are, you can still make us laugh."

"Well," said Cyrus, "and would you not give a great deal to have made these jokes and to have

---

[1] On the principle of opposites just described, the man who is ψυχρός ("frigid," "cold-blooded") should have a wife who is θερμή. In § 23 ψυχρός is used in another sense— "frigid" or "dull" in his humour.

ἀπαγγελθῆναι παρ' ᾗ εὐδοκιμεῖν βούλει ὅτι
ἀστεῖος εἶ;

Καὶ ταῦτα μὲν δὴ οὕτω διεσκώπτετο.

24. Μετὰ δὲ ταῦτα Τιγράνῃ μὲν ἐξήνεγκε
γυναικεῖον κόσμον, καὶ ἐκέλευσε τῇ γυναικὶ
δοῦναι, ὅτι ἀνδρείως συνεστρατεύετο τῷ ἀνδρί,
Ἀρταβάζῳ δὲ χρυσοῦν ἔκπωμα, τῷ δ' Ὑρκανίῳ
ἵππον καὶ ἄλλα πολλὰ καὶ καλὰ ἐδωρήσατο.
Σοὶ δέ, ἔφη, ὦ Γωβρύα, δώσω ἄνδρα τῇ θυγατρί.

25. Οὐκοῦν ἐμέ, ἔφη ὁ Ὑστάσπας, δώσεις,
ἵνα καὶ τὰ συγγράμματα λάβω.

Ἦ καὶ ἔστι σοι, ἔφη ὁ Κῦρος, οὐσία ἀξία
τῶν τῆς παιδός;

Νὴ Δί', ἔφη, πολλαπλασίων μὲν οὖν χρημάτων.

Καὶ ποῦ, ἔφη ὁ Κῦρος, ἔστι σοι αὕτη ἡ οὐσία;

Ἐνταῦθα, ἔφη, ὅπουπερ καὶ σὺ κάθησαι φίλος
ὢν ἐμοί.

Ἀρκεῖ μοι, ἔφη ὁ Γωβρύας· καὶ εὐθὺς ἐκτείνας
τὴν δεξιάν, Δίδου, ἔφη, ὦ Κῦρε· δέχομαι γάρ.

26. Καὶ ὁ Κῦρος λαβὼν τὴν τοῦ Ὑστάσπου
δεξιὰν ἔδωκε τῷ Γωβρύᾳ, ὁ δ' ἐδέξατο. ἐκ δὲ τούτου πολλὰ καὶ καλὰ ἔδωκε δῶρα τῷ Ὑστάσπᾳ,
ὅπως τῇ παιδὶ πέμψειε· Χρυσάνταν δ' ἐφίλησε
προσαγαγόμενος.

27. Καὶ ὁ Ἀρτάβαζος εἶπε, Μὰ Δί', ἔφη,

them reported to the lady with whom you wish to have the reputation of being a witty fellow?"

Thus, then, these pleasantries were exchanged.

24. After this he brought out some articles of feminine adornment for Tigranes and bade him give them to his wife, because she had so bravely accompanied her husband throughout the campaigns; to Artabazus he gave a golden goblet and to the Hyrcanian a horse and many other beautiful presents. "And you, Gobryas," he said, "I will present with a husband for your daughter."

25. "You will please present him with me, then, will you not," said Hystaspas, "that so I may get the collection of proverbs?"

Hystaspas receives the hand of Gobryas's daughter

"Ah, but have you property enough to match the girl's fortune?" asked Cyrus.

"Yes, by Zeus," he answered, "and several times over."

"And where is this property of yours?" asked Cyrus.

"Right there," said he, "in your chair; for you are a friend of mine."

"I am satisfied," said Gobryas; and at once stretching out his right hand he added: "Give him to me, Cyrus; I will accept him."

26. And Cyrus took Hystaspas by the right hand and placed it in the hand of Gobryas, and he received it. And then Cyrus gave Hystaspas many splendid gifts to send to the young lady. But Chrysantas he drew to himself and kissed him.

27. "By Zeus, Cyrus," cried Artabazus, "the cup

XENOPHON

ὦ Κῦρε, οὐχ ὁμοίου γε χρυσοῦ ἐμοί τε τὸ ἔκπωμα δέδωκας καὶ Χρυσάντᾳ τὸ δῶρον.

Ἀλλὰ καὶ σοί, ἔφη, δώσω.

Ἐπήρετο ἐκεῖνος, Πότε;

Εἰς τριακοστόν, ἔφη, ἔτος.

Ὡς ἀναμενοῦντος, ἔφη,[1] καὶ οὐκ ἀποθανουμένου οὕτω παρασκευάζου.

Καὶ τότε μὲν δὴ οὕτως ἔληξεν ἡ σκηνή· ἐξανισταμένων δ' αὐτῶν ἐξανέστη καὶ ὁ Κῦρος καὶ συμπρούπεμψεν αὐτοὺς ἐπὶ τὰς θύρας.

28. Τῇ δὲ ὑστεραίᾳ τοὺς ἐθελουσίους συμμάχους γενομένους ἀπέπεμπεν οἴκαδε ἑκάστους, πλὴν ὅσοι αὐτῶν οἰκεῖν ἐβούλοντο παρ' αὐτῷ· τούτοις δὲ χώραν καὶ οἴκους ἔδωκε, καὶ νῦν ἔτι ἔχουσιν οἱ τῶν καταμεινάντων τότε ἀπόγονοι· πλεῖστοι δ' εἰσὶ Μήδων καὶ Ὑρκανίων· τοῖς δ' ἀπιοῦσι δωρησάμενος πολλὰ καὶ ἀμέμπτους ποιησάμενος καὶ ἄρχοντας καὶ στρατιώτας ἀπεπέμψατο.

29. Ἐκ τούτου δὲ διέδωκε καὶ τοῖς περὶ ἑαυτὸν στρατιώταις τὰ χρήματα ὅσα ἐκ Σάρδεων ἔλαβε· καὶ τοῖς μὲν μυριάρχοις καὶ τοῖς περὶ αὐτὸν ὑπηρέταις ἐξαίρετα ἐδίδου πρὸς τὴν ἀξίαν ἑκάστῳ, τὰ δὲ ἄλλα διένειμε· καὶ τὸ μέρος ἑκάστῳ δοὺς τῶν μυριάρχων ἐπέτρεψεν αὐτοῖς διανέμειν ὥσπερ αὐτὸς ἐκείνοις διένειμεν. 30. ἐδίδοσαν δὲ τὰ μὲν ἄλλα χρήματα ἄρχων[2] ἄρχοντας τοὺς ὑφ' ἑαυτῷ δοκιμάζων· τὰ δὲ τελευταῖα οἱ ἑξάδαρχοι τοὺς ὑφ' ἑαυτοῖς ἰδιώτας δοκιμάσαντες πρὸς τὴν

---

[1] ἔφη yz, Edd.; ἔτι x (*I shall still be waiting*).
[2] ἄρχων MSS., Edd.; <ἕκαστος> ἄρχων Gemoll.

which you have given me is not of the same gold as
the present you have given Chrysantas!"

"Well," said he, "I will give you the same gift."

"When?" asked the other.

"Thirty years from now," was the answer.

"I shall wait for it, then," said he, "and not die
before I get it; so be getting ready."

And thus that banquet came to an end. And as
they rose to depart, Cyrus also rose and escorted
them to the doors.

28. On the following day he dismissed to their
several homes all those who had volunteered to be
his allies, except such as wished to settle near him.
To those who stayed he gave houses and lands which
even to this day are in the possession of their
descendants; these, moreover, were mostly Medes
and Hyrcanians. And to those who went home he
gave many presents and sent both officers and
privates well contented on their way.

29. Next he divided also among his own soldiers
the spoil that he had obtained at Sardis. To the
generals and to his own aides-de-camp he gave the
choicest portions—to each, according to his merit—
and then distributed the rest; and in assigning to the
generals their proper portions he left it to their dis-
cretion to distribute it as he had distributed to them.
30. And they apportioned all the rest, each officer
examining into the merits of his subordinate officers;
and what was left to the last, the corporals, inquiring
into the merits of the private soldiers under their

Cyrus and the allies

He divides the Lydian spoils

ἀξίαν ἑκάστῳ ἐδίδοσαν· καὶ οὕτω πάντες εἰλήφεσαν τὸ δίκαιον μέρος.

31. Ἐπεὶ δὲ εἰλήφεσαν τὰ τότε δοθέντα, οἱ μέν
τινες ἔλεγον περὶ τοῦ Κύρου τοιάδε· Ἦπου αὐτός
γε πολλὰ ἔχει, ὅπου γε καὶ ἡμῶν ἑκάστῳ τοσαῦτα
δέδωκεν.

Οἱ δέ τινες αὐτῶν ἔλεγον, Ποῖα πολλὰ ἔχει;
οὐχ ὁ Κύρου τρόπος τοιοῦτος οἷος χρηματίζεσθαι,
ἀλλὰ διδοὺς μᾶλλον ἢ κτώμενος ἥδεται.

32. Αἰσθόμενος δὲ ὁ Κῦρος τούτους τοὺς λόγους
καὶ τὰς δόξας τὰς περὶ αὐτοῦ συνέλεξε τοὺς
φίλους τε καὶ τοὺς ἐπικαιρίους ἅπαντας καὶ
ἔλεξεν ὧδε· Ὦ ἄνδρες φίλοι, ἑώρακα μὲν ἤδη
ἀνθρώπους οἳ βούλονται δοκεῖν πλείω κεκτῆσθαι
ἢ ἔχουσιν, ἐλευθεριώτεροι ἂν οἰόμενοι οὕτω φαί-
νεσθαι· ἐμοὶ δὲ δοκοῦσιν, ἔφη, οὗτοι τοὐμπαλιν οὗ
βούλονται ἐφέλκεσθαι· τὸ γὰρ πολλὰ δοκοῦντα
ἔχειν μὴ κατ᾽ ἀξίαν τῆς οὐσίας φαίνεσθαι ὠφε-
λοῦντα τοὺς φίλους ἀνελευθερίαν ἔμοιγε δοκεῖ
περιάπτειν.

33. Εἰσὶ δ᾽ αὖ, ἔφη, οἳ λεληθέναι βούλονται
ὅσα ἂν ἔχωσι· πονηροὶ οὖν καὶ οὗτοι τοῖς φίλοις
ἔμοιγε δοκοῦσιν εἶναι. διὰ γὰρ τὸ μὴ εἰδέναι τὰ
ὄντα πολλάκις δεόμενοι οὐκ ἐπαγγέλλουσιν οἱ
φίλοι τοῖς ἑταίροις, ἀλλὰ τητῶνται.[1]

34. Ἁπλουστάτου δέ μοι, ἔφη, δοκεῖ εἶναι τὸ

---

[1] τητῶνται Dindorf, Edd.; ἡττῶνται xz ; ἀπατῶνται yVG².

command, gave to each according to his deserts.
And so all were in receipt of their fair share.

31. And when they had received what was then
given them, some spoke concerning Cyrus in this
vein: "He must be keeping an abundance himself,
one would think, seeing that he has given so much
to each one of us."

"Abundance, indeed!" some others would say;
"Cyrus is not of the sort to make money for himself;
he takes more pleasure in giving than in keeping."

32. And when Cyrus heard of these remarks and
opinions about himself, he called together his
friends and all his staff-officers and addressed them as
follows: "My friends, I have in my time seen fellows The use
who wished to have the reputation of possessing *vs.*
more than they had, for they supposed that they the abuse of
would thus be thought fine gentlemen; but to me," wealth
said he, "it seems that such persons bring upon
themselves the very reverse of what they wish. For
if any man enjoy the reputation of having great
wealth and do not appear to help his friends in a
manner worthy of his abundance—that, it seems to
me at least, fixes upon him the stigma of being
a mean sort.[1]

33. "On the other hand," he continued, "there
are some who wish to keep it a secret how much
they do possess. It seems to me, then, that these
also are mean toward their friends. For oftentimes
their friends are in need and, because they are
ignorant of the truth, they say nothing to their comrades about their difficulties, and really suffer want.

34. "To me, however," he went on, "it seems

---

[1] Ἐλευθέριος and ἀνελευθερία have both a double meaning:
(1) of free or mean extraction, and (2) of free (liberal) or
miserly character.

τὴν δύναμιν φανερὰν ποιήσαντα ἐκ ταύτης ἀγωνίζεσθαι περὶ καλοκἀγαθίας. κἀγὼ οὖν, ἔφη, βούλομαι ὑμῖν ὅσα μὲν οἷόν τ' ἐστὶν ἰδεῖν τῶν ἐμοὶ
ὄντων δεῖξαι, ὅσα δὲ μὴ οἷόν τε ἰδεῖν, διηγήσασθαι.

35. Ταῦτα εἰπὼν τὰ μὲν ἐδείκνυε [1] πολλὰ καὶ
καλὰ κτήματα· τὰ δὲ κείμενα ὡς μὴ ῥᾴδια εἶναι
ἰδεῖν διηγεῖτο· τέλος δ' εἶπεν ὧδε· 36. Ταῦτα,
ἔφη, ὦ ἄνδρες, ἅπαντα δεῖ ὑμᾶς οὐδὲν μᾶλλον ἐμὰ
ἡγεῖσθαι ἢ καὶ ὑμέτερα· ἐγὼ γάρ, ἔφη, ταῦτα
ἁθροίζω οὔθ' ὅπως αὐτὸς καταδαπανήσω οὔθ'
ὅπως αὐτὸς κατατρίψω· οὐ γὰρ ἂν δυναίμην·
ἀλλ' ὅπως ἔχω τῷ τε ἀεὶ καλόν τι ὑμῶν ποιοῦντι
διδόναι καὶ ὅπως, ἤν τις ὑμῶν τινος ἐνδεῖσθαι
νομίσῃ, πρὸς ἐμὲ ἐλθὼν λάβῃ οὗ ἂν ἐνδεὴς τυγ-
χάνῃ ὤν.

Καὶ ταῦτα μὲν δὴ οὕτως ἐλέχθη.

V

1. Ἡνίκα δὲ ἤδη αὐτῷ ἐδόκει καλῶς ἔχειν τὰ ἐν
Βαβυλῶνι ὡς καὶ ἀποδημεῖν, συνεσκευάζετο τὴν
εἰς Πέρσας πορείαν καὶ τοῖς ἄλλοις παρήγγειλεν·
ἐπεὶ δ' ἐνόμισεν ἱκανὰ ἔχειν ὧν ᾤετο δεήσεσθαι,
οὕτω δὴ ἀνεζεύγνυε. [2]

2. Διηγησόμεθα δὲ καὶ ταῦτα ὡς πολὺς στόλος
ὢν εὐτάκτως μὲν ἀνεσκευάζετο, [3] ταχὺ δὲ κατεχω-

---

[1] ἐδείκνυε MSS.; ἐδείκνυ Hug.
[2] ἀνεζεύγνυε MSS.; ἀνεζεύγνυ Hug.
[3] ἀνεσκευάζετο E(?)F ; κατεσκευάζετο καὶ πάλιν ἀνεσκευάζετο
zDVC (in margin), most Edd. (*unpacked and packed up
again*).

the most straightforward way for a man to let the extent of his means be known and to strive in proportion to them to show himself a gentleman. And so I wish to show you all that I have, as far as it is possible for you to see, and to give you an account of it, in so far as it is impossible for you to see it."

35. With these words, he showed them many splendid possessions and gave them an account of those that were so stored away as not to be easily viewed. And in conclusion he said: 36. "All this, my friends, you must consider mine no more than your own; for I have been collecting it, not that I might spend it all myself or use it up all alone (for I could not), but that I might on every occasion be able to reward any one of you who does something meritorious, and also that, if any one of you thinks he needs something, he might come to me and get whatever he happens to want." *Cyrus exhibits his possessions*

Such was his speech.

V

1. When it seemed to him that affairs in Babylon were sufficiently well organized for him to absent himself from the city, he began to make preparations for his journey to Persia and issued instructions to the others accordingly. And as soon as he had got together in sufficient quantity, as he believed, everything that he thought he should need, he started at once. *Cyrus goes to Persia*

2. We will relate here in how orderly a manner his train packed up, large though it was, and how quickly they reached the place where they were *An oriental camp*

ρίζετο ὅπου δέοι. ὅπου γὰρ ἂν στρατοπεδεύηται
βασιλεύς, σκηνὰς μὲν δὴ ἔχοντες πάντες οἱ ἀμφὶ
βασιλέα στρατεύονται καὶ θέρους καὶ χειμῶνος.

3. Εὐθὺς δὲ τοῦτο ἐνόμιζε Κῦρος, πρὸς ἔω
βλέπουσαν ἵστασθαι τὴν σκηνήν· ἔπειτα ἔταξε
πρῶτον μὲν πόσον δεῖ ἀπολιπόντας σκηνοῦν τοὺς
δορυφόρους τῆς βασιλικῆς σκηνῆς· ἔπειτα σιτο-
ποιοῖς μὲν χώραν ἀπέδειξε τὴν δεξιάν, ὀψοποιοῖς
δὲ τὴν ἀριστεράν, ἵπποις δὲ τὴν δεξιάν, ὑποζυγίοις
δὲ τοῖς ἄλλοις τὴν ἀριστεράν· καὶ τἆλλα δὲ
διετέτακτο ὥστε εἰδέναι ἕκαστον τὴν ἑαυτοῦ
χώραν καὶ μέτρῳ καὶ τόπῳ.

4. Ὅταν δὲ ἀνασκευάζωνται, συντίθησι μὲν
ἕκαστος σκεύη οἷσπερ τέτακται χρῆσθαι, ἀνατί-
θενται δ' αὖ ἄλλοι ἐπὶ τὰ ὑποζύγια· ὥσθ' ἅμα
μὲν πάντες ἔρχονται οἱ σκευαγωγοὶ ἐπὶ τὰ τεταγμένα ἄγειν, ἅμα δὲ πάντες ἀνατιθέασιν ἐπὶ τὰ
ἑαυτοῦ ἕκαστος. οὕτω δὴ ὁ αὐτὸς χρόνος ἀρκεῖ
μιᾷ τε σκηνῇ καὶ πάσαις ἀνῃρῆσθαι.

5. Ὡσαύτως οὕτως ἔχει καὶ περὶ κατασκευῆς.
καὶ περὶ τοῦ πεποιῆσθαι δὲ τἀπιτήδεια πάντα ἐν
καιρῷ ὡσαύτως διατέτακται ἑκάστοις τὰ ποιητέα·
καὶ διὰ τοῦτο ὁ αὐτὸς χρόνος ἀρκεῖ ἑνί τε μέρει
καὶ πᾶσι πεποιῆσθαι.

6. Ὥσπερ δὲ οἱ περὶ τἀπιτήδεια θεράποντες
χώραν εἶχον τὴν προσήκουσαν ἑκάστῳ, οὕτω καὶ
οἱ ὁπλοφόροι αὐτῷ ἐν τῇ στρατοπεδεύσει χώραν
τε εἶχον τὴν τῇ ὁπλίσει ἑκάστῃ ἐπιτηδείαν, καὶ
ᾔδεσαν ταύτην ὁποία ἦν, καὶ ἐπ' ἀναμφισβήτητον
πάντες κατεχωρίζοντο. 7. καλὸν μὲν γὰρ ἡγεῖτο
ὁ Κῦρος καὶ ἐν οἰκίᾳ εἶναι ἐπιτήδευμα τὴν εὐθη-

due. For wherever the great king encamps, all his
retinue follow him to the field with their tents,
whether in summer or in winter.

3. At the very beginning Cyrus made this rule,
that his tent should be pitched facing the east; and
then he determined, first, how far from the royal
pavilion the spearmen of his guard should have their
tent; next he assigned a place on the right for the
bakers, on the left for the cooks, on the right for the
horses, and on the left for the rest of the pack-animals
And everything else was so organized that every one
knew his own place in camp—both its size and its
location.

4. And when they come to pack up again, every
one gets together the things that it is his business to
use and others in turn pack them upon the animals,
so that the baggage-men all come at the same time
to the things they were appointed to transport, and
all at the same time pack the things upon their
several animals. Thus the amount of time needed
for striking a single tent suffices for all.

5. The unpacking also is managed in this same
manner; and in order to have all the necessaries
ready at the right time, each one has assigned to
him likewise the part that he is to do. In this way
the time required for doing any one part is sufficient
for getting all the provisions ready.

6. And just as the servants in charge of the *Cyrus's per-*
provisions had each his proper place, so also his *fect organ-*
soldiers had when they encamped the places suitable *ization*
to each sort of troops; they knew their places, too,
and so all found them without the slightest friction.
7. For Cyrus considered orderliness to be a good
thing to practise in the management of a household

μοσύνην· ὅταν γάρ τίς του δέηται, δῆλόν ἐστι
ὅπου δεῖ ἐλθόντα λαβεῖν· πολὺ δ' ἔτι κάλλιον
ἐνόμιζε τὴν τῶν στρατιωτικῶν φύλων εὐθημο-
σύνην εἶναι, ὅσῳ τε ὀξύτεροι οἱ καιροὶ τῶν εἰς τὰ
πολεμικὰ χρήσεων καὶ μείζω τὰ σφάλματα ἀπὸ
τῶν ὑστεριζόντων ἐν αὐτοῖς· ἀπὸ δὲ τῶν ἐν καιρῷ
παραγιγνομένων πλείστου ἄξια πλεονεκτήματα[1]
ἑώρα γιγνόμενα ἐν τοῖς πολεμικοῖς· διὰ ταῦτα
οὖν καὶ ἐπεμέλετο ταύτης τῆς εὐθημοσύνης μάλιστα.

8. Καὶ αὐτὸς μὲν δὴ πρῶτον ἑαυτὸν ἐν μέσῳ
κατετίθετο τοῦ στρατοπέδου, ὡς ταύτης τῆς χώρας ἐχυρωτάτης οὔσης· ἔπειτα δὲ τοὺς μὲν
πιστοτάτους ὥσπερ εἰώθει περὶ ἑαυτὸν εἶχε, τούτων δ' ἐν κύκλῳ ἐχομένους ἱππέας τ' εἶχε καὶ
ἁρματηλάτας. 9. καὶ γὰρ τούτους ἐχυρᾶς ἐνόμιζε
χώρας δεῖσθαι, ὅτι σὺν οἷς μάχονται ὅπλοις οὐδὲν
πρόχειρον ἔχοντες τούτων στρατοπεδεύονται, ἀλλὰ
πολλοῦ χρόνου δέονται εἰς τὴν ἐξόπλισιν, εἰ μέλ-
λουσι χρησίμως ἕξειν.

10. Ἐν δεξιᾷ δὲ καὶ ἐν ἀριστερᾷ αὐτοῦ δὲ καὶ
τῶν ἱππέων πελτασταῖς χώρα ἦν· τοξοτῶν δ' αὖ
χώρα ἡ πρόσθεν ἦν καὶ ὄπισθεν αὐτοῦ τε καὶ τῶν
ἱππέων. 11. ὁπλίτας δὲ καὶ τοὺς τὰ μεγάλα
γέρρα ἔχοντας κύκλῳ πάντων εἶχεν ὥσπερ τεῖχος,
ὅπως καὶ εἰ δέοι τι ἐνσκευάζεσθαι τοὺς ἱππέας,
οἱ μονιμώτατοι πρόσθεν ὄντες παρέχοιεν αὐτοῖς
ἀσφαλῆ τὴν καθόπλισιν.

12. Ἐκάθευδον δὲ αὐτῷ ἐν τάξει ὥσπερ οἱ
ὁπλῖται, οὕτω δὲ καὶ οἱ πελτασταὶ καὶ οἱ τοξόται,

---

[1] πλεονεκτήματα Schneider, recent Edd.; τὰ κτήματα zV,
Dindorf, Breitenbach; ταῦτα (τὰ D) κτήματα xy.

also; for whenever any one wants a thing, he then knows where he must go to find it; but he believed that orderliness in all the departments of an army was a much better thing, inasmuch as the chances of a successful stroke in war come and go more quickly and the losses occasioned by those who are behindhand in military matters are more serious. He also saw that the advantages gained in war by prompt attention to duty were most important. It was for this reason, therefore, that he took especial pains to secure this sort of orderliness.

8. Accordingly, he himself first took up his position in the middle of the camp in the belief that this situation was the most secure. Then came his most trusty followers, just as he was accustomed to have them about him at home, and next to them in a circle he had his horsemen and charioteers; 9. for those troops also, he thought, need a secure position, because when they are in camp they do not have ready at hand any of the arms with which they fight, but need considerable time to arm, if they are to render effective service. The arrangement of his camp

10. To the right and left from him and the cavalry was the place for the targeteers; before and behind him and the cavalry, the place for the bowmen. 11. The hoplites and those armed with the large shields he arranged around all the rest like a wall, so that those who could best hold their ground might, by being in front of them, make it possible for the cavalry to arm in safety, if it should be necessary.

12. Moreover, he had the peltasts and the bowmen sleep on their arms, like the hoplites, in order that,

ὅπως καὶ ἐκ νυκτῶν, εἰ δέοι τι, ὥσπερ καὶ οἱ
ὁπλῖται παρεσκευασμένοι εἰσὶ παίειν τὸν εἰς χεῖρας ἰόντα, οὕτω καὶ οἱ τοξόται καὶ οἱ ἀκοντισταί,
εἴ τινες προσίοιεν, ἐξ ἑτοίμου ἀκοντίζοιεν καὶ
τοξεύοιεν ὑπὲρ τῶν ὁπλιτῶν.

13. Εἶχον δὲ καὶ σημεῖα πάντες οἱ ἄρχοντες
ἐπὶ ταῖς σκηναῖς· οἱ δ᾽ ὑπηρέται ὥσπερ καὶ
ἐν ταῖς πόλεσιν οἱ σώφρονες [1] ἴσασι μὲν καὶ τῶν
πλείστων τὰς οἰκήσεις, μάλιστα δὲ τῶν ἐπικαιρίων, οὕτω καὶ τῶν ἐν τοῖς στρατοπέδοις τάς
τε χώρας τὰς τῶν ἡγεμόνων ἠπίσταντο οἱ Κύρου
ὑπηρέται καὶ τὰ σημεῖα ἐγίγνωσκον ἃ ἑκάστοις
ἦν· ὥστε ὅτου δέοιτο Κῦρος, οὐκ ἐζήτουν, ἀλλὰ
τὴν συντομωτάτην ἐφ᾽ ἕκαστον ἔθεον. 14. καὶ
διὰ τὸ εἰλικρινῆ ἕκαστα εἶναι τὰ φῦλα πολὺ
μᾶλλον ἦν δῆλα καὶ ὁπότε τις εὐτακτοίη καὶ
εἴ τις μὴ πράττοι τὸ προσταττόμενον. οὕτω
δὴ ἐχόντων ἡγεῖτο, εἴ τις καὶ ἐπίθοιτο νυκτὸς ἢ
ἡμέρας, ὥσπερ ἂν εἰς ἐνέδραν εἰς τὸ στρατόπεδον
τοὺς ἐπιτιθεμένους ἐμπίπτειν.

15. Καὶ τὸ τακτικὸν δὲ εἶναι οὐ τοῦτο μονον
ἡγεῖτο εἴ τις ἐκτεῖναι φάλαγγα εὐπόρως δύναιτο
ἢ βαθῦναι ἢ ἐκ κέρατος εἰς φάλαγγα καταστῆσαι
ἢ ἐκ δεξιᾶς ἢ ἀριστερᾶς ἢ ὄπισθεν ἐπιφανέντων
πολεμίων ὀρθῶς ἐξελίξαι, ἀλλὰ καὶ τὸ διασπᾶν

---

[1] [οἱ σώφρονες] Hug.

if there should be occasion to go into action even at night, they might be ready for it. And just as the hoplites were prepared to do battle if any one came within arm's reach of them, so these troops also were to be ready to let fly their lances and arrows over the heads of the hoplites, if any one attacked.

13. And all the officers had banners over their tents ; and just as in the cities well-informed officials know the residences of most of the inhabitants and especially those of the most prominent citizens, so also in camp the aides under Cyrus were acquainted with the location of the various officers and were familiar with the banner of each one ; and so if Cyrus wanted one of his officers, they did not have to search for him but would run to him by the shortest way. 14. And as every division was so well distinguished, it was much more easy to see where good order prevailed and where commands were not being executed. Therefore, as things were arranged, he believed that if any enemy were to attack him either by night or by day, the attacking party would fall into his camp as into an ambuscade.

15. He believed also that tactics did not consist solely in being able easily to extend one's line or increase its depth, or to change it from a long column into a phalanx, or without error to change the front by a counter march according as the enemy came up on the right or the left or behind;[1] but he considered

Cyrus as a tactician

---

[1] " We learn from Aelian (*Tact.* 27) that this was either a countermarch by files (κατὰ ζυγά), in which the wings only changed places, or a countermarch by companies (κατὰ λόχους or στίχους) when the whole line turned and the rearguard marched in front, so that there was a change of front as well as of wings. The object of the last-named movement was to put τοὺς κρατίστους [the best men] forward." (Holden.)

ὁπότε δέοι τακτικὸν ἡγεῖτο, καὶ τὸ τιθέναι γε
τὸ μέρος ἕκαστον ὅπου μάλιστα ἐν ὠφελείᾳ ἂν
εἴη, καὶ τὸ ταχύνειν δὲ ὅπου φθάσαι δέοι, πάντα
ταῦτα καὶ τὰ τοιαῦτα τακτικοῦ ἀνδρὸς ἐνόμιζεν
εἶναι καὶ ἐπεμέλετο τούτων πάντων ὁμοίως.

16. Καὶ ἐν μὲν ταῖς πορείαις πρὸς τὸ συμ-
πῖπτον ἀεὶ διατάττων ἐπορεύετο, ἐν δὲ τῇ στρατοπεδεύσει ὡς τὰ πολλὰ ὥσπερ εἴρηται κατεχώ-
ριζεν.

17. Ἐπεὶ δὲ πορευόμενοι γίγνονται κατὰ τὴν
Μηδικήν, τρέπεται ὁ Κῦρος πρὸς Κυαξάρην.
ἐπεὶ δὲ ἠσπάσαντο ἀλλήλους, πρῶτον μὲν δὴ
ὁ Κῦρος εἶπε τῷ Κυαξάρῃ ὅτι οἶκος αὐτῷ ἐξῃρη-
μένος εἴη ἐν Βαβυλῶνι καὶ ἀρχεῖα, ὅπως ἔχῃ
καὶ ὅταν ἐκεῖσε ἔλθῃ εἰς οἰκεῖα κατάγεσθαι·
ἔπειτα δὲ καὶ ἄλλα δῶρα ἔδωκεν αὐτῷ πολλὰ
καὶ καλά. 18. ὁ δὲ Κυαξάρης ταῦτα μὲν ἐδέχετο,
προσέπεμψε δὲ αὐτῷ τὴν θυγατέρα στέφανόν
τε χρυσοῦν καὶ ψέλια φέρουσαν καὶ στρεπτὸν
καὶ στολὴν Μηδικὴν ὡς δυνατὸν καλλίστην.
19. καὶ ἡ μὲν δὴ παῖς ἐστεφάνου τὸν Κῦρον,
ὁ δὲ Κυαξάρης εἶπε, Δίδωμι δέ σοι, ἔφη, ὦ Κῦρε,
καὶ αὐτὴν ταύτην γυναῖκα, ἐμὴν οὖσαν θυγατέρα·
καὶ ὁ σὸς δὲ πατὴρ ἔγημε τὴν τοῦ ἐμοῦ πατρὸς
θυγατέρα, ἐξ ἧς σὺ ἐγένου· αὕτη δ' ἐστὶν ἣν
σὺ πολλάκις παῖς ὢν ὅτε παρ' ἡμῖν ἦσθα ἐτιθη-
νήσω· καὶ ὁπότε τις ἐρωτῴη αὐτὴν τίνι γαμοῖτο,
ἔλεγεν ὅτι Κύρῳ· ἐπιδίδωμι δὲ αὐτῇ ἐγὼ καὶ
φερνὴν Μηδίαν τὴν πᾶσαν· οὐδὲ γὰρ ἔστι μοι
ἄρρην παῖς γνήσιος.

20. Ὁ μὲν οὕτως εἶπεν· ὁ δὲ Κῦρος ἀπεκρίνατο,

it also a part of good tactics to break up one's army into several divisions whenever occasion demanded, and to place each division, too, where it would do the most good, and to make speed when it was necessary to reach a place before the enemy—all these and other such qualifications were essential, he believed, to a skilful tactician, and he devoted himself to them all alike.

16. And so on his marches he always proceeded giving out his orders with a view to existing circumstances; but in camp his arrangements were made, for the most part, as has been described.

17. As they continued their march and came near to Media, Cyrus turned aside to visit Cyaxares. And when they had exchanged greetings, the first thing Cyrus told Cyaxares was that a palace had been selected for him in Babylon, and official headquarters, so that he might occupy a residence of his own whenever he came there; and then he also gave him many splendid presents. 18. Cyaxares accepted them and then introduced to him his daughter, who brought him a golden crown and bracelets and a necklace and the most beautiful Median robe that could be found. 19. As the princess placed the crown on Cyrus's head, Cyaxares said, "And the maiden herself, my own daughter, I offer you as well, Cyrus, to be your wife. Your father married my father's daughter, whose son you are. This is she whom you used often to pet when you came to visit us when you were a boy. And whenever anybody asked her whom she was going to marry, she would say 'Cyrus.' And with her I offer you all Media as a dowry, for I have no legitimate male issue."

20. Thus he spoke, and Cyrus answered: "Well,

Cyrus visits his uncle

Cyaxares offers him his daughter's hand and all Media

403

Ἀλλ', ὦ Κυαξάρη, τό τε γένος ἐπαινῶ καὶ τὴν παῖδα καὶ τὰ δῶρα· βούλομαι δέ, ἔφη, σὺν τῇ τοῦ πατρὸς γνώμῃ καὶ τῇ τῆς μητρὸς ταῦτά σοι συναινέσαι.

Εἶπε μὲν οὖν οὕτως ὁ Κῦρος, ὅμως δὲ τῇ παιδὶ πάντα ἐδωρήσατο ὁπόσα ᾤετο καὶ τῷ Κυαξάρῃ χαριεῖσθαι. ταῦτα δὲ ποιήσας εἰς Πέρσας ἐπορεύετο.

21. Ἐπεὶ δ' ἐπὶ τοῖς Περσῶν ὁρίοις ἐγένετο πορευόμενος, τὸ μὲν ἄλλο στράτευμα αὐτοῦ κατέλιπεν, αὐτὸς δὲ σὺν τοῖς φίλοις εἰς τὴν πόλιν ἐπορεύετο, ἱερεῖα μὲν ἄγων ὡς πᾶσι Πέρσαις ἱκανὰ θύειν τε καὶ ἑστιᾶσθαι· δῶρα δ' ἦγεν οἷα μὲν ἔπρεπε τῷ πατρὶ καὶ τῇ μητρὶ καὶ τοῖς ἄλλοις φίλοις, οἷα δ' ἔπρεπεν ἀρχαῖς καὶ γεραιτέροις καὶ τοῖς ὁμοτίμοις πᾶσιν· ἔδωκε δὲ καὶ πᾶσι Πέρσαις καὶ Περσίσιν ὅσαπερ καὶ νῦν ἔτι δίδωσιν ὅτανπερ ἀφίκηται βασιλεὺς εἰς Πέρσας.

22. Ἐκ δὲ τούτου συνέλεξε Καμβύσης τοὺς γεραιτέρους Περσῶν καὶ τὰς ἀρχάς, οἵπερ τῶν μεγίστων κύριοί εἰσι· παρεκάλεσε δὲ καὶ Κῦρον, καὶ ἔλεξε τοιάδε· Ἄνδρες Πέρσαι καὶ σύ, ὦ Κῦρε, ἐγὼ ἀμφοτέροις ὑμῖν εἰκότως εὔνους εἰμί· ὑμῶν μὲν γὰρ βασιλεύω, σὺ δέ, ὦ Κῦρε, παῖς ἐμὸς εἶ. δίκαιος οὖν εἰμι, ὅσα γιγνώσκειν δοκῶ ἀγαθὰ ἀμφοτέροις, ταῦτα εἰς τὸ μέσον λέγειν.

23. Τὰ μὲν γὰρ παρελθόντα ὑμεῖς μὲν Κῦρον ηὐξήσατε στράτευμα δόντες καὶ ἄρχοντα τούτου αὐτὸν καταστήσαντες, Κῦρος δὲ ἡγούμενος τούτου σὺν θεοῖς εὐκλεεῖς μὲν ὑμᾶς, ὦ Πέρσαι, ἐν πᾶσιν ἀνθρώποις ἐποίησεν, ἐντίμους δ' ἐν τῇ Ἀσίᾳ

Cyaxares, I heartily approve of your family and your daughter and your gifts. And I desire, with the approval of my father and mother, to accept your offer."

Thus Cyrus answered; but still he made the young lady presents of everything that he thought would please Cyaxares as well as herself. And when he had done so, he proceeded on his way to Persia.

21. And when, as he continued his journey, he came to the boundaries of Persia, he left the main body of his army there, while he went on with his friends to the capital; and he took along animals enough for all the Persians to sacrifice and make a feast, and brought with him such gifts as were appropriate for his father and mother and his friends besides and such as were suitable for the authorities and the elders and all the peers. And he gave presents also to all the Persians, men and women, such as even to this day the great king bestows whenever he comes to Persia. *Cyrus arrives in Persepolis*

22. Then Cambyses assembled the Persian elders and the highest of the chief magistrates; he called in Cyrus also and then addressed them as follows: "Toward you, my Persian friends, I cherish, as is natural, feelings of good-will, for I am your king; and no less toward you, Cyrus, for you are my son. It is right, therefore, that I should declare frankly to you what I think I recognize to be for the good of both. *Cambyses's address to his people*

23. "In the past you advanced the fortunes of Cyrus by giving him an army and placing him in command of it. And at its head Cyrus has with the help of the gods given you, Persians, a good report among all men and made you honoured throughout

πάσῃ· τῶν δὲ συστρατευσαμένων αὐτῷ τοὺς
μὲν ἀρίστους καὶ πεπλούτικε, τοῖς δὲ πολλοῖς
μισθὸν καὶ τροφὴν παρεσκεύακεν· ἱππικὸν δὲ
καταστήσας Περσῶν πεποίηκε Πέρσαις καὶ πε-
δίων εἶναι μετουσίαν.

24. Ἦν μὲν οὖν καὶ τὸ λοιπὸν οὕτω γιγνώ-
σκητε, πολλῶν καὶ ἀγαθῶν αἴτιοι ἀλλήλοις
ἔσεσθε· εἰ δὲ ἢ σύ, ὦ Κῦρε, ἐπαρθεὶς ταῖς παρ-
ούσαις τύχαις ἐπιχειρήσεις καὶ Περσῶν ἄρχειν
ἐπὶ πλεονεξίᾳ ὥσπερ τῶν ἄλλων, ἢ ὑμεῖς, ὦ πολῖται, φθονήσαντες τούτῳ τῆς δυνάμεως κατα-
λύειν πειράσεσθε τοῦτον τῆς ἀρχῆς, εὖ ἴστε ὅτι
ἐμποδὼν ἀλλήλοις πολλῶν καὶ ἀγαθῶν ἔσεσθε.
25. ὡς οὖν μὴ ταῦτα γίγνηται, ἀλλὰ τἀγαθά,
ἐμοὶ δοκεῖ, ἔφη, θύσαντας ὑμᾶς κοινῇ καὶ θεοὺς
ἐπιμαρτυραμένους συνθέσθαι, σὲ μέν, ὦ Κῦρε,
ἤν τις ἐπιστρατεύηται χώρᾳ Περσίδι ἢ Περσῶν
νόμους διασπᾶν πειρᾶται, βοηθήσειν παντὶ σθένει,
ὑμᾶς δέ, ὦ Πέρσαι, ἤν τις ἢ ἀρχῆς Κῦρον ἐπιχειρῇ καταπαύειν ἢ ἀφίστασθαί τις τῶν ὑποχειρίων, βοηθήσειν καὶ ὑμῖν αὐτοῖς καὶ Κύρῳ
καθ᾽ ὅ τι ἂν οὗτος ἐπαγγέλλῃ.

26. Καὶ ἕως μὲν ἂν ἐγὼ ζῶ, ἐμὴ γίγνεται ἡ ἐν
Πέρσαις βασιλεία· ὅταν δ᾽ ἐγὼ τελευτήσω, δῆλον
ὅτι Κύρου, ἐὰν ζῇ. καὶ ὅταν μὲν οὗτος ἀφίκηται
εἰς Πέρσας, ὁσίως ἂν ὑμῖν ἔχοι τοῦτον θύειν τὰ
ἱερὰ ὑπὲρ ὑμῶν ἅπερ νῦν ἐγὼ θύω· ὅταν δ᾽ οὗτος
ἔκδημος ᾖ, καλῶς ἂν οἶμαι ὑμῖν ἔχειν εἰ ἐκ τοῦ

all Asia. Of those who went with him on his campaigns he has enriched the most deserving and to the commoners he has given wages and support; and by establishing a Persian cavalry force he has made the Persians masters also of the plains.

24. "If, therefore, you continue to be of the same mind also in the future, you will be the cause of much good to each other. But, Cyrus, if you on your part become puffed up by your present successes and attempt to govern the Persians as you do those other nations, with a view to self-aggrandizement, or if you, fellow-citizens, become jealous of his power and attempt to depose him from his sovereignty, be sure that you will hinder one another from receiving much good. 25. And that this may not befall you, but the good, it seems best to me for you to perform a common sacrifice and to make a covenant, first calling the gods to witness. You, Cyrus, on your part, must covenant that if any one sets hostile foot in Persia or attempts to subvert the Persian constitution, you will come to her aid with all your strength; and you, Persians, on your part, are to covenant that if any one attempts to put an end to Cyrus's sovereignty or if any one of his subjects attempts to revolt, you will come to your own rescue as well as Cyrus's in whatsoever way he may call upon you.

26. "As long as I live, the Persian throne continues to be mine own. But when I am dead, it will, of course, pass to Cyrus if he survives me. And as often as he comes to Persia, it should be a sacred custom with you that he sacrifice on your behalf even as I do now. And when he is away, it might be well for you, I think, that that one of our family who seems

XENOPHON

γένους ὃς ἂν δοκῇ ὑμῖν ἄριστος εἶναι, οὗτος τὰ τῶν θεῶν ἀποτελοίη.

27. Ταῦτα εἰπόντος Καμβύσου συνέδοξε Κύρῳ τε καὶ τοῖς Περσῶν τέλεσι· καὶ συνθέμενοι ταῦτα τότε καὶ θεοὺς ἐπιμαρτυράμενοι οὕτω καὶ νῦν ἔτι διαμένουσι ποιοῦντες πρὸς ἀλλήλους Πέρσαι τε καὶ βασιλεύς. τούτων δὲ πραχθέντων ἀπῄει ὁ Κῦρος.

28. Ὡς δ᾿ ἀπιὼν ἐγένετο ἐν Μήδοις, συνδόξαν τῷ πατρὶ καὶ τῇ μητρὶ γαμεῖ τὴν Κυαξάρου θυγατέρα, ἧς ἔτι καὶ νῦν λόγος ὡς παγκάλης γενομένης· [ἔνιοι δὲ τῶν λογοποιῶν λέγουσιν ὡς τὴν τῆς μητρὸς ἀδελφὴν ἔγημεν· ἀλλὰ γραῦς ἂν καὶ παντάπασιν ἦν ἡ παῖς.][1] γήμας δ᾿ εὐθὺς ἔχων ἀνεζεύγνυεν.[2]

VI

1. Ἐπεὶ δ᾿ ἐν Βαβυλῶνι ἦν, ἐδόκει αὐτῷ σατράπας ἤδη πέμπειν ἐπὶ τὰ κατεστραμμένα ἔθνη. τοὺς μέντοι ἐν ταῖς ἄκραις φρουράρχους καὶ τοὺς χιλιάρχους τῶν κατὰ τὴν χώραν φυλακῶν οὐκ ἄλλου ἢ ἑαυτοῦ ἐβούλετο ἀκούειν· ταῦτα δὲ προεωρᾶτο ἐννοῶν ὅπως εἴ τις τῶν σατραπῶν ὑπὸ πλούτου καὶ πλήθους ἀνθρώπων ἐξυβρίσειε καὶ ἐπιχειρήσειε μὴ πείθεσθαι, εὐθὺς ἀντιπάλους ἔχοι ἐν τῇ χώρᾳ. 2. ταῦτ᾿ οὖν βουλόμενος πρᾶξαι ἔγνω συγκαλέσαι πρῶτον τοὺς ἐπικαι-

---

[1] ἔνιοι . . . παῖς MSS.; omitted by Dindorf, Edd.
[2] ἀνεζεύγνυεν MSS., most Edd.; ἀνεζεύγνυ Hug.

to you the most worthy should perform that sacred office."

27. When Cambyses had finished speaking, Cyrus and the Persian magistrates accepted his proposal. And as they then covenanted, with the gods as their witnesses, so the Persians and their king still continue to this day to act toward one another. And when this had all been completed, Cyrus took his departure.

28. When, on his way back, he came to Media, Cyrus wedded the daughter of Cyaxares, for he had obtained the consent of his father and mother. And to this day people still tell of her wonderful beauty. [But some historians say that he married his mother's sister. But that maid must certainly have been a very old maid.] And when he was married he at once departed with his bride for Babylon.

Cyrus marries his cousin

VI

1. When he arrived in Babylon, he decided to send out satraps to govern the nations he had subdued. But the commanders of the garrisons in the citadels and the colonels in command of the guards throughout the country he wished to be responsible to no one but himself. This provision he made with the purpose that if any of the satraps, on the strength of the wealth or the men at their command, should break out into open insolence or attempt to refuse obedience, they might at once find opposition in their province. 2. In the wish, therefore, to secure this result, he resolved first to call together his

Cyrus institutes satrapies

ρίους καὶ προειπεῖν, ὅπως εἰδεῖεν ἐφ' οἷς ἴασιν
ἰόντες· ἐνόμιζε γὰρ οὕτω ῥᾷον φέρειν ἂν αὐτούς·
ἐπεὶ δὲ κατασταίη τις ἄρχων καὶ αἰσθάνοιτο
ταῦτα, χαλεπῶς ἂν ἐδόκουν αὐτῷ φέρειν, νομίζοντες δι' ἑαυτῶν ἀπιστίαν ταῦτα γενέσθαι. 3. οὕτω
δὴ συλλέξας λέγει αὐτοῖς τοιάδε·

Ἄνδρες φίλοι, εἰσὶν ἡμῖν ἐν ταῖς κατεστραμ-
μέναις πόλεσι φρουροὶ καὶ φρούραρχοι, οὓς τότε
κατελίπομεν· καὶ τούτοις ἐγὼ προστάξας ἀπῆλθον ἄλλο μὲν μηδὲν πολυπραγμονεῖν, τὰ δὲ τείχη
διασώζειν. τούτους μὲν οὖν οὐ παύσω τῆς ἀρχῆς,
ἐπεὶ καλῶς διαπεφυλάχασι τὰ προσταχθέντα·
ἄλλους δὲ σατράπας πέμψαι μοι δοκεῖ, οἵτινες
ἄρξουσι τῶν ἐνοικούντων καὶ τὸν δασμὸν λαμβά-
νοντες τοῖς τε φρουροῖς δώσουσι μισθὸν καὶ ἄλλο
τελοῦσιν ὅ τι ἂν δέῃ. 4. δοκεῖ δέ μοι καὶ τῶν
ἐνθάδε μενόντων ὑμῶν, οἷς ἂν ἐγὼ πράγματα
παρέχω πέμπων πράξοντάς τι ἐπὶ ταῦτα τὰ ἔθνη,
χώρας γενέσθαι καὶ οἴκους ἐκεῖ, ὅπως δασμοφορῆ-
ταί τε αὐτοῖς δεῦρο, ὅταν τε ἴωσιν ἐκεῖσε, εἰς
οἰκεῖα ἔχωσι κατάγεσθαι.

5. Ταῦτα εἶπε καὶ ἔδωκε πολλοῖς τῶν φίλων
κατὰ πάσας τὰς καταστραφείσας πόλεις οἴκους
καὶ ὑπηκόους· καὶ νῦν εἰσιν ἔτι τοῖς ἀπογόνοις
τῶν τότε λαβόντων αἱ χῶραι καταμένουσαι ἄλλαι
ἐν ἄλλῃ γῇ· αὐτοὶ δὲ οἰκοῦσι παρὰ βασιλεῖ.

chief officers and inform them in advance, so that when they went they might know on what understanding they were going; for he believed that if he did so, they would take it more kindly; whereas he thought that they might take it ill, if any of them discovered the conditions after being installed as satraps, for then they would think that this policy had been adopted from distrust of them personally.   3. And so he called them together and spoke as follows :

" My friends, we have in the subjugated states garrisons with their officers, whom we left behind there at the time ; and when I came away I left them with orders not to trouble themselves with any business other than to hold the forts. These, therefore, I will not remove from their positions, for they have carried out my instructions faithfully ; but I have decided to send satraps there, besides, to govern the people, receive the tribute, pay the militia, and attend to any other business that needs attention. 4. I have further decided that any of you who remain here, and to whom I may occasionally give the trouble of going on business for me to those nations, shall have lands and houses there; so that they may have tribute paid to them here and, whenever they go there, they may lodge in residences of their own."

The duties and privileges of satraps

5. Thus he spoke, and to many of his friends he gave houses and servants in the various states which he had subdued.   And even to this day those properties, some in one land, some in another, continue in the possession of the descendants of those who then received them, while the owners themselves reside at court.

6. Δεῖ δέ, ἔφη, τοὺς ἰόντας σατράπας ἐπὶ ταύτας τὰς χώρας τοιούτους ἡμᾶς σκοπεῖν οἵτινες ὅ τι ἂν ἐν τῇ γῇ ἑκάστῃ καλὸν ἢ ἀγαθὸν ᾖ, μεμνήσονται καὶ δεῦρο ἀποπέμπειν, ὡς μετέχωμεν καὶ οἱ ἐνθάδε ὄντες τῶν πανταχοῦ γιγνομένων ἀγαθῶν· καὶ γὰρ ἤν τί που δεινὸν γίγνηται, ἡμῖν ἔσται ἀμυντέον.

7. Ταῦτ᾿ εἰπὼν τότε μὲν ἔπαυσε τὸν λόγον, ἔπειτα δὲ οὓς ἐγίγνωσκε τῶν φίλων ἐπὶ τοῖς εἰρημένοις ἐπιθυμοῦντας ἰέναι, ἐκλεξάμενος αὐτῶν τοὺς δοκοῦντας ἐπιτηδειοτάτους εἶναι ἔπεμπε σατράπας εἰς Ἀραβίαν μὲν Μεγάβυζον, εἰς Καππαδοκίαν δὲ Ἀρταβάταν, εἰς Φρυγίαν δὲ τὴν μεγάλην Ἀρτακάμαν, εἰς Λυδίαν δὲ καὶ Ἰωνίαν Χρυσάνταν, εἰς Καρίαν δὲ Ἀδούσιον, ὅνπερ ᾐτοῦντο, εἰς Φρυγίαν δὲ τὴν παρ᾿ Ἑλλήσποντον καὶ Αἰολίδα Φαρνοῦχον. 8. Κιλικίας δὲ καὶ Κύπρου καὶ Παφλαγόνων οὐκ ἔπεμψε Πέρσας σατράπας, ὅτι ἑκόντες ἐδόκουν συστρατεύεσθαι ἐπὶ Βαβυλῶνα· δασμοὺς μέντοι συνέταξεν ἀποφέρειν καὶ τούτους.

9. Ὡς δὲ τότε Κῦρος κατεστήσατο, οὕτως ἔτι καὶ νῦν βασιλέως εἰσὶν αἱ ἐν ταῖς ἄκραις φυλακαὶ καὶ οἱ χιλίαρχοι τῶν φυλακῶν ἐκ βασιλέως εἰσὶ καθεστηκότες καὶ παρὰ βασιλεῖ ἀπογεγραμμένοι.

10. Προεῖπε δὲ πᾶσι τοῖς ἐκπεμπομένοις σατράπαις, ὅσα αὐτὸν ἑώρων ποιοῦντα, πάντα μιμεῖσθαι· πρῶτον μὲν ἱππέας καθιστάναι ἐκ τῶν συνεπισπομένων Περσῶν καὶ συμμάχων καὶ

6. "And then," Cyrus resumed, "we must take care that those who go as satraps to such countries shall be men of the right sort, who will bear in mind to send back here what there is good and desirable in their several provinces, in order that we also who remain here may have a share of the good things that are to be found everywhere. And that will be no more than fair; for if any danger threatens anywhere, it is we who shall have to ward it off."

7. With these words he concluded his address on that occasion; and then he chose out from the number of his friends those whom he saw eager to go on the conditions named and who seemed to him best qualified, and sent them as satraps to the following countries: Megabyzus to Arabia, Artabatas to Cappadocia, Artacamas to Phrygia Major, Chrysantas to Lydia and Ionia, Adusius to Caria (it was he for whom the Carians had petitioned), and Pharnuchus to Aeolia and Phrygia on the Hellespont. *Cyrus appoints the satraps*

8. He sent out no Persians as satraps over Cilicia or Cyprus or Paphlagonia, because these he thought joined his expedition against Babylon voluntarily; he did, however, require even these nations to pay tribute.

9. As Cyrus then organized the service, so is it even to this day: the garrisons upon the citadels are immediately under the king's control, and the colonels in command of the garrisons receive their appointment from the king and are enrolled upon the king's list.

10. And he gave orders to all the satraps he sent out to imitate him in everything that they saw him do: they were, in the first place, to organize companies of cavalry and charioteers from the Persians *Further duties of satraps*

413

ἁρματηλάτας· ὁπόσοι δ' ἂν γῆν καὶ ἀρχεῖα λά-
βωσιν, ἀναγκάζειν τούτους ἐπὶ θύρας ἰέναι καὶ
σωφροσύνης ἐπιμελομένους παρέχειν ἑαυτοὺς τῷ
σατράπῃ χρῆσθαι, ἤν τι δέηται· παιδεύειν δὲ καὶ
τοὺς γιγνομένους παῖδας ἐπὶ θύραις,[1] ὥσπερ παρ'
αὐτῷ· ἐξάγειν δ' ἐπὶ τὴν θήραν τὸν σατράπην
τοὺς ἀπὸ θυρῶν καὶ ἀσκεῖν αὑτόν τε καὶ τοὺς
σὺν ἑαυτῷ τὰ πολεμικά.

11. Ὃς δ' ἂν ἐμοί, ἔφη, κατὰ λόγον τῆς δυνάμεως πλεῖστα μὲν ἅρματα, πλείστους δὲ καὶ
ἀρίστους ἱππέας ἀποδεικνύῃ, τοῦτον ἐγὼ ὡς
ἀγαθὸν σύμμαχον καὶ ὡς ἀγαθὸν συμφύλακα
Πέρσαις τε καὶ ἐμοὶ τῆς ἀρχῆς τιμήσω. ἔστων δὲ
παρ' ὑμῖν καὶ ἕδραις[2] ὥσπερ παρ' ἐμοὶ οἱ ἄριστοι
προτετιμημένοι, καὶ τράπεζα, ὥσπερ ἡ ἐμή, τρέ-
φουσα μὲν πρῶτον τοὺς οἰκέτας, ἔπειτα δὲ καὶ ὡς
φίλοις μεταδιδόναι ἱκανῶς κεκοσμημένη καὶ ὡς
τὸν καλόν τι ποιοῦντα καθ' ἡμέραν ἐπιγεραίρειν.

12. Κτᾶσθε δὲ καὶ παραδείσους καὶ θηρία
τρέφετε, καὶ μήτε αὐτοί ποτε ἄνευ πόνου σῖτον
παραθῆσθε μήτε ἵπποις ἀγυμνάστοις χόρτον ἐμ-
βάλλετε· οὐ γὰρ ἂν δυναίμην ἐγὼ εἷς ὢν ἀνθρωπίνῃ ἀρετῇ τὰ πάντων ὑμῶν ἀγαθὰ διασώζειν,
ἀλλὰ δεῖ ἐμὲ μὲν ἀγαθὸν ὄντα σὺν ἀγαθοῖς τοῖς
παρ' ἐμοῦ ὑμῖν ἐπίκουρον εἶναι· ὑμᾶς δὲ ὁμοίως
αὐτοὺς ἀγαθοὺς ὄντας σὺν ἀγαθοῖς τοῖς μεθ' ὑμῶν
ἐμοὶ συμμάχους εἶναι.

13. Βουλοίμην δ' ἂν ὑμᾶς καὶ τοῦτο κατανοῆσαι
ὅτι τούτων ὧν νῦν ὑμῖν παρακελεύομαι οὐδὲν τοῖς

---

[1] θύραις Reiske, Edd.; θύρας MSS.
[2] ἕδραις Stephanus, Edd.; ἕδρας MSS.

who went with them and from the allies; to require as
many as received lands and palaces to attend at the
satrap's court and exercising proper self-restraint
to put themselves at his disposal in whatever he
demanded; to have the boys that were born to them
educated at the local court, just as was done at the
royal court; and to take the retinue at his gates out
hunting and to exercise himself and them in the arts
of war.

11. "And whoever I find has the largest number He gives
of chariots to show and the largest number of the them
instructions
most efficient horsemen in proportion to his power,"
Cyrus added, "him will I honour as a valuable ally
and as a valuable fellow-protector of the sovereignty
of the Persians and myself. And with you also, just
as with me, let the most deserving be set in the
most honourable seats; and let your table, like mine,
feed first your own household and then, too, be
bountifully arrayed so as to give a share to your
friends and to confer some distinction day by day
upon any one who does some noble act.

12. "Have parks, too, and keep wild animals in
them; and do not have your food served you unless
you have first taken exercise, nor have fodder given
to your horses unless they have been exercised.
For I should not be able with merely human
strength single-handed to ensure the permanence of
the fortunes of all of you; but as I must be valiant
and have those about me valiant, in order to help
you; so you likewise must be valiant yourselves and
have those about you valiant, in order to be my allies.

13. "Please observe also that among all the
directions I am now giving you, I give no orders to

δούλοις προστάττω· ἃ δ' ὑμᾶς φημι χρῆναι
ποιεῖν, ταῦτα καὶ αὐτὸς πειρῶμαι πάντα πράττειν. ὥσπερ δ' ἐγὼ ὑμᾶς κελεύω ἐμὲ μιμεῖσθαι,
οὕτω καὶ ὑμεῖς τοὺς ὑφ' ὑμῶν ἀρχὰς ἔχοντας
μιμεῖσθαι ὑμᾶς διδάσκετε.

14. [Ταῦτα δὲ Κύρου οὕτω τότε τάξαντος ἔτι
καὶ νῦν τῷ αὐτῷ τρόπῳ πᾶσαι μὲν αἱ ὑπὸ
βασιλεῖ φυλακαὶ ὁμοίως φυλάττονται, πᾶσαι δὲ
αἱ τῶν ἀρχόντων θύραι ὁμοίως θεραπεύονται,
πάντες δὲ οἱ οἶκοι καὶ μεγάλοι καὶ μικροὶ ὁμοίως
οἰκοῦνται, πᾶσι δὲ οἱ ἄριστοι τῶν παρόντων
ἔδραις προτετίμηνται, πᾶσαι δὲ αἱ πορεῖαι συν-
τεταγμέναι κατὰ τὸν αὐτὸν τρόπον εἰσί, πᾶσαι
δὲ συγκεφαλαιοῦνται πολιτικαὶ[1] πράξεις εἰς ὀλίγους ἐπιστάτας.][2]

15. Ταῦτα εἰπὼν ὡς χρὴ ποιεῖν ἑκάστους καὶ
δύναμιν ἑκάστῳ προσθεὶς ἐξέπεμπε, καὶ προεῖπεν
ἅπασι παρασκευάζεσθαι ὡς εἰς νέωτα στρατείας
ἐσομένης καὶ ἀποδείξεως ἀνδρῶν καὶ ὅπλων καὶ
ἵππων καὶ ἁρμάτων.

16. Κατενοήσαμεν δὲ καὶ τοῦτο ὅτι Κύρου
κατάρξαντος, ὥς φασι, καὶ νῦν ἔτι διαμένει·
ἐφοδεύει γὰρ ἀνὴρ κατ' ἐνιαυτὸν ἀεὶ στράτευμα
ἔχων, ὡς ἢν μέν τις τῶν σατραπῶν ἐπικουρίας
δέηται, ἐπικουρῇ, ἢν δέ τις ὑβρίζῃ, σωφρονίζῃ,
ἢν δέ τις ἢ δασμῶν φορᾶς ἀμελῇ ἢ τῶν ἐνοίκων
φυλακῆς ἢ ὅπως ἡ χώρα ἐνεργὸς ᾖ ἢ ἄλλο τι
τῶν τεταγμένων παραλίπῃ, ταῦτα πάντα κατευ-

---

[1] πολιτικαὶ Eichler, recent Edd.; πολλαὶ MSS., Dindorf,
Breitenbach.
[2] ταῦτα . . . ἐπιστάτας MSS., most Edd.; bracketed by
Lincke, Hug.

slaves. I try to do myself everything that I say you ought to do. And even as I bid you follow my example, so do you also instruct those whom you appoint to office to follow yours."

14. [And as Cyrus then effected his organization, even so unto this day all the garrisons under the king are kept up, and all the courts of the governors are attended with service in the same way; so all households, great and small, are managed; and by all men in authority the most deserving of their guests are given preference with seats of honour; all the official journeyings are conducted on the same plan and all the political business is centralized in a few heads of departments.]

15. When he had told them how they should proceed to carry out his instructions, he gave each one a force of soldiers and sent them off; and he directed them all to make preparations, with the expectation that there would be an expedition the next year and a review of the men, arms, horses, and chariots.

16. We have noticed also that this regulation is still in force, whether it was instituted by Cyrus, as they affirm, or not: year by year a man makes the circuit of the provinces with an army, to help any satrap that may need help, to humble any one that may be growing rebellious, and to adjust matters if any one is careless about seeing the taxes paid or protecting the inhabitants, or to see that the land is kept under cultivation, or if any one is neglectful of anything else that he has been ordered to attend to; but if he cannot set it right, it is his business to

Plans adopted for the visitation of the provinces

417

τρεπίζῃ· ἢν δὲ μὴ δύνηται, βασιλεῖ ἀπαγγέλλῃ·
ὁ δὲ ἀκούων βουλεύεται περὶ τοῦ ἀτακτοῦντος.
καὶ οἱ πολλάκις λεγόμενοι ὅτι βασιλέως υἱὸς
καταβαίνει, βασιλέως ἀδελφός, βασιλέως ὀφθαλ-
μός, καὶ ἐνίοτε οὐκ ἐκφαινόμενοι, οὗτοι τῶν ἐφόδων
εἰσίν· ἀποτρέπεται γὰρ ἕκαστος αὐτῶν ὁπόθεν ἂν
βασιλεὺς κελεύῃ.

17. Κατεμάθομεν δὲ αὐτοῦ καὶ ἄλλο μηχάνημα
πρὸς τὸ μέγεθος τῆς ἀρχῆς, ἐξ οὗ ταχέως ᾐσθάνετο καὶ τὰ πάμπολυ ἀπέχοντα ὅπως ἔχοι.
σκεψάμενος γὰρ πόσην ἂν ὁδὸν ἵππος κατανύτοι
τῆς ἡμέρας ἐλαυνόμενος ὥστε διαρκεῖν, ἐποιήσατο
ἱππῶνας τοσοῦτον διαλείποντας καὶ ἵππους ἐν
αὐτοῖς κατέστησε καὶ τοὺς ἐπιμελομένους τούτων,
καὶ ἄνδρα ἐφ' ἑκάστῳ τῶν τόπων ἔταξε τὸν
ἐπιτήδειον παραδέχεσθαι τὰ φερόμενα γράμματα
καὶ παραδιδόναι καὶ παραλαμβάνειν τοὺς ἀπει-
ρηκότας ἵππους καὶ ἀνθρώπους καὶ ἄλλους πέμπειν νεαλεῖς. 18. ἔστι δ' ὅτε οὐδὲ τὰς νύκτας
φασὶν ἵστασθαι ταύτην τὴν πορείαν, ἀλλὰ τῷ
ἡμερινῷ ἀγγέλῳ τὸν νυκτερινὸν διαδέχεσθαι.
τούτων δὲ οὕτω γιγνομένων φασί τινες θᾶττον
τῶν γεράνων ταύτην τὴν πορείαν ἀνύτειν· εἰ
δὲ τοῦτο ψεύδονται, ἀλλ' ὅτι γε τῶν ἀνθρωπίνων
πεζῇ πορειῶν αὕτη ταχίστη, τοῦτο εὔδηλον.
ἀγαθὸν δὲ ὡς τάχιστα ἕκαστον αἰσθανόμενον ὡς
τάχιστα ἐπιμελεῖσθαι.

19. Ἐπεὶ δὲ περιῆλθεν ὁ ἐνιαυτός, συνήγειρε
στρατιὰν εἰς Βαβυλῶνα, καὶ λέγεται αὐτῷ γενέσθαι εἰς δώδεκα μὲν ἱππέων μυριάδας, εἰς δισχίλια

report it to the king, and he, when he hears of it, takes measures in regard to the offender. And those of whom the report often goes out that "the king's son is coming," or "the king's brother" or "the king's eye," these belong to the circuit commissioners; though sometimes they do not put in an appearance at all, for each of them turns back, wherever he may be, when the king commands.

17. We have observed still another device of Cyrus to cope with the magnitude of his empire; by means of this institution he would speedily discover the condition of affairs, no matter how far distant they might be from him: he experimented to find out how great a distance a horse could cover in a day when ridden hard but so as not to break down, and then he erected post-stations at just such distances and equipped them with horses and men to take care of them; at each one of the stations he had the proper official appointed to receive the letters that were delivered and to forward them on, to take in the exhausted horses and riders and send on fresh ones. 18. They say, moreover, that sometimes this express does not stop all night, but the night-messengers succeed the day-messengers in relays, and when that is the case, this express, some say, gets over the ground faster than the cranes. If their story is not literally true, it is at all events undeniable that this is the fastest overland travelling on earth; and it is a fine thing to have immediate intelligence of everything, in order to attend to it as quickly as possible.

Cyrus inaugurates a postal system

19. Now, when the year had gone round, he collected his army together at Babylon, containing, it is said, about one hundred and twenty thousand

Cyrus completes his conquests

δὲ ἅρματα δρεπανηφόρα, πεζῶν δὲ εἰς μυριάδας
ἑξήκοντα. 20. ἐπεὶ δὲ ταῦτα συνεσκεύαστο αὐτῷ,
ὥρμα δὴ ταύτην τὴν στρατείαν ἐν ᾗ λέγεται
καταστρέψασθαι πάντα τὰ ἔθνη ὅσα Συρίαν
ἐκβάντι οἰκεῖ μέχρι Ἐρυθρᾶς θαλάττης. μετὰ
δὲ ταῦτα ἡ εἰς Αἴγυπτον στρατεία λέγεται γενέσθαι καὶ καταστρέψασθαι Αἴγυπτον.

21. Καὶ ἐκ τούτου τὴν ἀρχὴν ὥριζεν αὐτῷ πρὸς
ἕω μὲν ἡ Ἐρυθρὰ θάλαττα, πρὸς ἄρκτον δὲ ὁ
Εὔξεινος πόντος, πρὸς ἑσπέραν δὲ Κύπρος καὶ
Αἴγυπτος, πρὸς μεσημβρίαν δὲ Αἰθιοπία. τούτων
δὲ τὰ πέρατα τὰ μὲν διὰ θάλπος, τὰ δὲ διὰ
ψύχος, τὰ δὲ διὰ ὕδωρ, τὰ δὲ δι' ἀνυδρίαν δυσ-
οίκητα. 22. αὐτὸς δ' ἐν μέσῳ τούτων τὴν
δίαιταν ποιησάμενος, τὸν μὲν ἀμφὶ τὸν χειμῶνα
χρόνον διῆγεν ἐν Βαβυλῶνι ἑπτὰ μῆνας· αὕτη
γὰρ ἀλεεινὴ ἡ χώρα· τὸν δὲ ἀμφὶ τὸ ἔαρ τρεῖς
μῆνας ἐν Σούσοις· τὴν δὴ ἀκμὴν τοῦ θέρους δύο
μῆνας ἐν Ἐκβατάνοις· οὕτω δὴ ποιοῦντ' αὐτὸν
λέγουσιν ἐν ἐαρινῷ θάλπει καὶ ψύχει διάγειν ἀεί.

23. Οὕτω δὲ διέκειντο πρὸς αὐτὸν οἱ ἄνθρωποι
ὡς πᾶν μὲν ἔθνος μειονεκτεῖν ἐδόκει, εἰ μὴ Κύρῳ
πέμψειεν ὅ τι καλὸν αὐτοῖς ἐν τῇ χώρᾳ ἢ φύοιτο
ἢ τρέφοιτο ἢ τεχνῷτο, πᾶσα δὲ πόλις ὡσαύτως,
πᾶς δὲ ἰδιώτης πλούσιος ἂν ᾤετο γενέσθαι, εἴ τι
Κύρῳ χαρίσαιτο· καὶ γὰρ ὁ Κῦρος λαμβάνων
παρ' ἑκάστων ὧν ἀφθονίαν εἶχον οἱ διδόντες
ἀντεδίδου ὧν σπανίζοντας αὐτοὺς αἰσθάνοιτο.

horse, about two thousand scythe-bearing chariots and about six hundred thousand foot. 20. And when these had been made ready for him, he started out on that expedition on which he is said to have subjugated all the nations that fill the earth from where one leaves Syria even to the Indian Ocean. His next expedition is said to have gone to Egypt and to have subjugated that country also.

21. From that time on his empire was bounded on the east by the Indian Ocean, on the north by the Black Sea, on the west by Cyprus and Egypt, and on the south by Ethiopia. The extremes of his empire are uninhabitable, on the one side because of the heat, on another because of the cold, on another because of too much water, and on the fourth because of too little. 22. Cyrus himself made his home in the centre of his domain, and in the winter season he spent seven months in Babylon, for there the climate is warm; in the spring he spent three months in Susa, and in the height of summer two months in Ecbatana. By so doing, they say, he enjoyed the warmth and coolness of perpetual spring-time.

He locates his residences

23. People, moreover, were so devoted to him that those of every nation thought they did themselves an injury if they did not send to Cyrus the most valuable productions of their country, whether the fruits of the earth, or animals bred there, or manufactures of their own arts; and every city did the same. And every private individual thought he should become a rich man if he should do something to please Cyrus. And his theory was correct; for Cyrus would always accept that of which the givers had an abundance, and he would give in return that of which he saw that they were in want.

His personal popularity

421

VII

1. Οὕτω δὲ τοῦ αἰῶνος προκεχωρηκότος, μάλα δὴ πρεσβύτης ὢν ὁ Κῦρος ἀφικνεῖται εἰς Πέρσας τὸ ἕβδομον ἐπὶ τῆς αὑτοῦ[1] ἀρχῆς. καὶ ὁ μὲν πατὴρ καὶ ἡ μήτηρ πάλαι δὴ ὥσπερ εἰκὸς ἐτετελευτήκεσαν αὐτῷ· ὁ δὲ Κῦρος ἔθυσε τὰ νομιζόμενα ἱερὰ καὶ τοῦ χοροῦ ἡγήσατο Πέρσαις κατὰ τὰ πάτρια καὶ τὰ δῶρα πᾶσι διέδωκεν ὥσπερ εἰώθει. 2. Κοιμηθεὶς δ᾽ ἐν τῷ βασιλείῳ ὄναρ εἶδε τοιόνδε· ἔδοξεν αὐτῷ προσελθὼν κρείττων τις ἢ κατὰ ἄνθρωπον εἰπεῖν, Συσκευάζου, ὦ Κῦρε· ἤδη γὰρ εἰς θεοὺς ἄπει. τοῦτο δὲ ἰδὼν τὸ ὄναρ ἐξηγέρθη καὶ σχεδὸν ἐδόκει εἰδέναι ὅτι τοῦ βίου ἡ τελευτὴ παρείη. 3. εὐθὺς οὖν λαβὼν ἱερεῖα ἔθυε Διί τε πατρῴῳ καὶ Ἡλίῳ καὶ τοῖς ἄλλοις θεοῖς ἐπὶ τῶν ἄκρων, ὡς Πέρσαι θύουσιν, ὧδε ἐπευχόμενος, Ζεῦ πατρῷε καὶ Ἥλιε καὶ πάντες θεοί, δέχεσθε τάδε καὶ τελεστήρια πολλῶν καὶ καλῶν πράξεων καὶ χαριστήρια ὅτι ἐσημαίνετέ[2] μοι καὶ ἐν ἱεροῖς καὶ ἐν οὐρανίοις σημείοις καὶ ἐν οἰωνοῖς καὶ ἐν φήμαις ἅ τ᾽ ἐχρῆν ποιεῖν καὶ ἃ οὐκ ἐχρῆν. πολλὴ δ᾽ ὑμῖν χάρις ὅτι κἀγὼ ἐγίγνωσκον τὴν ὑμετέραν ἐπιμέλειαν καὶ οὐδεπώποτε ἐπὶ ταῖς εὐτυχίαις ὑπὲρ ἄνθρωπον ἐφρόνησα. αἰτοῦμαι δ᾽ ὑμᾶς δοῦναι καὶ νῦν παισὶ μὲν καὶ γυναικὶ καὶ φίλοις καὶ πατρίδι εὐδαι-

---

[1] αὑτοῦ Edd.; αὐτοῦ MSS.
[2] ἐσημαίνετε y, Hug, Marchant; ἐσημήνατε xz, Dindorf, Breitenbach, Gemoll.

VII

1. WHEN his life was far spent amid such achieve- The passing
ments and Cyrus was now a very old man, he came of Cyrus
back for the seventh time in his reign to Persia.
His father and his mother were in the course of
nature long since dead; so Cyrus performed the
customary sacrifice and led the Persians in their
national dance and distributed presents among them
all, as had been his custom.

2. As he slept in the palace, he saw a vision: a He is
figure of more than human majesty appeared to him warned in
in a dream and said: "Make ready,[1] Cyrus; for thou a vision
shalt soon depart to the gods." When the vision
was past, he awoke and seemed almost to know that
the end of his life was at hand.   3. Accordingly, he at
once took victims and offered sacrifice in the high
places to ancestral Zeus, to Helius, and to the rest
of the gods, even as the Persians are wont to make
sacrifice; and as he sacrificed, he prayed, saying: "O His prayer
ancestral Zeus and Helius and all the gods,
accept these offerings as tokens of gratitude for
help in achieving many glorious enterprises; for in
omens in the sacrifice, in signs from heaven, in the
flight of birds, and in ominous words, ye ever showed
me what I ought to do and what I ought not to do.
And I render heartfelt thanks to you that I have
never failed to recognize your fostering care and
never in my successes entertained proud thoughts
transcending human bounds.   And I beseech of you
that ye will now also grant prosperity and happiness
to my children, my wife, my friends, and my country,

1 Literally "Be packing up"; cf. Varro, de R.R. I. 1:
annus octogesimus admonet me ut sarcinas colligam ante-
quam proficiscar e vita.

μονίαν, ἐμοὶ δὲ οἷόνπερ αἰῶνα δεδώκατε, τοιαύτην καὶ τελευτὴν δοῦναι.

4. Ὁ μὲν δὴ τοιαῦτα ποιήσας καὶ οἴκαδε ἐλθὼν ἔδοξεν ἡδέως ἀναπαύσεσθαι[1] καὶ κατεκλίνη.[2] ἐπεὶ δὲ ὥρα ἦν, οἱ τεταγμένοι προσιόντες λούσασθαι αὐτὸν ἐκέλευον. ὁ δ' ἔλεγεν ὅτι ἡδέως ἀναπαύοιτο. οἱ δ' αὖ τεταγμένοι, ἐπεὶ ὥρα ἦν, δεῖπνον παρετίθεσαν· τῷ δὲ ἡ ψυχὴ σῖτον μὲν οὐ προσίετο, διψῆν δ' ἐδόκει, καὶ ἔπιεν ἡδέως.

5. Ὡς δὲ καὶ τῇ ὑστεραίᾳ συνέβαινεν αὐτῷ ταὐτὰ[3] καὶ τῇ τρίτῃ, ἐκάλεσε τοὺς παῖδας· οἱ δ' ἔτυχον συνηκολουθηκότες αὐτῷ καὶ ὄντες ἐν Πέρσαις· ἐκάλεσε δὲ καὶ τοὺς φίλους καὶ τὰς Περσῶν ἀρχάς· παρόντων δὲ πάντων ἤρχετο τοιοῦδε λόγου·

6. Παῖδες ἐμοὶ καὶ πάντες οἱ παρόντες φίλοι, ἐμοὶ μὲν τοῦ βίου τὸ τέλος ἤδη πάρεστιν· ἐκ πολλῶν τοῦτο σαφῶς γιγνώσκω· ὑμᾶς δὲ χρή, ὅταν τελευτήσω, ὡς περὶ εὐδαίμονος ἐμοῦ καὶ λέγειν καὶ ποιεῖν πάντα. ἐγὼ γὰρ παῖς τε ὢν τὰ ἐν παισὶ νομιζόμενα καλὰ δοκῶ κεκαρπῶσθαι, ἐπεί τε ἥβησα, τὰ ἐν νεανίσκοις, τέλειός τε ἀνὴρ γενόμενος τὰ ἐν ἀνδράσι· σὺν τῷ χρόνῳ τε προϊόντι ἀεὶ συναυξανομένην ἐπιγιγνώσκειν ἐδόκουν καὶ τὴν ἐμὴν δύναμιν, ὥστε καὶ τοὐμὸν γῆρας οὐδεπώποτε ἠσθόμην τῆς ἐμῆς νεότητος ἀσθενέστερον γιγνόμενον, καὶ οὔτ' ἐπιχειρήσας οὔτ' ἐπιθυμήσας οἶδα ὅτου ἠτύχησα.

---

[1] ἀναπαύσεσθαι Stephanus, most Edd.; ἀναπαύσασθαι xzV, Hug, Breitenbach; ἀναπαύεσθαι y.

[2] κατεκλίνη Cobet, most Edd.; κατεκλίθη MSS., Breitenbach.

[3] ταὐτὰ Zeune, recent Edd.; ταὐτὰ ταῦτα F; ταῦτα xzDV, Dindorf, Breitenbach.

and to me myself an end befitting the life that ye have given me."

4. Then after he had concluded his rites and come home, he thought he would be glad to rest and so lay down; and when the hour came, those whose office it was came in and bade him go to his bath. But he told them that he was resting happily. And then again, when the hour came, those whose office it was set dinner before him. But his soul had no desire for food, but he seemed thirsty and drank with pleasure.

5. And when the same thing befell him on the next day and the day after that, he summoned his sons; for they had accompanied him, as it chanced, and were still in Persia. He summoned also his friends and the Persian magistrates; and when they were all come, he began to speak as follows:

6. "My sons, and all you my friends about me, His last the end of my life is now at hand; I am quite sure words of this for many reasons; and when I am dead, you must always speak and act in regard to me as of one blessed of fortune. For when I was a boy, I think I He reviews plucked all the fruits that among boys count for the his life best; when I became a youth, I enjoyed what is accounted best among young men; and when I became a mature man, I had the best that men can have. And as time went on, it seemed to me that I recognized that my own strength was always increasing with my years, so that I never found my old age growing any more feeble than my youth had been; and, so far as I know, there is nothing that I ever attempted or desired and yet failed to secure.

7. Καὶ τοὺς μὲν φίλους ἐπεῖδον δι' ἐμοῦ εὐδαίμονας γενομένους, τοὺς δὲ πολεμίους ὑπ' ἐμοῦ
δουλωθέντας· καὶ τὴν πατρίδα πρόσθεν ἰδιωτεύ-
ουσαν ἐν τῇ Ἀσίᾳ νῦν προτετιμημένην καταλείπω·
ὧν τ' ἐκτησάμην οὐδὲν [οἶδα][1] ὅ τι οὐ διεσωσάμην.
καὶ τὸν μὲν παρελθόντα χρόνον ἔπραττον οὕτως
ὥσπερ ηὐχόμην· φόβος δέ μοι συμπαρομαρτῶν
μή τι ἐν τῷ ἐπιόντι χρόνῳ ἢ ἴδοιμι ἢ ἀκούσαιμι ἢ
πάθοιμι χαλεπόν, οὐκ εἴα τελέως με μέγα φρονεῖν
οὐδ' εὐφραίνεσθαι ἐκπεπταμένως.

8. Νῦν δ' ἢν τελευτήσω, καταλείπω μὲν ὑμᾶς,
ὦ παῖδες, ζῶντας οὕσπερ ἔδοσάν μοι οἱ θεοὶ γενέ-
σθαι· καταλείπω δὲ πατρίδα καὶ φίλους εὐδαι-
μονοῦντας· 9. ὥστε πῶς οὐκ ἂν ἐγὼ δικαίως
μακαριζόμενος τὸν ἀεὶ χρόνον μνήμης τυγ-
χάνοιμι;

Δεῖ δὲ καὶ τὴν βασιλείαν με ἤδη σαφηνίσαντα
καταλιπεῖν, ὡς ἂν μὴ ἀμφίλογος γενομένη πράγματα ὑμῖν παράσχῃ. ἐγὼ δ' οὖν[2] φιλῶ μὲν
ἀμφοτέρους ὑμᾶς ὁμοίως, ὦ παῖδες· τὸ δὲ προ-
βουλεύειν καὶ τὸ ἡγεῖσθαι ἐφ' ὅ τι ἂν καιρὸς δοκῇ
εἶναι, τοῦτο προστάττω τῷ προτέρῳ γενομένῳ καὶ
πλειόνων κατὰ τὸ εἰκὸς ἐμπείρῳ. 10. ἐπαιδεύθην
δὲ καὶ αὐτὸς οὕτως ὑπὸ τῆσδε τῆς ἐμῆς τε καὶ
ὑμετέρας πατρίδος, τοῖς πρεσβυτέροις οὐ μόνον
ἀδελφοῖς ἀλλὰ καὶ πολίταις καὶ ὁδῶν καὶ θάκων
καὶ λόγων ὑπείκειν, καὶ ὑμᾶς δέ, ὦ παῖδες, οὕτως
ἐξ ἀρχῆς ἐπαίδευον, τοὺς μὲν γεραιτέρους προτι-

---

[1] οἶδα MSS., Dindorf[3], Breitenbach ; [οἶδα] Dindorf[4], Hug,
Marchant, Gemoll.
[2] δ' οὖν Hertlein, recent Edd. ; δὲ νῦν xzVε, Dindorf,
Breitenbach ; οὖν y.

7. " Moreover, I have lived to see my friends made His services
prosperous and happy through my efforts and my
enemies reduced by me to subjection; and my
country, which once played no great part in Asia, I
now leave honoured above all. Of all my conquests,
there is not one that I have not maintained.
Throughout the past I have fared even as I have
wished; but a fear that was ever at my side,
lest in the time to come I might see or hear
or experience something unpleasant, would not let
me become overweeningly proud or extravagantly
happy.

8. " But now, if I die, I leave you, my sons, whom
the gods have given me, to survive me, and I leave
my friends and country happy; 9. and so why should
I not be justly accounted blessed and enjoy an
immortality of fame?

" But I must also declare my will about the dis- He defines the succes-sion
position of my throne, that the succession may not
become a matter of dispute and cause you trouble.
Now, I love you both alike, my sons; but precedence
in counsel and leadership in everything that may be
thought expedient, that I commit to the first born,
who naturally has a wider experience. 10. I, too,
was thus trained by my country and yours to give
precedence to my elders—not merely to brothers
but to all fellow-citizens—on the street, in the
matter of seats, and in speaking; and so from the
beginning, my children, I have been training you
also to honour your elders above yourselves and to

μᾶν, τῶν δὲ νεωτέρων προτετιμῆσθαι· ὡς οὖν παλαιὰ καὶ εἰθισμένα καὶ ἔννομα λέγοντος ἐμοῦ οὕτως ἀποδέχεσθε. 11. καὶ σὺ μέν, ὦ Καμβύση, τὴν βασιλείαν ἔχε, θεῶν τε διδόντων καὶ ἐμοῦ ὅσον ἐν ἐμοί.

Σοὶ δ᾽, ὦ Ταναοξάρη, σατράπην εἶναι δίδωμι Μήδων τε καὶ Ἀρμενίων καὶ τρίτων Καδουσίων· ταῦτα δέ σοι διδοὺς νομίζω ἀρχὴν μὲν μείζω καὶ τοὔνομα τῆς βασιλείας τῷ πρεσβυτέρῳ καταλιπεῖν, εὐδαιμονίαν δὲ σοὶ ἀλυποτέραν. 12. ὁποίας μὲν γὰρ ἀνθρωπίνης εὐφροσύνης ἐνδεὴς ἔσει οὐχ ὁρῶ· ἀλλὰ πάντα σοι τὰ δοκοῦντα ἀνθρώπους εὐφραίνειν παρέσται. τὸ δὲ δυσκαταπρακτοτέρων τε ἐρᾶν καὶ τὸ πολλὰ μεριμνᾶν καὶ τὸ μὴ δύνασθαι ἡσυχίαν ἔχειν κεντριζόμενον ὑπὸ τῆς πρὸς τἀμὰ ἔργα φιλονικίας καὶ τὸ ἐπιβουλεύειν καὶ τὸ ἐπιβουλεύεσθαι, ταῦτα τῷ βασιλεύοντι ἀνάγκη σοῦ μᾶλλον συμπαρομαρτεῖν, ἃ σάφ᾽ ἴσθι τοῦ[1] εὐφραίνεσθαι πολλὰς ἀσχολίας παρέχει.

13. Οἶσθα μὲν οὖν καὶ σύ, ὦ Καμβύση, ὅτι οὐ τόδε τὸ χρυσοῦν σκῆπτρον τὸ τὴν βασιλείαν διασῶζόν ἐστιν, ἀλλ᾽ οἱ πιστοὶ φίλοι σκῆπτρον βασιλεῦσιν ἀληθέστατον καὶ ἀσφαλέστατον. πιστοὺς δὲ μὴ νόμιζε φύεσθαι ἀνθρώπους· πᾶσι γὰρ ἂν οἱ αὐτοὶ πιστοὶ φαίνοιντο, ὥσπερ καὶ τἆλλα τὰ πεφυκότα πᾶσι τὰ αὐτὰ φαίνεται· ἀλλὰ τοὺς πιστοὺς τίθεσθαι δεῖ ἕκαστον ἑαυτῷ· ἡ δὲ κτῆσις αὐτῶν ἔστιν οὐδαμῶς σὺν τῇ βίᾳ, ἀλλὰ μᾶλλον σὺν τῇ εὐεργεσίᾳ. 14. εἰ οὖν καὶ ἄλλους τινὰς πειράσει συμφύλακας τῆς βασιλείας

---

[1] τοῦ Schneider, recent Edd.; τῷ MSS., Dindorf, Breitenbach.

be honoured above those who are younger. Take
what I say, therefore, as that which is approved by
time, by custom, and by the law. 11. So you,
Cambyses, shall have the throne, the gift of the gods
and of myself, in so far as it is mine to give.

"To you, Tanaoxares, I give the satrapy of Media,
Armenia, and, in addition to those two, Cadusia.
And in giving you this office, I consider that I leave
to your older brother greater power and the title of
king, while to you I leave a happiness disturbed by
fewer cares; 12. for I cannot see what human
pleasure you will lack; on the contrary, everything
that is thought to bring pleasure to man will be
yours. But to set one's heart on more difficult
undertakings, to be cumbered with many cares, and
to be able to find no rest, because spurred on by
emulation of what I have done, to lay plots and to be
plotted against, all that must necessarily go hand in
hand with royal power more than with your station;
and, let me assure you, it brings many interruptions
to happiness.

13. "As for you, Cambyses, you must also know
that it is not this golden sceptre that maintains your
empire; but faithful friends are a monarch's truest
and surest sceptre. But do not think that man
is naturally faithful; else all men would find the same
persons faithful, just as all find the other properties
of nature the same. But every one must create for
himself faithfulness in his friends; and the winning
of such friends comes in no wise by compulsion,
but by kindness. 14. If, then, you shall endeavour to make others also fellow-guardians of

His words
of counsel—
(1) to
Cambyses;

429

ποιεῖσθαι μηδαμόθεν πρότερον ἄρχου ἢ ἀπὸ τοῦ
ὁμόθεν γενομένου. καὶ πολῖταί τοι ἄνθρωποι
ἀλλοδαπῶν οἰκειότεροι καὶ σύσσιτοι ἀποσκήνων·
οἱ δὲ ἀπὸ τοῦ αὐτοῦ σπέρματος φύντες καὶ
ὑπὸ τῆς αὐτῆς μητρὸς τραφέντες καὶ ἐν τῇ αὐτῇ
οἰκίᾳ αὐξηθέντες καὶ ὑπὸ τῶν αὐτῶν γονέων
ἀγαπώμενοι καὶ τὴν αὐτὴν μητέρα καὶ τὸν αὐτὸν
πατέρα προσαγορεύοντες, πῶς οὐ πάντων οὗτοι
οἰκειότατοι; 15. μὴ οὖν ἃ οἱ θεοὶ ὑφήγηνται
ἀγαθὰ εἰς οἰκειότητα ἀδελφοῖς μάταιά ποτε
ποιήσητε, ἀλλ᾽ ἐπὶ ταῦτα εὐθὺς οἰκοδομεῖτε
ἄλλα φιλικὰ ἔργα· καὶ οὕτως ἀεὶ ἀνυπέρβλητος
ἄλλοις ἔσται ἡ ὑμετέρα φιλία. ἑαυτοῦ τοι κήδε-
ται ὁ προνοῶν ἀδελφοῦ· τίνι γὰρ ἄλλῳ ἀδελφὸς
μέγας ὢν οὕτω καλὸν ὡς ἀδελφῷ; τίς δ᾽ ἄλλος
τιμήσεται δι᾽ ἄνδρα μέγα δυνάμενον οὕτως ὡς
ἀδελφός; τίνα δὲ φοβήσεταί τις ἀδικεῖν ἀδελφοῦ
μεγάλου ὄντος οὕτως ὡς τὸν ἀδελφόν;

16. Μήτε οὖν θᾶττον μηδεὶς σοῦ τούτῳ ὑπα-
κουέτω μήτε προθυμότερον παρέστω· οὐδενὶ γὰρ
οἰκειότερα τὰ τούτου οὔτε ἀγαθὰ οὔτε δεινὰ ἢ
σοί. ἐννόει δὲ καὶ τάδε· τίνι χαρισάμενος ἐλπί-
σαις ἂν μειζόνων τυχεῖν ἢ τούτῳ; τίνι δ᾽ ἂν
βοηθήσας ἰσχυρότερον σύμμαχον ἀντιλάβοις;
τίνα δ᾽ αἴσχιον μὴ φιλεῖν ἢ τὸν ἀδελφόν; τίνα

your sovereignty, make a beginning nowhere sooner than with him who is of the same blood with yourself. Fellow-citizens, you know, stand nearer than foreigners do, and messmates nearer than those who eat elsewhere; but those who are sprung from the same seed, nursed by the same mother, reared in the same home, loved by the same parents, and who address the same persons as father and mother, how are they not the closest of all? 15. Do not you two, therefore, ever make of no effect those blessings whereby the gods have led the way to knitting close the bonds between brothers, but do you build at once upon that foundation still other works of love; and thus the love between you will always be a love that no other men can ever surpass. Surely he that has forethought for his brother is taking care for himself; for to whom else is a brother's greatness more of an honour than to a brother? And who else will be honoured by the power of a great man so much as that man's brother? And if a man's brother is a great man, whom will any one so much fear to injure as that man's brother?

16. "Therefore, Tanaoxares, let no one more (2) to readily than yourself yield obedience to your brother Tanaoxares or more zealously support him. For his fortunes, good or ill, will touch no one more closely than yourself. And bear this also in mind: whom could you favour in the hope of getting more from him than from your brother? Where could you lend help and get in return a surer ally than you would find in him? Whom would it be a more shameful thing for you not to love than your own brother? And who is there in all the world whom

δὲ ἁπάντων κάλλιον προτιμᾶν ἢ τὸν ἀδελφόν;
μόνου τοι, ὦ Καμβύση, πρωτεύοντος ἀδελφοῦ
παρ' ἀδελφῷ οὐδὲ φθόνος παρὰ τῶν ἄλλων
ἐφικνεῖται.[1]

17. Ἀλλὰ πρὸς θεῶν πατρῴων, ὦ παῖδες,
τιμᾶτε ἀλλήλους, εἴ τι καὶ τοῦ ἐμοὶ χαρίζεσθαι
μέλει ὑμῖν· οὐ γὰρ δήπου τοῦτό γε σαφῶς δοκεῖτε
εἰδέναι ὡς οὐδὲν ἔτι ἐγὼ ἔσομαι,[2] ἐπειδὰν τοῦ
ἀνθρωπίνου βίου τελευτήσω· οὐδὲ γὰρ νῦν τοι
τήν γ' ἐμὴν ψυχὴν ἑωρᾶτε, ἀλλ' οἷς διεπράττετο,
τούτοις αὐτὴν ὡς οὖσαν κατεφωρᾶτε. 18. τὰς
δὲ τῶν ἄδικα παθόντων ψυχὰς οὔπω κατενοήσατε
οἵους μὲν φόβους τοῖς μιαιφόνοις ἐμβάλλουσιν,
οἵους δὲ παλαμναίους τοῖς ἀνοσίοις ἐπιπέμπουσι;
τοῖς δὲ φθιμένοις τὰς τιμὰς διαμένειν ἔτι ἂν
δοκεῖτε, εἰ μηδενὸς αὐτῶν αἱ ψυχαὶ κύριαι ἦσαν;
19. οὔτοι ἔγωγε, ὦ παῖδες, οὐδὲ τοῦτο πώποτε
ἐπείσθην ὡς ἡ ψυχὴ ἕως μὲν ἂν ἐν θνητῷ σώματι
ᾖ, ζῇ, ὅταν δὲ τούτου ἀπαλλαγῇ, τέθνηκεν· ὁρῶ
γὰρ ὅτι καὶ τὰ θνητὰ σώματα ὅσον ἂν ἐν αὐτοῖς
χρόνον ᾖ ἡ ψυχή, ζῶντα παρέχεται. 20. οὐδέ
γε ὅπως ἄφρων ἔσται ἡ ψυχή, ἐπειδὰν τοῦ
ἄφρονος σώματος δίχα γένηται, οὐδὲ τοῦτο πέ-
πεισμαι· ἀλλ' ὅταν ἄκρατος καὶ καθαρὸς ὁ νοῦς
ἐκκριθῇ, τότε καὶ φρονιμώτατον αὐτὸν εἰκὸς εἶναι.
διαλυομένου δὲ ἀνθρώπου δῆλά ἐστιν ἕκαστα
ἀπιόντα πρὸς τὸ ὁμόφυλον πλὴν τῆς ψυχῆς· αὕτη
δὲ μόνη οὔτε παροῦσα οὔτε ἀπιοῦσα ὁρᾶται.

---

[1] ἐφικνεῖται Dindorf, Edd.; ἀφικνεῖται MSS.
[2] ἔτι ἐγὼ ἔσομαι x, Hug, Marchant, Gemoll; εἰ μὲ ἐγὼ ἔτι
xzVε, Dindorf, Breitenbach.

it would be a more noble thing to prefer in honour than your brother? It is only a brother, you know, Cambyses, whom, if he holds the first place of love in his brother's heart, the envy of others cannot reach.

17. "Nay by our fathers' gods I implore you, my sons, honour one another, if you care at all to give me pleasure. For assuredly, this one thing, so it seems to me, you do not know clearly, that I shall have no further being when I have finished this earthly life; for not even in this life have you seen my soul, but you have detected its existence by what it accomplished. 18. Have you never yet observed what terror the souls of those who have been foully dealt with strike into the hearts of those who have shed their blood, and what avenging deities they send upon the track of the wicked? And do you think that the honours paid to the dead would continue, if their souls had no part in any of them? 19. I am sure I do not; nor yet, my sons, have I ever convinced myself of this—that only as long as it is contained in a mortal body is the soul alive, but when it has been freed from it, is dead; for I see that it is the soul that endues mortal bodies with life, as long as it is in them. 20. Neither have I been able to convince myself of this—that the soul will want intelligence just when it is separated from this unintelligent body; but when the spirit is set free, pure and untrammelled by matter, then it is likely to be most intelligent. And when man is resolved into his primal elements, it is clear that every part returns to kindred matter, except the soul; that alone cannot be seen, either when present or when departing.

Cyrus on the immortality of the soul

433

21. Ἐννοήσατε δ', ἔφη, ὅτι ἐγγύτερον μὲν τῶν ἀνθρωπίνων θανάτῳ οὐδέν ἐστιν ὕπνου· ἡ δὲ τοῦ ἀνθρώπου ψυχὴ τότε δήπου θειοτάτη καταφαίνεται καὶ τότε τι τῶν μελλόντων προορᾷ· τότε γάρ, ὡς ἔοικε, μάλιστα ἐλευθεροῦται.

22. Εἰ μὲν οὖν οὕτως ἔχει ταῦτα ὥσπερ ἐγὼ οἶμαι καὶ ἡ ψυχὴ καταλείπει τὸ σῶμα, καὶ τὴν ἐμὴν ψυχὴν καταιδούμενοι ποιεῖτε ἃ ἐγὼ δέομαι· εἰ δὲ μὴ οὕτως, ἀλλὰ μένουσα ἡ ψυχὴ ἐν τῷ σώματι συναποθνήσκει, ἀλλὰ θεούς γε τοὺς ἀεὶ ὄντας καὶ πάντ' ἐφορῶντας καὶ πάντα δυναμένους, οἳ καὶ τήνδε τὴν τῶν ὅλων τάξιν συνέχουσιν ἀτριβῆ καὶ ἀγήρατον[1] καὶ ἀναμάρτητον καὶ ὑπὸ κάλλους καὶ μεγέθους ἀδιήγητον, τούτους φοβούμενοι μήποτε ἀσεβὲς μηδὲν μηδὲ ἀνόσιον μήτε ποιήσητε μήτε βουλεύσητε.

23. Μετὰ μέντοι θεοὺς καὶ ἀνθρώπων τὸ πᾶν γένος τὸ ἀεὶ ἐπιγιγνόμενον αἰδεῖσθε· οὐ γὰρ ἐν σκότῳ ὑμᾶς οἱ θεοὶ ἀποκρύπτονται, ἀλλ' ἐμφανῆ πᾶσιν ἀνάγκη ἀεὶ ζῆν τὰ ὑμέτερα ἔργα· ἃ ἢν μὲν καθαρὰ καὶ ἔξω τῶν ἀδίκων φαίνηται, δυνατοὺς ὑμᾶς ἐν πᾶσιν ἀνθρώποις ἀναδείξει· εἰ δὲ εἰς ἀλλήλους ἄδικόν τι φρονήσετε, ἐκ πάντων ἀνθρώπων τὸ ἀξιόπιστοι εἶναι ἀποβαλεῖτε. οὐδεὶς γὰρ ἂν ἔτι πιστεῦσαι δύναιτο ὑμῖν, οὐδ' εἰ πάνυ προθυμοῖτο, ἰδὼν ἀδικούμενον τὸν μάλιστα φιλίᾳ προσήκοντα.

24. Εἰ μὲν οὖν ἐγὼ ὑμᾶς ἱκανῶς διδάσκω οἵους χρὴ πρὸς ἀλλήλους εἶναι· εἰ δὲ μή, καὶ παρὰ τῶν προγεγενημένων μανθάνετε· αὕτη γὰρ ἀρίστη

[1] ἀγήρατον F, Photius, Edd.; ἀκήρατον xzV; ἄκρατον D.

21. "Consider again," he continued, "that there
nothing in the world more nearly akin to death
than is sleep; and the soul of man at just such times
is revealed in its most divine aspect and at such times,
too, it looks forward into the future; for then, it
seems, it is most untrammelled by the bonds of the
flesh.

22. "Now if this is true, as I think it is, and if the
soul does leave the body, then do what I request of
you and show reverence for my soul. But if it is
not so, and if the soul remains in the body and dies
with it, then at least fear the gods, eternal, all-
seeing, omnipotent, who keep this ordered universe
together, unimpaired, ageless, unerring, indescribable in its beauty and its grandeur; and never allow
yourselves to do or purpose anything wicked or
unholy.

He preaches the doctrine of reverence

23. "Next to the gods, however, show respect
also to all the race of men as they continue in
perpetual succession; for the gods do not hide you
away in darkness, but your works must ever live
on in the sight of all men; and if they are pure
and untainted with unrighteousness, they will make
your power manifest among all mankind. But if
you conceive any unrighteous schemes against
each other, you will forfeit in the eyes of all
men your right to be trusted. For no one would
be able any longer to trust you—not even if he
very much desired to do so—if he saw either of
you wronging that one who has the first claim to
the other's love.

24. "Now, if I am giving you sufficient instructions as to what manner of men you ought to be
one towards the other—well and good; if not, then

435

XENOPHON

διδασκαλία. οἱ μὲν γὰρ πολλοὶ διαγεγένηντα
φίλοι μὲν γονεῖς παισί, φίλοι δὲ ἀδελφοὶ ἀδελ
φοῖς· ἤδη δέ τινες τούτων καὶ ἐναντία ἀλλήλοι
ἔπραξαν· ὁποτέροις ἂν οὖν αἰσθάνησθε τὰ πραχ
θέντα συνενεγκόντα, ταῦτα δὴ αἱρούμενοι ὀρθῶ
ἂν βουλεύοισθε.

25. Καὶ τούτων μὲν ἴσως ἤδη ἅλις.

Τὸ δ' ἐμὸν σῶμα, ὦ παῖδες, ὅταν τελευτήσω
μήτε ἐν χρυσῷ θῆτε μήτε ἐν ἀργύρῳ μήτε ἐν ἄλλ
μηδενί, ἀλλὰ τῇ γῇ ὡς τάχιστα ἀπόδοτε. τί γὰ
τούτου μακαριώτερον τοῦ γῇ μιχθῆναι, ἣ πάντ
μὲν τὰ καλά, πάντα δὲ τἀγαθὰ φύει τε καὶ τρέ
φει; ἐγὼ δὲ καὶ ἄλλως φιλάνθρωπος ἐγενόμη
καὶ νῦν ἡδέως ἄν μοι δοκῶ κοινωνῆσαι τοῦ εὐερ
γετοῦντος ἀνθρώπους.

26. Ἀλλὰ γὰρ ἤδη, ἔφη, ἐκλείπειν μοι φαί
νεται ἡ ψυχὴ ὅθενπερ, ὡς ἔοικε, πᾶσιν ἄρχετα
ἀπολείπουσα. εἴ τις οὖν ὑμῶν ἢ δεξιᾶς βούλετα
τῆς ἐμῆς ἅψασθαι ἢ ὄμμα τοὐμὸν ζῶντος ἔτ
προσιδεῖν ἐθέλει, προσίτω· ὅταν δ' ἐγὼ ἐγκαλύ
ψωμαι, αἰτοῦμαι ὑμᾶς, ὦ παῖδες, μηδεὶς ἔτ' ἀν
θρώπων τοὐμὸν σῶμα ἰδέτω, μηδ' αὐτοὶ ὑμεῖς.

27. Πέρσας μέντοι πάντας καὶ τοὺς συμμάχου
ἐπὶ τὸ μνῆμα τοὐμὸν παρακαλεῖτε συνησθη
σομένους ἐμοὶ ὅτι ἐν τῷ ἀσφαλεῖ ἤδη ἔσομαι, ὡ
μηδὲν ἂν ἔτι κακὸν παθεῖν, μήτε ἢν μετὰ το
θείου γένωμαι μήτε ἢν μηδὲν ἔτι ὦ· ὁπόσοι δ' ἀ

ou must learn it from the history of the past, for this
the best source of instruction. For, as a rule,
arents have always been friends to their children,
rothers to their brothers; but ere now some of them
ave been at enmity one with another. Whichever,
herefore, of these two courses you shall find to
ave been profitable, choose that, and you would
ounsel well.

25. "But of this, perhaps, enough.

"Now as to my body, when I am dead, my He gives directions for his burial
ons, lay it away neither in gold nor in silver nor
anything else, but commit it to the earth as
oon as may be. For what is more blessed than
o be united with the earth, which brings forth
nd nourishes all things beautiful and all things
ood? I have always been a friend to man, and I
hink I should gladly now become a part of that
hich does him so much good.

26. "But I must conclude," he said; "for my
oul seems to me to be slipping away from those parts
f my body, from which, as it appears, it is wont to
egin its departure. So if any one wishes to take my
and or desires to look into my face while I yet live,
et him come near; but after I have covered myself
ver, I beg of you, my children, let no one look upon
y body, not even yourselves.

27. "Invite, however, all the Persians and our
lies to my burial, to joy with me in that I shall
enceforth be in security such that no evil can ever
gain come nigh me, whether I shall be in the
ivine presence or whether I shall no longer have
y being; and to all those who come show all the
urtesies that are usual in honour of a man

ἔλθωσι, τούτους εὖ ποιήσαντες ὁπόσα ἐπ' ἀνδρὶ
εὐδαίμονι νομίζεται ἀποπέμπετε.

28. Καὶ τοῦτο, ἔφη, μέμνησθέ μου τελευταῖον
τοὺς φίλους εὐεργετοῦντες καὶ τοὺς ἐχθροὺ
δυνήσεσθε κολάζειν. καὶ χαίρετε, ὦ φίλοι παῖδες
καὶ τῇ μητρὶ ἀπαγγέλλετε ὡς παρ' ἐμοῦ· κα
πάντες δὲ οἱ παρόντες καὶ οἱ ἀπόντες φίλο
χαίρετε.

Ταῦτ' εἰπὼν καὶ πάντας δεξιωσάμενος ἕνεκα
λύψατο[1] καὶ οὕτως ἐτελεύτησεν.

Chapter VIII can be considered only as a later addition t
Xenophon's work—a bit of historical criticism in a reviev
accompanying the book reviewed. It spoils the perfec
unity of the work up to this chapter: Cyrus is born, grow
to manhood, completes his conquests, establishes his kingdon
organizes the various departments of his empire, dies. Som
violent opponent of Medic influence in Athens could n

VIII[2]

[1. Ὅτι μὲν δὴ καλλίστη καὶ μεγίστη τῶν ἐ
τῇ Ἀσίᾳ ἡ Κύρου βασιλεία ἐγένετο αὐτὴ ἑαυτ
μαρτυρεῖ. ὡρίσθη γὰρ πρὸς ἕω μὲν τῇ Ἐρυθρ
θαλάττῃ, πρὸς ἄρκτον δὲ τῷ Εὐξείνῳ πόντω
πρὸς ἑσπέραν δὲ Κύπρῳ καὶ Αἰγύπτῳ, πρὸ
μεσημβρίαν δὲ Αἰθιοπίᾳ. τοσαύτη δὲ γενομέν
μιᾷ γνώμῃ τῇ Κύρου ἐκυβερνᾶτο, καὶ ἐκείνο
τε τοὺς ὑφ' ἑαυτῷ ὥσπερ ἑαυτοῦ παῖδας ἐτίμ
τε καὶ ἐθεράπευεν, οἵ τε ἀρχόμενοι Κῦρον ω

[1] ἐνεκαλύψατο Cobet, Hug, Marchant, Gemoll ; συνεκαλ
ψατο MSS., Dindorf, Breitenbach.
[2] Chapter viii came under the suspicion of Valckenaer firs

hat has been blessed of fortune, and then dismiss
hem.

28. "Remember also this last word of mine," he
aid : "if you do good to your friends, you will also
e able to punish your enemies. And now farewell,
ny children, and say farewell to your mother as from
ne. And to all my friends, both present and absent,
bid farewell."

After these words, he shook hands with them all,
overed himself over, and so died.

---

eave all this glorification of Persian institutions unchallenged,
nd so in this appendix he has supplied an account of the
legeneracy of the descendants of the virtuous Persians of the
arlier day.

The chapter is included here in accord with all the
manuscripts and editions. But the reader is recommended
o close the book at this point and read no further.

VIII

[1. THAT Cyrus's empire was the greatest and most *The empire
and its dis-*
glorious of all the kingdoms in Asia—of that it may *integration*
be its own witness. For it was bounded on the east by
the Indian Ocean, on the north by the Black Sea, on
the west by Cyprus and Egypt, and on the south by
Ethiopia. And although it was of such magnitude,
it was governed by the single will of Cyrus ; and he
honoured his subjects and cared for them as if they
were his own children ; and they, on their part,

it is rejected by most Edd.; it is defended by Cobet, Eichler,
Marchant.

XENOPHON

πατέρα ἐσέβοντο. 2. ἐπεὶ μέντοι Κῦρος ἐτελεύτησεν, εὐθὺς μὲν αὐτοῦ οἱ παῖδες ἐστασίαζον
εὐθὺς δὲ πόλεις καὶ ἔθνη ἀφίσταντο, πάντα δ
ἐπὶ τὸ χεῖρον ἐτρέπετο. ὡς δ᾽ ἀληθῆ λέγω
ἄρξομαι διδάσκων ἐκ τῶν θείων.

Οἶδα γὰρ ὅτι πρότερον μὲν βασιλεὺς καὶ οἱ ὑπ
αὐτῷ καὶ τοῖς τὰ ἔσχατα πεποιηκόσιν εἴτε ὅρκους
ὀμόσειαν, ἠμπέδουν, εἴτε δεξιὰς δοῖεν, ἐβεβαίουν
3. εἰ δὲ μὴ τοιοῦτοι ἦσαν καὶ τοιαύτην δόξαν εἶχον
οὐδ᾽ ἂν εἷς αὐτοῖς ἐπίστευσεν,[1] ὥσπερ οὐδὲ νῦν
πιστεύει οὐδὲ εἷς ἔτι, ἐπεὶ ἔγνωσται ἡ ἀσέβεια
αὐτῶν. οὕτως οὐδὲ τότε ἐπίστευσαν ἂν οἱ τῶν
σὺν Κύρῳ ἀναβάντων στρατηγοί· νῦν δὲ δὴ τῇ
πρόσθεν αὐτῶν δόξῃ πιστεύσαντες ἐνεχείρισαν
ἑαυτούς, καὶ ἀναχθέντες πρὸς βασιλέα ἀπετμή-
θησαν τὰς κεφαλάς. πολλοὶ δὲ καὶ τῶν συστρα-
τευσάντων βαρβάρων ἄλλοι ἄλλαις πίστεσιν
ἐξαπατηθέντες ἀπώλοντο.

4. Πολὺ δὲ καὶ τάδε χείρονες νῦν εἰσι. πρόσθεν
μὲν γὰρ εἴ τις ἢ διακινδυνεύσειε πρὸ βασιλέως
ἢ πόλιν ἢ ἔθνος ὑποχείριον ποιήσειεν ἢ ἄλλο τι
καλὸν ἢ ἀγαθὸν αὐτῷ διαπράξειεν, οὗτοι ἦσαν οἱ
τιμώμενοι· νῦν δὲ καὶ ἤν τις ὥσπερ Μιθραδάτης
τὸν πατέρα Ἀριοβαρζάνην προδούς, καὶ ἤν τις

---

[1] ἐπίστευσεν Hug, Gemoll ; ἐπίστευεν MSS., other Edd.

reverenced Cyrus as a father. 2. Still, as soon as Cyrus was dead, his children at once fell into dissension, states and nations began to revolt, and everything began to deteriorate. And that what I say is the truth, I will prove, beginning with the Persians' attitude toward religion.

I know, for example, that in early times the kings and their officers, in their dealings with even the worst offenders, would abide by an oath that they might have given, and be true to any pledge they might have made. 3. For had they not had such a character for honour, and had they not been true to their reputation, not a man would have trusted them, just as not a single person any longer trusts them, now that their lack of character is notorious; and the generals of the Greeks who joined the expedition of Cyrus the Younger would not have had such confidence in them even on that occasion. But, as it was, trusting in the previous reputation of the Persian kings, they placed themselves in the king's power, were led into his presence, and had their heads cut off. And many also of the barbarians who joined that expedition went to their doom, some deluded by one promise, others by another.

The decline in moral standards

4. But at the present time they are still worse, as the following will show: if, for example, any one in the olden times risked his life for the king, or if any one reduced a state or a nation to submission to him, or effected anything else of good or glory for him, such an one received honour and preferment; now, on the other hand, if any one seems to bring some advantage to the king by evil-doing, whether as Mithradates did, by betraying his own father Ario-

ὥσπερ Ῥεομίθρης τὴν γυναῖκα καὶ τὰ τέκνα κα
τοὺς τῶν φίλων παῖδας ὁμήρους παρὰ τῷ Αἰγυ
πτίῳ ἐγκαταλιπὼν καὶ τοὺς μεγίστους ὅρκου
παραβὰς βασιλεῖ δόξῃ τι σύμφορον ποιῆσαι
οὗτοί εἰσιν οἱ ταῖς μεγίσταις τιμαῖς γεραιρόμενοι.

5. Ταῦτα οὖν ὁρῶντες οἱ ἐν τῇ Ἀσίᾳ πάντες ἐπ
τὸ ἀσεβὲς καὶ τὸ ἄδικον τετραμμένοι εἰσίν· ὁποῖο
τινες γὰρ ἂν οἱ προστάται ὦσι, τοιοῦτοι καὶ οἱ ὑπ
αὐτοὺς ὡς ἐπὶ τὸ πολὺ γίγνονται. ἀθεμιστότερο
δὴ νῦν ἢ πρόσθεν ταύτῃ γεγένηνται.

6. Εἴς γε μὴν χρήματα τῇδε ἀδικώτεροι· οὐ γὰρ
μόνον τοὺς πολλὰ ἡμαρτηκότας, ἀλλ' ἤδη τοὺς
οὐδὲν ἠδικηκότας συλλαμβάνοντες ἀναγκάζουσι
πρὸς οὐδὲν δίκαιον χρήματα ἀποτίνειν· ὥστε
οὐδὲν ἧττον οἱ πολλὰ ἔχειν δοκοῦντες τῶν πολλὰ
ἠδικηκότων φοβοῦνται· καὶ εἰς χεῖρας οὐδ' οὗτοι
ἐθέλουσι τοῖς κρείττοσιν ἰέναι. οὐδέ γε ἀθροίζε-
σθαι εἰς βασιλικὴν στρατιὰν θαρροῦσι. 7. τοιγαροῦν ὅστις ἂν πολεμῇ αὐτοῖς, πᾶσιν ἔξεστιν ἐν τῇ
χώρᾳ αὐτῶν ἀναστρέφεσθαι ἄνευ μάχης ὅπως ἂι
βούλωνται διὰ τὴν ἐκείνων περὶ μὲν θεοὺς ἀσέ-
βειαν, περὶ δὲ ἀνθρώπους ἀδικίαν. αἱ μὲν δὴ
γνῶμαι ταύτῃ τῷ παντὶ χείρους νῦν ἢ τὸ παλαιὸ
αὐτῶν.

8. Ὡς δὲ οὐδὲ τῶν σωμάτων ἐπιμέλονται
ὥσπερ πρόσθεν, νῦν αὖ τοῦτο διηγήσομαι. νόμιμον γὰρ δὴ ἦν αὐτοῖς μήτε πτύειν μήτε ἀπομύττεσθαι. δῆλον δὲ ὅτι ταῦτα οὐ τοῦ ἐν τῷ σώματι

barzanes, or as a certain Rheomithres did, in violating his most sacred oaths and leaving his wife and children and the children of his friends behind as hostages in the power of the king of Egypt[1]—such are the ones who now have the highest honours heaped upon them.

5. Witnessing such a state of morality, all the inhabitants of Asia have been turned to wickedness and wrong-doing. For, whatever the character of the rulers is, such also that of the people under them for the most part becomes. In this respect they are now even more unprincipled than before.

6. In money matters, too, they are more dishonest in this particular: they arrest not merely those who have committed many offences, but even those who have done no wrong, and against all justice compel them to pay fines; and so those who are supposed to be rich are kept in a state of terror no less than those who have committed many crimes, and they are no more willing than malefactors are to come into close relations with their superiors in power; in fact, they do not even venture to enlist in the royal army. 7. Accordingly, owing to their impiety toward the gods and their iniquity toward man, any one who is engaged in war with them can, if he desire, range up and down their country without having to strike a blow. Their principles in so far, therefore, are in every respect worse now than they were in antiquity. *Financial dishonesty*

8. In the next place, as I will now show, they do not care for their physical strength as they used to do. For example, it used to be their custom neither to spit nor to blow the nose. It is obvious that they *Physical deterioration*

---

[1] Tachos; see Index, *s.v.* Ariobarzanes.

ὑγροῦ φειδόμενοι ἐνόμισαν, ἀλλὰ βουλόμενοι διὰ
πόνων καὶ ἱδρῶτος τὰ σώματα στερεοῦσθαι. νῦν
δὲ τὸ μὲν μὴ πτύειν μηδὲ ἀπομύττεσθαι ἔτι διαμένει, τὸ δ' ἐκπονεῖν οὐδαμοῦ ἐπιτηδεύεται. 9. καὶ
μὴν πρόσθεν μὲν ἦν αὐτοῖς μονοσιτεῖν νόμιμον,
ὅπως ὅλῃ τῇ ἡμέρᾳ χρῶντο εἰς τὰς πράξεις καὶ
εἰς τὸ διαπονεῖσθαι. νῦν γε μὴν τὸ μὲν μονοσιτεῖν
ἔτι διαμένει, ἀρχόμενοι δὲ τοῦ σίτου ἡνίκαπερ οἱ
πρωαίτατα ἀριστῶντες μέχρι τούτου ἐσθίοντες καὶ
πίνοντες διάγουσιν ἔστεπερ οἱ ὀψιαίτατα κοιμώ-
μενοι.

10. Ἦν δ' αὐτοῖς νόμιμον μηδὲ προχοΐδας
εἰσφέρεσθαι εἰς τὰ συμπόσια, δῆλον ὅτι νομίζοντες τὸ μὴ ὑπερπίνειν ἧττον ἂν καὶ σώματα καὶ
γνώμας σφάλλειν· νῦν δὲ τὸ μὲν μὴ εἰσφέρεσθαι
ἔτι αὖ διαμένει, τοσοῦτον δὲ πίνουσιν ὥστε ἀντὶ
τοῦ εἰσφέρειν αὐτοὶ ἐκφέρονται, ἐπειδὰν μηκέτι
δύνωνται ὀρθούμενοι ἐξιέναι.

11. Ἀλλὰ μὴν κἀκεῖνο ἦν αὐτοῖς ἐπιχώριον
τὸ μεταξὺ πορευομένους μήτε ἐσθίειν μήτε πίνειν
μήτε τῶν διὰ ταῦτα ἀναγκαίων μηδὲν ποιοῦντας
φανεροὺς εἶναι· νῦν δ' αὖ τὸ μὲν τούτων ἀπέχεσθαι ἔτι διαμένει, τὰς μέντοι πορείας οὕτω
βραχείας ποιοῦνται ὡς μηδέν' ἂν ἔτι θαυμάσαι
τὸ ἀπέχεσθαι τῶν ἀναγκαίων.

12. Ἀλλὰ μὴν καὶ ἐπὶ θήραν πρόσθεν μὲν
τοσαυτάκις ἐξῆσαν ὥστε ἀρκεῖν αὐτοῖς τε καὶ
ἵπποις γυμνάσια τὰς θήρας· ἐπεὶ δὲ Ἀρταξέρξης

observed this custom not for the sake of saving the moisture in the body, but from the wish to harden the body by labour and perspiration. But now the custom of refraining from spitting or blowing the nose still continues, but they never give themselves the trouble to work off the moisture in some other direction. 9. In former times it was their custom also to eat but once in the day, so that they might devote the whole day to business and hard work. Now, to be sure, the custom of eating but once a day still prevails, but they begin to eat at the hour when those who breakfast earliest begin their morning meal, and they keep on eating and drinking until the hour when those who stay up latest go to bed.

10. They had also the custom of not bringing pots into their banquets, evidently because they thought that if one did not drink to excess, both mind and body would be less uncertain. So even now the custom of not bringing in the pots still obtains, but they drink so much that, instead of carrying anything in, they are themselves carried out when they are no longer able to stand straight enough to walk out.

11. Again, this also was a native custom of theirs, neither to eat nor drink while on a march, nor yet to be seen doing any of the necessary consequences of eating or drinking. Even yet that same abstinence prevails, but they make their journeys so short that no one would be surprised at their ability to resist those calls of nature.

12. Again, in times past they used to go out hunting so often that the hunts afforded sufficient exercise for both men and horses. But since Ar-

Decline of the old disciplines

XENOPHON

ὁ βασιλεὺς καὶ οἱ σὺν αὐτῷ ἥττους τοῦ οἴνου ἐγένοντο, οὐκέτι ὁμοίως οὔτ᾽ αὐτοὶ ἐξῆσαν οὔτε τοὺς ἄλλους ἐξῆγον ἐπὶ τὰς θήρας· ἀλλὰ καὶ εἴ τινες φιλόπονοι γενόμενοι σὺν[1] τοῖς περὶ αὑτοὺς ἱππεῦσι θαμὰ θηρῷεν,[2] φθονοῦντες αὐτοῖς δῆλοι ἦσαν καὶ ὡς βελτίονας αὐτῶν ἐμίσουν.

13. Ἀλλά τοι καὶ τοὺς παῖδας τὸ μὲν παιδεύεσθαι ἐπὶ ταῖς θύραις ἔτι διαμένει· τὸ μέντοι τὰ ἱππικὰ μανθάνειν καὶ μελετᾶν ἀπέσβηκε διὰ τὸ μὴ εἶναι ὅπου ἂν ἀποφαινόμενοι εὐδοκιμοῖεν. καὶ ὅτι γε οἱ παῖδες ἀκούοντες ἐκεῖ πρόσθεν τὰς δίκας δικαίως δικαζομένας ἐδόκουν μανθάνειν δικαιότητα, καὶ τοῦτο παντάπασιν ἀνέστραπται· σαφῶς γὰρ ὁρῶσι νικῶντας ὁπότεροι ἂν πλεῖον διδῶσιν. 14. ἀλλὰ καὶ τῶν φυομένων ἐκ τῆς γῆς τὰς δυνάμεις οἱ παῖδες πρόσθεν μὲν ἐμάνθανον, ὅπως τοῖς μὲν ὠφελίμοις χρῶντο, τῶν δὲ βλαβερῶν ἀπέχοιντο· νῦν δὲ ἐοίκασι ταῦτα διδασκομένοις, ὅπως ὅτι πλεῖστα κακοποιῶσιν· οὐδαμοῦ γοῦν πλείους ἢ ἐκεῖ οὔτ᾽ ἀποθνήσκουσιν οὔτε διαφθείρονται ὑπὸ φαρμάκων.

15. Ἀλλὰ μὴν καὶ θρυπτικώτεροι πολὺ νῦν ἢ ἐπὶ Κύρου εἰσί. τότε μὲν γὰρ ἔτι τῇ ἐκ Περσῶν παιδείᾳ καὶ ἐγκρατείᾳ ἐχρῶντο, τῇ δὲ Μήδων στολῇ καὶ ἁβρότητι· νῦν δὲ τὴν μὲν ἐκ Περσῶν καρτερίαν περιορῶσιν ἀποσβεννυμένην, τὴν δὲ τῶν Μήδων μαλακίαν διασῴζονται.

[1] σὺν Dindorf, Hug; [καὶ] σὺν Marchant, Gemoll; καὶ σὺν MSS. (except Med. 55. 19).
[2] θαμὰ θηρῷεν Dindorf, Edd.; ἅμα θηρῷεν xyGV; μαρτυρῶεν ΑΗε.

taxerxes and his court became the victims of wine, they have neither gone out themselves in the old way nor taken the others out hunting; on the contrary, if any one often went hunting with his friends out of sheer love for physical exertion, the courtiers would not hide their jealousy and would hate him as presuming to be a better man than they.

13. Again, it is still the custom for the boys to be educated at court; but instruction and practice in horsemanship have died out, because there are no occasions on which they may give an exhibition and win distinction for skill. And while anciently the boys used there to hear cases at law justly decided and so to learn justice, as they believed—that also has been entirely reversed; for now they see all too clearly that whichever party gives the larger bribe wins the case. 14. The boys of that time used also to learn the properties of the products of the earth, so as to avail themselves of the useful ones and keep away from those that were harmful. But now it looks as if they learned them only in order to do as much harm as possible; at any rate, there is no place where more people die or lose their lives from poisons than there.

15. Furthermore, they are much more effeminate now than they were in Cyrus's day. For at that time they still adhered to the old discipline and the old abstinence that they received from the Persians, but adopted the Median garb and Median luxury; now, on the contrary, they are allowing the rigour of the Persians to die out, while they keep up the effeminacy of the Medes.

16. Σαφηνίσαι δὲ βούλομαι καὶ τὴν θρύψιν αὐτῶν. ἐκείνοις γὰρ πρῶτον μὲν τὰς εὐνὰς οὐ μόνον ἀρκεῖ μαλακῶς ὑποστόρνυσθαι, ἀλλ' ἤδη καὶ τῶν κλινῶν τοὺς πόδας ἐπὶ δαπίδων[1] τιθέασιν, ὅπως μὴ ἀντερείδῃ τὸ δάπεδον, ἀλλ' ὑπείκωσιν αἱ δάπιδες. καὶ μὴν τὰ πεττόμενα ἐπὶ τράπεζαν ὅσα τε πρόσθεν εὕρητο, οὐδὲν αὐτῶν ἀφῄρηται, ἄλλα τε ἀεὶ καινὰ ἐπιμηχανῶνται· καὶ ὄψα γε ὡσαύτως· καὶ γὰρ καινοποιητὰς ἀμφοτέρων τούτων κέκτηνται.

17. Ἀλλὰ μὴν καὶ ἐν τῷ χειμῶνι οὐ μόνον κεφαλὴν καὶ σῶμα καὶ πόδας ἀρκεῖ αὐτοῖς ἐσκεπάσθαι, ἀλλὰ καὶ περὶ ἄκραις ταῖς χερσὶ χειρίδας δασείας καὶ δακτυλήθρας ἔχουσιν. ἔν γε μὴν τῷ θέρει οὐκ ἀρκοῦσιν αὐτοῖς οὔθ' αἱ τῶν δένδρων οὔθ' αἱ τῶν πετρῶν σκιαί, ἀλλ' ἐν ταύταις ἑτέρας σκιὰς ἄνθρωποι μηχανώμενοι αὐτοῖς παρεστᾶσι.

18. Καὶ μὴν ἐκπώματα ἢν μὲν ὡς πλεῖστα ἔχωσι, τούτῳ καλλωπίζονται· ἢν δ' ἐξ ἀδίκου φανερῶς ᾖ μεμηχανημένα, οὐδὲν τοῦτο αἰσχύνονται· πολὺ γὰρ ηὔξηται ἐν αὐτοῖς ἡ ἀδικία τε καὶ αἰσχροκέρδεια.

19. Ἀλλὰ καὶ πρόσθεν μὲν ἦν ἐπιχώριον αὐτοῖς μὴ ὁρᾶσθαι πεζῇ πορευομένοις, οὐκ ἄλλου τινὸς ἕνεκα ἢ τοῦ ὡς ἱππικωτάτους γίγνεσθαι· νῦν δὲ στρώματα πλείω ἔχουσιν ἐπὶ τῶν ἵππων ἢ ἐπὶ τῶν εὐνῶν· οὐ γὰρ τῆς ἱππείας οὕτως ὥσπερ τοῦ μαλακῶς καθῆσθαι ἐπιμέλονται. 20. τά γε μὴν πολεμικὰ πῶς οὐκ εἰκότως νῦν τῷ παντὶ

---

[1] δαπίδων Dindorf, Breitenbach, Hug ; ταπίδων xyV, Marchant, Gemoll ; ταπήτων G ; ταπήδων AH.

16. I should like to explain their effeminacy more in detail. In the first place, they are not satisfied with only having their couches upholstered with down, but they actually set the posts of their beds upon carpets, so that the floor may offer no resistance, but that the carpets may yield. Again, whatever sorts of bread and pastry for the table had been discovered before, none of all those have fallen into disuse, but they keep on always inventing something new besides; and it is the same way with meats; for in both branches of cookery they actually have artists to invent new dishes.

The effeminacy of the orientals

17. Again, in winter they are not satisfied with having clothing on their heads and bodies and legs, but they must have also sleeves thickly lined to the very tips of their fingers, and gloves besides. In summer, on the other hand, they are not satisfied with the shade afforded by the trees and rocks, but amid these they have people stand by them to provide artificial shade.

18. They take great pride also in having as many cups as possible; but they are not ashamed if it transpire that they came by them by dishonest means, for dishonesty and sordid love of gain have greatly increased among them.

19. Furthermore, it was of old a national custom not to be seen going anywhere on foot; and that was for no other purpose than to make themselves as knightly as possible. But now they have more coverings upon their horses than upon their beds, for they do not care so much for knighthood as for a soft seat. 20. And so is it not to be expected that in military prowess they should be wholly

The modern knighthood

χείρους ἢ πρόσθεν εἰσίν; οἷς ἐν μὲν τῷ παρελ-
θόντι χρόνῳ ἐπιχώριον εἶναι ὑπῆρχε τοὺς μὲν
τὴν γῆν ἔχοντας ἀπὸ ταύτης ἱππότας παρέχεσθαι,
οἳ δὴ καὶ ἐστρατεύοντο εἰ δέοι στρατεύεσθαι, τοὺς
δὲ φρουροῦντας πρὸ τῆς χώρας μισθοφόρους εἶναι·
νῦν δὲ τούς τε θυρωροὺς καὶ τοὺς σιτοποιοὺς καὶ
τοὺς ὀψοποιοὺς καὶ οἰνοχόους καὶ λουτροχόους καὶ
παρατιθέντας καὶ ἀναιροῦντας καὶ κατακοιμίζοντας
καὶ ἀνιστάντας, καὶ τοὺς κοσμητάς, οἳ ὑποχρίουσί
τε καὶ ἐντρίβουσιν αὐτοὺς καὶ τἆλλα ῥυθμίζουσι,
τούτους πάντας ἱππέας οἱ δυνάσται πεποιήκασιν,
ὅπως μισθοφορῶσιν αὐτοῖς. 21. πλῆθος μὲν οὖν
καὶ ἐκ τούτων φαίνεται, οὐ μέντοι ὄφελός γε
οὐδὲν αὐτῶν εἰς πόλεμον· δηλοῖ δὲ καὶ αὐτὰ
τὰ γιγνόμενα· κατὰ γὰρ τὴν χώραν αὐτῶν ῥᾷον
οἱ πολέμιοι ἢ οἱ φίλοι ἀναστρέφονται. 22. καὶ
γὰρ δὴ ὁ Κῦρος τοῦ μὲν ἀκροβολίζεσθαι ἀποπαύ-
σας, θωρακίσας δὲ καὶ αὐτοὺς καὶ ἵππους καὶ ἐν
παλτὸν ἑκάστῳ δοὺς εἰς χεῖρα ὁμόθεν τὴν μάχην
ἐποιεῖτο· νῦν δὲ οὔτε ἀκροβολίζονται ἔτι οὔτ᾿ εἰς
χεῖρας συνιόντες μάχονται. 23. καὶ οἱ πεζοὶ
ἔχουσι μὲν γέρρα καὶ κοπίδας καὶ σαγάρεις ὥσπερ
οἱ[1] ἐπὶ Κύρου τὴν μάχην ποιησάμενοι· εἰς χεῖρας
δὲ ἰέναι οὐδ᾿ οὗτοι ἐθέλουσιν.

24. Οὐδέ γε τοῖς δρεπανηφόροις ἅρμασιν ἔτι
χρῶνται ἐφ᾿ ᾧ Κῦρος αὐτὰ ἐποιήσατο. ὁ μὲν γὰρ
τιμαῖς αὐξήσας τοὺς ἡνιόχους καὶ ἀγαστοὺς[2]

[1] οἱ Nitsche, Hug, Marchant, Gemoll; not in MSS., other Edd.
[2] ἀγαστοὺς Dindorf⁴, Hug, Marchant, Gemoll; ἀγαθοὺς MSS., Dindorf⁸, Breitenbach.

inferior to what they used to be? In times past it was their national custom that those who held lands should furnish cavalrymen from their possessions and that these, in case of war, should also take the field, while those who performed outpost duty in defence of the country received pay for their services. But now the rulers make knights out of their porters, bakers, cooks, cup-bearers, bath-room attendants, butlers, waiters, chamberlains who assist them in retiring at night and in rising in the morning, and beauty-doctors who pencil their eyes and rouge their cheeks for them and otherwise beautify them; these are the sort that they make into knights to serve for pay for them. 21. From such recruits, therefore, a host is obtained, but they are of no use in war; and that is clear from actual occurrences: for enemies may range up and down their land with less hindrance than friends. 22. For Cyrus had abolished skirmishing at a distance, had armed both horses and men with breastplates, had put a javelin into each man's hand, and had introduced the method of fighting hand to hand. But now they neither skirmish at a distance any longer, nor yet do they fight in a hand-to-hand engagement. 23. The infantry still have their wicker shields and bills and sabres, just as those had who set the battle in array in the times of Cyrus; but not even they are willing to come into a hand-to-hand conflict.

Inefficiency of infantry and chariots

24. Neither do they employ the scythed chariot any longer for the purpose for which Cyrus had it made. For he advanced the charioteers to honour and made them objects of admiration and so had

ποιήσας εἶχε τοὺς εἰς τὰ ὅπλα ἐμβαλοῦντας· οἱ
δὲ νῦν οὐδὲ γιγνώσκοντες τοὺς ἐπὶ τοῖς ἅρμασιν
οἴονται σφίσιν ὁμοίους τοὺς ἀνασκήτους τοῖς
ἠσκηκόσιν ἔσεσθαι. 25. οἱ δὲ ὁρμῶσι μέν, πρὶν
δ' ἐν τοῖς πολεμίοις εἶναι οἱ μὲν ἄκοντες[1] ἐκπί-
πτουσιν, οἱ δ' ἐξάλλονται, ὥστε ἄνευ ἡνιόχων
γιγνόμενα τὰ ζεύγη πολλάκις πλείω κακὰ τοὺς
φίλους ἢ τοὺς πολεμίους ποιεῖ. 26. ἐπεὶ μέντοι
καὶ αὐτοὶ γιγνώσκουσιν οἷα σφίσι τὰ πολεμιστήρια ὑπάρχει, ὑφίενται, καὶ οὐδεὶς ἔτι ἄνευ
Ἑλλήνων εἰς πόλεμον καθίσταται, οὔτε ὅταν
ἀλλήλοις πολεμῶσιν οὔτε ὅταν οἱ Ἕλληνες αὐτοῖς
ἀντιστρατεύωνται· ἀλλὰ καὶ πρὸς τούτους ἐγνώ-
κασι μεθ' Ἑλλήνων τοὺς πολέμους ποιεῖσθαι.

27. Ἐγὼ μὲν δὴ οἶμαι ἅπερ ὑπεθέμην ἀπειρ-
γάσθαι μοι. φημὶ γὰρ Πέρσας καὶ τοὺς σὺν
αὐτοῖς καὶ ἀσεβεστέρους περὶ θεοὺς καὶ ἀνοσιω-
τέρους περὶ συγγενεῖς καὶ ἀδικωτέρους περὶ τοὺς
ἄλλους καὶ ἀνανδροτέρους τὰ εἰς τὸν πόλεμον νῦν
ἢ πρόσθεν ἀποδεδεῖχθαι. εἰ δέ τις τἀναντία ἐμοὶ
γιγνώσκοι, τὰ ἔργα αὐτῶν ἐπισκοπῶν εὑρήσει
αὐτὰ μαρτυροῦντα τοῖς ἐμοῖς λόγοις.]

---

[1] ἄκοντες Muretus, Edd.; ἑκόντες MSS.

men who were ready to hurl themselves against even a heavy-armed line. The officers of the present day, however, do not so much as know the men in the chariots, and they think that untrained drivers will be just as serviceable to them as trained charioteers. 25. Such untrained men do indeed charge, but before they penetrate the enemy's lines some of them are unintentionally thrown out, some of them jump out on purpose, and so the teams without drivers often create more havoc on their own side than on the enemy's. 26. However, inasmuch as even they understand what sort of material for war they have, they abandon the effort; and no one ever goes to war any more without the help of Greek mercenaries, be it when they are at war with one another or when the Greeks make war upon them; but even against Greeks they recognize that they can conduct their wars only with the assistance of Greeks. *The barbarian helpless without Greek soldiers*

27. I think now that I have accomplished the task that I set before myself. For I maintain that I have proved that the Persians of the present day and those living in their dependencies are less reverent toward the gods, less dutiful to their relatives, less upright in their dealings with all men, and less brave in war than they were of old. But if any one should entertain an opinion contrary to my own, let him examine their deeds and he will find that these testify to the truth of my statements.] *Conclusion*

APPENDIX I

The manœuvre is not quite clear because Xenophon assumes that his readers will take it for granted where the light-armed troops ("the poorest") will be stationed. The first position is :—

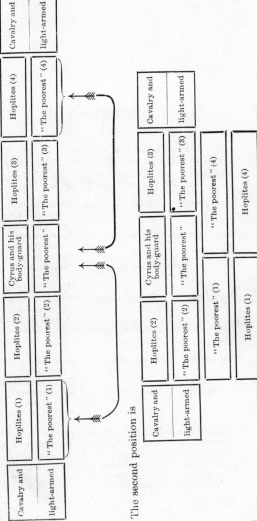

The second position is

455

APPENDIX II

To make clearer the relations between Xenophon's kings in Babylon and those of Bible story and the Babylonian inscriptions, the following tables of succession are added (the vertical lines denote sonship) :—

Nabopolassar	Ναβοπαλάσσαρος	Nabu-apal-usur (625–604 B.C.) (Nabu protect the son)
Nebuchadnezzar	Ναβουχοδονόσορος	Nabu-kuduri-usur (604–561 B.C.) (Nabu protect the boundary)
Evil Merodach	Ἀμιλμαρούδοκος	Amil-Marduk (561–559 B.C.) (Man of Marduk)
Neriglissar [1]	Νηριγλισσόορος	Nergal-shar-usur (559–556 B.C.) (Nergal protect the king)
Labosoarchod	Λαβασσοάρασκος	Labashi-Marduk (556 B.C.)
Nabonidus	Λαβύνητος	Nabu-naid (558–538 B.C.) (Nabu is exalted)
Belshazzar	Βαλτάσαρος	Bel-shar-usur (slain 539 or 538 B.C.) (Bel protect the king)

The relationship between Xenophon's "old king" and "young king" and the historical succession is not clear. His "old king" is slain in the first battle and can, therefore, be neither Nabonidus nor Belshazzar (for both (?)

---

[1] Neriglissar was brother to Evil-Merodach.

APPENDIX II

were in Babylon at its fall), but ought to be Labashi-Marduk. But if Labashi-Marduk were the "old king," the "young king" would be Nabonidus, and Nabonidus was not the "son" of his predecessor. By the "old king" Xenophon probably means Nabonidus, and by the "young king" Belshazzar, though the chronology is not in order, for Nabonidus was not slain in that earlier battle. There seems to be an inextricable snarl, in any case.

Cyrus's line, tabulated from his genealogy given by himself on his famous clay cylinder found in the ruins of his palace, from Xenophon's statements, and from well-known facts of history, is as follows:—

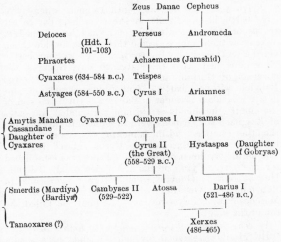

For the sake of further comparison the following striking parallels to Xenophon's story are added from two official documents of the kings themselves, discovered in the ruins of their palace:—

APPENDIX II

I. *The Nabu-naid Chronicle:* " 6th year. [His troops] he collected and marched against Cyrus, King of Anshan, to conquer him. . . . The troops of Astyages rebelled against him, and, taking him prisoner, they handed him over to Cyrus. Cyrus (went) to Ecbatana, the royal city. The silver, gold, possessions, property . . . of Ecbatana they carried away as spoil, and he brought (it) to Anshan . . .

" 9th year . . . In Nisan, Cyrus, King of Parsu, mustered his troops and crossed over the Tigris below Arbela. In Iyyar . . . he slew its king (and) took away its possessions. He stationed his own garrison there. After this time his garrison remained there with that of the king . . .

" 17th year . . . In the month Tammuz, when Cyrus gave battle in Opis (and) on the river Salsallat to the troops of Akkad, the people of Akkad he subdued (?). Whenever the people collected themselves, he slew them. On the fourteenth day Sippar was taken without battle. Nabonidus fled. On the sixteenth day, Gobryas, the governor of Gutium, and the troops of Cyrus entered Babylon without battle. Nabonidus, because of his delay, was taken prisoner in Babylon. Until the end of the month, the shields of Gutium surrounded the gates of Esagila. No weapons were brought into Esagila and the other temples, and no standard was advanced. On the third day of Marcheshvan Cyrus entered Babylon. The harine lay down before him. Peace was established for the city. Cyrus proclaimed peace to all Babylon. He appointed Gobryas, his governor, governor in Babylon . . . On the night of the eleventh day of Marcheshvan, Gobryas against . . . (and) he killed the son of the king."

II. *The Cylinder of Cyrus, now in the British Museum:* " He [Marduk] searched through all lands, he saw him [Cyrus], and he sought the righteous prince, after his own heart, whom he took by the hand. Cyrus, King of Anshan, he called by name ; to sovereignty over the whole world he appointed him. The country of Qutu, all the Umman-manda, he made submissive to him. As for the Black-headed People, whom he [Marduk] caused his [Cyrus's] hands to conquer, in justice and right he cared for them. Marduk, the great lord, guardian of his people, looked with joy on his pious works and his upright heart; he commanded him to go to his city, Babylon, and he caused him to take the road to Babylon, going by his side as a friend and companion. His numerous troops, the numbers of which, like the waters of a river, cannot be known, in full armour, marched at his side. Without skirmish or battle he permitted him to enter Babylon. He spared his city Babylon in (its) calamity. Nabonidus, the king, who did not reverence him, he delivered into his hand. All the people of Babylon, all Sumer, and Akkad, nobles and governors, prostrated themselves before him, kissed his feet, rejoiced at his sovereignty, showed happiness in their faces. The lord, who by his power brings the dead to life, who with (his) care and protection benefits all men —they gladly did him homage, they heeded his command. I am Cyrus, king of the world, the great king, the powerful king, King of Babylon, King of Sumer and Akkad, king of the four quarters (of the world), son of Cambyses, the great king, King of Anshan; grandson of Cyrus, the great king, King of Anshan; great grandson of Teispis, the great king, King of Anshan, of ancient seed-royal, whose reign Bel and Nabu love, whose sovereignty they regard necessary to their happiness. When I made my gracious entrance into Babylon, with joy and rejoicing I took up my lordly residence in the royal palace. Marduk, the great lord, [granted] me favour among the Babylonians, and I gave daily care to his worship. My numerous troops marched peacefully into Babylon. In all Sumer and Akkad, the noble race, I permitted no unfriendly treatment. I gave proper attention to the needs of Babylon and its cities . . . the servitude, which was not honourable, was removed from them. I quieted their sighing (and) soothed their sorrow. Marduk, the great lord, rejoiced over my

APPENDIX II

[pious] deeds, and he graciously blessed me, Cyrus, the king who worships him, and Cambyses, my own son, and all my troops, while we, in his presence, and with sincerity, gladly lauded his exalted [divinity]. All the kings dwelling in royal halls, of all quarters (of the world) . . . brought me their heavy taxes and in Babylon kissed my feet . . . I collected all their people and restored (them) to their dwelling-places . . ." [1]

---

[1] The translations are from *Assyrian and Babylonian Literature, Selected Translations*, by Robert F. Harper. New York : D. Appleton and Co.

INDEX

INDEX

463

INDEX

INDEX

---

[1] The walls of Babylon, according to Herodotus, were 40 miles in circumference, 335 feet high, 85 feet wide at the top, and were broken by 100 gates —25 on each side. His account and Xenophon's are in keeping with the documents of Nebuchadnezzar himself, who says in the Babylon, the Winckler, and the Grotefend inscriptions: "The great walls of Babylon I set in order, and I built the wall of its moat mountain-high with burned brick and bitumen and threw it around the city for protection. . . . In the upper . . . of the city gate of Ishtar from the bank of the Euphrates up to the city gate, for the protection of the sides of the city I built with bitumen and burned brick a mighty citadel, and I laid its foundation at the water's edge in the depth of clear water. I raised its turrets mountain-high and skilfully strengthened the watch-tower and thus protected Babylon."

INDEX

Chaldaea, a mountainous country between Armenia and the Black Sea, III. ii. 7; at war with Armenia, III. i. 34; III. ii. 4; subdued by Cyrus, III. ii. 1–17; reconciled to Armenia, III. ii. 17–25

Although confused by the earlier Greek writers and most modern scholars with the Chaldeans of Babylonia (in scripture), there was no connection, as is shown by the later Greek use of Χαλδία, by an entirely different form in the Armenian writings, and by the form Haldi instead of Haldu in their own writings. *See* Chaldaeans

Chaldaeans, the people of Chaldaea, a nomad tribe in the mountains on the borders of Armenia, III. i. 34; III. ii. 4; a martial folk, III. ii. 7; conquered in battle, III. ii. 10; poor, III. ii. 7; join Cyrus, III. ii. 25, 26; go to India, III. ii. 27; III. iii. 1; scale the walls of Sardis, VII. ii. 3; their insubordination, VII. ii. 5–8. *See* Chaldaea

Chariots of war, Arabian, II. i. 5; Assyrian, III. iii. 60; Median, VI. ii. 8; inaugurated by Cyrus, VI. i. 27–30; their position in the battle, VI. iii. 34–36; VII. i. 15, 16; their part in it, VII. i. 29–32, 47; races of, VIII. iii. 33

Chase, *see* Hunting

Chrysantas, a captain of the peers, his personal appearance, II. iii. 5; VIII. iv. 20–21; his sound common sense, II. iii. 5; discusses prize money, II. ii. 17–20; II. iii. 5–6; sent to invade Armenia, II. iv. 22–30; captures the Armenian fugitives, III. i. 4–5; discusses exhortations with Cyrus, III. iii. 48–55; gallant conduct in battle, IV. i. 3; promoted to a colonelship, IV. i. 4; eulogizes horsemanship, IV. iii. 15–21; leads the van to the defence of Gadatas, V. iii. 36, 52–56; helps Cyrus quell a panic, VI. ii. 21–22; master of the horse, III. i. 3, 8, 39; VIII. iii. 16; discusses with Cyrus the enemy's advance, VII. i. 6–9; his part in the battle, VII. i. 39; proposes to use the river against Babylon, VII. v. 8; proposes a royal home for Cyrus, VII. v. 55–56; declares for discipline in the empire, VIII. i. 1–5; a cavalry general, VIII. i. 16; his superior merit, VIII. iv. 10–12, 16; kissed by Cyrus, VIII. iv. 27; satrap of Lydia and Ionia, VIII. vi. 7. Known only from the Cyropaedia

Cilicia [Khilakku], the country at the northeast corner of the Mediterranean, I. v. 3; IV. v. 56; governed by Cyrus, I. i. 4; an independent tributary state, VII. iv. 2; VIII. vi. 8. Possibly a vassal-kingdom in the time of Herodotus, certainly in the time of Xenophon. Its chief city was Tarsus. *See* Cilicians

Cilicians, natives of Cilicia, I. i. 4; I. v. 3; II. i. 5; in the Assyrian army, VI. ii. 10; join Cyrus's army, VII. iv. 1. *See* Cilicia

Considerateness, in Cyrus's discipline, VIII. i. 27–28

Courage, how inspired, III. iii. 50–54; and a sharp spear, VI. ii. 33

Croesus, king of Lydia (560–546 B.C.), I. v. 3; a descendant of the shepherd Gyges, VII. ii. 24; joins the Assyrian, II. i. 5; VII. ii. 22; commands a division of his army, III. iii. 29; his flight, IV. i. 8; IV. ii. 29; seeks alliance with Sparta, VI. ii. 10; commander-in-chief, VI. ii. 9, 19; VI. iii. 11; VII. ii. 23; directs the battle, VII. i. 23; is defeated, VII. i. 26 ff.; flees, VII. ii. 1; as a prisoner before Cyrus (B.C. 546), VII. ii. 9–29; and the Delphic oracle, VII. ii. 15–20[1]; delivers

---

[1] Herodotus (I. 46–48) tells how Croesus put the various oracles to the test to see if they could tell the truth. He sent various envoys out from

467

Sardis on the same day to go to the various oracular shrines and ordered each one on the hundredth day thereafter to inquire of the oracle to which he went how Croesus was employed at the precise moment of their enquiry. The Pythian prophetess replied in hexameter verse : " I know the number of the grains of sand and of the drops in the sea ; I understand the dumb and hear the man who speaks not. A smell reaches my nostrils of a hardshelled tortoise boiled with lamb's flesh in a vessel of bronze—bronze is below and bronze is above." Croesus was cooking just such a stew and, amazed at the knowledge of the Delphian oracle, accepted it as infallible.

INDEX

INDEX

INDEX

worship on Mt. Parnassus in Phocis, VII. ii. 15, 18

Eagle, in Augury. *See* Omen
"Ears," the king's, VIII. ii. 10–12
Earth, the goddess, III. iii. 22; VIII. 24; the giver of all things good, VIII. vii. 25
Ecbatana [Hagmatana = the place of assembly (?); the Achmetha of the Bible], formerly the capital of Media, on the northeast slopes of the Orontes mountains, the summer capital of Cyrus, VIII. vi. 22. (Taken by Cyrus, B.C. 550)
Economics, household and army, I. vi. 12; VIII. i. 14–15
Egypt, the rich land of the Nile, I. i. 4; subdued by Cyrus, VIII. vi. 20; the western boundary of his empire, VIII. vi. 21; VIII. viii. 1
Egyptians, natives of Egypt, I. i. 4; mercenaries in the Assyrian army, VI. ii. 10; VI. iii. 19, 20; VI. iv. 17; in the battle, VII. i. 30–40, 46; VII. iii. 3; they join Cyrus, VII. i. 41–44; they settle in his realm, VII. i. 45
Embas, an officer commanding Armenian infantry, V. iii. 38
Enyalius, originally a name of a god of war, also an epithet of Ares, the god of war, VII. i. 26
Eros, the god of love, VI. i. 41
Ethiopia, the land of the Upper Nile, south of Egypt; the southern boundary of Cyrus's empire, VIII. vi. 21; VIII. viii. 1. (Ethiopia was not included in his realm; a small portion of Ethiopia was subdued by Cambyses, the son of Cyrus)
Euphratas, commander of the engines of war, VI. iii. 28
Euphrates [Ufrātu], the mighty river of western Asia (over 1,700 miles in length), rising in Armenia, flowing through Babylon, VII. v. 8; more than two stadia in width, VII. v. 8; diverted from his course, VII. v. 9–19; never called by name in the Cyropaedia

Europe, the continent, I. i. 4
Euxine Sea. *See* Black Sea
"Eyes," the king's, VIII. ii. 10–12; VIII. vi. 1β

Friends, how won, VIII. ii. 1–4; VIII. vii. 13; the richest treasure, VIII. ii. 19; the king's sceptre, VIII. vii. 13

Gabaedus, king of lesser Phrygia, II. i. 5; flees after the battle, IV. ii. 30. *See* note under Artacamas
Gadatas, a neighbouring prince subject to the Assyrian, prosperous and happy, V. iv. 34; emasculated, V. ii. 28; V. iii. 8; hatred of the Assyrian, V. iii. 10; V. iv. 35; drawn into secret alliance with Cyrus, V. iii. 9–21; VII. v. 51; the Assyrians invade his land, V. iii. 26, 27; the conspiracy against him, V. iv. 1–6; saved by Cyrus, V. iv. 6–8; gives him gifts, V. iv. 29; openly joins him, V. iv. 39; begs Cyrus to continue the war, VI. i. 1–3; promises a fort, VI. i. 19; artillery, VI. i. 21; at the obsequies of Abradatas, VII. iii. 7, 11; leads the way into Babylon, VII. v. 24–30; with Gobryas kills the king, VII. v. 30, 32; leads 10,000 horsemen in the procession, VIII. iii. 17; wins the race against the Syrians, VIII. iii. 25; chief mace-bearer and a grateful friend, VIII. iv. 2
Ge, mother-earth. *See* Earth
Gobryas [Gaubruva; Gubaru or Ugbaru, in the Nabunaid-Cyrus Chronicle], an Assyrian elder, IV. vi. 1; V. iv. 41; governor [of Gutium], IV. vi. 2; his story, IV. vi. 2–7; his compact with Cyrus, IV. vi. 8–10; V. i. 22; receives a visit from Cyrus, V. ii. 1; shows him his castle, V. ii. 3–7; invites him to dinner, V. ii. 14; joins his army, V. ii. 21, 22; VII. v. 51; is taken into his confidence, V. iv. 23; is rewarded, V. iii. 1; challenges the Assyrian king, V. iii. 5–7; envoy

471

INDEX

3-20; v. i. 22; v. iii. 24; VII. v. 50; assail the Assyrian camp, IV. ii. 31–32; bring in spoil, IV. iii. 3; IV. iv. 1; joint distributors of the spoils, IV. ii. 43; IV. v. 2, 11, 38–58; their king in Cyrus's confidence, v. ii. 22, 23; praised by him, IV. v. 23; on the relief-expedition to Gadatas, v. iii. 38; v. iv. 13; they beg Cyrus to continue the war, v. i. 28; VI. i. 1, 7; in Cyrus's procession, VIII. iii. 18, 25; at the banquet, VIII. iv. 1; they remain in Babylonia, VIII. iv. 28

Hystaspas [Vishtáspa], a Persian peer, IV. ii. 46; his story of bad manners, II. ii. 2–5, 15; preaches temperance, IV. ii. 46; brings Gadatas to Cyrus, VI. i. 1–5; commands a company of cavalry, VI. iii. 13, 14; VII. i. 19–20; his part in the battle, VII. i. 39; sent against Phrygia, VII. iv. 8–11; collects subscriptions for Cyrus, VIII. ii. 16–18; leads 10,000 horsemen in the procession, VIII. iii. 17; why inferior to Chrysantas, VIII. iv. 9–12; wins the daughter of Gobryas, VIII. iv. 15–16, 24–27. Father of Darius I. Satrap of Hyrcania in the time of Darius I

Illyrian, an inhabitant of Illyria, a Balkan state on the Adriatic, the modern Albania, I. i. 4; the king of Illyria, I. i. 4

India [Hindu], not the whole peninsula, but the Punjab, I. v. 3; sends embassy to Media, II. iv. 1–9; III. ii. 27; governed by Cyrus, I. i. 4. India proper was not added to the empire until the time of Darius I

Indian, an inhabitant of India, I. i. 4; I. v. 3; II. iv. 5–9; III. ii. 25; the king of India, III. ii. 27; his great wealth, III. ii. 25; Cyrus asks him for money, III. ii. 28–30; his ambassadors to Cyaxares, II. iv. 1–9; III. ii. 27; to Cyrus, VI. ii. 1; sent as spies, VI. ii. 2, 3, 9–11

Indian Ocean, with its two gulfs, the Persian Gulf and the Red Sea, the eastern boundary of Cyrus's empire, VIII. vi. 20, 21; VIII. viii. 1

Ingratitude, punishment of, I. ii. 7

Ionia [Yauna, Iyauna], the central division of Greek western Asia Minor, VI. ii. 10; a satrapy (with Lydia), VIII. vi. 7

Ionians, belonging to Ionia; serving perforce under Croesus, VI. ii. 10

Justice, in Persian education, I. ii. 6, 7, 15; I. iii. 16–18; I. vi. 31

King, the best man, VIII. i. 37, 40; Cyrus the best of all, I. i. 4; his idea of a good example, VIII. i. 12, 22; kings and shepherds, I. i. 2; fathers of their people, VIII. i. 1, 44; VIII. ii. 9; VIII. viii. 2; their pomp, VIII. i. 40

Labynetus [Nabu-naid], king of Babylon. See Appendix II

Lacedaemon. See Sparta

Lacedaemonian. See Spartan

Larisa, a city on the coast of Aeolis, assigned to the Egyptians, VII. i. 45

Libya, the northern province of Africa, with Cyrene as its capital, VI. ii. 8

Love, a matter of free will, v. i. 9–11, 13–15; a kind of slavery, v. i. 12; the gods subject to love, VI. i. 36

Lycaonia, a province in southeast Asia Minor, southwest of Cappadocia, VI. ii. 10

Lycaonians, belonging to Lycaonia; a wild and lawless tribe, who maintained their independence of Persia (An. III. ii. 23) and lived by plunder; in the Assyrian army, VI. ii. 10

Lydia, the middle province of western Asia Minor; the kingdom of Croesus, I. v. 3; II. i. 5; IV. ii. 29; subdued by Cyrus I. i. 4; a satrapy, VIII. vi. 7; the Assyrian king marches for,

INDEX

VII. iv. 8; joins the Assyrian, II. i. 5; subdued by Cyrus, I. i. 4; VII. iv. 8–11; a satrapy, VIII. vi. 7

Phrygian, a native of (1) *greater* Phrygia, I. i. 4; I. v. 3; in the Assyrian army, VI. ii. 10; in Cyrus's army, VII. v. 14; (2) *lesser* Phrygia, I. i. 4; I. v. 3; IV. ii. 30; in the Assyrian army, VI. ii. 10; the king of, VII. iv. 10; Phrygians in Cyrus's army, VII. v. 14

Postal system, inaugurated by Cyrus, VIII. vi. 17–18

Prayer, the secret of, I. vi. 3–6; Cyrus prays, II. i. 1; III. iii. 21, 22, 57; IV. ii. 12; V. i. 29; VI. iii. 11; VIII. vii. 3; Gadatas's prayer, V. iv. 14; Abradatas's, VI. iv. 9; the soldiers pray, VI. iv. 19; VII. i. 1; how one should not pray, I. vi. 4–6

Procession, Cyrus's royal, VIII. iii. 1 ff.

Red Sea, in the sense of the Indian Ocean, *q.v.*

Religion, Cyrus's, I. v. 6; I. vi. 1–6, 46; VIII. i. 23; a state institution, VIII. i. 23–25; VIII. iii. 11 ff.; ceremonies of, *see* "Prayer" and "Sacrifice" and "Magi"

Rhambacas, a Median cavalry officer, V. iii. 42

Rhathines, a Cadusian, winner of the horse-race, VIII. iii. 33

Rheomithres, revolting satrap, betrays his wife and children and friends, VIII. viii. 4. *See under* Ariobarzanes

Riches, true, IV. ii. 42–44; V. ii. 8–10; VIII. ii. 15–23; hoarding of, III. iii. 3; VIII. ii. 15 ff.; VIII. iv. 33; disregard of, IV. ii. 43; VIII. ii. 15; VIII. iii. 46–47

Sabaris, younger son of the Armenian king, III. i. 2; captured by Chrysantas, III. i. 4

Sacas (a Sacian, *q.v.*), cupbearer to Astyages, I. iii. 8–14; I. iv. 5

Sacia, a part of Scythia, next to Hyrcania, V. ii. 25; east of the

Caspian Sea, a country of nomads, governed by Cyrus, I. i. 4

Sacian, an inhabitant of Sacia, I. i. 4; enemies of Assyria, V. ii. 25; V. iii. 11, 22; in Cyrus's army, V. iii. 22, 24, 38, 42; V. iv. 13; VII. v. 51; beg Cyrus to continue the war, VI. i. 1; in Cyrus's procession, VIII. iii. 18, 25; the Sacian partner of Pheraulas, VIII. iii. 25–32, 35–50

Sacrifice, I. v. 6; III. ii. 3, 18; III. iii. 21, 22; VI. iii. 1; VII. i. 1; VII. v. 57; VIII. iv. 1; VIII. v. 21, 26; manner of, III. iii. 21, 34, 40; VII. vii. 1, 3; bulls to Zeus, horses to Helius, VIII. iii. 11

Sambaulas, a Persian lieutenant, and his ugly friend, II. ii. 28–31

Sardian, belonging to Sardis (*q.v.*), VII. ii. 3

Sardis, the wealthy city of Croesus, VII. ii. 11–14; the capital of Lydia on the Pactolus, VII. ii. 1–3; captured by Cyrus (B.C. 546), VII. ii. 3–4; VII. iv. 1; VII. v. 53, 57; Cyrus departs, VII. iv. 12; the spoils of, VII. iii. 1; VII. iv. 12; VII. iv. 29–31

Satrap [kshatram = kingdom; from ksha comes shah], VIII. i. 11; business of, VIII. vi. 1; Adusius, of Caria, VII. iv. 7; VIII. vi. 7; Tanaoxares, of Armenia, VIII. vii. 11; various appointments, VIII. vi. 7; none sent to Cilicia, Cyprus, or Paphlagonia, VII. iv. 2; VIII. vi. 8

Sciritae, a mountain tribe in the north of Laconia, furnishing picked troops for the left wing of the Spartan army and always given the post of extremest danger, IV. ii. 1

Scythia [Sakā], the vast country of southern Europe, on the Black Sea, the Caspian Sea, and along the Danube, I. i. 4

Scythian, an inhabitant of Scythia, I. i. 4; the king of Scythia, I. i. 4

Self-control. *See* Temperance

476

INDEX

Sham battle, II. iii. 17–20

Soul, V. i. 27 ; V. iv. 11 ; its dual nature, VI. i. 41 ; immortality of, VIII. vii. 17–22

Sparta, the great Doric city and province in southeastern Peloponnesus, at the time of Cyrus the greatest city of Hellas, sought as an ally by Croesus, VI. ii. 10

Spartan, a citizen of Sparta, IV. ii. 1

Specialization, advantage of, II. i. 21 ; VIII. ii. 5

Sun-god, the, Helius (identified with Mithra), honoured with sacrifice, VIII. iii. 12, 24 ; VIII. vii. 3

Susa (Persian, Shūs ; the Shushan of the Bible), the capital of Susiana, the country lying between the Parachoathras Mountains, the Persian Gulf, and the Tigris river ; the home of Panthea, IV. vi. 11 ; VI. iii. 14 ; capital of Abradatas, V. i. 3 ; VI. ii. 7 ; VI. iii. 35 ; the spring residence of Cyrus, VIII. vi. 22

Syria (shortened from Assyria [Ashur], which became to the Greeks the specific name for the countries about the Tigris, while Syria meant to them the Semitic Northwest, including Phoenicia and Palestine, as well as Babylonia, Assyria, and Mesopotamia), lower Syria, the country on the Mediterranean coast, [VI. ii. 11] ; subdued by Assyria, I. v. 2 ; subdued by Cyrus, I. i. 4 ; VIII. vi. 20 ; its wealth, V. ii. 12 ; used erroneously for Assyria, V. iv. 51 ; VI. i. 27 ; VIII. iii. 24 ; rich in produce, VI. ii. 22

Syrian, belonging to Syria, VII. v. 31 ; a native of greater Syria, I. i. 4 ; IV. v. 56 ; identical with the Assyrians, V. iv. 51 ; V. v. 24 ; VI. ii. 19 ; VII. iii. 15 ; VIII. iii. 25

Tachos, king of Egypt (fourth century, B.C.), supports a revolt against the king of Persia (B.C.

362), VIII. viii. 4. *See under* Ariobarzanes

Tactics, theory of, I. vi. 12–46 ; VIII. v. 2–16 ; in practice, V. iii. 36–45 ; V. iv. 19–23, 43–50

Tanaoxares [= strong in body; called Mardus by Aeschylus, Mergis or Merdis by Justin, Smerdis by Herodotus, and Bardiya by Darius in the Behistan inscription], Cyrus's younger son, VIII. vii. 5, 6, 8, 9 ; satrap of Media, Armenia, and Cadusia, VIII. vii. 11 ; quarrelled with his brother, VIII. viii. 2 (and slain)

Temperance, in the Persian discipline, I. ii. 8 ; IV. v. 1, 4 ; V. ii. 15–20 ; VIII. i. 30–32 ; enforced with tears, II. ii. 14 ; Cyrus preaches, I. iii. 10, 11 ; I. v. 9 ; IV. ii. 38–45 ; VII. v. 75–76

Thambradas, an officer commanding Sacian infantry, V. iii. 38

Thracian, an inhabitant of Thrace, the king of Thrace, I. i. 4 ; mercenaries in the Assyrian army, VI. ii. 10

Thymbrara, a city of Lydia, on the Pactolus, and not far from Sardis, VI. ii. 11 ; VII. i. 45

Tigranes [Digran = an arrow], crown-prince of Armenia, hunted game with Cyrus, III. i. 7, 14 ; his teacher, III. i. 14, 38–40 ; III. iii. 5 ; pleads his father's case, III. i. 14–30 ; married, III. i. 2, 36 ; regains his wife, III. i. 37, 41 ; joins Cyrus's army, III. i. 42 ; III. ii. 1, 3, 11 ; IV. ii. 9, 18 ; IV. v. 4, 35 ; joint-distributor of the Assyrian spoils, IV. ii. 43 ; his loyalty, V. i. 27 ; in command of his cavalry, V. iii. 42 ; promises artillery, VI. i. 21 ; wins the race against the Armenians, VIII. iii. 25 ; at Cyrus's banquet, VIII. iv. 1, 24. The great national historian of Armenia, the pseudo-Moses of Chorene, gives a long and fabulous account of the relation of Digran with Astyages. Compare also the later Tigranes who

477

INDEX